The Nordic Fae Series

THE NORDIC FAE SERIES

ELLE THRASHER

For my sexy trolls.

FROM THE AUTHOR

Dear reader,

Thank you for picking up this book and choosing to spend your time with these characters. I hope you have as much fun reading this as I did writing it. Lennie's story originally came to me one night as I was falling asleep. What if a human missed her cruise ship and stumbled upon magic and a hidden fae society? What if that was in Norway? Well, that idea ended up being this series.

During my childhood I had the great fortune of living in a small Norwegian village. A lot of my experiences have made their way into this story, some with a slight fantasy twist.

Buckle up. This is a fun one.

Best wishes,
Elle

Pronunciation Guide

Espen -- Ess-pen

Øyvin -- Oy-vihn

Alvdalen -- Alv-dah-len

Balder -- Bahl-derr

Bente -- Ben-the

Dagny -- Dahg-nee

Embla -- Emm-blah

Fjell -- Fyell

Freija -- Frey-ah

Gunvor -- Guun-vore

Halvar -- Hal-vahr

Herja -- Herr-yah

Ingeborg -- In-geh-bohrg

Jorunn -- Yoo-runn

Kjetil -- Sheh-till

Knut-Arne -- Knewt - Ahr-neh

Leif -- Layf

Oddvar -- Odd-vahr

Reuven -- Rew-ven

Salka -- Sall-kah

Skolvik -- Skoll-veek

Solveig -- Sool-vay

Stavanger -- Stah-vang-er

Torsten -- Torr-sten

Trygve -- Tryg-veh

Turi -- Tuu-ree

Unni -- Oo-nee

Veigar -- Vey-gahr

Vigdis -- Vigh-diss

Wilhelm -- Vill-helm

Ylva -- Yll-vah

Content Warning

Each book has slightly different content warnings. Please take care of your own mental health and feel free to dip out if something isn't for you.

The Fae of the Fjord:
Violence, graphic language, on page sex, loss of a loved one, and poisoning.

Christmas on the Fjord:
On page sex, alcohol use.

The Fae of the Forest:
Language, on-page sex, peril, violence, minor gore, mentions loss of loved ones.

The Fae of the Fjell:
Significant violence, graphic language, on page sex, gore, death, war, natural disasters such as wildfires, house fires, brief moments of ptsd and flashbacks.

TABLE OF CONTENTS

The Fae of the Fjord

1

LENNIE

Aiming the lens at the forest across the fjord, I lined up the shot, tightened the focus, and clicked. I pulled the camera away from my face and frowned as I peeked at the screen. Tall pines shot into the sky, blanketing the base of the cliffs that rose up on either side of the Norwegian fjord—the deep, watery inlet that stretched inland from the North Atlantic. Glancing up at the scenery I'd tried to capture, my heart stuttered as I took in the breathtaking blues and greens I'd traveled across the world to experience. While the photo was adequate, it didn't even begin to come close to the real thing. I could do better.

I readjusted the aperture and took a deep breath. Lining up the trees around a tiny clearing, I found what I wanted, and clicked.

It was a much better shot than the first—the composition was more balanced, and the foreground was less blurry—but there was a speck of silvery light in the clearing I hadn't noticed earlier.

A horn blared from the valley below. Startled, I dropped the lens cap and glanced toward the noise. A white ship shifted away from the dock in the village below, pointing its bow out of the harbor.

"Fuck," I muttered under my breath and started running down the mountainside I'd hiked up this morning toward the little village of Skolvik on the water.

The crew on the cruise-ship had warned me before—okay, maybe *several* times—that if I missed the designated check-in time, they would leave me behind. No exceptions. Those assholes waited for no one, and now I realized how true that was.

I'd zoned out during most of the lecture this morning as we debarked the cruise ship for our daily excursion, but now they came back to me as I hurried down the rocky path. Consequences like having to find my way back to the port where the cruise had started, Stavanger, collect my luggage from said dock, and deal with Customs and Immigration when they asked why I'd missed the boat. The latter were manageable, but the worst part would be figuring out a way back to Stavanger, which was over five hundred miles south of my current location.

Yeah, I was well and truly fucked this time, but I ran like hell anyway.

The crew's parting words rang through my head as I bolted down the hillside. "Do not be late, Ms. Martin. This is your final warning. The ship sets sail promptly at 5:00 pm local time, Lennie."

My legs pistoned and feet pounded against the rocky path as the chilled air buffeted against my face. The bag on my back smacked against me and my water bottle started leaking, spraying liquid across the arm of my rain-jacket. I did my best to keep my balance, grabbing onto tree-limbs a few times to save my ass and head. Was I fast and physically fit? Yes, decently so. Was I graceful? Nope, never a day in my twenty-eight years had I been labeled that.

When the terrain finally leveled out, I sprinted toward the dock. Rounding several small buildings, and dodging some of the locals—who scowled as my blonde-ish ponytail may have whacked them in the face—I reached the gang-plank at the tiny harbor. Or at least, where it should have been...

The boarding ramps had been pulled back, the water quietly lapped against the dock, and the ship... the small, white cruise-ship that was supposed to take me further north on a sightseeing tour of the Norwegian Fjords, was gone.

Well, not gone, but far enough along the watery passage that there was no way in hell I was getting on-board. Unless I found a dingy with an outboard motor strong enough to pull up alongside it, like a pirate. Breathing heavy, I quirked a smile at the thought of commandeering a vessel to take on a boat ten times the size. That kind of thinking had got me into trouble in the past, and no doubt would in the future too.

I scanned the little marina for something small and floaty, but all I could see were white pleasure boats and a derelict trawler that had probably been moored due to overfishing along the coastline.

A deep chuckle sounded behind me and I spun.

"Du kommer ikke til å finne noe brukbart der," a man muttered looking between me and the harbor, the wind playing with the wisps of gray hair that stuck out the sides of his wool-knit hat. The old man continued walking past me, shaking his head, his hands clasped behind his back.

"I don't speak Norwegian," I said, a bit too sassily considering my current predicament. I knew a few words, but they may have been: hello, thank you, yes, no, and two beers. Which, according to my app, were: *hallo, tusen takk, ja, nei,* and *to øl.*

The man laughed again and came to a stop, his shoulders rising and falling underneath his big rain-jacket. "You Americans never do." He had a thick accent, but I understood an insult when I heard it. You didn't live in South Boston for three years without hearing smack-talk and brutal honesty on the daily.

I sighed and glanced back at the cruise-ship that was now a blip between the mountains.

"*Følg meg*," the man mumbled, his voice a grumbly tone that sounded more at home in a troll than a little old man. "Follow me," he said sternly.

"Why should I do that?" I asked, rubbing my hand across my forehead as panic crept in. "There has to be a cab or a bus around here that can take me to the closest city."

I spun around, searching the harbor for any signs, scanning my surroundings. To my left was the path to the village where the man had started walking, in front of me was the main road into town and the mountain side that rose up beside it, and to my right was the tourist center... and a sign for a bus-stop. The blue-and-white logo for mass transit was a beacon of hope, and my lips tugged into a gentle smile.

"That will not be here for a while," the man said, following my gaze with a raised brow.

"That's fine. I'll just wait out here," I replied, pointing toward the wooden bench next to the small building with posters covering the windows—one of which advertised the cruise I had just missed.

"You will be waiting a long time."

I bit my lip and rolled my eyes. I was troubleshooting this mess and did not need his negativity. "When does the next bus arrive?"

He grinned, the scruff around his mouth and jaw twitching. "Three months."

I started. Three *months?!* That was ludicrous! These were modern times; there was no way buses ran that infrequently.

"No way," I countered, my stomach starting to churn with annoyance and a hint of anxiety. "It's 2023, you need buses for the tourists." I waved at myself as an example.

He shook his head again in frustration, and unclasped his hands, sticking them into his jacket pockets with force. "You are correct."

I smiled at my own little slice of victory.

"But," he continued, "when Autumn arrives and the last ship of the season leaves"—he pointed down the fjord behind me—"there is no need for the bus anymore. It only comes back one time or two times in the winter if we have little snow."

My smile faltered as the weight of my mistake set in.

"You might be able to convince someone to drive you down the fjord to Heimsund—a bigger town that has buses—but most of us will laugh at you." He grinned again, like he was quietly relishing in my misfortune.

My shoulders sank and I shuffled my feet. I just needed to regroup and figure out another plan. I could totally convince someone to give me a ride to wherever I needed to go... Admittedly, I knew almost nothing about Norway and had no idea where to go, other than this Heimsund that he'd mentioned, but I'd figure it out. I *always* figured it out in the end. Whether it was a problem with my camera or the boring documents at work, I could triage the shit out of a situation.

"Like I said," the man piped up again, and I dragged my attention back to him. "Follow me."

I took a deep breath and nodded, out of ideas for the moment. The man spun on his heel and started walking toward the village center. For only the eighth time in my life, I did as I was told, and followed.

2
LENNIE

The village of Skolvik was quaint and cute, sitting at the very end of the deep fjord. Bright, natural-toned buildings and homes dotted the water's edge as boats bobbed in the soft waves. Buttressed on all sides by steep hills that curved into sharp mountains covered in pines and birch trees, it was a picture perfect scene and exactly what I expected of Norway. Which is why I'd gone on the damn cruise in the first place.

I loved landscape photography. Ever since my parents gave me my first camera when I was nine, I'd spent my free-time perfecting my craft and exploring. That first camera was nothing special—a basic digital point-and-shoot camera, but I was obsessed. Then, when I graduated from high school, my grandmother had gifted me a DSLR camera—my first manual camera. I'd used that thing for years before saving up to buy my current baby, a state-of-the-art device with a lens that cost me almost as much as the camera itself. What started in the fields and gullies of Ohio, had continued after college in Boston, and then stayed my passion when I reluctantly moved back to Columbus, Ohio due to the insane cost-of-living in the city. Now, whenever I could, I saved up to go on trips around the world.

My latest trip-turned-current-disaster had been a spontaneous adventure. A well-placed ad on my phone had me sold instantly, especially since the tickets were deeply discounted for the last sailing of the season. If I hadn't captured some spectacular shots over the past week, I'd have said the whole trip was a damn mistake.

Now, I needed to rectify the error my tardiness had created.

"What's your name?" I asked, jogging to catch up to the old man as he walked down the street. He moved fast for the age his gray hair and curved stature portrayed.

"Oddvar," he said, his accent throwing the vowels and rolling the Rs into tones I could never hope to replicate.

"Okay, Oddvar," I said, overextending the A and, based on the rise in my new friend's wispy, gray-brows, absolutely butchering the name. *Oh well, points for trying.* "I'm Lennie. Where are we going?"

"My coffee shop. There you can figure out what you want to do next." He never slowed as we wove between the small wood-buildings with tiled rooftops, and I walked quickly to keep up. "And we will talk to my friend, Solveig. She can help you, too."

Cool. Great. Progress, I guess. His tone seemed put-out—either because I was an American or an annoyance, to be determined—but at least he was helpful. I could ignore the way he'd taken great pleasure in seeing me miss the boat. Hell, I could only imagine the faces I'd made as I watched the ship sail away without me. I would have been amused, too.

Rounding another corner and traipsing down a tiny road devoid of vehicles, I kept up with the Norwegian and his silence. A few minutes later, he stopped in front of a storefront on the corner and stepped up to the wood-and-glass door. The small shop had wooden walls with peeling white paint, a few windows on either side of the door in the center, and a simple sign that read: Kafé. A tiny road ran between the buildings, too narrow for cars, and appeared to be for pedestrians only.

A bell chimed as Oddvar opened the door and stepped inside. I followed closely behind him, taking in the café as Oddvar shucked off his jacket and hung it up on a stand by the door. The interior of the building was tiny, but the space was used effectively. Light wood tables and chairs lined the walls beside the windows, and at the back of the room, centered slightly to the right, was a counter and cashier-machine. Aside from the two of us, the shop was empty, seemingly closed for the day.

"You like coffee?" he asked as he busied himself behind the counter, pouring water and setting up a large coffee pot.

Does a bear shit in the woods? It was a little late in the day for the dark stuff, but I never turned down coffee. "Yes," I replied, taking a seat at the closest table and setting down my camera. Pulling off my backpack, I set it on the chair beside me, making sure the contents—including my laptop—didn't fall off.

Oddvar continued his silent treatment, and it didn't take long before the smell of a nutty, bitter caramel roast permeated the space. I shrugged out of my rain jacket, resting it over the back of my chair and grabbed my camera.

Shit.

The lens cap was missing. I thought back to my run down the mountain, and then further back to taking photos at the top, trying to figure out when I'd last had it. I tilted my head back with a sigh, remembering I'd dropped the damned lens cap when the ship's horn blared. I added re-hiking the mountain to my mental to-do list, but that was a problem for tomorrow-Lennie.

The sun had started to set while I sat in the shop. It was getting late, and I needed a place to stay tonight, then transportation tomorrow to a bigger city further down the fjord to get me toward Stavanger, and probably something from the American Embassy so I didn't get myself into trouble considering my passport was still in my luggage on a cruise ship without me.

With a groan, I grabbed my cell-phone out of my jacket and called the Norwegian Fjord Tour that had abandoned me.

After talking to the cruise company customer service—who not so graciously told me to figure my shit out and get my stuff before the end of the year or they'd donate it all—I called the person that would be the most likely to help me out of my current situation. The first call went to voicemail, so I tried again. The second call was picked up on the fourth ring.

"I need your help," I mumbled into the phone pressed to my ear.

A low grumble sounded across the line. "Do you know what fucking time it is?"

I glanced at the clock above the shop-counter and did the mental math. Six in the afternoon, minus seven hours, was eleven in the morning.

"It's eleven a.m."

"On a Sunday!" my brother exclaimed, his voice hoarse.

I bit my lip, but couldn't keep the sneaky smile at bay. The fucker was hungover. If I didn't need his help, I would have rubbed it in his face or played heavy metal music down the line. But as it was...

"I missed the boat."

Howls of laughter battered my ear-drum, and I pulled the device away from my head until he caught his breath.

"Your tardiness was always going to come back to bite you in the ass, sis," Ryan laughed down the phone. I growled like a toddler at his words and their truth. "I'm surprised Mom and Dad didn't take away that camera of yours in high school with the number of detentions you racked up for being late to math class."

"How do you know it was the camera's fault?" I asked, trying to play it cool, but my voice betrayed me by rising several octaves.

"When is it not?" I could hear my brother's signature smirk, and I didn't like it. Not one bit.

Ryan was the younger of my three older brothers, and currently gallivanted around Chicago. He was 32 and did something in public relations, and had the personality to be good at it. He was always the charismatic one, and when my high school teachers found out I was his little sister, I saw heart-emojis bursting out of their eyes. That same feeling did not transfer to me once they saw how many shits I gave about being in class—except art, that one I aced every year. Oh, and, some of my science classes I'd done okay in, but only when they focused on environment and earth sciences. The rest were boring, like my eldest brothers.

My two other siblings, Andrew and Jared, had both settled down after marrying their college sweethearts. It was kind of creepy how alike they were. Andrew was two years older than Jared, both now well into their thirties. Both had been good students, won football scholarships to The Ohio State University, and set the gold standard for all the Martin kids to follow. Which Ryan, at least, did.

Me, on the other hand, I'd always been the rebel. Ever since my mom and dad found out they were having a happy-surprise-accident-baby, I'd been the odd one out. But I was still their only girl, and I lorded that shit over my brothers to this day. The stuff I got away with was spectacular—

"Are you listening to me?" Ryan's voice dragged my attention back to the phone call.

"Partially," I admitted with a sigh, lazily brushing my fingers across the table.

"Well, get your partial shit together because this call is going to cost you a fuck-ton of money."

I shuddered at the thought of the cell-phone bill I'd find when I eventually got home. I wasn't even connected to wifi right now, so my data usage wasn't going to be pretty either.

"So, you missed the boat because the scenery was too beautiful and it had to be captured," Ryan said, mimicking my usual excuse for being late to just about everything.

"Pretty much," I replied. "And my luggage is on-board, along with my phone charger, and passport."

"How many times have I told you to always carry your passport on you when you're in a foreign country," he said with an exasperated sigh.

"I know, I know, I know." I waved away the lecture. I'd been an idiot. Wasn't the first time, and wouldn't be the last either. "Can you help me or not?"

Ryan groaned and debated it for a second. No doubt wondering how he could use this against me at future Thanksgiving dinners or the annual Martin family reunion next spring.

"Just don't tell Mom, please," I added, trying not to sound like I was begging. I was going to fix this mess, but if I could have my annoying brother working in my favor back in the US and making some calls for me, I might be able to solve this without too much damage to my already measly bank account.

"Fine," he conceded, and I sent down a quiet thank you to hell, which must have frozen over for my brother to so easily agree. "I'll call the embassy for you and see what we can figure out."

"Thank you," I said, my shoulders sagging in relief.

"Don't thank me yet," he scoffed. "This shit's gonna cost you, sis."

"I know."

"Good," he said, and then hung up.

I lobbed my phone onto the table and leaned back in the chair.

One problem down, three to go.

3
LENNIE

"Drink up," Oddvar said, his voice gruff, as he set a small cup of coffee on the table in front of me. Steam drifted up and the smell of straight black bean-nectar was an assault to my nostrils. *Had he heard of creamer?* By the lack of any around, and the man's firm gaze, I was going to guess it wasn't standard in Norway and would not be offered this evening.

"Thank you, Oddvar," I said, wrapping my hands around the beverage, feeling the comforting heat beneath my palms. He winced at my pronunciation, but I was too tired to try the throaty tongue-roll thingy like he did when he'd told me his name. It was time to tackle another part of my to do list. "Do you know of somewhere I can stay that isn't too expensive?"

I may have been able to afford the trip out here, but I'd used almost all of my money on the cruise. My emergency funds didn't plan for hotel stays. So, hopefully the local hotel was cheap, or there were other options, like a tent or a park bench out of the wind.

"Yes, as I said earlier. I will take you to Solveig," Oddvar replied, returning behind the counter and wiping it down with a rag.

I stared at him blankly, waiting for him to elaborate. Was Solveig a person? Or a place? This meant nothing to me.

His dark brown eyes assessed me before he continued. "She runs a guest house. A... what do you Americans call it? An inn, at her house." He rambled like he was trying to find the right word to describe the place. Fortunately for him, I'd take anything that didn't bankrupt me.

"A bed-and-breakfast?" I supplied as he waved his hand through the air, then pointed at me.

"Yes."

"Okay, thank you." I bobbed my head, hoping this Solveig had reasonable rates.

Oddvar nodded at the cup in my hands. "Drink, then we go."

"Yes, sir," I muttered and took a sip, then let out a wheezy gasp. Fuck, it was hot... and strong. I'd be wired for hours after this, I was sure of it.

Setting down the mug to cool, I grabbed my camera and started flicking through the pictures I'd taken today before things had gone to shit. They were gorgeous, part skill and part natural beauty that remained untouched by humans. Pointy pine trees in all shades of deep green swept across the terrain, and the fjord almost glittered in the gray sunlight. I clicked through some more and stopped when I reached the last photo.

It was similar to the one prior, but with one glaring difference. In the middle of the shot, peeking through the trees, was a flash of silvery light—as if a lens flare had appeared in the forest... a very unnatural beam of light. I'd never seen anything like it, and it most definitely did not come from the sun, which had been hiding behind the clouds.

The door chimed and someone entered the café, but I didn't bother to look up, too busy zooming in on the silvery-something on my camera.

"*Litt sent å være åpen?*" A thick and gravelly voice said.

"*Hun rakk ikke skipet i tide,*" Oddvar muttered from somewhere across the room.

I didn't pay attention considering I couldn't understand them, so I focused on the picture. It looked like there were two figures beneath the silvery light. I tried enlarging it, and the camera beeped at me, letting me know I'd reached maximum zoom. With a grumble, I continued staring at the human-shaped figures. *What the fuck was that? Were they wearing something to throw the light like that?* I'd heard of scarves and jackets that refracted light in weird ways, distorting images, so maybe that's what was happening.

Someone plopped down opposite me at my table and coughed.

I started at the sound and looked up.

The man across from me was big in every sense of the word. From his broad shoulders, to the sharpness of his jaw, to the sizable hands resting on the table between us. He had choppy dirty-blond hair, deep-blue eyes the color of the fjord, and pale skin. His full lips curved into an unwelcoming smile as I continued scanning him. Before I could ogle him further—and try to visualize what was hiding underneath his thick navy-sweater—I set down my camera and clicked it off.

"*Har du ekstra kaffe?*" the man said, not averting his eyes from me as I crossed my arms over my chest. Maybe the aggressive staring was a Norwegian thing, but sitting at my table while he continued to speak in a language I didn't understand was grating on my nerves. Sure, I understood that I was the foreigner here, but leering like this wasn't polite in any country.

"*Ja, men dette er alt jeg har i kveld,*" Oddvar said, not that I had a clue what that meant, but he uttered words the stranger in front of me understood. Then Oddvar brought over a little to-go cup of steaming coffee for the man, who thanked him with a nod, before Oddvar quickly disappeared behind the counter again.

The newcomer didn't move to grab the cup, but his eyes creased as he continued to stare. Whatever it was he found so interesting, I wasn't amused. I mean, who sits down at someone's table and starts glaring at them?

"You gonna keep staring, buddy?" I challenged, leaning back in my chair with the bravado of a woman who didn't have any more fucks to give.

He scoffed. "Any good photos?"

I glanced at the camera between us, before meeting his gaze again.

"Just mountains and trees," I said. Which wasn't a lie. The thing was full of photos of the fjords, mountains, and forests.

He flicked his brows and said, "Ah, American."

"What do you mean by that?" I narrowed my eyes at him.

"Nothing," he replied with a smarmy smile that had me clamping my palms together. "But here's what you need to do."

I leaned back and crossed my arms, biting my lower lip as I prepared for whatever this asshole was about to say. If there was one thing in the world that annoyed me the most, it was a man telling me what to do.

"Tourists are only needed here in Skolvik during the summer and early autumn season. Thereafter, we no longer require your *dollars.*" He said the currency like it was filth and tilted his head to one side. "Any continued influx of visitors, even just one, is a threat to the region's wellbeing, especially the fjord."

"Tell me how you really feel," I deadpanned, giving him a swift upward nod to continue while the blood in my veins started to boil.

He took a sip of his coffee, then leaned in, resting his forearms on the table. "The amount of pollution you alone can create is a problem. Even if you draw in extra financial benefit, ultimately, you're not wanted here. You're not needed here, so leave."

"Not even a please?" I seethed, reaching the end of my tether. I took a deep breath and then added, "I can't be the first tourist who's been stuck or decided to stick around a little longer."

He grabbed his coffee cup and scooted his chair away from the table, the scraping sound loud in the near-empty café. "Every season there is always someone who gets left behind or who decides they want to stay. They usually leave when the first storm arrives. It used to be people visiting from Germany, but lately it's always a dumb American." He finally stood from his chair, and I took in the full height of the beast, his arms filling out every inch of his sweater. *Why were the hot ones always dicks?*

I straightened up and ignored the insult as I realized the tidbit of information he just dropped. *Wait a second... Leave?*

"How do they get out of here?"

He sauntered over to the front door before turning back. I spun in my seat, keeping my eyes locked on him, waiting for his answer... a little glimmer of hope sparking in my chest at the thought of being able to get home.

"Boat," he replied curtly.

"Like, they ask someone with a boat or there is a ferry that takes them down the fjord?"

He shook his head and took a sip of his drink. "None of those."

"Then what?" I asked with an exasperated sigh that only seemed to amuse the guy even more. The tiniest hint of a smirk tipped his lips up, and I wanted to smack the look from his arrogant face.

"They go on the little ship with the town's deliveries."

"You mean, a boat delivers your groceries and stuff?"

He nodded. "Exactly. Cheapest and easiest way down the fjord."

"When does the next one arrive?" I asked quickly, almost stumbling over my own words as I tried to eke out more information from the man.

"In one week."

Fuck me sideways. I grumbled, and the man smiled at my misfortune. "You don't happen to know of anyone else that might have a boat or a car and be willing to help out a poor tourist?"

"No."

I groaned in frustration and brushed my hand across my forehead.

Meanwhile, the asshole nodded to Oddvar and said, "*God kveld.*"

"*Ja, god kveld,*" Oddvar replied while sorting something behind the counter.

The man left, and I said nothing else. My brain was already flying through plans to get myself on that goddamn ship.

My new to-do list now consisted of: locating lodging, finding my lens cap, buying extra clothes for the week, and getting my ass on that boat.

"You finished?" Oddvar asked, pulling his coat back on and nodding at my coffee cup.

I grabbed the cup and downed the black liquid. It warmed my throat and felt like jet fuel in my stomach. Nodding at the now empty mug, I stood up and crossed the room, placing it in the metal sink behind the counter, before grabbing my stuff and pulling my own jacket on. I wasn't sure how Oddvar felt about the exchange that had transpired between me and the blond guy, but if he had thoughts on the matter, he remained mum.

"To Solveig?" I asked, zipping up my jacket and hoisting my bag onto my back.

Oddvar nodded and we made our way through town to his friend's house.

4

LENNIE

Oddvar walked me through town, past small boutiques and businesses that were closing for the day, and around to the north side of the harbor. A five-minute walk down an asphalt path on this side of the fjord led us to three larger houses, one white, one red, and one blue with white trim. Oddvar—sprightly for his age—kept a brisk pace and aimed for the blue house that faced the fjord. As we got closer, I questioned how on earth you entered the thing, because at the front wasn't what appeared to be a main entrance. Upfront was a fenced-in deck that backed onto the small path, which, in turn, sat above the rocky drop into the fjord itself.

At the last minute, Oddvar pivoted and headed toward the rear of the house. I quickened my steps to keep up with the man, and found what he'd been aiming for. The front door was at the back of the house, which was fucking bizarre in my book. But, alas, on my travels I'd learned that not everything was as straightforward as a cookie-cutter suburban house with a white picket-fence or a three-story brownstone.

Reaching the door, Oddvar knocked twice and then we waited, him with his hands behind his back and me with my palms in my jacket pockets.

A ray of sunshine opened the front door with a smile and short white hair. *"God kveld, Oddvar,"* she said, which sounded like a greeting, but also a bunch of gibberish to my non-Norwegian ears.

"Ja, ja, good evening," my older companion replied before waving at me. "This is the young lady I mentioned in the text."

The woman nodded, her eyes crinkling at the corners. "Yes, the American who missed the boat." She stepped aside and waved us both inside.

I politely obliged, but quickly added, "I'm Lennie." I really didn't want to be known as 'the American who missed the boat.'

"I'm Solveig," the woman replied as she closed the door behind us, shutting out the cold. "You are welcome to stay with me until arrangements can be made for your trip home."

"Thank you. I really appreciate it. How much do you charge?"

Her soft and gentle smile grew. "How about fifty American dollars per night? I will include breakfast."

That sounded like a freaking bargain. I could practically hear my bank account begging me to take the deal. "That works," I replied, trying not to sound *too* relieved. "Thank you."

"Wonderful. How about I show you around?"

I nodded, and Oddvar mumbled something in Norwegian that I could barely hear. Thankfully, Solveig understood the sounds that came out of his mouth, and a moment later Oddvar left.

After his departure, Solveig showed me the living room, kitchen, then upstairs to the guest room and bathroom across the hallway. The entire house was constructed of light-colored wood with bright walls. Even with the sun gone for the day, the interior glowed and looked like something out of a minimalist architecture magazine—everything had its place, and there wasn't an ounce of clutter in sight. It was the polar opposite of my tiny apartment back home.

The guest bedroom was minimally appointed, but somehow still cozy. The small double bed was covered in a blue-striped duvet—oddly folded in half instead of draped across the width of the bed—and a wooden dresser sat beside a tiny closet built into the wall.

"Will this be all right?" Solveig asked, her voice heavily accented, but her English was impeccable.

"This is perfect. Thank you so much," I replied, setting down my bag and resting my hands on my hips.

"Well, I'm making dinner. If you want some stew, you are welcome to join me in an hour."

"That sounds amazing."

"Wonderful. I shall let you get settled," she said, and left the room, closing the door behind her.

I took a deep breath and stretched my neck from one side and then the other. *What a day.*

While I waited for dinner to be ready, I unpacked what few belongings I had in my backpack, and took a five minute power-nap before heading downstairs.

Our meal was delicious, and my conversation with Solveig was cordial and lighthearted. Apparently, she'd lived here her entire life and couldn't imagine living anywhere else. However, she asked me loads of questions about the places I'd visited around the world, with northern Italy being the one she wanted to know the most about. I politely indulged her, happy to share the tales from my travels—at least the ones socially acceptable to discuss at the dinner table. I may have been a bit of a rebel and had a few rowdy adventures along the way, but Mom had taught me proper table manners.

After dinner, I crawled into bed. With exhaustion weighing heavily on my limbs, and a full stomach warming me through, it wasn't long before I fell asleep.

The sound of my phone beeping and buzzing woke me up. I leaned over and grabbed it off the nightstand, blinking the sleep out of my eyes. It was a bit fuzzy, but the name of the person video-calling me was legible in my bleary state.

With a grumble, I accepted the call.

"Andrew, I'm trying to sleep."

My oldest brother smiled back at me, with his big toothy grin, short dusty blond hair in perfect position, and the dark brown eyes we'd both inherited from our mother filled with warmth and care.

"I didn't mean to wake you," he said, "but, I wanted to make sure you're okay."

"Ryan texted you didn't he?" I pushed my hair back and pulled the covers up higher, frustrated at their antics.

Andrew nodded. "As soon as he hung up on you, he texted me and Jared. But I thought I would give you some time to cool down after your chat with him. You two always get feisty after interacting for more than five minutes."

He wasn't wrong about my relationship with Ryan, but I wasn't going to tell Andrew he was right. His ego was boosted enough by Midwest society and the picture-perfect suburban neighborhood he called home.

"I'm fine, Andrew."

"Okay, good. Trust your gut and get your butt home," he said, a hint of parenthood seeping into his voice. "We'll keep this from Mom and Dad, for now, but if she starts asking questions, I will tell her."

"Could you be more of a first-born child?" I narrowed my eyes at him, annoyance lacing my tone.

Andrew chuckled. "Don't do anything stupid... and don't anger any Vikings."

"I'm going back to sleep now," I grumbled.

"All right. Love you, sis."

"Yeah, yeah. Love you too, Andrew."

I hung up, and flicked my phone to its home-screen. Sure enough, sitting there waiting for me was a text message from Jared, the last of my brothers. I was surprised he bothered, what with the demands of his new veterinarian practice.

After a knee-injury in his sophomore year of college, Jared's dreams of playing pro-football had been shattered. So, he pivoted and ended up continuing his education, becoming a vet. His job took up much of his time, and he rarely checked in with me. When he did, it was in the form of a quick text.

I opened the one he'd sent while I was sleeping.

Jared: Ryan told me what happened. You good, sis?

I typed out a quick response:

Lennie: Fine. Be back soon. Don't tell Mom.

Surprisingly, he texted back immediately.

Jared: K

I snorted. Typical Jared. It was shocking how he'd managed to find a wife with those communication skills. I opened another text that had come in while I was sleeping, this one from Ryan.

Ryan: Embassy says you're fine to stay without any repercussions for ninety days post initial arrival.

I sent him a thumbs-up emoji in reply and shut off my phone, throwing it back onto the nightstand. It was at 22% and fading. I would need to find a charger at the store tomorrow. Right now though, sleep took priority. I buried my head in the soft pillow and heaved the covers over my head, blocking any remaining light from my comfy cocoon.

5
LENNIE

Solveig was, honest to hell, one of the sweetest ladies I'd met on my travels. She was up early, already had coffee made for me—with milk to go in it—and had even prepared breakfast to-go. It wasn't my usual breakfast of oatmeal with random stuff on top, but it was delicious. A fresh bread roll, butter slathered over it, with smoked salmon and three thin slices of cucumber on top. I downed my coffee, and after thanking Solveig for the food and drink, wandered into the village, munching on the last of my yummy breakfast.

I'd worn my spare clothes today, which I always included in my backpack for emergencies. It wasn't the cutest outfit, but it was convenient, and fit nicely into a packing-cube, stuffed into my bag. The black long-sleeve shirt had some stretch to it, and worked with the jeans I'd worn yesterday and thrown on again today. Pair that combo with my hiking boots and my navy rain-jacket, and I almost looked like a local. At least, a very sporty local who had thrown her long blonde hair into a ponytail again for ease.

It wasn't a particularly warm morning, but the sun was starting to peek through the gray clouds, and the dew that hung over the little town made the entire place smell fresh and clean. There were no major pollutants here, except the cruise-ship that had abandoned me like a moldy husk of corn.

The town was barely waking, the curtains still drawn over many of the neighbors' windows, and no activity around the little white houses. It was quiet as I strolled toward the harbor, and realizing it was too early for any clothes stores to be open, I decided to knock something else off my to-do list instead: find my lens cap up the mountain.

Tightening the camera strap around my neck, I aimed for the trail beside the harbor, and started climbing like I'd done the day before.

The trail was completely empty compared to yesterday when fellow hikers had been out and about. The trek wasn't too long, but my thighs got a workout as I ambled up the rocky path, traipsing over moss-laden logs as I snapped another twenty photos of the flora and fauna. When I reached the clearing at the top where I'd been yesterday, I took a deep breath and started searching for my missing camera lens cap. It was black and shouldn't blend too much with the rocky ground. I scoured the terrain, and trod as lightly as possible in case I accidentally stepped on it. Which, admittedly, wouldn't be the first time, but would be seriously inconvenient considering current circumstances. Unlike a phone charger, I highly doubted I'd be able to replace a lens cap here in this little town.

"Looking for something?"

I jolted at the male voice and straightened before spinning around to face the owner.

Leaning against a large, mossy boulder was a man with a mop of dark hair, pale skin, a short beard, and a cocky smirk that said he knew exactly what I was looking for. He was wearing a black jacket and what looked like black rain-pants with a checkered reflective-stripe around the calf of each leg.

I gave him a winning smile and said, "It's probably the piece of plastic in your hand, Sunshine."

The man chuckled, and his amber eyes shimmered in a way I'd find attractive if he weren't pinching my lens cap between his fingers.

"Littering is heavily frowned upon in Norway. Some might even fine you for it," he said, his English perfect with barely a hint of an accent.

I stepped forward and plucked the lens cap from his grasp, careful not to look too closely at him. "Thank you. I'll be sure to remember that." And I wouldn't intentionally litter—I valued the nature around me too much to even consider it. What had happened yesterday was an accident.

"Get any good photos?" The man asked, still perched against the boulder. That was the second time in two days a hot stranger had bombarded me with this question.

Rubbing the black disk on my shirt and then blowing some air across it for good measure, I made sure it didn't have any debris on it before I clicked it onto the end of my camera—where it belonged. "Yes, mostly trees and waterfalls. You have a lot of them here."

"We do," he chuckled again. The noise was kinda sexy—husky and warm—it did things to my insides that shouldn't be allowed around a stranger. I shook my shoulders and took a deep breath through my nose. "They really are majestic, some might even say *magical*."

"Sure." I scoffed and glanced toward the area I'd photographed yesterday. The spot where I'd seen the silver flare was back to its regular gray-and-green coloring. Not a flicker of weirdness in sight.

"Haven't you heard of the legends and tales about the magical creatures that call this fjord home?" he asked, as I turned my back on him, fully entranced by the view.

But even facing away from the man, I couldn't hide my snort. Yes, they'd told us the stories on the cruise ship about monsters akin to the Loch Ness Monster that lived beneath the surface, but... "They're bullshit," I replied and turned my focus to the rocky ground and the moss trying to creep between the individual stones. "But, you might want to check out the clearing across the way, saw some weird silver shit over there yesterday. Caught it on camera, too. Could have been someone littering more than a misplaced lens cap."

"What exactly did it look like?" he said over my shoulder, suddenly right behind me.

Spooked, I spun on instinct and landed a swift punch in his ribs. He let out a grunt. Before I could retract my fist, his hand wrapped around my wrist and we both stilled—shock in our eyes. Or, at least, that's what he could likely see on my face, because I'd spotted the word printed across the top left of his jacket in a silvery font that matched the reflective material on his pants. It was only six letters:

Politi.

Fuck me sideways. I was 99% certain I'd just punched a cop.

I bit my lip and held my breath, unsure how I was going to get myself out of this one. Panicked flashes of Norwegian prison cells ran through my mind. Were they as bad as the ones in the US, with metal bars, a bucket for my shit, and crappy little beds? Or dungeons hidden in the middle of nowhere with ship-planks to sleep on? Maybe they had fancy wooden doors and flat-pack furniture like an IKEA display? I was about to find out, and then probably get shanked by a Viking when I inevitably opened my goddamn mouth and said something stupid.

The man breathed steadily, but said nothing, his amber eyes boring into mine with a ferocity that made my skin tingle.

I'd never punched a cop before—drunk dude at a bar that was getting too handsy? Sure. With three older brothers, I learned to swing hard and fast. But even I wasn't dumb enough to punch law enforcement. Now, looking at the man before me, I realized I'd gone too far, even in self-defense. A Viking's shank was in my future, and I'd never be heard from again. My mother would be beside herself.

"Ummm, so, how much trouble am I in right now?" I finally asked, my voice wavering slightly.

He dropped my wrist and took a step back, the rocks crunching under the weight of his black boots. "None," he said. "If you show me what's on your camera from yesterday."

Was he for real?

I blinked at him, confusion racing through my mind as the thought of meatball-only prison meals subsided. "I'm sorry for hitting you... but you really shouldn't sneak up on people like that."

He shrugged and bobbed his head from one side to the other, as if actually considering my suggestion. Which was lunacy, because my mouth got me into more trouble than out of it, so I highly doubted it would get me out of accidentally hitting a cop.

"Maybe," he said, then bit his lower lip and continued thinking, narrowing his eyes at me.

"Okay..." I waved my hand requesting his name in the international signal for *insert info here.*

"Espen."

"Okay, Espen. How about I show you my photo with the silver litterers, and we forget about this whole punchy situation?" This was a long-shot, but I'd give it a try if it meant I didn't get in trouble.

At the mention of the silver light, Espen straightened and nodded.

Thank fuck.

I sighed and grabbed my camera, clicking through to the weird photo and passed it to the cop.

He stepped closer again, holding my camera. I could feel the heat radiating off him, and see the specks of dark-brown in his amber-colored eyes as he inspected the image. He smelled like moss and leather. Up close, I could make out his short lashes and the muscles in his jaw jumping. I was starting to feel tingly around the man—almost attracted. I mean, he was good-looking. Hell, I'd even go so far as to classify him as hot-as-fuck.

His jacket brushed against mine as he said, "Your name?"

"Lennie Martin," I said, discreetly splaying my fingers to rid myself of the ache in my knuckles.

"And you took this yesterday?"

"Yes."

"Anyone else seen it?"

"No," I replied, then shifted my weight away from him slightly. No one had seen the photo... except, maybe that guy at the café last night. He could've easily looked over my shoulder when he walked in. But why would that matter?

"Are you sure?" Espen asked, probably sensing my hesitation. He side-eyed me, waiting for a response.

I sighed and rested my hands on my hips. "There may have been one guy last night at the café. But, I can't be sure he saw anything. My back was to him when he entered."

Espen handed back my camera and I draped it back over my neck while he let out a low hum. "What did he look like?" he asked, invading my personal space with his odd authority and messy hairstyle.

I turned off the camera and let it rest against my chest, the strap around my neck taking the weight. Having him this close had my throat tightening, and goosebumps skittering across my arms.

"Well?" he said, drawing my attention back to his question and stopping my thoughts from considering the size of his hands as he crossed his arms.

I shook my head, refocusing. "Tall, blond hair, minor scruff, broad shoulders, grumpy with an attitude of asshole, and a hell of a staring problem."

Espen grumbled. "I know the man."

Why the annoyed tone, though? Was it such a problem if someone else saw the photo? Deciding not to be argumentative, and considering I'd just punched Espen, I asked, "I take it he might be problematic?"

"No." Espen rubbed his hand across his face and through his hair, messing it up even more. "But he's a pain in the ass."

"Ha! Glad I'm not the only one who thinks so. Don't put him on the town's welcoming committee. Seriously, bad for tourism." If given the chance, I wouldn't have been surprised if the Asshole had tried to drop-kick me out of town.

Espen let out a bubble of laughter that made something in my stomach flutter. "He hasn't been for decades."

I chuckled, and stopped. *Decades?* The man I'd met had been forty, at most. "Wait, what?"

Espen stilled. "What?" He raised his thick brows.

"I could've sworn you just said—"

"Nevermind," he quipped and stepped back, resting his hands on his hips. "Thank you for showing me the photo. Do you like yoga?"

Give me whiplash or what bro?

"Yeah. Sure." I shook my head at the sudden pivot, but decided to roll with it considering I was miraculously off the hook for punching him. So, I circled back to our original topic. I was still curious about it. "You know what that silver thing is?"

"Ye—," he started, before quickly switching to, "no."

I blinked, giving him a deadpan stare. Here I was thinking men were pretty straightforward creatures. Turns out they made them a little differently in Norway. Must be all the fresh air or something.

"You really gonna lie to me?"

He sighed. "You wouldn't believe me."

I tilted my head, eyes squinted in challenge. "Try me."

He smirked, and the fire in his eyes gave me the feeling he wanted to *try me* in more ways than one. I squirmed a little, standing straighter, but wasn't wholly opposed to the idea, either.

"You've already said you don't believe in magic."

"Yeah, because it's animated crap that only happens in movies." I snorted.

He widened his gaze, leaning in closer to me as he whispered, "Are you sure?" Standing this close, it was impossible not to notice the way the dark flecks in his eyes flickered, like a silvery light briefly replaced them. It happened so fast, I almost didn't catch it, but... what the fuck *was* that? I took a step back and sucked in a gulp of air. It was a trick of the light, nothing more than the sun playing with colors.

"Magic is bullshit," I reiterated, shaking my head as I took another deep breath. "What's in the photo?"

Espen backed away and settled on the big boulder again. Resting one of his boots against it, he recrossed his arms and sighed. "I may as well tell you." He shrugged. "You've seen too much already, and I can't have you telling people about it around the village... or elsewhere, for that matter."

"Clearly," I said with a pound of venom and sass in my tone that had always landed me in trouble as a kid. Kinda like punching a cop in a foreign country. Some things apparently never changed.

He took a deep breath and locked his gaze with mine. "What you photographed was likely the illegal transfer of magic from one fae to another."

I stilled.

My knees buckled.

And then I laughed. Full on, hunched over, belly-meet-thighs, laughed. Because, oh man, did they need to take this guy off the roster down at the station.

"They won't fire me," Espen said.

I steadied myself by placing my hands on my knees. Apparently I said that last bit out loud. Oops.

Espen laughed, too. But it didn't sound as warm as it had earlier. This chuckle was more jovial and slick. He lifted his hand and placed it on his shoulder. I watched as his police jacket and black pants flickered and were replaced with a dark-green military-style coat with tubular collar, a short cape over one shoulder, and brown leather straps criss-crossing the front. Beneath that was a pair of gray pants and tall brown boots. He looked like some medieval warrior with ancient camouflage.

It was as if he'd...

It was like...

It was... magic.

I passed out.

6
LENNIE

Blinking open my eyes, I strained to see through the brightness invading my senses. Minimalist decor and light-wood tones glowed in the light as my brain caught up with the rest of my body and woke up. I was on my back, on what appeared to be the sofa in Solveig's living room.

"Oh good," a voice trilled, and I shifted to see Solveig walk into the room from the adjacent kitchen. She set a jug of water and a glass on the coffee table and poured me a drink. "Glad you're awake. We were a little worried."

"We?" I asked, sitting up and taking the glass from her outstretched hand.

"*Ja*. Me and Espen. He brought you back here. Said you were light-headed after hiking up the mountain where he found you."

Espen.

The cop.

The man who'd mysteriously changed outfits like some mirage had washed over him. The same man who said magic was real.

I stared at the water in my hand, and promptly put it back on the table. My mouth was dry, but after what I'd witnessed this morning, I wasn't entirely sure the local water was safe to drink. Hallucinogens were the only answer to whatever had happened, right? Solveig, thankfully, didn't remark on my actions.

"What time is it?" I asked, adjusting my disheveled ponytail and glancing toward the window. The sun had come out, and the fjord shimmered in the rays of light.

"Just after lunch," Solveig replied. She pulled the sleeves up on her cream sweater and smiled. "Would you like something to eat?"

The answer to that question was always yes. But, I did feel a little queasy. I twitched my nose. "How about just a light snack?"

"Of course," she said, and made for the kitchen.

I nodded and thanked her before she left the room. I'd hit the jackpot staying with her—I should be paying triple for this kind of care and service from my gracious host. Not that I could afford to do so, though.

My crazy morning aside—which I didn't want to think too hard about—I had a long list of things to do today. First and foremost, hit up the local boutiques for some clothes and toiletries. I could live without makeup, but underwear and a few more outfits would be needed if I was staying here until that supply-ship showed up on Sunday. That was my ticket out of here, and I just needed to get by until it took me up the fjord to the bigger city where I could get some form of transit south to Stavanger where my cruise-ship would finally dock.

Solveig gave me a sweet roll with icing drizzled on top. I'd drooled a little while I watched her make the topping—powdered sugar and water—simple as hell, and delicious, too. It was the perfect mini-meal while I walked to the clothing store she'd suggested in town.

The village was now awake, with people milling about the streets. I stared in fascination, especially at the man zipping through town with long roller-blade looking things on his feet and ski poles in his hands, while wearing an all-in-one skin-tight suit that was *not* family friendly. I was so caught up in what the man was doing that I missed the arrival of another "thing" and startled at their greeting.

"He's summer skiing," Espen said, appearing beside me.

With a shrug and acceptance of what was apparently normal around here, I turned to the dark-haired cop. His eyes shone with something like glee, and I spun on my heels, avoiding him as I headed toward the store Solveig had mentioned.

"Thank you so much, Espen, for bringing me down the mountain when I fainted," he said with a high pitched tone, keeping pace beside me. "Thank you for saving me. The wolves would've eaten me whole—"

I scoffed. "Are there seriously wolves up there?"

Espen grinned. "It's rare, but yes."

"Are you one of them? A werewolf perhaps?" I asked, even though I didn't believe he was a wolf. Or that magic was real. Or that whatever happened this morning had actually happened. Because... no, it most definitely wasn't worth thinking about anymore. Magic was bullshit, illusions for kid's birthday parties, and traveling fairs. Total bullshit.

"I'm not," Espen replied and clasped his hands behind his back in a move I'd seen Oddvar do yesterday. "And, by the way, you missed the turn for the clothing store two streets ago."

I pulled to a stop with a grunt and finally looked at him fully. He was still in his black uniform, the large jacket shielding him from the light breeze off the fjord. A head and a half taller than me, Espen was a lithe but sturdy build, with a friendly smile and mischief in his eyes. The latter were amber in color and so much brighter than my plain brown ones.

"And you weren't going to mention this sooner?" I asked, my usual snarky sass bubbling to the surface.

He beamed. "I thought I would see how far you would go before you realized, but I also feel a little guilty after the way we left things this morning."

"Really?"

"Yes and no." He pointed back the way I'd come, and I pivoted, heading in the new direction. Espen stayed by my side, guiding me toward the store whether I wanted his company or not. Passersby waved and nodded, greeting him happily as we walked. Clearly, everyone in this town knew him.

A few minutes later, we arrived at a storefront with mannequins and a tent in the window. When Solveig had said this was the perfect place, I hadn't expected all-terrain gear and boots, but I wasn't in a position to complain.

Espen was a gentleman and opened the door for me to enter. An electronic bell chimed, and a woman with short, bottle-blonde hair smiled as we crossed the room toward the women's clothing section.

"Do you not need camping gear?" Espen asked with a chuckle.

"No." My reply wasn't harsh, but certainly efficient, as I started perusing the racks of shirts. The stock was varied from athletic materials to knitwear and I pulled aside a dusty-pink t-shirt made out of stretchy material, a basic black cotton-shirt, and a dark-blue quarter-zip sweater that was big and cozy-looking.

Espen continued to trail me as I moved on to pants. "Are you going to follow me for the rest of the day?" I asked, slightly bothered by his proximity.

The man brushed his fingers over a pair of shorts before facing me. "Maybe. Thought you might need a friend, especially if you keep fainting."

My shoulders slumped, and I took a deep breath through my nose. "You know why I passed out," I whispered, hoping the woman up front couldn't hear us.

"No," he said, meeting my gaze. "I don't." A smirk grew on his lips, and he stepped up in front of me. With only a few paces between us, he reached out and touched my shoulder. "All I did was this."

A wave of warmth washed over my skin, and he removed his hand. I glanced down. My outfit from this morning was missing, replaced by a copy of the dusty-pink t-shirt I held and a pair of black yoga pants that had a slight flare at the bottom. I sucked in a breath, my heart pounding, and felt my eyes widen.

Looking up, I found Espen smiling and a sneaky gleam in his gaze. I did my best not to hyperventilate. Or move. Hell knew I didn't need to accidentally smack a cop again... like ever. But the rational, logical part of my brain couldn't keep up with what I was seeing.

"How are you doing this?" I mumbled, staring down at my body again. It didn't feel any different from what I had been wearing, but it appeared as if I had put on an entirely new outfit.

"Magic," Espen replied quietly.

"Is bullshit," I said, finishing his sentence on a whisper, even though what was happening could only be described by the word he'd just uttered. Which was madness. "Make it stop."

"Okay," he said, and placed his hand on my shoulder again. The wave of warmth returned, and I watched as my appearance shifted back to what I'd been wearing two minutes ago.

"Do you still think it's bullshit?" he asked, taking a step back and leaning against the display table of pants.

"Yes."

"Are you sure?"

"No," I replied honestly, scrunching the clothes in my hands. Either someone had slipped me drugs when I wasn't paying attention, or magic was real. I couldn't quite believe my eyes, but I'd also felt the shift, the... *magic*... fall over my skin when Espen changed my clothes. "Explain."

He grinned like he'd caught a fish in his net. "How about you find some clothes for the week, and I'll tell you over dinner."

Hesitating, I took a deep breath. "Hypothetically, if magic is real, why are you telling me about it?"

His smile faltered and he cleared his throat before replying, "Because in this situation, I believe it is wiser to have you in the know and on my side, than a loose cannon creating larger-than-life fabricated stories about what you saw and share that photo with the world. America has Area 51, England has Stonehenge... Skolvik will not become the Norwegian equivalent."

Okay, he had me. That was a decent explanation for the hypothetical. I narrowed my eyes at him and his frustratingly handsome floppy hair. "How do you know I need clothes... and how did you know I was staying with Solveig, by the way?" I didn't recall telling him where I was staying, or how long I'd be here for.

"Small town," he shrugged. "And I'm a police officer. It's my job to know what's going on, including when a mysterious American tourist missed their boat."

I drew my lips into a firm line and glared at him.

"So, dinner tonight?"

"And why should I trust you?" I waved my hand at him. "Whatever you are?"

"I'm a fae," he whispered with a gentle smile that had the corners of his eyes crinkling.

"Okay," I said, sounding very much not okay. "You're like a magical troll?"

He smiled. "I prefer *sexy* troll."

Rolling my eyes and picking up a pair of yoga pants like the ones he'd *magicked* onto my body from the display table beside us, I said, "Fine. I'll go to dinner with you, but I want more information about this magic nonsense."

"Deal."

He looked way too happy with himself. "Tonight, dinner, tomorrow... who knows... perhaps you'll join me for yoga in the woods."

I squinted, trying to see if there was some sort of innuendo or if this dude was really serious. Were we talking about yoga or *yoga*? "Don't get your hopes up."

"I already have." He winked. "You looked good in those tight yoga pants."

I scowled at him, but couldn't help the smile that grew on my face. This guy was slick and friendly as hell. Randomly grabbing another pair of pants, I spun toward the dressing room. "Where should I meet you for dinner?"

"Fisken," he replied instantly. "The restaurant by the public docks."

I threw my items into the dressing room and spun around, holding the long curtain in my hand. "I'll meet you there at seven."

Espen beamed, and a warmth settled in my chest at the sight. "It's a date."

I slammed the curtain shut and set about trying on the clothes I'd selected, heat radiating from my chest and an anxious energy coursing through my veins. Because, apparently, fae and magic were real.

7

LENNIE

Espen left while I was in the changing room, which finally gave me the peace I needed to find underwear, another tee, a couple extra sports bras, and socks. Solveig had graciously offered her laundry machines to clean my current outfits, but it was still wise to grab some more stuff so I wasn't constantly having to clean my clothes.

I grabbed a five-pack of long socks and mulled over the magic nonsense that Espen had shown me as I looked for some comfy sports bras, the rest of my future purchases slung over my arm—yoga pants included. In the woods, Espen had mysteriously changed his outfit from his police uniform into attire that looked like it belonged in *ye olde times*. I mean, who wore a cape outside of attending a Renaissance fair?

That shift was ludicrous, but then, this afternoon, in this very store, he'd changed my clothes without so much as yanking my pants off me.

I snatched a bra in my size off the hanging rack and shoved it between my arms and chest where I was stashing the rest of my purchases.

The whole concept of magic being real and not in movies was overwhelming, and too much to take in. So, it was bullshit. Complete and utter bullshit. It was probably all in my head, right? I'd been eating a lot less processed sugar during my trip so far, and getting a lot more fresh air than I'd get on a normal day in Ohio. Maybe that was the reason why I was seeing things? Because, if it wasn't, and magic was in fact real, that would be fucking absurd.

Confused and determined to get some answers out of Espen that evening, I wandered over to the checkout, paid for my new stuff, and headed back to Solveig's house.

I arrived at the restaurant and bar called "Fisken" at seven for dinner with Espen. The drizzle outside made my hair frizz, but the soft warmth inside the building would certainly dry it out quickly, even if I did look a bit frazzled now.

A low hum of chatter rose from the few occupied tables, but it wasn't too busy. Taking a moment to gather my bearings, I looked around the space. The walls were made of dark wood with photos of fishing boats and mountains hanging on them, exactly what you'd expect in a little town on the water. To my left was the bar, and to the right were tables facing the bank of windows that looked out over the public harbor, boats bobbing up and down on the water.

I spotted Espen sitting at one of the old wooden tables near the back of the room and shucked off my rain-jacket as I approached him. He smiled as I rolled up the sleeves on my black shirt, slung my jacket over the back of a chair, and joined him.

"Glad you made it," he said, his eyes flickering with glee again. He'd replaced his uniform with a long-sleeved black sweater, dark green pants, and a pair of dark boots that might have been the same ones he'd been wearing this morning. The more casual look suited him, with his dark-brown hair a mess on top, but cut shorter on the sides, and I couldn't help but realize how attractive he was. It was sorely tempting to reach out and run my fingers through... I shook my head away from the thoughts that were bubbling up and refocused on the table between us.

"I'm looking forward to some explanations." I picked up a menu from the middle of the table and ignored Espen's quiet chuckle when I realized the entire thing was in Norwegian. Any trace of a smile faltered when I looked over the unfamiliar words. My app of basic Norwegian phrases hadn't prepared me for this, and all the other places I'd been to on my trip so far had their menus in English, or at least photos of the dishes so I knew what I was ordering. Plus, I'd forgotten to buy a fucking phone charger, again, and it was deader than dead. My app couldn't save me, nor could a quick internet search.

"Would you like me to translate?" Espen offered kindly after I'd stared at the menu for entirely too long, hoping magic *was* real, and it would translate itself for me.

I sighed and, because it was the easier and quicker option and I was starving after my shopping adventure, I decided to do the unthinkable. "Can you just order for me?"

Espen nodded politely, his smile not concealing any sort of victory. When the waiter came by for our order a few moments later, Espen muttered something about "*pølselapskaus* and *øl*." The former sounded completely garbled, the latter I knew exactly what I was getting—beer.

When the waiter left, I dared to ask, "What exactly did you just order other than beer?"

"A potato-based stew of sorts with vegetables and sausage. It's served with a snappy flat-bread," he said, before quickly adding, "very tasty. Loved by kids, locals, and tourists."

I snorted and placed my napkin across my thighs. "Thank you for not ordering me something outlandish. The cruise-ship staff already tricked me into trying some gelatinous icky *loo-tee-fisk* that tasted disgusting."

Espen chuckled as the waiter returned with our beers, setting them down and wandering off again. "You mean *lutefisk*. Yes, that is an acquired taste for some, but certainly a lot more palatable when served with bacon."

Now there was something we could agree on. Give me bacon any day of the week, for any meal, and I was a happy camper. I took a sip of my beer and relished in the taste, leaning back in my chair. More chit chat followed, mostly about the village and the weather, and then our food arrived, smelling damn delicious.

"Tell me about yourself," Espen said as he dove into his meal. He really was treating this as a date of sorts, which made me slightly skeptical... but only slightly. I had been the one to ask for more info, and if this was what I needed to do to get it out of him, then so be it.

"What do you wanna know?" I replied, taking a bite of the stew. The hot potatoes, carrots, and what I thought tasted a bit like rutabaga, were perfection and super hearty after a long day. The snappy flat bread—that looked like a large cracker—was also a fantastic vessel for pieces of sausage.

"The usual. Family, friends, hobbies." He gave me a friendly grin between bites of stew, and I couldn't help feeling relaxed around the guy. Maybe he was onto something with that forest yoga he'd mentioned earlier if it made him chill like this.

After swallowing my own mouthful of hot stew and a piece of the cracker-bread, I gave him a quick rundown of my life: Lennie Martin in 5-minutes or less.

"Mom, Dad, three older brothers. Born and raised in the state of Ohio. Twenty-eight years old. I enjoy hiking, photography, and exploring the world. Lived in Boston for three years after college, until it bankrupted me and I moved back to Ohio—Columbus, specifically. Now, I have a desk job that puts food on the table and money in my account for trips like this one." I took another bite of my dinner before adding, "Small group of friends from high school and college who I still hang out with on a regular basis, but most of them are married or have kids. How about you?"

Espen leaned back in his chair, his bowl empty as he'd practically inhaled his meal. He took a sip of his golden beer and said, "Parents died a while ago—old age. Two sisters, both older and live quite a bit further north of here, where we grew up. I see them and their kids a few times a year when I can get away from work. My job, as you know"—I bit my lip at the smirk and teasing look he gave me—"is a police officer. I help the town, but my primary duties lie in the forest. We are a small unit, so I serve as our forest ranger, too."

"Like a yoga-loving park ranger?" I said, and took a final bite of my delicious and filling dinner.

"Yes, I guess you could say that," Espen replied. "I like hiking, foraging for mushrooms, exercise, and yes, yoga." He finished with a wink.

I smiled back at him, still not entirely sure if he was serious about the yoga part or if it was a dirty innuendo, but I was at ease with the conversation. Plus, still curious about the magic stuff and... "How old are you?" He'd failed to mention that so far.

He stared at his drink and shifted minutely in his seat, eyes locked on the tiny bubbles floating up through the liquid. "Thirty-ish."

I leaned back in my chair and took him in. "Oh really?"

He nodded and without looking at me directly, he whispered, "A fae never reveals his age."

I wasn't entirely buying it. He certainly looked like he might be in his thirties, but I had a sneaking suspicion that was far from the truth. Weren't mythical beings supposed to be ancient or something? "Why do I think you're lying to me, Espen?"

A hint of a smile graced his lips, but a feminine voice said, "He's 225."

I turned and found a short woman chuckling as she circled us and pulled up a chair. Espen let out a long sigh as she sat down, resting her forearms on the table.

Mentally, I was trying to process Espen's old age and attempting to match that with the man—creature—who most definitely looked like he was in his mid-thirties, at most. Physically, I was openly staring at the woman who'd joined us. She had a round face, brown hair cut into a bob, rosy cheeks, and eyes the color of a mountain—somehow gray and brown at the same time. If this woman knew Espen's age, then what were the odds she was one of these fae thingies, too?

"Hey, I'm Nora," she said in perfect English.

"Lennie," I replied, giving her a gentle nod.

"Nice to meet you," she added with a small smile before turning to Espen, who was still intently studying his beer. "Why is she not laughing at your age, Espen?"

Espen glanced up, but didn't reply. His dark lashes brushed across his pale cheeks.

"What happened, Espen?" Nora asked, half-stern, half-playful.

The police officer shook his head, and I thoroughly enjoyed watching him squirm a bit. Apparently, I was a problem—which most definitely wasn't a first for me. This magic stuff though, that was new.

"We ran into an incident," Espen said. "And Lennie captured it on camera."

"What?" Nora paled slightly, her eyes widening, but Espen continued, blatantly ignoring her look of panic.

"Looks like another illegal transfer. I'm already looking into it."

She took a deep breath, her chest rising sharply before her eyes darted to me briefly. "We can't have that happening again. You know what happened last time. You know what could happen—"

"I'm well aware of the consequences," Espen practically growled, and Nora's nostrils flared at his sharp words and shift in tone.

"*Og hvorfor har du fortalt et menneske om oss? Er du gal?*" She continued with what sounded like a scathing whisper through her clenched teeth.

"I'm not crazy, Nora. I've had enough of a scolding from my Council, I don't need to hear it from you too."

"*Hvorfor gjorde du det?*" She muttered, leaning back and crossing her arms over her chest.

"I had to make a decision on the spot. She'd seen enough already. The Council may not fully support my actions, and I may have lost some trust with them because of it, but they agreed that the image could not get out into the world."

Nora shook her head and muttered something that sounded vaguely like "Men."

I looked between the two of them, feeling restless. Espen still hadn't explained anything about his magic, and I didn't like being left out of the loop. "Would you two care to explain what's happening? Kinda rude to talk around me like this, don't you think?"

Espen turned to me and bit his bottom lip as he playfully flicked his thick brows upward once. It was a move that screamed challenge accepted. He opened his mouth, but Nora jumped in.

"Not in here," she said rather formally, cutting him off. "Too many humans."

So, she *was* one of them. Clearly there were more of them than just Espen. He'd mentioned a council, so there must be quite a few more than just these two. But why was it okay for them to tell me about the fae and this illegal magic stuff and not the others in here? Was it really only because I'd taken the photo? If that were the case, Espen should've just stolen my damn camera, or even just the memory card. I mean, I'd have hunted him down for it, but if he asked nicely, I probably would've just deleted the picture. He must've had some alternate reason to tell me about them, which, admittedly, made me feel even more curious.

I glanced around the restaurant, noticing it had indeed filled up. Almost all the tables were full; the only vacant seats were the big booths at the very back of the space.

I turned back to the two fae. "When *can* you tell me?" That had been the whole point of this dinner-date, after all. Espen was supposed to explain his magic voodoo stuff. Instead, it had felt like a real-ish date with him trying to get to know me.

"Tomorrow," Espen replied.

Nora shrugged like it was a satisfactory answer.

I still wasn't entirely sure I could trust the guy, or whatever he was planning in that head of his. "When, where, why?"

"That's what I would like to know, too?" A strong voice said, and I glanced up into a pair of blue eyes that raged with the power of a midnight storm.

8
LENNIE

The tall, blond behemoth strode across the room, aiming for our table. Espen straightened in his seat, while I leaned back and took a sip of my beer. It was the rude man from Oddvar's café, wearing a navy jacket, black jeans, and a holier than thou attitude.

He nodded slowly to Nora, almost like a bow, then turned to Espen.

"Espen," he said in greeting, his tone flatter than a pancake.

"Øyvin."

The man gave me the up-down. "American."

"Asshole," I replied with a smarmy smile.

"No, thank you."

"You'd enjoy it." I winked, taking his salacious pivot and rolling with it. I wasn't lying either—I'd had nothing but rave reviews. Øyvin grimaced like he'd never entertain the idea.

Espen spluttered into his beer glass and drew my attention from the beast. "Before you two start a brawl, maybe you could tell me why you're here?" he said to Øyvin.

Nora had remained silent during the entire interaction, but her smirk was visible from the corner of my eye. She reached out her hand and lightly tapped my wrist, sending a sharp sting across the skin there, like I'd swatted a bug zapper. I retracted my arm and brushed my palm across the spot that she'd touched. The prick wasn't painful, but was strong enough to notice. Before I could ask her what the fuck she was playing at, Asshole started talking.

"Balder sent me to speak with you. One of our scouts found markings in the woods—"

"They wouldn't happen to be in the forest on the north side of the fjord?" I asked, interrupting him.

His eyes widened, and Espen turned with a matching look of surprise on his face.

"What?" I quirked a brow in confusion at their expressions.

"He said that in Norwegian," Espen replied, and I suddenly understood their reaction. He spun toward Nora with a glare. "What did you do, Nora?" Nora chuckled once.

I glanced down at my wrist, checking it for any marks. Where she'd shocked me was blank, no scarring, no discoloration, nothing. "You mess with my hearing?" I asked her, blunt but curious as to how I could suddenly understand every word of a language I knew next to nothing of ten minutes ago.

She bit her lip, then said, "Might flicker on and off, but I thought it could be useful."

"Thank you." Now, *this* was magic I could get behind. My Norwegian wasn't even rudimentary, and now I understood everything that was said around me... without anyone else knowing either.

I smirked at the thought. *This'll be fun.*

I'd just have to watch people's lips closely when they spoke so I could discern when someone was actually talking Norwegian and it was being translated by whatever magic tomfoolery this was, or English. Wouldn't do me any good to be responding to people in English when they were speaking to me in Norwegian, especially strangers.

"Oh, and he's 237," Nora whispered with a cheeky grin, subtly pointing toward Øyvin. "We age slowly once we hit eighteen."

My eyes widened, and I tilted my head in manner that said, *thank you for that tidbit.* She nodded back like we were now compatriots, in league against the two males. And I didn't mind that one bit.

Espen slowly shook his head, his dark locks shifting with the movement, and turned back to the broody Asshole. "You were saying?"

Øyvin sighed and restarted his monologue. "Balder's scouts found markings in the forest on the north side of the fjord." He shot a glare at me, and with a quick glance over his shoulder, continued. "It looks like another transfer was made. As it was in your territory, I thought it best to inform you. I wasn't aware you already knew."

"Have you told Halvar?" Espen asked.

"No."

Espen sighed, his shoulders slumping. "You're going to ask me to do it, aren't you?"

Øyvin tilted his head slightly in agreement, a deep frown taking over his face. "Halvar's not a fan."

I scoffed. "I wonder why?"

I got an eye-roll for that quip, but I took another sip of my beer. From the sound of this conversation and Nora's information about his age, it seemed a safe bet to assume Asshole was another one of these fae things. How many of them were around here? We were now up to these three plus a council, scouts, and whatever Nordic names had just been uttered.

Espen turned to Nora, a pleading look in his eyes. "Can you tell Halvar?"

"No, you know I don't get involved in my sister's business," she replied with a shake of her head. "Especially not her Head Guard."

Espen let out a long sigh and rubbed his hands across his short beard. "Fine. I'll head up there tonight," he conceded, settling back into his chair. He turned to Øyvin and added, "You can tell Balder that I'm looking into it and will report it to the Fjell."

Øyvin gave him a brief nod of acceptance, then fell back into his broody asshole-ish state by glaring at me. I gave as good as I got, and glared right back.

"Tomorrow we'll take a closer look, and I'll tell you about our people," Espen said to me. I was about to thank him and ask why on earth I would be needed, when I was interrupted.

"You cannot be serious," Øyvin grumbled.

Espen and I glanced up at the man, while, out of the corner of my eye, I spotted Nora swipe Espen's beer and take a long sip.

"She's seen too much already, and I could do with the help keeping things... classified." Espen's usually friendly demeanor took on a new tone—darker, firmer, like that of a leader who was done messing around.

"Fine," Øyvin said, sounding anything but fine. "Let me know if there are any problems." And, with that, he bowed his head to Nora, again, and left in a huff. I decided, there and then, that Øyvin was a douche-canoe-extraordinaire that needed to chill the fuck out. Or, at least, pull the stick out of his ass.

I turned to Espen, who had just noticed his missing beer and was glaring at Nora as she finished the drink. "So, you need me tomorrow? And will explain everything then?"

He shook his head at the short-haired woman—who grinned at him—and focused on me. "Yes, I will need to photograph the area, and could use your help to..." his voice dropped to a whisper, "keep this out of the office." He gave me the universal look for *wink-wink, nudge-nudge.*

"On one condition," I said, taking some control of the situation and working it to my favor. "If I help you, you need to make sure I get on that boat to get down the fjord and back to Stavanger."

"Deal," Espen said, extending his hand across the table.

I took his palm in mine, the heat of which was comforting, and shook it. I would be his camera-woman and help him keep the investigation away from prying eyes—which likely meant the humans at the police station—and he would help me get the fuck out of here on Sunday.

"Good," I replied before quickly adding, "I still don't understand why someone in town can't just give me a ride down the coast where I might find other transit options."

Espen bit his bottom lip, and Nora let out a loud laugh. "That's because everyone thinks your misfortune is funny," she said. "And no one wants to drive over six hours along the zig-zag roads to help you."

9
ESPEN

The American was a problem and a delight. The former, because she'd somehow photographed fae magic, which in itself should've been impossible. And the latter, because her wily mouth and luscious curves captivated me, and I couldn't tear my eyes away. Fortunately, she was warming to me after our altercation in the woods this morning, and had accepted my dinner invite. Unfortunately, Nora and Øyvin barged in and ruined what was turning into a nice evening.

The tall Fjord Fae did have a point though. The fae in our area were broken into three sections—Fjord Fae who dwelled in the water, Fjell Fae under the mountain, and my own people, the Forest Fae—and, while independent, we watched out for each other when it concerned the potential exposure of our world. All day I'd avoided heading up the mountain to inform the Fjell Fae of the magic transfer, but I couldn't put it off any longer. Queen Freija, her Head Guard Halvar, and their people, needed to know. I owed it to them as part of the Forest Fae's alliance with the Fjell Fae, too.

So, after saying good night to Lennie downtown, I walked up the mountain road and swept into the forest with Nora. Between the light rain and the dark night sky, the trails were free of humans, making it easy for us to stay hidden as we took one of the hundreds of trails that led into the cliffside itself.

"I like her," Nora said, her voice breaking the silence between us and the birch trees standing sentry in this part of the woods.

I agreed. There was a lot to like about our lost tourist. Lennie was fiery, spoke her mind, and could throw a hell of a punch. That hit she got in this morning had taken me by surprise and knocked the wind right out of me. "I like her, too."

"Just make sure she understands the secrecy she needs to keep about everything she sees," Nora said sternly. "You know what will happen if word got out that could harm my sister."

I nodded, fully aware of the subject she was referencing. Halvar, Freija's Head Guard and my counterpart for the Fjell Fae, would likely rip any threat to shreds before burying them in a stony grave. He was old and powerful, and would do anything to protect his Queen. Something I wish I could do, but would never have the chance to after what happened twenty years ago.

Our steps slowed as we reached the hidden cave entrance that led into this part of the mountain. The opening was shielded by a magical veil that appeared as moss and rock, no different than the scenery around it. Magic discouraged humans from approaching it, but if a human happened to try walking through it without the approval of the Fjell Queen, they would be rebuffed—like walking into a wall.

Nora and I slipped inside. The drizzle ended, but the temperature within the cave-like hallway dropped, sending a chill across my cheeks where my beard couldn't protect me.

"This is where I leave you," Nora said, turning left down another hallway. "Good luck," she added over her shoulder as she sauntered deeper into the mountain.

"Thanks," I muttered, knowing full well I'd need all the luck I could get.

The maze of hallways within the mountain was vast and lit by magical lanterns. Torsten, a friend of mine and the partner of Leif, one of my own Forest Fae, was in charge of the lighting within the mountain. Lanterns were mounted on the rocky walls every few meters, casting a warm glow throughout the tunnels. I took a deep breath and admired Torsten's work, the immense effort that went into keeping the lights on in here. He had a sunny disposition, which was probably what had drawn Leif to him in the first place. Both were rays of sunshine, but with one belonging to the Fjell and the other the Forest, it had taken a few decades—and the new alliance—for them to be comfortable living between the two places. Previously, intermingling had been frowned upon, but not outright banned. Yet, it still had made many uneasy in declaring their true feelings for a member of another faction.

I put a hand to my shoulder and transformed my human attire into my formal uniform as I'd done in the forest to show Lennie my magic. The transformation was quick, and my trousers and sweater disappeared, replaced by my gray wool jacket, a short green cape over one shoulder, gray pants, and brown boots that matched the pieces of leather on the ensemble. While I was more comfortable in my more human attire, there was a possibility I'd be seeing the Queen tonight, and I should pay her the respect she deserved by wearing the pesky thing.

Taking a deep breath, I squared my shoulders just as a voice came down the hallway.

"Making a late-night report?" Torsten said, his tawny hair, tied into a bun on his head, and stout form coming into view as he lifted his hand. Within his grasp was a tiny ball of silver light—the magic he used to keep these tunnels' lanterns lit for the Fjell residents. He was in his uniform, on duty, the dark gray-and-black outfit similar to my own.

"Yes. Is Halvar in the throne room?" I asked, following Torsten down the hallway to my right.

"Last I saw him," he nodded beside me.

"And the Queen?" I asked, wondering if Freija was still awake. It wasn't late by any means, but the woman was older than she looked and tended to retire early.

Torsten shrugged, his own cape jostling with the movement. "You'll see for yourself." He veered down another smaller tunnel that was dark. "Good night!"

"Say hello to Leif for me."

Torsten beamed, his eyes crinkling at the corner. "Will do."

I strode deeper into the behemoth mountain that housed over seven-hundred fae and stretched for miles in all directions. A few minutes later, I turned down a crystal lined hallway with silver markings dancing across the dark walls. The heart of the mountain glowed, matching the majesty of the woman who reigned here.

Stepping past two guards and into the throne room, I was greeted by a silver-haired brute. Halvar wore a uniform similar to Torsten's, with an empty sword belt at his hip, and stood before the throne—protecting it, even though it was empty. He was a big fae, a son of the mountain, and had seen more life and death than I ever wanted. With sky-blue eyes and a silvery beard, he looked fit but wisened. No one knew exactly how old he was, but he was a lot older than my 225 years.

"Espen." His voice rumbled across the space as I stopped before him.

"Halvar," I replied with a slight tip of my head. We'd been in an alliance ever since my own Queen of the Forest died, but I always showed this man respect. One, because he deserved it as Head Guard of the Fjell Fae, and, two, because I never wanted to be on the receiving end of his wrath. Rumor had it he fought alongside the Vikings, and that they'd held him in such reverence that stories were told of his might on distant shores for centuries.

"I came to share a report. A situation has occurred that I thought you and Queen Freija should be aware of."

Halvar nodded. "Proceed, and I shall inform the Queen."

I took a deep breath and shared what had happened. From Lennie's unfortunate photograph, to the report from Øyvin, I left nothing out.

"You are running an investigation, too?"

"Off the books," I replied. "I will have Lennie assist with photography so we aren't using anything that belongs to the government or the station." Halvar nodded, and I quickly added. "I'll make sure she doesn't share our existence with anyone else."

"How will you ensure that?" he asked, crossing his arms over his broad chest, signs of the beast beneath peeping through his guarded veneer.

"She wants to leave here. I'll make sure she gets on the next cargo ship on the promise that she never speaks of us or this area ever again. I already plan on talking to Oddvar tomorrow to help coordinate her passage."

Halvar didn't move, his face still in its usual stoic state. "Make sure she does, or the threat to our secret will be removed."

I gaped in surprise, but should have seen this coming. "You've taken up killing humans now?"

His stern gaze didn't waver. "I will do whatever is necessary to secure the safety and wellbeing of the Fjell and its inhabitants," he said, crossing his arms and giving me the sinking feeling that he would, indeed, follow through on his threat.

Unwilling to stay another minute longer, or anger the old-man, I gave him a curt nod and retreated. "Give my regards to the Queen," I said as I exited under the white-and-blue crystalline archway that matched the style of the throne.

Halvar replied with a low grumble.

I left the mountain, changed back into my human attire, and walked home to my little cabin. The whole journey home, I mulled through the investigation and thoughts of the American woman that had landed herself in the middle of it all.

LENNIE

The sky was overcast when I woke up the next morning. I frowned at the cloud cover through the window, thinking through the plans for a hike with a fae to take photos of magic something or other. While I loved hiking and photography, I couldn't say this was my usual itinerary. Given the lack of transportation out of this little town, I didn't have much choice but to take Espen up on his exchange. I needed to get back south so I could get my stuff from the cruise ship—including my passport—and fly home to the US before I lost my job and drained my bank account. I just had to survive the next five days investigating fae magic with a local cop until the cargo ship could hopefully take me back down the fjord.

If my brother's caught wind of this shit, they'd think I was high. Good thing my phone was still dead and they couldn't reach me. Honestly, that thing needed to stay off as much as possible so I didn't rack up an obscene phone bill.

Once I pulled on some of my new clothes, I grabbed my backpack, camera, and reusable water bottle, and made my way downstairs. My bright and kind hostess was at the kitchen-table, drinking her morning coffee when I walked in.

"Good morning, Lennie," Solveig trilled with a warm smile on her face.

"Good morning, Solveig," I replied, finally nailing the pronunciation of her name. Fourteenth time's the charm. She beamed, recognizing the little win.

"Where are you off to today?"

"I'm going on a quick hike with Espen," I said, filling up my water bottle at the sink.

"Ah, he is a good man," she said, and I bit my lip as I tightened the lid on my drink. From the little I gathered last night at dinner, the fae were secretive amongst the humans here. Solveig likely wasn't aware that Espen wasn't a "man"—at least not by her definition. And it wasn't my place to reveal their secret. "He's so nice," she added. "A good tour guide for you."

"Yeah, I hope so." I threw my bottle into my bag and slung it over my shoulders.

"There is a bread-roll with ham and cheese in the fridge if you would like that for breakfast, or I can recommend some options in town?"

Honest to hell, this woman deserved the world for how well she took care of her guests. I mean, feeding me would always win you favor, but Solveig seemed to go above and beyond.

"I'd love the bread-roll to go, thank you."

She pointed to the fridge, and I helped myself.

With a nod and a thank you, I sauntered out of the kitchen to the front door. Slipping my feet into my hiking boots—and holding my breakfast between my teeth while I tied the obnoxious laces—I prepared for departure. I grabbed my coat, secured the camera strap around my neck, and headed out the door to find a magic-wielding police officer that liked to do yoga in his free time.

I finished my breakfast as I walked to our meeting point. The trail-head was a little further down the paved path that Solveig's house backed onto. With the fjord to my left and rounded shrubs to my right, I breathed in the fresh morning air during my pleasant five minute stroll. I'd left the house with what I thought was plenty of time, but knowing my habits, there was a good chance I was already late.

As if to prove my point, I reached the trailhead to find Espen leaning against a large sign in the shape of a log cabin with a moss-covered roof. He was back in his black uniform, the reflective word "Politi" emblazoned on his left breast, pretty damn visible even in the dull light of the day. So visible, you'd think someone might notice it before they decided to punch the wearer. Maybe I needed glasses? Or self-control?

I stepped up beside him. Espen smelled like moss, leather, and pine, blending in with the forest around him. I'd bet he could stand in close proximity to a doe and it wouldn't even know he was there.

"Morning," he said, slowly taking me in from boot, to head, to tip of my ponytail. "You'll be pleased to know that I've spoken to Oddvar, and he has secured your passage on the supply boat on Sunday."

"Thank you," I said, giving him a grateful smile, but immediately thought about my bank account that was turning into nothing but mothballs. "Do I owe him anything?"

Espen shook his head, and I relaxed my shoulders. "Oddvar's son is the captain of the boat. You don't owe him anything."

I breathed a sigh of relief. "Thank you." I didn't know what I'd done to deserve such luck, but I most definitely appreciated it. Shaking my hands toward the device hanging around my neck, I pivoted to today's task. "Well, I've got my camera. You ready?"

"Let's go then," he smiled.

We traipsed into the woods along the rocky dirt path, tall trees rising on all sides, and dewy ferns tapping at our ankles. The smell of moss and pine drifted around me, and the crunching of our footfalls was the only sound aside from the light chirping of birds somewhere in the distance. The landscape was so different from that in Ohio, steeper for one, but also teeming with luscious greenery that I couldn't help but fall in love with.

The trail zig-zagged upward and narrowed the higher we hiked. We were on the north side of the fjord, the deep inlet just visible between the trees and foliage, its waters glistening in the soft morning light. Espen kept pace beside me, stepping back to let me go in front of him when the path got too small for us to walk side-by-side.

After about ten minutes of peaceful silence, I decided it was time for Espen to start filling me in on the details he was supposed to share at dinner last night.

"So, start explaining what you are and this whole magic business."

"Only if you promise to never speak of it to any human... ever," he said with a stern look in his eyes. "Because if you do, I myself won't kill you, but others likely will."

A shudder ran through me and I nodded. "Deal." Then I waved my hand at Espen, requesting that he answer my initial request, doing my best to ignore the second-hand death threat I'd just received.

"First of all, we've already established that magic is not bullshit."

"Debatable," I scoffed, as he settled in beside me, slowing his pace so we could chat more easily.

He bit his lip playfully before he said, "Second of all, there is a bit of history to unpack."

"I like history." I shrugged. Sure, I'd almost failed my American History class in high school, but I wouldn't mind a story. As long as it detailed what the hell this guy was. "Go on."

Espen took in a big breath, hesitating, and I wondered how much trouble he'd get in for disclosing information about the fae. But he began his tale about them and their magic as we trudged deeper into the verdant forest.

"The fae have lived in Norway for centuries. We are wardens of the natural resources, protecting them from harm, and, in turn, receiving power from them."

"Like a magical ecosystem?"

"Exactly. Our magic is given to us from earth, and we use it to help life flourish."

"So, you're like an elf?" I looked over at him, taking in his rakish hair, thick brows, and solid physique that screamed I-like-the-outdoors. "Do you have pointy ears?" I asked unabashedly. Which was probably rude, but to hell with it. I wanted to know and right now I was picturing—

Espen placed his hand to his left earlobe and a short point appeared. The tips of his ears were indeed sharper than those of humans.

My eyes felt like they were going to pop out of my head and roll down the hill into the fjord as I blatantly stared. "How does that work?"

"Think of it as layers. Most fae have the ability to shift their attire by manipulating a layer of magic over their clothes. The same applies to our ears, but only our ears—like magical evolution to keep our species hidden from threats. This base-level ability is drawn from the air, and can be used by all of us. Some of us, however, are a little stronger and can manipulate more layers. Nora is one such fae. She can manipulate the layer of not only appearance, but some sounds and light."

That would explain how she altered my hearing so I could understand snippets of Norwegian.

"But her sister, Queen Freija, is much stronger in that regard. Each fae faction has their own abilities, too. Forest Fae, like myself, can use magic to help the trees and animals thrive." He stopped walking and I pulled to a halt. Crouching down, he placed his palm against the mossy soil beside the trail. A minuscule flicker of silver light glowed from beneath his hand and he lifted it away. A few seconds later, a tiny speck of green breached the surface—the start of a new plant. My breath caught in my throat, and Espen watched my face closely. I glanced into his eyes, the amber warmth calming and caring. "It will become a skinny birch tree one day."

"That's... amazing," I admitted, in awe of what I'd just witnessed. This wasn't bullshit. Not at all. "What about the others—Øyvin and Nora? Can they do that, too?" I asked, still watching the tiny sapling as it shook off the remaining soil holding it captive.

"Not really," Espen said as he started walking once more. "Each faction has a specialty. Fjell Fae—like Nora—have magic that is rooted in the ground and mountain. Fjell means mountain in Norwegian. And then there are the Fjord Fae, like Øyvin. Their element is water. They can manipulate the element, move it around, breathe underwater, but their primary objective is to keep the fjord clean for the wildlife here."

I took it all in. Shocked and amazed at the magical world that existed beside the one I knew and loved. Plus, their ability to protect nature spoke to a part of my soul that loved every iota of the environment—my photography muse. "What about the stuff I caught on camera?"

"The silver flare you saw is our magic made visible. You can see flickers of it from time to time, but during a transfer there is no way to hide the power."

"Why would someone transfer their power to another?" I asked, stepping over a mossy log that had fallen across the path.

"It's a good question," he replied, pressing on through the dense woods. "One we asked ourselves twenty years ago when it first happened. But the best theories are to harm the Queen of the Fjell or the King of the Fjord. The royals' magic is intertwined with the wellbeing of the entity and fae they protect, so by attacking said entity, it would be slightly easier to overthrow a monarch.

"Last time," He paused, his head down. "Last time things didn't end well. Forest Queen Ragnhild was weakened by illegal transfers and then killed in battle by a southern faction of the Forest Fae—relatives of ours from the southern coast of Norway. The uprising was unusual, but not unheard of, in our history. What *was* alarming was the speed with which they attacked and how easily she was killed. It was as if someone had drained her and her forces before the war began. Both Queen Ragnhild and my mentor, Mads, died in the battle that also took out two hundred Forest Fae."

Espen's shoulders had slumped, his steps faltering slightly, as he spoke. The weight of what happened had clearly taken a toll on him. Inhaling a gulp of damp air, I said, "I'm sorry for your loss."

He nodded, his eyes somewhat distant as he waved his hand, dismissing my words.

"Did the Forest Fae catch whoever was behind the uprising?" I asked gently, curious but cautious of the subject matter. War was never a palatable subject, but the information might be helpful to this investigation.

Espen stepped out into a tiny clearing off the side of the trail and I followed, brushing aside some pine tree limbs.

"We didn't." He traipsed across the open space covered in mossy boulders and clusters of tall grass then paused. The sun seeped into this slanted spot, giving us a slight view of the fjord and the mountain on the other side—where I'd taken the troublesome photo.

"What happened afterward?" I rested my butt on a rock and watched him gaze into the treeline behind us.

"I brought the living back home, and, with the guidance of some Forest Fae elders—the Council—our faction formed an alliance with Queen Freija and the Fjell Fae."

I swallowed the lump in my throat at his insinuation, and my chest tightened. He'd been there. He'd witnessed the slaughter of 200 of his people, the death of his Queen and mentor. Fucking hell.

"Is she the Queen of the Forest now, then?"

He shook his head. "We aligned with the Fjell for greater protection from this happening again, and as thanks for the assistance they provided after the battle. You could say we have a close friendship instead of assimilating our two factions. We coexist harmoniously."

"What about leadership? Was your Queen... Ragnhild... replaced?" This had to be the most attentive I'd ever been during a history lesson, but I couldn't stop—I wanted to know more. I was intrigued by their powers, leadership system, and how they'd resided within human society without being exposed.

"No," he said firmly, turning his warm gaze to me. "There is no ruler. We have the Council and my people placed their trust in me to be a representative and protector for them. Mads, the previous Head Guard of the Forest Fae, was training me as his successor. The role was handed to me upon his death," Espen explained, a hint of melancholy in his tone.

He shook his head, then his arms, as if shaking away the weight on his shoulders alongside the heavy memories. "Enough of that. What is your favorite yoga pose?"

The whiplash again. But Espen smiled like it was his usual tactic to throw people off or pivot the subject to a happier one. He kept bringing up yoga though, so maybe he was serious about doing it in his free time... or perhaps he was obsessed with a different kind of *yoga*. Either way, I chuckled and thought through the poses I knew from watching videos online. I wasn't overly flexible, but there was always one position that I enjoyed more than the others. "Corpse."

Espen snickered and licked his bottom lip.

"What about you?" I asked, tearing my eyes from his mouth.

He took a step back and lifted one foot, resting it against his other thigh. Then he brought his hands to his chest in a perfect prayer position. "Tree pose." He beamed.

I let out another bubble of laughter, the mood around us officially lifted. "Should have guessed. You're a tree hugger aren't you?"

"I am," he admitted with a smile, still holding his balance, not even swaying slightly. "You should try it. Really good for the complexion."

"Tree pose or hugging trees?"

"Both."

"How is hugging a plant good for my skin?" I stood from the boulder.

He pointed to a thick pine tree and raised his brows.

I sighed and conceded to his madness. Rolling my eyes, I wandered over to the large tree and wrapped my arms around its trunk. The bark was rough beneath my cheek and it smelled earthy and damp.

"See? Doesn't that make you feel good?" he said, not moving an inch.

"Sure, but what the fuck is it supposed to do for my wrinkles and adult acne?" It should be illegal to have *both* acne and wrinkles simultaneously. If hugging this thing would rid me of those suckers, I'd sleep out here. I pulled away from the tree, glanced at its rough outer layer, and stopped breathing for a second.

Silver.

Silver marks, like knife slashes, were etched into the thick brown bark.

"Espen, this is the spot I photographed, isn't it?"

"Should be, yes."

"Look at this."

He appeared behind me. Reaching over my shoulder, he ran his hand over the markings. "Shit."

11
LENNIE

Espen's warm breath tickled against my ear as he pulled his hand away from the tree. Waves of tension rolled off him, and the change in his easy-going personality was jarring. I didn't dare move. Standing at my back, he scanned the tree trunk's silver scars. The marks were thin—practically invisible at a distance—but deep. At this vantage point you could easily see them criss-crossing the thick bark.

I glanced over my shoulder, lifting my eyes to Espen's face. Gone was the playful yogi I'd come to know. That bubbly man had been replaced with the warrior from today's history lesson—one who had seen far more death than I could comprehend. His thick eyebrows were drawn into a firm line, jaw clenched.

"How bad is it?" I whispered into the few inches between our bodies, the warmth from his chest shielding me slightly from the damp air around us.

His darkened eyes met mine. "As bad as it was twenty years ago."

My stomach muscles tightened and I swallowed the lump that had formed in my throat.

"Can you take a photo of this, please?" Espen asked softly, taking a step back into the clearing.

With a nod, I removed the lens cap from my camera, slipping it into my jacket pocket so I wouldn't lose it again. I started snapping away, making sure I got some wide shots, and turned on the macro function for more detailed close-ups.

While I documented the evidence on the tree, Espen scanned the other flora in the clearing—checking for more scars.

"Over here," he said, crouched down beside a boulder and a tree on the other side of the open space. Beside the gray rock was a bolt of ferns he held to one side to reveal his findings. Across the base of this withering tree were more tiny silver scratches. I took some more photos, making sure to get a couple from different angles, in hopes that it might help Espen's investigation.

"Can you heal them?" I asked, nodding at the marks.

Espen tilted his head from one side and then the other, like he was uncertain. He brushed his palm over one of the lines. My heart rate sped up, hopeful to see his magic work wonders again. I watched closely as a faint glow emitted from his hand, then petered out. Espen pulled away and rose to his feet with a sigh, and my shoulders fell as air whooshed out of me. The sliver he tried to heal had puckered, like it wanted to close up, but couldn't quite do it.

He shook his head lightly as he stared at the marks. "If it needs more energy than that, then I'm afraid the marks are permanent... again."

I stilled, my breaths an even tempo as I took in what he was saying. History was repeating itself, and someone—or some*thing*—was out there in the woods harming the land and attempting to harm the fae. Just the thought had my veins humming with anger.

"These scars are a result of the immense amount of magic that was illegally transferred from one fae to another," Espen explained, wiping his hand across his short beard. "That flare in your photo was basically an explosion of magic that left marks on things around it." He pointed back to the injured tree.

"What can you do?"

"Catch them before—" He spun, amber eyes darkening as his gaze swept over the clearing.

A bush rustled to my left, and a flurry of nervous energy took over my body as I turned toward the sound. I dropped my camera, letting it hang around my neck, so I could free my hands.

Espen stepped toward the noise.

Another rustle sounded from behind me, and I spun, putting my feet into a ready-position like I was about to tackle one of my brothers in a full-blown wrestling match in the living room. As the only girl in a family of football players, I had my fair share of practice.

"You found them, then," a low voice rumbled as someone stepped out from the shadows in front of me.

The someone was the shape of a behemoth Asshole.

"What the fuck are you playing at?" I grumbled at Øyvin as I dropped my fisted hands back down to my side, adrenaline still pumping into my veins. He gave me a minute smile that most certainly wasn't friendly. Nah, that shit was definitely an "I don't care" half-grin I'd seen my brothers' ex-girlfriends give me when I was a kid and trying to get the boys' attention. It was belittling and dismissive, and I despised it. Those feelings were pretty damn accurate for this guy, too.

He wore his large navy rain jacket, cargo pants, and big hiking boots that looked like they could cause severe damage to the terrain.

Espen leaned against the large boulder again as Øyvin stepped into the light of the clearing, leaving me near the shadows. "You're brave for sneaking up on her like that."

Øyvin scoffed. "Why?"

"Lennie punches first, asks questions later. And she can throw a hell of a punch."

Øyvin leered at me. I gave him my best "fuck you" smile—the same one I'd given the ladies at church before my Mom decided I should stay at home on Sunday mornings. "Espen learned first hand."

He glanced over at Espen, who was beaming from ear to ear.

"She hit you?" Øyvin raised a brow before returning his icy glare to me. "You should lock her up for that."

"I considered it," Espen replied. "But I couldn't have her spouting about silver shiny things in the woods, now could I? Figured I'd keep an eye on her myself, have her help with the investigation."

And for that I was grateful as I wasn't excited to see the inside of a Norwegian prison.

"What are you doing up here anyway?" I asked Øyvin, my sass level as high as a fucking eagle on the hunt. I pulled the lens cap out of my pocket and clicked it back into place on the camera.

"I came to see the marks for myself," Øyvin said matter-of-factly. "I wanted to see if our scouts' report was true."

"It was," Espen said with a hint of gloom. I kind of missed the happy-go-lucky version of him. Not that there was anything wrong with this Espen, but, for some reason, I liked his smile and bubbly attitude.

Espen nodded at the tree behind me and then to the one I'd hugged on the other side of the clearing. "Someone stood there and the other stood there," he said. "There are some other marks, but the largest clusters are at those two points."

"Do you have any idea who would do something like this?" I asked, aiming my question at the blond-haired jerk.

Øyvin's blue eyes snapped to mine, and I felt an onslaught of animosity and annoyance from his gaze. The feeling was mutual.

He raised his large hands and said, "It wasn't me or my men."

My men? Was this dick the King of the Fjord?

"Does King Balder know how bad it is?" Espen asked, and I was relieved that this Øyvin-schmuck wasn't fae royalty.

Øyvin shook his head, his short sandy hair barely shifting with the movement. "Balder sent me to confirm the findings from our scouts. I'll make my official report today. He knows I'm here to have a look." He strode across to the tree I'd hugged and grazed his large knuckles across the lacerated bark.

Espen and I watched him closely as he surveyed the damage there, poking and prodding at the scars. Øyvin then backtracked to where I was standing, passing me as if I didn't exist, and scanned the other marks. He said nothing while conducting his own research of the evidence. After five minutes of pure silence, Øyvin let out a low grumble and ran his hand through his hair.

"I thought the same," Espen said, as Øyvin moved to stand between us, his back toward me.

"Care to enlighten the human?" I said, feeling slightly weirded out by using the word "human." Sure, it was accurate, but it still felt odd talking to these creatures that also looked human, but were very much *not*.

I couldn't see Øyvin's response to my snarkiness, but knowing what little I did about the asshole, it was probably an eye roll or a grunt.

Espen, on the other hand, gave me a brief smile, as if he were happy to have me there, but not so happy about the information he was about to share. "The amount of fae magic that was transferred was enough to cause lasting damage to the surroundings and the perpetrators," he said, reminding me of the fact that he couldn't heal these scars. "It was a big transfer that is likely trying to weaken one or both of the remaining fae royalty—or my own people, again—by taking magic that is meant for healing our environment. Think of it as a break in the ecosystem."

I nodded, recalling the magic process he'd mentioned earlier—how the fae were wardens of the natural resources.

"The illegal transfer is one or more fae cycling power *away* from where it is supposed to go—the forest, mountain, or fjord—and funneling their magic elsewhere instead, thus weakening its intended environment."

"Can you tell who did it from these marks, or maybe from the photos?" I pointed at my camera.

"Maybe." Espen shrugged. "I can't be certain until I see the photos and can zoom in."

Øyvin straightened and strode to the trail at the south end of the little clearing. "Our source of magic is the same. It's our abilities and how we use the magic that makes us different."

Espen nodded, confirming Øyvin's statement. "We should go see if there is anything else on those photos. It might tell us more about the culprit."

"Okay," I agreed, equally curious as to what we would find when I uploaded the images to my computer.

"Perhaps we can grab your laptop or cables and head to my house to look at them. That way we can keep Solveig out of this. I can make us lunch, too." Espen stood from the boulder and motioned toward the trail head.

I nodded, never one to turn down a free meal.

"I'm heading back to the fjord," Øyvin grumbled, already striding back into the woods.

"Give my regards to the King," Espen said, as the Fjord Fae trudged off through the trees, leaving us to our work.

12

ØYVIN

The American was a problem and infuriating. The former, because she'd been exposed to our world, even before Espen had dragged her into it head-first. And the latter, because of her fucking attitude. I didn't like it.

Irritation fueled me as I walked away from where I'd left her with Espen, reaching the edge of the fjord at a point where it bent out of sight of the town. The thick brush here along the shore hid me from any onlookers and was an ideal entrance point to the Fjord Fae domain beneath the surface. I stepped into the cold, my boots sloshing into the slate-blue waters. Once I was waist-deep, I pushed off from the bank and dove under. The fjord enveloped me in her chilly embrace, the cool temperature having no effect on me thanks to my being a Fjord Fae, and my muscles finally relaxed after my run-in with Espen and Lennie.

Instantly, my senses changed. Gone were the sights, smells, and sounds of the human world above. Instead, the fjord sang her song to me—a quiet melody of swishes and movement from the creatures that called it home. The area closest to the surface was clear, tiny fish the size of sardines scuttling behind rocks as I passed, but the deeper I went, the darker and murkier the water became.

I pushed the water around me with a gentle nudge of my power, having already created a thin layer of air that would keep me dry. Descending deeper into the profound abyss, the sun no-longer reaching these dark depths, I swept my hands forward and then back, helping me reach my destination quicker than merely propelling myself with power. While I could swim like humans did, using my Fjord Fae powers in tandem with the usual swimming motions tripled my speed—pushing me on faster than any land-dwelling creature.

After a few minutes, a litany of cave entrances came into view. Wholly invisible to the human eye or any fishing sonar—thanks to a layer of magic from King Balder—the subterranean pockets were the entrances of homes and the royal household. Not all of the Fjord Fae lived underwater here—some made homes out in the open under bubbles of air made to look like rocks on the fjord bed and some lived above the surface, like me—but most lived in the rocks along the jagged edges of the deep water, where the mountain above met the watery valley below.

Silvery lights flickered near the entrances to the caves, and I aimed for the largest one which had rugged carvings of aquatic figures and animals above the archway. A carving of a scaled serpent curled around the entry with fish of all shapes and sizes dancing around it, desperately avoiding its sharp maw. The entire artistic display was a show of power fit for royalty. Balder and his ancestors had lived here for centuries. It always left me in awe of how this home—a veritable palace—could survive not only the pressure of the fjord, but the weight of the mountain above it.

I brushed my hands across the top of the entry and swung my legs into the pocket of air as I'd done so many times before. The motion sent me flying inward, and I landed on my feet, thumping onto the dry ground within the hall. The soldiers guarding the entrance nodded to me in greeting, standing straighter in their gray and navy-blue uniforms, their short capes draped from one shoulder. I was their boss's boss, and had been for the past century. I expected the utmost respect from my men, and always got it. In turn, I respected and would always thank them for their willingness to serve their King and fellow Fjord Fae. We rarely saw battle anymore, but the threat of instability always lingered.

I shook off the droplets of water that seeped into my pants when I first submerged, and strode into the King's home, completely dried off.

People bustled past, each one busy with their work for the day as I wove deeper into Balder's domain. The hallways down here were similar to the tunnels in the mountains above in Fjell Fae territory, but where they had rocky walls, ours were polished smooth. Specks of white quartz shimmered within the mottled stone walls, and rugged wooden artwork, from eels hiding in reeds to salmon jumping, decorated the space. A minute later, I reached my destination—the king's chambers. I strode into the wing that housed the throne room, Balder's offices, a meeting room, and my own office when I wanted to get some work done down here. I'd decided long ago that I preferred living above the water. It wasn't so much that I didn't like living beneath the surface—I did, it was homey—but I liked having the separation between where I lived and worked.

I found Balder in his study sitting behind his large wooden desk that looked like something he'd plundered from an old ship, like a lot of the furniture did here in our underwater world. The king leaned forward in his chair, reviewing some charts and had an antique atlas open on his desk, not bothering to look up when I entered.

I stood just inside the doorway, waiting for his cue to speak. Balder was one of the oldest fae of the entire fjord region, but you'd never know it from the way he looked or moved. With a thick scraggly blond-and-silver beard, eyes the color of algae, sharp features, and the countenance and build of a warrior, Balder was a fae that shouldn't be crossed.

Still studying the charts in front of him, Balder said, "Did you see the marks for yourself?" His voice had a low rumbling timbre that could set off waves.

"Yes, sir," I replied as he looked up and pushed aside the papers he'd been examining. "And it is as we suspected. There was indeed an illegal transfer from one fae to another. The scars on the trees were thin, but deep. Looked like Espen or some other Forest Fae had tried to heal one of them. The line had puckered, but didn't close."

Balder twitched his nose. "That is concerning."

I nodded in agreement. If the Forest Fae couldn't heal the trees, then no one could. "I haven't received any reports from my men of weakened shields or power failures in our territory."

"That's good," Balder sighed, leaning back in his chair with his hands steepled in front of him. "We can't let the pollution wall down. We can't allow the humans to find us down here. Let them think any blips on their radar are their beloved creatures from folktales and myth."

I nodded again. Humans had a tendency to explain the unexplainable with tales of beings that would haunt their dreams. From the creepy Nøkken that would lure you into bodies of fresh-water, to the trolls that dwelled within the dense woods that would eat wayward children who couldn't answer a complicated riddle. While slightly inaccurate, these stories helped us stay hidden.

Taking a deep breath, I steadied my resolve to ask my next question. I doubted it would see my head severed, but Balder had moods, and my predecessor had found an unsavory one the day I was appointed Head Guard. "Have you felt any weakening of your powers?"

Balder sucked on his teeth and glanced around the room full of bookcases and trinkets, even a chessboard abandoned mid-game. "No, I haven't noticed anything. But, I'm forever battling the tainted sources in the waterways to our west. Those humans and their oil," he grumbled.

At the far entrance to the fjord, kilometers upon kilometers away from Skolvik, where the ocean met the country, the humans had shredded the shore-line, replacing the pristine land with equipment, refineries, and factories for their oil. Much of the inky-liquid was brought in from the oil rigs in the North Atlantic, but there were often little spills and the human element caused immense damage to the waterways. It was a never ending fight for us to keep the waters running clean, and stop the pollution from flowing further down the fjord. We'd even erected a magical wall beneath the surface to buffet any pollutants and keep the inner fjord untainted.

"Glad to hear that you are okay, but please let me know if you want me to increase our efforts on the wall to keep the pollution at bay. While none of us are as strong as you, we can pair some of our soldiers up. I will not have you weakened with this transfer business happening."

Balder nodded, his eyes slightly distant, as he considered my suggestion. As the most powerful of the Fjord Fae, he used layers of his magic every day in an effort to keep the pollution out of our waters. Paired with the power from the Fjord soldiers stationed along the western front, and we were almost insurmountable to pollutants, but if we could ease some of the load on our monarch, then I'd gladly move some soldiers around.

"Do it," he said eventually. "If this transfer nonsense escalates, I don't want to find myself unable to protect my people."

"Yes, sir." I gave him a curt nod and made for the exit but stopped as he spoke again.

"And Øyvin." He stood from his chair, his large form towering over the furniture. The fact that he fit into dwellings down here was astonishing—the humans wouldn't be wrong for thinking he was one of their myths if they ever saw him wandering the streets. He rarely left the fjord though. "Let me know about any new developments with the transfer business."

"Of course," I replied and strode from the room, ready to inform my soldiers of their new positions.

13
LENNIE

On our way back to the village, Espen and I stopped at Solveig's house to pick up my laptop and camera cable so we could go over the photos I'd taken of the magical scars on the trees. Then, with the promise of lunch hanging over my head, we wandered back through town toward Espen's house. We passed Oddvar's café, which was bustling with customers, a boutique with silver nordic jewelry in the window, and started to climb a trail that meandered up the hill on the southern side of the fjord.

"There's no road to your house?" I asked, half-jokingly while taking in our surroundings—a copse of pines, curling ferns, and not a hint of gravel or asphalt.

"No," Espen replied from beside me. "I live in a cabin. No roads in or out up here. Just me, nature, and the local wildlife."

I was about to ask him more about the type of animals that lived around here, when we cleared the treeline and our destination came into view. I couldn't contain the gasp that escaped me.

Nestled beside three slim birch trees in a small meadow was a modest log cabin made of dark timber. Its roof was covered in grass, a little chimney jutted up at the back, and tiny square windows looked out over the area. The entire scene was straight out of a fairy tale.

"Yeah, okay, I get the no roads thing," I said as we wandered up the well-trodden path to the front door. I could feel Espen's sense of peace beside me, and that, or the fresh air, had my shoulders and muscles relaxing, too. I wouldn't want anyone to find me up here either.

As he unlocked the door, I turned toward the fjord and gawked at the view from up here. It hadn't felt like we'd climbed that high as we'd hiked away from town, but what I saw took my breath away.

Espen's home offered a clear view of the village and fjord, the water glittering in the dull gray light. You could almost see the entire valley from up here. Even though I'd seen views from my hikes, every time I took in the beauty of my surroundings here I could hardly breathe.

"I know," Espen whispered behind me. "It's beautiful."

I nodded, at a complete loss for words, my fingers itching to photograph the stunning vista. Pictures could never do this view justice, though. It was stunning.

"You hungry?"

I nodded again, drawn by the lure of lunch, and followed him inside.

Espen's home smelled like the forest had taken up roots indoors, and I kind of liked it. Inside the cabin was a small sofa with knitted throw pillows, a tiny wooden dining table with two chairs, and a compact kitchen with shelves full of mugs, plates, and spices. Beside the kitchen was a short hallway that looked like it led back to a bedroom and bathroom.

We both unlaced our boots by the front door and pulled them off, setting them on a floor tray to avoid tracking in too much dirt. I shucked off my jacket and hung it beside Espen's on a hook on the wall.

Espen made for the kitchen as I flung my backpack off and set it on the sofa. I retrieved my laptop and cable to the sound of clattering noises. Glancing over to the kitchen, I watched with curiosity as Espen pulled out a pot while holding a can of something. I shook my head and set my gear up at the table, putting aside a small potted fern to make room for my stuff.

"Tomato soup?" Espen asked, holding the red-labeled can in one hand and a ladle in the other.

"Yes, please," I grinned.

"Great," he said, setting to work. "Do you like egg in your soup?"

I leaned back in the dining chair and blinked a few times. "Can't say I've ever had egg in my soup." Pho? Sure. Tomato soup? No.

"It's hardboiled," Espen said, dumping the can contents into the pot on the stove. He opened the short refrigerator beneath the counter and retrieved a bowl of brown and white eggs. "I make them ahead of time. Easy snack or I have them in my breakfast sandwiches." He held one up and cast an inquisitive look at me, one brow cocked.

"Ummm, yes, thank you." A sexy man was cooking for me. So, yeah, I'd try whatever he wanted to feed me.

While Espen prepared our lunch, I tightened my ponytail and started transferring today's photos off my camera. As they loaded, I decided to grab the silver flare photo, too, just in case he wanted that for evidence as well.

Espen brought over our meal and included some whole-wheat bread beside the bowl of soup. The hardboiled egg had been sliced, and the yellow-and-white discs floated on the surface. My stomach grumbled at the sight as I pushed aside the laptop—which was still downloading the files—and we dug in.

We ate our lunch in relative silence, hunger getting the best of both of us. While the sight of the egg bobbing in the soup was strange, I couldn't deny the egg-in-soup thing was delicious and perfect after a morning hike.

Once finished, Espen grabbed our bowls, plonked them into the sink, and returned to the table. He pulled his chair around and sat beside me, our knees touching ever so slightly. My breathing hitched at the small contact, and a teasing warmth rose from my chest up my neck, likely tinting my cheeks rosy.

"So, what do we have?" he asked with a slight twinkle in his eyes.

"Not a lot." I shrugged, shaking off the tingling sensation in my hands as I pulled up one of the macro-shots of the silver scars we'd found on the trees today. This zoomed in, the thin, but deep, lines etched across the bark were painful to look at.

One image after another revealed the detailed view of the damage. If I hadn't known about the fae and their magic, I would've thought some animal had come through and marked their territory, but after inspecting the photos, I could tell this was much more sinister. The scar that Espen had tried to heal had puckered, and the bark around it—as well as the other scars—was a withered gray. This tree was dying. The surrounding landscape seemed unharmed though—the ferns and brush were lush and green in comparison.

Any lightness that had exuded from Espen before now faded away as we reviewed each image. My eyes danced back and forth between the images on the screen and Espen sitting at my side, seemingly making mental notes based on his narrowed eyes and the fact he kept biting his bottom lip.

"This is not the norm," he said absentmindedly, his gaze never wavering from the screen.

I reached the last one and was about to ask him if he had any ideas on who might be behind the illegal magic transfer, when a pop sounded behind me and my ponytail fell, my blonde hair brushing across my shoulders. *For fuck's sake.*

Letting out a slow sigh, I reached down and found the broken hair-tie. The elastic had given up completely, and even if I tried tying it in a knot, there was no chance this thing would ever hold my thick-ass locks again.

"Here, let me take that," Espen said, plucking the detritus from between my fingertips. He stood and sauntered into the kitchen, tossing the broken elastic into the garbage. Opening a drawer, he retrieved a ball of cooking rope and a pair of scissors. With a quick glance over his shoulders, he measured out a few lengths of the string, cut it, and returned to the table. "May I?" he asked, standing behind me.

"Sure." Fuck yeah he could play with my hair. That shit was bliss on steroids. I always accepted whenever my nieces wanted to play hair stylist, even after they'd tried to give me bangs a couple of years ago.

Espen gathered my strands into his palms, lightly brushing his fingers across the base of my neck. I held it together and refrained from quivering at his touch, but it was difficult. The way he swept his hands across my hair, gently tugging it all into a bundle, sent little feverish sparks across my skin and I curled my toes.

"I don't think it's someone within the Forest Fae faction," Espen said, drawing me out of my slight arousal.

"Because?"

He fastened the rope around the low ponytail he'd created, the material pulling softly as he looped it into a small bow. Sitting back down, he added, "We wouldn't voluntarily harm the forest like this. I suppose a Forest Fae could've been forced to do so against their will, but... I don't know. There's also a chance that someone, an outsider, an old rival from the Southern or Northern factions may be trying to infiltrate. They'd be foolish to do so, but...." He let out a long sigh, resting his elbow on the table, looking at me with a half-distant gaze.

"Well, at least we've narrowed it down somewhat."

He chuckled, the sound warm and inviting. "Are you always this positive?"

I let out a single laugh. "Fuck no. But it seemed like your usual rays of sunshine had dimmed, so I thought I'd be kind for a moment. Don't expect this to be my norm." I gave him my best smile, and got one in return.

"We don't always have a lot of sunshine around here—it's gray for a large portion of the year—but when we do, it's spectacular." He smiled, but the look didn't reach his eyes, and I wanted to reach across the small space between us to hug him, but I held back. "I try my best to be positive, for myself, for the Forest Fae, for the fjord." He glanced toward the window, and a heaviness settled over his features.

In that moment I saw the leader side of Espen. The one who watched over everything like an eagle in flight, as if he alone was the one to bear the burden. And I guess, in a way, he was. From what he'd told me, I knew he'd been elected defacto leader in his Head Guard role for the Forest Fae after his queen and mentor were both killed in the last war they fought—the last time an illegal transfer like this had gone down.

"You'll figure it out," I said reassuringly. "Do you need these photos transferred to your laptop?"

He shook his head, defeat sagging his shoulders. "Please take care of them for now. I'll let you know if I need to look at them again. Thank you for your help."

I nodded and closed my laptop. "Thank you for telling me about the fae and for helping me catch that ship out of here in five days."

He smiled again and dipped his head, his luscious brown locks falling across his forehead before he swept them back. I twisted my fingers in my lap at the sight.

"You like hiking, yes?" he said, randomly pivoting the subject—which seemed to be a habit of his.

"Yes," I replied, dragging out the vowel.

"Do you want to go hiking with me tomorrow? It's my day off," Espen said as he brushed his fingers across the wood table, removing some invisible lint.

"Sure." It wasn't like I had anything else going on while I waited for the supply boat, and hiking for photography had been the initial plan for this trip all along. "Where should I meet you?"

14

LENNIE

"Coffee? Right before a hike?" I asked Espen as I met up with him outside Oddvar's café, pulling my jacket tighter to shield from the morning chill.

"There's *always* time for coffee," Espen replied with a grin, and my heart skipped a beat, because that was *the* answer—the only statement one should ever mention in regards to a cup o' joe. He handed me a reusable mug, and I took it, welcoming the warmth on my hands in the chill of the morning.

I was glad I'd bought a few new outfits as I looked down at my new pants and dark-blue quarter-zip sweater, plus my rain jacket. Espen wore a pair of dark cargo pants and a dark green jacket that made his eyes pop.

"Is this black?" I asked, recalling the way Oddvar had served it to me before I dared to take a sip of the hot beverage. It also gave me an excuse to look away from the comforting heat in Espen's gaze.

He chuckled. "No, I added a bit of milk and sugar."

"Thank you," I replied, and tested a sip. It was perfect—just the right amount of sweet and roasted caffeinated nectar. "Where are we off to then?"

"I thought we'd head up behind the village into the woods. There are some nice spots that would be perfect for photos." He nodded at my camera hanging around my neck.

I smiled, waving him forward as I took another sip, thankful for the coffee and the company.

We traipsed through the village, headed past little white houses made of wood with slate tile roofs I hadn't seen before, and followed a road with no markings save for a speed limit sign with the number 40 on it. A few minutes outside town, a trail entrance appeared between some bushes, and Espen pointed to it. I wandered toward the path, lost in my thoughts about the Forest Fae.

Espen was a conundrum. Fae, yogi, and magic stuff aside, he always made a point of walking beside me or fell behind, never in front.

He *never* led.

I'd never experienced anything like it with any other guy I'd hung out with before. It was as if he always wanted to be at my side, watching my reaction to the countryside from the corner of his eye. Honest to hell, I didn't mind it. It made me feel like an equal, even if I didn't have magical powers like him.

The trail was wide enough for two, but significantly rocky and gave my thighs a good work out as we climbed higher into the Norwegian forest. The smell of pine, earth, and morning dew wrapped me into a state of awe and comfort. The trees in this part of the forest were covered in a thick layer of moss, but only on one side—the bark on the other side strained to reach the few rays of sunlight that poked through the clouds ever so often.

As the terrain got steeper, I drained the last of my coffee, wanting my hands free in case I fell. Espen took my cup and placed it inside his own before stuffing them into the pouch on the side of his backpack that was vacant.

"You like it here?" Espen asked, filling the serene silence that had fallen between us.

I laughed softly. "I mean... it's not the worst place to get stuck." I waved my hand at the thick forest around us, mesmerized by the majesty of this part of the world. "And I seem to have made friends... kind of."

Espen grinned. "Am *I* the friend? Please say I'm your friend," he added, batting his eyelashes innocently.

I took a moment, pretending to think about it, before saying, "Sure, but let's just say I wasn't expecting to make any friends on this trip. Especially not one with," I waved in his general direction, "*abilities.*"

The look on Espen's face was pure glee as he beamed at me. The mischievous expression made me think he probably thought the abilities I mentioned weren't the magical ones he'd already shown me. Typical guy. I eyed him, wondering what it would be like for him to kiss me, for this tension that was building between us to pull me under.

"You were not what I was expecting when I heard a tourist missed the boat."

"What were you expecting?" I asked, stepping onto a rocky outcrop near a wood-and-rope bridge. I glanced down into the deep ravine below, the sound of crashing water drifting upward with the mist.

"I was expecting a cheerleader," he said, drawing my attention away from the sharp drop. "The typical American stereotype."

I scoffed and took a few steps back to where Espen stood beside the bridge. "Well, I was a cheerleader for a little while. My Mom desperately wanted me in a skirt with pom poms at my brothers' football games. They all played at one point, and adding a cheerleader would complete her perfect little sporty family."

"A little while?" He arched a brow in question.

"I got kicked off the team for unsportsman-like conduct." I shrugged. It wasn't my finest moment, but you know, whatever. Shit happens.

Espen chuckled, shaking his head. "What did you do?"

I scrunched my nose as the memory came back to me. "The head cheerleader, Melissa, used a nasty word for me and my friend, saying we belonged at the bottom of the pyramid because of our size."

"That's mean," Espen replied, but narrowed his eyes at me. "What did you do, Lennie?"

I let out a long sigh. "I cut off her ponytail." Even in my memories, I could hear the screaming voices of both Melissa and her mother as I did it, see my mother's appalled expression as she apologized profusely, dragging my smug ass off the field. But really, Melissa had looked better with a bob and I doubt she ever called anyone fat again. I did that bitch a favor.

"Wait, how old were you?" Espen asked, pulling out his water bottle and taking a sip.

I crossed my arms. "Eight."

Espen coughed, choking on his drink. "Remind me to never let you near sharp objects," he said, waving his index finger at me.

"You're fine. Just don't ask me to be the base of the pyramid."

"I would never do such a thing. You always deserve to be on top." He winked, and something fluttered in my stomach. I grabbed my own water bottle and occupied my mouth by drinking and avoiding saying anything else that might get me into trouble... or into his bed.

We were just friends.

I didn't have the hots for a sexy-troll-magic-fae-thing.

After our quick stop for a drink, we continued over the bridge and eventually reached a clearing. The forest thinned, parting to reveal a farm and field, right there on the slopes of the damn mountain. I'd grown up in farm country, but the flat fields in Ohio did not look like this.

I grabbed my camera off my chest and prepared to take some photos. Espen stepped up to the old wooden gate nestled between the rocky wall-turned-fence that contained a flock of sheep. I took a quick photo of him before angling the camera at the fluffy livestock that grazed peacefully in the lush green grass.

"You coming?" Espen asked and I glanced over to where he was now standing on the other side of the rock-wall!

"What the fuck are you doing?" I yelled, frantically looking around for anyone that could claim he was trespassing.

"Hiking." He shrugged. "Why the panic?"

"Because you're trespassing on farmland," I whisper shouted as my heart raced. One didn't grow up in rural America without a healthy fear of being shot in the ass for trespassing.

He furrowed his brow, narrowing his eyes at me, before nodding in realization. "Doesn't work the same way here."

"What the fuck are you talking about?" I asked, stepping up in front of him, staying on the correct side of the barrier. This trip had gone off the rails already, and I didn't need any other problems—like a bullet to the butt.

He crossed his arms and tilted his head. "Here in Norway we have a rule called *allemannsretten*."

"The what now?" I raised my brows, blinking rapidly. Nora's magical layer of translation didn't work on that last bit I guessed, because all I heard were garbled letters and noises.

"*Allemannsretten* gives people the right to roam or, in more legal terms, the right of access to nature. Essentially, the land belongs to all the people of Norway, and everyone has a right to use it without harming it. We are all taught to respect property, especially farmland. Usually, agricultural fields are not part of the law, but lucky for us, part of my job with the local police includes acting as the Ranger for this area. I also know the owner." He beamed, shifting his head toward a small wooden building across the meadow. "As long as we respect his land, do not disturb the animals, and close the gate, we may walk through."

That was a concept that did not exist at all in the US, and definitely not in Ohio.

"So, you can walk and hike anywhere you want?" I asked, still somewhat skeptical of the idea and wary of the odds that I could get in trouble... even if I was hiking with a magical-yogi-cop.

"Within reason, yes." Espen nodded. "You must pick up after yourself, do no harm to nature, and do not camp within five hundred feet of a residence or building." He rattled off the facts like he'd memorized the law, which he probably had considering his line of work as both cop and ranger.

"That simple?"

"That simple." He set his hands on his hips, and a slow smirk spread across his face. "Now, are you going to join me, or do you not have enough stamina to continue to our destination?"

I turned off my camera and let it hang against my chest before replying with a smug grin of my own. "Oh, honey. I've got stamina for days."

Espen quirked a brow, his amber eyes gleaming. "Let's go then."

The rest of our walk to Espen's secret destination was pleasant, but sneakily uphill in a lot of places. One second I thought the terrain had leveled out, the next my thighs were burning. We wandered—carefully—through a few more tiny fields, remembering to close the gates we used, and narrowly avoiding piles of sheep shit. The entire time, Espen pointed out little hidden gems for me to photograph or showed me berries that were safe to pick, and which were best left for the animals.

It wasn't long after his lecture about the tart but tasty cowberries that I heard a rumbling noise—like a boulder continuously tumbling down a rocky facade. Curiosity drove me forward until we turned past a thick copse of trees and found the source of the noise.

A massive waterfall.

Gallons of water crested over the cliff high above us, crashing down into a rocky ravine. Espen pointed to a little outcrop beside us that was slightly sheltered from the mist that now coated me from head to boot, and I aimed in that direction.

Retreating away from the edge, I plonked down on the mossy soil, removed my backpack, and grabbed my raincover for my camera. It had taken years of saving to buy this camera—the love of my life—to replace the old one that my grandmother had given me, and I treated it like the precious piece of equipment that it was. My baby could handle some moisture, but the amount of water in the air here wasn't safe. I buttoned it up to protect it from the elements and grabbed a few shots from this vantage point before putting the camera away again as my stomach grumbled. It had been several hours since we set-off, and the uphill hike had left me starving.

Following my same train of thought, Espen pulled out the picnic spread that he'd prepared for us. The two granola bars I still had in my backpack were measly in comparison, so I shoved them back into my bag. I grinned as Espen handed me a sandwich with butter, ham, and cucumber. It was surprisingly delicious, and, once devoured, Espen pulled out a small chocolate bar for each of us.

"Chocolate? On a hike?" I said, taking the sugary goodness with gratitude. Chocolate was right up there with coffee for me in the "never turn it down" category.

"It's a tradition in Norway." Espen tore into his own bar. "Plus we need the sugar high for the hike back down."

The bar was only three small squares, but I wasn't complaining as the dark chocolate melted in my mouth.

After our lunch and some more water, I snapped some photos of the waterfall, capturing how the dim light reflected off the mist casting rainbow effects through the haze. Espen watched me from his spot on the ground, and, while I'd normally find it annoying to have someone monitoring me that closely while I photographed, for some reason I liked his attention.

Once we'd packed up, we headed back to the trail and started our descent.

"How'd you get into yoga?" I asked, breaching the comfortable silence between us.

Espen kept pace beside me, matching my smaller strides even though he had long legs and was a good five inches taller than my five foot six stature. "My sisters always liked yoga, so that's where it initially started. But, once I joined Ragnhild's guard, I started doing it more regularly as part of my training regimen. It keeps me calm and grounded, helps me focus too," Espen explained. "I always enjoy a good workout. How about you?"

My brows flew skyward. "Do I like working out?"

He nodded, motioning me to answer the question.

"Yeah, I'm not a regular at the gym, but I couldn't grow up around my brothers and not be into sports and athleticism in some form." I let out a low chuckle. Growing up with Andrew, Jared, and Ryan had most definitely shaped me into an athlete... but I rebelled a bit there, too. I never stuck to a sport very long. "I tried soccer for a year, swimming for a week, and softball for a couple of years. My Mom refused to let me try gymnastics after the cheer debacle."

Espen shook his head and laughed. "Your childhood sounds a lot different than mine."

"I mean, you're old, and magic, so I'd imagine it was."

He flicked his brows at the mention of his age. "Yes, my 'childhood' was a couple hundred years ago during an era that was vastly different than the one we live in now."

"Horse drawn carriages and shit?" I asked, half teasing, half curious.

"Try horse drawn sleighs and dinner by candlelight," he replied, tilting his head as if recalling the memories from long ago. "But you're not wrong about the differences. As children, we are raised with growing responsibilities. Everyone contributes to the Forest, learning from it as we both grow and change. Children are given more freedom, but we don't do sports the way you do. Sure, some kids these days join the humans for games of *soccer*," he said, intonating the word we Americans used for the sport known as football in the rest of the world. I rolled my eyes at him, before he laughed and continued his story. "But it isn't as common. We still spend a lot of time outdoors until we are of age to take on fae jobs or further integrate into the human world."

"What kind of jobs do your people have?" I asked, stepping around a slick boulder.

"It varies based on abilities and level of power." He shrugged. "Some are healers, some plant new specimens, others become guards or farmers or wildlife rangers."

"Did you have a job before you became a guard?"

Espen nodded. "I was originally a healer as the forest responded well to my magic. Then, when I enlisted in the guard, word got out regarding my skills." He waggled his brows at me, and I chuckled. "Queen Ragnhild personally requested that I be mentored by her Head Guard." Espen stepped behind me as the bridge we'd returned to was too narrow to cross side-by-side.

"So, Mads became your mentor and you trained with him to one day take on the role?" I said as I walked onto the bridge.

"Exactly," Espend replied. "Well done for remembering his name."

Honestly, I was just as shocked as he was that I'd remembered his mentor's name. I'd never been good with names—usually, they went in one ear and out the other, never getting caught by memory cells within my brain. Why this one stuck, I had no idea.

"Well, don't expect miracles. What's your name aga—"

My words cut off as I dropped, falling between two wood boards that snapped beneath my feet.

Air was sucked from my lungs, and I couldn't even scream as something caught my wrist before I fell into the misty ravine below.

Gasping, I looked up. Espen lay panting on his stomach, his head and shoulders peeking through the broken board I'd just fallen through. He tightened his grip around my wrist, knuckles white, eyes wide.

"Don't wriggle," he said through gritted teeth.

I didn't dare nod or move, but my heart beat so hard I was surprised my whole body didn't jerk with each beat. I just hoped he could see my agreement in my eyes, because they felt as wide as the chasm I now dangled above.

Slowly and steadily, Espen began to peel himself off the wood-planks on the bridge, carefully lifting me with one arm—which was wholly impressive, no matter my size—but I didn't dare say a word. He reached his other hand down. "Grab on, gently."

I lifted my right arm and grasped his hand, wrapping my fingers around his wrist. He continued pulling me up in movements so slow, they felt like a lifetime. Surely my ribs were bruised from the slamming of my heart. As my head reached the hole I'd fallen through, Espen grunted and pulled quickly. I was hoisted up, lightly scraping my ass across the boards that remained before he set me on my feet. Not waiting a second longer, I was suddenly enveloped in Espen's arms. I clung to him, hitching my legs around his torso, as he leaped across the hole and sprinted across the rest of the bridge.

We reached the other side, both of us panting and holding on to each other for dear life. He didn't stop until we stood with my back against a tall pine. Seconds ticked by as we caught our breath, Espen with his legs spread into a triangle, one hand braced against the tree, while his other hand held my thigh. My calves were still firmly crossed behind his back, as I sucked in lungfuls of air, and my camera was safely nestled between us.

"Are you okay?" he asked, his warm gaze meeting mine.

"I will be... but I might have pissed my pants." I couldn't feel anything warm and wet down there, but the adrenaline coursing through my veins was numbing me to all sensations, except Espen's hand that was seriously close to cupping my butt.

"I don't smell anything," he said, his lips curving into a cheeky smile.

"Fae have heightened smell, too?" I panted.

"In some cases."

I bit my lip and hoped I didn't reek of sweat.

Espen flicked his gaze to my lips, then let out a throaty grunt and set me down on my feet. He took two steps back and ran his hand through his dark hair. "Ummm... I need to secure the site."

I nodded, swallowing the tight lump in my throat and shaking off the tingly sensation in my limbs.

Espen straightened up and pulled off his backpack. He retrieved a knot of neon-pink rope and began to untie it. Creating a loop in one end, he slid the circle of rope over one of the bridge posts before crossing down to the base of the other post, letting the bright fiber block the entrance to the passage. By the time he was done, the entrance was cordoned with a big neon-pink X that would hopefully stop anyone from using the bridge.

"That should be okay until we can send a crew up to fix it," he said, returning to me and hoisting his bag onto his back again.

I agreed. "Let's get back to town before it gets dark or I get eaten by a bear."

Espen nodded. "Or a wolf."

The hike back down was considerably quicker and we made good time. The setting sun's rays bounced off slate rooftops and windows as we left the trail and entered the far end of the village. Sweat beaded at my neck and I unzipped my jacket to let in the light breeze. I was hyper-aware of how desperately I needed to shower and wash my armpits after almost dying. I pulled my hair into a ponytail to stop it from sticking to my cheeks.

As we traipsed through town toward the harbor where we'd part ways, the sound of sirens met my ears. I glanced over at Espen in question. His brow was furrowed and he picked up his pace, striding ahead of me—for the first time today—toward the noise. I followed, staying right on his heels, until we found the reason for the siren.

On the edge of town, near the tourist center by the harbor, was a massive rock slide.

15

ESPEN

Boulders the size of small cars were strewn across the southern road, blocking it entirely as they piled against the steep incline of the mountain. The swath of material was as tall as a building at its highest point, with trees and debris scattered all around.

I ran up to the scene, Lennie right behind me, and found my colleagues securing the area.

"Stay here," I said firmly to Lennie. She did as requested, which was rather miraculous considering her obstinate personality. But, then again, the place was teeming with police officers, and she'd already made it clear how often she landed in trouble.

I strode over to the chief of police, Bente, a stoic no-nonsense woman with a shock of white hair and a dark sense of humor that was only on display during night-shifts or at the bar when she had the day off. She was always a joy to spend time with, and a great boss. "Any injuries?" I asked.

"Espen." She nodded in greeting. "No, thankfully not."

"When did it happen?"

"About twenty minutes ago," she said, her eyes landing on me briefly before she continued surveying the area and the other officers corralling bystanders. They were using one of the police cars, white with neon-yellow stripes, as a makeshift barrier until better barricades could be put up.

"What can I do?"

"It's your day off, but I need everyone's help." She gave me a tight smile that was more of an apology than anything else.

"That's okay. This is bad," I said, because it really was. This was the main road in and out of town. With this blocked, and the hillside insecure, we had a serious safety issue on our hands. Plus, the size of the rockslide would take a week or more to clear.

Bente gave me a quick nod. "Thank you. Help the boys move the people further back, and block any entry to the tourist center. I cannot have anyone going in there in case there are more landslides into the fjord."

"Yes, boss." I spun on my heel and headed back to Lennie, who was tinkering with her camera and completely oblivious to the other man walking up behind her. I should've probably warned her, but I also wouldn't mind watching her punch Øyvin in the stomach if he caught her off-guard.

"Lennie," the Fjord Fae said, unfortunately announcing his presence before the American could take a swing.

She turned and glared at him.

"Øyvin," I said in greeting as I joined them. "Any damage below?" From what I'd seen, the landslide had washed slightly into the fjord.

"Not too bad," Øyvin replied, his straw-like hair fluttering slightly in the light breeze. "Some fish habitat was damaged, but the material seems to have settled near the water line with minimal damage further beneath the surface." He spoke firmly, but not too loud. Most of the humans recognized him as a quasi-harbor master, but he didn't have an official job in the human world. King Balder kept him on a tight leash, and his work to secure and protect the fjord waters was a daily challenge with the number of pollutants further down the passage.

"Good," Lennie and I said at the same time. A small smile graced her lips briefly, before it turned back into a snarl as she watched Øyvin.

"Well, looks like you definitely won't be leaving town by car," Øyvin said, aiming his comment at Lennie.

She rolled her eyes at him, but he was right. With the road blocked, her only option really would be the supply ship that arrived in four days.

"I need to stay here and help," I said, turning to Lennie. "Thank you for joining me on a hike today. I'm sorry our day ended like this."

She smiled softly. "More like thank *you*."

"Of course." I grinned, glad that I'd been able to save her from falling to her death when the bridge broke. The entire incident had left me on edge. Thankfully the panic had subsided from the sheer terror I'd felt when I saw her drop in front of me. I couldn't remember another time I'd been so glad I had fast reflexes.

Lennie stepped back and straightened up, almost like she was shaking free of something. The memory of us pressed together against the tree perhaps? Because that vision had been playing on repeat in my mind the entire trek back to town. "I'm gonna head home and shower," she announced. "Good luck."

She spun, sneered at Øyvin, and walked away, blonde ponytail swishing behind her.

"You think this is related?" Øyvin asked, referencing the magic investigation and drawing my focus away from Lennie's backside.

"Maybe," I said, running my hand through my hair. "But it's not like it's unheard of around here either."

He huffed and crossed his arms. We surveyed the scene for a moment in pure silence before he said, "I don't like it."

Admittedly, neither did I. Either it was sheer coincidence that the timing of the rockslide had happened so close to the illegal transfer that had damaged the woods, or something else was going on. "Whatever it was, I need to get to work. I'll let you know if I find anything... interesting."

Øyvin grunted—never one for many words or lengthy goodbyes—and wandered back into the village.

The next few hours were spent herding humans away from the debris, erecting blockades and fencing to stop people entering the area, and calling the various agencies that needed to be notified and brought in to assist with the clean-up.

By the time I was able to stand still for more than two minutes, the sun had set and I was exhausted. The hike we did this morning wasn't easy, and I'd now been on my feet almost all day. While fae didn't tire as quickly as humans, I was still drained from the events of the day—almost losing Lennie when the bridge gave way beneath her feet, and then the fear for my people and the humans had set in as soon as I heard the sirens.

I glanced over the scene. Thankfully the rockslide had settled completely. The local police force had done an excellent job at blocking off the site, and the public had been pushed back a safe distance. There weren't many onlookers left—most had probably gone home for supper, but a few remained with their phones out trying to take a photo. I recognized every single one of them, including Halvar...

Halvar?

Shit.

The broody, giant Fjell Fae stood off to the side in the dark, the blue lights from the patrol car bouncing ominously off his stoic face.

He never left the mountain. *Ever.*

This couldn't be good.

Steeling myself, I walked over to him and braced for the worst.

"Queen Freija has requested a meeting with you, the young lady, and Øyvin," Halvar said in his natural gruff tone. His body was relaxed beneath his thick brown waxed-cotton jacket, and I was pretty sure this was the first time I'd ever seen him in jeans instead of his usual uniform or black attire.

"Has something happened?" I asked.

He stared at the tumble of rocks and debris behind me, and quirked a single brow.

"Aside from this?" I added with a wave of my hand.

"We can discuss tomorrow morning at her office." Since Queen Freija didn't *have* an office—at least not one that I'd ever seen—that meant we were being summoned to the throne room. "There are... concerns."

My brow drew down at his word choice. There were gaping holes between the lines, and any assumption that could be slotted between wasn't good. "Is the Queen all right?"

Halvar stared into my eyes. "No."

16
LENNIE

"Ah, good. You left your camera at home," Espen said, striding toward me in his police uniform the next morning. I was heading to Oddvar's café for coffee before I went to the store to buy a phone charger I still hadn't grabbed. After the life-threatening events yesterday, I needed a calm day to recover.

I didn't stop walking, but I looked his way. "Why does that matter?"

"We have a meeting to go to," he said just as Øyvin stepped around the corner and ruined my morning with his presence. "Perfect timing," Espen greeted the brute. I scowled at Øyvin's thick gray sweater and blue jeans, which, unfortunately, almost matched my own. I'd picked out my dark gray fleece jacket and navy jeans—which Solveig had graciously thrown in the laundry for me last night so I had some clothes to wear today. Mistakes were clearly made, though, as the Asshole and I looked ready for a family portrait session.

I huffed and crossed my arms. "What are you talking about, Espen?"

"We've been ordered to meet with"—he glanced around and gently touched my elbow, pulling me aside, away from passersby—"Queen Freija. All three of us."

"She wants to talk to me? A human?" I asked as a tingly and not unpleasant sensation ran up my arm where Espen's fingers still pressed against me.

"Apparently. And, before you ask, no, I don't know why."

My mind reeled, coming up blank as to any reason why the queen of *anything* would be interested in me. "Is it the investigation? Is the rock slide related?"

Espen shrugged and removed his hand. "Maybe."

"Did Nora come find you or call you?" Øyvin asked, stepping up on Espen's other side, both of them now towering over me.

Espen shook his head and said, "Halvar."

"He left the mountain?" Øyvin's blond brows hit his hairline. I glanced between the two men, but didn't have time to question who this Halvar was. "Shit. Let's go."

We strode out of town and up into the woods, Øyvin leading the way as we followed yet another trail—how many trails could one little town have?—between pines, ferns, and birch trees. It wasn't an unpleasant morning; the sun had even deigned to show its face between the clouds. But today I was sans coffee, and it was a damn shame. Jet fuel was needed if I was going to get through the day, especially if I had to spend it around the Asshole.

No one spoke as we steadily climbed up the mountain-side, listening to the sounds of the woods and its inhabitants. Far too quickly, my thighs began a minor protest. Yesterday's hike with Espen wasn't excessive, but it had done a number on my muscles.

At one point, the trail widened, and we were able to walk all three side-by-side. Unfortunately for Øyvin, this put me right beside him, and I took the opportunity to poke the bear a bit.

"So, what does a big brute like yourself do for fun? Steal candy from children? Throw barrels of ale like a shot put? Crochet? Fishing? Crochet *while* fishing?"

A flicker of something happened at the corner of Øyvin's lips, and I honed in on it, ignoring Espen's snickering.

"Come on big guy, what's your poison?"

"Sometimes reading, sometimes music," he said firmly, his lips falling back into a solid line again. "No fishing."

I blinked but tried to hide my surprise at the rather tame list of hobbies. He didn't need to know he shocked me with his admission. "Next you're going to tell me you don't eat fish because they're your friends."

He said nothing and kept looking forward.

"Seriously?" My brows shot skyward at having nailed the guy's eating habit. Then I gasped. "Are you one of the sharks from *Finding Nemo*? You're Bruce, aren't you? A reverse pescatarian?"

Øyvin rolled his eyes. "No, I don't eat fish. I protect them and the fjord from idiots like you who think going on a cruise is a good way to spend your free time, never thinking about the damage it does to the planet and waters."

"Would you prefer I drive all around the coastline instead?" I snapped, matching my strides to his obnoxiously large ones.

"I'd prefer it if you weren't here at all."

I scoffed, but his harsh words egged me on. "You know, not everyone can live in such a beautiful place. If I can capture that beauty in my photos for others to enjoy, then I'm happy."

He glared at me, walking faster, but I picked up my pace to meet his. No way was I backing down now. "Your happiness and frivolity will only lead *more* people to this region, causing more damage."

I couldn't entirely disagree with him, but travel in Norway was wildly expensive. If I hadn't got the cruise tickets on sale, I wouldn't have come. "Well, you don't need to fucking blame me for the behavior of others. I'm not wholly responsible for the polar ice-caps melting, you dick!"

"Bitch."

"Asshole."

Espen slid between us, his back to me as he met Øyvin's glare. "Perhaps we should lower the volume and put on smiles for our meeting?" His upbeat tone and the way he shimmied his shoulders barely hid the warning beneath his words. Our chat with Queen Freija was important enough for him to revert to police-officer-Espen, not his usual carefree-and-jovial-Espen.

I breathed through my nostrils, trying to calm my temper and the rage coursing through my muscles.

Øyvin quirked his brow and strode ahead of us, heading straight through the rocky mountain wall up ahead without another word.

My eyes bulged at the sight of him nonchalantly—but also with his signature fuck-the-world swagger—strolling straight through the stone facade. He didn't even flinch or go splat. He just disappeared.

"Please tell me there's a train to a wizarding school on the other side of that wall."

Espen chuckled. "Let me explain."

I nodded, keeping my eyes on the mountain, my mouth hanging open. I couldn't look away from where Øyvin had just disappeared. Sure, I'd seen Espen use his magic in the woods and change outfits, but this... this was another thing entirely. "Yeah, that would be great."

He huffed and if I'd been capable of looking at anything other than the spot where Øyvin had been, I'd probably find Espen's usual cheeky grin plastered across his handsome face. "The Fjell Fae live in the mountain," he started. "There are maybe a hundred entrances around the area that are hidden from the humans using layers of magic. This is one of the main entrances."

He waved his hand against the rocky disguise and it rippled slightly, like wind brushing against the surface of a pond. "It won't hurt. You won't feel a thing."

I eyed him and the magic warily.

"Do you trust me?" He asked, holding out his hand to me.

Now that was a good question. If he'd asked that forty-eight hours ago, I probably would have said no. But, after yesterday, when he'd saved my life and carried me to safety, I guess I could trust that he didn't want me dead.

"Yes." I nodded. "I trust you."

He smiled as I placed my hand in his and we walked into the mountain. We stepped through the mirage—which felt like walking through a puff of air from a heating vent—and entered a well-lit cave. The inside of the mountain looked like someone had chiseled their way through the stone with gargantuan picks and hammers, the jagged edges catching the light from nearby lanterns. It wasn't cold in here, but there was a slight damp chill now that we were out of the sunlight and surrounded by rocky walls.

"We should change clothes to meet the Queen," Espen said, turning me to face him before dropping my grasp. "May I?" He held his hand above my shoulder, close but not touching.

"Knock yourself out." I shrugged. He scrunched his brow, then shook his head—probably confused by the American phrase—before touching my shoulder. As soon as he did, a warm shift settled over my skin like a heated blanket. It wasn't painful by any means, but definitely noticeable.

Feeling a little like Cinderella after the fairy godmother transforms her, I looked down at the dress that had appeared on my body. The skirt and bodice were made of a thick dark-green wool with silver embroidery—almost like celtic markings—woven into the hem and the fabric that rested across my breast. A white undershirt covered the tops of my boobs, and was clasped shut by a silver broach at my neck. It was a gorgeous outfit and matched the one I'd seen him magically change into the first day I met him.

"Is this okay?" he asked, scanning me from top to toe, before flicking his gaze back to mine.

"Yeah, it's hefty, but mobile," I said, sinking into a squat. "I can move in it. Could probably even tackle a guy." I crouched forward into a perfect ready position, the same one my older brothers had taught me decades ago when Mom finally let me play football with them.

Espen chuckled and tilted his head, watching me closely as if trying to understand the way my brain worked. Good fucking luck—I was a mystery even to myself.

He pressed his hand to his own shoulder and his police uniform disappeared, replaced with the jacket with dark green cape combo he'd previously spooked me with. This time though, his ears shifted too, slight points appearing at the top of each. My traitorous body warmed at the sight of his cheeky grin, something fluttering in my stomach.

Shaking myself free from his knowing gaze, I asked, "So, where exactly are we going?"

Espen opened his mouth to reply—

"Throne room," Nora said, strolling up behind him in a long dress like my own. Her's was a dark gray, though, with the same silver embroidery. "Best not to leave my sister waiting."

"She's not wrong," Espen said, pointing down the hall.

Nora, walking backward like a tour guide, led us through a winding maze of tunnels, all lit by little orbs of light in lanterns at carefully marked intervals, roughly every six feet. It certainly brightened the space and distracted me from the fact that I was walking within a fucking mountain.

"How many Fjell Fae live in here?" I asked, doing my best not to butcher the Norwegian name for *mountain* in front of a royal fae who called one home.

Nora gave me a proud smile. "Over seven hundred fae, with more in other mountains around the country. This mountain stretches far down the side of the fjord and is almost 30 kilometers wide at its broadest point. We have everything we need in here—light, water, food, clean air—all thanks to our own people and their abilities."

"Nora here can tell you everything you need to know about the Fjell," Espen interjected. "She's both their historian and a painter."

Nora winked and continued her monologue. "The Fjell Fae have lived here for centuries under my family's reign. My sister, Queen Freija, has been on the throne for over two hundred years. Any questions?" Nora asked as we turned another corner, slowly descending into the mountain, the chill non-existent in my magic dress.

I mulled through some ideas while we continued our walk, and landed on one that might prove helpful to ask now rather than later. "Is there anything I should be aware of before meeting with the Queen?" Like how to stay out of trouble.

A wide grin spread on Nora's face. "Let her speak first and do not disrespect the Fjell. Do those two things and she will like you."

"Okay," I said. That should be easy.

"Anything else?" Nora asked Espen as we came to a stop before a shimmering blue stone archway. The rocks in the walls here were almost clear, but glowed and cast a pale blue light across all three of us.

"Don't anger Halvar," he said, and Nora chuckled before she left us, waltzing through the archway and into a room made of the glowing stones.

"How do I know which one is Halvar?" I asked as Espen extended his arm, motioning me through with him.

A low chuckle rumbled from his chest. "You said you trust me. You'll know."

17

LENNIE

My eyes blew wide as I looked around the throne room. It was spectacular, something out of a damn movie. Whatever rock it was made out of shone like the insides of an ice cave, glittering whites and blues dancing in the low light. At the center of the room was a throne of the same pale blue stone, its tall back blending into the mountain itself. A forty-something-year-old woman perched in it, her hands gently placed in her lap. Her dark blue dress, covering almost every inch of her, brushed the slate-colored floor.

Something shifted to her left, and I glanced at the movement. A beast of a man stepped beside the throne, his gigantic form shadowing the bronze-haired woman beside him. The fae-man-beast-thingy wearing all black stared at me, his gaze narrow and unwelcoming, and my breaths grew shallow. Espen was right; it was easy to guess this was Halvar.

The Queen's welcoming smile was the opposite of the harsh cold wafting off the man to her left. She nodded to Øyvin as he stepped up beside me, as if appearing out of thin air, wearing his own gray-and-navy uniform. Nora had taken up a seat along one of the walls in the chamber where benches were carved into the glossy rock.

Glancing between her and the Queen, it was easy to see that they were sisters. Where Nora's short brown bob haircut framed her round face, Freija had more chiseled features, as if the fullness had slowly chipped away over the centuries. Freija's hair was also more gilded than Nora's, a wave of coppery brown swept up into a bun with small tendrils brushing against her pale cheeks. But the stand-out feature that revealed their relation was their eyes. Both fae had sharp brown-and-gray eyes that shimmered almost unnaturally. It was eerie, but beautiful, and I couldn't stop staring. I'd never seen anything like them.

"Thank you for coming today," Freija said, her voice a gentle timbre. "I appreciate the reports I have received thus far, but thought it wise to meet and discuss the matter at hand."

Both Espen and Øyvin bowed their heads lightly in a reverent display of grace. I hesitated momentarily, not sure if I should do the same, but no one had said anything about needing to bow on our walk here. Instead, I stood still and kept my mouth shut.

"Øyvin, is all well with King Balder?"

"Yes, Queen Freija. He sends his regards, but, as you know, we are fighting our own battle with the pollution further down the fjord," Øyvin replied, sounding like a soldier giving a report to his superior, his hands clasped behind his back.

"Indeed. It is a challenge and I commend his efforts," Freija said with a flicker of a smile. "We appear to be facing a challenge of our own." She cast her eyes to Espen, who didn't move. His hands were relaxed by his side, and his breathing was steady. "Did you see anything unusual in the rock slide?"

"Not at first," Espen responded, and all three Fjell Fae in the room raised their eyebrows. Halvar's features quickly returned to a stoic scowl though, and Espen continued, "I went back last night when all the humans had gone to sleep and sent my colleague back to the station, taking over his duties as watchman. I pressed some magic into the debris. After a minute, there was a reverberation in the rocky-soil, and I caught a glimpse of a silvery scar on one of the largest boulders."

The room stilled, and Nora muttered something under her breath that I could only assume was an expletive based on the cutting glare she received from her sister.

Freija reset her dainty shoulders and took a deep breath. With a quick glance at Halvar, she said, "Well, it is as we feared, then. Someone is trying, once more, to bring down the monarchs."

I swallowed the lump in my throat, unsure why it was there in the first place, but certain that whatever was going on here, was bad. Both Espen and Øyvin straightened up, but didn't move an inch.

"And you, young lady," the Queen said, her unearthly gaze landing on me.

Ah shit. Here we go. I was probably about to get my mind wiped for being human and knowing too much, or locked up in a dungeon never to be heard from again.

I took a deep breath and braced for her next words.

"Thank you for capturing the evidence with your camera," she said, and I nodded, giving her a tight smile sans teeth—just in case that was offensive or Halvar thought I was a threat. I certainly hadn't missed the size of his hands, and didn't want to be on the receiving end of them. Freija continued, "Without it we might not have been able to act as quickly. So, thank you."

My shoulders slumped in relief, and I tipped my head slightly. "It was sheer fuc—"

Øyvin's hand clapped over my mouth before I could finish my sentence. I glared up at him, and thought better of punching him in the balls in front of the nice Queen. Instead, I pried his fingers from my face—ignoring the way they brushed against my lips—before finishing my answer. "You're welcome. I'm glad it was helpful." I felt rather than saw the pride emanating from my right side where Espen stood.

Freija looked between the three of us, a slow smile forming on her face and crinkling the corners of her eyes. "We will be increasing our security measures, closing some of our entrances, and securing any parts of the mountain that may be loose." Her missive was firm and clear as she stood from her throne. "I have also instructed Halvar to prepare for my birthday in two weeks time."

Nora coughed and looked up at her sister. "You can't go through with the event. Not now. It's too dangerous."

Freija took a deep breath, not turning to the other fae. "I shall use the annual celebration of my birth to draw out any suspects. It has already been agreed upon," she said with a quick nod to Halvar.

He bowed his head ever so slightly, the glow from the stones shining off his silver hair and beard.

"In that time," she continued, turning back to the three of us. "I expect you to hunt down the culprit and, should you find them, bring them to me." Her eyes darkened and, for the first time since entering the room, I actually feared the woman and whatever power lurked beneath the surface of her calm exterior.

The guys beside me nodded, gruff remarks coming from Øyvin in thanks as we were dismissed.

We spun in unison and strode out of the throne room, entering the maze of hallways once again. While we wound our way back to the entrance, Espen and Øyvin chatted, making plans for what to do next.

Thankfully, none of this was my problem, because I was leaving in three days. I'd do what I could in the meantime, if only to make sure Espen lived up to his bargain and got me on that damn supply ship that Oddvar had secured my passage on. Other than that, my work here was done.

18

LENNIE

After finishing a nice sandwich for lunch that afternoon, I stomped out of Oddvar's café, a piping hot cup of coffee—with milk and two sugars—in my hand, and a Forest Fae at my back.

"It's just for today," Espen pleaded as I strode down the street toward the store so I could finally buy a charger for my phone. Could I borrow one from Solveig or someone else? Probably, but I wanted to troubleshoot this problem myself. Plus, the longer I left my phone off, the smaller my cell phone bill would be when I got home. I just needed to call my brothers to make sure they hadn't told Mom, and check for any messages from the cruise ship.

Espen kept up beside me, matching my strides with his longer legs. We were back in our human clothes: me in my dark gray fleece jacket and navy jeans, him in his black police uniform with reflective strips.

"I don't need a babysitter, Espen." I was a grown ass woman who could take care of herself.

"But what if you fall over or get attacked by a bear?" he asked, and I stopped, my lips pursed.

"I'll punch it in the nose."

Espen chuckled, a warm sound that sent flutters into my stomach every time I heard it. His smile wasn't bad either. Maybe it was the short beard, or the dark mop of hair that made me feel this way. Hell only knew. "I'm quite certain that only works with sharks," he said.

I shrugged and continued walking toward the grocery store, hoping they stocked chargers. "Nobody likes being punched in the nose. I bet it would work with a bear, too. I'll make sure to report back." When he didn't leave my side, I said, "Don't be an asshole, Espen. The village already has one of those; you don't need two."

As if speaking his name had summoned him, the fae in question stepped around the corner and almost plowed right into me. "I'm here," Øyvin grumbled, as displeased with today's babysitting plan as I was.

"Wonderful," Espen said, way too chipper about all of this, before turning back to me. "I figured he could take you on a sightseeing tour of the fjord or something."

Øyvin and I wore matching deadpan expressions, and damn it, I hated having anything in common with the man.

Espen rolled his eyes. "Why, what a wonderful idea, Espen," he said with a high-pitched voice, swaying as he spoke. "It will be so nice to spend the day on the water, seeing the beauty that is Norway. We'll have such fun together."

A short sigh left my chest, and I took a sip of the jet fuel in my hand. "I'm not getting out of this, am I?"

"Not at all," Espen replied, giving me a toothy grin.

"You know too much. We can't have you wandering around and getting into trouble or telling anyone," Øyvin added, giving me the straight truth, which seemed rather miraculous for the grouch. Then again, he wasn't a fan of mine and liked to annoy me with his presence. So, maybe he said it to push my buttons. Either way, I took another sip of coffee to calm my aggravated nerves.

"Yes, exactly," Espen said, backing away from us. "On that note, I'm going back to work. Try not to kill each other." He spun on his heel and sprinted down the road, turning toward what I could only assume was the police station that I most definitely did not want to visit.

A low rumble emanated from behind me, and, instead of turning toward it, I waltzed in the other direction back toward the shore and the path to Solveig's house. Plan A: join Øyvin on a tour of the fjord. Plan B: go home and try to buy a charger tomorrow, avoiding the Fjord Fae and his awful personality. The second option sounded so much more palatable.

Unfortunately, Øyvin had a broad stride and caught up to me as I reached the edge of the harbor.

"You know, you could just go home," I said, heading away from the downtown core with the last of the white-colored, wooden buildings to my right, and the fjord to my left. Boats of all shapes and sizes bobbed on the nearly smooth surface, and the breeze shifted the smell of the water and pine through the village.

"I need to make sure you don't do anything stupid," Øyvin practically growled, and tugged on my arm, spilling some of my coffee onto the asphalt.

"Asshole!" I ripped my hand out of his grip and stumbled closer to the shoreline, following the path out of town that didn't have any buildings alongside it until you reached the collection of houses where Solveig lived.

"You have quite the mouth on you," he snarled.

I chugged the rest of my drink, unwilling to let it go to waste should he decide to jostle me again. It tasted heavenly, but burned my mouth. When I was done, I threw away the cup and recycled the lid in the garbage station that sat along the walkway.

"I'm aware. Haven't had any complaints about that either, though," I said, swaying my hips to provoke the bull.

He grumbled and muttered something under his breath that sounded like "stupid human," but I couldn't be sure.

"You know, you really should get laid. It would probably help take the edge off whatever bullshit—"

Before I could finish my sentence, Øyvin stormed toward me and pushed me into the fjord. I landed with an almighty splash, narrowly missing the rocks, and sank. My ass touched the bottom, and, thankfully, it was shallow enough that my head stayed above the cold water. Based on the grimace on the Asshole's face, submersion had been his initial plan.

"What the fuck was that for?" I yelled, water sweeping around my stomach.

He shrugged and folded his arms across his chest. "I was asked to show you the fjord." He waved his hand at me. "Done."

With a huff and an expletive that my mother's friends would balk at, I rose to my feet. Water dripped from every part of me, the cool droplets returning to the fjord where they belonged. "Manhandle me one more time, buddy," I said, climbing over the rocks, pulling myself back onto the pathway, and shifting to a standing position in front of him. "And I'll kick you in the balls."

Øyvin grumbled, his cobalt eyes turning stormy, and grabbed my shoulders, spinning me on the spot. Before I could yell at him again, he wrapped his wide arms across my front, pressed my back against his torso, and dove into the water. I was practically a mermaid bust on the prow of a pirate ship as we careened, face first, into the fjord. I held my breath as the water closed over our heads, completely submerged in the icy water.

If I survived this, I'd be *severing* his balls instead.

Øyvin held me tight against his chest as we were propelled forward by what I was assuming was his magic. Espen had mentioned something about Fjord Fae being able to manipulate the water. So, being able to push it aside and swim like a fucking torpedo kind of made sense. Surprisingly, an air bubble settled around us, keeping us dry and letting us breathe beneath the surface. Or, at least, it kept *Øyvin* dry. I was still very much soaked from my prior dip into the fjord.

I scanned my surroundings, my eyes growing wide and my heart hammering at the sight before me. The light was dim beneath the surface, but I could clearly see schools of fish hiding in the rocks near the shore, and little cave-like structures dotted into the mountain where it fell beneath the water. As we pressed on further down the fjord, I dared to glance over my shoulder. It was a mistake, though, as Øyvin's light stubble grazed against my cheek, sending a shiver down my spine. Whether he noted the touch or not, he said nothing, and we plowed on further along the fjord.

After a solid twenty minutes below the surface—which, for my human mind that needed to come up for air regularly, was fucking wild—the water grew murkier. Øyvin shifted his weight, and our bubble rose above the darker patches until we eventually broke the surface. Still wrapped tightly in his arms, Øyvin showed off by launching us out of the fjord and onto a tiny pebbled beach. He landed on his feet and set me down, before stepping away from me like I was a live-wire. Usually a wise move, but in this case, I could have used the support. My legs felt like jelly and I wobbled on the spot.

"Follow me," Øyvin grumbled, stalking up a rocky trail between some skinny trees like a mountain goat.

With a huff, I followed the Asshole, doing my best not to slip as my feet and clothes were still soaking wet. The air temperature was mild-ish, but the slight breeze at this end of the fjord had a cutting chill in it. I shivered, water squelching in my boots as I scrambled up onto an outcrop where Øyvin had stopped to take in the view. "Any chance you could magically dry my clothes?" I asked, sitting down on the cold cliff.

His stormy gaze raked over me before his eyes rolled so hard I was shocked they didn't get stuck in the back of his head. With a wave of his hand, a blanket of heat swept across my clothes and I was miraculously dry again. I gave him a brief nod in thanks, not wanting to be *too* kind to the Asshole. I didn't want him to think I'd changed my mind and started to tolerate his presence. Shaking off *that* unlikelihood, I turned my focus away from my annoying companion, and looked out over the fjord.

The water gleamed in the foreground, with a sparse layer of trees on the opposing hillside giving way to patches of gray rock jutting up behind it. A simple, but majestic display. However, perched on the other side of the fjord beneath a bluff was what looked like some sort of factory. Warehouses dotted the immense dock space and large ships were moored to its flank. Further back from the shoreline sat silos—not too different from the grain silos we had in Ohio—and miles upon miles of meandering pipes. At this distance, the people working over there were mere specks, ants compared to the size of the equipment around them.

"What is that?" I asked, nodding toward the gray-and-brown cluster of buildings and metal.

"Poison."

I glanced over my shoulder to judge if his comment was sarcastic, but seeing the stoic Fjord Fae's expression, I didn't laugh. He'd tightened his jaw and his fists were clenched at his sides, his eyes locked on the scene across the fjord.

"It's one of several oil refineries you'll find along the Norwegian coastline," he explained. "You humans rely on oil, and the North Atlantic will gladly provide it to those brave enough to weather her storms. But, it comes at a cost." I wanted to argue with him for lumping me in with his general distaste of humans, but held myself back—then wondered if maybe the dip in the fjord had rattled my brain. His eyes darkened and his voice turned more grumbly than his normal timbre. "They've become better at avoiding oil spills, but the damage comes from the ships, the destruction of the shoreline, and past malpractice that has polluted the ground and surrounding waters."

"Well, fuck," I mumbled, glancing back at the operations.

Øyvin grunted in agreement before sitting down beside me, leaving a gap so we most definitely could not accidentally bump into each other. Which I appreciated, even as my breath caught temporarily in my throat at the movement. This close I could see the different shades of blond in Øyvin's hair, the way his stubble curved over his chin, and how extremely long his eyelashes were. *Why did men always have such enviable lashes?* It wasn't fair to womankind.

He turned toward me and flicked his gaze to mine.

I sucked in a quick breath and looked away, brushing my hands across my jeans while mumbling, "How far down the fjord are we?"

"A little over half-way."

Hold up.

I turned slowly, my eyes squinted as anger rose in me. "You mean you could've torpedoed me down the fjord this entire time?" My voice reached an exasperated crescendo as I peered over at the grumpy fae. The same guy who could've saved me from a week of waiting and a near-death experience.

He rolled his eyes and shook his head. "There's quite a bit further to go, and two very good reasons why I can't do that."

"Go on."

"Number one: I'm King Balder's Head Guard. I do not have the time to forsake my duties to help a wayward human get home. I have people I'm accountable for and a fjord to keep clean."

"And this annoying babysitting operation slash fjord tour is not a dereliction of duty?"

Øyvin grumbled, resting his hands on his knees. "Today is actually my day off, but even then, I don't stray far from the fjord."

I let out a huff but conceded that he kind of had a valid point. "What's the second reason you couldn't save my ass and help me down the fjord?"

His lips twitched into a minuscule grin, and I did a double-take wondering if my eyes were deceiving me. "I don't want to."

I scoffed in reply and let out an expletive that would've had me grounded if I still lived with my parents. "Why do you hate me so much?" I asked, brushing my fingers across the tufts of lavender that stuck up between the cracks in the rock.

"You're annoying and you clearly don't understand the impact of your actions."

I snarled at him. "Is this about saving the world from pollution again? What the fuck do you want me to do? I want to see the world and photograph it."

He stood up, brushing off his pants, his sapphire gaze boring into mine. "Take photos of the world around your home."

"I don't want to."

"And why not?"

"Because... Because I don't want to." I said, partially avoiding his question. It wasn't that Ohio was ugly—quite the opposite, the gullies and trails were gorgeous—but I was bored with my surroundings.

Travel and photography were ways for me to escape the mundane parts of life, to live a little and capture the beauty around me. From trips to Hawaii to see the beaches and volcanoes, to hikes in Peru (where I needed a special tea to stop the altitude sickness and accompanying headaches), I wanted to experience what the world had to offer and document it. I wanted to see everything mother nature had created, and I couldn't do that by staying in the fields of Ohio. My carbon footprint was probably substantial because of my frequent flights, but I alone couldn't be blamed for global warming. I could do better, find more eco-friendly ways to travel, but...

"Why are you so grouchy, anyway?" I asked, pivoting the topic away from me.

"I'm responsible for the health and safety of the Fjord Fae on a good day. Good days do not include the illegal transfer of magic."

He did have a point about the silvery-magic-stuff. Even Espen and the Fjell Fae seemed remarkably alarmed by it. Plus, the new landslide just seemed to make matters worse for the Fae... and they still didn't know who was behind it or why these attacks were happening.

"Do you have any clue who might be behind the transfer?" I asked, rising to my feet and stepping back from the cliff-edge.

Øyvin shook his head and ran his hand through his short hair. "The landslide complicated matters."

"How so?"

"I've only ever seen magic like that done by a Forest or Fjell Fae."

My eyebrows hit my hair-line and I let out a choked cough. "You mean, someone like Espen might be behind it?"

"No, not him, but I've seen Forest and Fjell Fae shift the earth in battle before," he said, reminding me that he was old enough to have fought in the war that Forest Queen Ragnhild had died in.

"What if someone was mimicking the power?" I asked.

Øyvin looked me in the eyes, his gaze darkening. "It would likely be stolen powers, if so. The Forest and Fjord Fae seem fine, but Queen Freija did not look like her usual self. I fear something may be weakening her."

I shoved my hands into my jacket pockets and shuffled from one side to the other, careful to avoid trampling the wild lavender. "What... what would happen if she died?"

Øyvin swallowed audibly and his voice dropped even lower. "If the King or Queen dies, this region will fall into ruin. Animals and plants will die, rock slides will become the norm, and the waters would be filled with filth, killing marine life."

"The forest is fine after Queen Ragnhild died, isn't it?"

"Only because Espen had the power to heal large swaths of it and protect it from further harm. He may not look it, but he is extremely powerful."

"Work together, then. Build a new alliance where all three factions work together, and fight back against whatever or whoever is doing this."

"Easier said than done when you're also fighting outsiders and their damaging actions." He nodded toward the refinery and warehouses across the water.

I grumbled and let out a long winded sigh.

Øyvin shook his head and took a step toward me. "But you're right," he said, and my eyes widened at the statement. "Life on the fjord would be a lot easier if we could all work together." Taking yet another step closer, he brought us chest to chest. Before I could throw another comment or question at him, he wrapped his thick arms around me and plunged us into the fjord below.

We breached the fjord's surface just outside the village, away from prying eyes, on a narrow rocky beach surrounded by tall pine trees. Øyvin dropped his arms from around my waist and set me down less than gently. My footing faltered on the slick rocks, and my head spun like I'd had too much tequila. Before I could topple onto my ass, a hand at my shoulder steadied me.

"Easy there," Øyvin said, retracting his hand like he'd just realized what he was doing.

"How does your torpedo swimming not give you the spins?" I asked, glancing over my shoulder at the completely dry Fjord Fae, his tawny hair shifting lightly in the chilly breeze.

"I've had over two centuries to grow accustomed to the sensation, and I was born beneath the surface, so the pressure doesn't bother me," he remarked and then strode past me.

I rolled my eyes at his back, but followed him through the grove of trees and onto a pine needle-covered trail that I assumed led back to Skolvik. The more I thought about his remark about being born underwater, the more questions popped into my head. One question in particular bothered me enough to voice it, even though I wasn't sure if the grumpy Asshole would consider answering.

I caught up and fell in beside him, making sure I didn't trip on any of the rocks that jutted up from beneath the crunchy forest floor. "Do you draw your powers from the water?" I asked.

He narrowed his eyes at me and furrowed his brow.

"What I mean is, do you need to be near the water to have your powers?"

He relaxed his features and pressed his lips together briefly before shaking his head. "You're asking if I need to be *near* the fjord to have the water powers?"

I nodded.

"No, there is water in the air." He waved his hand around us. "That's enough to assist us in doing certain things like making it rain."

I blinked twice and almost walked into a tree. *Make it rain?* Damn. That was some next level shit.

Øyvin caught my arm and steered me back onto the trail before I was taken out by a pine. He swiftly released me as we emerged from the woods and stepped onto a paved pathway with a sign noting a short distance back to the village. "I always *prefer* being close to the fjord because of my duties, but also because of my affinity for water. I like being near it—the sound, the feel, it makes me content."

My lips curved into a smile at his confession. I knew that feeling well. "The state I live in back in America—"

"Ohio," he said, sounding out the vowels like all the other people I'd met on my travels that had never heard of the state before.

I nodded, tucking my hands into the pockets of my fleece jacket. "That's the one. It doesn't have a lot of water. There is a huge lake at the top of the state, but other than that, we're landlocked."

"You don't have other lakes or rivers?" he asked, coming to a stop and turning to me. His eyes widened like the mere thought of no waterways was an unspeakable disaster.

"Oh, we do," I laughed and halted. "The rivers and gullies in Ohio are beautiful." In fact, they were my favorite thing to photograph when I couldn't afford to travel outside the state. "But there are no other large bodies of water, nor ocean. So, I've always enjoyed being near the water." I gestured to the fjord at our right as it gently lapped against the brush covered boulders along the shoreline. "It was a rarity growing up and brings me joy, too."

He gave me a lopsided grin, and my chest tightened at the sight. I gazed into his eyes and, for a split second, saw a happiness I'd never witnessed from Øyvin. My mouth and brain emptied of any words that could fill the growing silence, and heat spread over my cheeks. Øyvin lifted his hand and swept a stray piece of hair from my forehead, his fingers lightly brushing across my skin before he tucked the strand behind my ear. My eyes fluttered shut and I leaned into his touch, the warmth of—

No. No, no, no, no. Not the Asshole.

My eyes flew open and Øyvin's smile disappeared, his hand falling back to his side like he'd been burned. We both reared back from each other, looking anywhere but at the person across from us. Just because we had one thing in common didn't mean I *liked* the oaf.

"So, don't take you out to a desert then. Noted," I said with a cough, trying to pivot us back to our prior topic of conversation as my lungs fought to regain control of my breathing.

"Mm-hmm," he mumbled, brushing his hands across his pants, and moving again, increasing his pace toward the village.

I shook my arms and followed after him.

What the fuck just happened?

No, it wasn't worth thinking about.

Øyvin was an asshole. We hadn't bonded over a joint admiration for H_2O. There was no way in hell. He'd verbally thrown me on my rear when I'd missed the cruise ship, then literally thrown me in the fjord earlier today.

We despised each other.

Loathed, not liked.

Whatever had just transpired was a momentary lapse in judgment. Nothing more.

We reached Solveig's house that sat along the path by the water—the enclosed back porch facing the fjord—and I practically bolted for the front door on the other side of the building. "Okay, bye. Thanks for the tour," I yelled over my shoulder, catching him nod once and then briskly continue along the footpath.

I speed-walked to the door and unlocked it with shaky hands, the key giving me trouble that was wholly unnecessary. Stepping into Solveig's house, I slammed the door behind me and fell against it, my back pressing into the wood and glass. My chest heaved again, and I set my palms on my knees.

"Are you all right, Lennie?" Solveig asked, stepping out of the kitchen in her Nordic-patterned sweater and black pants. "Do you need a glass of water?"

Water... Fjord... Øyv—

"Nope." I straightened and waved away her offer. "No, I'm fine. Thank you."

She shrugged and retreated back into the kitchen.

I sucked in another breath and mentally reassured myself that I was fine. Totally and utterly, fine.

19
ØYVIN

I gave her a curt nod goodbye, acknowledging her swift departure before I spun on my heel and strode toward town, not daring to glance back over my shoulder. A dim glow settled over the wooden buildings of the village, the late afternoon autumn light dwindling faster as we got closer to winter. I kept my pace steady as I lost myself in my own thoughts.

What had I done? Why had I touched her? Had she really leaned into it?

I'd had a moment of madness. It likely settled in when she laughed and shared her fondness for water. Then I'd smiled. *Ancestors save me, why had I smiled?*

Perhaps she was right—which I was loathe to admit—but it had been a while since I'd seen any... action. I hadn't met a fae I'd been interested in recently, nor met any pretty little things I could enjoy for a night.

Lennie is pretty, though.

I shivered at the intrusive thought and drew my shoulders closer to my ears as I swept past Oddvar's Café on my way home.

Yes, she was attractive—with those curves, that unruly mane of hair, and brown eyes that always looked like she was calculating some sort of scheme. But therein lied the problem with her: she was trouble, and a human who knew the secret of our world, knew about the fae. Plus, there was her attitude.

I *hated* her damn attitude.

I let out a short huff. Lennie was trouble with a capital T, and she would be leaving here on Sunday.

A few minutes later, I reached for the key in my jacket pocket and unlocked the front door to my house. Wrenching the knob and pushing inside, I let out a deep breath before slamming the door shut.

Whatever had just happened between us was a momentary lapse of judgment—an inconsequential blip—and I would forget it had ever happened by tomorrow morning.

20
LENNIE

"Any threes?"

"Go fish," I replied, and Espen let out a low grumble of frustration as he drew another card from the pile between us. The collection of cards in his hand was steadily growing and his patience was dwindling. I loved to see it.

It was a quiet Friday night playing card games with a magic fae creature that looked like a handsome guy—you know, a typical way to end the work week—and I'd donned my navy quarter-zip sweater and leggings for the occasion, while Espen was in jeans and a sweater. Tomorrow was my last full day in Skolvik. The supply ship would be here on Sunday, and I'd finally be heading south to get my luggage from the cruise that had abandoned me like a sack of moldy corn husks.

Tendrils of Espen's dark hair fell across his eyes as they'd done all night, which only seemed to aggravate him more. Instead of brushing them away with his hand or a flick of his head, he'd set his lips askew and blow it out of the way. This cycle was repeated again and again and again as we continued our card game.

"Any tens?" I asked, one brow raised.

He sighed and handed one over. That card gave me a full set and I beamed at him. His hair settled back across his brow once more, and I scoffed. "Why don't you just tie that back?"

Cutting it would be stupid. His shaggy hair did, admittedly, look really good on him. But a cute little toddler-style ponytail that made him look like a unicorn wouldn't do any harm to his luscious locks.

He shook his head, but an idea crossed my mind at the same moment. "Where's that ball of string?" I asked, recalling the material he'd used to tie up my hair a few days ago when my hair-tie decided to quit while on the job.

Espen narrowed his eyes. "What are you thinking?"

I set down my cards and stalked over to the kitchen. Scanning the shelves, I found nothing but plates and crockery.

"Top drawer on the left," Espen said with an exasperated sigh.

I opened the drawer—an everything-but-the-sink one based on the array of contents—and found what I was looking for. Grabbing the small ball of twine and a pair of scissors, I returned to the sofa.

The string was soft but strong—perfect for lashing together a makeshift scrunchie. I wrapped a few loops around my fingers, and cut off the piece. Putting aside my tools, I glanced over at Espen who was sitting at the other end of the couch, watching me warily.

Sidling up next to him, I motioned for him to dip his head and lean closer. "Do you trust me?"

"Depends on where you left the kitchen scissors. I don't want to end up with a haircut, or does that only apply to cheerleaders?" he remarked with a sneaky grin.

"Fuck you." I chuckled and nudged his knee.

His smile didn't falter as he leaned forward, and I lightly brushed my fingers through his silky hair. Honestly, what conditioner did this guy use? Bringing the dark brown tresses into a soft peak, I looped the string around the bundle and pulled, tightening it before finishing up with a mini bow to hold it all together. Leaning back, I took in the sight before me: Espen biting his lower lip, looking ridiculous but with his hair well off his brow.

"It should hold," I muttered, a warm sensation curling up my leg from where our knees touched. "Now, you really *do* look like a sexy troll. Should we give you a bedazzled belly button, too?"

He squinted at me. "A bedazzled belly button? You mean to match my sparkling personality?" A slow smirk spread across his lips, and Espen wobbled his head, the little ponytail shifting but not unraveling. "Or do you just want to undress me?"

I licked my lips, pleased with my work on his hair, but all too aware of how hot my cheeks were starting to feel. Just the thought of undressing him had my fingers itching to pull off his sweater and brush across the hard planes of his abdomen. I knew he was strong—he'd saved me from falling into the ravine—but how many muscles was he hiding under there? How would they feel beneath my palms?

Shaking myself free of the intrusive thoughts and refusing to respond to his question, I slid back to my spot on the other end of the sofa before allowing another quick glance at Espen. His eyes flicked to my mouth, then returned to his cards.

He coughed softly. "Any twos?"

I shook my head, feeling slightly victorious, among other things. "Go fish."

Espen let out a frustrated grumble and picked up another card, sorting it into his ever growing collection.

"Øyvin wouldn't be caught dead doing this on a Friday night." I chuckled, trying to ease the tension in the room.

Espen snorted, a bubble of laughter escaping his chest. "No, he's probably playing his piano or cleaning his boat."

His WHAT?

I stilled and the room grew silent, the specks of dust too scared to flit about the space for fear of triggering my wrath. "What did you just say?"

"Øyvin has a piano."

"The other part," I said, my voice dropping to an icy tone.

"His boat?" Espen waved his hand toward the window. "He lives in his boathouse on the fjord. One of the red ones at the curve of the harbor. Didn't he show it to you yesterday on your tour?"

"No," I huffed. "He did not."

"What? Then how—"

"He took me on a tour *in* the fjord," I said, and Espen's eyes widened. "Not *on* it. I was a human submarine!"

I clenched my teeth, tossed my cards onto the coffee table, and stomped to the small window at the front of Espen's cabin. Pushing aside the little checkered curtain, I glared at the fjord below.

"Where?"

"What?"

"Where is his house?" I growled.

Espen appeared at my side and slid the curtain shut.

"Why do you need to know? I thought you liked visiting me?" He winked, but clearly didn't take the hint.

I didn't respond. Instead I shoved my feet into my boots, threw open the door, and traipsed outside leaving my jacket behind.

Espen muttered something behind me, but I kept walking down the rocky path toward the fjord, toward the bastard fae that had lied to me. I'd asked Øyvin in the café if he knew of anyone with a boat, and he'd said no. Had that question been phrased as 'a person with a boat'? Yes, but he'd still withheld information. I didn't have time for fucking *loopholes*.

This whole time the prick had a boat and could've helped me. Yes, he probably couldn't leave the area because of his job or whatever, but he could've let me or someone borrow the boat. Hell, I could probably have asked Oddvar to skipper the vessel and help me get down the fjord.

"He didn't mean it."

I glowered as Espen ran up beside me, keeping a steady pace. I raised my brows and pulled my hair into a ponytail—which was impressive considering the uneven terrain beneath my feet. "You knew?"

"Knew what?"

An exasperated groan left my lips, and I stomped into the forest, following the trail down the hillside. "You knew he had a boat this whole time? You knew he could've taken me down the fjord days ago."

"Ah, that," Espen said, looking only slightly guilty. "I knew he had a boat, but I honestly thought you knew and that he'd laughed in your face when you asked for help."

He basically had—and yesterday he'd even mentioned the two reasons why he hadn't swum with me down fjord—but that was beside the point. Right now, I was angry at the Asshole and a little bit annoyed at the handsome thing dodging trees like a pro as he wandered beside me downhill.

"Which one is it?" I asked when we reached the small collection of boathouses. Each one was red with white trim and a slate gray roof. All five of them sat over the water, but were built on the rocky edge of the fjord. The boulders led right up to the stilted foundations where the water lapped at the pylons.

"I—I'm not entirely sure I should tell you," Espen hesitated, running his hand across his short beard.

I set my hands on my hips and narrowed my gaze. "You have two balls, yes?"

Espen's lips quirked, amusement shining in his eyes. "Yes."

"You want to keep both?" I pincered two of my fingers like a pair of scissors.

He shook his head like I was too much to handle. "The last one," he revealed with a sigh. "Don't do anything stupid. We're all on edge. We just want to help our people."

I grumbled, unwilling to listen to reason right now.

I left a smirking Espen on the shore as I stomped across the wood dock that led to Øyvin's front door. It wasn't a small building, but it wasn't overly large either—it looked like a garage with a floor above it. There was a door that faced the street, with a window on either side and a little square window near the triangular roof. I also spotted a side door along the broadside of the red house. That was where I aimed my anger.

Twisting the handle, I threw the door open and stormed inside, then was instantly assaulted by damp air and the sound of water lapping against a hull. To my left was an open garage door letting in cool air, the fjord visible from where I stood. And right in front of me, moored and roped within the water inlet inside the building, was a perfectly sea-worthy white speedboat.

"What are you doing here?" A cold voice skittered across my skin and I spun, slipping on the wet wood beneath my feet. Øyvin grabbed my arm before I fell onto the boat and hurtled me across the room. I landed with a thud against the wall, not far from the door I'd just entered through.

Before me stood one angry Fjord Fae. His eyes were wide and his jaw was as tight as my own.

"You fucking... lying... piece of shit," I seethed.

A grumble emanated from his chest, which was only covered by a thin white shirt, the sleeves rolled up his forearms exposing thick muscles that jumped with tension. "I have never lied to you."

"Lies by omission are still lies, Asshole," I snarled, my lungs heaving for air. Glancing to my left, I grabbed the first thing I saw—a plastic buoy—and threw it at Øyvin's head. He ducked, and it landed in the boat with a dull thump. "Try being nicer to visitors."

Øyvin grumbled and lunged toward me. I shifted back into the wall behind me as he pressed his hands on either side of my head, caging me in. "You break into my house and expect me to be *nice* to you?" The lines on his forehead deepened, and his chest lightly brushed mine. The air between us warmed and swelled, ready to explode.

"You could've gotten rid of me days ago," I hissed. "Found someone to float me down the fjord in your boat and been done with me once and for all. I wouldn't have had to wait until Sunday. You wouldn't have had to babysit me yesterday."

He grimaced, his nostrils flaring, breaths sawing in and out of both of us. "Like I said, you aren't—"

"Wanted here, *needed* here," I interjected on a whisper, using the words he'd told me the day we'd first met at Oddvar's café when he'd so rudely pointed out that I was unwanted. "I'm a problem and a threat to the fjord and faes' wellbeing, aren't I?"

He let out a low grumble, letting me know exactly how he felt with the anger raging within his eyes. "You're trouble. Thankfully, the supply boat arrives in less than 48 hours."

"You know what we do with troublesome problems in the US?" I asked, not leaving him time to answer. "We handle them. We remove them as quickly as possible. You could've done so when you had the chance. You could've helped yourself."

He growled—straight-up *growled* like an animal. I returned the sentiment with a grunt of my own, and then, without thinking it through, I kicked him in the shin. He stumbled back, removing his arms, and freeing me from my temporary confines.

"Bitch!"

"Asshole!"

"Why don't you just fucking walk away from the fjord then?" he yelled, sweeping his arms wide. "Go climb some mountains to get back to your cruise ship in Stavanger?"

"With that kind of logic, I may as well fucking swim!"

"Fine!" he replied, and before I had a chance to catch my breath, I was flying into the water behind his boat, through the open garage archway, landing outside the building entirely.

The freezing cold fjord closed above my head for the second day in a row, and my lungs contracted from the blow. Keeping my eyes shut tight, I righted myself and kicked upward through the water, using my hands to carve through my frigid captor.

I broke the surface only a few seconds after being submerged, and dragged in a deep breath. The air above the water was almost as cold as the fjord. Sucking down more oxygen, I blinked away the droplets on my eyelashes and spun around.

Øyvin leaned against the side of the boathouse, a wicked grin on his face, his blond hair rippling lightly in the evening breeze.

I swam toward the ladder by his feet, muttering a new expletive with every stroke.

Øyvin didn't move, and he most definitely didn't offer a hand to help me out of the water. I grabbed onto the top rung and hauled myself up and over the edge of the dock. My chest heaved as I caught my breath, and I raised my arm, giving Øyvin the middle finger.

"Stupid." He scoffed.

"Y-you threw m-me in the d-damn fjord!" I stuttered, unable to stop the shaking from entering my voice. My clothes were soaked through, plastered to my body, and chilling me to the bone. "*Again.*"

"You said you wanted to swim. Seemed appropriate since I needed to throw a human out of my house for breaking and entering."

I put up my other middle finger in response.

A flicker of a smile twisted Øyvin's lips as he added, "Like you Americans say, I had to take out the trash."

I shouldn't have gone for his shin; I should've aimed higher when I had the chance.

I rolled onto my stomach and pushed off the now wet dock that wrapped around the side of the building. Stepping up in front of him, I lifted the end of my ponytail and twisted it. A stream of water fell from my soaking tresses and landed on his feet. He bit his lip and hissed, now the proud owner of wet socks.

"Fuck. You," I growled and stomped off, back down the road to Solveig's house. The entire trek I mulled over ideas to get revenge on the Asshole. I had one day to do it, and wringing my hair out over his feet was not enough—I had to think bigger. Perhaps I could sneak lutefisk—the slimy, fishy *delicacy*—into his house and stink up the place. Or maybe I could throw neon pink glitter all over his boat. A smile crept across my face as I strode through the village, the white-colored buildings of the downtown core standing sentry against the inky waters of the fjord that lapped against the hulls of the boats in the marina.

His boat.

21
LENNIE

I devoured my early lunch, the ham-and-cheese sandwich and hot coffee from Oddvar's a treat as I watched locals wander past the café window. After bundling up in jeans and a fleece sweater this morning, I'd thrown my hair into a ponytail and had traipsed back up to Espen's to retrieve my rain-jacket, before strolling through the village to hatch my afternoon plan. Was this idea going to be somewhat stupid? Yes, which was why I'd gone to Oddvar's first to consume some courage and calories.

I was going to commandeer Øyvin's boat, drive it out a little ways, and set it adrift down the fjord. I already had it on good authority—also known as Espen—that Øyvin was working today. So, sneaking in undetected shouldn't be too difficult. Espen had rolled his eyes at me when I mentioned that I'd be paying a visit to Øyvin's house. I hadn't even revealed what I was going to do, but he'd still said, "Don't end up at the police station."

Clearly, the male didn't know me very well at all. I had no intention of getting caught.

I'd had all night to ruminate on my idea, picking my course of action, and then spent my lunch hour building myself up to pull it off. Fully aware that I was going for a swim, I'd left my camera at Solveig's. There was no need to cause severe damage to my baby while completing this prank, however much I wanted photo evidence to look back on.

After finishing up my lunch, I paid Oddvar and gave him a quick nod as I strolled out the front door of the café. Outside, the clouds had come out, blanketing the entire region in a gray cloak. I pulled my zipper up, stepped out of the way of the "summer skier" as he glided past in his skin-tight suit that highlighted *everything*, and headed toward Øyvin's boathouse.

I arrived to perfect silence. Not a single noise emanated from the red building on the shoreline. It was just me, the fjord, and the sleek white boat inside. *Perfect.*

I checked the front and side door, jiggling the handles, both locked. Taking a deep breath and steadying my pulsing heart rate, I crept along the little dock to the back of the building that faced the fjord. The garage door was half-closed, but there was enough of a gap that I could potentially squeeze around and under.

Where was the *Mission: Impossible* theme song when I needed it?

Sidling up against the wall, I squatted and gripped the white trim that lined the entire portal to the garage. With a prayer to the guy downstairs, I swung my left leg down and around, hitching it onto the wooden-platform on the other side of the wall. My muscles spasmed and my fingers got a workout for the ages as I quickly shifted underneath the metal door, using my momentum to crash, butt first, onto the interior planks with a thud.

Letting out a small chuckle of victory, I quickly surveyed my dark surroundings. Water lapped against the boat's white hull, buoys and rope hung on the far wall, and a tiny lamp was on above the side door casting a glow across the space. Without waiting a second longer, I untied the thick ropes from the cleats and stepped onto the boat. It wasn't large by any means but had a bench at the back, two seats in the middle including the captain's chair and steering mechanisms, plus two small seats up front. Luckily, the key was in the ignition, and with a few sputtered starts, the engine roared to life.

Now to open the damn garage door.

I searched around the control console and found a clicker that looked a lot like the garage door opener my parents had. Since it wasn't a red button with warning labels around or an image of a skull and crossbones, I clicked it. A motor high above me started whirring and the large white door lifted upward, letting in a cold breeze and the smell of pine and water.

My lips twitched into a wicked smile, and my heart thrummed in my chest, victory another step closer. I successfully reversed out of the boathouse, thankful for the summers on a little boat with my family on the Great Lakes and the bumpers that helped me avoid a disastrous collision or scraping the patina. I didn't have a death wish: I was fairly confident Øyvin would murder me if his boat came back damaged. I just wanted to yo-ho-ahoy it down the fjord a little ways, for the sake of making his life difficult.

Once I'd cleared the building and was safely out into the fjord, I shifted the throttle into drive and coaxed the boat in a westward direction. Wind whipped at my ponytail as I stood in front of the captain's chair, hands on the wheel. Nobody else was out on the water, which was exactly why I'd opted to do this in the afternoon. Most people were at work or school, and as the lone tourist in town, I had zero responsibilities to tie up my day.

It was just me, the fjord, and the boat.

With towering evergreens and slivers of silver birch trees climbing up the mountainside, I wished I'd brought a camera. The fjord was gorgeous from this vantage point on the water. The clouds hung close to the tops of the hills, and the town grew smaller as the boat continued humming along slowly, barely a trace of a wake behind it. The water was a beautiful mottled blue, green, and gray as it reflected its surroundings like a choppy mirror or mosaic of stained glass. The majestic—

Thud.

I gripped the steering wheel and slowed the engine to idle, my knuckles turning white, my breaths coming hard and fast. "What the fuck?"

Thud.

The noise was definitely coming from the left side of the boat. I glanced over but saw nothing untoward. *Had I hit something underneath the surface?* There was nothing on the little monitor thingies on the dash, but I also hadn't paid any attention to them. This wasn't a fishing trip.

Thud.

A pale hand reached out of the water and slapped against the boat's railing. I jumped, letting out a strangled scream as the Asshole hoisted himself onto the boat. His denim button-down shirt and black pants were soaked and clung to him, little droplets of water filling the boat—he'd clearly been too angry to create that bubble thing he used the other day. The boat rocked from side to side as he narrowed his eyes, a low rumble emitting from his chest.

I took a step back, and eyed the odds of me making it into the water before the Fjord Fae killed me. He was one big motherfucker, and had just swam upside the boat like a humanoid submarine—I didn't have a chance. So, I settled on deflecting. "Fancy seeing you here," I said with a toothy grin.

His scowl somehow turned down further. "What the fuck are you doing with my boat?"

My smile faltered, and I pushed my ponytail off my shoulder. "Joy ride?"

He took two steps toward me, bringing us chest to chest, his grimace unyielding.

"What are you, a shark?" I scowled at his annoyed face, his blue eyes conveying how badly he'd love to kill me. "Should I punch you on the nose to make you go away?"

"Sharks don't live in this fjord."

"Just assholes, then. You'd think the water would be a lot browner." I crossed my arms, and he nudged me out of the way of the captain's console. Wrapping one hand around the steering wheel and the other over the throttle, Øyvin took control of the boat and pointed it home. I let out a long vexed sigh at my own failure, slumping into the chair next to him.

"What were you hoping to achieve?" he grumbled as the boat glided toward his house.

"A damn sight more than *this* shambles," I huffed, disappointed in myself.

"Why don't you just go home?"

"That's kinda what I've been *trying* to do. I could've left a lot quicker if you weren't such a selfish prick." Both of us increased our volume with every sentence, the blood in my veins pumping harder and harder. "The supply ship arrives tomorrow, though, so I'll be gone soon."

"Good." He didn't look at me, just scowled and steered the boat back to his house.

I let out a harrumph and averted my gaze, focusing instead on the calm waters ahead of us and the reflection of the trees across them. My plan had gone to shit. I'd barely made it out of eyesight from the village, and already I'd been busted. Young Lennie would be appalled by my inability to pull this off.

Maybe I should've gone with the lutefisk idea. My hands would've smelled for days, but at least it would have been more successful.

We cruised to the outer-edges of the village and into the boathouse.

"Stay there," Øyvin said and jumped out of the boat, landing smoothly on the internal dock like he'd done this a thousand times.

I watched for a few seconds as he tied up the boat to the cleats before hoisting myself off the vessel. Øyvin turned to me, groaned and muttered something rude under his breath, then continued his work.

Conceding to my own failure, I shrugged and headed for the door. It wasn't the first time one of my pranks had been foiled, and I highly doubted it would be the last. Turning the knob and then yanking the side door open, I made to step out of the boathouse—

Øyvin slammed the door shut, his hand plastered against it above my head. "What were you thinking?"

I turned on the spot, my face level with his chest, and glanced up into his darkened gaze. "That payback's a bitch."

He scoffed.

"How did you find out anyway?" I asked, narrowing my eyes at him before glancing at his lips.

"A friend below"—he tilted his head toward the water—"noticed my boat out on the fjord and informed me."

Fuck. I hadn't even considered the Fjord Fae beneath the surface. Rookie mistake.

"I can either report you to the chief of police," he said, making a point of *not* mentioning the yogi-fae-cop that'd probably let me off the hook... again. "Or you can wash down my boat."

"How about neither?"

"One or the other."

"No."

"Yes."

"Bite me."

With a frustrated growl, he surged forward and pressed his lips against mine. My heart slammed in my chest at the sudden move, but within seconds I was grasping his shirt in my hands, clutching him to me as he crowded me against the door. My back rubbed against the weathered wood and he lifted my leg, running his palm down the underside of my thigh. Wrapping my calf behind him, I pulled him in closer, chest to chest, and moaned as he deepened the kiss with a vicious fervor.

Damn it, why is he so good at this?

The thought flitted through my head as we used our mouths to devour each other in an anger-infused haze. I was too caught up in the sparks of pleasure that sang through my veins and the throbbing in my core to care about hating the fae right now. The way his length hardened against my stomach, his large hands palmed my ass, his teeth tugged on my bottom lip—he blissfully overwhelmed my senses.

I pushed against his chest, fingers fumbling as I started unbuttoning his shirt. I got three unfastened before he pulled back and ripped it open, sending the little buttons skittering across the floorboards. I skimmed my hands down the muscled planes of his torso before flicking my eyes up to his. Unadulterated lust and hunger shone through, his pupils blown wide. With how my core spasmed and begged to be touched, I didn't doubt that my own gaze looked very much the same.

I rolled my lower lip between my teeth, and he growled. Lifting me up, I hooked my legs around his waist and my arms around his neck as he grasped my ass and walked to the other door. He kicked his boot against it, and the door flew open, crashing against the wall inside.

I didn't get a chance to survey my surroundings before I was thrown onto a brown leather couch. Lying on my back, Øyvin hovered above me with one hand on the sofa-top, the other on the armrest, and his knee between my thighs.

"Tell me to stop."

"Not a fucking chance," I groaned, desperate for the hate-sex that was about to go down.

He mercifully obliged, unfastening and removing my boots in record time before yanking down my pants, pulling my underwear with them.

A groan escaped from low in his throat and I unzipped my jacket, pulling it and my sweater off and dropping them onto the floor. His eyes flicked up to my chest before returning to the apex of my thighs. Tantalizingly slow, he swept his fingers up the inside of my legs, and a deep shudder ran through me. My synapses fired and my core pulsed as he trailed two fingers across my soaking center. I moaned, and, without further warning, he plunged those digits into me. I swore at the sensation, arching my back for more.

"Greedy," Øyvin muttered, his eyes bright with approval.

"You fucker."

He chuckled and curled his fingers inside me, sending a fiery jolt of pleasure up my spine. A whimper left my lips, and the corner of his mouth curved into a spiteful smile. After swiftly removing his fingers and popping them in his mouth, he disappeared for a few seconds before returning and ripping open a condom wrapper—the zipper on his pants undone. He freed his cock and rolled on the condom, watching me closely the entire time.

In that moment, I didn't care how I felt or who he was. I wanted and needed release—to rid my body of the pent up tension that had been riding me for the past twenty-four hours and stoked into a frenzy in the past ten minutes.

Returning his hands to my legs, Øyvin shifted and settled between my thighs. Without further fanfare, he lined up and plunged into me. I let out a guttural sound and clung to his shoulders, loving the stretch of his invasion. He roughly pressed his lips to mine, devouring me yet again. I opened my mouth, taking as much of him as I was giving of myself. With a groan from both of us, he increased the aggressive pace of his thrusts, pounding me into the cushions. Raking my nails across his back, I bucked against the cresting waves of pleasure. Electricity hummed through my veins, overpowering my senses, as the ache in my core grew and grew and grew. A wave of pleasure finally washed over me, bathing me in euphoric bliss. I dug my heels into Øyvin as he stilled and shuddered, finding his own release.

We lay there for a minute, wrapped up in each other, panting and spent. He pressed his forehead against mine, letting our breaths intermingle, before swiftly pulling back and out of me. Another spasm rocked through me at the removal, and I swallowed a whimper.

Øyvin scrambled off the sofa and left, heading through a small door by the kitchen. As the sound of water met my ears, I sat up fully and a sinking feeling settled over me.

I just hate-fucked a creature several hundred years older than me.

I shook my head, swallowed the conflicting emotions, and frantically searched for my discarded clothes. Locating them on the other side of the wooden coffee-table, I straightened up and took the moment to take in his home. A small kitchen sat in the back corner to my left, then there was the little bathroom Øyvin had disappeared to, the sofa in front of me and a small tv hanging above a fireplace at my back. I pulled on my clothes as my eyes bugged out at the final piece of furniture in the room. To my right, beside the door to the boat, was a gorgeous, old upright piano. Before I could run my fingers over the keys, Øyvin sauntered back into the room, all tidied up—save for his now broken shirt that hung open, revealing the abdominal muscles of a fae-creature-asshole-thingy that would definitely *never* feature in any of my daydreams. Ever.

"Don't think this means I like you," I said, pointing a finger at him before sliding on my boots.

He leaned against the small kitchen counter, messing up his blond hair with his hand. "Wouldn't dream of it, even in my nightmares."

"Good." I nodded, not uttering another word. Crossing to the front door, I unlocked it and wandered back toward Solveig's house, feeling aftershocks from my nerve-shattering orgasm the whole way home.

22

ESPEN

I awoke in the middle of the night to a muffled rumbling sound and the earth shaking minutely beneath my bed. Ever since Lennie arrived in the village, I'd had vivid dreams—most featured her in all her sassy glory, and in a few she was even doing yoga with me. Whatever the thundering noise was, it must've been a dream, too, because Norway didn't get earthquakes.

Rolling over and burying my head into the pillows, I began to drift off again to the thoughts of Lennie joining me on the mat until—

A heavy-metal tune—the ringtone I'd assigned to my boss, Bente—sounded from my bedside table and I bolted upright, scrambling to reach across the bed to answer. "What happened?"

"Another landslide," Bente said, her no-nonsense tone traced with a hint of sadness that had my stomach flipping upside down. "There are injuries."

I launched out of bed, nestled the phone between my shoulder and ear, and started pulling on my uniform that hung on a hook beside my closet. "Where was it?"

"The East Road, near the trail."

Shit. That was where I'd hiked with Lennie the other day. If that road was blocked, too, then the entire town would be trapped—no entry, no exit, except by boat. "Did it block the entire road?"

"Yes."

Shit. Shit. Shit.

"Report to the site in fifteen minutes."

"I'll be there in five," I replied and hung up.

Earth and boulders were strewn across the road, the land having given way and shifted like a collapsed sandcastle. It wasn't unlike the last landslide, but, as Bente had mentioned, this one apparently had injuries. A police car was parked and pointing its headlights at the debris as another officer set up the floodlights. But even in the dark and drizzle, it wasn't hard to miss the shattered taillights of a car poking out beneath the rocks.

The firemen arrived a moment later, three of which ran directly to the car, seemingly unafraid of the potential risks of more movement from the earth. While they did their job, attempting to find signs of life and extract the vehicle from the chaos, I assisted my fellow officers with securing the area by setting up more barricades. The entire time, I focused on my work, my duty as a "human," and avoided using my fae powers to lift or remove the boulders from atop the car. While I could have eased the weight of the soil above the stranded humans, I couldn't shift the whole thing without outing myself as *other*. It was the worst kind of torture—being unable to help when help was needed the most.

But it wouldn't have made a difference. One of the firemen turned back to us and shook his head, and my stomach turned over at the gut-wrenching reality of what had occurred.

For hours I assisted other officers and the firemen at clearing the debris enough to fully access the crushed car. By the time the sun rose, casting an eerie glow on the scene, we'd removed enough material to safely extract the deceased occupants from the car.

It was Mr. and Mrs. Anderson—a local older couple, both in their late fifties, who enjoyed a late dinner at Fisken every Saturday night. I'd known them both for almost a decade and was heartbroken at the loss.

My stomach turned at the gory sight, the likes of which I hadn't seen since the war in the south. I stepped away, letting the firemen finish retrieving the bodies and turned to where Bente stood beside the police car, overseeing the scene and keeping back the few people from the village that had woken early to see what all the commotion was.

"It's the Anderson's," I said quietly, making sure no one else heard the name until we'd notified their next of kin—their daughter who lived in the capitol city, Oslo.

Bente sighed and shook her head, her white hair damp from the dreary rain. "I'll call Emma Anderson. Can you monitor the people while I head back to the station to notify her?"

I nodded, and she departed, striding back into town toward the police station.

"I heard what happened," a female voice I immediately recognized said from the gathered crowd. Lennie squeezed her way between two villagers that had been practically camped here for the past three hours. They grumbled at her, but she just rolled her eyes at them. Their responding snort fell short of gaining her attention as her forlorn gaze met mine. "Are you okay?"

I nodded. The shock of what happened had worn off, that telltale tingling sensation in my bones easing away slowly as the morning dragged on. Seeing her here also soothed something in me. Like everyone else in the crowd, she was wearing her rain jacket and a pair of jeans. Her blonde hair hung down, brushing the top of her chest and framing her face perfectly. "Your boat is today. Are you ready to leave?"

A beat of silence went by as we stared at each other before she answered, "Yeah, I've packed my stuff. It's at Solveig's waiting to go this evening."

"Good," I said and shuffled on the spot. "Umm, the supply ship should've arrived an hour ago. Oddvar let them know earlier this week to expect you. All you need to do is meet them at the docks at 8 p.m. tonight."

She scrunched her brow and crossed her arms. "That's kind of late."

I couldn't hold back the tiny chuckle that escaped me, amused by her reaction to such a common-place thing in my world. "The crew like to grab dinner at Fisken before they head out. The captain is Oddvar's son, remember?"

She tilted her head and nodded gently. "Yeah, that makes sense, then." She matched my stance and shuffled her feet a bit, before adding, "You gonna see me off or should I say my goodbyes now?"

"Do you want me at the docks?" I asked, sincerely hoping I'd get another chance to see her.

She shrugged. "I wouldn't mind it. If you can get away, that is." She nodded at the chaos behind me.

I glanced over my shoulder, before turning back to her. "I'm sure I can step away for a bit."

She smiled, her cheeks flushing a tad pinker than usual, before she shook her arms and straightened up. "Okay then. I'll see you later. Gotta go say goodbye to Oddvar and get one last cup of coffee."

I returned her grin, and nodded. "I'll see you later, Lennie."

She spun and sauntered back through the thinning crowd, dodging past the two grumbly guys again. With each step she took away from me, something inside my chest spasmed.

23
ØYVIN

Espen rubbed the top of his chest with his fist when I emerged from the crowd, narrowly avoiding bumping into the American that plagued my dreams. Her moans had left a mark, as had her fingers where they'd scratched up my back yesterday.

Shaking off the memory, I stepped in front of the Forest Fae.

He jolted at my sudden appearance, and I smiled at the impact I had on him, the inner thoughts I'd clearly just disturbed. Based on where he'd been looking, I could easily guess who they'd been about.

He cleared his throat. "Good morning. Everything okay?" He didn't mince his words, keeping them brief and to the point with humans within hearing range, and I appreciated that about him.

"All fine this time, but I had a visitor this morning."

"If you want to invite me to join your escapades, you need only call," Espen said with a quick grin.

I rolled my eyes and shook my head. "Not that kind of visitor. Halvar stopped by."

Espen's gaze widened, and his eyebrows hit his floppy hair that was in need of a comb.

"Freija has requested another meeting—"

"Should we grab, Len—"

I waved my hand. "Just us. Halvar was very adamant that it was just you and I meeting with her this time."

"When?" Espen asked, glancing around, likely reassuring himself that the onlookers were staying behind the police barriers.

"Her office. After lunch. Can you attend?"

He nodded. "I'll have someone take over."

"Good." I spun on my heel and walked back to my boathouse.

Several hours later I traipsed up the hillside and into the mountain. As soon as I crossed the threshold, I placed my palm against my left shoulder and shifted my appearance, my ears elongating slightly and my Fjord Fae Guard uniform materializing—formal attire was always favored when meeting with one of the royals, especially when said meeting was happening in the throne room. It wasn't my preferred choice of clothing—I liked more casual knit sweaters and jeans—but at least I could use my fae powers to mimic my uniform over my body like a mirage. Clothes shifting was one of the powers I used the least, but it was always helpful when you needed to avoid any humans spotting your unusual attire or ears.

I strolled into the mountain, nodding to the guards I passed along the way. As I reached the entrance to the throne room, I found Espen already inside, conversing with Queen Freija.

The noble and her Head Guard, Halvar, lifted their heads at my arrival. Espen, wearing his green Forest Fae uniform, glanced over his shoulder giving me his signature beaming smile, albeit more sluggish than usual. I'd never understood that fae's unrelenting joy, and probably never would.

With a bow of my head, I approached the trio. Halvar was in gray-and-black attire, his uniform looking ready for battle, while the Queen wore a long emerald dress of thick material that swallowed her delicate frame. Her hair hung down neatly on either side of her face, the dark brown tresses brushing across her chest.

"Øyvin, glad you could join us," Freija said respectfully, as we both knew I was exactly on time. Espen had just been early, which wasn't surprising. "We were just discussing last night's landslide."

"Any news?" I quirked a brow as I stepped up beside Espen.

He shook his head. "I haven't been able to search the scene. With the death of the Andersons, there are too many people around."

I shrugged. He had a fair point.

"I think it's safe to assume this was a repeat of what happened the other day," Halvar said, his burly timbre echoing off the sky-blue quartz of the glistening throne room.

"Agreed," I replied, my tone echoing the displeasure I felt within.

"Have you seen any other impacts internally?" Espen asked, not shifting when Halvar narrowed his eyes at the Forest Fae.

Halvar glanced to his left, looking at the Queen for a quick second, before turning his light-blue eyes back on us. Crossing his arms over his chest, he said, "There is nothing that you need concern—"

"Halvar, please," Freija interjected, lifting her hand, and her Head Guard stopped and clenched his jaw. "What he *meant* to say is that I have felt weaker; the magic of the mountain seems to be weakening with every one of these natural events. Whomever is behind this is targeting me as they did my dear friend, Queen Ragnhild, two decades ago."

Espen and I froze to the spot, our chests barely moving as the Queen uttered words I'd been dreading. Words I knew would hit hard for the fae beside me. Words that stirred an unwelcome emotion inside my own chest.

Freija continued, "But I shall not be drawn asunder. Øyvin, I know we have no formal alliance with the Fjord Fae, but has Balder informed you of any weakening of his magic, any pollution increase in the waters?"

I shook my head. "None, your Majesty. King Balder's magic does not appear weakened at this time, but he is constantly challenged by the humans and their pollution of the fjord."

She took a deep breath and tilted her head slightly. "I understand. If Balder should see fit to do so, please inform me if anything changes. As you both know, it is the monarch's duty to worry for our people, and my concerns are great at present." I nodded, and she continued, "With that said, we are proceeding with my birthday celebrations in two weeks' time."

Halvar grunted, not saying anything to disagree with his monarch, but it was evident he very much did not agree with this decision. Sensing the tension in the room, Espen and I stayed silent, unmoving.

"All Forest Fae and Fjord Fae are welcome to attend the event in the great hall. The festivities will commence at dusk." Freija turned to me before adding, "Please extend the invitation to King Balder."

Halvar grunted again.

I bowed my head. "I shall."

Freija smiled and rose from her seat before tilting her head in thanks, then left the room. Halvar followed closely behind her, exiting through a side entrance, but not before he cast a glare over his shoulder. I refrained from reacting, even though that look sent a brief pang of fear into my chest as he departed.

"Well, could've gone worse," Espen piped up, bouncing on the balls of his feet, seemingly unaffected by the death-glare we'd just received.

Rolling my eyes, I turned for the entrance to the throne room, making my own exit. I needed to get back to work and check in with my scouts for updates on the oil that was supposed to be delivered to the refinery tonight.

Espen caught up with me, and we walked in relative silence until he almost crashed into a rushing Nora.

"Gentlemen," she sputtered, her breaths labored as if she'd been running from a troll.

"Nora," Espen said by way of greeting, while I just stared at the short Fjell Fae with rosy cheeks.

"Here to see Freija, I presume?" she asked.

We both nodded, but she barely paid us any attention, her hands full of books and what looked like a quill, the likes of which I hadn't seen in decades.

"I have to get to work. Another fae needs their story documented. Dinner tonight, though? Fisken?" Nora asked as she whirled around the corner, ducking into the opening of another tunnel.

"How about tomorrow?" Espen said. "I already have plans."

"Ah... saying goodbye to someone?" A knowing glint shone from her eyes, and she flicked her eyebrows once.

Espen nodded, and I swallowed hard.

"I'm on duty at the western coast, another time perhaps," I replied, my voice frustratingly strained.

"I'll see you at Fisken tomorrow at seven, then," Nora said and disappeared down the glowing passage, heading deeper into the mountain.

Espen and I walked toward the main exit in silence, both mulling over the words of the Queen and the events of the past week.

"Are you sure there aren't any scars or problems in the fjord?" Espen asked on a sigh, breaking the peace.

I took a deep breath, steadying my annoyance at the invisible finger being pointed at the Fjord Fae. "If there was, my scouts would have informed me."

Espen held his hands up as his fae uniform slowly faded until he stood before me in his black-and-silver police uniform. "It was just a question. We still don't know who is behind all of this, but—"

"There is evidence it could be someone from any of the three factions."

"Yes, I agree. But the worst damage appears to have been above the waterline. And I don't believe a Forest Fae would do this sort of harm without being coerced."

I lifted my hand to my shoulder and slowly removed the magic mirage of my Fjord Fae uniform, the gray-and-navy material vanishing into thin air, leaving me once again in my cream-knit sweater and dark jeans. "You clearly haven't been down the fjord in a while."

"You know I've been busy," Espen sighed. "Getting out west isn't easy when I have responsibilities here among the humans."

I refrained from scowling but whatever look crossed my face had Espen shaking his head.

"I know it's bad; the pollution will never get better unless humans rely less on fuel and its byproducts."

With a grunt I sauntered out of the mountain, Espen following closely behind.

"You going to the docks to say goodbye?" he asked, not making eye contact or even stopping for that matter.

"Already did."

Espen let out a humm that sounded very much like he didn't believe me. He was right though, I hadn't.

I didn't want to say goodbye.

We may have slept together, but it hadn't meant anything. Lennie was leaving, heading home to America, where she would go on with her human life, taking her precious photos, and never returning to our little village at the end of the fjord.

"You okay there?" Espen pried as we traipsed through the woods, the breeze keeping us company, and the afternoon sky barely visible through the canopy.

I grunted a reply, which had Espen chuckling.

"I know she got under your skin—"

"I'm going home," I grumbled, cutting him off as we reached the edge of the village. I didn't want to talk about her any more. She was leaving. End of story, end of trouble, end of whatever this ache was in my chest.

24

LENNIE

A light breeze flitted around me and the stars had begun to twinkle in the clear night sky. I waited on the pier with my over-stuffed backpack by my feet, watching the large supply ship bob on the inky water. The ship's hull was a menacing black—ready to carve through the waters—and aboard lay short stacks of pallets where crates had sat earlier in the day.

"So... this is goodbye," someone said behind me.

Turning slowly, I took in the Forest Fae ambling down the dock. Espen was still in his police uniform, eyes a little darker than usual, heavier—probably from what had happened last night. I couldn't blame him.

"This is it," I said, my voice a little chipper in hopes of seeing him smile again.

He came to a stop in front of me before rocking on the balls of his feet and looking me over like he was memorizing the image. My skin tingled in response as if he could see beneath my layers of clothing, *truly* see me. It was heartwarming, and something I wasn't accustomed to feeling, something I couldn't quite name, washed through me.

"It was nice to meet you, Lennie," he said, stepping closer and wrapping his arms around me.

After a second of hesitation, I melted into his hold and let out a deep breath. "It was nice to meet you too, Espen. Good luck with everything." I leaned backward and looked up into his amber-colored eyes. "I hope you find the culprit of all this chaos."

He sighed and stepped back, releasing me from his arms and letting his hands fall to his sides. "Thank you for your help."

"No problem," I replied, pushing a wayward hair behind my ear as my chest tightened with each word. "Thanks for not shoving me in jail when I punched you."

He scoffed a laugh, his lips quirking into that cute smile of his as he ran his fingers through his dark hair. "You're welcome. Try not to do that anymore."

"I'll do my best."

For a moment we just stared at each other, the gentle lapping of water against the nearby boats the only thing keeping us company. I was at a loss for words, which was unusual for me. But there I stood, unable to utter a single syllable because none of them felt good enough to encapsulate this departure.

With a drawn out exhale and a gentle smile, Espen said, "Goodbye, Lennie."

I returned the grin with one of my own, though it didn't fill my face. "Bye, Espen."

He sauntered backward, his hands still firmly in his pockets until he reached the start of the pier. There he turned and disappeared into the village without another glance in my direction.

Watching, waiting, as if expecting him to return, I stood there for a while, the wind sending errant strands of hair brushing across my cheeks as my heart beat harder than it had five minutes ago. Why had saying goodbye to Espen felt so difficult? I'd only known him a week, yet now I rubbed my fist across the top of my chest, trying to soothe the pang there.

"Are you ready?" a gruff voice said, startling me.

I spun and looked at the man behind me, his wool hat sitting slightly askew atop his head. He had weather-worn features and was a younger version of Oddvar with thick brows and a gravelly tone.

"Almost," I said with a sigh. Turning around again, I took one last glance across the village that I'd called home for the past week, mentally photographing the scenery. From the little lights in the windows of the white houses, to the tall pine trees that blanketed the mountainsides. Skolvik was a beautiful little oasis. A magical sanctuary for both humans and those creatures that I'd somehow befriended.

"Are you waiting for someone else?"

Was I? Øyvin had made it quite clear that he didn't like me when I first arrived, but over the past few days things had taken a turn between us. From the moment he showed me what lay within the fjord, to the way he gently tucked my hair behind my ear like he couldn't stop himself, I could feel him warming to me. Then there was the explosive hate-sex—which had been stellar. But, what stuck in my mind now, wasn't how good it felt to have him inside me; it was the way he'd pressed his forehead against mine afterward. When our throes of passion had waned, our climaxes reached and diffused, he'd rested his forehead against mine and breathed us in, that moment filled with more emotion than I'd been prepared for.

"Miss?" A voice seeped through my thoughts, dragging me back to the present.

I shook my head, freeing myself of the memories with the Fjord Fae, and shoved my hands into my jacket pockets. My right hand brushed against something soft, and I pulled the material out gently. Lifting it up, I held the piece of string in front of my face, and then chuckled at the sight of my makeshift hair tie. The one Espen had used to hold my hair back. I studied the small rope and the way it danced in the wind. My mind whirled and my chest spasmed as I chewed on my bottom lip.

Of course there was also the Forest Fae that had clearly gotten under my skin. Falling for one's hero seemed so cliché, but with Espen, how could anyone blame me for developing a soft spot for the ray of sunshine? Not only had he saved my life, but he'd been warm, welcoming. Hell, he'd even put his neck on the line with his own people by telling me about their secret world. No guy I'd ever previously met, let alone dated, had ever done so much for me in such a short space of time.

"Are you all right?"

I scoffed, not looking in the man's direction. "Depends on who you ask."

The Norwegian captain behind me snorted. "Well, are you coming or not?"

I returned the string to my pocket and glanced around again, taking a steadying breath.

I should leave. I'd wanted to for the past week. It'd been almost all I could think about, the goal I'd been chasing when I wasn't helping the local fae solve a mystery. But... something felt off. In me, in the air, who the fuck knew. Something seared in my chest and it wasn't heartburn. Maybe there was something in the water I'd been drinking for the past week, because I didn't feel right. It was like standing on the edge of a cliff—a stupid idea—just to get a photo of a major attraction. Adrenaline flooded my system and I shook my head.

"Pull yourself together, Lennie," I muttered to myself, ignoring my audience.

I looked toward the cabin on the hill, invisible from this angle, but I knew it was there. Espen was probably there by now, worried for his people, for the fate of the fjord... What would happen to them after I left?

After everything I'd experienced here, would I be able to return home to my day-to-day routine?

Did I want to?

My life at home was good: I had my family who loved and supported me, and a small group of friends I hung out with ever so often. They would certainly miss me if I stayed a little while longer.

My job would definitely miss me—probably fire me. But, that didn't bother me nearly as much as it probably should. I'd taken the boring desk job to put food on the table and enough money in my account to afford my photography excursions around the world. What harm would there be if I pushed out my departure date?

I could cancel my flight and hopefully recoup the cost or reschedule my flight back to the US. And, if I stayed, I could potentially see even more of the country. Hell, now that I thought about it, I'd even be willing to put down my camera and stop constantly photographing the environment around me and actually help it thrive instead. Maybe, just maybe, I could stay and help the fae solve the illegal magic mystery?

"Miss, last chance. Are you coming aboard?"

I shook my head, and the captain let out a frustrated sigh. Looking around once more, I took in the majesty of the scenery even as it was cloaked in darkness. The breeze shifted, sending my hair into my eyes, and I brushed it back, thinking of the rope in my pocket, but not reaching for it.

Then...

"Fuck it," I mumbled, grabbed my backpack, and walked off the dock toward the village.

25

LENNIE

My breaths came out in steady puffs as I reached the front door of Espen's cabin. The lights were on inside, and my heart hammered at the thought of what I was doing, what I had done... again. But damn it, leaving on that boat just didn't seem like the right thing to do. These people, this land, needed help. And, if I was being introspective, maybe I did, too. So, I set down my backpack and knocked on the door.

A few stomps sounded before the door swung open and a bleary-eyed Espen answered. He'd changed out of his uniform and into a plain green sweater and jeans but looked just as handsome as he always did. His watery gaze landed on me and widened, his jaw slackening slowly.

"What are you—"

I lifted the string from my pocket and brought it into the light streaming out of the house.

Espen flicked his eyes from my face to the little rope and back to me again. He braced one palm against the door frame and ran his other hand across his jaw, disturbing his short beard.

I quirked a brow after several beats of silence went by. "Are you breathing?"

"I—I'm not sure."

I tilted my head and returned the string to my pocket, securing it shut with the zipper.

Espen licked his lips and shifted, turning to look back into his cabin then back at me. "I'm not dreaming am I? I was lying on the sofa and there was a knock—"

I poked his chest, the pectoral muscle firm beneath my touch. "I'm here."

He shook his head again, then cupped my face and pressed his lips to mine.

My heart hammered and a fluttering sensation coursed through my veins as he stole my breath. Just before I melted on his doorstep, he pulled back. His eyes were dilated and his lips split into a big smile.

"I couldn't get on the boat," I whispered as he removed his palms from my cheeks. A slight chill crossed them in the absence of his warmth.

His chest heaved and he pressed his thumb against my bottom lip, as if reassuring himself that I was real, that he'd just kissed me to the point where air decided to permanently vacate my lungs. Without thinking, at least not with my head, I flicked my tongue out across the tip of his thumb.

He let out a low rumble from the back of his throat, and I smirked.

"Wait here," he said and disappeared into the cabin. I picked up my bag and stepped inside, setting it down next to some of Espen's shoes by the front door. Before I had time to wonder where he'd gone, Espen came hurtling around the corner with a dark green yoga mat in one hand then shoved his feet into a pair of boots.

My forehead scrunched in confusion. "Where are you going? This sounds presumptuous when I say it out loud, but I was thinking more along the lines of taking clothes *off*, not putting shoes on when I came to see you." He stepped in closer, our faces mere inches apart, and his eyes shimmered with happiness.

"Do you trust me?"

I let out a deep breath and tried to stifle a smile, but something about Espen made that damn near impossible. "Yes."

With a spark of victory in his gaze, he grabbed my hand and dragged me outside, shutting the door behind us with his yoga mat under his arm. We wandered into the field beside his cabin, the wild grass short in some spots and longer in others. I tried to tamp down my disappointment that Espen was more interested in *literal* forest yoga than bedroom *yoga,* but I couldn't help but be happy in his presence. Once we reached a clearing between the woods and the house, Espen stopped and let go of my hand. With a flick of his wrists he unfurled the yoga mat.

"Please tell me that's for the good kind of forest yoga," I said, pointing at the green mat.

He turned to me with a mischievous smirk and I rolled my bottom lip between my teeth. Stepping into my personal space, he invaded my senses with his strong form and the sumptuous smell of moss and leather with a dash of evergreen in there, too. Our breaths came in steady waves, our chests rising and falling in tandem as he brushed an errant hair off my cheek.

"I'm so glad you stayed," he whispered, cradling my head with one hand while sliding his other around my waist.

At that exact moment, I couldn't help it. I was glad I'd walked away from the harbor, too. "Make it worth my while," I said, my voice huskier than I'd ever heard it.

A low, satisfied rumble emitted from Espen's chest in answer. "Oh, I definitely will."

He pressed his lips to mine in a soft but firm kiss that sent a wave of heat crashing through my body, promising a helluva lot more. I sank into his hold and wrapped my arms around his neck, needing to be closer. He swept his tongue across my mouth, requesting entrance, and I happily relented, falling further under this magical feeling that was brewing inside my chest.

After a few minutes of the best kiss of my life, I pulled back, desperate for air.

Espen gave me a rakish grin, like he knew exactly what he was doing. And, honest to hell, he really did. "Lie down," he said, nodding to the mat at our feet.

I sure as fuck wasn't going to say no. For only the tenth time in my life, I did as I was told, and laid down on the yoga mat.

Looking up, my breath left my lungs again. Not just at the sight of Espen pulling off his sweater, but at the starry sky above us, a hint of green light dancing above the mountain across the fjord. Espen, now completely shirtless, glanced up at the northern lights and smiled.

As our eyes met again, he crouched down on his knees by my feet. Achingly slow, he started untangling my laces and pulled off my boots, gently placing them in the grass beside us. Next up went my socks, which he carefully slipped off my feet. Cold air brushed across my toes as he wrapped his fingers around my ankle.

I slowly unzipped my jacket, fully aware of his eyes locked on my every movement, the heat of his gaze visible thanks to the light of the stars and the aurora borealis shifting above us.

His hands slid along my rib cage, pushing up my shirt and then my sports bra. Fingers traced over my nipples and I sucked in a breath at the feel of the cold air mixed with his hot touch.

"Perfect," he said, and I almost combusted at the sound of his voice, every nerve alight. He leaned above me, resting on his forearm, as he unfastened the button on my jeans.

"We're gonna freeze," I murmured.

"I promise to keep you warm," he said before his hot mouth latched over my nipple, sucking lightly, drawing a moan from deep in my throat.

Pulling my jeans and panties down my legs, Espen marked every inch with a kiss, and the spot where I desperately wanted his mouth grew needier by the second. Pull, kiss. Sweep, kiss... until he reached my feet and expertly tugged my pants over my toes, setting the clothes aside.

With a sly grin and a shimmer in his gaze, Espen undid his pants revealing no boxers or briefs. His dick was hard, and looked exactly the same as any human dick I'd had the fortune of meeting, which shouldn't have been surprising after my encounter with Øyvin. But, in Espen's case, he was significantly more endowed than any of my priors. I rolled my lip between my teeth again and flicked my eyes up to his. His smile widened and he leaned over me where I squirmed, wanton and needy.

"Are you on birth-control?" he asked, hovering above me, bracing his palms on either side of my head.

I nodded, my breath sawing in and out of my lungs, desperate to take things further. He hadn't even touched me, but my core was already dripping. "Yes. Are you clean?"

"Yes."

"And things don't work differently because—"

He smirked, notching his dick at my entrance. "Same equipment, same process. I'm just magical."

"Well, that's yet to be—"

He thrust inside me and cut off the end of my sentence as my mouth fell open. I wrapped my legs around him, groaning at the fullness as he pushed in deeper, waiting for my body to adjust before he started moving. I grabbed his hair as he traced kisses down my neck, holding him to me until I couldn't take it any longer. "Move, damn it."

Needing no further instruction, Espen pulled back, then slammed back in, drawing noises from my mouth I'd never heard before. Encouraged by the sound, he kept up an unrelenting pace, surging inside me, again and again and again, hitting all the right spots. His fingers tangled in my hair as our lips found each other and continued kissing, claiming, devouring.

With each move, my core fluttered around him, desperate for more. He must have sensed my need, because two seconds later his fingers found my clit and he started caressing the bundle of nerves. I shuddered in response, the sensation building and building until I detonated, moaning into his mouth.

He was still hard, and smiled against my lips as I came down from my high.

"Do you know the move, downward dog?"

I nodded and let out a satisfied sigh, because I'd happily take more of that, thank you very much.

He winked, and I chuckled, pulling my jacket from my arms and yanking my shirt and bra over my head before I rolled onto my stomach and pushed my ass toward the starry sky. Grabbing onto my hips, Espen kicked my legs wider, stretching my trembling muscles.

"Where's your hair tie?" he asked, his voice heavy and husky.

I braced my weight on one shaky hand, and quickly reached into my jacket pocket next to me, pulling out the makeshift one he'd created for me. Holding it up, he quickly took it and I placed my hand back down, redistributing my weight across the mat. Cool air drifted across my rear as he stepped beside me. He pulled my hair back and fastened it with the loose bit of rope. It sure as hell wouldn't hold it in a ponytail, but it would keep the strands out of my face.

I stretched deeper into the position as he returned to his spot behind me. Wiggling my ass in his direction, I heard a throaty chuckle before he slapped his hand across my ass cheek. My core clenched at the sharp sting, and I moaned, my knees buckling slightly.

"Oh no you don't," Espen said, gripping my hips and returning my legs into the spread out yoga position. In this stance I was completely at his mercy, angled slightly by the gentle slope beneath us, but still vulnerable to whatever he wanted to do with me. "Don't move."

"Wasn't planning on it," I mouthed, sure as hell not going anywhere.

"Good," he replied, before leaning over, pressing his slick cock against me, and grabbing my hair. With a gentle tug, he pulled my head back and wrapped my hair around his fist so I stared up the grassy hill. I groaned as he rubbed himself between my entrance and clit, then back again. Wiggling once more, hoping for another slap, I got what I asked for and then he thrust inside me. The sting on my scalp and ass sent shivers down my spine, the sounds of our bodies slapping against each other filling the otherwise quiet night.

At this angle, Espen hit all the right—and deep—spots to have my nerves sparking. He dropped my hair, and his hands gripped my hips, holding me in position as he pounded into me, keeping an even tempo that left me breathless, yet aching for more. My legs quivered, arms burned, knees wobbled—if I didn't explode in the next five seconds, I was going to my knees. Espen must've sensed that I couldn't hold the position much longer as he slowly lowered us to the mat without removing himself.

"Press your chest down," he said, sliding his palm down my spine and gently applying pressure between my shoulder blades.

With my knees on the mat, I sank deeper into the modified pose, feeling the stretch in my upper back, the fullness between my thighs, and let out a satisfied groan. Espen took that as his cue and started pounding into me again, only this time, much harder and faster.

My breaths sawed in and out of my mouth, the euphoric precipice closing in. The stretch, the fullness, it was all too much, and I shattered. I moaned through my release as Espen chased his own. He shifted both hands back to my hips, tightening his grip, the bite of it so much more in my current state of bliss. With a few more deep surges, he exploded inside of me.

My legs shook as I slowly lowered to my stomach, removing his dick from my swollen core in the process. I collapsed onto the yoga mat, spent, happy, and definitely interested in more once I could feel my thighs and arms again.

Espen curled up beside me, our noses nearly touching. I caught his satisfied grin before he shifted, nuzzling against my neck. "Told you I'd keep you warm."

"You certainly are a man of your word."

He chuckled, pulling me onto my side and into his arms.

Staring at the sky, watching the green-and-teal lights dance above us, I relaxed into his hold. While I certainly had been mad that I'd missed the cruise ship, I most definitely was happy I'd chosen to not get on the supply boat. And, not that I'd tell him to his face, but that might have been some of the best sex of my life.

26
LENNIE

I awoke in a tangle of sheets by myself, the sound of a shower shutting off greeting me in my sleepy haze. The scent of my second round of *yoga* antics last night lingered in the air and the satisfied ache between my legs was a welcome sensation as I stretched my limbs.

Espen wandered into the bedroom, a white towel slung low around his hips, beads of water slowly descending his torso. He caught my gaze and gave me a cheeky smile. "Good morning, Lennie."

"Morning."

"How are you feeling?" he asked, his gaze raking over me and the sheet I'd pulled up over my chest.

I took a mental inventory, assessing every limb and extremity, plus the state of my blissed out mind. "Fine."

Espen's eyes widened in panic. "When women say 'fine' it usually means the opposite. Are you sure you're all right? I didn't hurt you, did I?"

His concern was adorable, so I let him sweat it for a moment as I pretended to think it over. When he looked ready to combust, I said, "I'm feeling really good, Espen. Don't worry."

He let out a long breath, his shoulders sagging as relief washed over his features.

"Where are you staying?" he asked, pivoting the topic with a shake of his head.

I rolled my shoulders and the joints popped before I sat upright. I doubted I could stay with Solveig again—that seemed too imposing, especially considering my departure date was very much unknown. "Hadn't thought that far ahead."

With his back to me, Espen dropped his towel and tossed it to the side. "You could stay with me."

I vaguely caught the smile he threw over his shoulder considering my attention was drawn down to his perfectly toned ass. "Are you sure?"

"Of course." He nodded, slowly pulling on a pair of boxers.

"I don't want you to think that what we did last night suddenly means something," I remarked, pointing between us.

He shook his head and crossed the room. Pressing his fists on either side of my hips on the bed, he brought his face to mine. "I don't expect it to. But I like you and if you need a place to stay, you're welcome here. This can be whatever you want it to be." He tilted his lips into a smile. "And if you want to *go* again, you need only ask."

My core spasmed at the look in his eyes and the words on his tongue. Before I dragged him back into bed, I swallowed hard and asked, "How angry will your boss be if you're late for work?"

"Very," he replied before planting a kiss on my lips and pushing off the bed. He crossed the room and started pulling on his uniform. "There's coffee in the cupboard above the kitchen sink, and eggs in the fridge. Make yourself at home."

Later that morning, I sauntered down to the village and stopped by Oddvar's for another cup of coffee. The bell chimed as I stepped inside, and Oddvar's wispy eyebrows hit his hairline. I gave him a quick smile which he vaguely returned with a twitch of his lips before spinning around and filling a mug with coffee.

"Morning, Oddvar."

"I see you don't know how to climb aboard boats," he said, turning back and proffering the steaming cup of nectar with my desired milk and sugar already added.

"Apparently not." I accepted the drink with a chuckle and thanked him.

"So, you are staying then?" Oddvar asked as I took my usual seat by the window.

I sighed and nodded. "For a little while."

"Okay." And that was that.

The old man went back to his work—fetching beverages and sandwiches for other patrons—and said nothing more than a clipped goodbye when I paid and left for the convenience store in hopes of finding a charger for my phone.

I returned to Espen's house with my successful shopping trip completed. After letting my phone charge for ten minutes, I started it and connected to the wi-fi using the password that Espen had given me before he left for work. Messages started pinging like crazy, and I opened my texts. Majority of which were from my dear brothers.

Ryan: Answer your fucking phone, Len.

Andrew: You okay? We're starting to get worried over here.

Jared: Andrew asked to check in. Text Y if alive.

Having an overprotective older brother to look out for you was nice sometimes, but three was overkill. They were cute when they were worried but also seriously annoying. They'd been like this when I was in high school too—not trusting any of the boys, especially the ones on the football team. Which was fair, but damn did it prove problematic when I wanted some D after a Friday night game. None of the players would go near Andrew and Jared Martin's little sister. Fucking ridiculous is what it really was.

Andrew: Evelyn, this is serious. Please call us or I'll have to tell Mom and Dad.

Ah shit. The full name from Andrew was never a good sign.

*Jared: *skull emoji**

Ryan: Brace yourself.

Andrew: I told Mom and Dad. They're really worried. We all are. If you don't call us back, I'm calling the embassy.

I grumbled. Opening my chat-app, I clicked Andrew's smiling face, and video called him. Hoping this would be cheaper than an actual phone call, I prepared for the polite tirade I was about to receive from my eldest brother.

"Thank God, you're alive," Andrew said, his face popping up on my screen. He was the male older version of me, with dark blond hair and ochre eyes. Wearing a collared shirt, he looked ready for work, and I could hear his two daughters giggling in the background.

"My phone died. Sorry."

"For *days*? We were starting to think you'd done the same. For Christ's sake, Evelyn."

I sighed and started groveling. "Andrew, I'm sorry. I'm fine. I just got caught up in some stuff and didn't get a new charger until today. I called you as soon as I could."

His brows knit together and he pinched the bridge of his nose. It was a move I'd seen my Dad do countless times too—mostly in response to something I'd done. "At least you're on your way home."

My stomach dropped and I grimaced.

"You *are* on your way home, right?"

"About that...."

"Lennie, please tell me you're in Stavanger about to get on a flight back to Ohio."

"No."

Andrew let out an audible sigh through his nose and ran his free hand across his jaw. "Do I want to know?"

"Probably not."

He shook his head. "You know Mom worries about you when you travel alone." Ugh, now he *sounded* like Dad too.

"I'm well aware, but things didn't go according to plan."

"They never do with you."

He had me there. My adventures had a tendency to go off the rails, but this one had seriously veered off track.

"Look, Lennie," Andrew continued. "I'm glad you're okay, but I need to get to work and you need to call Mom immediately."

"I will. I promise."

"Good. All right, love you, Sis."

"Love you too," I said and then he hung up, leaving me to my next task. Calling Mom.

I set my phone back down on the kitchen table, letting it charge while I mentally prepared myself for the reprimand I was about to endure. Mom definitely had a right to be angry with me. I had gone too far this time, but I'd still followed her rule: always inform her and Dad when I was traveling somewhere. They'd put it in place after I went to the Grand Canyon with my brother Ryan one spring break. We hadn't bothered to tell them, and Mom lost her cool when she found out afterward, claiming that so many hiking accidents happened there—true—and that it was always best to tell someone when venturing on hikes or entering certain terrain—fair enough, also true. So, I'd followed the rule ever since. However, my communication skills once I was on the road had never been the best, and this instance was clearly not helping matters.

Taking a deep breath, I picked up my phone again and video called my Mom. It was early back in the US, but she'd have been awake since six anyway.

It rang three times and then... "Oh thank the heavens, you're all right."

"Hi Mom."

"I'm very disappointed with you for not having your phone on and missing your cruise ship."

"I know, and I'm sorry."

"As you should be. Your Dad and I have been extremely worried. When your brother told me you'd missed your ship, I thought I'd misheard him. Then I find out that all three of your brothers knew before me...." She shook her head, her dark brown locks shifting across her shoulders as she patted her palm against the top of her chest.

"Again, I'm sorry. I'll do better." I mean, I was a grown-ass woman, but I did appreciate their love and care for me.

"You certainly will. Now, when does your flight land? Are you flying through Chicago to Columbus or Cincinnati? Do you need Dad to come pick you up at the airport?"

"Soooo, about that."

Her eyes widened slowly and her lips pinched together. "Evelyn."

"I'm staying in Norway for a little while longer."

"Why? How long? With what money? When—"

"I'm not sure how long, but probably another few weeks. I made some friends here and they are letting me stay with them."

"But *why*?" she asked, her tone escalating toward panic.

Now there was a good question. Because I felt some sort of need to stay and help. Because this town was adorable, and I met two guys and a whole host of other characters that I liked (but also didn't like). Because the fjord needed to be saved from whatever chaos was bearing down on it. Because the thought of going home now to my boring life in Ohio after knowing that so much else existed out there sounded absolutely fucking miserable.

I still wasn't sure about the *why*. Maybe it was all of the above. Whatever the real answer, I'd made my decision and I was going to stick with it.

"Because I had the opportunity to stay and help out a local community with some photography stuff," I replied. It wasn't exactly a lie, but it most definitely wasn't the entire truth. The latter was something I couldn't exactly share with anyone or I'd get in serious trouble with the fae.

"Is this because of a man?"

"Really, Mom?" I deadpanned.

"Did you meet someone?"

It dawned on me what she was struggling to say. "I've met several guys, Mom. But I'm not staying because of one of them." The words felt odd coming out of my mouth for some reason I didn't want to analyze too closely. "You won't be getting a wedding out of me any time soon."

"A mother can dream," she said with a sigh.

I shook my head. "I'll let you know when I've booked my flights home," I said, pivoting from one of her favorite discussion topics.

"Good, and please check in with me more often, at least every Sunday."

"Will do."

"I love you, Evelyn. Please stay safe."

"Love you too. And I'm always safe."

She scoffed. "We both know that's a lie."

I laughed as I ended the call and set the phone back down on the table. Stretching my arms above my head, I eased the tension out of my muscles and decided I'd call the airline company next and try to get a refund for my flight before heading out for dinner this evening.

But, I had one other task to complete first. As I launched myself onto Espen's sofa, I typed out a quick message to my brothers.

Lennie: I'm alive. Staying in Norway for a few more weeks.

*Andrew: *heart emoji**

Ryan: Don't have too much fun. You owe me for waking me up early last week.

Jared: K.

27
LENNIE

Monday night Espen and I wandered into town for dinner, then bolted into Fisken to avoid the rain that had started hammering the village. I shivered as we both pulled off our jackets and hung them on the old-fashioned coat rack by the door, water dripping onto the wood floor beneath them. Rubbing my arms, I took in my surroundings, noticing how crowded it was as Espen waved to a woman at a table across the restaurant. A waiter spotted us and motioned us forward, and I followed Espen toward his friend. We wandered over to the table, its inhabitant giving me a welcoming smile as I took a seat.

"This is Ylva," Espen said, motioning toward the woman as he sat down in one of the vacant chairs. My head tilted to the side as I studied her, noticing her dirty blonde hair that fell below her shoulders and sharp features. She was slim in stature and wore a wool sweater with Nordic patterns across the chest. "A good friend of mine," he added with a knowing look, which led me to believe she was a Forest Fae like him, "and my second in command."

I nodded to her. "It's nice to meet you."

"Espen has told me about you," Ylva said with a tip of her beer glass.

Part of me was surprised Espen had mentioned me, but I had been working with him lately, so it wasn't shocking. "Has he now?"

"Mm-hmm," she murmured, her eyes glittering with mischief.

"Only nice things," Espen said, leaning toward me. "I promise."

Considering my usual behavior, and the fact that I'd punched him—a knee-jerk self-defense reaction—when we'd first met, I highly doubted his sentiments had been solely good. I glanced back at Ylva and saw her barely contained grin. Yeah, she most definitely knew about the first time I'd met Espen.

"Anything to report this evening?" Espen asked, looking at Ylva, whose amused gaze broke away from mine.

She let out a long exhale and surveyed the room. Seemingly satisfied with whatever she saw, she said, "There was an issue with wolves north of the Langholm farm."

Espen stilled, his jaw tightening.

"Myself and a few others sent them away without any harm to livestock or farmland—"

"But?" Espen interjected.

"—but, the locals are now a bit spooked." She narrowed her eyes at him. "I'm surprised you weren't notified at the station."

"If they did call it in, I wasn't informed." Espen wiped his palm across his jaw before settling back in his seat.

"Care to explain why these big bad puppies are a problem?" I asked, looking between the two of them before turning to Espen.

He sighed and clasped his hands together, resting his wrists on the table edge. "They're only a problem if they start picking off the sheep or any other animals, which always causes a ruckus with the *locals*," he said, that last word sounding more like a codeword for *humans*.

"Can't you just monitor the fields or have them moved to a safer location, like a sanctuary?" I asked, waving my hand toward the windows.

Espen and Ylva looked at each other, a silent conversation briefly passing between them. "It can be a bit more of a complex situation than that," Espen replied, choosing his words carefully.

"I'll go get us some drinks then," I said, sensing this conversation would include a lot more information that I wouldn't understand. I rose from my chair and turned toward the lightly packed bar, chatter rising from the high stools that were occupied. As I crossed the room, I was intercepted by Nora with two full glasses in her hands, wearing a brightly patterned sweater and black pants.

"Beer?" she asked, pulling up alongside me and proffering a tall glass of amber liquid.

"Thank you." I accepted the drink and swallowed a large gulp while watching Espen laugh with his second in command. Something warmed my chest at the sight, but I tried to shake it off.

I wasn't one for emotions or attachments—I'd always been a *wham, bam, thanks man*, kinda gal—and hadn't ever really pictured myself settling down. And, even though Espen was single and older than me—honestly too old for *any* human—he seemed like the kind of yogi-fae-cop thingy that *would* settle down and have a family. I wasn't sure how I felt about the spark between us, if it could even be called that...

I took another large swig of my drink as Espen looked over and gave me a gentle smile and a nod to Nora. I smiled back, the corners of my eyes crinkling.

Nora looked at me, then Espen, then back to me, letting out a low humm before gasping. "You didn't?"

I turned to her, catching her widened gaze with my own. "Didn't what?"

She looked between me and Espen again, her mouth dropping open and an excited look washing across her features. "Oh, you *totally* fucked Espen. Is that why you stayed? Which, I'm glad you did, by the way, but—"

I clamped my free hand across her mouth. "Shut up, right now."

Her lips shifted into a grin beneath my palm, eyes alight with laughter at my reaction.

Just then, the door opened, and Øyvin walked in, his gaze lingering on me for a second too long before he rolled his eyes, brushing past me. "Trouble."

"Øyvin," I replied, dropping my hand from Nora's face. The tension in the room rose swiftly, and I swallowed down the lump that was forming in my throat at the sight of the Fjord Fae. The way that damn cream-colored sweater of his hugged his shoulders and arms had my skin flushing, and memories of what lay beneath clouded my thoughts.

Like he could hear me thinking, he glanced over his shoulder and the corner of his lips twitched as he reached Espen's table. Nora inhaled loudly.

"Nooooooo," she gasped, her eyes darting to the big blond fae and back to me, a wide grin taking up her face. "You didn't."

"I don't know what you're talking about." I busied my mouth with my drink and made an attempt to escape the deteriorating situation. Nora's hand shot out and grabbed my upper arm, not letting me leave. For such a small thing, she was strong as fuck—her grip like an iron shackle as she pulled my attention solely onto her.

"Part of me wants every gory, smutty detail, and the other part of me wants to shove my fingers in my ears. I've known them both for over a century."

I quirked a brow at her comment and remained silent.

She didn't back down though. A second later she was in front of me. "Please tell me you're staying in town for quite a while. We haven't had this much excitement since—well. Not a good kind of excitement, anyway." With a shake of her head, she dismissed the somber thought and went back to the topic at hand, unfortunately. "So, who did you do first? Or was it a dueling swords situation? Now that I say that, I could see—"

"Nora!" I hissed, leaning toward her as my eyes bugged.

The others looked over at us, but Nora waved them away and pulled me into an empty booth. Unable to shake her hold on me, I sidled onto the leather seat and she plopped down beside me, blocking my exit, but keeping an eye on the other fae in the room. And, more specifically, the two fae that I had indeed fucked.

"Your cheeks are bright red and your hand trembled minutely after my first accusation, so don't bother lying." She propped her head into her palms, resting her elbows on the table. "Now, please, tell me the story."

I stared at my half empty glass, trying to decide what to say, if anything. While I wasn't embarrassed about my actions, I also wasn't sure what the future held with either of the males.

Did I want a repeat performance? Abso-fucking-lutely. But was there more to my magnetism to them than just sexual chemistry? I wasn't sure I was ready to think too hard on that.

Nora's eyes were wide in anticipation and her lips were spread into a tiny smile. "Espen does yoga. I'd imagine that helped you get into all kinds of *positions*," she said, not holding back at all as she leaned into my space. Even as I pulled away from her, my mind shifted to the angles he'd hit last night and heat washed over my skin at the thought. Nora grinned like she'd caught a massive fish. "There it is."

"Fine." I stalled by taking another sip of my beer, shaking my head as I set it back down. It had been a while since I had a girlfriend to chat with, and I was coming to like Nora. "Yes, yes, and *hell yes*."

Nora clapped her hands excitedly, bouncing in the booth. "I'm going to need more details than that."

"Why?"

She glanced over her shoulders before lowering her voice. "I'm a three-hun-dred-and-fifty-two year old fae historian that doesn't get out of the mountain enough. Give an old lady some good gossip. Also, we're friends. Friends share."

I shook my head, but her words meant something to me. While I didn't know her well yet, she'd been welcoming and hadn't completely shunned me when she found out I was a human that knew about her world. It was like we were in a secret club together, and slowly getting to know one another, on our way to becoming friends for real. And, clearly, Nora liked to hear about cock.

"Lennie..." she said, tapping her fingers on the table as she eyed me hopefully.

"Nora...."

"I'll live for at least a few more centuries." She crossed her arms with a wicked look on her face. "I have time to wait."

"Fine," I relented, and she sat upright like a puppy getting a treat. "I hate-fucked Øyvin at his boathouse after trying to steal his boat."

She snort-laughed and almost fell out of the booth. "H-his boat? You didn't?"

"I did," I said, taking another sip of my beer. "Failed because someone ratted me out."

Her eyebrows shot up, a broad grin taking over her face. "And then he thanked you by fucking you?"

I pursed my lips, glancing over at the male in question. "Not exactly. Heated words were exchanged and then sex happened."

"I love it." She downed the rest of her drink before grabbing mine and chugging that too. "Now, what about Espen?"

"What about me?" the fae said, sliding into the booth across from us, and I started at his sudden appearance.

"We were just discussing how nice you are for letting me stay at your house," I said with a forced smile, hoping Nora understood my unspoken words to keep her damn mouth shut. Friends could chat about cock, but not tell the cock that they did so. It was girl-code or some shit.

"I *am* a gentleman." Espen placed his hand over his heart and grinned.

"Yes, well," Nora said, tapping her fingers on the table, her eyes darting sideways at me briefly, "always nice to have it both ways."

I practically growled at Nora for the innuendo and for stealing my beer—I needed that safety blanket to avoid this conversation. Just then, the others joined us—Øyvin taking a seat at the end of the table, while Ylva set down a tray of ten shot glasses filled with light, amber liquid and then sidled into the booth beside Espen. I squirmed in my spot, considering sitting on my hands, and choosing to shove them under my thighs when Espen gave me a pointed look like he understood exactly what kind of conversation we'd been having.

"Aquavit?" Ylva asked, breaking the tension and pointing at the arrangement of shots.

Without saying a word, I lunged forward and grabbed one, then downed it. Liquid fire sluiced down my throat, and my eyes widened in panic. *What the fuck was that?* I sat back and placed my fist in front of my mouth, coughing and sputtering, trying to catch a breath that didn't make me feel like a dragon about to set the building ablaze.

Nora took the glass from my hand as the rest of the group grinned at me—except Øyvin, but he bit his lip which was just as much of a similar reaction.

"It's a sipping liquor," Ylva piped up, giving me a tentative smile. "Sorry."

I waved away her apology, but couldn't voice anything other than an "mm-hmm."

The others picked up a small glass each and took a genteel sip.

"It's made from potatoes and caraway," Espen said, passing me another shot glass of the stuff. "A bit like vodka."

I winced and leaned away, wrinkling my nose at the beverage.

"It's not as bad if you sip. I promise," he added, nudging the drink in my direction.

Deciding I could trust him—and would pace myself this time—I pulled the little glass closer but waited a few minutes before taking a dainty-ass sip.

Thankfully, Espen was right, it wasn't as bad. It most definitely still burned, but I could taste the nutty and earthy notes of caraway this time around.

"What were we talking about anyway?" Ylva asked, glancing around the table.

"Nora's job," I said, finally feeling able to speak without spewing fire. "That was my next question." And a much better subject than my sex-scapades when both parties sat at the table with me.

"I record stories for *my mountain people*. From major events to the last tales from the dying," Nora said, taking a sip of the liquor and lowering her voice so no one but those at our table could hear.

"That seems like a very important job... and kind of sad," I said.

She smiled briefly, pushing some of her short brown locks behind her ear, all of her excitement from our previous conversation gone. "Yes, on both counts. But, I'm glad I can capture the dying *individual's* memories and record them for posterity."

"They have a wall," Øyvin butted in, and Nora nodded.

"What do you mean?" I asked, taking a tiny sip of aquavit like the lady I was. I could practically hear my mother's derisive snort at the thought.

"Most stories, like those I write down from a dying *mountain people*, are recorded in large tomes that we keep in the library. But major events, battles, births of royals, those are all recorded the old fashioned way. Those tales are magically carved into the mountain by me." She downed the remnants of her shot before saying, "Would you like to see some of them?"

I choked on my own shot of aquavit, the burning sensation coating the back of my throat unpleasantly again even as excitement raced through my veins. "Y-you can let me see that? It's not forbidden or some shit?"

She shifted her head from one side and then the other, her lips set in a firm line. "Well, you've already been inside and met my sister—"

"And Halvar," I added, a wary shiver running up my spine at the memory of the beast of a fae.

"—and him. So, I don't see a problem with it. Just don't take any pictures or tell anyone about it."

My mouth gaped slightly, glancing at the table full of fae around me. "And just like that, I get to see this stuff?"

Nora shrugged, a small smile playing across her face. "I *am* the Fjell historian and sister to the Queen. It comes with some benefits."

I bet it fucking did. "Okay, deal."

"Great," she said, standing from the booth and dragging me with her. "Let's go."

28
LENNIE

Nora and I traipsed up the hillside, heading straight for the main entrance of the mountain—the same one I'd entered through with Espen and Øyvin when we'd visited the Queen. The rain had let up to a light drizzle, the clouds blocking the light of the moon, putting me and my very human eyesight at a severe disadvantage. I moved as swiftly as I could under the cover of darkness, tripping over logs and rocks every fifth step. Nora, on the other hand, didn't seem to have any trouble navigating the terrain, moving with the ease of a cat.

Like last time, we stepped through the magical entry that looked like a sheer rock face. A ripple of warm air washed over me and my skin tingled more than it already was thanks to the alcohol I'd consumed. The world wasn't quite spinning, but aquavit was no fucking joke and I could feel the buzz.

Even though I'd seen the tunnels before, I couldn't help but gawk at the lanterns hanging every few feet, casting a sparkling glow over the rough-cut rock walls. Before I could reach out and touch the walls, exploring it like I hadn't been able to the first time, Nora started walking and I was forced to follow as we wound through tunnels, descending deeper into the belly of the mountain.

"Nora, you're great and all, but you need to slow down or you're gonna lose me. And, I don't ever like to admit weakness, but seriously cardio after shots is a bad idea at any age," I said between heaving breaths, gripping my side. Damn, that alcohol had done a number on me. Or perhaps I was exhausted after last night's exercise with Espen? I shook off the thought. "This one time in college I thought drunk baseball sounded like a fun idea, but seeing double while balls flew at my face wasn't nearly as exciting as it originally sounded. At least not like that, anyway."

Nora laughed, the happy sound bouncing off the walls around us, then thankfully slowed and hooked her arm through mine. "No more shots for the human."

I shook my head. "Not after beer, and not before hiking up that hill."

She chuckled, and we continued walking for another several minutes, winding deeper into the mountain. Eventually we turned a corner and wandered through a low archway into a cavernous space with blank rock walls.

A chill swept over my face, the air in here slightly colder than that of the tunnels as I looked up. Pair that with the darkness—only dismal rays from the entryway enlightened the space—and this was the perfect recipe for eeriness. At least, that would explain the creepy sensation that skittered up my spine until Nora unlooped our arms and placed her hand against the wall.

A moment later, silver swirls started to appear on the cave walls, casting an ethereal glow as they grew and morphed into images. I wasn't sure what I was expecting—maybe primitive cave paintings like from ancient times, which some definitely were—but most were far more detailed. The pictures were indiscernible at this distance, but looking at the ones closest to the entry, they almost looked like ancient runes and engravings.

My mouth hung open as I sauntered deeper into the space, taking it all in. One image was of a boat with little stick figures in it, large fish swimming beneath them. Another drawing had figures wielding hatchets, swords, and shields—Vikings. One after the next, each told a story, even if I didn't understand the context. Nora remained silent as I surveyed the shining marks, each revealing another layer of the Fjell Fae history.

"How long have the fae existed?" I whispered, any other volume feeling too loud for what appeared to be hallowed space.

Nora pushed off the wall and stepped closer, her gaze tracing over the images. "No one knows exact numbers, but at least several millennia."

I checked my face to make sure my eyes were still where they were supposed to be, feeling my brain implode at this new information. "Are you serious?"

She nodded. "Ages and lifetimes vary wildly. Some Fjell Fae live to be five-hundred-years-old, others double that. Many start to lose track though."

"Do you know who's the oldest?"

She shook her head. "But I'd wager that Halvar has been around for a long time. He served in my father's army, and may have even fought for my grandfather, but I'm not sure. Every time I ask, he just grunts and walks away."

I snickered, fully able to picture the hulking fae of few words. I cast my eyes back to the carvings, inspecting them more closely—the intricate marks glowing like the lanterns that dotted the tunnels.

"How do you draw these?"

Nora stepped forward, eyes roving over the wall as she moved. "The Royal line has some light magic from our ancestors. I'm able to use that to carve the scenes into the rock."

"So, you're also the one who lights all the tunnels?" I asked, looking around the room, taking it all in, trying to understand how they could create light in such a dark place, so far underground.

Nora let out a gentle laugh, turning back toward me. "No, I don't. There's one particular Fjell Fae that has similar magic to mine and Freija's. He is in charge of all the lighting within the fjell."

Overwhelmed by the sight of so much history before me, something so few humans had ever seen, I stood in silence—rare for me.

"The power I use to make these drawings is just like his magic, although mine is much more diluted," Nora continued, stroking her palm across the cave wall, seeming lost in her thoughts. "My sister and I have a blend of all the powers of the Fjell Fae. From creating and lifting boulders, to healing cracks, and even shifting appearance and sounds. Our power stems from the mountain, and we, in turn, take care of it and our people. We do what we need to do to make sure the Fjell Fae live long and prosperous lives."

"Like the Forest and Fjord Fae do for their realms?" I asked.

"Yes, exactly." She shoved her hands into her back pockets, offering me a small smile. "All our powers have an elemental skew. It's our responsibility to use those abilities to protect the natural resources around us."

"And as royals you inherit more power than others?"

Nora let out a breathy sigh and wrung her fingers. "In a way. The history books are inconclusive on where the royal line started, but Freija and I inherited more power than normal fae upon our birth. Fae power is a gift from earth, and in return we use it to help our domain. When we were born, we got a little extra, like the magic I used to rewire your hearing, making you understand Norwegian." She nodded to my ears, and I brushed my fingers across them. That party trick sure had been useful.

"For the Fjell Fae, when the first born of the first born ascends to the throne upon the monarch's passing," she continued, staring at the shimmering stories on the wall, "they are gifted the deceased's power so they may continue to lead the Fjell Fae."

I followed her gaze, trying to make sense of what she was telling me. "So, basically, the mountain—earth—recycles the monarch's power to the new monarch?"

Nora nodded. "Exactly. There's a whole private ceremony after the coronation," she added with a wave of her hand.

A sudden chill went up my spine and I hugged myself, running my hands up and down my arms. While I was still wearing my jacket, the chill within the cave still seemed to seep into my skin, my bones. Or perhaps it was the room and the history around me. I yawned and then quickly snapped my mouth shut as Nora laughed, her full cheeks growing wider with her smile.

"Looks like it is well past someone's bedtime," she remarked, placing her hand against the wall by the entrance, shutting off the carvings like that particular spot served as an on/off switch for the room.

I nodded and moved over to her, using the light from the tunnel to guide me. "Alcohol hits a little harder after twenty-five."

"I wish I could relate, but seeing as I was under 25 over 300 years ago, it all seems a bit foggy," she replied, grabbing my arm and looping it through her own. "Let me walk you back to the entrance. You think you can make it back to Espen's by yourself?"

I nodded. "Just keep talking to me until we get to the entrance." I'd need the extra motivation to stay alert until the night air outside could smack me in the face.

Thankfully, Nora obliged, regaling me with stories of her drunken escapades as a much younger fae—the ones she could remember at least. A lot of the stories had taken place within the confines of the mountain, but the funniest ones, by far, were when she'd had to dunk her head into the fjord to wash away the severe buzz only to then walk back to the mountain and have her hair start to freeze.

Giving me a quick once over by the entrance to the mountain, Nora patted me on the shoulder and sent me on my way. I thanked her, and stepped out into the night.

29

LENNIE

I stumbled off the path from the mountain, wandered onto the street, and headed across the village toward Espen's house. My breath fogged the air in front of me as I walked under the sporadic street lights through the sleepy town. The cold air had settled across the buildings, leaving a layer of frost on the windows of the houses I passed. All the stores and most residents had turned off their lights for the night already, but some homes still cast a warm glow across the narrow streets. I shoved my hands into my jacket pockets, wishing I'd brought gloves and a hat.

"You stayed," a voice said, startling me as I rounded the corner by Oddvar's Café. Øyvin stepped out into the soft beam of a street-lamp, his hands firmly planted in the pockets of his rain jacket and his eyes brimming with a warmth I could barely look away from.

Why'd he have to be so stubbornly handsome? And, dammit, why am I calling him handsome? I blame the alcohol.

"What a keen observation," I replied and kept walking as my throat tightened. It was oddly nice to see him again, and I was annoyed with the flush I felt creeping across my cheeks.

A low grumble emanated from his chest as I sauntered past him.

"Why?"

"Because I wanted to," I said as he caught up and matched his pace with mine. In all honesty, I still wasn't entirely sure of the answer to that question. Why *had* I stayed? In the moment I'd wanted to stay and help, but now it was starting to feel like I'd stayed because I had unfinished business here. What was happening out here was so much more exciting than my life back home. Norway was rife with color and opportunity, whereas Ohio just didn't seem as important right now. Either way, when it came time to leave, I couldn't find it in me to climb

aboard that damn supply ship I'd spent a week waiting for. I couldn't go home...
at least, not yet.

Silence brewed between us before he spoke again. "We should talk."

My brows rose, but I didn't bother turning toward him. "Since when are you
talkative?"

That question was met with another growly noise that sounded like an
expletive, and I smiled to myself, stopping to turn toward where he'd paused in
the road. "Fine, you want to talk? Let's go back to your house and we can discuss
the investigation. *That* is why I stayed."

I don't know why the words came out of my mouth, why I'd suggested going
to his house. Nothing good could come of it. We'd either end up at each other's
throats again or...

I swept my tongue across my bottom lip and shook the intrusive thought
away.

Øyvin ran his fingers through his hair and sighed, looking up at the dark sky.

"Well, if you don't want to hear about my list of suspects—" I added, making
to move on with my journey.

The Fjord Fae encroached on my space, bursting my happy bubble by bringing us chest to chest. "Don't talk about it out here," he seethed.

"So, you *do* actually want to talk about the investigation?" I peered up at him,
daring him to suggest something else. *Go on then, tell me what you really want?*

He took a deep breath, his shoulders shifting with the effort. "Yes. That is
what we should talk about."

Honest to hell, that aquavit had gone to my head because I couldn't control
myself around him. The need to touch him seared through me, pushing me on.
"You sure? There isn't something *else* you want to get off your chest?" I poked
the beast, his pecs rock hard beneath my finger.

He glared at the offending appendage, looking ready to bite it... or suck it.

"Come on then, Sharky," I said, stepping back and sauntering past him
toward his house on the fjord, "we've got things to discuss."

I didn't look back, but I knew he was watching. My spine tingled as if I was
in the presence of a predator, and I exaggerated the sway of my hips in response.

We entered Øyvin's boathouse and shucked off our jackets and shoes. This time
I took a second to appraise the space, which had been the furthest thought from
my mind the last time I was here. His main living space was sparsely decorated,

but featured blond hardwood floors and white cabinetry in the tiny corner kitchen, giving it a *Scandinavian coastal* style. A small circular dining table sat to the left, with four wooden chairs dotted around it—all of which had been pushed in to allow walking space. To my right was the living room area, with that leather sofa we'd previously *enjoyed*, a bookcase beside the small fireplace, and a piano against the far wall.

"I'll text Espen," I said, because he should be here if we were indeed going to discuss the investigation. I reached into my jeans for my phone... and found nothing. I tapped each pocket and my backside, coming up empty. I'd left it at Espen's to charge.

"Problem?"

"Damn it." I crossed my arms as I sat down on the piano bench. "Can I borrow your phone? You have Espen's number, right?"

He rolled his eyes and pulled his cellphone from his pocket, tossing it into my outstretched palm without a word.

"Brave," I said with a flick of my eyebrows.

He tilted his lips into a tiny smirk, his blue eyes darkening into bottomless oceans. "You try anything stupid and I'll throw you into the fjord again."

I guffawed at his insinuation and threat. "Your phone would get wet if you did."

He shrugged and sat down beside me. "Yes, but I can dive in and create an air pocket around it so I don't have to put it in rice for a week."

"And you'd let me sink to the bottom and get soaked?"

"Yes."

I shoved his shoulder, but he didn't move, didn't even budge from his spot beside me on the piano bench. Finding Espen's name in the contacts, I typed out a quick message that would get him over here pronto.

Øyvin: Been kidnapped by the beast from below. Send help to his house. —Lennie

Before I gave it back, I took a quick selfie, giving the camera the middle finger and a mischievous grin. Lennie Martin at her fucking finest—my Mom would be so ashamed.

Øyvin snatched the phone from me before I could do any other damage—like set the image as his background—and stashed it away.

"What do you want to do while we wait?" I asked.

His jaw twitched and he ran his palms across his jean-clad thighs. Without saying a word, he spun around and faced the piano, settling his thick fingers above the ivory keys. As he started to play, I turned around too, watching him move with a grace and fluidity that was shocking considering his size.

The melody was somewhat sombre, a tune filled with swells and valleys that conveyed more than any lyrics could. It kind of reminded me of landscape photographs—pictures that said a thousand words without anyone ever having to open their mouth to impart them. The tune drew me into a mesmerizing trance, where the only things around me were the trilling notes, the smell of clean linen, and the warmth of Øyvin's arm and thigh brushing against mine. My breaths grew more ragged, and I crossed my ankles to avoid my toes curling. Øyvin spotted the movement out of the corner of his sight and a minuscule smirk quivered upon his lips. That alone drew me out of my haze and I tapped a random key, ruining his perfect melody.

Øyvin tightened his jaw at the invading *dummm*, but didn't stop.

"I wanted to..." he started, drawing my attention away from the ivories even as he continued to play. "I wanted to apologize for the way I spoke to you last week."

I stilled, my breath catching in my throat and my eyes going as wide as satellite dishes. When I said nothing, he continued, "I was being overprotective and my choice of words was unkind. I also appreciate you staying to help with the investigation."

I pressed my lips together, unsure what was happening or how to respond, because the last thing I ever expected to hear out of the stoic Asshole's mouth was an apology. *Is this really happening, or have I passed out in a ditch thanks to the late night and aquavit?* Øyvin continued to play the beautiful tune, turning every so often to check on my facial features—which probably resembled the shock I was feeling—and eventually I conceded an, "Okay."

The acceptance earned me one of his lopsided grins that made him look like he'd won some sort of prize, and that just didn't sit well with me. So, being the respectful lady that I was, I pressed one of the keys again... and then once more for good measure, ruining his beautiful song.

Before I could make an additional attempt, Øyvin grabbed my wrist and lifted it above my head. I wobbled on the bench and he steadied me, stopping me from falling off. My breath caught in my throat, and his chest shuddered.

"You really are trouble."

"You have no idea." I grinned.

He surged forward and pressed his lips against mine, guiding my hand and letting it settle on his shoulder. I looped my other arm around his neck, dragging him as close as I could. Running his palms down my arms, sides, and stopping at my hips, he squeezed my curves and a low hum escaped from his lips.

With an animalistic grumble, he shifted me so I sat astride the bench, and then rose while dragging my ass to the edge of the seat. My heart hammered within my chest and my breathing turned ragged and needy, matching the pulsing between my thighs.

He pressed me down over the length of the bench, the soft cushion taking my weight. Spreading my legs, he knelt before me, then swept his hands up my thighs. My breaths quickened as, with deft fingers, he slid the top of my pants down. I lifted my hips to ease his endeavor, and he slowly pulled them over the curve of my ass. Øyvin continued shifting the fabric down my legs, taking my underwear with it. His eyes met mine, deep pools filled with lust.

Exposed and wanting, a shiver ran through my spine and heat welled at my core. A hint of a smile graced Øyvin's face, like he was soaking in every second of my need.

Leaning over me, and not wasting another second, he swept his tongue across my center. My toes curled, and I grabbed his hair, keeping him where I so desperately needed him. Caressing my calves, he continued worshiping my core—sucking, licking, giving me everything and then some.

"Øyvin, fuck," I groaned as sparks shot up and down my spine.

A grumble was all I got in return as he detached himself and rose to his feet. With one hand, he pulled his sweater off, keeping his eyes locked on me the entire time. The move was probably the hottest thing I'd ever seen, and the view afterward wasn't bad either.

Before I could request his return to my swollen clit, he lifted me off the bench, kicked it out of the way, and laid me down on the floor. I followed his lead, ripping my shirt and bra over my head, desperate to be rid of any barriers between us. The wooden boards were cold beneath my back and in stark contrast to the burning fae who settled above me. Not wanting to wait a moment longer, I unzipped his pants, pulled him out, and lined him up, rubbing the tip of his dick against my entrance, both of which were slick with desire. He pressed his forehead against mine and then pushed inside.

Fucking hell.

I swallowed thickly, heat pooling at my core and a desperate need zipping down my limbs. My head lolled to the side and I moaned as he picked up the pace, rocking against all the right spots, bringing me closer to that pleasure-filled precipice. As my back arched involuntarily, I grasped at his shoulder blade and the piano keys above us, sending a low note reverberating through the room. The resonance matched the chaos unfurling between my thighs.

Øyvin pressed on, pushing me over the edge and groaning through his own release with shuddered bursts and shallow breaths.

Both of us fully sated, he relaxed above me, keeping us in an entangled embrace. My lungs heaved, and the smell of our actions permeated the air around us. With wavering hands, I ran my fingers down Øyvin's spine and he shuddered, his dick twitching inside me as his head dropped to my neck.

"Don't stop on my account," Espen's voice sounded from the doorway to the boathouse, and I stilled. I grabbed Øyvin's hair and tilted his head out of the way so I could see our surprise guest.

"How long have you been there?" I asked.

Espen grinned slowly, his gaze on fire. "Yeah, Øyvin, how long have I been here?"

I took a deep breath, then pulled Øyvin's head away from my neck so I could look him in the eyes. He peered up from beneath his golden brows, a salacious sparkle in his gaze. My heart hammered in my chest, the waves of pleasure slowly subsiding in my limbs and between my thighs where his cock remained buried. I must have missed Espen's arrival, I certainly hadn't heard him over the noise of Øyvin's thrusts, my moans, and my hands grabbing across the piano keys.

"Let's just say, I caught most of the show." Espen leaned against the door-frame, his arms crossed, the material of his shirt tight across his shoulders and chest.

I tilted my head back, staring up at the wooden beams on the ceiling. My veins were humming, my thoughts spinning so much that I didn't have any comeback. I was swimming in bliss and had nothing to say.

Slowly, painfully so, Øyvin pulled out of me, rising to his full height. His jeans hung loosely off his hips, his cock still exposed. He extended his hand to me and I took it, only to be hauled off the floor and into his arms. Shocked by the sudden shift, I wrapped my legs around him, and he grabbed my ass in his broad palms while Espen watched us, saying nothing.

"How about we take this upstairs?" Øyvin asked.

I let out a shaky breath and surveyed Espen, who tilted his head and gave me a look that said he was game if I was.

Biting my lip and sliding my arms around Øyvin's neck, I nodded. "Fuck yes." A threesome, with these two? I was definitely in a ditch having some sort of fever dream, or my body was about to be rocked into blissful oblivion.

A low rumble of approval rolled from Øyvin's chest, and he strode out of the room, heading for the loft above us.

Øyvin dropped me unceremoniously onto his large bed, and I was immediately hit by the smell of clean linen and rain. His room was minimally decorated, as if only the essentials were necessary, plus an exceptionally comfortable duvet and sheets.

Øyvin stood beside the bed, while Espen shucked off his jacket and pants, his eyes locked on my body the entire time. My skin pebbled under their attention and my nipples were rock hard. Being naked in front of either of them set my senses on fire, but being bare with both of them in the room was like a fucking inferno raging beneath my skin. Hot and bothered didn't even come close to describing how I felt.

I laid down to watch the two specimens, both of whom were eying me like ravenous wolves. "So, you two are okay with sharing?" I asked, hoping to hell they'd say yes.

They both smirked and glanced at each other.

"Is... is this something you two have done before?"

Espen chuckled and Øyvin rolled his eyes. Grabbing my arm, he spun me on the bed so I was lying across it at an angle where my ass sat close to one edge and my head lolled across the end near him. The position brought me face to face with his cock, and I wasn't entirely mad about it. Not one bit. "No," he replied. "But when you've lived as long as we have, pleasure is pleasure."

Espen clamped his hands around my ankles before slowly letting his fingers drift up toward my thighs, leaving gentle caresses as he went. My core throbbed at the sensation, and I closed my eyes, basking in the pleasure until a low grunt sounded behind me.

I opened my eyes to find Øyvin, now in all his naked glory. *Fuck me sideways.*

"Open wide," he said with the faintest smirk, his eyes shimmering with the lust I'd seen downstairs.

I quirked a brow in challenge. *How was he hard again already?*

Øyvin narrowed his eyes, then nodded to Espen.

A sharp pinch on my thigh and then the slide of a finger against my clit had my mouth falling open in a moan, and next thing I knew I was groaning around Øyvin's girth. I could taste myself on him, and beads of pre-cum slid down my throat. I wanted more.

Espen slid his fingers across my center, before plunging two inside me. I arched my back at the sensation while Øyvin took the opportunity to push deeper into my mouth.

I couldn't see what was happening at the other end. I could only feel what Espen was doing to my body, and somehow, that heightened everything. My senses were all on high alert. The sound of our breaths, the smell of our actions, the feel of every nerve-ending between my thighs sparking like the fucking Fourth of July.

Espen pressed the tip of his cock against my entrance, teasing, then slowly pushed inside. I groaned around Øyvin, who started slowly pumping in and out of my mouth. Grabbing onto him, my hands dug into his thick, muscular thighs, and I took control of his motion and tempo, setting a slow but steady pace.

It was all overwhelming, but fucking spectacular. The in-and-out on both ends had me aching for more, the stimulation of both my core and mouth almost unbearable. Espen's thrusts increased in pace, and before I could stop to catch my breath, Øyvin clamped his hands over my arms, keeping me in place. The sensation spiraled and my skin felt like it was burning. My core spasmed, and the telltale sign of impending euphoria built and built and built until I exploded around both of them.

Øyvin popped himself out of my mouth, ferociously fisting himself as Espen continued pumping deeper and deeper, my body quivering around him as he worked me through my orgasm. Both males were breathing hard and the sight of them both working toward their undoing was almost enough to have me orgasm again, but my body merely continued tingling with aftershocks. With a groan from both of them I watched as Espen finished inside me, then witnessed Øyvin cumming all over my chest—the white ribbons of cum trailing between my breasts.

Espen pulled out and flopped down on the bed next to me before he began tracing patterns across my hip. Øyvin backed away and settled on a wooden stool beside his dresser. He tilted his head back against the wall, but kept his darkened gaze on me. Holding his stare, I licked my lips and then swept my fingers through the mess he'd left on my body. Not a single muscle on his relaxed form moved, except a minute twitch in his jaw, as I curled my tongue around my fingers, tasting him.

"We should do that again some time," I said, bringing my hand back down to the rumpled sheets while I tangled my other hand into Espen's hair. "You two interested?"

Espen let out a throaty groan. "Fuck yes."

I chuckled as he leaned over and kissed my cheek. Shifting slightly onto my side, I glanced over at Øyvin—this time looking at him right way up. "And will you be joining us?"

Øyvin took a deep breath, watching his mess slide down my chest, then rose from his little chair. He opened the dresser beside him and pulled out a plain white t-shirt, then strode across the room in a few short steps. As he reached out, grabbed me, and pulled me to my knees, I wet my lips with my tongue. The sheets tangled around my feet, my breathing stuttering as he stared down at me and began to wipe up his cum, starting near my belly button and making his way across my breasts. Before I could say anything, he pressed his lips to mine and stole my breath. Pulling away sharply, he brushed my hair behind my ear, threw the dirty t-shirt across the room, then nodded—accepting the offer for a part two to this escapade. My lips curved into a satisfied smile as thoughts of what else we could do together drifted through my mind.

"Good," Espen said, shifting across the bed and leaning against the headboard with his eyes closed, "give me twenty minutes."

30

LENNIE

The next morning, I awoke between two fae—one snoring lightly in his sleep, the other sleeping like a rock—both shockingly virile for their age. Honestly, if you'd told me how old they were I'd laugh in your face. Both Espen and Øyvin looked like they belonged in the Roman statue section of a museum. Although... their combined ages would actually put them... *Don't do math, Lennie. Just, don't do it.*

I shook the thought free and turned onto my side, facing Øyvin.

"Good morning, Trouble," he muttered, his voice husky with sleep as he cracked his eyes open.

"Morning, Asshole."

He grinned. "We can try that next time."

"You mean, you want me to find a strap-on?"

He scoffed, and an arm yanked me backward into something very similar to such a device.

"I think he means you," Espen whispered into my hair, and I shivered in response.

"Well, I'm game if you two are," I said, looking between the two of them. A serene warmth settled over me, and I felt the sudden need to say something else—juuuust in case their subtle smiles were signals of thoughts progressing too far ahead. "While I enjoy both of you, I'm not interested in any definitions at this time," I said as diplomatically as possible considering my state of undress. "But, I also wouldn't mind continuing *this.*"

Øyvin gave me a lopsided grin, and Espen chuckled before saying. "We can let *this* be whatever you want it to be. Right, Øyvin?"

The Fjord Fae nodded, his eyes locked on mine, and a sense of peace eased through my limbs. I valued my freedom and independence, and wasn't ready for any *settling down.* "Good," I said. "Wouldn't want you two to think I was suddenly your—"

A knock sounded from the front door, and all three of us stilled.

Øyvin creased his brow and shook his head, clearly not expecting visitors. Letting out a deep breath, Øyvin got up, yanked on his jeans, and grabbed a clean sweater from his dresser, throwing that on too as he left the loft. Since the loft was walled in we couldn't see him, but we could just about hear him as he crossed the room downstairs and greeted the visitor with a low grunt.

Espen removed the bit of sheet between us and pulled me flush against his chest, my ass firmly planted against his cock.

"Who is it?" I asked, unable to hear exactly what was being said downstairs.

Instead of grinding against me, Espen wrapped his palm across my mouth, silencing me. "Shhhh," he whispered into my ear, his breath tickling my neck.

I wriggled, but he just tightened his hold—his arms constricting my movement like a damn anaconda. After a few more hopeless squirms, I relented, mumbling against his hand instead. "What are they saying?"

Espen's heart was beating fast against my back as he quietly replied, "The investigation."

I stilled completely, my chest shuddering as I swallowed the shock that invaded my system.

"I don't know who it is, but it sounds like one of the Fjord Fae councilmen—the king's council."

I digested the information by refraining from moving. I didn't need to land myself in more trouble with fae of the fjord, especially not a representative of the king. Nor did I really want Øyvin to get busted for having us up here... however appealing that thought might also be.

Espen continued, "The councilman is asking about the wall down the fjord... and the wildlife... something about concerns with the fish upstream."

I was amazed Espen could actually hear anything. All I could make out were low grumbles, probably from Øyvin, and the sound of my own pulse. It wasn't like this was the first compromising position I'd almost been caught in—I was famous for terrible ideas—but this, for some reason, felt different. The consequences of getting caught were bigger—more was at stake. Perhaps it was the investigation and my knowledge of the fae... or perhaps it was the two fae I'd fucked last night. Either way, it was a helluva way to start my morning. Fuck, I hadn't even had coffee yet and my heart was already racing.

The mumbling downstairs concluded and the front door clicked shut. A moment later, Øyvin leaped back upstairs and appeared in the doorway. Espen slowly removed his hand from my face, and I took the chance to talk.

"Who was that?" I asked.

"The King's Chief Advisor," Øyvin replied, his jaw tight and his arms crossed as he leaned against the door frame.

Espen flopped onto his back and let out a long sigh.

"And he has concerns about the wall and the fish upstream?" I questioned, not bothering to cover up when Espen pulled at the sheets. So be it if I was naked. It might be a bit distracting for the grumpy Fjord Fae, but it might also get him to vocalize more than his usual grumbles.

Øyvin quickly glanced at my tits before flicking his eyes back up to mine. "The King and the Council have some concerns about the fish upstream in light of the recent landslides. They want me and some soldiers to check on them today."

"And the wall?" Espen asked, rolling out of bed and pulling on his pants.

"Just the usual concerns, but I'm going to do a full inspection as I do every week."

"Perfect," Espen said. "Shall we have breakfast?"

My stomach rumbled in answer, and Espen smiled, tugging me from the bed to my feet.

"So, let's discuss our leads," I said, plopping onto the couch with my morning coffee that Øyvin had made—it was sans creamer and sugar, and definitely an inferior roast compared to whatever Oddvar brewed, but after last night's shenanigans, I needed the liquid energy. Breakfast had been good, the bread rolls with salami filling up my starving belly, but coffee was what I ultimately required to get on with my day.

"I think we can safely say Queen Freija is not to blame for this," Espen said, sitting down beside me.

"Are you *sure*?" I asked, not entirely certain of the history or politics of the three factions, and not ready to dismiss anything yet.

"Positive," Øyvin replied, taking a seat on his piano bench but facing us, firmly grasping his coffee mug. The object seemed so small and fragile in his large hands.

"I'm just playing devil's advocate." I raised my empty palm and shrugged. I didn't necessarily disagree with them, but I felt like it needed to be said. Just in case. "I guess that means Halvar is out of the running for culprit, too?"

Both fae nodded, and I agreed. Based on the behavior I'd seen in the throne room, I doubted Halvar would ever do anything to jeopardize the health and wellbeing of his Queen and her people. No, that man would protect his flock at all costs.

"Do either of your factions have enemies?"

The Fjord and Forest Fae looked at each other for a while as if silently communicating or, at the very least, having a staring competition. I poked Espen in his side when no one responded after a while.

Espen sighed. "There are always threats from different regions, fae who are angry and decide to take it out on others."

"And they regularly choose to attack Skolvik?"

Espen tilted his head from one shoulder then to the other, as if saying 'sometimes.'

"Why?"

"Stories claim this fjord as the birthplace of our kind," he replied, taking a sip of his own coffee. "Fae have allegedly lived here for millennia, and there are claims that this area is as close as one can get to the ancestral power as possible, where we may be our strongest."

"It's nonsense," Øyvin chimed in with zero exuberance.

"Okay, so there are threats to both the Fjell, Fjord, and Forest Fae from other factions. Like there was twenty years ago? When this happened last time to the Forest Fae?"

Both nodded.

"But no one ever found out who it was that killed the Forest Queen, right?"

"Correct," Espen said solemnly and took another sip of his drink, staring toward the window by the front door.

I placed my mug on the tiny coffee table and pulled my legs onto the sofa, curling them under my ass and facing the two fae.

"It could very easily be someone from the south again, trying to pull power from us," Øyvin said, downing his drink and setting the empty mug beside mine.

"Then we mark them as our main suspect for now. Any particular individual?" I asked.

Øyvin glanced over at Espen who took another very large gulp of his drink, like he was avoiding the question.

I raised my brow at Øyvin, hoping he could fill me in on whatever tension just rocked up next to me. But, as per usual, he remained mum.

"Espen, is there anyone in particular—"

"It would have to be their descendants," he muttered, wholly lost in a trance.

"What?"

"It would have to be the descendants of the people who fought for the southern factions twenty years ago."

"Why?"

"Because they were obliterated on the battle field," Øyvin finally chimed in, an ounce of something I couldn't quite place—sadness perhaps—lacing his words.

"Do I want to know how?"

I glanced at Øyvin who looked at Espen again. I turned to the Forest Fae beside me, who'd gone very still. After a minute, he shook his head. "No, you don't want to know."

However much I wanted to dig for more details, I let it be. The subject was clearly painful for him, and considering he lost his Queen and mentor that day, I didn't want to bring back those memories.

"They'd have to be working with someone here though, right?" I said, pivoting the subject minutely. "They're pulling magic away from the area, so someone around here must be helping them. There *were* two human-like shapes in that initial photo I took. Maybe someone around here was working with one of those descendants from the south?"

"It could be anyone," Espen said with a nod, and a solemn mood settled over us.

31
ESPEN

A week after my initial tryst with Lennie and Øyvin—and a few more sessions in between—we still hadn't found any new leads for our investigation, but that hadn't stopped the problems from spreading in the region. Early this morning an entire school of fish had been found floating along the banks of the fjord by the marina—too many for this to have been just an ecological problem. Øyvin and his men were dealing with it, as were some of the more weathered fishermen in town.

Meanwhile, my job for the day was assisting with the final roadside clean up from the first landslide. The terrain needed clearing of some of the smaller debris and detritus that could incapacitate regrowth or become a potential hazard should it end up in the road.

When I'd told Lennie about the group of volunteers and what we'd planned to do, she'd jumped at the opportunity to help—not even bringing her camera along. Lennie and I worked alongside Solveig and two of her knitting club friends—Jorunn and Dagny. We were all in our rain gear, the Norwegian autumn in full swing with its vacillating downpours and drizzle. We'd also brought with us brooms, gloves, and bins that we could store branches in that could either be returned to the woods to decompose or thrown into a machine and turned into mulch for the village gardeners.

While Lennie helped the ladies clear broken branches and rocks out of the drainage areas, I swept the ground for any signs of fae magic—any scars, any marks that could be a clue or needed healing—making sure I removed debris as I went so I didn't look too suspicious.

"Lennie here was staying with me for a while, you know," Solveig said to her friends in English, brushing some smaller rocks off the road with a thick-bristled broom she'd brought from home.

The white-haired duo nodded, and Lennie glanced at me, flicking her eyebrows in a flirtatious manner. She knew what was coming next. So did I but I did nothing to stop it. I didn't want to.

Solveig continued, "And, instead of heading back to America, she decided to stay for a while longer."

"So, where is she staying now?" Jorunn asked.

"With Espen," Lennie replied, joining their morning gossip session.

All three let out an "oooooh" and I felt their gazes on my back. Leaving my search, I wandered over to them before things could get really out of hand.

"It's nothing to get all excited about," Lennie said, sounding a little snarky, and I had to bite my lip to keep from smiling even as I wanted to reach out and pull her into my side. Lennie had mentioned more than once whatever was going on between us was casual—no-strings-attached fun while she was here—but that didn't stop the way my heart beat faster in her presence.

"Lennie, dear, we live in a small village. Either everything is exciting or nothing is." Solveig set her hands on her hips, and her friends giggled and nodded.

"If it's excitement you've been looking for all these years, you should've said something," I said, sauntering up beside the women as I grabbed the pile of gathered material Solvieg had swept up, dumping it into the closest bin.

"Oh, you're *much* too young for the three of us," Solveig chuckled.

Lennie coughed and stifled a laugh into the crook of her elbow, then waved them off when the ladies cast concerned looks at her.

"Age is but a number, ladies." I grinned, knowing full well the effect it had on them.

I caught Lennie rolling her eyes before turning back to some rocks that were blocking one of the drain pipes where water ran down the hill and back into the fjord.

"How long are you staying, then?" Solveig asked Lennie.

She shrugged, lifting the rocks one at a time and moving them to the side. "Until I get kicked out."

Solveig smiled knowingly, turning to me with a wink.

I returned her grin with one of my own as a pang of concern skirted up my back. She likely was only alluding to Lennie staying with me and that something was clearly going on between us, but I'd always wondered if Solveig knew, if someone had told her about the fae. She was a wise woman, always in the know about the town's happenings—good friends with all, and always kind to tourists like Lennie. It made her dangerous in regards to our secret, my people's wellbeing.

For those of us who intermingled with humans, it was common to move regularly so as to not raise wariness or doubt. When you don't age as quickly as humans, they started to get suspicious. I'd been born in the north, but had spent a lot of time in Skolvik when I joined Queen Ragnhild's Guard and always returned when I could. However, every thirty years or so, I needed to move. The way Solveig eyed me made me wonder if it was time to move again soon. As they got back to work, the ladies switched to Norwegian, probably so Lennie couldn't understand them. The only problem was, Nora had tinkered with Lennie's hearing, so she could understand everything the women were saying.

"I saw her bickering with Øyvin. Thought there was something going on there," Dagny said.

"I remember you telling me that. Who stands outside Oddvar's and argues like lovers?" Jorunn added.

"Now, now, be nice," Solveig tutted, leaning on her broom. "If you were her age, you'd both be climbing that man like you were being chased by a bear."

The women chuckled and nodded, Dagny even adding, "I still might. Think he's into older women?"

I bit my lip and got back to work, carefully watching Lennie as she listened in on the conversation happening nearby fighting back a smirk of her own. I wasn't sure what Øyvin's stance was on older women but I knew first-hand that Lennie didn't require a bear to be chasing her to climb Øyvin *or* myself.

Having finished our work and parted ways with the trio of ladies, Lennie and I wandered back into the main part of town, heading toward Oddvar's for lunch. As we reached the waterfront by the public docks, I pinched my nose and Lennie gagged, then started spluttering.

"I thought Øyvin and the fishermen were cleaning up the fish?" she asked, cupping her hands over her nose and mouth to block out the rancid stench of rotting fish permeating the chilly air. "The smell wasn't this bad down the road."

It was admittedly less than what we'd been met with this morning but, likely thanks to the way the wind and air circulated around the end of the fjord, the fishy smell lingered in the village instead of moving out quickly. I shrugged and opened the door to the café, holding it open for her. She practically bolted past me and took a deep breath once inside—tilting her face upward and looking relieved.

Oddvar gazed across the counter, far less amused by Lennie than I was, then he quickly grumbled, "Close the door!" I swiftly obliged, making sure it was secure.

Lennie motioned to an open table and yanked off her jacket, hanging it over the back of the chair before sitting down. I joined her, removing my own coat and doing the same.

"What do you want for lunch?" I asked, peering at the little plastic menu that stood atop our table. "My treat as a thank you for helping us this morning."

Lennie smiled. "I don't need a thank you for volunteering but I do like carbs, so I'm not going to say no."

I let out a chuckle and ran my hand through my hair, pushing it off my forehead. Lennie watched the movement, then quickly looked away, a blush rising in her cheeks when she realized she'd been spotted.

"How about a ham and cheese sandwich with cucumber, lettuce, and mustard?" I asked with a smirk, feeling slightly giddy at the effect I had on her.

She nodded. "Sounds good. Thank you."

"No, thank *you*," I replied, placing my hands on the table, shamelessly letting the muscles in my arms flex as I leaned down and toward her. "You didn't have to join us this morning, but I'm glad you did. It was nice to have you there."

She snorted, crossing her arms and leaning back in her chair, but her eyes raked over my body just as I'd intended before meeting my own, full of her signature sass. "You mean as a buffer between you and the ladies?"

I shrugged, challenging the look she was giving me. "Someone needs to keep them at bay. You heard how they talked about Øyvin—if I hadn't been standing there, they would have said the same about me."

"And you think I'm the woman for the job?"

"Based on how quick you are to sass everyone and desire to be *on top* of things, I think you'd do perfectly."

"Oh, really?" She rolled her lip between her teeth, her gaze dropping down my body again, and I had to steady my breathing. "Tempting."

I let out a slow shuddered breath, ready to launch across the table and carry her back to my cabin. "Choose your next words wisely, or I'll punish that mouth of yours later."

"You know what my mouth *really* wants?" she whispered, leaning forward. I angled toward her across the table, giving her a nod to continue that sentence. "Food."

I hung my head and rubbed my hand across my jaw as I straightened up. Just then a chair scraped across the floor, the air grew rather pungent, and someone sat down at the end of our table. "I'll have what she's having," Øyvin said.

"I don't think you want what we were just discussing," Lennie said, raising her brows and giving him a knowing look. "By the way, you stink. Consider showering."

Øyvin rolled his eyes. "I will have whatever *sandwich* she is having."

I smiled and stood from my chair. "Three sandwiches, coming right up," I said, then strode across the room to the counter, giving Oddvar our order.

As per usual, the sandwiches at Oddvar's were delicious—simple local ingredients paired with freshly made bread would always be a win in my book, and the same appeared to be true for Lennie considering how quickly she devoured it. Øyvin ate quickly too but was frequently interrupted by glares from other customers who were unamused by the smell still clinging to his clothes. I did my best to ignore it but Lennie had been right—he should've gone home first to shower or, at the very least, changed out of his cream-knit sweater and jeans.

"So, all the dead fishies are gone?" Lennie asked, wiping her fingers on a napkin.

Øyvin nodded, chewing on his last bit of sandwich. "All of them have been removed from the marina, taken to the local landfill to be dealt with."

"Gross," Lennie said, her lips turning into a grimace. "Any idea what caused it?"

I leaned back in my chair, equally interested in what might have caused the large school of fish to die so suddenly. This type of thing wasn't entirely unheard of, but it was usually as a result of a pollutant and I hadn't heard of any recent spills.

"Oxygen starvation," Øyvin replied, and I furrowed my brow. "As the water gets hotter, the less oxygen there is available for the fish to absorb. It's usually a sign of pollution and global warming, but..." He cast his gaze around the table, his blue eyes speaking volumes.

I grimaced. "But it could also be related to other *things*?"

He nodded.

"You think the culprit is mimicking global warming problems to throw us off their trail?" Lennie asked, her voice barely above a whisper.

Øyvin and I both nodded. Honestly, it was a smart—albeit, awful tactic to hide the trace of magic in the fjord. Like so many other places around the world, pollution was a problem here—if we hadn't already been looking for magical problems, we might not have dug deeper into the issue to discover the root cause. This entire situation grew more frustrating by the day. All I wanted to do was protect the Forest Fae, the inhabitants of our region, but I constantly felt like I was behind or being caught off guard.

"I think it's safe to say," Øyvin piped up, checking over his shoulder to make sure none of the other customers were listening, "that whoever is behind this *definitely* lives here."

"What makes you say that? They could be visiting from the south?" Lennie tilted her head and widened her eyes.

I was curious what he had to say to that too, because my guess still remained on retaliation from the south for what had happened twenty years ago... that day that would haunt me for the rest of my life.

"First, the damage to the forest, then the mountain with the landslide, and now this. All three are regular occurrences here naturally. Whoever is behind this knows exactly how to hide their tracks, making these seem like unfortunate events. They must live here—or have been here for a long time—and know the area well. They're too consistent, too good at going undetected."

"Save for my photographic brilliance," Lennie said, wiggling her eyebrows.

Øyvin sighed and crossed his arms. "Yes, except for that hiccup. But you still didn't capture their faces."

Lennie huffed and mumbled "Asshole." I did my best not to chuckle at her reaction. Øyvin had a point though. From the rock slides to the dead fish, whoever was behind this mess was always one step ahead—they must know the area and understand its natural weaknesses.

"Any changes *elsewhere*?" I asked, making sure not to mention the fjord and inhabitants therein as we were within earshot of humans.

"None that I am aware of at this time," Øyvin replied with a long sigh. "But, I am going to do my usual rounds tomorrow morning, which includes checking on the wall."

32

ØYVIN

I pressed the button and opened the boat-garage door until it was a quarter of the way up. The wind from the morning storm rushed in, whipping around me and brushing against my navy wool-knit sweater. Taking a deep breath, I stepped toward the edge of the internal dock and dove into the water, creating an air pocket around myself as the water enveloped me.

Beneath the choppy surface, the Fjord was a blissful silence that comforted me as I propelled myself east toward the frontlines. I needed to check in on my soldiers and spend some time bolstering our protections against the oil refinery and bustling waterway.

Several of my fellow Fjord Fae inhabitants nodded as I zipped past and a couple schools of fish wholly ignored me as I dodged them, doing my best not to disturb the creatures. With the great deal of strength from my power-stores, my journey wasn't long. After about fifteen minutes underwater, the wall my men held against the pollution a third of the way down the fjord came into view.

Stretching from the fjordbed to the surface, the immense shimmering shield stretched two kilometers across. The thick wall of water and power was see-through, but buffeted anything deemed a pollutant. Marine life could easily swim through it, but should a trail of oil or pieces of human debris drift up against the wall, the object would be disintegrated by our magic.

Standing at regular intervals along the base of the sheer barrier were Fjord Fae soldiers in their uniforms, albeit without the capes as this wasn't a formal occasion.

I landed against the ground with a dull thump, sediment billowing up around my feet, and was greeted with a nod from the closest fae. The water down here on the fjordbed was murky, but with our specially attuned eyesight, the haze was easy to see through. As a Fjord Fae, I had the ability to not only swim at high speeds through the water, but also walk on the waterbed. Where other beings, like humans, would float without proper SCUBA equipment or weights, we could traverse down here by adjusting our buoyancy at will—unencumbered by the pressure. Talking beneath the water was a trait Fjord Fae were born with, too. While we could have air pockets around ourselves, our ability to communicate wasn't hindered by the water between us. We could translate the reverberations, so no words were lost. It was similar in some ways to what Nora had done with Lennie's hearing—the Fjell Fae Princess had royal powers that could help with translations, whereas ours were granted to all Fjord Fae and specifically targeted toward underwater communication. Without it, we wouldn't be able to live down here, nor protect the fjord as well.

"Report?" I asked the fae next to me, Sigurd, as I scanned the wall for breaches and leaks.

"All clear this morning," the black-haired fae said as he held his hands against the wall, holding it up with his magic, the same as each soldier did down the entire stretch. "But there was a disturbance in the middle of the night."

"What happened?" I crossed my arms as a wave of anger swept through me. "And why didn't anyone inform me?"

The fae swallowed, but didn't falter. "It was a minor situation. Two of the young soldiers got into a fight—"

"About what?"

"A bad joke." Sigurd shook his head. "They're kids."

"They are soldiers in the Royal Fjord Guard that should act like it. Do I even want to know what the joke was about?"

"It's a waste of time and energy to even utter the words, sir."

My lips quirked into a minuscule grin. This was why I liked Sigurd. He was always honest and knew the importance of his job. "Thank you, Sigurd. Where are they?"

"Back on the wall." He nodded to the north. "Half a mile down. One with red hair, the other blond. Scrappy things."

Yeah, I appreciated Sigurd. At a hundred years old, with fifty of those defending the fjord, Sigurd was well versed in the activities of the Royal Guard. He even knew that I didn't ever bother with names. It was a rarity for me to remember the names of Guard members, and with a force of over three hundred fae, it was easier to just keep track of who the captains were.

"Thank you," I said with a bow of my head and left him to continue his work fortifying the wall with his power.

While swimming over to the miscreants would be faster, I decided to walk along the barrier instead. With my long strides, it took me merely five minutes to reach the two troublesome soldiers. Sigurd had been correct; based on their stature and lean limbs, these two fae were extremely young—probably part of the recent cohort of graduates from our training programs.

The blond one spotted me first and flinched. A split second later the red-haired fae grew a sickly shade of green.

"Gentlemen." It wasn't the words I wanted to use for them at that moment, but from experience, calling my troops *pieces of shit* by way of greeting wasn't always effective. At least not in times of peace.

Both bowed their heads as I came to a halt between them. The idiots were standing too close, out of position, and it took every gram of patience I had left to not immediately reposition them.

"Would either of you care to tell me what happened last night?" I asked, spreading my feet wide and crossing my arms.

Neither spoke nor made a move.

"Nothing?"

Silence.

"Well, if neither talks then both will be punished."

"He insulted my mother!" The blond one piped up, pointing at his colleague.

The red-head glared past me. "You joked about my sister!"

I rubbed my hand over my face. *Ancestors give me the strength not to kill them both right now.*

"—she came to me!"

"She'd visit Satan before she ever bothered with you!"

They continued yelling at each other while I contemplated my next course of action. As was usually the case with rookie soldiers, they needed fear shot through their veins a few times before they could show the respect I needed from them. These two were no exception. So, before they decided to start punching each other, I grabbed both of them by the collar, spun us to the other side of the barrier, and shucked them away from me. Propping my back against the magic wall, I pushed my power into it, not letting it falter now that the two imbeciles weren't supplying it with their energy.

"If either of you step out of line again, insults will be the least of your worries," I said, crossing my arms again. "Do I make myself clear?"

They both nodded and cast their gazes down.

"I said... Do I make myself clear?"

Both instantly straightened up, eyes wide, and their hands behind their backs. "Yes, sir."

"Good. Now you"—I pointed at the red-haired fae—"take up position down that way beside the boulder."

He glanced at the large rock about thirty meters from where we currently stood and nodded.

"And you stand here silently until your shift is over," I said to the blond one, who nodded continuously like the troll bobblehead toys I'd seen in the tourist center gift shop.

"If either of you steps out of line again, you'll be out of the Guard."

Once they were in position, I leaned off the wall and then left, not wasting my time with any other statements or pleasantries that had no place down here.

The rest of my inspection was calm, the soldiers manning the wall contributing enough magic to sustain the barrier that was primarily fed by the King's well of power. Without King Balder's power and immense strength, the whole thing would crumble or be weakened to a point that would render it almost useless in protecting the waters of the inner fjord. Thankfully, the serene state continued along the length of the wall... until I reached the very northern end.

The fae manning the part of the wall that brushed against the mountain was visibly struggling. He'd created a bubble around him to keep himself dry, but his feet were left out and beads of sweat marred his wrinkled forehead.

I stepped up beside him and pressed my hands against the vacillating barrier, shocked by what I found. Something pushed back—some energy that felt like hail buffeting against my palms. Taking a deep breath, I focused on my well of power, the pool of magic that churned away within my chest, granting me the ability to manipulate the aqueous element. I gathered up an extra cup of energy and poured it down my veins, sending it into the wall. The fae beside me grunted and I tightened my jaw as my power shot upward through the barrier like a reverse waterfall.

But even with my magical boost, my gut told me we had a weak spot. The power that now stabilized the wall at this point was merely gauze over a wound.

Did this have anything to do with the illegal transfer of magic? Or the recent landslides?

"How long has the wall been shifting like that?"

"Half an hour at most, sir," the fae said, his voice strained from exertion.

"Anyone else know about it?"

He shook his head. "The next watch guard isn't due for another ten minutes. I haven't had a chance to inform anyone yet."

I nodded. Watch guards walked up and down the frontline constantly, monitoring the soldiers and communicating problems back to the captains, so I must've arrived at the right time if I was the first on the scene.

"Good job holding it for as long as you did," I said to the soldier who looked ready to collapse. "I can take it from here. You head back to base and send me two more fae as soon as you get there."

He nodded and I felt his magic ease out of the wall.

"Thank you, sir."

"Thank you for your work. Please take tomorrow off and rest. I'll make sure your shift is filled."

He took a weary step back and gave me a gentle smile. "I appreciate it." With a nod, he lightly kicked off from the ground and swam down the fjord, heading toward the outpost office I'd set up a few decades ago.

After two fae and a watch guard had taken up position on the problematic part of the wall, I'd headed back to the Royal household to report to King Balder. Some of his magic flowed within our barrier, so he'd likely already felt a shift, but it was best to inform him about what was happening. Especially in light of what had occurred above the surface recently.

I knocked on the door to Balder's office and shifted into my Fjord Fae uniform. Balder wasn't usually a stickler for formalities—at least not from me—but considering the situation, it felt necessary.

"Come in," a low voice bellowed from inside, and I entered.

Balder was sitting behind his desk poring over a pile of documents with an antique green reading light casting a warm glow across the pages in his hands.

"King Balder."

"Øyvin. Do you have a report for me?" he asked, setting aside his work, his bright green eyes lifting to mine as he sat back in his chair.

"I do, sir."

With a wave of his hand, he said, "Proceed."

"As you may have felt, there was a problem with the wall."

His brow furrowed as he nodded. "I did feel a minor disturbance, but nothing more than what I feel if there is a small leak."

I sighed and prepared my words, knowing the news I carried was more concerning than that. "It wasn't a leak. I'm not even sure what it was, but it felt like something invisible was scratching away at the wall at the northern edge by the mountain. I was able to use some of my powers to patch the spot, but I don't know how long that will hold. The soldier manning the location..." I paused, remembering how exhausted the fae had been. "Sir, he looked depleted."

"Depleted?" Balder said, straightening in his seat and leaning forward over his desk.

I nodded and thought back on the fae's appearance. He was an older, stronger fae, but he was losing control of his magic, his abilities markedly frail compared to what was required of a soldier at the wall.

I handpicked soldiers for wall-duty. If a soldier didn't have the strength to help, they were assigned elsewhere. So, this soldier should've been able to handle his job—he'd certainly done so in the past—but it was as if the wall had been draining the man of his powers.

Balder clasped his hands, and the sound of him moving brought me back to the present moment. "I've never heard of anything like this but I'll alert the Fjord Fae Council and see if anyone else has."

"When is the next meeting?" I asked, wondering if I should attend this one and see what the King's advisors had to say.

"It starts shortly, actually," Balder replied as he glanced at the clock on his bookshelf. "I'd like you to be there and share your report."

"Of course, sir."

"Who did you leave guarding the problem spot?"

I straightened up and clasped my hands behind my back. "Two soldiers are powering the wall at the weakened spot, and I have a watch guard holding a permanent position there with orders to report directly to me with any issues."

"Good—"

A knock sounded at the door.

"Come in," Balder said, and I turned to see who would interrupt my meeting with the King.

In stepped Kjetil, Chief Advisor to the King, with his copper hair cut closely to his head, piercing crystal eyes, and his jacket collar popped so tall that it ensconced his entire neck like a scarf.

"Kjetil," I nodded in greeting.

"Øyvin," he replied with a brief smile before turning to the King. "King Balder, the council is assembled in the chamber next door. We are ready for you."

"Good." Balder rose from his seat, his frame almost too large for the room. "Øyvin will be joining us today, too. He has an interesting report from the wall."

I strolled into the council chambers behind Balder with Kjetil by my side. The rest of the council—eight other Fjord Fae—took their seats around the long wooden table as Balder sat at the head, his chair larger than the rest to accommodate his position and stature. I sidled into my seat at his right, while

Kjetil took up position to the King's left, still standing as he called the meeting to order.

"We have several pieces of information to discuss today, including the recent request for more housing closer to Skolvik Harbor, but first"—he glanced at me before turning to the King—"should we discuss the security matter brought forth by General Håland?"

I refrained from wincing at my rarely-used but official title. Head Guard was the more common term, and people rarely used my last name, but Kjetil had a flair for the formalities of our world.

Balder nodded once, at which the entire room focused their attention on me, and Kjetil finally sat down.

I cleared my throat and rested my hands on the table. "A disturbance was found along the wall today at the far northern end where it meets the mountain. An energy was pressing, scratching against it. The soldier manning it prior to my arrival was under significant strain and has since been replaced by two rested fae and a permanent Watch Guard who is reporting back to me on any changes."

I scanned the room, the looks on the council's faces were grave and concerned—even Kjetil had furrowed his brow. "Has anyone here heard of a power or fae that would attack the energy in the wall? Deplete the power of our soldiers as they fight against it?" I asked, hoping one of the elder council members might have any information.

Several shook their heads, and a few more shrugged as my eyes passed over them. Out of the corner of my eye I could see Balder doing the same, his chin resting on his fist as he leaned back in his chair.

"There was one instance that comes to mind," Valdemar, one of the older council members, started and my attention whipped to him as he continued. "But that was about twenty years ago and not here, not in our fjord."

Balder let out a low cough before requesting more information with a wave of his hand.

"It was a rumor, really. Chatter from some cousins of mine in the southern fjord. Their protections were quietly attacked a few weeks prior to the battle breaking out above the water."

The battle that had killed Queen Ragnhild and her Head Guard—Espen's mentor. The battle that I didn't ever like to think about, not after what happened to—

"Did their barricades fall?" the King asked, drawing me out of my thoughts and back to the present.

"Briefly," Valdemar replied with a solemn look across his weathered features. "But no one ever found out exactly what caused it and no official report was rendered." Which would explain why we'd never heard about it. I sighed as he turned to me and added, "My cousins described it in the same way, like something scratching at the wall, trying to break through."

My stomach curled into a bigger knot but I kept my features guarded. This was bad, really bad. Far worse than I'd initially imagined—a threat to us, the rest of the fae factions, and even the humans.

The room quieted as we all pondered the new information and waited for Balder to say something. After a few moments of silence, the king straightened up and clasped his hands together, resting them on the table.

"We continue Øyvin's current plan, doubling up guards at this location, but I want a continuous rotation of fae on the wall so no two fae are significantly depleted after a shift. Should we activate the reserves, too?" he asked, turning to me.

"Yes," I replied immediately, relief coursing through my veins that he took this threat as seriously as I did. "I don't want any soldiers running low."

"Not if another battle is heading our way."

The room collectively stilled at Balder's words but I responded to his warning. "Yes, sir."

Balder's gaze darkened slightly as he tilted his head toward me. "Good. But promise me this: word of these events shall not be reported to the Fjell Queen, nor our friend in the woods."

I straightened and took a deep breath. Refraining from telling them would be difficult, especially when trying to be diplomatic about the ongoing investigation, but orders were orders, and I had a duty to the fjord.

"Yes, sir."

33

LENNIE

"So, any last things I need to know before you throw me to the wolves in there?"
I asked Espen as we walked into the mountain for Queen Freija's birthday ball,
the magical barrier granting us passage into the behemoth.

Espen chuckled and glanced around at the other fae who were arriving for the
party and shifting their attire within the tunnels. "Pretty sure you're prepared
but maybe brace yourself for lots of questions and stares."

"Depends on what you're planning on dressing me in," I retorted.

He flicked his eyebrows, and a wicked look crossed his features. "What if I
just removed your clothes?" He leaned in and whispered, "Naked looks good on
you."

"I'd rock it," I said, giving him a daring look in return. "But can you actually
do that?"

He stepped closer and I backed up against the rocky wall as other revelers
sauntered past, shifting into their finery. My body hummed as he raked his gaze
over me and grinned. "Haven't tried in a while, but I've seen you naked several
times now, so it shouldn't be that hard..."

"Go ahead, buddy," I replied, my voice sounding breathy and seductive as I
leaned in to whisper back, "And we'll see who ends up *hard*."

He brushed his tongue across his bottom lip and then shook his head as he
pulled away from me. "You'll be the death of me, Lennie."

"You had a good run." I smirked.

With another shake of his head he placed his palm against my left shoulder
and a wave of warmth swept over me. Glancing down, I watched as my leggings
and black long-sleeve sweater disappeared and were replaced by a spectacular
emerald green dress made of floaty material and embroidered with delicate silver
threads in an almost branch-like pattern. The sleeves were a sheer fabric with the
same silvery motif continuing across my shoulders and encircling my wrists.

I looked up at Espen, who'd shifted into his Forest Fae uniform—cape and all—and he smiled. "Green okay? Or would you prefer black?"

"Like my heart?"

He chuckled. "Your choice."

I shook my head and surveyed the finery once more, noticing the way I matched Espen. "It's perfect. Thank you."

With a wink, he proffered his arm, and I looped my hand through it before he guided me toward the ethereal music floating down the tunnels.

I was expecting the party to be held in the throne room I'd visited before, but boy was I wrong. Espen led me deeper and deeper into the mountain until the revelry noises grew louder and we stepped into what could only be classified as an enormous cavern. The space was made of the same sky-blue stone as the throne room but was probably twenty times the size, big enough to contain the hundreds of people already in attendance and the large tables of food and drink that had been laid out. Like in the throne room, there was a dias at the end of the large hall with Queen Freija's throne—or another rendition of the one I'd previously seen her in. To the left sat a band of twenty fae playing some instruments that I recognized—violins and a piano—plus a few others I'd never seen before that looked reminiscent of banjos.

"Come on, let's make our rounds," Espen said, and gently pulled me into the melee.

We wandered around the immense room and Espen greeted just about everyone. I glanced around the hall, taking in all the fae in their finery—some in sparkling dresses, others in bespoke suits, and guards in their uniforms, each one matching the faction they belonged to. The entire scene was a jewel-toned vista that I wished I could photograph, but knew better than to expose these fae to the world.

Almost every fae we passed looked at me with narrowed eyes before swiftly pasting a pleasant smile on their face when they glanced at Espen. A smirk full of challenge and mock nicety settled on my face, and I chose to ignore the stares of the party-goers, instead focusing on the feeling of having my arm looped through Espen's. The warm and pleasant sensation that filled my chest from being on his arm swelled within me, giving me the extra boost of confidence I needed to keep my head up and move through the room with as much grace as I could muster.

"Where's Øyvin?" I asked, looking around for the brute.

"Queen Freija and King Balder don't have the best relationship," Espen explained, squeezing my hand where it rested in the crook of his arm. "There was uncertainty of whether the Fjord Fae would make an appearance. Some will probably sneak in but as for an official group of visitors from the royal in question?" He shrugged. "I'm not entirely sure."

"That's a shame. I was hoping to see Øyvin in his uniform again." What could I say? That thing hugged his ass and shoulders nicely, and Øyvin's shoulders and ass were a thing of beauty. While I hadn't been his biggest fan to start, I'd never turn down an opportunity to sneak a peek at that outfit when given the chance.

Espen scoffed and chuckled. "He's never been one for parties. As you know, he likes to stay home and play his piano on a Friday night."

That, I did know. Intimately.

Some sort of look must've crossed my face because before I could continue revisiting my memory of what I'd done to those ivories the last time he'd played for me, Espen pulled me onto the dance floor. "Care to dance?"

His knowing smirk and dilating pupils spoke volumes. He knew exactly where my head had been, and I knew he'd enjoyed *that* show.

I nodded. "Lead the way, yogi-cop."

He swept us into the middle of the elegant crowd, their attire casting shimmering light across one another and the blue stone walls. Releasing my hand from the crook of his arm, he spun me around and then gently pressed me against him. With one hand at my lower back and the other grasping my palm, he guided me to the waltz-like music of string instruments. My dress swished around my ankles, and I felt very princess-y but didn't wholly despise it. The gentle turns, the festive ambiance, the handsome uniformed fae leading me—it was all mesmerizing and, before I knew it, the band moved on to a new tune. I glanced around, taking in the couples around us, and my eyes landed on a handsome pairing in crisp suits.

"Who's that?" I asked, nodding toward the stout man with his sandy hair tied into a perfect man-bun. He kept monitoring the lamps and candles, and if one went out, he quickly reignited it with a silvery ball of light from his hand.

"That is Torsten, Leif's husband, one of my men."

"Is Torsten a Fjell Fae?"

Espen nodded and spun me around again, before we continued swaying gently to the violin music. "Married to a Forest Fae. Both are great men. Very kind."

I smiled as the couple continued dancing, only stopping now and then to pilfer a sweet treat off a passing platter. "But if he's a Fjell Fae, how does he have powers to help with lighting?"

"He has a rare ability that the ancestors only bestow upon one Fjell Fae at a time. No one quite knows how or why any one specific fae is granted that blessing, but not long after one such-gifted Fjell Fae dies, another is chosen."

Oh, so that was who Nora referred to when we visited the story cave. "So, he's special?"

"We're *all* special," Espen said with a salacious wink.

I rolled my eyes but couldn't entirely disagree. Not that I would tell him that. His ego was big enough already.

"I mean, his powers differ from those rocky, earthy ones of the other Fjell Fae?"

Espen dipped me slowly before pulling me back up to face him, his eyes ablaze as my chest slowly rubbed against his. "Yes and no. He's more similar to the royal Fjell Fae—their powers are more closely aligned with the ancestors. It's said that the ancestors—those who have passed on—relinquish their powers back to earth and gain control of the air element. But somehow, parts of that power seep into the strongest of fae or appear in the form of skill sets like Torsten's as gifts."

Fascinating.

My mind wandered over the many fae I'd met, all far more powerful and unique than the rest of the humans I'd ever known, while the music slowed and then shifted to something upbeat, more like a jig than a waltz.

Espen stepped back and smiled, releasing his hold on me. "Would you like a drink?"

"I'd love one," I replied as we moved off the dance floor.

"Great. I'll be right back," he said and disappeared into the crowd, heading for the drinks station.

I was about to partake in some sort of fluffy, white meringue dessert that was carried past on a tray when a commotion at the hall's entrance had me freezing on the spot.

The chatter in the room died down and the music petered out as the crowd parted, revealing new arrivals. Whispers of the name Balder echoed around the cavernous chamber.

A group appeared between the parted masses. At the head of the spear of fae was a man as big as Halvar, with a warrior-like presence but that's where the similarities ended. Unlike Halvar, this man looked like a Viking just returned from battle—long scruffy blond-and-silver beard, small scars across his face, and piercing green eyes that looked like they'd seen centuries of war. This was not a guy to be messed with. If I punched this guy like I did the first time I met Espen, I wouldn't end up at the police station. No, I'd be chained to the bottom of the fjord.

Yeah, I was an idiot for ever thinking Øyvin was King of the Fjord, because this man sure as fuck was the keeper of that title.

To Balder's right was Øyvin, and to his left was another man with light-red hair. The entire contingent, ten large fae, wore the Fjord Fae uniform—gray and navy materials, gray boots, and short capes that clung to one shoulder. The King's cape fastened to both his shoulders and the entire underside of the thick material was covered in silver embroidery of marine life and reeds.

I glanced to the other end of the chamber and, sure enough, Freija had appeared on her throne. A regal smile graced her face, her hands neatly clasped in her lap. To her right stood her ever-loyal guard, Halvar, his stoic gaze and stance not yielding any tells on how he felt about the sudden arrival of the Fjord Fae. An arrival that had the room collectively holding their breath.

"King Balder," Freija said with a nod, never taking her eyes off the new guests.

Balder swept his arms wide and gave her a toothy grin. "Happy Birthday, Queen Freija. Apologies for our late arrival."

He didn't look sorry at all. He and his guards swaggered further into the room, stopped, and then his men bowed their heads deeply while he didn't budge further.

As the party straightened, Øyvin's eyes flicked to mine and he quirked a brow.

I gave him a small smile as Torsten and Leif appeared on either side of me, their earlier grins faltering slightly as Balder bestowed more pleasantries.

"So, you're the American," the one with the man-bun said.

I puffed out my chest before replying quietly. "That, I am."

"I'm Torsten," he added before tilting his head to his husband, but never taking his eyes off the throne. "This is Leif."

I glanced up at Leif, the tall, slender Forest Fae. His dark hair was cut short and his bright green eyes were in stark contrast to his thick brows, slightly tan skin, and black suit. It looked like he'd stepped right out of the forest and into a men's tailor shop. Leif turned and the corner of his mouth twitched when he caught me gawking.

"You two know who the red-head is?" I whispered, turning my attention back to the group of Fjord Fae in the middle of the dance floor.

"Kjetil, King Balder's chief advisor."

"So, he's like second in command?" I asked, keeping my voice as low as humanly possible.

Leif shook his head. "Kjetil is the head of Balder's advisory council. Those other Fjord Fae with them are councilors and soldiers. Øyvin is in charge of security and soldiers, whereas Kjetil and the council bestow advice."

Glancing back at the group, I refocused just in time to catch Freija rising from her light-blue throne, her eyes twinkling even from this distance. "I'm glad you could attend, old friend. Please, do enjoy yourselves." She gave a graceful nod to the band, and they swiftly started playing again—a joyful tune to combat the crazy energy that had swept through the party at the King's sudden arrival.

Balder grinned and stepped off the dance floor, most of his men following after him but a few defected, including Øyvin. He strode toward me with assured strides and a playful smirk on his lips.

"Trouble," he said, coming to a stop before me.

"Asshole." I gave him a wink which he returned with a flick of his eyebrows.

"Torsten, Leif." He nodded to each of the fae beside me with a respectful manner that was curt but enough to be considered somewhat kind.

"Come with me?" Øyvin asked, proffering his hand. "You don't mind me stealing her, do you?" He glanced at my new compatriots who grinned like they had a secret burning on their lips.

"Not at all," Torsten replied.

"It was nice to meet you, Lennie," Leif added with a genteel nod.

I returned the gesture. "It's been a pleasure gentlemen."

With that, Øyvin pulled me away and back onto the dance floor where the earlier crowd had returned after Balder's council dispersed. Øyvin guided me into the same position Espen had held me in and started moving us gracefully about the space, carefully dodging other revelers like it was second nature. His timing was impeccable and with each flourish within the tune, he executed perfect movements—from spins, to dips, to swift footwork that I almost stumbled over—it was as if he could feel the music, the vibrations.

"That dress looks good on you," he said, his voice barely a whisper. "Espen did well."

"Can't say I disagree with you. It might actually be the most elegant thing I've ever worn." Which was likely, considering the last fancy event I'd been to was my brother Jared's wedding and I'd worn a satin burnt-orange travesty of a bridesmaid dress I had yet to forgive my sister-in-law for. The clingy fabric in the Midwest summer heat and humidity had been *far* from elegant.

"Well, I like it too, although it might look better in blue," Øyvin said, pulling my focus back to the present.

I rolled my eyes but couldn't keep the small chuckle that escaped me contained. "Don't start an incident, Øyvin. Sharing is caring, remember?"

His lips quirked up at one corner. "Oh, I remember." He pressed me more firmly against him, letting his hand dip a little lower on my back. "Speaking of, where is Espen?"

"Gone to get some drinks," I replied, glancing around the room. Nora stood to our right in a sleek silvery dress with long sleeves talking to a group of women who appeared to be doting on her. The forced smile on her face told me she wasn't pleased with the attention but I didn't know how to help my new friend out of that situation. I continued my search, but couldn't find Espen.

My footsteps slowed as I kept coming up empty and Øyvin brought us to a stop before guiding me off the dance floor.

"I'll go see what is taking him so long," he said, noticing my concerned frown. "I'm sure he's just got caught up talking to people. You know what he's like—"

"Honorary mayor," I interjected.

Øyvin chuckled. "Exactly. Far too friendly. I'll be right back." With that, he sauntered into the crowd toward the drinks table. With how tall he was, he towered over a lot of the other fae, so hopefully he could spot Espen more easily than I could.

I gazed across the dazzling room, watching the Forest and Fjell fae dance away. Many had openly stared at me while I'd danced with both Espen and then Øyvin—a few straight up gawked—but I ignored them, enjoying the experience.

"You'll forgive my people for staring at you," a serene voice said, and the Queen herself stepped up beside me. "It's been almost two centuries since we've had a human in our midst." Her long navy dress made of velvet with gold motifs threaded into the bottom was spectacular, and made even more regal with the matching cape that was cinched at her shoulders and fell to the floor, pooling behind her.

My eyes widened at the timespan she mentioned, realizing how rare my acceptance here was. "That's quite a long time. Who was the last human allowed inside the mountain?"

She smiled, her lips parting gently. "He was a young man, not much older than yourself. One of my people fell in love, and, although it was quite the scandal and to-do at the time, the human man and fae woman were permitted to marry and remain part of the Fjell Fae."

"And they were happy together?" I asked, glancing around the room for no one in particular.

Freija sighed. "Until he passed. Unfortunately, he had no magic, and thus lived for only forty years after the union."

"How sad," I said, unsure of what else to say.

Queen Freija hummed in agreement. "It was inevitable, but they were happy together."

"That's the important thing in the end."

"It most certainly is," she replied, tilting her head slightly toward Halvar at her side. "I'm glad you're here," she added with a gentle nod toward me, pivoting the subject. "I wished to thank you again for your assistance. The photograph you captured was invaluable, and I dare say we'd be in a great deal of trouble without it. Because of you, we knew about the problems in the area much sooner than we might have otherwise."

I looked over to her, finally taking the opportunity to face her. She was slimmer than the last time I'd seen her, back when we'd first been summoned to the throne room. Now her cheeks were less full, her already high cheekbones much more pronounced.

"I'm glad I was able to help. If there's anything else I can—"

She shook her head and raised her hand, giving me another soft smile. "By all means, Lennie, please just enjoy yourself."

"Happy Birthday, Queen Freija," I said with a gentle nod that felt appropriate in the royal's presence. She gave one in return before her and Halvar moved on into the crowds of fae.

I glanced around the room again, noting the faces that turned away quickly as if they'd been watching my interaction with the Queen. Which, considering the guilty blushes on more than two of the fae, I'd bet money—that I didn't have—was true. With a sigh, I straightened up and headed toward the drink table. I made it all of two steps before screams pierced the air.

The band stuttered to a stop.

A commotion built within the crowd before the refreshments.

My stomach sank.

Before I knew what I was doing, I was sprinting forward, pushing my way through the throngs of chaos. When the fae finally parted, I found my yogi-fae-cop convulsing on the ground. I fell to my knees in front of him, avoiding the shattered glass and liquid beside us. Espen's skin was pale, he was gasping for air, and I didn't know what the fuck I could do.

Øyvin, or someone else with a deep baritone voice like his, barked orders. Others were yelling. The crowd shifted and moved, but Espen closed his eyes and stilled.

"No, no, no," I whispered, reaching for him—

"We need to move him, now," a female voice said, and someone hooked their hands under my arms, lifting me back to my feet.

I spun around, dazed and bewildered, my heart hammering in my chest and my hands shaking.

This can't be happening.

34
LENNIE

Øyvin stormed past with King Balder and the contingent of Fjord Fae. The grumpy fae gave me a stern look and pointed at Espen. "Stay with him," Øyvin mouthed before he disappeared into the crowds. While I'd never been one for commands, that was one I'd definitely be following.

A group of Forest Fae lifted Espen up on a stretcher of birch trees and linen and were swiftly followed by a slim fae with long tawny hair wearing a green and brown uniform. I rushed after Ylva, who was giving orders to Forest Fae left and right, her petite stature draped in authority. Keeping up with the brigade carrying Espen out of the mountain, crowds parting to give the group speedy passage, I asked, "Where are you taking him?"

She spun around, not stopping her brisk pace toward the exit, her stern eyes narrowing slightly before she sighed. "The healers hut east of the village."

"I'm coming with you."

She took a deep breath, screeched to a halt, and then placed her palm on my left shoulder. A soft wave of heat washed over me and my beautiful dress disappeared, giving way to my leggings, sweater, and boots from before. "That should make things easier. Just keep moving."

I nodded and followed her, my movement unencumbered now that I was out of the evening wear.

The fae carrying Espen ducked and dodged through the forest with ease and preternatural speed. It was difficult to keep up with them, but I somehow managed, spurred on by my own erratic pulse and anxiety every time I caught a glimpse of Espen's still form.

The healer hut was indeed just east of the village, not far from the farm Espen and I had hiked past a few weeks ago. The hut blended seamlessly into the surrounding terrain. With a grassy rooftop and short stone walls, the entire thing looked like an overturned Viking-ship, and I wondered if it was old enough to have actually housed Vikings at some point. It must have, if Espen and Øyvin were as old as they said they were. Their grandparents, or great-grandparents, may have even taken up the raiding profession to blend in with the humans of their time. I shuddered at the thought of magical Vikings and the destruction they could've caused.

Ylva pushed through the door to the hut and our group followed her inside. The long-ship building was open, formed around a central hearth, and I was instantly assaulted by the musty scent of herbs and earth, while feeling like I'd stepped back in time.

The soldiers set Espen atop a workbench on the far side of the room. Two fae women, their slightly pointy ears visible, jumped into action, their long skirts swishing around them the only noise beside the crackle of the fire in the middle of the space. The wooden plank wall beyond Espen was bedecked with vials, bottles, and roots of all shapes and sizes. There were also stacks of wood, some with the papery bark that I recognized from the birch trees that littered the landscape of this country beside their kindred pines, others looking like pieces that had fallen off charred logs.

Ylva and her team of fae left after a brief chat with one of the healers. I settled on a bench in the corner of the hot room, carefully watching as the two healers started stripping Espen of his clothes save for his pants and giving him all manner of concoctions. One was as clear as water, another was the color of dark cherries.

"What are those?"

One of the women looked up, her dark eyes sweeping over me before she shook her head. I didn't realize I'd spoken aloud, but the question still stood. The last thing they poured down his throat looked more like tar than water.

They flipped Espen over on his side, using pillows to stop him rolling over onto his back.

I watched as he retched, his dinner and drinks returning into the bucket they'd prepared at his bedside. Even as the sight and scent made my eyes water, I didn't look away. I couldn't tear my eyes away from the happy, bubbly yogi-fae-cop thing that had brought so many smiles to my face, now devoid of any emotion as he fought for his life.

Even with the elixirs the women had given him, he didn't wake up. It was as if his body was doing what it needed to, ridding itself of the poison while he slept. His eyes remained shut, not even a flutter of an eyelash, no twinkling in his amber eyes. *Why is it always the good ones?*

"What was it?" I asked aloud as he stopped, and the women began cleaning both Espen and the surrounding area.

"There are a plethora of poisons across Norway—berries, algae, mushrooms, the list is endless," the elder healer said, washing and drying her hands before coming over to me. "My name is Heidi," she added, her dark gaze scanning me from head to toe. "I take it you are the human we've heard whispers about. The one who missed two boats?"

I chuckled at the description but couldn't seem to make myself react more than that. "That's me."

The younger healer washed up and then bid us goodnight before swiftly departing. The silence in the space began to consume me, and when I didn't say anything else, Heidi nudged me with her elbow. "He's going to be all right."

"How can you be sure of that, Heidi?" I snapped.

She scoffed, and I glanced over at her to find her eyebrows meeting her hairline like I'd said some sort of joke.

"Well?"

She rolled her eyes and leaned against the post beside me. "I heard you had a sharp tongue."

Now it was my turn to scoff. I mean, she wasn't wrong, but damn did they gossip in this town.

I crossed my arms and looked her in the eyes. "Will he recover?"

She nodded gently. "We got to it quickly, but I can't be sure how much damage was done by the poison until he wakes."

"How long will he be out?"

She sighed and looked over at Espen. "Until his body is ready."

"That's not really a time frame," I quipped.

"It could be hours or days—"

"*Days?*"

"—or weeks." She raised her palms in a motion that said it was out of her hands. "We can only keep him comfortable and watch for fever spikes until he wakes."

I let out a deep breath, trying to still my racing heart. In an effort to pivot my thoughts from the unpleasant ones that were trying to make themselves at home in my head, I said, "You're English is really good, by the way."

Heidi let out a rolling laugh that bounced joyously around the room. "I've been speaking Norwegian this entire time, young lady."

My brain short circuited. "What?" I must've been too worried about Espen to notice the way her lips moved hadn't matched up with the words I heard.

She smiled, her full cheeks flush with color, her silvery up-do shimmering in the firelight.

"But I've been speaking English—"

"Oh, I fully understand English, but I don't like speaking it," Heidi interjected. "*Your* English is really good, too."

"Now who has the sharp tongue?" I retorted, quirking a single eyebrow.

Her smile didn't falter as she pushed off the pole and sauntered across the room. "Sit down over here, I'll make you some tea to calm your nerves."

"Oh, I'm—"

"You will sit or you will leave."

"Yes, Ma'am." For whatever reason, I did as I was told. Heidi had a motherly aura around her that permeated the space with a warmth that had nothing to do with the roaring hearth. It was endearing and, for some reason, I didn't want to aggravate her any more than I already had—Espen *was* under her care, after all. So, I took a seat at the sturdy wooden table near the kitchen area, sneaking looks at Espen every time a log popped in the fire.

I watched as she prepared the tea, using a whole bunch of leafy bits I couldn't name. As she set the drink down in front of me, a question formed in amongst the chaos of my brain. "What do we do about his work? Won't the police grow suspicious when he doesn't show up?"

Heidi nodded and sat down across from me, bringing her tea cup to her lips and lightly blowing across its steaming surface. "Ylva is handling that problem for us."

"How?" I asked, and took a sip. The tea was earthy, slightly herbaceous, and had a hint of sweetness to it that reminded me of honey. It was good. Not as delicious as coffee, but I needed something in my system after the shock I'd just endured.

"Ylva will mention to the Chief of Police, Bente, that Espen had a family emergency and needed to visit his sisters in the north."

"And this Bente will believe that?" I wrapped my hands around the teacup, letting it warm my fingers.

Heidi nodded. "Ylva is acquainted with Bente, and Bente knows that Ylva and Espen are good friends."

"Does Bente know...?" I waved my hands at my ears, and then around the room, referencing the fae as best I could.

"No. Definitely not," she replied before narrowing her gaze at me. "And it must stay that way. We cannot have humans finding out about us or we'll be hunted to extinction. All creatures crave power to survive and eventually rally against those perceived as more powerful than themselves. If humans found out about us, they'd ignore our true purpose to protect nature, and, instead, do their best to use us to their own advantage—be that in capitalism, politics, or war."

I raised my hands. "Hey, you won't have any trouble from me." Which was saying something considering my penchant for trouble.

She chuckled like she didn't quite believe that, but took another sip instead of challenging me on my sincerity.

The rest of my time there was met with companionable discussion, mostly me asking Heidi what the different things on her shelves were, punctuated with furtive glances at Espen and hoping he would stir. After what must've been a solid hour and the tea in my cup vanishing, I let out a long yawn and rubbed at my eyes.

A gentle smile graced Heidi's lips. "Let me send for someone to escort you back."

I yawned again and nodded, grateful for whatever she was saying as my eyes threatened to seal themselves shut for the rest of the night. It probably was time to get some sleep.

35
LENNIE

I entered Espen's little cabin and vigorously brushed my hands over my arms. With only the gentle glow from the moon to light the cabin, and me the only inhabitant, the space felt too empty and quiet. It was as if the cozy cabin was mourning.

Kicking off my shoes, I stumbled through the living room and into the bedroom where I flopped onto the bed. With my clothes still on, I curled up into the sheets and inhaled the smell of moss and leather. My muscles screamed at me from all the exertion today, but as I let the warmth beneath the covers grow, I settled into a peaceful calm. It was the same feeling I felt after I'd been on long hikes, a feeling of satisfied exhaustion. However, the satisfaction was missing tonight. Instead, it was replaced by a knot in my stomach and an ache in my chest.

Why did shitty things always happen to good people? The Espen I knew hadn't deserved this, hadn't deserved to be poisoned. Anger and sadness swelled inside my chest, exasperating the pain there, and I rubbed my palm against my sternum. It dawned on me how much I truly cared about Espen. It had been a long time since I'd cared about anyone in such a way—in fact, I wasn't quite sure my feelings for Espen, or Øyvin for that matter, could even compare to any of my prior mediocre relationships. Not that I was officially in a relationship with either of the fae, but...

Images of the two fae men flitted through my mind: Espen and his beaming smile and positivity, that mop of hair constantly falling across his brow, and Øyvin with his stoic no-nonsense attitude that was fortified by his sense of duty to the fjord. Both of them tugged on something deep inside me.

I didn't think I'd ever felt this way about anyone before, let alone for *two* men—a sense of happiness and belonging that made me excited to see them. It was a sensation that oozed comfort like a warm hug on a cold winter's morning.

Espen was certainly that reassuring warmth, while Øyvin was the chilled breeze that swept across my cheeks making me so attuned to his presence.

With another yawn, I let the thought of those sensations drag me under into a fitless sleep.

Later that morning, I was back at Heidi's, having decided that my time was better spent here than sitting in the quiet shell of a house by myself. After a quick coffee pit stop at Oddvar's, I'd miraculously found my way back to the healing hut deep within the forest. And by miraculous, I meant I'd asked Øyvin for directions when we briefly crossed paths that morning outside the café.

Now safely ensconced in the secluded building, I removed the lid from the paper cup and wafted my hand over the steaming coffee, aiming the scent under Espen's nostrils. Maybe this would help wake him up? It sure as hell would work if I were the one laying unconscious instead.

"That better not be what I think it is," Heidi muttered from across the room where she was busy tending to some herbal concoction.

"Not at all," I replied, quickly replacing the lid and trying to hide the cup behind my back.

"That stuff is not allowed in here."

I frowned, my shoulders sagging. "But, coffee is human magic."

She scoffed and threw a sprig of something into the mixture. "It leads to high heart rates and headaches. It does not heal."

"It heals the *soul*, Heidi."

"Well it can *heal your soul* outside until you have drunk the entire thing." She waved her hand toward the entry.

"What?" I looked at the door and shivered. It was freezing outside, the sun completely hidden by cloud cover on the gloomy day.

"Now, out you go," she said, shooing me out the door, but leaving it open.

"You're throwing me out into the cold?"

"You may come back inside once you've finished your drink, young lady," she said with her hands on her hips like she was ready to corral me.

With a shudder, I exited and then leaned against the side of the building. Peering between the dense forest, I watched the morning fog slowly ascend from the valley. Mixed feelings washed through me as I took in the majestic scenery—part of me wished I'd brought my camera, the other part knew I couldn't risk exposing Heidi's home. I'd just have to commit this picture to my internal memory: the gray sky, the tall pines, and the chilly air. I took a deep breath before taking a sip of my coffee. It was delicious, as always, with a splash of milk and sugar in it.

"What are you doing in there?" I asked, breaking the sounds of the breeze and the creaking forest.

"Preparing concoctions for the winter," Heidi replied, her voice slightly muffled by the rocky wall between us.

"What are they for?" I took another gulp of my drink, relishing in its warmth.

"Burns and infections."

"Fae can't magically heal themselves?" I asked and furrowed my brow. All the magical creatures I'd seen in movies and read about in books had the miraculous ability to heal themselves quickly. Perhaps the fae were different though?

"Depends on the injury or malady. Broken bones will heal more quickly in fae than humans, and infections clear up swiftly, but poisons like the one Espen ingested are dangerous."

"How dangerous?" My voice wavered slightly and I swallowed a lump in my throat.

"I ran some tests overnight. He had water hemlock in his system," she said with a grave tone. "If he wasn't as strong a fae, he would have died at Queen Freija's celebration."

I shook involuntarily at the thought and tried to peer inside to where Espen lay bundled up in a comatose state but I couldn't quite see him from this angle.

Turning my gaze back to the forest, I was about to take another sip of my coffee when movement between two pines caught my eye. A moment later two fae appeared carrying another between them. The middle fae had his arms slung over the others' shoulders, and all three were wearing Forest Fae uniforms. They hobbled toward the hut and I spun toward the door.

"Uh, Heidi..."

"Wait a minute."

"Heidi!"

The elder fae woman appeared in the doorway but swallowed her retort and swore as she spotted the arrival. The middle fae's pant leg was ripped open, deep gouges in his calf covered in blood and matter I couldn't stomach to look too closely at.

The trio stormed past me and followed Heidi inside.

Not wanting to miss what was going on—and curious if this was related to our investigation or Espen's poisoning—I downed my coffee. After setting the empty cup aside next to the wall to take home and throw away later, I straightened up and walked inside.

Back within the warm healing hut, Heidi was already tending to her new patient set up on another exam table near Espen. He was grumbling and exclaiming in agony as she prodded, and honest to hell, I couldn't blame him. Something had carved open his leg.

"Hold him down," Heidi ordered, and the two healthy forest fae soldiers jumped into action. Meanwhile I settled by the entrance, keeping my distance and staying out of the way, but still close enough to hear any chatter between the fae.

The soldiers shackled the injured one to the table, one restraining his feet, the other restraining his hands. He was by no means a large fae—definitely more svelte compared to Espen and Øyvin—but from the way he shifted and the muscles in his forearms contracted, I could tell he was strong. His eyes almost bugged out of their sockets when he spotted Heidi with a dark-brown salve. She shook her head gently before resting the little glass jar on a work bench beside the table. The bench was small, holding a variety of medicinal objects as well as a small bowl that she'd filled with water. She grabbed a cloth and dabbed it in the basin. While wringing it out, she muttered something and the fae heaved a breath.

As she set to cleaning the wound of debris, the injured fae hissed but said no more, like he was trying to contain his pain. He breathed hard through every swipe and it wasn't long before Heidi was dropping a red-soaked cloth back into the bowl.

"Brace yourself, young man," Heidi said with a voice that conveyed her next actions would hurt like a bitch, and I grimaced on the fae's behalf.

She lifted her palms and set one on his knee and the other by his ankle. Taking a deep breath she closed her eyes, and, a split second later, a light glow emanated from her hands.

I watched in awe as she used the same magic I'd seen Espen use on the scarred tree weeks ago. The light slowly swept down the fae's calf and started knitting together his wound until two puckered red lines started to form.

"Wolf," Heidi muttered as she watched her magic stitch the leg back together.

The fae on the table nodded weakly, his face having gone severely pale as his whole body flexed under her touch, damn near convulsing in pain.

My stomach knotted and my throat constricted. I knew dog bites could be bad, but fucking hell.

"What are they doing this far south?" Heidi asked, turning her head from one of the soldiers to the other.

"Espen had us keeping watch, and Ylva doubled our shifts recently." The fae at the head of the table glanced at the sleeping leader in the room. "But one of the wolves attacked randomly this morning before retreating back to the small pack that has been prowling around the farm on the hill."

Heidi shook her head and a look of disgust settled across her features. "Lennie, can you pass me the bottle with the red liquid?"

I glanced over at the counter space she'd been working at this morning and panicked. There were so many bottles in different shades of red, reddish-brown, and reddish-pink, let alone the blacks and greens. How the fuck was I supposed to know which one she was—

"The one closest to the sink," she supplied.

I nodded and did as I was told. Passing her the small vessel, I stepped back and watched as she administered the tonic. Lifting the fae's head, she tilted a few drops of the liquid between his chapped lips. He stared up at her, his eyes growing heavy with thanks and the power of the concoction. She stoppered the bottle and put it aside on the work table before gently setting his head back down and patting him on the shoulder. "Get some rest."

He closed his eyes and his breathing quickly evened out until he was indeed fast asleep.

Just as swiftly as they'd arrived, the other two soldiers thanked Heidi and then made their way to the door that still stood propped open, the sound of rain now drifting in.

"I'll send word to Ylva about his recovery," Heidi said softly, a firm and genuine kindness seeping into her words. "You two be careful."

They nodded and took their leave.

I skirted around the newest patient and wandered over to Espen. Even with all the commotion, he was still fast asleep. I glanced between the two injured fae, resting my hand on Espen's bed. There was no way these two instances could be related, not unless some fae was poisoning other fae and controlling the wolves. Was that even a thing fae could do—control animals? The former seemed more realistic, and the latter sounded outlandish in my mind. No, they couldn't possibly be related. Could they?

"Do you think—"

"That these are related?" Heidi interjected as she washed up.

"Yeah."

She took a deep breath and shook her head. "Highly unlikely. Someone clearly had a grudge against Espen, or someone else at that party, and Espen was an unfortunate accident. As for the wolves, they aren't unheard of around here, just rare. I wouldn't go wandering around the forest alone anymore. If there are wolves attacking other beings, it won't be long before the humans notice something is amiss and more of them start scouring these woods with rifles in an effort to eradicate the beasts. The humans have done so before and they will do so again if the need is there. There is a massive debate in this country around wolves and hunting them, I'd advise you don't get caught up in it."

"Duly noted," I mumbled, brushing my hand across my forehead.

Heidi finished cleaning up and pulled a small flip-phone out of the pocket in her long wool dress.

"*You* have a cellphone?" I exclaimed.

She rolled her eyes. "I don't live in the 1800s anymore."

I swallowed my laugh but couldn't hide the smile. "You know, if I didn't know about all of this"—I waved my hand around—"then I'd think you were being real funny, Heidi."

"Oh, I am very funny, Lennie. But getting eaten by wolves is no laughing matter. So, I'll call for an escort."

I gave Espen's hand a gentle squeeze before crossing the room to her. "I don't need a babysitter, Heidi."

"I insist."

I shook my head. "No, Heidi. I'll be fine. I'll leave now, though, so I'm at least out in the daylight."

She returned her phone to her pocket. "Fine."

"Thank you for helping him." I glanced over my shoulder at Espen, wanting nothing more than for him to wake up and make a joke about yoga positions.

"Give him time," Heidi replied with a sigh. "He'll be back on his feet soon."

I certainly hoped so. I kinda missed the bundle of sunshine.

36

ESPEN

My head pounded and my body felt like it was on fire, as if I was burning from the inside out. I could smell coffee, though... and something that reminded me of a fruity cocktail.

Light flickered on the other side of my eyelids, but they were so heavy that I couldn't open them.

Someone was talking in English, while another person responded in Norwegian—the two carrying on a conversation I couldn't quite grasp.

So sleepy.

Sleep sounded good... really good... maybe the fire would go out if I just slept it off?

Yes, that sounded right...

LENNIE

Frustrated by the lack of movement from Espen as he lay unconscious and sitting around for so long, the next afternoon I decided to blatantly ignore Heidi's advice to avoid the woods and the wolf threat. Wolves were generally crepuscular or nocturnal animals, and I had no intention of provoking them like the fae soldiers probably had. What Heidi didn't know wouldn't hurt her. I needed to get outdoors, to take some photos, and to do something of value to distract myself from the endless waiting. So, I grabbed my camera, pulled on my boots, and set off on a hike.

The drizzle-filled air clung to my rain jacket and hair as I trekked up the trail by the mountain, away from town. With the need to be productive coursing through my veins spurring me on, I made my way back toward the clearing where Espen, and I had found the illegal magic transfer scars, feeling like an eternity had passed since then.

I took my time retracing my steps, capturing photos of the fjord and all manner of flora. From the white-and-black birch trees, to the little mushrooms pushing through the moss at the base of a fallen pine, nothing was left undocumented. My hands were steady, but my pulse beat to a happy rhythm. It felt good to be behind the camera again—as easy as breathing. I couldn't remember the last time I'd gone more than a week without snapping a few shots, but here I was having picked it back up.

I continued my trudge toward the clearing and when I finally reached it, I sat on one of the boulders, taking a swig of water from the bottle I'd stashed in my backpack.

The area was devoid of any other creatures, but creaks and skitters between the trees told me I wasn't entirely alone. For some, hiking by themselves was scary and too dangerous. For me, it was a chance to clear my head, an escape from reality so far removed from the frustrating and mundane parts of life. And, it wasn't like I was ever a complete moron when hiking alone—I had a first aid kit in my bag, provisions, and proper footwear. Honestly, the number of people I'd seen hiking in flip-flops in the US was ridiculous.

Hydrated and ready to keep moving, I returned my bottle to my bag and wandered over to the scarred tree. The bark was still marred with small slashes as it was the first time we'd seen it, time having done nothing to heal them. I brushed my hand across one, the tough layer scraping against my palm. A pang of annoyance and anger rippled through me. *Why would anyone want to harm this area and the fae who live here?*

With a hefty sigh and no answers, I straightened and decided to keep moving. The days were growing shorter, darkness encroaching quickly, and I wanted to be back in the village before nightfall but had time to explore a little more. I continued further into the forest that blanketed the steep mountainside next to the fjord, following a trail that wove into more dense wood, and I got distracted by the scenery once again, snapping picture after picture. Water droplets hanging off the edge of a light-green fern, a thick layer of moss draped across a slate-colored rock, and the trickle of a tiny stream that crept down the mountainside—I captured it all. Framing my shot, adjusting the focus, and clicking away, it was blissful. At the rate I was going, I would run out of space on the memory card I'd put in the camera this morning. But, I continued anyway, until a snapping noise caught my ear and I looked up...

Shit.

The sun was almost gone.

How did I miss the shift in the light?

Another cracking noise rent the air, and a shiver ran down my spine. In classic Lennie Martin fashion, I'd been distracted by my camera again. My brother Ryan would laugh in my face when he heard about this.

I carefully put the lens cap back on my camera, making sure it clicked securely into place—I didn't want to lose that again. Something shifted between the trees to my right, and I swallowed the brief lump of panic in my throat. I spun around to retrace my steps and halted.

Blocking the trail back down to Skolvik was a man right out of a Viking movie. With short hair, furs and leathers draped across his body, and a wicked grin, he looked like an animal ready to pounce.

"Going somewhere?" he asked, his voice rumbling with a threat that had me clenching my fists and shifting my feet into a tackle-ready stance.

"I was thinking home, but if you wanna play, big guy...?"

He flinched, blinking as if I'd startled him.

"You're not Norwegian."

"Nope."

A crunch escaped from the forest and another man emerged, equally clad in a weird-ass outfit. In the remnants of light, I spotted the shape of the newcomer's ears—pointed, a fae. *But what faction?* Whichever group they belonged to, my fight or flight senses were screaming foe.

"How do you understand me?" the first one asked, his brow furrowing into deep lines. "I'm not speaking English."

I grinned and flicked my eyebrows. "Magic."

They both narrowed their eyes at that and then snarled.

Bracing for a fight and incapable of keeping my mouth shut, I asked, "So, you two from around here or is this your fave vacay spot? Let me guess, it's the smell of the pine and the fresh air that *really* gets you going? Was I interrupting a tryst? Don't stop on my behalf."

My opponents smirked and tilted their heads in unison, the small motion raising every hackle I had. My skin pebbled at the sight, and my heart thundered against my ribs. Then, in the same way Espen would change the appearance of our clothes, the two fae touched their left shoulders. However, instead of shifting into new attire, they morphed into another form. I watched with my stomach in my throat as joints cracked, snouts pushed out from their faces, and fur sprouted across their bodies. Wolves.

Shit.

"What big teeth you have," I muttered, and then bolted away from their jaws.

My legs pistoned and my breaths came in jagged puffs as I careened through the dense forest, adrenaline pushing me faster than I'd ever moved. Branches whacked me in the face and thighs, and I narrowly avoided tripping over numerous rocks and slipping on the damp moss. Unfortunately, my split-second lead was disappearing as the two wolves bounded after me and howled with what I could only assume was delight.

Trust me to land myself in a shitty situation... again. First the boat, now this? I really should start to listen to authority figures. Heidi had *just* mentioned not to walk alone in the woods, especially at night, and I'd ignored her, just like I always did.

Tripping on a damn twig, I tumbled to the ground—tucking and rolling to protect my precious camera. I landed with a thud, my back taking the brunt of the blow as the air whooshed out of me. The sound of footfalls slowed and, before I could get back up, two sets of snarling teeth were a mere inch from my face.

What a way to go. I took a shallow breath, gulping down the lump in my throat as I stared up at the razor-sharp teeth. *Mom's gonna be pissed.*

One of the wolves reared back and opened its jaw, the rancid smell from its mouth turning my stomach. I squeezed my eyes shut as he lunged for my head, nicked my chin, and then yelped... never fully making contact. I blinked rapidly, hands rising to protect my face as I watched as the beast and its friend were tossed aside.

My heart hammered in my chest, and a wave of relief washed over me as a behemoth fae grumbled at the wolves. Halvar was practically cloaked in darkness, as if the shock of silver hair on his head and face were the only parts of him the moonlight was allowed to touch.

I scrambled to my feet as the wolves circled back, glaring at my savior.

"Be gone!" Halvar bellowed, his voice like rolling thunder.

The wolves sneered in reply as I stepped closer to the Fjell Fae, keeping him between me and them.

"Leave this mountain, and never return, or it will be the last one you climb."

At that, the wolf closest to Halvar lunged... but never made contact. Halvar caught the beast, wrapping his large hands around its neck. The wolf whimpered, but swatted at him with its paws, trying to use its back legs to scratch Halvar's chest.

I took a step back to avoid being trampled as Halvar growled, "Leave."

The wolf snapped back, its eyes full of a deathly ferocity.

That was apparently the wrong answer because, before I could take my next breath, Halvar grabbed the wolf's snout with one hand, the other locked on its neck, and twisted. A sickening crack echoed around us, and the wolf went limp. Halvar chucked the beast toward its accomplice who'd stilled. "May that be a warning to you. Take him, head north, and do not return."

The wolf that remained alive slowly shifted back to his fae form. Cracks and snaps were the only noises that emanated from the forest as the fae morphed from four legs to two. His furs and leathers returned to his shoulders, and his ears formed small points at the tops. With an ashen face, he carefully stepped forward and hoisted the body of his friend into his arms. Without another word, look, or nod, he turned and retreated into the forest.

After a moment of silence, and once I was certain the wolf-fae-thing had left, I muttered. "Well, fuck me sideways. That was close."

Halvar glanced over his shoulder with an unamused look and something inside me panicked a little.

"Uh... thanks, by the way." I smiled briefly, swiping the back of my hand across my chin and coming away with a smear of blood.

"It's just a scratch," he said matter-of-factly. "You're okay."

"Well, that's usually debatable." I shrugged and scoffed. "Physically? Yes. Mentally? Probably not. I *did* just witness two humanoid-like creatures snap, crack, and pop into big dogs. That shit is prime material for some gnarly nightmares, my friend." And therapy. A fuck-ton of therapy. *I wonder if the fae have therapists that I could talk to about all of this?* If I tried to tell a human therapist, they'd probably ask me to lay off the Twilight marathons while they prescribed a nice fitted straight jacket.

Halvar crossed his arms, clearly in no mood for my jokes.

I swallowed hard and took a deep breath.

"Come with me," Halvar said—an order, not an option—and started walking back toward Skolvik.

"If you could just escort me to Espen's, that would be greatly appreciated. You know, just in case that wolf decides to test their luck."

"It won't." Halvar pushed aside some branches for us to pass through without being swatted in the face.

"Well, either way—"

"We will go to Espen's to get your things. Then you'll come to the mountain with me."

I frowned, glaring daggers at the big scary fae's back. "I'll be fine at the cabin."

"Queen's orders," he grunted.

"Don't get me wrong, I really like Freija, very nice fae. But, she can't exactly order—" The glare Halvar shot at me had my mouth zipping shut faster than a farmer shucking a corncob, and I silently followed Halvar all the way back to Espen's cabin.

38
LENNIE

Halvar loomed in the kitchen as I packed my shit once more. It was weird to see the Fjell Fae outside of the mountain, and especially in Espen's cabin. His frame felt too big for the space, like he was built differently, of rocks and boulders that had no place indoors.

After putting a lackluster Band-Aid over the gash on my chin, I found a rumpled old duffel bag under Espen's bed and unceremoniously shoved my stuff inside it. Feeling the pressure from the brooding fae in the other room, I moved as quickly as possible. I couldn't be sure what living conditions I would be in thanks to Queen Freija's orders, so I borrowed some of Espen's clothes. I grabbed a green knit sweater with a Nordic pattern across the top, a fleece jacket that kind of fit me, and a pair of woolly socks. Worst case scenario, these would keep me warm, especially with the temperatures dipping every day since I'd arrived.

I threw the duffel through the doorway into the kitchen and living area, then set my sights on grabbing the last minute things I would normally forget—my toothbrush, my backpack, and my phone charger. Although, I wasn't entirely sure if where I was going would have outlets.

"Okay, we're good," I said, stepping out into the kitchen area with the last of my things.

Halvar leaned against the counter and glared at my stuff. With a silent nod, he pushed off and strode over to the front door.

I shook my head at his verbosity, slung my backpack across my shoulders, grabbed the duffel, and locked up behind us.

Halvar led me into the mountain through the same entrance I'd used previously. Instead of shifting my attire, he waved for me to follow him through the tunnels in my very distinct human hiking gear. I didn't stand out too much but a lot of the residents threw inquisitive glances in my direction as we marched deeper into the mountain.

The side of my neck tickled and I instinctively wiped at it, feeling something slick. Pulling my hand away, I found a scarlet smear of blood across my fingers. *So much for my little Band-Aid.*

"Ummm, when you said scratch," I muttered to Halvar three large strides ahead of me, "you didn't say bleeding significantly." I swept my fingers across my chin only to find more blood. "Any chance you've got a Heidi where you're taking me?"

Halvar glanced over his shoulder, but barely slowed. His eyes narrowed, assessing me, before he nodded and turned back. "Bad scratch. It will heal."

"So, you don't have a healer or some medical stuff?" The first-aid kit in my backpack was substantial, but if I needed stitches... I shuddered at the thought. There wasn't much that scared me, but needles? No thanks. Hard pass.

"We do," Halvar said, never breaking his brisk pace. "I'll send for them to clean you up."

Sensing this was as friendly as Halvar got, I said a quick, "Thank you."

We turned down another narrower corridor lined with little sconces of flickering light—magic light considering the lack of flame within the glow. The air around us grew slightly warmer somehow, as if the mountain was insulated. After another minute of walking, Halvar turned to his left and opened a large wooden door that looked straight out of a medieval castle.

Inside the room was a small bed with blankets and a single pillow, a table and chair beneath a light-orb lantern, and a worn out armchair in the corner. It couldn't be more basic, but I wasn't sure what I'd expected from a glorified cave dwelling. How should I know, I hadn't exactly spent a lot of time living within a mountain.

"Thank you," I said again, scanning the room and Halvar.

"There's a bathroom three doors down on the left," he said, making to leave. "I shall find the healer for your scratch. Stay here." With that order, he departed, closing the door behind him.

Deciding I'd neglected to follow the wise words of authority figures once already today—and learning the consequences—I did as I was told. Plus, I got the feeling upsetting Halvar might be worse than getting cornered by crazy wolves. I carefully shucked off my backpack and sat it and the duffel bag down by the table before plopping down on the bed. The mattress sank heavily beneath me, but wasn't wholly uncomfortable.

I waited only a few minutes before a knock sounded at my door and Halvar entered, followed by a young male fae with dark hair who wore a slate apron and carried an old-fashioned doctor's bag like the Mary Poppins of the mountain.

"Hi, I'm Lennie," I said with a gentle smile.

The newcomer smiled in return before turning to Halvar. "Can you translate for me?"

Halvar shrugged and crossed his arms, leaning against the wall by the door. "She understands Norwegian. Nora tinkered with her hearing."

The fae's dark eyebrows flicked upward before his lips curved again. "I'm Trygve. It's nice to meet you, Miss Lennie. You appear to have a big scratch on your chin. May I examine it?" He approached me carefully, like I was a bull that might charge him at any second. And I guessed, to him, I *was* a foreign entity that was worth being wary of. How often had he treated humans?

"Have at it." I waved at the wound.

He nodded, then gently tipped my chin, tilting it to have a closer look at the underside. With a tut, he pulled away my Band-Aid and said, "Good thing Halvar found you and stopped those wolves."

"Mm-hmm," I mumbled, his fingers still holding my head at an angle.

"The cut is small, but not too deep. I shall clean it up with alcohol, then apply a glue and bandage to hold it shut. It might leave a small scar though."

"Meh, I'm alive, so thank you and do what you need to do." While a scar could be bothersome, it honestly didn't agitate me. Would my mom have an absolute meltdown about it? One thousand percent yes, which I was kind of excited to see. It would certainly make the holidays fun if I went back to Ohio in time.

Trygve nodded again and got to work, disinfecting the cut and patching me up.

"Aside from the one on your wrist, is this your first scar?" Trygve asked, making small talk while Halvar loomed on the other side of the room.

"What do you mean 'the one on my wrist?'"

"The magic one," he said, pressing a small gauzy bandage across my wound.

"I don't have any other scars, Trygve," I replied, probably butchering his name.

He tapped my wrist and stepped back just as Halvar piped up, "Nora's magic would have left a mark when she tinkered with your linguistic hearing."

I glanced at my wrist. *It can't have.* I'd felt a slight sting when she'd done it, but hadn't seen a damn thing... And yet... Sure enough, there on my wrist, almost as small as a freckle was a tiny white dot. "Well, fuck me sideways," I muttered.

"Magic leaves scars, not unlike the one you're going to have on your chin. But these," Trygve waved his hand at my wrist, "are slightly more silver in the light."

I twisted my forearm, tilting it toward the lanterns on the wall. The little mark shimmered, barely noticeable—you'd have to know exactly where to look in order to see it.

"Is that normal?" I asked, looking between the two fae and the mark on my wrist.

Trygve turned to Halvar, as if asking for permission to speak, and Halvar gave him a gentle nod to proceed. "Again, magic can leave scars. The stronger the magic, or the greater the amount, the bigger or deeper the scar. Take your altered hearing. That is generally a power only the Royal Fae can do, and for them, is considered more of a party trick compared to their other abilities."

"If magic is given or taken by force," Halvar piped in, his voice low and serious, "then deep scars are left behind, like slashes through whatever material is acted upon. No one has ever quite understood exactly why, but it's commonly agreed upon that the scars are a repercussion from the ancestors for not using our magic for good, nor its intended purpose—to protect the natural resources of our world."

"So, what about the trees in the clearing where the illegal magic transfer happened?" I asked, tilting my head, the image of the damaged trees still fresh in my mind from earlier in the day.

Halvar nodded, following my line of thought. "Those were a side effect from the explosion of a large amount of magic transferred from one entity to another. It's a heinous act that would've left similar scars on the perpetrators, too."

"It's not natural," Trygve added quietly, pursing his lips and shaking his head. Then, with a sigh he glanced up at me. "Is that all your injuries, or do you have more that I need to look at?"

I shook my head, feeling a little overwhelmed by the amount of information they'd just shared, and then shouting sounded from the other side of the door—muffled, but growing louder by the second.

Halvar shifted just as the door burst open and two soldiers barreled after a seething intruder. Øyvin shadowed the threshold, his chest heaving, nostrils flared, his eyes as dark as the bottom of the fjord. He took one step forward and Halvar blocked his path. Then the idiot actually growled at the Fjell Fae. In response, Halvar grabbed Øyvin by the front of his wool sweater and spun, slamming him against the rocky wall. The soldiers and Trygve wisely cleared the room. I, on the other hand, sat back and watched the show—a warmth growing within my chest.

Øyvin held up a ball of water in his palm before smashing it into Halvar's face. The Fjell Fae grumbled and then started spouting water like a cherub fountain—a very large, angry cherub fountain. Water spewed from between his lips, falling in a graceful arc to the rocky floor where it began to pool around their boots. His eyes widened, and he slipped his hands around Øyvin's throat, starting to squeeze. I pressed my lips together, stifling a laugh that threatened to bubble out, and then winced when the movement pulled at the skin on my chin.

Øyvin's gaze flicked to mine, concern etched across his features.

That split second was enough time for his magic to subside, and the water spewing from between Halvar's lips slowed to a trickle. Øyvin's face was turning red from strain and lack of oxygen where Halvar now held him by the throat. When the fountain dried up, Halvar snarled, "Don't use your tricks on me, boy."

Øyvin was released with a small shove, and he brushed off his shoulders like nothing had happened. He squared up to the older fae, glaring at him. "Don't get between me and her again."

My heart skipped a beat at Øyvin's statement, and Halvar bit back, "Don't come storming into my mountain—"

"This is *Freija's* mountain," Øyvin said, cutting him off, and I let out a hiss. Wrong words to say, buddy. I'd only known Halvar for a hot second, but even *I* knew that shit wouldn't sit well with the big guy.

"She will be staying in the mountain until Espen wakes up," Halvar said with the authority of a Viking who was obeyed and never questioned.

"She'll come back to the boat house with me—"

"Where you'll have time to watch her and keep her from wandering through the forests where she could be attacked?"

Øyvin crossed his arms and took a deep breath, but didn't reply.

"Exactly. You serve the King; you have enough responsibilities."

"And you don't?"

"I have a fortress to protect our inhabitants—"

"You know," I interrupted, "I can take care of myself. So, when you two decide to stop bickering like two little old ladies fighting for the best pew at church, let me know." I leaned back on the bed and kicked up my feet, resting my arms behind my head.

Deep sighs filled the room and the two fae backed off their dick-measuring session.

I glanced over at Øyvin, who looked wracked with anger and something I couldn't quite place. "I already agreed to stay here until Espen wakes up. I'll be fine. Perhaps you could even come visit when you get off work," I suggested, wiggling my eyebrows and hoping he got the hint.

Øyvin tilted his head and furrowed his brow, but Halvar clearly understood. He scowled, grumbled something I couldn't quite hear, and with one final glance at Øyvin, left the room, slamming the door as he went.

"I was talking about sex," I stage-whispered.

Øyvin snorted and shoved his hands in his pockets, giving me a pointed look.

At the sight, I realized it hadn't just been about sex. While the Asshole was an annoying grouch, I'd also come to enjoy our sparring matches. And, if I thought really hard about it, he wasn't the worst company on the planet, which was a revelation indeed. Perhaps there had been some sort of hallucinogenic in the wolf scratch? Or maybe the sight of him storming in here had done more to my heart than just ignite a spark of warmth within my chest.

I shifted and turned my head, starting to feel drained after the day's events.

Øyvin's gaze landed on my chin and he stilled. "Are you okay?"

"I'll be fine," I replied with a resigned sigh, and sat up again, setting my feet on the floor.

"I don't like seeing people hurt," he muttered, stepping up beside the bed, his signature scent of fresh linen joining him. He sank onto the mattress next to me, our thighs lightly brushing against each other, the sensation sending a bubble of warmth through my veins. "It's my job to protect the fae of the fjord. It's been my family's responsibility for centuries and something we take great pride in. So, when I heard..." he nodded toward me, then shook his head and shoulders, as if trying to rid himself of the emotions that were seeping out of him.

"You can talk to me."

He raised a single brow and tilted his head in such a way that I knew what his internal monologue was.

"You *can* trust me."

"Somewhat, but you don't always take things seriously."

"I know, but when it comes to family and protecting those I care about, I will be the most serious woman on the planet. You can trust in that. Scout's honor."

"I have a hard time believing you were ever a Scout."

"That's beside the point."

An exasperated sigh left him as he shook his head, but he couldn't hide the way his lips tipped up in a grin, and I loved that I made him smile. Those grins were so rare that it felt like I'd won a little piece of treasure anytime I could get one out of him. He clasped his hands together and leaned forward, resting his elbows on his knees. With a deep sigh, my grumpy fae started opening up. "My father was in this role before me. He and my mother were so proud when I took up the mantle. They passed not long after, which was tough but also a blessing in disguise, as twenty years ago my only sibling, my brother, who'd moved to the south, died, too."

A lump settled in my throat hearing of his losses and that twenty year marker—the one that kept popping up again and again.

"We weren't sure if he was part of the rebel uprising," Øyvin continued, "or if he was merely a bystander, but he died in the battle that killed Queen Ragnhild. There was nothing my forces could do for him. He was gone when they arrived."

He stared at the wall across the room, dazed and lost in memories. I felt a pang of sadness at his story, and the realization that he was probably the only member left of his family had a tear welling at the corner of my eye.

"So, that's why you're so protective of the fjord," I said, voicing my thoughts and brushing away the tear before it could fall.

"I'm protective of family and the resources that my people were created to protect."

"That's fair." I gently placed my hand on his thigh, and he gazed down at it before biting his lower lip.

He brushed his fingers across the top of my hand, lightly trailing small patterns around my knuckles. Tiny sparks shot up my arm at the soothing sensation, and I pressed closer to his side. "I'm glad you're safe," he said, his voice barely above a whisper. My heart stuttered at the sentiment, the care laced through every note, every word.

He swept a strand of my hair off my shoulder and let his hand settle between my shoulder blades. The warmth from his palm sent a shiver down my spine.

"Øyvin," I whispered his name, and his eyes flicked to mine.

"You're a stubborn, troublesome woman," he uttered, gently turning my face to his and pressing his forehead against mine, our shallow breaths intermingling. "But..." he sighed like he was struggling to find the words. "I'm glad you're here."

The next thing I knew his lips were pressing against mine, and I was lifting my arms, wrapping them around his neck and pulling him into me. The kiss stole my breath, and he swept his tongue against the seam of my lips, asking for entry, which I slowly granted him, savoring the moment. My heart beat wildly in my chest, my brain losing all sense of focus on my surroundings, zoning in on the feel of the man pressed against me instead.

When I finally thought I might succumb to the feverish kisses, Øyvin pulled back, his lips now puffy and his eyes full of lust.

I ran my hands down his chest, the brush of his jacket smooth beneath my palms. *What was that?* And why did it feel so good?

Taking a deep breath in through his nose, Øyvin straightened up and rose to his feet. I scooted back but didn't feel offended by the loss of his warmth or touch. The fact that Øyvin had shared as much as he had seemed like a damn miracle. And the kiss was full of passion and acceptance—something I didn't realize I wanted from him, but was happy to have received.

He strode to the door, his face blank and his lips pursed into a fine line. "I'm glad you're all right."

"You're such a grouch," I said with a chuckle and a wink as he opened the door.

He spun in the doorway, a hint of a smile on his lips. "No, I'm a fae of the fjord."

And with that he walked out, wholly unaware of the flame within me that started to burn a little brighter. It was an unfamiliar feeling that had me wondering what the hell kind of turn my life had taken and where we would go next.

39
ØYVIN

I swallowed the lump in my throat—the annoying thing had lodged itself there while I told Lennie about my family, but finally disappeared as I left the fjell. Taking one deep breath after another, I began to rein in my breathing—in through my nose, hold for a few seconds, and then out through my mouth. This continued as I traipsed down the mountain trail toward town, the dark of night enveloping me in her shadows.

Hearing of the wolf attack on the Forest Fae soldier the other day had surprised me. Receiving word that Lennie had been attacked rattled me to my core. It was a vulnerable feeling I didn't like the taste of. She may have been a pain in the ass and could handle herself in the woods, but she was still human. A bite from one of those Forest-Fae-shifting-shits from the North wouldn't just scar her, it could flay her to pieces.

The amount of problems going on in the fjord right now wasn't just concerning, it was like a pot of water about to bubble over. I could sense it in the air and I was sure the humans could, too. But they could at least brush it off as an impending bad winter or a storm on the horizon that set all the creatures of the fjord and the forest on edge. They didn't know what truly lurked beneath the surface and skulked between the trees. Their legends and folktales were never too far from the truth, but I hoped, for everyone's sake, that they never found out the reality they really lived in.

I sauntered past Oddvar's, locked up and closed for the night, and aimed toward my home. As I approached the line of red boathouses, I spotted someone leaning next to my front door.

"Sir," the man said, tilting his head toward the porch light so I could see his face.

Sigurd. The captain from the wall.

"What are you doing here?" I asked as I approached and began to unlock the door. I refrained from opening it though. This was my sanctuary, and I didn't like inviting work across the threshold.

"There's been a change. Kjetil sent me—"

I jerked upright, turning toward him. "Kjetil?"

"Yes, sir. When you didn't answer your phone"—*damn the mountain and its thick rock walls*—"the King's Chief Advisor was notified. He's down at the site already."

"Tell me what happened," I said sternly, crossing my arms in preparation for more bad news.

"The wall, sir, it keeps falling. The pressure is becoming too much for merely two fae to control."

"Let's go." I spun quickly, re-locked the door, and strode toward the waterline beside my house that was hidden from view of the street.

Sigurd was right. The northern part of the wall was flickering like a faulty light bulb and disappearing sporadically, letting through detritus. A collection of Fjord Fae, including Kjetil, were gathered around the opening, re-erecting it continuously. People were yelling, power straining to hold the line, chaos and panic flooding from the group.

"Press harder!"

"Steady men!"

"Where are the others?"

I landed on the fjord-bed with a dull thump, and immediately pressed my hands and shoulders into the wall, adding my power and strength to our barricade. The magic of the wall pulsed beneath my palms, pressing back with equal measure, like the whole thing was about to come down. I closed my eyes and focused on the well of energy within me. Calling forth some extra strength, I pushed the added power into the wall and opened my eyes. The flickering slowed, and the fae at my side relaxed their shoulders slightly while Kjetil stood back and nodded—not contributing his power to the effort. *And Lennie thought I was an asshole.*

"We've already sent for more reinforcements," he muttered.

I nodded. "Thank you. You all right, soldiers?" I asked, glancing down the line of fae who were aiding in keeping the wall stable.

They looked worse for wear, but all nodded—sweat staining their brows within their pockets of air as they leaned on the wall, giving it their energy, same as I did. My own brow was starting to bead with sweat but I pushed through the strain and focused on the problem before me.

"Has the King issued any new orders?" I yelled over my shoulder to Kjetil.

"None," he replied. "Only to keep the wall up."

Right, well, that was starting to become more and more difficult. With six of us channeling power into this part of the wall, and it still threatening to collapse, I needed to make a decision and fast.

"Break the wall. Reroute it south of the disturbance—"

"That would encroach on protected territory," Sigurd said, coming up to my side.

"It would, but we can't have that disturbance siphoning all the power out of our soldiers. This much energy could kill them, and I won't have that during peacetime."

"Yes, sir." Sigurd stepped back again, as if giving me leave to make the next steps.

My breaths deepened and my muscles spasmed as I thought through the steps that would do the least amount of damage and risk the fewest injuries or threats to my men. It wasn't going to be easy but, with this number of fae, we should be able to do it.

"All right," I yelled, my voice carrying through the water. "Sigurd and you two." I nodded to the two fae closest to me, "You press your energy into the edge of the wall to my left."

They nodded and shifted swiftly to my other side. As they moved, I felt that same scratching sensation against my power—what I'd felt during the previous inspection—and was relieved when it subsided as they repositioned themselves, refueling the wall.

"You three," I said to the remaining fae, "on the count of three, I want you to shift twenty paces back with me. Keep your line, but move as swiftly as you can without swimming—we can't allow whatever this invisible threat is to get beneath our feet."

They nodded and responded with a unified, "Yes, sir!"

I leaned away slightly from the wall and rolled my neck before glancing over my shoulder.

"You'd better move out of the way, Kjetil," I grunted, and the fae shifted back and to the side, where he could watch without getting trampled by us.

"One..."

"Two..."

I took a deep breath.

Please work.

"Three!"

The wall shimmered beneath my palms as we started to drag it backward. My fellow soldiers grunted and strained, but it was working, the wall was moving and not breaking—

One of the fae stumbled and fell, but jumped back to his feet quickly. However, the brief loss of power was enough to see his part of the wall collapse entirely. The pressure around us mounted, and I felt the air pocket I'd created around myself strain. I pressed more power into the barrier as we continued sliding it backward and the gap refilled where it had just fallen.

"Almost there!" I yelled, glad it was nearly over, starting to feel depleted and exhausted, my muscles aching like they hadn't been used in a decade.

"Three more steps."

Three.

Two.

One.

"And stop!" I yelled.

We'd done it. *Thank the ancestors.*

"All right, you three step back one step, let's see if this will hold, but be prepared to step in on my orders."

The three fae to my right nodded and then, in unison, they stepped away from the wall.

The pressure against my palms mounted and I pressed my shoulder against it, but there was no scratching sensation—no hail-like pelting that had besieged the wall previously. At that moment, a corps of reinforcements arrived and reported to Sigurd who pointed them in my direction. Five fae split from the contingent and joined me, pressing their hands against the wall and taking the strain.

I pushed off the wall that was now more heavily guarded and powered than it had ever been, hoping it would hold and that our monarch was all right. Without a doubt, Balder would've felt that strain on his own power.

A gentle clap sounded from my left. "Well done, General," Kjetil said, not a drop of perspiration or anxiety marring his brow. "Shall we report to the King?"

The only answer was yes, and however tired I now felt, I had a duty to uphold, one I'd sworn an oath to. With a deep breath, I nodded and we started to swim toward the King's quarters.

My head stung but the memories of piña coladas and blonde hair had me internally humming a happy tune. I liked the smell of the drink... and the blonde... both were nice and fruity but could seriously punch you in the gut... or ribs.

The fire in my veins had subsided, but I was so sleepy, my eyes remaining firmly shut.

Five more minutes wouldn't do any harm...

LENNIE

I wandered down the mountain tunnels toward the exit, my camera hanging around my neck. After a long rest this morning, I'd decided to spend my afternoon doing some photography around town and pay a quick visit to see if Espen was improving. I'd thrown on my jacket and boots, prepared for the cold and gray day outside, but when I stepped up toward the entrance, someone blocked my path.

"You can't go that way, young lady," the male in a gray Fjell Fae uniform said.

I pulled to an abrupt stop in front of him, a scowl settling across my features. "And why is that?"

"Orders," he replied and settled into a wider stance, like his body could ultimately stop me from leaving—which was likely true, it wasn't like I'd been working out lately or could take on any of Freija's soldiers, but still... The simple shift of his feet was annoying.

"From who?" I challenged, matching his irritating stance.

"From me," a gravelly voice said from the tunnel behind me.

I turned and found Halvar striding toward us, his silvery hair shining in the intermittent magical lighting. He was in gray fatigues and a thick knit sweater, but somehow still looked intimidating.

"Why am I being treated as a prisoner? I agreed to stay here, sure, but I didn't agree to being kept in a cage." I crossed my arms as he stopped in front of me.

"We'd need to escort you everywhere and, with the threats as they are, I cannot afford to send soldiers to babysit you out there for extended periods of time."

He had a point. I certainly didn't want to cause too many problems for Freija—it was clear she had a lot going on—but I hated being cooped up. I wanted to be outdoors, taking photos of the way the rainclouds settled over the fjord like a blanket. "Will I be able to see the light of day at some point during my stay at least? Humans need fresh air and a chance to stretch our legs or we go stir crazy."

Halvar pinched the bridge of his nose, his brow furrowing. "I can take you to see the sunset this evening. That will be worth photographing." He waved his hand toward my camera. "Just wait a few hours and refrain from taking any photos inside the fjell while you wait."

"Fine." I nodded, acquiescing to his *orders.*

The soldier at my back seemed to relax a little at that, and Halvar almost smiled. Almost. Okay maybe it was a figment of my imagination, but there was movement at the corner of his lips.

"Pick me up at four then," I said before wandering back down the maze of tunnels, toward where I hoped my room was. It was kind of difficult to remember.

"Where exactly are you taking me?" I asked as Halvar led us through the dense forest and up the switchbacks of the mountain's steep cliff side. The skies were clear, but the cold breeze stung my cheeks as it swept by.

"Only twice a year does the sun set perfectly between the two sides of the fjord. Today is one of those days," he replied.

All I could do was shrug, because, yeah, that did sound pretty epic and something I'd want to catch on camera. I'd just have appreciated a heads-up that we were hiking to the top of the mountain... at least the weather had cleared up and the clouds had dissipated.

We climbed further and further up the side of the fjell, Halvar expertly navigating us across boulders and through thickets, until we eventually reached the top. My chest heaved and my lungs ached but in a good way, like they'd needed the exercise as we traversed an open field, the terrain rocky and uneven.

"Is this really the easiest way to get wherever we're going?" I asked, narrowly avoiding twisting my ankle in a deep divot. Halvar glanced back at me and nodded.

"The other way would be a lot... steeper," he replied.

"Could it really get steeper than that?" I pointed over my shoulder with my thumb.

He nodded, and then motioned with his hand, directing it straight upward. My eyes widened, and I swallowed hard. "Well, thanks for taking me the easy route."

Halvar snorted and returned his focus to our path ahead. Or, at least, whatever path he knew, because there wasn't a visibly marked walking trail anywhere across this field. In fact, I doubted people ever came up here based on the rugged terrain and the steep drop down to the fjord on my left.

I followed Halvar as he stepped through a copse of trees at the far end of the field and onto what looked like a version of pride rock from the *Lion King* movie I'd grown up watching.

Halvar stepped aside and nodded toward the spit of rock.

"You gonna push me off?"

That earned me an eye roll.

Deciding he was unlikely to end my life here, I gingerly walked forward and then stopped in my tracks at the view before me, awe settling into my limbs.

The setting sun cleaved the sky in two, rendering the fjord gold in its waning light. It was a majestic sight to behold. I was blown away by the absolute majesty of the view, the spectacle Mother Nature was performing for us—a composition for this sliver of the world to witness and applaud. This right here—the sparkling rays, the blanket of fiery color—this was as close to a religious experience as I would ever have.

I pulled the lens cap off my camera, carefully stashing it in my jacket pocket, turned on the device, and set up my shot.

Photographing the galaxy's biggest light source was always a complicated endeavor. Capturing the sun itself and the surrounding landscape while trying to get the focus and depth of the composition right was a challenge because you always lost the detail surrounding your subject. But I did my best, making necessary adjustments and trying different things to get a decent photograph, wanting to remember this sight forever.

The mountains rolled into the fjord, the trees brushing the shoreline set alight by the fiery rays of the waning glow. The water glistened, tiny ripples forming where the wind swept down the passage and up toward me, sending tendrils of hair across my cheeks.

I snapped photo after photo, the rush of getting behind the camera filling my veins with a giddiness that brought a smile to my face.

When I felt somewhat satisfied with the shots I'd got, I turned back to Halvar and the forest where he waited, leaning against a tree like being exposed and out in the open was a threat.

"You got fresh air," he grunted as I joined him at the treeline. "We can go home now."

I took another look at the fjord below, inhaling deeply, the smell of pine and dew settling on the breeze around me. "Thank you."

I wished I'd been able to share this moment with Espen and Øyvin. I wished Øyvin could see how majestic his fjord looked in the setting light, and for Espen to see the peace that cloaked the entire scenery, the forests all along the water reaching toward the golden sky. The desire to have them here swept through me and somehow comforted me. It wasn't a surprising revelation—they'd become such prevalent figures in my life over the past weeks—but certainly a pleasant and welcomed feeling. One that warmed me from my head to my toes and found me smiling one last time toward the horizon.

Our trek back down the mountain was silent but punctuated by my grunts whenever I stubbed a toe on a rock or almost lost my balance. With the sun now fully set below the horizon, the only remaining light guiding us home was the silver glow of the moon and the weak-ass headlight I'd found in my backpack and strapped to my forehead. I was pretty sure only one battery inside it was still working based on the fragile and flickering beam.

"Don't worry your pretty, big head, I'm totally fine," I said after taking a tree branch to the face that Halvar had expertly dodged up ahead.

A low rumble emanated from the Fjell Fae, and I couldn't quite tell if it was a sigh, growl, or combo of the two. Either way, an unusual longing had settled in my limbs, and I kind of missed my bubbly Forest Fae. Espen had been a much better hiking companion.

"Can't you just take me to see him?" I asked.

"No."

"You're a stubborn troll," I grumbled.

Halvar let out an exasperated sigh as we continued to trudge through the forest back toward the fjell entrance. "Haven't you noticed how quiet it is since he was poisoned? How little has happened to worsen our circumstances since?"

I swallowed hard and thought about it for a second. He kind of had a point... but it also didn't sit right with me.

"Espen isn't the one causing all the problems," I said before quickly adding, "He isn't the one hurting *your* Queen." I hadn't missed the way Halvar looked at Freija, those tiny glances and constantly protecting her back like he was her shadow. It was the behavior of a man who was protecting his woman, not just a Guard protecting his Queen.

Halvar stopped and cast his gaze over his shoulder, his sky-blue eyes meeting mine and narrowing at my pointed remark. "Are you so certain? How well do you really know him?"

"Well enough to trust him." Espen had saved my life when I fell through the bridge on our hike. I'd watched him care for the people of the village when the landslides occurred, and, damn it, he'd taken care of me—the abandoned tourist—when he could've just left me alone. "He was with me when the first landslide happened, so it couldn't have been him," I added, pulling up in front of the behemoth fae, standing toe-to-toe with a creature that was at least several centuries my senior, if not a millennia. "Plus, I haven't seen any scars on him, and I've seen *a lot* of Espen."

Halvar sneered, lowering his voice to a gravely whisper. "You know him so well, he even told you what he did twenty years ago?"

I flinched. There was that number again. *Twenty.*

Halvar seemed to sense my hesitation. "Queen Ragnhild wanted Espen, not for his healing skills but for his ability to destroy. Every century or two, a fae comes along with the power of royalty, of a god as you humans would say. Espen can heal almost anything but he can equally tear the earth asunder. Which is exactly what he did when Ragnhild, her Head Guard, and company of soldiers were torn apart and killed. In response, he turned that battlefield into a wasteland."

I shuddered at the imagery and struggled to picture Espen in the throes of battle. He seemed so bubbly and happy all the time, like a little ray of sunshine. I couldn't imagine him being so destructive. Not my tree-pose-loving fae.

"Even if that's the case, can you really believe that he is behind all of this?" I asked, because I sure as hell couldn't. It didn't add up. If he were doing this, he'd have to be healing his own scars, which I'd already witnessed him unable to do with the scars on the trees in the clearing. I'd also seen the difference between regular healing magic—when Heidi had stitched up the Forest Fae soldier—and attempts to heal illegal magic transfer scars. The latter wasn't possible.

Halvar continued walking, as if trying to evade the question.

"Well, can you?" I challenged, following after him. There wasn't a chance in hell I was going to let him make such an accusation and run away from it.

After another moment of silence, he responded. "He's always a possible threat."

I sighed, clearly there was no reasoning with the big guy. So, instead of debating him, I shut my mouth and remained quiet for the rest of the trek to the mountain entrance.

Deep down I knew Espen wasn't behind this. And it wasn't just because I kind of cared about him. Espen *cared*. I'd seen the way he reacted when he saw the photo I'd taken that started all of this. The flash of silver in the image I'd captured had rocked him. And now knowing *why* that would concern him, there was no doubt in my mind, Espen was not illegally transferring magic. He cared so much about the Forest Fae, hell even the Fjell Fae and the villagers of

Skolvik. He wouldn't ever want to cause harm to any of them. I would continue to believe that even after he eventually woke up and could tell Halvar himself.

42
LENNIE

Later that evening, I wandered through the tunnels inside the mountain aimlessly, my mind caught in the maelstrom of my own thoughts as I tried to figure out who the fuck could possibly be behind all the chaos, all the destruction of the land around Skolvik, the area which these fae called home and had sworn to protect, heal, and help. No matter what Halvar had said, there was no way Espen was behind this, and I needed to find some way to prove that to Halvar without stripping the Forest Fae in a comatose state naked to reveal his lack of scars.

I really missed the bubbly Forest Fae, too. The loss of his sunny presence was starting to sink in even more, and I chewed on my bottom lip, hoping he'd wake up soon.

As I passed another cave entrance, something flickered and caught my attention. *The story cave.* Soft beams floated out of the space like someone had left the lights on, but I couldn't immediately hear anyone within.

Curiosity pulled me to a stop, my boots grinding against the rocky floor, and I backtracked and went inside. The room was silent as I peered around the space but found no one else in sight. I hesitated slightly before walking deeper into the room. Here by myself without Nora to guide me it felt kind of like I was intruding, but the guilty sensation that ran across my skin subsided when I saw the glorious images that speckled the walls of the cavern.

Pieces of the Fjell Fae's history glowed in the rock walls, telling me their stories, one magical carving at a time. Viking ships shimmered to my right, the stick figures on-board raising their fearsome swords to the starry sky above them. To my left were reindeer being chased by other figures bearing large spears. Right beside it was yet another image but, unlike the others, this one glowed a little brighter—like it was fresh. Swirls wrapped in and around boulders, like a melody of rocks and waves playing with one another. It was almost harmonious in the way the light shifted, as if twinkling lights had been set to phase within the cavern wall itself. I stepped closer, in awe of the beautiful carving, seeing the way the two clashing forces were so intertwined as if in a lover's embrace. If I had to put a name to this particular image, it would be *love*. Love in its purest and simplest form, between two entities that wanted to be near each other at all times.

I lifted my camera on instinct, barely aware of what I was doing, when a hiss sounded behind me, and I stilled.

"What do you think you're doing?"

Busted.

I spun, letting my camera hang against my chest, and found Nora in the doorway, her brow furrowed and arms crossed over her chest.

"I, um..." My throat tightened and the back of my neck heated uncomfortably at the thought of what I'd almost done. "I..."

I had nothing. This was hallowed ground, and I shouldn't even have brought my camera in here out of respect for their history and their secret. This was like getting pulled over for speeding when you knew you shouldn't be driving that fast, but worse. Oh, so much worse. I'd broken Nora's trust in me. The one thing all of them had said, time and time again, was to not take any photos inside the mountain. And here I stood having almost done exactly that. I deserved the hatred in Nora's eyes.

"Have you been taking photos in here?" she asked, accusatory venom lacing every syllable, the easy friendship between us gone as her arms crossed over her chest.

I shook my head, but knew she'd seen me with my camera in my hand, aiming and ready to snap.

Nora's shoulders trembled and she pursed her lips, giving me a look of utter betrayal. A look I felt deep into my core. *Yeah, I fucked up.*

I reached forward, grabbing Nora's forearm as she shifted back from me, and her shirt-sleeve rode up a bit at my touch. "I'm sorry—" I gasped, seeing the skin beneath my fingers. Her arm was riddled with scars, silvery-white that matched the color of the tiny dot she'd magically placed on my wrist all those weeks ago. The sheer volume of criss-crossing marks looked painful. It looked like... Shit. They were deep scars like the ones we'd seen on the trees in the clearing. Halvar's words regarding the illegal transfer of magic rang through my mind, *"It's a heinous act that would've left similar scars on the perpetrators too."*

I sucked in a breath, my hand trembling as it held onto hers and my stomach flip-flopping. "Nora, what happened?" Nora shucked her arm out of my grip, and quickly pressed her shirt back down with a snarl.

"What d-did you do?" I asked, my voice quivering as Nora, a Royal Fjell Fae—the woman I'd thought was becoming a friend, someone I could confide in—sneered at me, her eyes full of dismay. .

"Leave it," she bit out, glancing momentarily toward the wall beside us.

I looked over at the swirling image of rocks and water that her eyes had flicked to—the image that looked so new compared to the others, outshining those around it. Drawings that she was in charge of carving into the mountain as its resident historian...

My stomach dropped as the puzzle pieces connected—the stories, the scars, the new picture. "Nora, what have you done?"

"Nothing." She stepped back, and straightened her shoulders, blocking the exit.

I shook my head as my body began to shake, not believing her words. "This... this isn't nothing."

Fucking shit, *Nora* was the one stealing magic. Nora was behind all of this chaos. But who was she... I quickly glanced at the new drawing again, before looking back at her. Water. Water and boulders.

"Have you been working with someone from the fjord?" I asked, not quite believing the words that were coming out of my mouth.

Shouts rose from further down the tunnels, and she peered toward the noise before turning back to me with a grimace. "You'd never understand. Balder cares about me."

Shit. She was working with the damn King of the Fjord.

"More than himself and his own people?" I snapped, my natural instinct to protect family welling up inside me and spurring me on against a fae that was centuries my senior. "Is he making you do this? How long has this been going on?"

She shook her head. "She'd never let us be together. She'd never join our cause."

"She, who?" I asked, not following her words. "What are you talking about, Nora?"

Nora didn't answer, glancing behind her nervously. A chill ran down my spine as the echoes from the tunnels grew louder—incoherent shouting ringing through the mountain.

Before I could react, Nora grabbed my camera and yanked it into her grasp, the straps snapping at the hinges and separating from the camera, the neck strap hanging limply around my neck.

"What the fuck!" I roared and lunged after her. That was my baby! What the hell did she think she was doing? "Give that back!"

She dodged my perfect tackle, her chest heaving, my camera clutched in her hand.

My gut tumbled upside down like a rollercoaster inverting and rose back up into my throat as she stared me straight in the eyes and threw my camera against the rock wall.

A piercing scream broke free from my lips as I watched my baby shatter, falling to pieces and scattering across the cave. I fell to my knees and scrambled across the floor, picking up shards in a frenzied attempt to put it back together. But none of the fragments would fit, not even the cracked lens cap. I tried, and tried, and tried, but the pieces wouldn't stick back together. The sharp edges scratched my fingers and palm as I tried to gather them in my hand, but it was of little use.

My camera was gone. Irreparable.

How could she?

I dropped the useless remnants and looked over my shoulder expecting to find Nora sneering at me but the entrance to the cavern was empty. With my shaking hands, I covered my mouth, trying to hold myself together. Taking a deep breath to moderate the grief that surged through my heart, I tried to calm down. I wanted to curl up and cry, mourn my loss. I'd saved my money for a long time to buy that camera, and it had been like a friend to me, going with me on countless adventures around the world, capturing not just photographs, but memories, too. Memories of freedom that I wanted to sit here and grieve. However, I knew I couldn't hang around. I needed to warn Freija and Halvar. I needed to tell my boys. I needed to move, *now.*

With one last look at the remains of my beloved camera, I grabbed my SD card and ran.

43
LENNIE

I bounded down the tunnel that led toward the exit, my hair streaming behind me, my camera strap lost somewhere along the way. I dodged between Fjell Fae merrily going about their day and crashed against the wall as I tried to make a sharp turn. A dull pain spasmed through my shoulder as it took the brunt of the blow but I kept moving. Kept running until I crashed right into Torsten.

He grasped my shoulders, steadying me as my breaths came in sharp bursts, my chest heaving.

"Throne room... where... is it?"

A crease formed across Torsten's brow. "Is everything all right?" he asked, removing his hands from me and finishing up lighting the lantern on the wall beside us.

"The Queen... danger... warn Halvar."

Torsten's eyes widened at every word and thankfully didn't dismiss my obvious distress. "Follow me," he said, spinning and breaking out into a run.

I took a big gulp of air and bolted after him and his man-bun.

I still couldn't wrap my mind around Nora and Balder being behind the illegal magic transfers and all the problems that had faced the fjord area recently but the carving on the wall in the story cave, the marks on her arm, paired with what she'd just said, all pointed directly at them. I had to warn the Queen and Halvar, I had to make sure she was safe. She'd been so kind and Halvar had saved me—the very least I could do was return the favor by giving them a heads up.

Torsten and I barreled down endless tunnels and, after a few more minutes, the arched halls started to turn from slate to the crystalline blue that adorned the entire throne room. My heart hammered in my chest as we slowed and walked through the ornate entrance to the large room where Freija held court but my stomach plummeted when I saw the scene inside.

I was too late.

Freija's navy-clad form lay collapsed in Halvar's arms, her dress pooling around her and her fingers barely clutching at his shirt sleeve. He gently pushed her hair off her cheek, settling it behind her ear, as he whispered something to her. She nodded and a tiny smile crossed her lips.

"Sir," Torsten said hesitantly.

Halvar glanced over his shoulder and I flinched at the venom in his eyes—a promise to avenge her in the most horrific manner. "The tea was poisoned," he said. The shattered remnants of Freija's tea cup lay strewn across the floor before the throne where he knelt.

Freija took a rasping breath and her head lolled back.

Halvar shifted to hold her, pulling her into his chest. "Seal the mountain, and fetch Trygve, now!" he roared, the fae turning into the beast that always lurked beneath his controlled surface as he clutched the dying monarch.

Torsten nodded and disappeared.

I glanced at the couple, my hands shaking. "Halvar, it was Nora. She's the one behind the illegal transfers. I just caught her in the story cave. There's a new carving there of water and boulders. She said something about never being allowed to be with Balder and joining a cause, plus she has scars—marks all across her arm."

Halvar's face paled even further and Freija mumbled something before staring straight into my eyes. Her eyes crinkled at the corners, that otherworldly coloring surrounding her pupils shimmering as she lifted her face to Halvar.

"Noooo..." he mumbled, holding her delicate head in his large palm, stroking away her tears that had started to fall.

She closed her eyes and, with gargantuan effort, she raised her dainty hand to his chest. Sparks of silvery light exploded from her palm and Halvar let out a pain-filled growl. The glow grew, Halvar's jaw tightened, and all I could do was watch in fearful awe as I took a few steps closer.

A large hole opened in Halvar's shirt where her hand lay, revealing a hint of muscle beneath, and the light swelled to a blinding crescendo. I raised my hand to shield my eyes but it wasn't enough—the light too bright as it arced from Freija to Halvar. I turned away just as Halvar roared, grabbing Freija's hand and laying her down in front of her throne.

Pressing my palms against my eyes, I shielded myself from the worst of the magic. However, the rising temperature in the room and the pressure building at my back was unavoidable.

"Lennie!" Halvar yelled and I peered over my shoulder, scrunching my face against the barrage of light.

Halvar's body was practically glowing, a dense cloud of sparking silver surrounding him like a halo. Thick branches of light snaked up his neck toward his beard as he panted. He held out his free palm to me. "Hand. Now," he grit out.

I hesitated for a split second, glanced at the dying Queen, and, with a silent prayer to Hell, grabbed his hand.

Scalding pain blasted through my left hand where it connected with Halvar, shooting up my arm. A scream pierced the air and it took me several moments to realize it was my own. My breaths shallowed by the second, my arm felt like it was on fire, and my head throbbed like a rock concert on steroids. With my right hand, I yanked up my sleeve and found white lightning carving a path to my shoulder, scarring the skin.

Halvar roared in agony again, his features scrunched up and his body trembling with the overwhelming amount of power flowing through him. A moment later he let go of my hand and we both wobbled at the loss of contact. The room swirled, my vision flickering in and out of focus, and I hunched down beside Halvar and Freija's lifeless body, hoping to hell I wasn't about to pass out or die myself.

Halvar and I both panted, regaining our breath as the light around us subsided and the temperature in the room dropped back to its normal chill.

A noisy commotion drew my attention to the entrance of the throne room just before a group of Fjell soldiers in their gray-and-black uniforms ran in. Their eyes widened as they took in the sight before them: the empty throne, the grieving guard, and the human tourist. One of the soldiers stepped forward and unclasped his cape, before handing it to Halvar. He accepted the material with a nod, and, after taking a deep breath, he laid it over the fallen Queen.

A lump formed in my throat at the sight and I rose to my feet again, taking a step back out of respect.

The soldiers pressed their fist over their hearts with a thump and sank to one knee, bowing their heads in reverence.

Halvar straightened up to his full height and rolled his shoulders. "Freija, Queen of the Fjell, daughter of Erik and Astrid, has fallen," he proclaimed, his voice carrying through the large room and out into the tunnels where it echoed. "Long live the Queen."

"Long live the Queen," the soldiers replied, and I mumbled the words with them, staring in a daze at the shrouded figure on the floor.

Why would Nora do this? Why would she hurt her only family? I couldn't fathom why anyone would turn on their sibling. Sure, I hated my brothers from time to time, but I'd still do whatever I could for them if they needed me. I would move mountains for them if they asked.

I pushed my hair behind my ear—

Pointy. Why the fuck is my ear pointy?

"Nooo," I gasped, running over to the glassy wall of the throne room. Sure enough, staring back at me was my usual blonde-self but with a few new amendments. "Fuck off."

44

LENNIE

"Halvar," I half yelled, half mumbled in disbelief, my voice wavering as I turned toward where the Fjell Fae stood among his soldiers by the throne. "We have a slight problem here." I pointed to my ears with both hands.

His face didn't betray a single emotion—as if he'd locked that shit down after being vulnerable with Freija in her last moments—but I could have sworn I saw his right eye twitch.

"What the fuck happened?" I pressed my hands against my forehead, my heart rate starting to run another marathon. "I can't go back to Ohio looking like this!"

What the fuck would my parents say? My brothers would laugh until they shat themselves if they even believed me, but my parents... *Fuuuck.* How could I explain myself out of this one? I lightly tapped my fingers against the points and whimpered, wondering how on earth this was happening to me.

Halvar wandered over and examined my arm without touching it, then peered at my pointy ears. "I needed your help," he said quietly so no one else could hear us. "Her magic was too much for me to contain. I needed to transfer it into another being. You were the—"

"Bullshit."

He stilled, and his top lip quirked. "You were the only living being in the room. Trust me, I wasn't aware Freija's magic could"—he waved his hand at my newly acquired ears—"transform you into a fae."

I snort-laughed at how preposterous it sounded.

"You mean to tell me I am now some sort of Demi-Fae, a Demi-Fjell-Fae? What do you even call me? A f-uman? A hum-ae? That sounds terrible. Not that one. Help me out here, Halvar, I'm spiraling."

He bit his lower lip in a contemplative manner and crossed his arms, glancing back to where Freija lay covered in a cloak on the floor behind us. "Either her powers or mine."

"Did you..." I swallowed the shock, my body not only trembling but fully reverberating. "Did you just say I have powers, too?"

Halvar sighed, his large hand rubbing across his forehead in a very human gesture that told me he was just as overwhelmed as I was. "Fjell, or those of Fjell royalty. I can't be certain until we test your skills, see if you can create rocks, fuse cracks, and... more," he trailed off.

I stared down at my hands in disbelief, the backside of the left one lightly scarred with a silvery-white lightning pattern that, after checking under the collar of my shirt, I realized extended all the way up to my shoulder. Two scars in less than twenty-four hours... I really was doing well for myself on this trip.

"So, if I'm part Fjell Fae now, do I have to take *Fae 101* with you to understand how to use this magic?" I waved at my scarred arm, trying to dismiss the rising panic that threatened to pull me under. I needed to gain back some level of control.

Halvar shook his head, his hands dropping back to his sides. "Let's take things one day at a time."

"Yeah, okay, deal," I replied, sitting down on the cold bench that had been built into the wall on this side of the room as my legs all but gave out on me. Then quickly added, "Y'all have a welcome basket or some shit, too?"

Halvar had turned to the Queen and his men there, then looked back at me, consternation written in every line of his face. "Not unless you want a hat made for a baby? I dare say it wouldn't fit over your head."

My brows rose in shock, a hysteric bubble of laughter threatening to escape me. "Did you just crack a joke, big guy?"

"No," he replied and sauntered back to the soldiers who had now taken up position around Freija's body, guarding her. I snorted and leaned back against the crystal-like wall.

At that moment, Trygve came sprinting into the room, practically flying in his simple shirt and pants attire and apron covered with countless pockets. He let out a small whimper when he noticed the guards and the body, but Halvar distracted him by pointing at me. "Check her arm."

Trygve nodded and scampered over to where I'd settled.

He flinched when he spotted my ears.

"You think they make my ass look big?" I asked mockingly, not sure whether I was distracting him or myself.

Trygve blinked and stuttered. "U-umm... you... you have a nice bottom, Miss Lennie."

"Thanks, Trygve."

"May I ask you to remove part of your shirt so I can see your entire arm? We can go to another room, if you wish?" he said, clasping his hands together.

I waved him off, then shrugged completely out of my jacket and pulled up the side of my shirt, removing my left arm from its sleeve.

Trygve set to work examining my newly acquired scars and carefully avoided staring at my chest that was thankfully covered by a tank top and bra. The markings wound up my arm in a mesmerizing pattern that reminded me of lightning. It no longer burned but I'd be lying if I said it didn't feel a little numb. I told Trygve as much when he inquired, and he gave me a contemplative nod in response.

"So, what's the verdict, Doc?"

"Well, I dare say the marks are permanent but I can give you a cream that should cool the skin and reduce any potential swelling."

"Swelling?"

He tilted his head from one side and then to the other. "I can't say for certain as you're our first case of a human being transformed into a fae."

"You mean, this has never *ever* happened before?"

"Not in recent memory, and certainly not since I've been around these past three-hundred odd years."

I rubbed my right hand across my mouth, stifling a guffaw at his age, and wondering if I would live beyond a hundred now too... or would I age and become saggy? Because I was only half fae, would only parts of me age? Would only one boob sag while the other remained full and perky? Would I lose the wrinkles but keep the damn adult acne?

"Let me find that salve," Trygve said, drawing me out of my catastrophizing thoughts.

The healer fae dug around in his apron, pulling out random tubes from his pockets and examining them. He grabbed one, sniffed it, grimaced, then returned it, retrieving another tube instead. He unstopped this one, its dark molasses-like content dripping out onto my arm when he tipped it. My skin cooled where it landed and an instinctual shiver ran down my spine from the chill. With a gentle touch, Trygve began rubbing the cream into my arm and it started to slowly dissolve into my skin, disappearing without leaving any discoloration or residue. It was as if my new magical scar absorbed every ounce and the numbness began to subside.

"Thank you, Trygve."

"You're welcome, Miss Lennie. Let me know if there is anything else you may need or if you want more of the salve."

I nodded in thanks, and pulled my arm back through my shirt before throwing my jacket back on, too.

"Now, I must speak with Halvar," Trygve said, glancing over his shoulder where the Head Guard stood beside the fallen Queen and her throne. He scurried over to the group and I followed, hanging back a bit and staying out of the way—which was a somewhat novel concept for me, but crazy times called from crazy antics.

"Halvar, sir, I know it's not a good time, but I have an important report from the healing chambers—specifically the hospice room and morgue."

Halvar narrowed his eyes and crossed his arms. "Go on."

Trygve wrung his hands, his knuckles cracking as he began. "While preparing recently deceased bodies for their burial ceremony, I noticed that quite a few had limited magic remaining in their forms. This obviously isn't entirely un-usual—we all have differing levels of magic within us—but it started to become a pattern." He hesitated for a second, unable to meet Halvar's eyes. "I want to say this is only a hunch, especially during such a *delicate* time, but most of the patients had formerly had their last stories recorded by Nora." He stopped and waited for a response from Halvar, who in turn gave none except for waving his hand to get Trygve to continue.

"You know how we all gain scars over the centuries?"

Halvar nodded and I blinked at the use of the term *centuries*. That word apparently would never not be shocking.

"Well, these Fjell Fae all seemed to have the exact same scar in the crook of their arm." He demonstrated on himself, pointing at the inside of his elbow. "A deep silver gash that appeared rather recent. I-I don't want to be presumptuous here, but I do wonder if Princess Nora perhaps was stealing magic from the dying fae?"

Ding ding ding, winner right here! Step on up and grab your prize! You want a stuffed bear or perhaps a troll doll with neon green hair?

"I don't think we need to be, as you say, presumptuous, Trygve," Halvar started. "There have been similar reports of Nora's misdeeds today, and I dare say she and King Balder are behind the death of the late Queen," Halvar said, speaking with reverence and leadership that had everyone in the room listening to him. "It isn't the first time a King of the Fjord has made attempts to unsettle the delicate balance of the region. But, this one has been successful."

A shiver of energy seemed to reverberate through the room, the soldiers and myself remaining silent as the truth settled in. Balder and Nora were behind this. *Did Øyvin know?* More importantly, where was my Fjord Fae right now?

I turned away from the gathered fae and faced the shining wall once more. Watching my reflection as I ran my fingers across my newly acquired ears, I lost myself in a trance-like state. A barrage of information and images flitted through my brain, like a highlight reel of my trip. One picture after another, snippets of facts that, when strung together, painted a gruesome portrait of a power struggle I'd wandered into with my camera, blissfully unaware of the consequences.

In typical Lennie Martin fashion, I'd landed myself squarely in the middle of the mess. A mess that went so far beyond taking photos of the gorgeous scenery and accidentally capturing magic with my lens, and instead focused on the careful balancing act of protecting those stunning natural resources.

A rumbling noise broke through my daze and the stone floor began to shake minutely.

I raised my hands up like I was being caught stealing cookies from the cookie jar, and an instinctual desire to curl into a ball and protect my head sank in.

The other fae in the room started murmuring just as a crack fissured across the wall in front of me—sharp white lines forming like broken glass—and I stepped back before turning wide-eyed to Halvar. "That wasn't me," I said, pointing my thumb over my shoulder, my body starting to visibly tremble.

Halvar's usual grimace turned even more sour as another low rumble shook the mountain. It felt like an earthquake or someone shaking a beehive.

"Earthquake?" I asked, lowering my hands and hoping I wasn't about to get squashed by an entire mountain.

"We don't have big earthquakes in Norway," Trygve replied, casting a wary glance to Halvar.

The Head Guard looked around the room as more thin fractures appeared in the sky-blue stone around us, the tiny rifts reaching toward the empty throne.

Halvar took a deep breath and then began barking orders, soldiers springing into action at his words. "Deep Unit, clear the dungeons and lower levels. Evacuate to designated areas north of the Fjord and away from the town." He pointed at two fae, who in turn nodded and ran from the room. "Central Unit, evacuate to your designated area, too." Another fae bolted, his cape fluttering as he went.

The floor shook again and Halvar grumbled while I swallowed my increasing anxiety and nerves.

"Defense Unit, take up positions and send me Torsten and a battalion to the field atop the mountain. Upper Unit"—he nodded to another fae soldier—"I want you to mobilize the strongest residents to use their powers and reinforce the top of the mountain. I don't want any cave-ins." The fae nodded and charged like the others, leaving Trygve, myself, and a couple soldiers left in the throne room.

"Trygve—"

"Yes, sir," the healer fae replied, standing to attention.

"Have the Queen removed to her rooms and prepare her body. Then set up a field hospital near the northern field atop the mountain but keep your distance. Hide within the forest if you have to."

Trygve nodded like he knew exactly what all of this meant while I stared on in bewilderment, still in shock at what had happened let alone what was currently going on.

"Lennie," Halvar yelled.

"Yup," I replied, saluting him before realizing what I'd done and quickly shoving my offending hand into my jacket pocket.

His top lip twitched as he strode past me toward the exit, his soldiers following closely on his heels. "You're coming with me."

I flinched, straightened, and then scurried after him. "And where exactly are we going?"

His voice dropped several octaves as he ground out his reply. "To war."

45

LENNIE

We strode down the tunnels, the lights along the walls flickering with every shake and rumble as more soldiers fell in behind us, and Torsten—the man behind the light magic—stepped up beside Halvar. The two fae spoke briefly in hushed tones but after a few more paces Torsten glanced over his shoulder and smiled. "Welcome to the club."

I snorted and missed a step, almost falling flat on my face. Clearly obtaining new magic and becoming some form of fae hadn't improved my grace and balance.

We left the mountain through an exit I'd never seen before, its rocky archway more dusty and jagged than the smooth and clean main entrance I was used to. Stepping out into the pitch dark, I expected to be assaulted by the autumnal chill that had settled over the region recently but was instead met by slightly warmer temperatures—still cold enough to require a jacket but something in the air held a warmth the promised trouble. It was similar to the spring storms we'd get in Ohio, where the weather would suddenly shift and you could tell based on the humidity that a storm was brewing.

The soldiers around me, about thirty in total, seemed to sense it too, as each of them shifted or readjusted their uniform, preparing for something.

Halvar spun around and they all stood at attention, watching his every move, not a single syllable slipping from anyone's lips. Counter to character, I followed suit, remaining quiet and matching their rigid stances.

"Each unit of ten," Halvar began, his voice low but commanding. "Approach the field atop the mountain from your designated direction. Northeast, East, and Southeast." With each compass designation, he pointed at another fae—the unit leader I assumed—and they each nodded once. "Torsten, you're with me. Lennie, you too."

I nodded and refrained from saluting him this time.

"Our goal here tonight is to eviscerate Balder," he ground out between his clenched teeth, "and if any of you find Nora, capture her."

More nodding passed through the group, and I swallowed the lump in my throat before shaking my arms free of the tension that was building in my muscles.

Halvar continued, "As always, keep clear of the village. If any humans are in the woods, you know your cover story—"

"Costumed bachelor party on a drunken hike seeking shelter from the impending storm?" I said half under my breath, then clapped my hand over my mouth when I spotted a few of the soldiers smirking in my direction. I cast a furtive glance at Halvar who betrayed no emotion save for a tick in his jaw. Lifting my palm from my face, I mouthed an apology in his direction before shoving my hands back into my jacket pockets.

Torsten leaned over and whispered, "You're not far off. The humans tend to stay indoors when 'major storms'—our battles—whip up around here... but best stay quiet, baby fae." He winked down at me as Halvar began barking more orders and a few moments later, soldiers split off into their groups and we pressed forward through the dark forest.

Our journey through the densest part of the woods grew sluggish as the clouds above began to drizzle on us, making the moss covered ground and rocks dangerously slick. By grasping onto tree limbs and giving my thighs a serious workout, I was able to keep up with the male and female Fjell Fae soldiers, all of whom pressed on like they were indefatigable.

The ground grew steeper as we made our way up the side of the mountain, winding through trees and brush—keeping clear of any designated paths while also not inflicting damage on the wilderness around us. I grew antsier the higher we climbed, the blood in my veins humming with both excitement and nerves. Somewhere along the line I probably should have felt fear or hesitancy about walking into battle against centuries-old fae, but the shock of recent events jumbled my thoughts.

As the terrain flattened out, a rumble from above had our crew of soldiers glancing to the sky and Halvar's brow creasing into even deeper lines. Just then a creak sounded from our left and, before I could react, Halvar raised his hand, magically created a small boulder out of thin air, and threw it toward the noise. A ball of water swatted the rock and sent it tumbling to the ground and down the steep hill.

The sound of a low laugh met my ears and a warm shiver ran across my skin as a voice I recognized said, "I'm not your enemy, Halvar." Øyvin stepped out from behind a tree with a smirk on his lips as more Fjord Fae in their navy uniforms—sans cape—appeared from behind the pines. "The wall has fallen. Our King has betrayed us."

A little spark ignited in my chest, happy to see Øyvin alive and here. But the tone in his voice hinted at a raw and emotional wound within him, something I'd only heard once before, when he was telling me about the loss of his family after I'd been attacked.

"How did you know of his betrayal?" Halvar demanded.

Øyvin's lips turned into a scowl and he clenched his fists. "It wasn't difficult to guess when the wall collapsed entirely, the floorbed of the fjord began to shake, and large fissures formed across the deepest depths. No other Fjord Fae has the strength to pull that off, plus it has been *his* magic, fortified by our soldiers' power, that has held that wall intact for decades." He stuck his hand beneath the lapel of his uniform, pulling out his cellphone and waving it. "And your troops are quick to share information within your alliance. Ylva of the Forest Fae texted me about Nora and Freija. My condolences for your loss."

Halvar grunted in reply and all the soldiers remained unmoving, their preternatural stillness somewhat unnerving. It was as if they were all hovering and readying to pounce and the energy around us matched that feeling.

"Myself and a legion of my soldiers officially request an alliance to protect the fjord as a whole and bring down the King of the Fjord," Øyvin said, his shoulders squared and his posture imparting the formality of his request even as we stood at the precipice of a battle.

I looked from one Head Guard to the other, watching for any reaction from the Fjell Fae.

Halvar's ability to reveal nothing from his facial expression was amazing. Not a twitch of a brow hair, not a quiver of his lips, he had full control of his body, and I wasn't surprised in the slightest that this being—this beast of a fae—had been made Head Guard of the Fjell Fae.

The two stood there assessing each other, locked in a silent stalemate, as the appeal was considered.

"Your steadfast loyalty to the fjord and this region is noted, and your request to form an alliance is accepted," Halvar eventually replied.

Øyvin nodded slowly. "Thank you. We defer to your leadership."

More nods and looks were shared among the different soldiers at this. Moments later, Halvar and Øyvin had their fae moving into positions side by side, shifting forward and preparing. What *exactly* they were readying for, I had no fucking clue, so I just stood there like a lemon trying not to get in the way.

The earth shook once more as a roar of noise sounded from somewhere up ahead and I braced myself against a tree, my knees wobbling with the trembling ground. Halvar glanced over his shoulder at Torsten and raised his fist. The soldiers all responded by coming to a stop, their stances a clear ready position.

Halvar then nodded to Torsten and, at this signal, Torsten clapped his hands together vertically, then swiftly pulled them apart revealing a blinding ball of light the size of a soccer ball. I leaned further against the tree and watched him, my mouth agape at the blatant show of magic. He thrust his arms forward, and the ball of light shot ahead illuminating its surroundings.

The orb wove between the pines and breached the treeline, light shining brightly as it then skittered across the grassy field that could only be described as craggy and rock laden, before it crashed against a shield of water. It exploded and exposed a blockade of water-shields—like something out of a Roman war movie. I squinted and noticed more of these groupings, little squares of water across the far side of the field where rectangular shields had been erected both around and above clusters of Balder's forces. A lump lodged in my throat—based on the number of cubes, there must've been several hundred fae on the other side. *Fuuuuuuck.*

I spun on my heel and scoffed, "Hard pass. I'm out." Now seemed like a really good time to high-tail it out of here, find a boat or steal someone's car, and head back to Ohio.

An arm whipped across my middle and hauled me back, picking me up and planting me firmly beside the tree I'd been touching earlier. "Oh, no you don't."

I wiggled out of Øyvin's hold and pressed away from him. "No, you see, I really think my time has come." He stepped back, fighting a smile as Halvar called out more orders. "I've had my fun and I honestly prefer my chances in that prison cell down at Espen's police station. Speaking of, where is Espen? Still with Heidi?" *He would be really helpful right about now.*

Øyvin shook his head and lifted his hands. "No word from Ylva." He stepped closer again, his brows briefly knitting together as he scanned me from head to toe. "You're actually going to leave now, when your friends need you? When the Fjord needs you?"

"I'm pretty sure the Fjord needs me to stay out of the fucking way and keep my hands to my damn self." I gave him my best jazz hands gesture before clasping them together.

Øyvin chuckled as someone called his name and he whipped his head in their direction. His features immediately hardened and he was back to business.

"Stay hidden, Trouble," Øyvin whispered as he passed me, then flicked my ear. "And we'll talk about these later."

"Ow, Asshole!" I whisper-yelled at him, brushing the spot he'd hit. Note to self, those pointy bits were really sensitive.

He didn't look back as he and two other Fjord Fae soldiers got into position but I heard a faint laugh from him.

Doing as I was told for the... *shit*, I'd lost count of how many times now. I shook off the shock of *that* character growth and crouched down in the shelter of a large pine, its thick trunk hiding me and acting like a shield. The smell of rain and sodden earth invaded my senses and I watched in awe as our soldiers pressed forward onto the field of battle. It was, indeed, right atop the mountain, with a sheer drop down to the fjord below on our left and the treeline that swept to the right before descending into undulating hills and jagged mountains. It was the field Halvar and I had crossed on our hike earlier this evening.

Øyvin and Halvar began to work in unison, firing rocks and balls of water at the enemy forces. As the rain transformed from a drizzle to a downpour, Torsten stepped up and started throwing bolts of lightning toward Balder's forces. All together, the fae were creating a veritable thunder storm. It was mesmerizing.

Ylva and a group of Forest Fae emerged from the woods on the right, where the trees swooped around the field. Roots shot up out of the ground where her forces moved, weaving together and shielding themselves from the watery arrows shot in their direction. They in turn shot wooden arrows, branches fashioned from those around us, at the liquid blockades. Some of the shots penetrated the water-shields and they flickered and fell, but were quickly replaced by another. The Forest Fae kept up their barrage though as rocks were also pelted at the opposing forces from the Fjell Fae, and water lashed across the field in waves from our Fjord Fae.

Snap.

I flinched at the noise behind me and grit my teeth together. The hairs on the back of my neck flickered up and an instinctual shiver ran down my spine.

Still crouched, I slowly turned around and found two leather boots, black pants, brown leathers criss-crossing a chest... I choked down a breath as I finally glanced up into a pair of sharp brown-and-gray eyes that shimmered with an eerie malice.

46

LENNIE

I scrambled away from Nora, almost tripping as I took in her disheveled appearance. Her hair was a mess, twigs and leaves sticking out of it, but the look in her gaze was pure anguish, like she was simultaneously angry and in agony.

Pushing up from the ground, my hands slicked with water and pine needles, I rose to my feet, making sure the big tree was still at my back and shielding me from the battlefield.

"What happened to you?" Nora asked, narrowing her eyes at me.

I snorted and brushed my palms against my jeans, ridding myself of the debris on them. "I'm not even sure I have a proper answer for that one myself." I looked at her again, my eyes landing on hers, the ones that had matched her sister's. The marbled effect within them that seemed so unusual and yet was clearly a family trait... My heart hammered in my chest as I thought of what she'd done to said sister, and a warmth within me started to build as my lips turned into a snarl. "Why'd you do it?"

"You don't understand," Nora said, shaking her head and her hands as if she could dispel what she'd done.

"Oh, I sure as hell don't understand how you could kill your sister, your family."

She began burbling. "S-she wasn't supposed to get hurt. H-he promised it wouldn't kill her."

I scoffed at the absolute lunacy of the fae in front of me as she cornered me between the trees and boulders. "You really believed him? You never for a second asked yourself: hey, does this mo-fo have some sort of ill will toward the Fjell Fae?"

"He loves me. He didn't want anyone hurt," Nora continued, opening and closing her fists—fists I knew could likely create a boulder in a split second and then catapult it at my face the next.

But still, I snickered at her response.

"He didn't," she insisted, clenching her hands and holding them shut as she turned sideways and leaned forward. She was shifting into a ready position, and yet, I couldn't keep my damn mouth shut.

"Bitch, please."

"Fuck you!"

A loud roar erupted on the battlefield and Nora cast her gaze in that direction while I maintained a vigilant watch on her every move.

"How is he still alive?" she muttered, then turned back to me and added, "The sheer volume of power remaining in Freija should have felled Halvar if he tried to take it on."

"Yeah... about that." I stepped away from the tree, shifting a few paces to the right, and hoping to hell I could pull off the crazy stunt that had just crossed my mind.

She narrowed her eyes at me. "What?"

"I got a really cool thing from the tourist gift shop."

I slapped my hands together like I'd just seen Torsten do... but nothing happened.

Nora threw her head back and laughed. "First you're calling me a bitch, now you're giving me a round of applause—"

"Oh for fuck's sake, give me a damn second."

She sneered and backed up two steps before falling into a launch position. I stopped what I was doing and instinctively brought my arms down, bent at the elbows, shifting into a tackle-ready stance I'd been trained to do by my brothers.

Nora launched and I returned fire, dropping my shoulder and barreling into her. Our bodies met with a powerful thump, and my legs scrambled to push her backwards and down to the ground. She countered by twisting her upper body and grabbing my jacket. I hooked my hands into her leathers and used our falling momentum to throw her away from me. We landed on the ground with a thud, but my last-minute movement to push her away had worked, and I scrambled to my knees and then my feet, putting as much space between us as possible. Moss and pine needles clung to my hair and clothes, the damp air within the woods acting like glue for the detritus.

Nora rose to her feet and shook her arms. Brushing her equally disheveled hair from her face, she began to pace in a semi-circle, assessing the situation. She probably hadn't been expecting me to fight back, but alas, I'd grown up playing tackle football with my brothers. Emphasis on the tackle.

Straightening my shoulders, I refocused on drawing from that weird well of energy within my chest. Holding my hands out in front of me, I took a deep breath, focused on that new sensation, and clapped.

A large ball of light formed between my palms and my lips broke into a smirk.

Nora's eyes blew wide and her skin ashened in the glow of my new light source.

"Isn't it pretty?" I asked, my tone full of mocking and bitchiness. When the dumbfounded Nora didn't reply, I added, "Want some?"

She spun on her heels and darted into the trees, heading deeper into the forest.

I lifted the orb higher before thrusting it in Nora's direction like a dodgeball. The white sphere flew after her but she dodged and it crashed into a pine tree, disintegrating.

I let out a tiny whoop before I spotted the scar I'd left on the tree trunk. *Shit.* I clambered over to it and brushed my hand across the jagged indent. "I'm sorry," I said to the tree, wishing I knew how to heal the damage I'd caused and wondering why the hell I was talking to a tree. Was this what it was like when power went to your head? No, it couldn't be.

A weathered palm settled over mine and I screeched as someone pressed against my back.

"That was brave," Espen whispered into my ear. I let out a sigh of relief and glanced over my shoulder as he gave an order and a Forest Fae darted past me after Nora.

Espen stood behind me in all his fae glory, wearing his Forest Fae uniform sans cape. He looked healthy, alive, and like he hadn't been comatose for the past week. There was a slight rosiness to his cheeks, and a warmth in his chest as he gave me a gentle smile and nodded to the tree. "Stand still."

I didn't move, not even an inch. Somehow, in the middle of a battle, ensconced in his arms, with his palm atop mine against a tree, I felt safe. I felt like I belonged.

Espen spread our fingers wide over the injured part of the tree and, before I could blink, a flaring sensation grew beneath my hand, the tree bark around it glowing with a soft white light. It lasted mere seconds and when the magic subsided—withdrawing back inside Espen... or me—I lifted my hand to see what remained underneath. The bark that I'd damaged with my beginner's light bubble had healed, stitching itself back together with barely a puckering where the mark had originally been.

I turned in Espen's hold as he wrapped his arms around me, settling his hands against my lower back.

"Glad to see you alive," I muttered, staring up at him.

His lips quirked into a gentle smile. "Me too. Although, I appear to have missed a lot."

"If you'd woken up about twenty-four hours ago, there wouldn't have been as much to catch you up on."

"Oh, don't you worry. Heidi had enough stories to tell me before Ylva called about this." He nodded toward the battlefield where more skirmishes had broken out. "The healer even mentioned a few anecdotes about a recurring visitor. Any guesses who that might've been?" He tilted his head and gave me a knowing look.

I shrugged and shook my head. "Fuck if I know."

"Mm-hmm," he mumbled, pushing me against his chest.

The moment was broken when another loud roar and a clattering of lightning sounded, snapping the increasing tension between me and Espen. He let out a long breath, the muscles in his jaw tightening as he glanced toward the battle.

"Stay here and, whatever you do, don't run out onto the field," Espen said, planting a chaste kiss on my lips. "Can you do that?"

I slowly licked my bottom lip, feeling the need to challenge him but choosing not to. "Yes."

"You sure?" He quirked his brow and his lips tilted at one corner.

"I'm trying something new," I replied, pointing to my ears. "Thought obedience would go well with my newly acquired features."

A low chuckle escaped from Espen and he leaned in, pressing a gentle kiss against my cheek. "Oh, I look forward to discussing *that* news and showing you more of our world... just need to save it from a crazy man first." He stepped back and glanced toward the battle field, which we could just see the fringes of. "I'll be right back."

47

LENNIE

Standing in the shadows of the pines, I watched as Espen stalked onto the battlefield, Balder's men monitoring him wearily but with sly grins on their faces.

"No one needs to be hurt, Balder," Espen roared across the rocky field, his voice an authoritative thunder I'd never heard from him before. "Stand down."

Yeah, that was fucking hot.

Balder tilted his head with a smirk, his eyes glowing beneath his brow as he glared at our forces. "You'll be hard pressed to challenge me now, young man."

Øyvin shook his head minutely and Espen rolled his shoulders, anger rippling off him in waves as he started to press forward. He moved with a preternatural gate, slowly lifting his hands at his sides, and my stomach flipped when I noticed what he was doing. The earth rose around him, like a blanket being carefully peeled off the face of the world. Thick portions of soil, grass, and rocks rose up like an impending wave, matching the movement of Espen's hands. As he brought his palms to chest height, he quickly drew them together and clapped. Earth and debris crashed together like a tsunami on land and hurtled toward the line of Fjord Fae protecting Balder.

They lifted watery shields in response, using the barrier to protect themselves from the onslaught, but it was useless. The line fell and arrows quickly shot from the forest to our right, Ylva screaming orders over the rumble of thunder and the torrential rain.

I fist bumped the air at their momentary victory, but never got the chance to retract my hand as it was grasped tightly and I was spun into a choke hold. I took a large gulp of air and scratched at the thick band of muscle tightening around my neck. My captor shifted me back, gaining control of my footfalls and movement as I scrambled for freedom that was unlikely to come.

I glanced over my shoulder and caught sight of the sharp jaw and red hair of my assailant. *Kjetil, the King's Chief Advisor.*

"Nowhere to run to now, tourist," he said, the sly tone to his voice sending goosebumps across my skin. While I would've loved to inform him that I wasn't a fan of running, I couldn't exactly voice that right now. He grinned like he could tell what I was thinking though—that I wanted to challenge him but couldn't. Which was the most manly dickish thing, and set the blood in my veins to boiling.

I tried to stomp on his foot but he shifted out of the way at the last second. So, I attempted to reach his eye balls, which didn't work either. He banded his other arm around my middle and half-lifted, half-moved me forward under my own steam—my feet automatically moving forward in an effort to stay upright. I could barely breathe, my lungs heaving in protest as my vision began to blur.

He pushed us through the treeline and onto the battlefield. Before I had a chance to scream for help, he let out a sharp whistle that carried across the expanse. The soldiers closest to us turned and I watched my boys look back, their eyes wide in horror.

Kjetil tightened his hold around my neck, squeezing the last remains of air within me. I scratched at his arm and bucked in a last ditch effort to ease the pressure and escape. A blubbering whimper escaped my lips—

Something whizzed past my head and the stranglehold loosened. I desperately sucked in air before wobbling, taking a shaky step back, and then falling, spinning and crashing to the ground on my stomach. My entire body trembled with adrenaline and I cast my eyes over to my captor.

A branch-shaped arrow, knots and all, was embedded in Kjetil's forehead, his bright eyes staring into the dark rainy skies.

I bit down the bile that rose in my throat and looked away just as two pairs of hands scooped up my arms and yanked me to my feet. I barely registered Torsten and Leif on either side of me as we ran back to the treeline—water bombs dropping all around us, targeting us. One of them caught Torsten's leg with a hiss and he grumbled in pain.

We reached the edge of the battlefield and bolted behind the thick pines, shielding ourselves from the chaos. I took the moment of calm to assess Torsten's calf and found the fabric on his leg singed, the skin beneath quickly turning to red welts.

"Poison?" I asked, wiping my dirty hands across my pants with little success at rendering them wholly clean.

Leif knelt down beside his love's wound, examining it with delicate fingers. He shook his head. "Looks more like a burn."

"Feels like it's burned," Torsten grit out, the usually kind fae looking ready to shred someone to pieces instead. "I could—" He snapped his head to the right, looking past the trees and out onto the field again.

Leif and I followed his gaze and found the Forest Fae forces away from the main battle, circling around Nora. Ylva was in the mix, a large wooden sword in her hand that I imagined had one of Heidi's little potions on it. The other Forest Fae in the group had whip-like weapons and bats and Nora lunged at one after the other, physically fighting them and launching balls of light at their faces. She hit several of them, but wasn't paying attention to the fury-filled fae at her back. In one swift move, Ylva swung her sword across the back of Nora's thighs and the Fjell Fae let out an agonized scream. She fell forward and shuddered before all movement stopped and the other Forest Fae soldiers stepped back, save for one. Ylva hovered over Nora, blade at the ready again, her gaze continuously snapping from the captive at her feet and the rest of the battlefield.

I couldn't tell if our other soldiers had noticed the skirmish we'd just witnessed on the far side of the clearing, but neither Øyvin nor Espen looked in that direction. They were too focused on the shifting Fjord Fae forces working for the King, many of whom had now stepped out from behind their shields and launched physical attacks—some even fighting the Fjord Fae that had allied with Øyvin. Meanwhile, Balder's attention was solely on himself and those in front of him as he stalked back and forth behind his lines with a smarmy sneer on his face.

"I am the beast within the waters," he yelled, spreading his arms wide, his long cape flapping behind him in the wind. "I am the troll beneath the mountain. I am the dawn of Ragnarok, come to create anew." Balder's chest heaved as he spoke, his voice echoing in chorus with the thunder rumbling above us. "Join me and we shall form a greater, more prosperous union without the threat of the human race!"

Honestly, if anyone was the troll from the mountain it was Halvar, but now didn't seem like the time to point that out. Right now we had bigger fish to fry, like this over-sized trout with a misguided hero complex.

The two sides closed in on each other and chaos broke out as the ground rumbled again. Øyvin roared and volleyed attacks, aiming for the King behind his soldiers, while Espen unleashed more of his destructive powers, lifting the soil and roots beneath the opposing soldiers, then pulling them down and burying them alive. A shiver ran down my spine at the sight. Halvar had said Espen was powerful, I just never expected *this*. Hell only knew where Halvar had disappeared to and part of me sincerely hoped he hadn't met his demise.

Just then, a ripple of energy shot across the field from behind Balder's forces, sending them to their knees. The line of power fizzled out as it reached our soldiers, and I watched in shock as the water shields of the Fjord Fae came crashing down. Balder shuddered and spun before a large fist shot out, smashing his jaw and sending him to the ground, too.

The entire field stilled and watched as Halvar loomed over the King, his eyes a shimmering silver that was so bright it was visible even at this distance. A split second later, Halvar was wrapped within a vortex of water, pebbles and debris buffeting him as he snarled. Thrashing against the whorl with more silvery power, Halvar brought it crashing down and raised his hands with a roar. Rocky shackles wrapped around Balder's neck and wrists, forcing him down on his knees, anchored by monstrous boulders that hadn't been there seconds ago.

Everyone came to a stop, no one shifted, no one dared launch another attack—it was as if everyone was holding their breath, waiting for Halvar's next move. My stomach roiled and the weird warmth that lingered in my chest since the magic transfer a few hours ago simmered in anticipation. It didn't have to wait long.

A moment later, Halvar began moving his hands in an infinity pattern, his silver and gray powers swirling between his palms. Slowly, and with an almost ceremonial calm, a stone axe began to form. From the sharp double-sided head all the way down to the end of the shaft, the weapon looked extremely heavy and capable of cleaving the world in two. Halvar gripped the handle and raised the blade. Balder squirmed and yelled, unable to break his rocky chains. Halvar said something and began—

Leif grabbed my shoulder and spun me around, facing us away from the scene.

The earth shuddered, a guttural scream rent the air, and murmurs drifted across the dark field and through the woods.

"Did he just..." I asked, covering my mouth with my palm in hopes that would help me not up-chuck.

"Yes," Leif replied, wrapping his arm over my shoulders, stopping me from turning around. "No need to see that on repeat every night."

"I'm surprised he didn't go for his head," Torsten chimed in, still watching the field. "But I'm sure it will be useful to have it attached to his neck while being questioned. Oh look, here comes Trygve to stop the bleeding and grab the arm—"

"Spare us the gory details, my love," Leif said with a light chuckle. "The baby fae is turning green."

He wasn't wrong. The adrenaline was starting to wash out of my system, rapidly being replaced with exhaustion and the reminder that it was well past my bedtime. The thought of what was happening behind me had my stomach flip-flopping.

Torsten hobbled over and stepped in front of me, tilting his head to one side, giving me a gentle smile. "War not to your liking?"

I shook my head, my hair sticking to my cheeks but didn't dare open my mouth as bile rose in my throat.

Torsten nodded, then cast his eyes over my shoulder.

"Thank you, gentlemen. We can take her from here," Espen said behind me.

Leif's arm slipped from my shoulders and looped it with Torsten's as the two fae headed back onto the field. Their presence was replaced by two bruised fae, their uniforms torn in places, but their gazes locked firmly on me.

"You are exceptionally good at getting yourself into sticky situations," Espen said with a chuckle as Øyvin crossed his arms.

"Shit finds me," I replied, my lips quirking into a smile as the rain started to ease and relief washed through me. I looked between the two of them, all three of us weary and tired, but still breathing. Their show of strength had been mesmerizing, but also alarming, especially Espen's.

"Espen, did you really bury those soldiers alive?" I asked, brushing my hair behind my ear.

He nodded slowly. "Yes, I did."

Damn. I swallowed hard, pushing down the lump that had formed in my throat. It was at that moment I realized Espen probably didn't just do yoga for flexibility and mad *yoga* skills. No, he likely used it to calm his mind and keep his powers in check. I shuddered at the revelation.

"But, you should know, I left them a gap to breathe. They can claw their way out and answer to Øyvin's men."

Visions of fae rising like zombies out of the soil crossed my mind and I shook my shoulders and arms, trying to rid myself of that nightmare. Fuck, that was cold and brutal.

"My captains will handle the young defectors. Most appear to have been from our recent class of graduates, likely groomed by Balder," Øyvin said, the muscles in his jaw ticking.

I let out a long sigh, and Espen opened his arms for a hug. I stumbled into them.

"Let's go," Espen murmured, placing a gentle kiss on the top of my head. "We've been invited to the interrogation, but I want to stop by Heidi's before we head over."

"Sounds good," I said, momentarily raising my arm and giving them a thumbs up. "Any chance you can carry me down the mountain?"

Øyvin snorted and started walking away, mumbling something about going to inform the fjord residents, as Espen chuckled. "You're at least part fae now," he said lightly smacking my butt. "You'll find the energy to keep moving for a little while longer." He slipped his hand into mine, the warmth there somehow soothing, and started pulling me alongside him. "Come on, you can do your favorite corpse pose later."

"Deal."

48
LENNIE

Espen and I stood vigil outside Heidi's place, the motherly healer working her magic on the assortment of injured fae within as the sun began its ascent. There had only been a handful of deaths, mostly on Balder's side, but a lot of Forest Fae had been burned by boiling water bombs like the one that had caught Torsten. Ylva had evacuated most of her forces down here to the healer hut and then, with the assistance of some Fjell Fae, she'd escorted Nora back to the mountain. The Fjell Princess had been knocked out and still hadn't roused when they'd come past here. When I asked Ylva why, she gladly informed me that her blade had been laced with some water hemlock. And I honestly felt a pop of glee at that. Payback was a bitch.

Espen stood to my right, still covered in dirt and debris, specks of mud stuck in his wet hair. I'm sure I didn't look much better.

"You feeling all right?" I asked as we leaned against the grass-covered building.

"A little depleted but I'll be okay," he replied with a gentle smile, brushing his thumb over the back of my hand.

"Uh, yeah. Those stunts you pulled were scary. Why'd you never mention you could do that whole ground tidal-wave shit?"

His shoulders sagged and he pushed his hair off his forehead. "I don't like it," he admitted with a grimace. "I don't like that destruction. I was always meant to be a healer, a helper, but for some reason the ancestors thought I should also be gifted the power to destroy."

"That's why Queen Ragnhild recruited you to join her forces?" I asked, now knowing that what Halvar had told me on our way back from the sunset photo shoot was true.

Espen nodded solemnly, like the weight of that still hung around his shoulders. "I may be able to tear the earth apart, but I choose to heal and help. She requested my help and I gave it." He let out a long sigh, gazing across the clearing toward the trees. "I can't take back the actions of my past, but I can continue to help and protect the Forest Fae and those we are in alliance with."

"That's very noble of you."

He chuckled, shaking his head. "I don't wish to be anyone's king nor pawn, but I will lead where I can and answer to the Forest Fae and our council of elders."

That sounded fucking noble to me. Before I could think about what I was doing, I pressed a quick peck to Espen's cheek and pulled back.

He looked over, his eyes warming as his lips twisted into a sneaky grin.

Heidi interrupted the moment when she stepped out of the hut, searching for something or someone. Her eyes landed on me as she finished wiping her hands on her apron. "I heard you'd undergone some changes, young lady."

Before I could respond she stormed over, grabbed my left hand, and yanked up my jacket and shirt sleeve, revealing the crisscross of silvery-white scars there. She tutted thrice, turning my arm over and then back before dropping my hand and pushing my hair out of the way, glancing at my ear. "Well, shit, it is true."

Espen chuckled, ducking his head while I refrained from moving, still kind of in shock from Heidi's attention.

"I'd say demi, not full," she said, taking a step back and setting her hands on her hips. "Until you do any training, we won't know for certain how much magic you have within you."

I raised my brows and pulled my sleeves back down. "Can you tell who's magic I have?"

Espen shifted, and I could sense his interest in the topic from where he stood beside me. He was just as curious as I was. Was this only Freija's magic or had some of Halvar's seeped in, too? And what was the difference?

"It's definitely Fjell," she said, crossing her arms and nodding to my scars. "I'd wager more royal than Halvar's based on those markings."

"So, someone told you about what happened in the throne room?"

She nodded. "Leif and Torsten are inside getting that burn tended to. Torsten told me when I asked about you."

"You asked about me?" My voice pitched higher and I brought my hand to my heart, a sarcastic smirk forming on my lips.

She waved and set her hands on her hips again. "Only curious in case we had a dead human to attend to. You wouldn't believe the amount of paperwork and tomfoolery we must manage to make it look like an *accident*."

Espen snort-laughed and doubled over.

My jaw fell open. "Heidi! Really? Here I was thinking you cared for me."

She brushed her hands together and turned back to the door. "Glad to see we don't have that mess and that the cut on your chin is healing. Stop by for a visit some time but leave the coffee at home." Without waiting for an answer, she breezed back inside.

Espen straightened up beside me and his laughter subsided as his eyes narrowed in on my face. "How *did* you get that scar?"

I reached up to my chin, brushing across the site and grimacing when I realized my little bandage had fallen off. Must've happened during one of the many scuffles I'd had in the past twenty-four hours. Espen shifted closer and stepped in front of me, our eyes locking on each other. "It's just a scratch," I found myself mumbling, mimicking the words Halvar had used, and dropped my hand back to my side.

Espen tilted his head and gently lifted my chin with his thumb and finger, his touch warm and gentle against my cold skin. His jaw tightened as he examined the little cut. "Please tell me who did this to you." His breaths came in long exhales, like he was trying to control himself through yogic breathing.

I licked my lips, eyes still glued to his. "Some fae shifted into wolves and attacked me while I was hiking. Compared to those inside, I'm fine."

His nostrils flared and his eyes went as wide as tractor wheels. "Wolves?" he bit out.

I nodded and brought my palm to rest on his chest. His heart beat wildly beneath my hand, and he shifted his fingers from my chin to the back of my head, pulling me closer to him.

"I'm fine. Halvar came to the rescue."

That still didn't seem to satisfy Espen as his grip in my hair tightened. "They shouldn't be down this far. I should—"

"You don't *need* to do anything, Espen." I stepped into him, allowing him to wrap his arms around me, which he did. That smell of moss and leather that was so intrinsically him invaded my senses. "I'm okay, and the fae that jumped me was killed by Halvar."

"Good," he said between clenched teeth as the tension in his shoulders slowly eased out. "I'll talk to the Council of Elders and handle that."

"Problem for another time," Øyvin said from our left, and I turned to find him striding out of the woods toward us. He'd cleaned up slightly, removing the muck and debris from his face, but missing the bits of forest and mud that still clung to his uniform.

"Oh, and don't worry," I remarked to Espen. "Øyvin lost his shit enough for both of you when he found out."

Espen quirked a brow and looked over at the Fjord Fae. "Did he now?"

"Oh yeah," I replied. "He tried to fight Halvar and turned him into a little fountain."

Espen chuckled, his eyebrows climbing as he looked at Øyvin. "I'm surprised you still have teeth left after doing that."

Øyvin grunted and shrugged once, crossing his arms. "Speaking of the Fjell, we should head over there before we miss the interrogation. You ready to leave?" he asked, nodding toward the healing hut behind us, clearly aiming his question at Espen.

"Yeah, let me just do a final check on the injured and we can head over," Espen replied and released me from his hug. "Everything okay down in the fjord?"

Øyvin rubbed his palm across his chin. "It will be. The King's Council appears to have had no idea. For now, it sounds like Kjetil may have been the only one Balder confided in. The Council is assessing the situation and informing the Fjord Fae of what has happened. I've tasked one of my guards, Sigurd, with erecting the wall again with whatever power we can amass between us all without the King, and I'll do a greater assessment on our forces in the next couple of days. But first, the Council want me in attendance for Balder's interrogation."

"And they'll just let Halvar and the Fjell Fae march off with the King like that?" I asked, shoving my hands into my jacket pockets to keep them warm.

Øyvin nodded and flicked some errant moss off his sleeve. "He was captured in a battle for actions that threatened the safety of the entire fjord. While the Council and Fjord Fae tend to put themselves first—"

"You don't say," I interrupted with a smirk.

Øyvin glared in response before continuing, "—they see the tremendous value in having all factions working in harmony, with no single unit exerting hegemonic rule."

"Which is part of the reason why the Forest Fae opted to retain only a Council of Elders when Queen Ragnhild died," Espen chimed in. "Glad to hear things are okay down there."

Øyvin bowed his head gently in thanks and I nodded in agreement.

"I'm going to check on Heidi and the injured again. I'll be right back," Espen said, stepping away from me and heading inside.

Øyvin moved after him. "I'll come with you. We have a few people in here, too."

Together they moved inside, then Espen popped his head out of the doorway when I didn't follow. "You coming?"

I shook my head and stepped back against the side of the building again. "I think I've seen enough for today."

We walked back down the hillside, the guys magically shifting out of their uniforms and into human clothes as we got closer to the village just starting to stir under the low light of the rising sun.

"Where's Nora, by the way?" I'd seen her captured by Ylva and escorted back to the Fjell but I had no idea what they intended to do with her.

"She's been sent to the dungeons where she will remain," Øyvin answered.

"*Those* are prison cells you really don't want to see the inside of. Waaay worse than the ones down at the station," Espen supplied, leaning over and nudging my shoulder.

"That bad?" I asked, then yawned, the exhaustion of the past twenty-four hours and staying up all night starting to weigh on me more heavily.

Espen nodded, his eyes wide. "Let's just say, Nora will never see the sun ever again."

Shit. Yeah, hard pass. No thanks. I needed the fresh air and outdoors to thrive, always had growing up, too. The thought of being banished to a lightless cave sounded awful.

"And word has it," Øyvin added, "Halvar himself ordered her to be given a solution that will inhibit her powers and stop her from escaping."

"A solution? Like one of Heidi's potions?" I asked, looking up at him.

Øyvin nodded. "I've heard it might be diluted water hemlock."

Espen and I both sucked in air at the mention of the poison that had almost felled him and what killed her sister, and a shiver ran down my spine. While it didn't really come as a surprise, Halvar was fucking cold and brutal.

We strolled past Oddvar's where the man himself stood on the stoop, unlocking the shop for the day. He glanced over at us as we walked in his direction, his eyes narrowing at us. "You three are up early," he remarked, taking us in, and I was glad the guys had shifted their attire... *Shit.* I frantically pulled my hair forward, shielding my ears, hoping Oddvar hadn't noticed. "It'll take me some time to get the coffee machines running."

Espen glanced over at me and his eyes widened when he realized what I had just remembered. We hadn't used any magic to hide my new ears. He quickly turned back to Oddvar as we continued walking, picking up our pace a bit. "I'm afraid we're on police business this morning, Oddvar. Øyvin and Lennie agreed to assist me with a matter but we'll certainly stop by later for some coffee," he said, giving the man a genuine smile.

"Very well," Oddvar opened the door to the café and mumbled a 'good day' as he stepped inside.

As soon as he was out of sight, Øyvin grumbled and placed his hand to my left shoulder. A light wave of warmth brushed against my ears and I breathed a sigh of relief. "That was too fucking close."

Both guys let out a "mm-hmm," their chests rising and falling a little quicker than they were a few minutes ago.

"That is going to take some getting used to," Espen said, nudging his shoulder against mine as we strode through the rest of the village.

"No kidding," I replied with a swift smile, my own heart-rate dropping down to its resting level.

"We'll teach you how to hide them," Øyvin supplied, his gaze locked on the path ahead of us as we reached the edge of town and the trail that led up into the woods—the trail that would lead us directly to the main entrance of the mountain. "But first, we need to see what the King has to say for himself."

"How long?"

The angry shout echoed against the rock walls as we neared our destination. The lights in the tunnels leading to the dungeons were fewer than those above, the flickering casting an eerie glow on the place, and the air down here was much colder, damper, than other parts of the mountain. I shivered in my jacket, glad to have it on, even if it was still slightly wet from the rain on the battlefield.

A wicked laugh echoed through the hall as we approached, Espen by my side and Øyvin a few paces ahead with a Fjell Fae soldier who was guiding us down into the dungeons. Rounding a corner, we found soldiers lining the wall outside the room where Halvar interrogated Balder. Nods flitted between Espen, Øyvin, and the Fjell soldiers—all of whom looked a little worse for wear. Several had pieces of their uniform torn open, others looked like they had been nicked but spared from the boiling bombs of water. We came to a stop and the guys flanked either side of me, their gazes locked on the prison cell.

The room Balder was held in could only be described as a cave with a large boulder slid aside to reveal the entry. The fallen king knelt within, his lone arm shackled to the ceiling, blood dripping from his crooked nose. His shirt was gone and his chest—I sucked in a breath—his chest was covered in layers of deep silver scars, slashes on top of more slashes. I shook my head at the results of his misuse of the magic he'd sworn to use for good and focused on his shackles.

"Can't he just *'Open Sesame'* himself out of that?" I whispered to Øyvin, pressing up onto my toes to reach his ear.

He shook his head and then leaned down so I didn't have to stay on my tippy-toes for the answer. "There's either something within the manacles stopping him, or he is conserving his energy for his wounds, or something else."

"Hence the reinforcements," I said, looking over my shoulder at the Fjell Fae soldiers that were gathered.

Øyvin nodded, his emotions hidden behind a stoic facade that appeared impenetrable.

I glanced back at the fallen king and winced, hoping he didn't unleash a tidal wave that would drown us within the dungeon. That would be a shitty way to go.

"How long have you been stealing power from Nora? How long have you been doing this?" Halvar's voice was low, gravelly, and altogether murderous as he waved a hand toward Balder's scar-riddled chest.

"Twenty years," Balder spat.

Espen flinched beside me and Halvar narrowed his eyes at the king, blood and saliva flecking the dirty rock-floor beneath him.

"Shame Freija couldn't have been by her dear friend's side during the skirmishes in the south twenty years ago," Balder taunted Halvar, a wicked gleam in his bloodshot eyes. "Where was she anyway?"

Halvar tightened his jaw and fists but didn't respond.

"And Nora?" Halvar asked instead. "What part did she play in your grand plans?"

"A means to an end." The king smirked.

What an ass.

"She loved you," I blurted out, getting a silent glare from Halvar in response. "Sorry," I mouthed, but stared back at the one-armed king.

Balder snorted and looked directly into my eyes, those algae colored pools filled with malice and a delusional belief that he was more powerful than those who had fought against him and his ideals on that battle field. "She was a foolish young girl. Corrupting her loneliness and longing was a pleasure, believe me."

My gut tightened at his remarks. On one hand, I despised everything Nora had done, her betrayal and involvement with Freija's death. But after hearing Balder's words, I felt slightly sorry for her. Slightly.

He continued. "While I'm saddened she accidentally killed the Queen with the tea, instead of just incapacitating her like I'd planned, it saved me doing so later." His eyes shifted to Espen before glancing back at Halvar who was circling him. "And it did eliminate a player from the board, leaving me the clear ruler."

Silence hung in the chilly air, like the truth was muffling any noises as we all waited with bated breath for someone to say something.

"What part did you play in the uprising twenty years ago?" Halvar asked and I felt Espen still, bracing for the answer.

A slick grin slowly spread across Balder's face, his eyes darting quickly to the Forest Fae beside me again. "King."

Halvar grimaced, raising his right hand and slowly clenching his fist. In response, the band of rock around Balder's remaining wrist tightened, a grinding noise emanating from the handcuff. The King panted through the pain, a line forming between his brows as he clenched his jaw.

"What part did you play?" Halvar repeated and I sucked in a breath waiting for the answer.

"One cannot easily win at chess with two opposing Queens on the board," he ground out in reply. "Remove one, and your chances improve dramatically."

Espen took a step forward but I grabbed his arm, holding him back. While I wouldn't mind seeing my yogi-fae-cop deck the prick, Halvar seemed to have things covered. Meanwhile, Øyvin didn't move a muscle; he just stared at the monarch, his boss, the leader who had betrayed his people—him included.

"Why remove Queen Freija from the board, too?" Halvar asked, no hint of sadness lacing his tone.

"She would never have joined forces, knelt at my throne, deferred to me and the opportunity to make our region stronger, better, by uniting under one ruler."

We all knew that was true. Hell, I hadn't been here long, but even in that short period of time, I had seen the love and care Freija had for her people and the mountain. She would never have bowed down to him if she didn't think it was for the good of her people.

"Even if she knew," Balder continued while Halvar loomed behind him, "deep down, that gifting her power to me would be the wisest choice she could ever make, would strengthen the fae against the vile humans." Balder glanced at me, and a shiver ran down my spine at the hatred I saw in his eyes. "But then again, why go for the crown when you can steal from the princess?" His lips curved into a wry smile.

Choking sounded from behind us and I spun to find several soldiers coughing up water. The mountain shook and I stumbled, Øyvin's hand shooting out to steady me before he withdrew. A chuckle rent the air, and I looked back to the prison cell just as Balder's shackle crumbled to the ground, releasing him from his bonds.

Halvar lunged forward, gripped the King's head, one hand beneath his jaw, and ripped it sideways. Blood splattered and I spun into Øyvin's chest as a wet thump sounded behind me. Then came another bump, which I guessed was the rest of Balder's body falling to the floor.

"What in the *Game of Thrones,* big guy?" A warning would've been greatly appreciated, as my stomach now roiled and threatened to soil Øyvin's uniform.

Øyvin's chest shuddered and Espen brushed his palm across my back in small circles. I tried to take deep breaths, inhaling in through my nose and exhaling through my mouth, but it wasn't working. The air began to smell like copper and I pressed harder against Øyvin, trying to inhale his usual fresh linen scent instead.

The wet coughs in the tunnel subsided but a few other grunts sounded from the line of soldiers behind us where they stood against the wall. I was glad I wasn't the only one struggling to stomach what we'd just witnessed. I knew Halvar was brutal, had been warned as such and seen it with my own eyes when he saved me from the wolves, but this was a whole other level of cut-throat.

"I think I need to leave," I mumbled, hoping the guys could understand my muffled words as I began to feel lightheaded.

"Okay, we are no longer needed here anyway," Espen said, his tone authoritative but kind.

Espen shifted me from Øyvin's hold, the latter unmoving as we took a few steps down the tunnel. "You coming?" Espen asked and I glanced back, making sure I looked only at Øyvin and not within the bloody cave.

Øyvin stood stock still, his chest rising and falling in a steady rhythm as he stared into the room. He glanced down, nodded once, then straightened up and cast his eyes toward us. "Let's go."

He stepped back and moved over to us just as Halvar emerged, his black-and-gray clothes darkened and his hands covered in scarlet. "You three." We halted at his words, and a flicker of panic thrummed through my veins. "Meet me in the throne room."

50

LENNIE

We were escorted out of the dungeon to the throne room, the air-quality and temperature within the tunnels returning to a more comfortable level, and my stomach slowly stopped doing somersaults as we entered the sky-blue room. Freija's body had been removed along with her tea cup, and the only sign that anything was amiss were the cracks that marred the walls where Balder had shaken the mountain. The three of us hung about, not saying a word to each other as we waited. A few minutes later, the sound of footsteps approaching had us turning.

Halvar strode into the room, two soldiers fanning out at the entrance behind him, taking up their positions. Gone was the Head Guard's bloodied attire, replaced with a clean black-and-gray uniform with the cape draped across his shoulder glinting with silver threads as it floated around him. Seeing him in clean clothes made me hyper-aware of the fact that I hadn't washed or changed in well over twenty-four hours, and I was suddenly desperate for a scalding hot shower.

The guys fell in beside me, their stance matching that of the soldiers by the entry—legs in a triangle shape, hands clasped behind their backs.

I didn't bother with such a show of militant respect or precision but I did keep my mouth shut for once, which I was sure would please the big guy who took up a position before the throne.

"Thank you both for your assistance," Halvar said, his voice a little more hoarse than his usual gruff timbre. "I believe we need to discuss an alliance that would benefit us all."

"I'm certain the Council of Elders for the Forest Fae will gladly maintain our alliance with the Fjell Fae," Espen supplied, sounding like a diplomat.

Halvar nodded once, then cast his eyes to Øyvin.

The Fjord Fae rolled back his shoulders before responding, "I will have to consult with the former King's Council, but I believe they'll be amenable to a formal alliance that extends beyond the agreement we struck last night."

"And there aren't any more traitors among the Council?"

Øyvin shook his head. "I don't believe so. When I spoke to them this morning, all appeared to have been kept in the dark. The only person Ki—" he halted, taking a deep breath before continuing, "Balder only confided in Kjetil."

"And you trust them?" Halvar asked, narrowing his eyes at the Fjord Fae.

Øyvin paused for a moment, as if considering the question with detail and care. "Yes." He nodded. "But I shall inform you both if that were to ever change." He turned to Espen, who bowed his head in return before they both focused back on Halvar.

"Good," Halvar replied. "I shall meet with our Queen's Council to discuss this matter further and we'll formalize the agreement in the coming days."

"Will you be changing to a Council-run model?" Øyvin asked, which didn't seem like an out of turn question but Halvar appeared to blanch slightly at the words.

"That is another matter I must discuss with the Council as soon as possible."

"You have contingencies in case both sisters were," Espen paused as if choosing his words carefully, "incapacitated?"

The knot in Halvar's throat bobbed sharply. "Of a sort," he replied, then shook his head and focused his steely eyes on me. "Now, let's discuss you."

Ah shit, here we go.

"Take a seat, gentlemen," Halvar said, dismissing the guys and motioning to the bench carved into the side of the room. They strode away, Espen giving me a gentle nudge with his elbow before departing.

I stood there feeling like a lemon, unsure what to do or say—which was rather unusual. So, I clasped my hands together in front of me and braced for impact.

"How are you feeling?" Halvar asked, the concern in his voice taking me a bit by surprise. Nothing about this fae screamed kindness and caring, especially not what I'd witnessed in the past few hours. But, then again, I'd seen a hint of vulnerability when he'd held Freija in his arms.

I sighed. "Well, I'm *physically* fine. Mentally, disturbed. I'm also kinda hungry. Would kill for a coffee, shower, and a piss—not necessarily in that order."

Snickers rose from the side of the room, and I dared to look in that direction before Halvar spoke again, regaining my attention immediately.

"I meant your arm, the magic." He pursed his lips, crossing his arms again, wholly unamused by my honest answer.

I shrugged and rubbed my hand across my bicep. "Fine. Still slightly sore, but fine. Trygve's salve really helped."

"Good." Halvar nodded, then continued plainly, getting straight to the point. "You must make a decision. Forsake your human world and live here, or learn how to hide your gifts and ears and go home to your Ohio."

I flinched and glanced at the two fae who perched on the bench against the wall, the same bench I'd sat on yesterday after my arm had been scored and Halvar had given me parts of his or Freija's magic—likely the latter considering the light magic I'd thrown at Nora last night.

Øyvin shrugged, and Espen smiled, raising his hands in a gesture as if saying, "the choice is all yours."

"What'll it be, Lennie?" Halvar pressed, drawing my attention back to him. "Will you go back to your old life, or will you stay here and help us protect the fjord?"

I took a deep breath and considered my options. There were so many pros and cons to account for. Without a doubt, life here was more exciting than the one I led in Ohio, but there were so many new variables that would have serious consequences for the decision I made. I now had magic in my system—a warm ball of something that sat in the middle of my sternum, waiting to be used. I had the ears, which could ultimately be hidden or brushed away with a "this is how I was born" remark. The white scars up my arm could easily be described as a tattoo. Yet, there was so much more that could never be explained.

What would happen when my family aged and I didn't? There was no way my brothers wouldn't notice, especially Andrew. My eldest brother had always watched over the rest of us kids like a hawk, as if it was his duty as the first born to protect the rest of us from harm. And he had daughters, what would happen when my nieces suddenly looked older than me?

"How does the aging process work?" I asked, looking around the room.

"Slower," Espen said, capturing my attention. "We age like humans but the process is significantly slower. Female fae, for example, will have a longer fertility period and won't reach menopause until they are many hundreds of years old. Many fae won't lose their hair or start turning gray until they are five centuries old, too."

I nodded in thanks and cast my gaze to the silver-haired fae by the throne, wondering, not for the first time, just *how* old Halvar was. But, as a demi-fae, I likely wouldn't have such longevity... or perhaps I would? As Trygve had mentioned, nothing like this had occurred in a very long time, if ever.

"There's no way to know how long you will live, until you do just that... Live," Espen added, and I pressed my lower lip between my teeth. He was right. We had no data, no variables, no stories or history to take guidance from. This decision, this life, was mine to choose what to do with. And, honest to hell, that was an intimidating prospect.

On one hand, I had really enjoyed my time in Norway. I'd made some friends, met some guys whose company I *thoroughly* enjoyed, and found a location that honestly made me excited to get out of bed every morning. On the other hand, I had a life back in the US. I had a family back there. I had my photography excursions...

The thought of photography reminded me of my shattered camera and a tremor of sadness shuddered through me. I'd gained a lot on this trip and suffered some losses, which was what life was like—it ebbed and flowed, changed.

I began to pace, carving a rectangular shape with my footsteps across the throne room floor while maintaining my distance from any of the fae in the room.

I had a good life at home: a family that loved me dearly, an albeit small group of friends that I saw on occasion, and a job that, while not ideal, put food on the table and helped me afford my travel obsession. Ohio was great, but over the past few years I'd admittedly grown bored of the scenery. I'd found myself yearning for freedom, abroad more and more, spending less time in the state I'd called home for so long, the place where I'd grown up. But... a home should be where *I* was, it should be what I created for myself, and, most importantly, it should make me happy.

I'd certainly been happy here in Skolvik. And not just because of the two fae who were perpetually on my mind. There was the village that urged me to wake up earlier to witness every facet of its beauty. There were the people—the majority of whom were grumpy and set in their ways, but quite pleasant if you didn't take their attitude personally. And there was the fjord itself, with waters so teeming with magic and life that it brought a smile to my face just looking at it.

Yes, I had definitely been happy here.

With all that in mind, the decision before me felt easier to make than I'd first anticipated...

I stopped my pacing, and stared up at the Fjell Fae by the throne.

"I'll stay," I announced with a firm nod. "On one condition."

A little whoop came from my right, and I quirked my lips into a smile as Halvar waved his hand for me to proceed.

"I want that baby fae hat you mentioned. I want to know if it'll actually fit on my head."

Halvar brushed his hand across his temple and sighed. "Handle whatever affairs you need to get in order and we'll start your training as soon as I am done with the Fjell Council." He faced Espen and Øyvin, adding, "You two make sure she doesn't reveal herself to the humans."

"Halvar, really! I'm not gonna start mooning the village." Okay, so it wasn't an entirely inconceivable act but certainly not something I was planning on doing in the foreseeable future.

Halvar's deadpanned gaze met mine briefly before he turned back to the guys. "Make sure she knows how to hide her ears," he said without inflection, waving at his own pointy ears, and then left the room, his two soldiers following closely behind him as he headed through the back door to the Queen's chambers.

I turned to the guys sitting against the wall, one of whom was trying his hardest to hide a smile, the other beaming from ear to ear. I hadn't made my decision based on the way I felt about them—happy, intrigued, attracted—but, however much I'd always said I'd never make a life-changing decisions based on a man, these two had factored into my process today.

"Don't think I made my decision because of you two," I said as my heart pattered in an excited rhythm.

"Wouldn't dream of it," Øyvin said, a sly smirk on his lips, while Espen mouthed "bullshit" and winked.

A bubble of laughter escaped from me and I stepped up in front of them, an idea forming in my head that would probably cause trouble.

"Before I officially move here," I said, the thought of immigration paperwork, job hunting, and cardboard boxes briefly crossing my mind. "I'm gonna need to take care of some things back in the US." I set my hands on my hips and widened my stance, unable to stop the sneaky grin spreading across my face. "Either of you ever been to Ohio?"

51
EPILOGUE

LENNIE

Winter had officially arrived in Ohio. Blistering cold wind whipped down the streets and the threat of ice and snow lingered in the air when we stepped out of the airport and hopped into a ride-share that would take us back to my apartment.

Thankfully, we'd caught a ride with the supply ship and found transportation back to the port city of Stavanger on the southwest coast of Norway. Once there, and before we caught our flight, I'd been able to retrieve my luggage from the cruise ship, which I unceremoniously dumped onto my bed once we got inside my dusty home. While I desperately needed to clean my apartment, there was a whole slew of other stuff that needed to be dealt with.

I needed to pick up my things from the office and clean up my desk at the job that had fired my ass for being gone for so long. Once that was taken care of, I would have to pack up all the shit in my apartment and shove what I could in some extra suitcases to take back to Norway. There was no way in hell I was shipping stuff out there—I'd almost had a heart attack when I saw the cost to mail a single box. So I settled on buying two more obnoxiously large suitcases and calling it good. I could always buy new things in Skolvik.

Before I could move out though, or even take action on my next step, there was a pressing issue that needed attending to: meeting the parents.

We pulled up to my parents' house covered in twinkly lights, my dad having gone all out for the holidays. It was one of his favorite hobbies—some years he even set the lights to music. While it was fun and festive, it was also obnoxiously bright.

We got out of my car, Espen and Øyvin silent behind me, taking it all in as we reached the front door of my picture-perfect suburban, childhood home. I knocked twice, then let myself in. "Hello! Anyone have a pair of sunglasses? I think I need them if I go outside again."

Peels of laughter met my ears, my nieces in full-energy mode, barely visible as they ran past the entrance to the kitchen at the other end of the hallway. I kicked off my shoes—motioning for the guys to do the same—lest we get salt and ice-melt on my Mom's hardwood floors.

"The prodigal daughter returns," a male voice said, and I looked up to find my brother Ryan sauntering down the hallway, his arms open wide and wearing a button-down shirt and jeans. "Glad to see you're alive, Sis." I stepped into his hug and gave him a quick squeeze.

"One of us has to give mom and dad something to worry about. Better it be me than you, right?" I raised my brows at Ryan.

He snorted a laugh. "Most definitely." He glanced behind me and gave the guys a bro-nod, tilting his head up quickly in their direction. "What's up, I'm Ryan."

"Espen."

"Øyvin."

"And you two are...?" Ryan prodded, crossing his arms with a conspiratorial grin that had my heart fluttering in panic.

"Friends," I chimed in quickly. "These are my friends from Norway."

"Uh huh." He smiled. "Do you speak English?"

I smacked my brother in the stomach with my hand. "Shut up, yes they do."

"It's nice to meet you, Ryan," Espen piped up. "Thank you for having us over."

"Well, don't thank me. Thank Mom."

Espen smiled in response, while Øyvin was giving us all his usual silent treatment.

I pulled off my jacket and grabbed the guys' coats too, hanging them up in the already stuffed hallway closet.

"Nice tattoo," Ryan said, nodding toward my left arm. I glanced down and found my sleeve had rolled up when I'd removed my jacket.

"Don't tell Mom," I replied, quickly pushing the material back into place and hiding the lightning-shaped scars.

"Sure. How big is it?"

I shrugged, hoping he'd let it go.

"Go on, Sis, you can tell me." I fucking doubted that would be wise but he'd already seen it, so I was shit out of luck.

"Sleeve-ish," I mumbled, and Espen chuckled before trying to hide the noise with a not-so-subtle cough.

"Seriously? Damn that must've taken hours, and a lot of money that you don't have." Ryan glanced at Øyvin and Espen before continuing. "But I've heard white tattoos are the in thing nowadays in Europe. I also heard the white ink tends to change color pretty quickly though. Some even turn gray or yellow with time."

I stilled. He was rambling. Ryan only ever rambled when he was trying to deflect.

"You know a lot about tattoos all of a sudden. Do *you* have something to share, brother dearest?" I crossed my arms and started tapping my foot, giving him a challenging glare.

He paled and swallowed hard. "No."

Gotcha.

"I'll show you mine if you show me yours."

"Nothing to share." He shook his head and pushed his hand through his dark brown hair.

"On the count of three. One..." I held up a single finger, starting my visual countdown.

"Honestly, Lennie, this is how you behave in front of your boyfriends?"

"Yes. Two..."

"No, I can't."

"Why not?" I dropped my hand down, a little annoyed that he wouldn't let me finish. "I'll tell Mom about that time in college when you were supposed to—"

"Because it's on my ass," he hissed before glancing over his shoulder to make sure my parents hadn't heard him from the other room.

"What?" My eyes widened in shock.

Espen and Øyvin both stifled coughs behind me.

"I put PhD on my butt, so I could forever be a smart ass."

"You don't even have a PhD!" I yelled, raising my arms. "Were you drunk?"

He flipped me off and waltzed away, shouting toward the kitchen, "Mom, Lennie got a tattoo and brought home two Vikings."

Wonderful. Happy Holidays to me!

"Lennie, what's this about a tattoo and—" my mom rounded the corner, wiping her hands with a kitchen towel, then stilled, staring at the two fae behind me, taking in their broad stature "—oh my."

"Hi, Mom. I'm back. Kind of."

Christmas on the Fjord

52
LENNIE

I stretched my arms above my head, fingers grazing the wood headboard as a cozy warmth enveloped me from both sides. Not an ounce of sunlight streamed in through the curtains, but that wasn't surprising—sunrise in mid-December in Norway was after 8 a.m. and full daylight only lasted from nine until three in the afternoon. What *was* surprising was that I was the first one awake.

Rolling onto my side and bringing my arms back under my duvet, I stared at Espen—normally, the early riser—and watched as sleep relaxed his features, a smile still perpetually plastered across his face. His dark hair fell over one eye, giving him a childlike innocence I couldn't help but admire. No matter where we were, including here in Øyvin's bedroom, the centuries-old fae always seemed at ease.

Øyvin on the other hand... Well, the Asshole was forever slightly grumpy and testing my nerves, but I paid him back in kind by getting into trouble as often as I could. I shifted to my back and looked at the Fjord Fae on my other side. His blond hair was mussed up and his short lashes barely brushed across his cheeks, Espen's opposite in every way.

"Are you going to stare all morning?"

I startled at the question, but he didn't see it, his eyes still firmly shut. "Wasn't sure you were alive. You sleep like a log."

Øyvin opened his eyes and gave me a challenging look, those blues swallowed by the darkness of his pupils. "At least I don't thrash around like a fish caught in a net."

"Perhaps I needed saving from a bad dream?" Not true. I had a very pleasant *yoga* dream last night where they had me in all kinds of positions, one of which was a modified version of bridge pose that I was *very* interested in testing out some time soon.

"Espen can save you," he said, rolling out of bed and sauntering across the room in nothing but a pair of boxers that clung to his muscular thighs.

"Uh-huh," I muttered, bewitched by the Fjord Fae's ass. Despite his surly personality, or maybe to make up for it, Øyvin was the most attractive male I'd ever seen and it was hard to look away. "Sure."

Øyvin threw a knowing look over his shoulder before he grabbed his clothes for the day and headed to the bathroom.

Espen meanwhile, nestled up against my side, kissing me on the shoulder as he murmured, "I'll save you. Always."

My heart stuttered and I brushed my fingers through his luscious dark-brown locks. He let out a low moan and scooted even closer, his body now firmly tucked against me.

I didn't know how the three of us had fallen into such a comfortable living arrangement—residing primarily at Øyvin's since returning from Ohio, even having dinners together when they weren't working late—but, surprisingly, I didn't mind it. I'd never been one for any sort of long-term relationships, placing high value on my freedom and independence. With each passing day, these two slowly chipped away at that resolve, and while it was scary, I also kind of liked it.

Whatever this situationship currently was, it made me happy. There wasn't any loss of independence like I'd felt in relationships before in the US. Here in Norway, I didn't feel like Espen and Øyvin were tying me down to a particular lifestyle. Already, this arrangement felt so much better than my old life.

My connection to them wasn't holding me back from the things I wanted most: adventure, spontaneity, family and friends. I could have those things and more. I could do what I wanted, when I wanted to. New powers and fae-ness aside, my life now felt rife with opportunity and I wasn't going to let go of that. Especially after I'd spent the better part of my 28 years searching for it, even if I hadn't known exactly what *it* would look like.

I was ready to *live,* and these men made me feel alive.

As I prepared my morning oatmeal, throwing some chocolate chips and cinnamon on top to liven it up, Espen stepped up behind me in his police uniform and wrapped his arms around my torso. Nuzzling into my neck, he murmured, "Have I mentioned how much I like living with you?"

I couldn't help but smile at the sentiment and my body flushed from his proximity, the spoon in my hand shaking softly. That these men still affected me so easily after a month with them was both exasperating and thrilling.

"Well," I started, a teasing tone in my voice. "Do you like me less since you haven't moved in full-time?"

He chuckled against my neck, the vibrations sending goosebumps down my arms. Stepping back, he let out a deep sigh and I looked over my shoulder to see his eyes roving over my sweatshirt and leggings combo, leaving a tantalizing warmth in their wake. "There's a lot to like. Especially when you wear these." He pinched my butt.

I let out an undignified squeak and dropped the spoon into the bowl. "You mean my leggings?" I wiggled my ass, showing off the tight black material, and he pinched me again, this time a little harder, and let out a low groan.

"Yes," he replied, his voice thick and heavy. "You should wear these all the time."

"Will you pinch my butt every time I wear them?" I spun around and leaned against the kitchen counter, the cool stone biting into my lower back.

Espen looked ravenous, his pupils blown wide, a flush to his cheeks, his lips slightly wet like he'd swiped his tongue across them. "I'll want to touch your ass every single time you put those on."

I scrunched my face like I was repulsed by the prospect of his hands on my ass all the time. I wasn't. "Lighten up on the pinching and we'll be good."

"Fine." His lips quirked into a cheeky grin and he flicked his eyebrows once. "I'll save your ass from too many marks."

"That's my job," Øyvin said, striding into the room and adjusting his thick, cream knit sweater around his broad shoulders. The heated look he gave me sent tingly zings down my spine and I curled my toes. How could he have such an effect on me with one simple look?

"And you do excellent work," I teased, giving him a wink that earned me a slight twitch from the corner of his lips.

"Speaking of jobs, I need to go to mine," Espen said before leaning forward and planting a kiss on my cheek. "I'll see you two later." He bounded over to the front door and yanked on his chunky, black boots. "Don't kill each other while training."

"Training?" I straightened up and crossed my arms over my chest. What had I missed now? Had they told me about this or was this one of Øyvin's throw-her-into-the-deep-end plans? "What training?"

"He'll fill you in," Espen remarked with a quick wave and was out the door in the next instant.

I turned to Øyvin who reached into the fridge and pulled out the carton of eggs. "Care to explain?"

He set the eggs beside the stovetop and rolled up his sleeves. Leaning against the counter a few feet from me, he glanced over and gave me a lopsided grin that had my stomach flip-flopping in a bad way.

"Today you start learning how to hide your ears by yourself."

Ah, shit.

I'd been doing just fine having them help me hide them every morning before they went to work for the last few weeks. I'd tried several times already, but never successfully. Usually, I ended up creating half a mirage that lasted about three seconds and failed to hide the very top points of my ears completely.

"We have four days until Christmas," he added. "So, you have four days to learn."

"Five. We have *five* days until Christmas." Numbers might not have been my forté, but I could count to five.

He shook his head. "In Norway we celebrate Christmas on Christmas Eve. Haven't you been paying attention? Espen is super excited about it."

He wasn't wrong, but Espen was like a puppy who got excited about everything, which I liked about him. I'd been so caught up in trying to learn how to speak and read Norwegian for the last month that my focus was all over the place lately.

"Let me get this straight. You want me to learn how to hide my ears in *four* days? Why the rush?"

He nodded and cracked an egg into the pan on the stove. "Exactly. It can be your Christmas present to us. Plus, there is a caroling event downtown on Christmas Eve that Espen wants to drag us to, which would be a great time to test it out, ergo *rush*."

I groaned and rubbed my hands across my face. There were so many ways this could go wrong. But... Deep down I wanted to learn how to hide my ears by myself. It would also make the guys happy and was, as Halvar, the Fjell Fae Head Guard had once put it, *the basics* of my magic.

I hadn't tested my powers much, just little snippets here and there while the guys were home or on the weekends when we'd head up into the forest away from the village so no one would spot us and I didn't accidentally cause an incident. But even then, we'd only tinkered with the light magic that I'd previously used and avoided anything to do with the Fjell Fae powers—mostly because neither Espen nor Øyvin were Fjell Fae and didn't know what to ask me to do. Rumor had it Halvar was going to train me at some point, but the stoic fae had been busy with Fjell Council business after Queen Freija died and was going to get back to me in the new year. Until then...

I let out a long sigh, knowing I couldn't get out of this. "When do we start?"

"After breakfast. Now, hurry up and eat. We've got a lot to do."

53
LENNIE

After breakfast, I showered and pulled on warmer clothes for the chilly winter day. I swept my long blonde hair up into a ponytail so we could easily see my ears, and brushed my teeth.

I'd slowly made myself at home the last few weeks, buying a new electric toothbrush and toiletries I preferred. I was grateful Øyvin let me move in, but I wasn't naive enough to believe it wasn't in part due to his anxiety that I might reveal myself as fae if I lived anywhere but with him or Espen. With the little knowledge I had of my fae powers so far, I couldn't blame him.

During the days when I hadn't been testing out my powers, I'd been on excursions with my phone, wishing I still had my old DSLR camera. The photos were great, but not the spectacular shots I used to get with my baby that had been destroyed. Losing my camera felt like losing an extension of myself, but I couldn't afford to replace it yet.

I'd also been practicing speaking and reading Norwegian in the past few weeks, and could even say Merry Christmas (*God Jul*) now too. Thankfully, my translation magic still worked and I could understand Norwegian spoken around me, but I was getting frustrated that I couldn't respond in the language myself. Everything was different, even the extra three letters Norwegians had in their alphabet, but I was determined to master it. While the guys were at work, I downloaded apps and watched videos online to teach myself, then practiced each night with them.

I stared at myself in the mirror, studying the pointed ears I'd sported for a whole month as unease gnawed at me. As the vanilla latte, basic-of-basic level of magic, creating a mirage-thing over my new pointy ears shouldn't be too troublesome. In theory.

But, this was me, Lennie Martin. According to Øyvin, Trouble was my middle name. It was actually Louise, but that was neither here nor there.

It was time for me to start truly learning how to use my new powers, not just testing things out like a science experiment to be examined.

"So, how are we going to do this?" I asked as I waltzed into the living room, shoving any worry I felt aside. Water lapped against the hull of the boat in the bay garage, soft light reflecting off the water below the house and shining through the windows by the fireplace in the late morning. Both the piano and fireplace sat dormant, while the checkered throw pillows were neatly set on the leather sofa in the orderly fashion that Øyvin preferred in all aspects of his home. The space was cozy and lived in, but if you looked closely, everything had its place. Even the Christmas decorations. The tree twinkled in the corner beside the black, stove-top style fireplace and paper snowflakes hung in the living room window.

Øyvin stood in the middle of the living room area, pushing aside the coffee table. I helped him move it and set down the small mirror I'd brought from the bathroom, thinking I'd need it to see if the magic was working or not.

"We start simple. Focus on this one task, and avoid any and all distractions."

I pursed my lips at his words. While that wasn't an impossible task, I'd definitely have to close my eyes. The way his cream sweater hugged his shoulders and arms was distracting, especially since I knew in vivid detail what lay beneath the woven fibers.

"Trouble..."

"Yeah." I cleared my throat and straightened up as I entered the space he'd made in front of the couch, shoving aside my sexy thoughts. "I'm here and focused."

"Mm-hmm." His deadpan stare told me he knew exactly where my thoughts were focused.

"I'm serious." I set my hands on my hips, determination setting in under his doubtful gaze. "I can do this." *If I said it out loud, would that make it true? Perhaps even easier?* Worth a shot. "I can totally do this."

He stepped in front of me and flexed his fingers at his sides, like he was trying to tamper his frustration with me or stop himself from reaching forward to touch me. Honestly, with how hot and cold the emotional energy between us vacillated on any given day, either was possible.

"Focus on that well of power, the warmth that sits right here." He pointed to the spot right underneath my boobs in the middle of my chest. "Close your eyes and picture your ears the way they used to look."

"I can't say I ever paid much attention to my ears." *Seriously, who looked at their ears on a regular basis?*

He groaned, and I bit my bottom lip to stifle a laugh. Frustrating Øyvin had quickly become one of my favorite pastimes. He made it entirely too easy.

"Picture your old ears as clearly as you can. Imagine your ears without points."

"Got it." Rounded, fairly normal looking ears, with holes pierced in the lobes for earrings I hardly ever wore. "What next?"

"Now, imagine pulling that warm power up through your spine and deposit some of it at your ears."

That sounded crazy, but crazier shit had happened lately. Like traveling to Norway, accidentally photographing an illegal transfer of magic, and then becoming a demi-fae when a Fjell Fae named Nora decided to commit regicide along with her bat-shit crazy boyfriend, who also happened to be the King of the Fjord Fae.

"Can you do that?" Øyvin asked, crossing his arms and giving me a look that said he had his doubts. Nothing ignited my stubborn streak faster.

"I can do this," I repeated with more conviction as I rolled my shoulders.

He waved his hand, urging me on.

With the picture of my human ears firmly in mind, I closed my eyes, placed my hand on my left shoulder like I'd seen the guys do countless times when using their magic, and focused on the well of power that swirled within my chest. I deepened my breaths, pulling air in through my nose and out through my mouth, relaxing into the posture. Slowly and steadily I pulled tendrils of power through my torso, feeling it glide upward and brush along my spine, then my neck. I let the little lump of power settle at the back of my head, picturing it gathering there before spreading it toward my ears. My breaths grew quicker—

"Steady," Øyvin said, his voice barely a whisper.

I tilted my head from one shoulder and then over to the other, encouraging the magic to disperse evenly. A warm, tingling sensation grew where it moved and a wave of heat swept across my head and down my neck.

I cracked open one eye and peered at Øyvin. His brow furrowed as he stared intently at my ears.

"Anything?" I asked, hoping I'd nailed it on the first try.

"Almost," he replied, his gaze never straying from my head. "Keep going."

I closed my eyes again and pushed harder, pressing the warm power upward. "What about now?"

"Yes!"

My eyes flew open and heat washed down my spine, the power returning to my chest as I raised my hands in victory. *Fucking crushed it.*

Øyvin's smile dropped and his shoulders slumped.

"What?" I reached for the mirror on the coffee table and inspected my ears. Damn it! The pointed tips were still there.

"You had it for a few seconds."

"I doubt that counts as success, though."

He shook his head, and I let out an exasperated sigh.

"It might take some time to hold it for extended periods," he added. "But the more you try, the more you successfully create the mirage, the easier it should become. One day it'll be instinct and you'll barely have to think about it."

"You mean *'practice makes perfect?'*"

He nodded and crossed his arms. "Building stamina."

"I do have decent stamina." I snapped my fingers and winked, which earned me one of his signature eye rolls.

"How does this mirage thing even work? Is it like when Espen changed my clothes for the ball?" I asked, setting my hands on my hips and recalling how, in the blink of an eye, I'd gone from leggings and a sweater to the gorgeous silver-and-green dress he'd put me in.

"Yes," Øyvin replied, "but mirage may not be the best word for it."

"So, it's more like a shift those wolves did?" That snap-crackle noise their bones had made as they shifted from fae to wolves still haunted my dreams. Seriously, some things you couldn't unhear or unsee, and it was a damn shame those doggos would never vacate my memory.

"Somewhere in between," Øyvin sighed before continuing. "They're evolutionary physical mirages. Think of it like a blanket of magic covering what's truly there. Take that dress of yours. You were wearing your normal clothes underneath, but the magical layer—the dress—was wrapped over you, and the main thing you could feel and touch. It wasn't only the appearance of the clothes, like a mirage, but more tangible than that, even if it was only temporary."

That magic existed was still wild to think about, but his explanation was straightforward. I'd lifted the skirt of my dress and moved about in it as if it were on my body properly, not able to feel the casual clothes underneath. It had *felt* real. "And the ears are the same type of magic?"

Øyvin nodded. "The magic was gifted to all fae by our ancestors to help us hide when the human population started to swell. That was a very long time ago."

I had a feeling 'a long time ago' was many centuries...

"Try again," Øyvin commanded, drawing me back to the present.

I did as requested, focusing on the well of magic in my chest and pulling it up like I'd done before. Again and again and again. Each time I held it for a few seconds longer than the last, but it still wasn't good enough. I needed to hold it for hours, if not a full day, while around humans in town. I couldn't suddenly have it drop while I was at Oddvar's or visiting with Solveig. At the thought of my ears suddenly changing before them, I imagined Oddvar keeling over from a heart attack, and Solveig calling her best friends. Before I'd make it home, the whole town would know thanks to those gossips.

After a bajillion attempts and two cups of coffee for both me and Øyvin, I was ready to give up.

"One more, and then we can be done for today," Øyvin said, mirroring my frustration with my lack of progress. Clearly his patience had a limit, which was decidedly longer than I'd expected.

Clenching my teeth, I pulled the power up my spine again, letting it settle at the top of my neck before dispersing toward my ears. The telltale warmth spread from one side of my head to the other, and I pictured my human ears, willing the mirage-like magic into being.

The shift registered with me and I brushed my fingers across the rounded ends, shuddering at the sensation. Øyvin's brows rose slightly.

"Thousandth time's the charm?"

"Perhaps," Øyvin conceded with a twitch of his lips, which was generous for the grump. "But how long can you hold it?"

"You really don't think I can last long?" I asked, flicking my eyebrows once, my tone filled with challenge.

"No." He took a step closer, testing me. His voice dropped to a low timbre that skated across my skin, leaving goosebumps in its wake. "I really don't."

"Ye of little faith."

His tongue swept over his bottom lip as he stopped a mere inch in front of me, and I couldn't stop myself from tracking the movement. "Trouble by name," he said, the words twisting the muscles in my core. He leaned in, and my entire body tensed at his proximity, his breath skittering across the sensitive skin on my neck and shattering my concentration as my mind shifted to parts of me that were decidedly not my ears. "Trouble by nature."

"You don't play fair."

"Never," he replied, then pulled back, taking the delectable air with him. "But neither will Espen. You really think you can keep it together in public with him leaving little kisses on your cheek or whispering his happy, sweet words in your ear?"

Fuck. The Asshole had a point.

I glanced into the little mirror on the coffee table and, sure enough, thanks to his distraction, my ears had reverted to their pointy demi-fae state.

Øyvin reached out with his thumb and forefinger, tilting my head up so our eyes could meet. "You'll get there eventually, just not with me this morning.

I need to head below the surface." He dropped his hand and I shuddered at the loss of his touch, shaking off the heady sensation that had taken up root within me. We were always like this around each other—like a fire that ebbed and flowed from embers to bonfire and back again. It was overwhelming, but part of me didn't mind it one bit.

As he stepped toward the front door and pulled on his boots and jacket, he asked, "What are you doing with the rest of your day?"

I yanked the coffee table back into position in front of the sofa, and sauntered over to the Christmas tree we'd put up in the corner of the living room. The smell of spruce permeated the space, sending all kinds of nostalgia through me. "I'm going to finish decorating the tree," I replied, leaning down to grab the box of ornaments Espen had left for me to finish adding to the branches.

"Sounds cozy," Øyvin said, sounding more like he wanted to run in the other direction than assist, which was fair. Decorating trees wasn't for everyone, and honestly it didn't surprise me considering how grumpy and standoffish Øyvin could be. You'd never find him humming Christmas tunes, watching cheesy Hallmark movies, and donning an ugly sweater while drinking cocoa anytime soon. Espen, on the other hand...

"Espen asked me to finish adding the last of the decorations." I reached into the box of round wooden tree slices with the bark still on the edges, each with festive scenes or sayings burned into them. I pulled a few of them out and did my best to pronounce the Norwegian phrases on them. "This one says *God Jul*. This one says *Jeg Elsker Deg*." Øyvin flinched, but I continued. "And this one says something about *Juletiden*." I glanced over at Øyvin again, hoping I hadn't completely butchered the phrases—the only one I really knew well was *God Jul*. His pupils were blown wide and he looked like he'd seen a ghost.

"Is my Norwegian really that bad?" I looked back at the ornaments, trying to remember my lessons to recognize any of the words. Had I offended him? Accidentally called his grandmother ugly? Besmirched his ancestors?

He shook his head and brushed his hand across the light stubble on his chin. "It's not atrocious."

I beamed and gave myself an imaginary pat on the back. "Step in the right direction, then."

He nodded, looked at the door, and then back at me.

"You all right there? Forgetting something?" I asked, narrowing my eyes at his hesitation.

"Yeah, I'm fine." He nodded again, then grabbed the handle and sauntered out the door.

"Not even a goodbye," I chuckled to myself as I pulled more ornaments out of the box and set them down on the coffee table. Like the wooden tree slices, all of them were made of natural materials, including straw reindeer and little knitted mittens. It was cute and cheerful, and a far cry from the shiny rainbow baubles and tinsel I'd grown up with on my parent's Christmas tree.

With a contented sigh, I put some festive music on my phone and started merrily decorating our tree.

54
ØYVIN

Jeg elsker deg.

Those three words had just left Lennie's lips without a single care in the world, as if they meant nothing. From her lack of reaction, it was obvious she had no idea what she'd just said, only reading the words on the ornament, but *I* knew what they meant. I paced outside the front door of the boathouse, desperately needing to get to work, but unable to jump into the fjord, surprised by my own reaction to the simple phrase.

The sun hid behind a thick cloud cover, lending a dull glow to the street and water. While it hadn't snowed yet—and we usually didn't get snow until January and February—there'd been enough chilly days and the scent of snow in the air on several occasions, signaling winter's imminent arrival.

Christmas music started inside, Lennie singing along as some woman belted out what she *really* wanted underneath the tree.

Jeg elsker deg.

The words rang in my head, burning a hole through my defenses. She hadn't meant to say it, and I knew she didn't mean it yet. She'd made it perfectly clear she wasn't ready for "labels", and I wasn't ready to define anything either. What we had, what we were doing, clearly had all three of us happy, so there was no need to rock the boat or upend our joy. At least, not beyond what Espen had planned, which I wholly agreed with, and hoped she would, too. Not just for her own sake, but for the fae.

I shook my shoulders, trying to shake off the shock that had set in. Even in her muddled Norwegian, those twelve letters had still knocked the air out of my lungs. I vigorously brushed my hands through my hair, making a mess of it, and headed for the water, hoping a cold dip and the swim to the Fjord Fae palace would clear my racing thoughts.

Do I want her to mean those words?

Do I want to say them back?

It'd been over a century since I'd uttered those three words, and that had ended poorly. So much so, that I'd devoted myself wholly to the fjord and my career. That is... until Lennie missed her boat and brought her chaos into my life.

She has no idea.

I shook my head and dove into the fjord.

LENNIE

Training with Øyvin had left me hungry, both for food and for success in this new endeavor. After I decorated the tree, I spent the rest of my Wednesday practicing the ear magic in front of the bathroom mirror and quizzing myself on food items we had in the fridge, trying to say the names for them in Norwegian.

Thursday morning I wandered over to Oddvar's café to grab lunch with Espen before we went to the woods for a quick practice session during his break. Even though I'd been here for weeks, the sight of Skolvik was still magical, even more so as Christmas neared. Most of the buildings were white, but some had been painted a sunny yellow or traditional, Norwegian red. Residences and businesses alike had decorated for the holidays. Wreaths hung on doors and bunches of oat sheaves to feed the birds were fastened to porches with red ribbon. Some windows had a single light-up star hanging in them, while others had seven tiered candles on a wooden triangle-base lighting their windowsills. The Christmas decorations in Norway were beautiful and simple, and miles different from the inflatable Santas and light up reindeer you'd find in the US.

A cold breeze zipped across the fjord and into town, leaving the village slightly frosty. The overcast skies lent the whole place an eerie ambiance, as if we were cocooned in a chilly blanket. I'd bundled up in layers, my jacket, and my scarlet-and-gray hat. While the hat covered my ears, Espen also used his magic this morning to hide the tips.

Surprisingly, I arrived at Oddvar's before Espen. He was usually early to everything, but I didn't allow myself to worry. He was probably caught up saying hello to everyone he passed between the police station and the café. Seizing the moment alone, I strolled across the café and rested my forearm on the counter where Oddvar, the owner, stood awaiting customers, ready to ask the question I'd been thinking about for weeks.

"So, Oddvar," I tapped the counter, "any chance you have a job vacancy?"

I held my breath as I grinned, probably showing too much teeth, but since I still wasn't one hundred percent sure how I planned to work in Norway, I needed to try. While the guys didn't seem put-out to be hosting me, it would be nice to have a job to help put bread and butter on the table, and maybe save up for a new camera.

Oddvar let out a deep and long sigh, his wispy eyebrows twitching on a phantom wind, as he narrowed his eyes at me. He crossed his arms, and the material of his sweater, the color of which matched his gray hair, bunched around his elbows. "You know how to use a coffee machine?" he asked in his heavily accented and slightly mismatched English.

"Sure." Put hot water in a container, let steep, add accoutrement. Pretty simple.

He pointed to the fancy Italian espresso machine with all the shiny knobs and dials, including a milk frothing wand. "Do you know how to use *that*?"

I pursed my lips. Admittedly, he had me there. I was more of a stop at Starbies or Dunks (depending on what state I was in) kind of gal, but I could always learn. And the café seemed like the best fit for me out of all the businesses in town.

"No, but I'm sure I could find a good teacher around here," I replied, giving him an obnoxiously obvious wink followed by my brightest smile. The same smile I'd used with my mother any time I got in trouble growing up. "And I make a mean sandwich."

He huffed through his nose like a bull, the corners of his mouth remaining in a straight line. "I will think about it." He turned his back on me and started washing something in the sink.

Taking his words as a dismissal, I turned back to the room, refusing to abandon hope. It wasn't an outright no.

Espen still wasn't here, so I sat at one of the vacant tables and perused the little menu that I'd already memorized.

"Sorry I'm late," Espen said as he planted a kiss on my cheek a few minutes later, a chilly breeze following him in through the door. "Neighboring police station called and had some questions."

My smile faltered and a lump grew in my throat, thinking back on all of the drama that had happened earlier this fall. "Is everything all right?"

"Absolutely perfect. They just wanted to review some logistics to prep for next year's tourist season." He briefly glanced over his shoulder to the counter, and my nerves eased. "Have you ordered yet?"

I shook my head.

"How about a quick sandwich here and then coffee to-go?"

"Sounds perfect. Goat cheese with jam, please." I'd become addicted to the brown-colored goat cheese, caramelized whey tasting both sweet and salty at the same time. Paired with some nice bread and a dollop of strawberry jam, the simple dish was heaven for the tastebuds. For some reason, it reminded me of peanut butter and jelly sandwiches.

"Whatever you want, Lennie." Espen smiled.

Now, that was one of my favorite sentences.

After we'd finished our lunch, we grabbed our to-go coffee and sauntered up the hillside toward Espen's little cabin. He still lived here, but it was significantly smaller than Øyvin's boathouse, so it had become more of a little getaway space for us. Most nights Espen joined us at Øyvin's, unless he was working a late shift and didn't want to wake us up. How we'd fallen into such an easy living situation, I wasn't quite sure. But it likely had something to do with their protective instincts... and as I was still jobless, I wasn't going to say no to free rent. Not in this economy.

The area near the cabin was a grassy field with tufts of bushes and random boulders that looked like a Norse god had errantly chucked onto the landscape like salt crystals. The forest at our backs was still green thanks to the plethora of evergreens, but a few spindly and bare trunks dotted the treeline. I clutched my coffee cup to my chest, relishing in the warmth seeping into my hands and the steam brushing across my chin. The temperature had dropped overnight, and I'd overheard rumblings at the café that snow was on the way. Just the thought of seeing the village blanketed in a layer of snow had me giddy with excitement. Paired with this picturesque scenery of the mountains rising high around the edges of the fjord, Skolvik was bound to look like a snowglobe.

"This seems like a good spot to practice," Espen said, bursting my thought bubble. He bent down to set his coffee cup on a wooden table outside his cabin. Each of the four stools surrounding it were stumps and the table itself was the center beam of a larger log, befitting the Forest Fae.

I let out an exasperated sigh and took a swig of my coffee for moral support, needing more caffeine in my system. Using the magical energy wasn't physically draining, at least not to the extent that *I* was using the magic, but training with the guys was mentally exhausting.

"You ready?" Espen asked, rolling his shoulders like he was about to spar with me in a ring.

I set my coffee beside his and pulled off my hat, tucking it away in my jacket pocket. "Could I interest you in a quick *yoga* session instead?" It was part-joke, part-serious, refusing to admit nervous energy was eating away at my stomach with each failed attempt. I only had a few days left to master this skill if Espen's Christmas Eve plans were to be fulfilled, and I didn't want to let him down.

Espen flicked his thick brows, eyes roving over my body and leaving a heated trail behind. "Tempting, tempting, but we need to do this. The sooner you learn how to shield your ears, the better."

I huffed, but couldn't disagree.

He stepped forward and placed his hand on my left shoulder, dropping the mirage he'd magicked over my ears this morning before he left for work. "Now, stand over there"—he pointed to the field where we'd once done some very enjoyable *yoga* underneath the night sky and aurora borealis—"and let's use yesterday's lesson with Øyvin as a starting point."

I let out a deep breath and wandered into the field before turning on my heel to face him.

He nodded for me to proceed, watching me closely like I was a student or one of his Forest Fae soldiers.

I closed my eyes and focused on the mental picture I'd conjured up of my human ears like Øyvin had instructed yesterday. Pulling on the energy in my sternum, I placed my hand on my shoulder and dragged a piece of it up toward my ears, imagining it curling up my spine and depositing it at my ears.

"Well done," Espen exclaimed, and I fluttered my eyes open.

He was beaming, and the sight made my heart pitter-patter.

"Now, let's see how long you can hold it for." My stomach sank at his words, but he was right. I needed to be able to hold the magical mirage for hours on end without giving it much thought. "Ask me a question."

"How long did it take you to learn how to do this?" I asked, waving my hand at my head.

He leaned back against the table edge and crossed his ankles. "To hold it consistently? A couple of years. To hold it for a few hours at a time?" He tilted his head from one side to the other. "Maybe a few weeks."

I shifted on my feet and shoved my hands in my jacket pockets, hiding them from the cold air. "How old were you then?"

He took a deep breath and wiped his hand across his forehead, pushing aside his dark floppy hair. "About five years old."

I groaned. Yeah, this really was the basic of basics in the magic fae world.

"Don't worry," he said. "You'll get there quickly. I don't doubt it for a second. And look, you've been able to hold it while we've been talking without any flickering."

My ears did indeed still feel a little warmer than usual—maybe only by a degree or two, but it was noticeable. I took another deep breath and let it out through my mouth, watching as it fogged in the cool air.

"Keep asking me questions. Let's see if you can hold it until I have to go back to work."

"You mean keep distracting myself?"

He nodded.

I brushed an errant hair away from my face. "What do you normally do during the festive season? Do you stay in Skolvik or...?"

A soft, happy look crossed Espen's face and his amber eyes warmed. "It depends. Sometimes I take the Christmas shifts so my colleagues can enjoy the festivities with their families, and other times I head north to visit my sisters and my nieces and nephew."

"What was your original plan for this year? Before I showed up?"

He tilted his head and assessed me, before pushing off the table and taking a few steps closer. "I was going up north to see them."

My heart stuttered and my eyes widened, guilt seeping in. "I took you away from your family?"

Espen shook his head gently. "It's all right. I *want* to be here with you. I've had countless Christmasses with them and will have hundreds more. I'll video call them. Ingrid and Turi have already scheduled a time."

My shoulders dropped and I let out a small sigh of relief. If there was one thing in this world that I could classify as the most important thing in my life, it would be my family. No matter how far removed I was from them, I'd be lost without them—even my Mom and her incessant worry for me and interest in getting me married off. Part of me was a little sad that I was missing Christmas with them—the food, hanging up all the lights with Dad, and watching my nieces tear into their presents early in the morning while the rest of us adults chugged coffee to wake up. The other part of me was excited to experience my first Norwegian Christmas and make new traditions, new memories.

Espen took a few steps closer, his smile never faltering, and my heart did that weird fluttering thing it had been doing lately. I continuously ignored it whenever I was in his or Øyvin's presence, even if it had been happening more often over the last few weeks.

"Well, I'm glad I'll get to spend the day with—"

"Night," he interjected. "We celebrate on Christmas Eve."

"Night, right." I mumbled as he took another step closer, like a predator homing in on his prey. A pleasant shudder ran through me, but I shook it off. "I'm glad I'll get to spend the *night* with you."

A sly grin spread on his lips and my mind drifted to *other* nighttime activities, warmth drifting down and settling low in my abdomen. *Perhaps I should get Espen a Kama Sutra book for Christmas. Win, win.*

Espen's eyes dipped from mine and landed on my chest. He swept his tongue across his bottom lip before his gaze leisurely drifted back up to mine. He took a few steps closer, bringing us almost toe to toe.

"What?" I asked, my voice more breathy than I'd intended as I studied his expression.

He looked down and back up again, his eyes turning molten, and I glanced down.

For fuck's sake.

"How long?" I asked with a shake of my head, peering back up at Espen.

His grin turned wicked.

"How long have my tits been out, Espen?" Because sure enough, at some point during our conversation I must have accidentally magicked myself half-naked thanks to my R-rated wandering mind. My jeans were still on, but from my shoulders down to my hips, I appeared stark naked. Thankfully, it was a weak mirage and I actually had my jacket on so I wasn't cold or nipping hardcore. But, still...

Espen let out a throaty chuckle and leaned in. "Not too long." He trailed his fingers up both of my arms, leaving goosebumps in his wake. "Did you get distracted?"

"Maybe." Yes. Definitely. 100 percent. Dammit.

He tucked a lock of my hair behind my ear and dipped his head, brushing his lips across my cheek, then down my neck. "If I didn't have to go back to work," he whispered, sending tingles down my spine as his words caressed my skin.

"What would you do?"

He swallowed hard and let out an audible groan. "I'd treat these with the care and attention they deserve."

I tilted my head, breathing in his smell of moss and leather. He rested his hands on my shoulders, then slowly swept them down—

Beep, beep, beep.

He let out a dissatisfied grunt and stepped back, pulling his phone out of his jacket pocket. "Duty calls."

An annoyed sound escaped from my throat as I shook off the heady sensation coursing through my veins.

He turned off his phone alarm and sauntered back to the table, picking up our coffees. "Well, this has been good progress. You held your ears there for roughly twenty minutes. I dare say, if you focus, you may be able to hold it for a couple of hours when we go to the caroling festivities on Christmas Eve."

He handed me my drink, and I took a sip of the coffee and straightened up. *I could definitely do that.* I just needed not to think about getting naked, or the guys getting naked, or *yoga*.

Espen sauntered back down the hillside toward the woods that separated his cabin from the village.

"Ummm, Espen."

"Yeees?" He turned and gave me a sly grin.

"Are you forgetting something?" I motioned to my boobs which were still on display.

He took a sip of his drink and tilted his head. "I don't think so."

"Espen Solbakke..."

"Okay, okay, okay." He traipsed back up to me and placed his hand on my shoulder. A moment later my nudity mirage was gone, replaced by the clothes I was actually wearing. He turned and took two steps before he said over his shoulder, "You should try that trick again later, though."

I narrowed my eyes at him. "Only if you're a good boy and eat your veggies at dinner."

"I'm always a good boy." He winked and gave me his signature sunny grin.

I chuckled and swatted his ass. Together we walked back into the village—him breaking off to head back to the police station, and me back to the boathouse to continue practicing.

56

LENNIE

Tonight was the night: Little Christmas Eve, as they called it in Norway. The day before Christmas Eve, which I couldn't help thinking of as Christmas Eve Eve.

After my training session with Espen yesterday lunchtime, I'd spent the rest of the afternoon and this morning practicing holding the ear mirage at the boathouse in front of a mirror. Slowly but surely, I'd increased my total time. The guys had encouraged me to get my time above an hour and, so far, I'd been able to hit that, but not longer.

Tonight, the guys set a new challenge—Espen would drop his magic over my ears, then I would need to pull it back in place and walk through town without anyone noticing. The guys would meet me back at home.

Nervous energy threatened to distract my shaky hold on my magic since I still hadn't quite mastered using it, but it was nearly midnight. The only thing wending its way through the village was a cold breeze that nipped at my nose and cheeks, so, if I failed, the odds of me running into a human were pretty slim.

My breath fogged in the air as I tightened the scarf around my neck and removed my scarlet-and-gray hat, stuffing it into my jacket pocket. The fjord lapped gently against the rocks beside us on the north side of town, near the path that led to Solveig's house. Diffused moonlight shone down on the landscape, painting everything in a soft glow, and all of the plant life was fully entrenched in its winter slumber.

Espen set his hands on my shoulders and turned me to face him. "Are you ready?"

"You tell me, Coach."

Øyvin snorted as he watched our exchange with his arms crossed.

"You're going to do great." Espen swept his arms down my own, my jacket rustling from his touch. He placed my hands in his before adding, "I know you can do this. I believe in you."

I couldn't help the pitter-patter of my heart at the sentiment, hearing the warmth in his words. If this were a romantic comedy movie, this would be when I swooned and hearts would flutter around me like butterflies. But, instead I was in Norway, about to test run my newly acquired magic in a public space for the first time.

"I commend your positivity," I replied, squeezing his hands, wanting to believe him.

"Just don't fuck up," Øyvin added with a shit-eating grin that I wanted to wipe off his face.

Yeah, that look triggered some of the Martin Family competitiveness, and, knowing him, he'd said it for that exact purpose. "Is that a challenge, Asshole?"

Espen stepped between us, blocking my view of the Fjord Fae and his now surly expression. "I'll drop the current mirage and we'll leave you here. Ready?"

I nodded and straightened up, determination overtaking the last of my nerves. It was go-time.

Espen placed his palm against my left shoulder and let out a long, steady breath before removing his hand. A tiny wave of warmth swept over the sides of my head, and I instinctively reached up, feeling the sensitive points. *Still so bizarre.* I'd probably never get over the fact that I'd been born human, but was now part fae, too. Thanks, Halvar.

Espen planted a swift kiss to my cheek, before he headed into town. Øyvin playfully pinched my ass as he sauntered past with a smirk. He clearly didn't believe I could do this, but damn did that spur me on to prove him wrong.

With the two of them strolling into the village and out of sight, I was alone. Just me, the cool wind, a frosty smell, and my very fae features.

I shook off any lingering doubts and paced in a quick circle, focusing my thoughts and energy. I could do this. I'd done it for the last few days, and it was magic that was easily used by all the fae—an evolutionary tactic they'd been using for centuries to stay hidden among the humans. If all of the fae before me could do it, then dammit, so could I, even if I was a brand new demi-fae.

I took a deep breath and placed my right hand on my left shoulder, right above the end of the lightning-shaped scar that ran up the entirety of my arm—the one that had been left behind when Halvar transferred magic into me as Queen Freija died.

Closing my eyes, I focused on picturing my ears as they'd once been; rounded, human, normal. With the image firmly in mind, I pulled at the well of power within me, dragging it up my neck and leaving some at my ears. Warmth tingled under my skin, the tell-tale sign I was doing it. I was actually doing it. *I can do this!*

I shimmied with excitement, thoughts of how I'd make Øyvin repay me for his snarky comments later tonight filling my head. A wash of warmth swept down me, like the magic was whooshing back into place but missed its mark and hit my toes. I leaned over and glanced into the fjord to my right, checking my appearance on the water's surface, and brushed my fingers across my ears. Still pointy. Damn. Then I peered down.

"Shit."

From my collarbones down to my pinky toes, I was as naked as the day I was born. Or at least, it looked that way. I knew it was just a strong, physical mirage, but no one else would know that. If I stumbled across someone, they'd see me ready for the Polar Bear Plunge in my birthday suit.

I scuttled behind a nearby (thankfully empty) trashcan, ducking down to curl my body over itself before any late night walkers spotted me. I could triage this situation. Unfortunately, my magic hadn't ever stayed in place long enough for me to practice undoing it, so I had no idea what to do. Fuck me sideways, why was nothing ever easy?

Assuming undoing magic was the same as engaging it, I let my mind dial in on the clothes I'd been wearing—was technically *still* wearing beneath my accidental exposure—and closed my eyes. Feeling the warmth of my power in my sternum swirling around, I drew on some and tried to pull it across my body, like drawing the blinds shut or pulling a blanket over myself. My skin tingled and the wind nipped at my cheeks, but I held my concentration until I estimated enough time had passed. Opening my eyes to the fog of my own breath, I peeked down and...

I was still butt naked.

Fantastic.

The guys were going to laugh themselves to death when I walked through the door looking like this. I could picture it now, Espen curled up on the floor gasping for breath, while Øyvin leaned against the kitchen counter trying to hide his laughs behind his hand.

Brushing my free hand across my other arm, I shuddered at the weird sensation of feeling skin against skin, my mind battling with the conflicting senses. No goosebumps formed and my arm hairs didn't stand on end in the cold December air since I technically still had my jacket and pants on, but it *felt* like my skin to my touch. And yet, everything was visible, from my tits and bits, to the gnarly lightning-shaped scar that ran the length of my left arm. *Can't I go five minutes without landing myself in a chaotic situation?*

I looked around, wondering what else I could do. There was a wooden bench to my left, a metal bicycle rack on the other side of the path, and a signboard a few paces away with notices about tomorrow night's caroling event plastered all over it. Lights were off in the few light-colored buildings that marked the start of town, the small shops having closed for the day hours ago. There wasn't anything to save me.

I was going to have to streak.

With a sigh, I straightened up from my hiding spot and ran.

57
LENNIE

My arms pumped at my sides and my legs moved faster than ever before as I bolted into the downtown core of the village. The clouds hung heavy in the fjord, the smell of imminent snow lingered in the air, and almost all the houses and storefronts had turned their lights off as we closed in on midnight. I was a veritable Cinderella. Only, in my case, I'd lost a whole lot more than a shoe.

I wound around the corner, past the large, twinkling town Christmas tree, and sprinted into the village square by the harbor front. Strings of lights surrounded the cobble-stoned area, wreaths of greenery hung on lampposts lending a faint smell of pine to the air, and a band-stand was half-erected beside the obnoxiously large evergreen. If I had a spare moment to admire it all, I would, but as it were...

The lights suddenly turned off at Fisken, the local restaurant that looked out onto the square and harbor. The front door swung open and I immediately ducked behind a large, boxlike cement planter with a skinny tree in the middle. Crouching and panting heavily, I watched as Solveig and her two friends, Jorunn and Dagny—the old ladies I'd volunteered with to clean up after the landslides this past autumn—stepped out of the establishment arm-in-arm. Their broad smiles and bubbling laughter had my stomach sinking to my toes. Shit. Had they seen me?

Solveig did a stutter step between her friends, which had them teetering and sent them into further fits of giggles. I relaxed my shoulders and bit my lip, unable to fight the grin though. The three friends were tipsy, chattering away in Norwegian. Thankfully, the magic trick that Nora had pulled on me earlier this year still worked, so I understood everything they said.

"Watch out for the lamppost," Solveig snickered, shifting her white-haired friend out of the way at the last second. Dagny bowed her head to the street light in apology, then grabbed the hem of her long puffer-jacket and curtseyed.

"We shall have to dance another time. The aquavit has given me two left feet," she muttered to the lamppost, then spun to her friends with a wobble. "I wouldn't mind a dance with that Øyvin, though. So handsome. So dreamy."

I scoffed a laugh that came out a little louder than expected. All three of them whipped their heads in my direction and I ducked, hoping they hadn't spotted me. My heart pounded against my ribs and my hands started to feel clammy. *Shit, shit, shit, shit, shit.* I was going to end up naked at the police station where all of Espen's colleagues would see me, including his boss. I would be the talk of the town... *again.*

"Did you see that?" one of them said.

A loud hiccup echoed through the empty town square. "I saw you drink your weight in aquavit, that's what I saw."

"Are you sure your bifocals are working, dear?"

"My eyesight is perfectly fine, Solveig. Perhaps it was a *nisse.*"

I frowned, trying to remember the story Espen had told me last week. *Nisse* were elf-like creatures from Norwegian folktales that lived on farms and helped take care of the animals. On Christmas Eve the farmers would set out a rice pudding called *grøt*, which he'd described to be like oatmeal with cinnamon and sugar on it, plus a small square of butter. Did the tipsy trio really believe in *nisse*? Or maybe, just maybe, the tales about *nisse* were really stories about the fae who took care of the environment, including the animals?

"It *is* almost Christmas Eve, perhaps a *nisse* wandered down from the Langholm farm for a swim?" Solveig said.

Another hiccup. "I could do with a swim right about now."

"Oh no, you don't." Scuffeling and grunting sounded, and I peeked around the corner to watch them yank their friend away from the harbor. I mean, I couldn't blame her for wanting a dip after drinking aquavit—that stuff was pure fire—but it *was* the middle of December and the fjord was freezing cold. Unfortunately, I knew this firsthand since I'd taken an unscheduled plunge last week after asking Øyvin to pull the stick out of his ass.

I stayed hunched over, leaning against the cement planter, and waited for their chatter to die off as they sauntered home through the village. After several minutes of silence and no other sightings of humans, I rose and ran.

My lungs heaved, and I cursed myself for this unplanned cardio, especially in the middle of the night. Why, of all the times I'd tried to use my magic, did it decide that *now* was the right time for it to work properly and stay firmly in place? *Figures.*

Skolvik at night glowed under the dim beams of its street lights in a blur of festive reds, whites, and greens as I streaked through town. Reaching a turn in the road, I leaned against the building beside me and peered around the corner to make sure the coast was clear. The street was empty, the glow from storefronts' night lights the only thing in the roadway. A skittering noise sounded back the way I'd come from, but I didn't see anyone. *Probably just a cat.* With a deep breath, I pushed off the wall and bolted up the main street, hoping none of the stores had security cameras—and, if they did, that I was fast enough to be considered a ghost.

I pushed one foot in front of the other, my breaths sawing in and out of my lungs, cold air nipping at my face. Two short blocks to go and I would be on the road toward Øyvin's house with minimal street lamps and enough darkness to hide my nu—

An arm reached out from the side street to my left, and yanked me aside. It all happened so fast I didn't have time to scream or yelp or piss my invisible pants.

I grappled with my captor, but was spun around and landed with a *thud* against the wood wall of the white building. My assailant lightly pressed their forearm against my collarbone, both of my wrists ensnared and held above my head.

I glanced up into a pair of blue eyes full of glee.

"Hello, Trouble."

58

LENNIE

Before I could thrash out of his hold, Øyvin removed his forearm from my collarbone and tilted my chin up with his finger and thumb. He gave me a smug lopsided grin and swept his tongue across his bottom lip as he surveyed my state of undress.

"I had a feeling things would take a turn," he said, a large dollop of victory lacing his tone. "You have an uncanny ability to land yourself in troublesome situations."

"Good thing my middle name is Trouble, then, isn't it?" I goaded him, wholly unwilling to address the elephant in the room, so to speak. *Tatas who? Never heard of them.*

He stepped forward and pressed his body into mine as he squeezed my wrists pinned above my head, a reminder of who was in control. I sucked in a breath and swallowed hard, the tension between us pulsing. My nerve-endings sparked from the streaking adrenaline, plus having Øyvin so near, and my head filled with the lusty haze that always seeped in whenever he stood this close to me.

Øyvin's gaze dipped to my mouth and his palm rested on the side of my neck as he brushed his thumb across my bottom lip. It took every ounce of self-control I had to not press my tongue to the tip.

He shifted, his muscles taught, jaw tight as he gave me more of his weight. Every time we were alone together I wanted to push his buttons, see how grumbly he could *really* get, and then climb him like a tree. It was that never-ending fire again—flitting from inferno one minute to soft embers the next.

Before I lost all sense of composure, I cleared my throat. "Where's Espen? Has he been hiding along the route back to the boathouse waiting to jump scare me, too?" He definitely wouldn't do that; Espen was too kind, but I wouldn't put it past him to take up position and watch the events unfold.

"He had faith in your ability." Øyvin let out a mocking snort.

I scowled. "And you didn't?"

"I most certainly did not."

"Ye of little faith."

"I trust that you'll get into trouble whenever an opportunity presents itself." He pushed his hips into mine, and I returned the favor rolling my lower abdomen across him, heat spiraling up through me. His length pressed against me, and my breaths came harder, my core reacting to him. Needing him. *So much for that composure.*

"Espen's at home?" My words came out breathy and wanton, a clear signal that my head was taking a nap and my hormones were now in the driver's seat.

"He's waiting there ready to give you your reward."

"A reward?" I asked, wiggling my hands to signal I needed him to release them from where he had them pinned above my head or I'd lose all feeling in them.

He immediately dropped my wrists, but shifted his free hand to my hip and continued holding me firmly in place. "You shouldn't get anything for this disaster of a test." He tilted his head back toward the part of town I'd just run through.

"What? You don't think successfully streaking through the village deserves a reward?"

He let out an exasperated groan and, before I could make a move, pulled us away from the wall and hoisted me over his broad shoulder, my butt pointing toward the sky.

"You most definitely do *not* deserve a *reward.*"

I squeezed my thighs together, but was pretty sure I was now more exposed than ever. "But you're going to give me one anyway?"

That earned me a smack to the ass.

"You're not even going to fix my nudity?" I asked.

"I don't mind the consequences of your actions," he grumbled. "In fact, I prefer you like this."

"At your mercy?"

"Exactly."

Øyvin set me down outside the boathouse's front door and pushed it open, corralling me through.

"How'd you do?" Espen asked as we strolled inside, the lingering smell of linen and pine making it feel homey here. Since Øyvin hadn't bothered to help me with my state of undress, Espen's eyes bugged out when he spotted me in my birthday suit. "What happened?"

I placed my hands on my hips and beamed victoriously, done attempting to cover up. "I successfully streaked across the village." Focus on the positives, right? I could practically *feel* Øyvin's eye roll behind me as he pulled off his boots and set them neatly on the shoe rack by the door. "I'm here to collect my reward."

Yeah, I was pushing it, but don't blame a girl for trying.

"She thinks she deserves a reward for failure," Øyvin huffed as he sauntered past me into the kitchen. He leaned against the clean and tidy kitchen counter, a partially amused look spread across his face.

"Failure is in the eye of the beholder," I retorted, tipping my chin up.

Espen chuckled and drew my attention as he slowly stepped closer. His gaze roved over me from my toes to the tips of my ears, heat flaring in his eyes.

"Did anyone see you?" he asked, briefly looking toward Øyvin before turning his focus to me.

I shook my head. The only person that had spotted me was in the room with us and not a threat. Well, at least not to *us*. I'd seen what Øyvin could do on the battlefield—hell, I'd even witnessed him try to drown people on the spot—but I doubted he'd ever pull any of those tactics on me... unless I tried commandeering his boat again.

Espen stepped in front of me, eyes brimming with heat. Before I could utter anything, he placed his hand on my left shoulder and I felt the magic shift through me, removing the naked mirage. My clothes were back where they belonged and where they'd been hiding underneath the magic.

A slow smile swept across Espen's face and I squirmed under his heady stare. "You want a reward?"

I nodded and shifted my weight to one side, popping my hip.

His smile grew bigger and my pulse started humming faster. "Well then. We'll have to play a game and see if you win."

That stubborn competitive switch turned on in my brain once more. "A game?" I asked, my voice sounding all coy.

Espen brushed his hand across his beard and winked. "A game."

"What are the rules?"

"We make the rules," Øyvin said from the kitchen, and the low tone of his voice sent a shiver down my spine that landed at my core.

A look passed between the two fae before Espen turned back to me and beamed. I got the feeling I'd be both winning and losing this game. "Go on then, what's round one?"

Espen grabbed hold of the zipper on my jacket and stared into my eyes. I swallowed hard as he spoke. "Did you run past Fjordland Gullsmed?"

The silversmith-slash-jewelry-store was one of the first buildings I'd passed on my mad naked dash, but it was closed, like all the other stores in the village. I nodded.

He yanked down my zipper and I let out a guffaw as he pushed my jacket off my shoulders and arms before throwing it over the back of the sofa.

"They have a security camera on the corner of the shop," he said, and my stomach sank. *Shit.* I'd hoped that the locals didn't have heightened security on their buildings, but I should have guessed a jeweler might secure his wares. The store owner was going to have a nice video of my tits and bits on his camera footage.

"Did you run past the toy store?"

I scoffed. Of course I had, it was two doors—*Oh no.* My breath hitched as it dawned on me. Another camera. Espen's lip twitched. "They have a camera, too?" I asked.

He nodded and grabbed the hem of my sweater, then unceremoniously pulled it up and over my head before throwing it aside.

Øyvin snickered, and I gave him the middle finger. I could think of worse games than strip whatever-this-was, even if I was about to lose terribly. Maybe winning would come after I was naked?

"How about the library?"

I sighed. "Yes, I ran past *biblioteket*," I said, trying out the word I'd recently learned in Norwegian. I'd probably butchered it, but now was not the time for lessons—at least not that kind. "Let me guess. They have a handy-dandy camera, too?"

Espen nodded again and then tackled the long-sleeved t-shirt under my sweater. As soon as that landed beside the kitchen table, he leaned in and swept one hand around my back. Before I could ascertain what he was doing, the clasp on my bra sprung free and it fell down my arms. I shook it off and cast it aside, wholly impressed by his skill.

I arched a brow as I stared up into Espen's amber eyes that had gone molten at the sight of me half-dressed in the middle of the living room. "They have two cameras?"

"Mm-hmm."

This was torture. I wanted to lean in and return the favor, but as I lifted my hands to do just that, Espen tutted and gently tapped them away. "Hands down. No touching."

I clenched my fists and rolled my shoulders as heat swirled in my core, my nipples hardening in the cool air.

"Get on with it," Øyvin grumbled and I chanced a look at him. The blue in his eyes had darkened and his knuckles were white where he gripped the counter behind him. He was as tortured as I was. Good.

Espen knelt down and started unlacing my shoes.

"What are those for?" I asked, wondering what other cameras I'd accidentally mooned tonight.

"Speed," he practically choked out and I was glad I wasn't the only one overwhelmed by the heady tension in the room. My nerves tingled in anticipation, and it took every ounce of effort I had to maintain any sense of composure, let alone ability to keep my hands off him. When he finished with the laces, he helped me out of my shoes, then immediately unbuttoned and pulled down the zipper on my jeans.

"Hey!"

Espen grinned and peered up at me through his lashes, and I almost melted from that one look alone. Achingly slowly, he brushed his hands up my calves, thighs, and stopped at my hips right at the waist of my pants. I sucked in a breath and waited for his next move, desperate to rake my hands through that floppy hair of his, to hold him to the spot that desperately wanted attention.

"Did you run past the Christmas tree by the harbor?"

"She did," Øyvin grumbled before I could confirm that I had indeed run through the town square by the waterfront.

Cold air bit at me as Espen yanked down my jeans and underwear in one swift move. I let out a whimper, my core needing this to move along quicker, my desire to have this man inside me unfurling through every limb. "Are there security cameras to guard the tree?"

Espen let out a throaty chuckle and rose to his feet, skimming his hands up my thighs, waist, then sides as he stood. "No." His reply came out on a shuddered breath. "There's a web-cam that live streams the harbor to the town website."

Fuck me.

"Why did you even have me try the ears thing and walk through town knowing there were so many cameras?" I reached for Espen's chest, but he grabbed my wrists and held them in the space between us.

"It's one thing to explain away the ears as a *nisse* costume. It's a whole other thing to explain public nudity," he said.

"What if someone spotted Øyvin carrying me home?" I challenged.

"*She had too much aquavit and lost her clothes*," Øyvin said, pretending to give a hypothetical excuse to some poor witness.

Okay, that was a viable explanation considering the potency of the beverage and the effect it had on me, aside from making me feel like a fire breathing dragon.

"We may have to increase her magic lessons," Øyvin said as he sauntered over, opening and closing his fists. "If she's to master the basics—"

"Oh, I agree," Espen interjected, narrowing his eyes at me, and my stomach flip-flopped at the rolling tone in his voice. "But will she be a good student?"

"Unlikely," Øyvin muttered, his finger tracing across my pointed ear and down the side of my neck.

I squirmed, my heart hammering in my chest as a desperate desire for both of them took over. "Teach me a lesson, then."

Espen dropped to his knees and Øyvin came up behind me.

Not holding back, Espen didn't tease me anymore, grabbing my thigh and lifting it to his shoulder as he swept his tongue over my center, while Øyvin pushed my hair aside and kissed up the side of my neck. Unable to restrain myself any longer, I plunged my fingers into Espen's hair and held him where I needed him. He obliged by grazing his teeth across my sensitive clit and sent shocks of pleasure through me.

Øyvin swept his hands across my front and palmed one breast in each hand, gently kneading them. The pull and pressure from him was enough to have me panting already, moaning for more.

I lifted my arms and entwined my hands behind Øyvin's neck, pressing my breasts more firmly into his palms. He teased and tugged at my nipples until they hardened, sending bliss through my veins. The feel of his hands sweeping across my skin had me writhing against his body, his cock pressing against my rear.

I gasped as Espen pressed a finger to my opening, drawing lazy circles around my entrance. My knees buckled and Øyvin wrapped a muscled arm around my middle, holding me upright. As Espen pushed his finger inside me, I let out an agonized moan, my head falling back against Øyvin's chest from the waves of pleasure.

I wasn't going to last much longer at this rate. They knew every button to press, every part of me that was currently walking a tightrope awaiting the crash into oblivion. They were the puppet masters and I was theirs to wield—and damn, did I love it.

Espen picked up the pace, adding a second finger to his ministrations and I let out an undignified noise. A second later, with Øyvin's lips on my neck and Espen's tongue swirling around my clit, I shattered.

My breaths came in shuddered pants, my entire body convulsing through the bliss. A pleasurable feeling I never wanted to end.

Espen shot up to his feet and pressed his lips to mine, and I tasted myself on him. Øyvin didn't back away, leaving me sandwiched between the two fae, heat and hedonism filling the air around us.

"Well, that was..." I couldn't even finish the sentence. Words and breath evaded me.

Øyvin wrapped his arms around my middle while Espen swiped his thumb across my mouth. "Let's take this upstairs," Espen murmured, tilting my head so our eyes met. The passion and need in his eyes sent another tingling sensation down my legs and I was glad Øyvin still held me upright.

"Yes, please," I responded, my voice barely a whisper.

"I love it when you're polite," Øyvin mocked, his smile pressing against my shoulder.

"Do more of that and I'll not only be polite, I'll start begging."

"Perfect."

59

LENNIE

Øyvin deposited me on his bed, the white sheets soft and cool beneath my heated body. "Lie down," he murmured, and I did as requested, my eyes never drifting from his. He reached behind his head and, in one swift move, pulled off his cream-knit sweater, leaving his torso bare. Out of the corner of my eye, I caught Espen doing the same, dropping his shirt on the floorboards.

Before I could say anything, Øyvin wrapped his hands around my thighs and pulled me to the edge of the bed, lining me up perfectly with the seam of his jeans. Meanwhile, Espen climbed up on the bed beside me, kneeling near my head.

Øyvin unzipped his jeans and pulled out his cock, the length hard and ready. My heart raced as a condom packet flew over me and landed at the edge of the bed. Øyvin nodded to Espen, and I looked back to find the Forest Fae returning the nod. Somehow the two of them were on the same wavelength and, with my toes curling and core already dripping in anticipation, I wanted in on whatever they were planning to do to me, as soon as possible.

Øyvin rolled on the condom and notched himself at my entrance. Slowly, inch by teasing inch, he entered me. My breath caught as I squirmed with each tiny push, wanting and needing more, even as my core spasmed around him.

Once he'd fully settled inside me, Espen bent over me and took one of my nipples in his mouth, cupping my other breast with his warm hand. The feel of his tongue drawing circles around my peaked nipple had me losing all sense of composure, and I let out a throaty moan.

That was enough to get Øyvin moving, pulsing in and out of me in languid strokes. Together, the two of them worshiped my body. Espen explored every inch of my breasts with both his hands and his lips, while Øyvin worked me into a frenzy with each slow and unforgiving thrust. It didn't take long before my breaths shuddered and I gripped Espen's hair in both hands, holding onto him as my orgasm rocked through me, shattering every nerve ending in my body.

When I finally regained my breath, I mumbled, "Lesson learned," with a satisfied smile gracing my lips.

Both men chuckled, and the sound sent an eerie chill through my spine.

"Oh, Trouble," Øyvin said, pulling out and slamming back into me, my tender core clamping down around him once more. "We're just getting started."

Fuck.

60
LENNIE

The next morning, I'd just finished wrapping the guys' presents when a knock sounded at the bedroom door.

"All clear to enter?" Espen asked from the tiny hallway.

I frantically dove off the side of the bed and shoved the wrapped gifts under it, hiding them from view. "Come on in."

Espen opened the door and stuck his head around the corner, his dark-brown hair brushing across his forehead as I righted myself, sitting back on the bed. "Wow, you made a mess."

I scoffed and looked around at the parchment-style wrapping paper, some spools of red ribbon, and a single roll of green wrapping paper that I could only assume Espen had bought because it had trees on it. He wasn't entirely wrong about the mess, but this was tame compared to Martin Family Christmases, where my parents' bedroom was turned into 'Santa's workshop' for a day, and, one by one, we'd all take turns wrapping our gifts for one another. As the youngest, I was usually last and, by the time I got in there, it looked like drunken elves had run amok with sticky-bows, ribbon, and wrapping paper of all different colors.

This chaos was much more subdued.

"Did you need something?" I asked, nudging aside the parchment paper and watching it fall off the mattress with a thunk.

"I had an idea," Espen said, stepping into the room and closing the door behind him. His dark-green knit sweater hugged his shoulders and, for a split second, I wished he was wearing gray sweatpants instead of black jeans.

"What kind of idea?"

"Hiding your ears. I may have a different method that might be easier to conceptualize and hold for a longer period of time."

"Okay." I drew the word out hesitantly. "Proceed."

"We keep having you start your magic transition by touching your shoulder."

I nodded. "Yeah, because that's what you and all the other fae I've seen shift their appearance do."

"Right. But you don't *have* to do that."

"What?" I furrowed my brow as I crossed my arms, trying to follow his logic.

"We do that because that's how we were trained when we were little. Think of it as an ingrained motion or habit." He stepped across the room and sat down beside me, the bed shifting slightly under his weight. "You don't *have* to do that exact motion. In fact, to help you hold the mirage for longer, I want you to use a more specific movement."

My lips pursed, still not fully understanding what he wanted me to do instead.

"Instead of touching your shoulders, I want you to touch your earlobes when you try to shift the magic over your ears." He reached up and brushed his own thumbs and forefingers across his earlobes. "By doing that, you can focus or picture the magic going down your arms and directly into your ears instead of up and down your spine."

My mouth shifted into an *oh* expression. "I see where you're going with this. You want me to direct my magic away from my core to avoid any accidents of it 'falling' and taking my clothes with it."

He nodded. "That's a good way of thinking about it, yes. You want to give it a try?"

I mean, there was only one way to find out if it would work better than the shoulder method—not that said method hadn't been successful, but it hadn't been faultless either.

I shifted on the bed to face him, pulling my legs up underneath me.

"You have to want it," Espen coached, looking as hopeful as a puppy begging for a treat. "Truly focus on that image of human ears and *want* them to stay that way. Command the magic to stay there until you order it to relinquish its hold."

I took a deep breath and shut my eyes, shaking my arms at my sides in an attempt to get them and myself to relax and focus. "Think of it as putting on a hat," he added. "Keep the hat on until the end of the day."

"Or like earmuffs," I said, clenching my eyes shut and thinking about a set of fuzzy, pink earmuffs.

"Exactly."

Why hadn't I thought of this sooner? This was a much easier concept to grasp.

I closed my eyes and let my mind zero in on that thought, picturing my ears how they used to be as best as I could. With that image firmly in mind, I placed my hands on my earlobes and started pulling a tiny bit of my power from that well in my sternum, shifting it up my arms and onto my head as if I was putting on a pair of earmuffs I'd had as a child.

The heat tingled but settled nicely around my ears, warming them slightly.

"Well done," Espen said, and I opened my eyes to find him beaming at me.

"Now let's see how long I can hold it."

He patted my knee. "Come downstairs, fill in your immigration paperwork, and help me finish decorating the tree. Øyvin is working on tomorrow's dinner."

"Paperwork?" I knew I had adult shit to take care of, but in the past few days, that had completely slipped from my mind.

Espen nodded. "Yeah... uh. We need to have a conversation."

I followed Espen downstairs and he took a seat at the circular dining table, a stack of paper piled in front of him, while Øyvin chopped something at the kitchen counter.

"Are you ready to fill in your immigration documents?" Espen asked, a more serious tone in his voice and his usual smile missing.

"How bad can it be?" I countered, hoping this wouldn't take days or be too complex. I wanted to stay in the country, but also knew that immigration was a complicated matter. One that, in typical Lennie Martin fashion, I hadn't thought too much about when deciding to move here. "What do I need to do?"

The chopping stopped, and Espen straightened.

"Here's the thing." He patted the seat beside him and I took it, my stomach sinking lower and lower at the guys' hesitant expressions and actions. "You have two options really."

Øyvin coughed.

"Okay, you have one main option, but I want you to have a choice," Espen amended. My heart beat faster and I crossed my arms to steady myself, braced for whatever he was about to say. "Option one: you are a self-employed photographer that can prove an income of a certain, albeit quite significant, amount."

"Not an option," Øyvin grumbled from the kitchen counter, his back still turned to us, but clearly part of the conversation.

"Why is it not an option?" I challenged. It seemed quite reasonable to me. I mean, setting up a business wasn't easy and photography barely paid, but I could do family portraits and the like. The fact that my camera had been destroyed was certainly a problem I'd need to remedy in order to make it happen, but Øyvin's flat-out refusal to admit it was a possibility irked me.

Espen sighed and brushed his palm across his forehead, pushing his dark locks aside. "It's more of a challenge because the income level you have to prove is extremely high. If you don't meet it, you'll be forced to leave the country on very short notice."

I winced. Yeah, that didn't sound ideal. I'd hate to start feeling comfortable here only for the rug to be pulled out from underneath me. "What's option two?"

Øyvin set down his knife and turned, resting his lower back against the kitchen counter and crossing his arms. His eyes bore into mine and I shifted, clasping my hands together in my lap.

"What's option two, Espen?" I asked again, uneasiness settling in as I looked at the abnormally quiet and subdued Forest Fae.

"Option two is marriage."

I blinked twice.

My heart skipped three beats.

Did he just? No, I'm hallucinating. Too much sex would probably do that to a woman. Shattered nerve-endings and all that.

I glanced at Øyvin who didn't betray any emotion aside from his usual stoic grumpiness, then turned back to Espen and swallowed hard.

"Marriage?" I asked, my voice thick with a variety of emotions.

The word sounded foreign on my lips. I understood the *concept*, having watched two of my brothers tie the knot. But me?

Married?

I'd told my mother for years not to hold out hope and to quit asking when I'd be bringing a boy home for Thanksgiving. Then, this Autumn I'd brought home *two*, and they weren't exactly humans. Not that she knew that, but both her and Dad had liked them and thought they were very nice gentlemen. Everyone refrained from commenting on the fact that there were two though, which I appreciated considering we hadn't defined the relationship yet.

I wasn't ready, not then and not now.

Even after over a month together, I wasn't sure what *this* was entirely, other than that it made me happy. And that's what life was about right? Living in a way that made you happy and didn't cause harm to others.

Espen nodded slowly and scooted closer, taking my clammy hands in his as I looked back at him, eyes bugging like I'd seen a ghost. "Option two would see you marry me," he explained, his tone cool and calm in a way to encourage me to trust him. "I'd sponsor you as I have a human job that meets the income levels required by the Norwegian government. In order to make it legal, we'd have to have the signing or celebration within six months of approval."

Six months?

Six months from now it'd be June, and I still wouldn't have known these two an entire year. That seemed both outlandish, but also a little on-brand for me. Spontaneity was the name of the game.

I looked to Øyvin, who stood stock still, his gaze locked on me. "And you're okay with this arrangement?" I asked, not wanting him to feel left out. Was I even contemplating this?

"This is the only option that keeps you here long term, and I want you here," Øyvin replied, shoving his hands into the front pockets of his jeans that hung deliciously low on his hips. "However much trouble you cause."

A sharp, single syllable laugh escaped me, because, well, facts. Trouble seemed to find me 24/7. But my head and heart didn't miss those important four words in the middle. The stubborn and grumpy Fjord Fae had gone from hating my guts, to tolerating me, to wanting me here. I could pretend it was only to protect the fae secret, but his eyes betrayed a deeper emotion—one that sent warmth from the tips of my fingers to the ends of my toes. However much I annoyed the grouch—whether from purposefully putting things away in the wrong kitchen cabinet, or challenging him on the virtues of Beethoven—he cared about me, and I liked it.

"Øyvin suggested we hide you beneath the surface of the fjord," Espen continued, drawing my gaze away from the heat in Øyvin's. "But seeing as we don't know the full extent of your powers, but *do* know those powers came from the fjell and not the fjord, that didn't seem like a viable option. Plus, I'd like to follow the rules and give you an option to reject our proposal."

I stilled, because that's what this moment really was: a proposal. For immigration purposes, but it was still a proposal.

Did I want to marry him, though?

I'd be 29 this spring, which seemed an acceptable age to marry in my book. By Ohio standards that was practically ancient. In their eyes I was well on my way to spinster status and should've had three kids, a house, a poodle-mix, and a minivan with stick-figure family stickers on the back window announcing to the world how much procreating I'd done by now.

But I didn't live in Ohio anymore, nor did I want to return.

"If we do this"—I stood from my chair and rested my hands on the back, letting my eyes drift between the two of them—"I want it to be because we're trying to have me stay. I want this because it's for the safety of the fae secret and to help me better understand what the extent of my demi-fae powers are. If we decide this"—I waved my hand between the three of us, panic seizing me as I avoided the words *marriage* and *husband* like the plague—"whatever this is, isn't working even after we tie the knot, then I'm free to go."

That was the one thing I never wanted to give up: my own freedom. I'd been an independent person for so long. Doing what I wanted whenever I wanted to, and I enjoyed that lifestyle—the life I'd built for myself. But, then again, change wasn't always a bad thing.

I'd been through a literal and physical life change recently, one that would see my years extended for an unknown amount of time. Perhaps being a demi-fae could have me changing my preconceived plans? Maybe it already had?

"You will always be free to do whatever you want, Lennie," Espen said and Øyvin nodded in agreement. "We won't hold you here against your will."

"This doesn't mean we're *actually* defining the relationship," I said. A statement, not a question. "Only on paper."

I wasn't quite ready to make labels. It had only been a month or so. And while we'd decided not to sleep around or entertain anyone else, I didn't want to dive in head first; I wanted to slowly dip my toes and be happy, taking the days as they came.

"This is to keep you here legally." Espen nodded. "Nothing will change between us."

"Safer," Øyvin added. "You're right, it will keep you close to the fjell while we find out the extent of your powers and can keep you safe."

I bit my lip, refraining from remarking on his comment that 'I was right' which sounded like heaven to my ears. Instead, I took a deep breath and set my hands on my hips, trying to slow the galloping of my heart.

I was happy here.

I was building a new life for myself.

I had new powers that needed honing and protecting, and a local environment that needed that magic to help it thrive.

And I had two guys who cared about me. It was an unconventional situationship, but I liked what we had and if I didn't care about them, I wouldn't be here.

Fuck it. Fake marriage here I come.

"I'll go with option two, then."

Øyvin smirked, while Espen beamed and let out a massive sigh of relief, his head falling back briefly like he'd been holding his breath. Then he shifted out of his seat and got down on one knee. I sucked in a breath, my eyes widening at the sight.

"Lennie Martin of the humans and Fjell Fae, will you do me the honor of becoming my wife for immigration purposes, fae purposes, and for the sake of really good *yoga*?"

I snorted, but my lips curled into a smile. One couldn't not be happy around Espen.

"Espen Solbakke..." I paused and let him sweat a bit. "Yes."

Espen launched from his feet, picked me up and spun me around. Setting me back down, he planted a firm and passionate kiss against my lips that promised a celebratory *yoga* session. Before I lost my breath, he pulled back, grasped my shoulders and steered me to the mountain of documents on the kitchen table.

"Now, Ms. Martin who has been able to keep her ear magic up this entire conversation," he said, beaming from ear to ear. "Time to start signing these."

He landed a soft peck on my cheek, and my heart roared in triumph at holding the mirage the entire time, especially considering the distracting conversation, thoughts, and Espen's kisses. I didn't mind his little kisses, even when he did them in public. It was like he couldn't help himself, and just the thought of someone feeling that way about me, had my heart warming to temperatures I'd never felt before.

With the two fae watching on, I signed the paperwork.

ESPEN

She'd said yes.

My heart almost beat out of my chest when I'd suggested the idea of marriage knowing full well her feelings on *definitions*. But it was the only way to safely keep her in the country and close to Skolvik where we could help her and monitor her magic. As the first ever documented demi-fae, she was precious cargo.

Ultimately, she could always decide to go back to America. Even Halvar had given her that option this autumn. But if she chose to return to Ohio, we couldn't be there to help her should something go amok, which was bound to happen considering her proclivity for troublesome situations.

But, she'd said yes.

I stood in the kitchen after lunch with Lennie and Øyvin, helping with the prep-work for tonight's Christmas Eve dinner. Chopping away at the red cabbage, I couldn't stop myself from humming a happy little tune.

She'd said yes.

And I wasn't excluding Øyvin from this. He'd even agreed to it, without any counter-arguments or hesitation. Since the Norwegian government didn't have records of him, it had to be me. They *did* have me on record, albeit slightly modified to avoid any questions about my age, as I was employed by the local Police. Since I was a legal resident in human eyes, when Lennie eventually signed the marriage license, she could stay here legally and we could continue this thing the three of us had together.

She'd said yes, and I continued humming Christmas songs all afternoon, daydreaming about introducing her to my older sisters.

62
LENNIE

Bundled up to protect against the chilly weather—but sans hat so we could test my ability to keep my ears hidden—we sauntered into the village and headed toward the town square by the harbor I'd streaked through the night prior. Unlike last night, the entire esplanade was cordoned off tonight. Small tables were scattered around the space, covered in red and white tablecloths and booths lined the square, each one strung with twinkly lights. More people than I'd ever seen in Skolvik milled about under the night sky in their warmest jackets, crowding the sidewalks. The majority of folks had also donned red Santa hats with red tassels at the end, instead of white pom-poms that you'd see back in the US.

The smell of cocoa, pine, and a hint of smoke wafted through the air as we wandered past different booths, making our way toward the shimmering Christmas tree by the water where a small band was set up. The first booth we passed had men handing out flaming torches to adults and older children. I eyed the torches hesitantly, glancing around at the amount of wool people were wearing. Compared to the four-inch candles I was used to from Christmas Eve service in the US, this was a wild concept. It didn't escape my notice that neither of the guys offered me a torch, and I couldn't blame them—Trouble was my nickname, after all.

The scent of sugar and butter drew my attention to the second booth, eyeing the piles of several different types of cookies, none of which I recognized.

"Seven Types," Espen said, noting the platters and making a beeline for the table draped in red.

"What?" I asked, following and bumping into him as he came to a stop. Øyvin was thankfully paying more attention than me and didn't make this a sandwich situation by coming to a halt a few steps behind me. Ever since we'd reached the crowded street, he'd been on high alert, quietly peering over the masses, taking a few peeks at my ears, too. Probably making sure they hadn't accidentally turned pointy again.

"It's a Norwegian tradition," Espen said, drawing my focus back to the cookies that smelled so sweet, my mouth watered. "You make seven different varieties of cookies for Christmas."

"Only seven?" Don't get me wrong, that was a lot of cookies, but I'd grown up in a household with three older brothers who'd devoured anything and everything they could. Mom was constantly baking cookies over the holidays to accommodate our appetite for the sweet treats.

"Well, that's the thing." Espen perused the selection on the table that Solveig and her friends, Jorunn and Dagny, were manning. "There are no specifics around which seven to bake. So, each family has their own recipes and picks."

"And which is your favorite?" I asked, scoping out the platters on display, each with a little card at the front listing the name of the baked good.

Espen pointed to a golden, diamond-shaped one with crumbly bits of something on top. "Syrup snaps." The little sign beneath them said *Sirupsnipper*. Not that I knew how to pronounce the word, but the part of my brain that cared about the Forest Fae decided to commit that little nugget to memory.

"How about yours, Øyvin? What's your poison?"

"Too soon," Espen muttered as Øyvin replied, "Chocolate."

I bit my lip at the slip up, but appreciated Øyvin's choice. I too loved any cookies with chocolate in them.

"Good evening, Solveig. May we have one of each to take home for dessert?" Espen asked the older woman. She was wearing a festive Norwegian knit sweater beneath her open jacket and a white-and-green nordic hat that knitters around the world would want to emulate.

"Merry Christmas," she replied in accented English, giving us her brightest smile as her eyes crinkled at the corners. "One of each coming right up." She grabbed a bag and tongs, and set to work. Her and Espen traded the bag for some cash after which she motioned for me to come closer and briefly ducked beneath the table, coming back up with a neatly wrapped gift.

She smiled at me and held out the parcel. "A little something for your first Norwegian Christmas."

My heart lodged in my throat as I accepted the present, remembering the woman's kindness when I'd first arrived in town.

"Go ahead, open it. It may come in handy," she said, and her little old lady friends, Jorunn and Dagny joined her, having finished up helping other customers. They both motioned to go ahead, their eyes wide with excitement, wool headbands pulled down over their ears and wispy white hair.

With trembling hands I gently pulled apart the paper, careful not to accidentally litter. My fingers brushed across a soft material and my breath caught for a beat. Inside was the most beautiful pair of mittens I'd ever seen. White with an eight-pronged, red snowflake and the ends knitted into a point. The craftsmanship was immaculate.

"Thank you so much," I said, pulling them on and my hands instantly warmed. "They're gorgeous."

Solveig grinned, joy radiating off the kind woman. "You're welcome. I'm glad you like them."

Emotions clogged in my chest as I stared at the heartfelt gift, unsure what to say to express my gratitude for everything she'd done for me.

"Did you knit them yourself?" Øyvin asked, breaking the silence.

"I did indeed." Solveig nodded, before pointing to her friend, Dagny. "It's her pattern, but my handiwork."

"Very nice," Øyvin said, giving them all a congenial smile.

Espen agreed and with another thank you from me, we set off to see the rest of the town's festive setup.

As we stepped away from the white-haired trio, a blushing Dagny glanced over her shoulder and gave Øyvin a little finger-wave. To which he responded with a simple raised hand, and I bit my cheeks to stifle a laugh. I mean, don't get me wrong, I understood the appeal, and I couldn't blame her for trying to shoot her shot. But if she knew he was actually a fae... In fact, if she ever found out that Øyvin was more than a man, she might have a heart attack and die. So, it was probably best to leave her wanting and unknowing.

We meandered further into the throngs of people and Espen aimed for Fisken. On the street that ran beside the restaurant and up toward the main road through town, a couple of horse drawn carriages (in this case, sleighs with wheels put on them) with deer pelts covering the seats sat awaiting customers. The light beige horses whinnied and stomped their feet, their short and stick-straight white and black manes rustling.

"Norwegian Fjord Horses," Espen said, his warm breath tickling my neck as he leaned in close. "The breed has been around for eons, used by Vikings, too."

I scuttled closer to him and whispered back, "You mean they're older than Halvar?"

Espen snorted. "Not those horses in particular, but the breed? Most likely."

"You've known how old he is this whole time? I've been wondering—"

"No, no," he cut me off and pulled back, his eyes widened. "I have no idea how old Halvar is. I dare say, the only one who knows how old Halvar is, is the man himself."

Fair enough. The quest to figure out the ancient Fjell Fae's age continued. My current guestimate was somewhere in the 800s, but I could be wrong... Either way, I needed to find out what the guy's skincare routine was, because *damn*.

Two buildings down from the local restaurant, I spotted my favorite old curmudgeon serving up hot drinks at his stand and aimed in his direction.

Oddvar was busy and not one for small-talk, so we grabbed a hot chocolate each and a massive gingerbread heart—*pepperkakehjerte*—with a stiff, swirly, iced sugar pattern piped onto it. The cookie was the size of my head, but tasted delicious and made a snapping noise when I took a bite.

While paying, Oddvar passed Espen an envelope and then glanced over at me. "Merry Christmas," he said with a curt nod. I replied swiftly with a "*God Jul*" having noticed the way Oddvar's lips had moved meant he hadn't spoken English. He nodded again and set back to work, assisting customers as they ordered their own hot chocolate and gingerbread hearts.

"Come on," Espen said with a pep in his step, his eyes wide with excitement. "The singing is about to start."

We joined the gathering masses as they crowded around the large evergreen, a bright white-colored star glowing atop it, and a little band started to play. The predominantly brass instruments sent echoing sounds around the harbor and the crowd began to sing, instantly recognizing the Norwegian song.

"And Christmas with the joyous and desire..."

Standing between my two guys, I winced and hunched my shoulders, refraining from being rude even though I wanted to clap my hands over my ears.

I'd finally found a fault with Nora's magic trickery that translated Norwegian for my brain.

Mass singing was a problem. A few of the words made orderly sense, but most of it sounded like jumbled words sprinkled with Norwegian. I cringed, wishing there was an on-off switch for it, but there wasn't. At least not one I knew of. I was doomed to listen to mismatched wording and an out of tune chorus.

Øyvin narrowed his eyes at me, then widened them and gave me a lopsided grin.

"Don't even."

"Don't what?" he pried, wiping his hand over his mouth and chin as if that would mask his glee.

"Enjoy this too much."

"*We are so happy, so happy,*" the carolers continued, grinning from ear to ear. "*We are clapping, are clapping.*" A second later, half the crowd—those most actively singing—spun in a circle, curtseyed, and bowed. My eyes bugged at the sight, wondering how a caroling event could turn into a flash mob with flaming torches, all dancing in unison. Had Oddvar slipped something into the cocoa?

"Is Skolvik secretly a cult?" I asked, turning to Espen who was bobbing and clapping in time to the band.

He grinned and gave me a joking wink. "Only us *folk*. Do you not have songs like this back in America?"

I shook my head, staring out over the gathering while finishing off my gingerbread cookie with one large final bite. "Not quite like this."

Sure we had caroling events—often at churches or choral groups at theaters—but nothing similar. I was pretty certain this display of jubilation and tradition was what many of the Christmas markets around the world tried to achieve, but ultimately felt more like commercial cash-grabs with mulled wine that tasted like dog piss. Boiling wine really was an affront to the grapes—they didn't deserve that.

Espen bumped his shoulder against mine, glancing over with a smile that swiftly turned to a look of panic. "Your ears," he mouthed, his eyes wide as he quickly blocked my view of the stage.

Shit. Terror lanced through me, putting me on high alert, the cocoa shaking in my clutches.

Espen reached out his hand, aiming for my shoulder.

Øyvin grabbed his wrist from behind me and tossed it aside with a low growl. "Do it yourself," he bit out quietly, the words meant only for me. "Fix it."

Espen's worried gaze sent a shudder of fear through me. We were in public, in a huge crowd, and anyone could turn around right now or deviate their attention away from the carols and spot me and my fae ears.

A stuttered breath left my lips, panic taking over.

I couldn't expose the fae secret only a few months into becoming one myself. Halvar would kill me and then bury me somewhere deep within the mountain, probably in the tombs where they interred their dead. But I wouldn't get some fancy shrine-come-coffin with an effigy atop it like Queen Freija. No, no. I'd be deposited there in a nondescript stony box marked with: *Here lies the tourist-turned-demi-fae who betrayed our secret to an entire village of humans. On Christmas Eve, no less. Twenty-eight years old. Constant troublemaker. RIP.*

I shook off the maudlin thought and refocused. There was no use dwelling on that right now when I could still rectify the situation. I could do this. Espen nodded as if he could hear my thoughts, and Øyvin pressed his thumb and forefinger against my lower back providing an ounce of support.

I could totally do this. I just needed to focus and pull that magic swiftly up to my ears again.

I tugged lightly on my left earlobe, willing the power in my sternum to return to its spot, all while closing my eyes and picturing my non-pointy ears. The telltale warm energy swirled up my scarred arm, brushing through each prong of the lightning-shaped mark, and settled at my ear. I imagined it moving across to the other ear too, the warmth slowly following my request. I was putting on my magical earmuffs and it needed to stay there.

"Well done," Øyvin grumbled lightly behind me, rubbing a circle over my spine with his fingers before stepping back.

I opened my eyes to find Espen brushing his palm over his short beard and swallowing hard. "You did it. Now please keep it there or you'll give me an aneurysm." He stepped back beside me, exposing me to the crowd once more instead of blocking their view. Only a few people were peering in our direction, including Dagny, but they all swiftly looked back at the stage when I caught them.

Crisis averted.

A few songs later a woman with short white hair, wearing a long gray wool coat and authority that silenced the entire crowd, stepped onto a little platform in front of the tree. Thankfully, now that the singing had stopped, my Norwegian translation magic reverted back to its normal self, and I could understand what the woman was saying.

"Merry Christmas, Merry Christmas, and thank you all for being here this evening. On behalf of the mayor and—"

"That's my boss," Espen leaned down and whispered in my ear. "At least you didn't flash *her* with your ears."

I let out a single snort laugh. So, this was the chief of police. Part of me wanted to say hello, the more rational part knew not to go near the woman with my track record. In fact, it was probably best if I was never invited to any of Espen's work gatherings unless it was his fae job.

She continued her speech, wrapping up swiftly with more *God Jul*'s and reminders to grab cookies and goodies from the different stands. I was glad Espen had thought to grab some before the caroling began; with how many people were gathered here, there was about to be a post-singing rush on the cookie stands. I couldn't blame them. The treats looked delicious and I couldn't wait to try them later.

"You did it!" Espen exclaimed, fitting his hand in mine and swinging them through the cool night air as we sauntered along the deserted road just outside the village back to Øyvin's for dinner. "Not without hiccup, but you held the ear magic for ninety percent of the time!"

I shimmied my shoulders with joy and glanced back at Øyvin. "See, I'm not always a troublesome failure."

"Debatable," he huffed.

"You know what," I doubled down. "I think this deserves a reward." I wiggled my brows at Espen, hoping he'd get the hint.

"Dinner and presents first, then we can discuss any further rewards." He squeezed my hand and spun me in a circle as I let out a trill of laughter.

"I can work with that," I said, just as something landed on the tip of my nose. I stopped in my tracks and brushed my finger across it. Pulling my hand away from my face, I found a tiny snowflake clinging to the fibers of my new gloves. "It's—" I looked up and more flakes fell lightly across my cheeks. "It's snowing."

Espen chuckled and brushed his hand over his beard, taking in the whimsical scene unfolding around us, while Øyvin stepped up beside me, emitting a contented rumble from his chest.

"Snow for Christmas. It's been threatening frosty showers for weeks," Espen said, turning back toward the village behind us. "Look, Lennie."

Øyvin and I both spun around, and I sucked in a sharp breath.

We stood at the perfect spot on the road to capture Skolvik's beauty. Snowflakes fell gently across the town, dusting everything from the dark inky waters of the harbor, where boats bobbed and the lights from town shimmered across the ripples, to the Christmas tree and storefronts that sparkled under the glow of decorations.

The entire place looked like a snowglobe, and the magical scene took my breath away.

63
LENNIE

Logs popped and crackled in the stove fireplace, white lights flickered from the tree like fairies were hidden within the boughs, and the smell of a hearty home-cooked meal permeated the entire living room and kitchen, giving the boathouse a decidedly Christmassy feel.

Espen and I set the table when we got back from town, including little sprigs of fir and tealight candles in small glass votives dotted around the circular surface. Meanwhile, Øyvin carved the pork he'd roasted and completed the final preparations to his masterpiece—a meal, he'd mentioned, that was one of his favorites to cook. Dinner consisted of golden fingerling potatoes, pork belly with a crackling top, carrots, red cabbage, and a lingonberry jam that I wanted to smother over everything, including Espen.

Between trying everything and then sneaking one of Espen's favorite cookies—the *sirupsnippe* snapping then melting on my tongue—I was stuffed.

After helping wash dishes and put away leftovers, I practically rolled myself into the living room area. Curling up on the sofa, I tucked my feet beneath me and pulled one of the checkered throw pillows into my lap.

"Ready for some presents?" Espen asked, shoving an all-red santa hat onto his head.

"Ready!" I beamed, happy to see him happy, but still a little weirded out about opening presents on Christmas Eve. The Martin Family kids had been getting up to open presents at 7:00 a.m. on the dot for years, even when we were in high school and college. It had become a family tradition with all six of us in the living room, opening gifts together. By the time we were done, it always looked like a Hallmark store had exploded inside with wrapping paper and sparkly stick-on bows everywhere, the latter usually stuck all over Dad's head. That had shifted quite significantly post-college, but ever since my nieces were born, we were up early again, the adults chugging coffee to stay awake.

Espen leaned over and gave me a small satchel that fit in my palm.

"Is this from you?" I asked, shaking it lightly then tilting my head when a waft of something I couldn't quite name, but smelled herbaceous, drifted past my nose.

He shook his head. "That's from Heidi."

In that case...

I held the little pouch from the Forest Fae Healer further away from myself and lightly pulled at the drawstrings to open it. Nothing immediately jumped out, so I leaned in and pinched the fragment of parchment sticking out of the top. Unfurling the tiny piece of what looked like ancient papyrus, I read aloud the scrawling script, "For pleasure."

I scrunched my brow as I set aside the cryptic note. Reaching into the bag again, I pulled out a sachet of herbs and leaves and hell only knew what. It almost looked like a *ye olde poultice* that I'd seen on *Outlander*. "What the hell kind of tea bag is this?" I asked, holding it away from me, just in case the Forest Fae healer had decided to play a prank on me. I wouldn't put it past her as payback for the number of times I'd tried to bring coffee into her house in the forest.

Øyvin tilted his head and narrowed his eyes, but didn't move from where he perched on the piano bench, the sleeves of his navy sweater rolled up, exposing his forearms. Espen reached for the oversized gauzy tea bag and I handed it over for him to inspect. Lifting it to his nose, he took two short sniffs before a slow and steady smile grew on his lips.

"Not certain, but from what I can smell, this will make you feel all kinds of tingly and happy." He chuckled and handed it back.

"You mean it's weed?" I took a sniff. It didn't smell like weed. It smelled a hell of a lot nicer, but also earthy and somehow spicy, too. Green even, if green could be considered a smell. I placed the herb pouch back into the little gift bag and tightened the strings again before setting it on the coffee table.

"It's not marijuana, but it'll certainly make you feel good," Espen remarked, rolling his bottom lip between his teeth. "What did that note say: *for pleasure*?"

My stomach dropped and I looked between the two guys, eyes wide. "Holy shit! Is that for better orgasms?"

Øyvin snorted, but his eyes heated as they roved over me. Meanwhile Espen snickered, before giving in to a full-on belly laugh.

I chuckled, my cheeks hurting from smiling so much today. "Okay, don't laugh too hard." I jabbed my elbow into Espen's side. "You'll both be happy if that has me moaning your names in under two seconds."

They both stilled, and the air in the room heated—or maybe it was my body warming under their heady stares.

"You already moan our names in a few seconds," Øyvin said, leaning his elbows on his thighs, looking ready to launch himself at me to test the theory.

Goosebumps skittered across my arms under his intense gaze. Yeah, I wouldn't mind taking things upstairs once we were done here.

"Before we try this out," Espen said, clearing his throat in the process. "This is from Oddvar." He pulled an envelope from his back pocket and handed it over.

I made a surprised noise, opened the envelope, and unfolded the piece of paper only to find that the letter was unreadable. "It's all in Norwegian," I said, furrowing my brow and attempting to read the first line, but failing spectacularly as my Norwegian comprehension wasn't that advanced.

"Let me see," Øyvin said, his hand outstretched.

I passed the letter to him for translation.

"Dear Lennie, I have taken your request under consideration,"—Øyvin scrunched his brow, and I realized I'd forgotten to tell them about my brief chat with the café owner—"and, while I feel you have much to learn, I wouldn't mind your assistance at the café this summer for the tourist season. Part-time. We start training in May. Merry Christmas, Oddvar."

My eyes widened and I looked between the two fae in slight bewilderment. *Had I just been offered a job?* My mouth hung open like a goldfish as I tried to come to terms with the contents of the letter. *Had that actually worked? Holy shit!*

I had to learn how to use the fancy Italian espresso machine. Would probably need to watch some videos online to learn how to use all the gadgets and gizmos... then learn all the names for all the different things in the coffee shop *in Norwegian.* I rose to my feet, clutching one of the throw pillows to my chest as realization dawned on me.

I had to basically be somewhat fluent in Norwegian... in five months. All oxygen left my body. Why hadn't I thought of that before asking Oddvar about the job? "I need to learn Norwegian as fast as human-fae possible."

Someone tugged on my arm and I glanced down to find Espen staring up at me, his smile encouraging. "It'll be all right. We'll help you, won't we, Øyvin?"

I looked to Øyvin who peered up at me, his head tilted slightly to one side like he was preparing a challenging remark. But he shook his head, keeping whatever snark he'd planned to himself, and grunted, "Sure."

"Wonderful." Espen beamed and gently pulled me back onto the sofa where I settled in closer to him, curling up with my feet touching his thighs. "Now, onto the next presents."

If there was ever a time for Espen's quick subject pivoting tendencies, this was it. I didn't want to think too hard about the mess I'd inadvertently put myself in. Instead, I wanted to focus on enjoying my first Christmas Eve in Norway. My first festive season with these guys.

Our gift exchange continued and I opened a Norwegian wool sweater from the guys. It was white with a frosty-blue pattern across the top in the shape of snowflakes, and I couldn't wait to wear it.

I gave them both wooly hats, each with an obnoxiously large pom-pom on the top. I knew Espen would appreciate it, but Øyvin... Well, I just really wanted to see how much the thing irked him and if he'd actually wear it. Was he the kind of guy who would wear something once to be polite and then shove it into the back of a drawer to be forgotten about, or would he continue wearing it regardless?

"Try it on," I motioned to Øyvin who stared at the pom-pom with a flat smile. Espen meanwhile was already bobbing his head back and forth, the hat secure on his head and a grin plastered across his face. "Go on. I bet it'll bring out your eyes."

He gave me a deadpan stare, let out a deep sigh, and pulled the hat over his head. Tufts of blond hair stuck out the sides and a little across his forehead. "Happy?" he asked, his lips in a firm line but his eyes warmed as he looked over at me.

I clapped my hands together and brought them to my lips. "Ecstatic."

His mouth quivered into a miniscule lopsided grin, like he couldn't quite stop himself, and that alone made my heart beat a fraction faster.

"Well, that's it for presents," Espen exclaimed, shifting to face me on the sofa, and I broke my gaze from Øyvin's.

I peered across the little living room toward the tree. "What about that? Who's that one for?" I asked, nodding to the box wrapped in blue paper with silvery snowflakes on it. It was the only present remaining, shining like a beacon from beneath the twinkling tree in the corner.

"That's for tomorrow," Øyvin said as he pulled off his hat, stood, and offered me his hand. "Do you think you can wait that long?"

"Depends." I took his hand and rose from the sofa. "You two have any other festive activities you want to partake in this evening?"

Espen flicked his brows as Øyvin replied, "I'm sure we can think of a few."

64

LENNIE

"So," I started, stretching in my seat at the kitchen table, feeling sufficiently full from the leftovers we'd devoured for breakfast along with eggs. "What's the plan for today?" Normally, back in the US, after breakfast and presents we'd go on a walk in a park or watch movies with hot cocoa. "Please tell me there's no more caroling. Don't get me wrong, that was fun and a new experience for me, but I don't think my ears can handle translating more Norwegian singing."

Espen chuckled and planted a kiss on my forehead as he grabbed our plates and loaded them into the dishwasher. "How about the presents from us?"

"But you already gave me the sweater," I said, my voice a little wobbly as I hadn't got them two presents. The hats were it from me.

"This is your main gift from us," Øyvin replied. "The sweater was your Norwegian Christmas Eve present."

"What are you talking about?" I asked, rising from my seat and moving toward the Christmas tree, eyeing the last present we hadn't unwrapped last night. "That one?"

"Take a seat," Espen said, and I acquiesced without complaint, curling up on the sofa. Øyvin strolled over and took up his same spot from last night on the piano bench, his shirt sleeves rolled up to reveal his forearms. The sight, in itself, was a present. "First, this one." Espen plucked a tiny green velvet pouch that I hadn't noticed last night from one of the branches. He handed me the bag and plopped down beside me, the leather sofa sinking with his weight.

"Is this another gift from Heidi?" I asked, holding it at a safe distance just in case. Don't get me wrong, the 'tea' she'd gifted had been great—ten out of ten, would recommend. But I still didn't wholly trust the woman.

Espen shook his head. "This is from us, but isn't necessarily for Christmas."

Bringing the pouch closer, I scrunched my brows and untied the gold drawstring. *What on earth is this?*

I upended the bag over my palm. Something small and decidedly ring-shaped fell out, landing gently in my cupped hand. I swallowed around a lump that took up residence in my throat and eyed the piece as my heart rate picked up speed.

Holy shit.

"I-I..." I stuttered, unable to get the words from my brain to my mouth as I blindly set aside the empty bag.

In my palm was a stunning ring with a teardrop-shaped sapphire. The stone glinted from where it sat nestled between silver branches with tiny leaves on them. I may not have been a girly girl, nor very emotional—in fact my Dad often likened me to an ostrich with my head always in the sand when it came to feelings—but damn if I couldn't appreciate the sparkle and clear meaning behind the ring in my palm.

The branches and leaves on the engagement ring represented the Forest Fae and Espen, and the water droplet represented the Fjord Fae and Øyvin. My heart thumped in my chest and my hand shook minutely as I stared at the tiny, beautiful object.

"If the powers that be in the human world need to believe we're really engaged, we figured it might be wise if you had a ring."

He was right. I'd agreed to marry Espen—for immigration purposes—but, based on the way my heart clenched as I looked between both of them, I suspected it might one day be more. Not that I was ready to fully and officially define the relationship, but... I shook my head.

This was bigger than just me. This was about the fae magic within me and the region and people that magic belonged to. I was both human and fae. A demi-fae who needed to learn how to fully control her powers. This fake engagement—*fae-gement* if you will—was necessary for so many reasons, and I was surprisingly okay with that.

Norway really was changing me. I'd gone from never listening to authority figures to obeying (sometimes), and now here I was committing to stay, not just for myself, but for others too. What was next? Would they anoint me as their Chosen One? Or vote me in as their leader? Only time would tell, I guessed.

The room remained silent, but as I slid the ring onto my finger, two relieved sighs drifted past.

"It's gorgeous," I remarked, shifting my hand and watching as the light from the kitchen and tree bounced off the facets of the sapphire.

"Good," Øyvin said, taking a deep breath, just as Espen replied, "I'm glad to hear it."

The latter jumped up from the sofa and went back to the tree returning with the final gift. "This is from both of us," Espen said, sidling up next to me again and handing me the box with the blue paper. "We hope you like it."

Tearing noises filled the room as I shredded the paper. Then my heart stopped beating.

"Wha—what?" I could barely get the word out, could hardly breathe. The world stopped spinning as I took in the sight of a brand new DSLR camera. "Guys."

"We thought you could use a new one," Espen murmured.

"Just don't take photos of fae areas," Øyvin added. Ever the dutiful and protective guard.

My hands trembled as I shoved aside the wrapping paper and opened the box. The new camera smell hit me—that odd aroma of cardboard, foam, and metal—and my heart started thumping again, quickening in pace.

They'd bought me a new camera to replace the one that had been destroyed by Nora. They'd known I couldn't afford to move out here *and* buy a new one, so they'd gone ahead and...

I couldn't even think straight. Tears welled in my eyes. I wasn't one for grand displays of emotion, but I couldn't hold back the happy tears as my lips curved into a smile. "Thank you so much."

Espen reached over and squeezed my thigh lovingly. "You're welcome."

I placed my hand over his and swept my thumb back and forth in gentle caressing motions. With a glance toward Øyvin, I found him smiling. He didn't need to say anything. For however grumpy the Fjord Fae could be, there was one thing I could always count on with him: he showed his emotions through his eyes. Right now, they were filled with a contented warmth that had me feeling loved.

We hadn't put any labels on this *situationship*, but through these gifts and all of their actions over the past few months, I could truly say they cared about me. A lot. And the feeling was mutual.

I let out a quick breath of air, and straightened up, not interested in getting even more emotional. Shifting my hand away from Espen's, I shut the lid with a contented sigh and let my heart rate settle down again, my mind drifting.

I wasn't entirely sure what the next five months would entail—except perhaps training with Halvar, but I didn't want to think about that frightening prospect right now.

In the meantime, I'd fill my days with practicing Norwegian so I could work with Oddvar this summer, hike with my new camera, and spend time with two guys whose company I was coming to adore and whose world I wanted to learn more about.

It was a commitment, but I wasn't worried about it. In fact, it might actually be nice to fully commit to something for once. Surprisingly, the thought of staying in Norway and making a life here wasn't daunting at all.

I glanced down at my sparkling left hand as it rested on the camera box. Thoughts of all the places we could go where I could take photos filled my head, all the nature I could capture, all the trips. A smile spread across my lips and my heart thumped happily in my chest.

I couldn't wait for the fun adventures this camera and I were about to go on.

The Fae of the Forest

65

LENNIE

An orb of effervescent white light no bigger than a tennis ball floated between my palms. I let out a long breath and steadied myself. This was progress from my first day of training with the light-wielding Fjell Fae, Torsten, a few weeks ago, but having magic flow from me still felt like a fever dream.

"She can do it, yes she can." Espen, dressed in his police uniform and green wool hat with wobbling pom-pom, cheered from the wintry sideline of the clearing within the forest above the fjord. I glared at him, his peppy attitude annoying this early in the morning, especially considering I'd only had one cup of coffee. Oddvar made a strong brew, but it wasn't enough for the crack of dawn on a gray, snowy day in the middle of winter in Norway.

Looking back down at the fae power gathered in my hands, I did my best to ignore the gentle breeze winding across the clearing, brushing aside the top dusting of snow. My layers and jacket shielded me from the worst of the late-January chill, but my face was still exposed to the elements. Snot slowly descended through my nostrils as a not so pleasant reminder of the cold weather. I bet I was super attractive right now. One snotty hot mess express, anyone?

"Rah, rah, gooooooooo—"

"Do you mind?" I asked through gritted teeth, failing to keep my eyes from straying up to his obnoxiously handsome face. "That's not helping me concentrate."

Nothing about Espen ever helped me concentrate, but watching him do little jumping jacks and wave around invisible pom-poms was definitely not helping. With his floppy brown hair, short beard, and loving gazes at the hibernating flora, the Forest Fae looked at home in the wilderness.

"Would meditation help instead?" Espen replied, and the suggestiveness in his tone drew my attention. He brought his hands down and into prayer position in front of his chest, a smirk on his face as one dark eyebrow climbed. "Perhaps a gentle morning yoga routine?"

The glowing between my palms stuttered, but the ball of light remained as I strained to focus. "You should have let me continue my corpse pose in bed this morning."

Espen snorted. "We all know bridge pose is your new favorite."

I scoffed, but a low chuckle behind me agreed with Espen's assessment. Something in my stomach fluttered at the noise, and the orb wavered.

"You did seem fond of it," Øyvin said, his deep voice scratchy this early in the morning. I peered over at the broad-shouldered Fjord Fae with blond hair. Decked out in his signature navy-blue-colored winter gear, he perched on a boulder, keeping guard at the edge of my mini-forest-arena while I practiced using my new magic powers. Trees towered around us, blocking the view of the fjord and the town below. We didn't need anyone seeing this—including fae, because my entry-level abilities were embarrassing—nor anyone accidentally getting a ball of light to the face. Øyvin had a few close calls with some of my magical orbs recently, and had subsequently decided to be on watch duty while Espen "coached."

"My current favorite yoga pose-meets-sex position doesn't matter right now, does it guys?"

The ball of light evaporated, and I let out an exasperated groan, my hands falling to my sides. It was hopeless. I'd inherited these new powers several months ago, but couldn't do jack shit with them other than summon a ball of light. Considering I'd been human last fall, that wasn't nothing, but we'd been at this for weeks now, and I wasn't making measurable progress. Maybe we needed to change up my training regimen?

"Focus on your breathing." Espen sidled up behind me and rubbed his hands over my shoulders in a soothing motion. The tension in my muscles diffused and a tender warmth settled over me.

I filled my lungs and angled my face toward the sky.

"And out," Espen whispered into my ear, the warmth of his words skittering across my cold cheek. He slid his hands down my arms and lifted them slightly, lining up their height with my sternum. "Breathe in," he murmured once more, and I did, the cold air tickling my lips. "Now, focus on the light again, bring that power up from your chest. Visualize it in your palms."

I focused on that new-constant, the warmth that radiated between my ribs, the something extra I'd been gifted by Halvar when Queen Freija was dying and transferred magic to him, only for it to be too much for the Fjell Fae. As the only other "vessel" in the room, I'd been the lucky one to get some of that power too, enough to turn me into a demi-fae—half-human, half-Fjell Fae.

I closed my eyes and a gentle tickle swept down my arms, pressure formed between my hands, and a glow swept across my eyelids.

"There you go," Espen said, his voice matching the church-like stillness around us. He moved his hands to my waist and pressed his chest against my back, and I pushed my rear against the top of his thighs, reveling in the warmth he provided. "Keep breathing."

Taking another deep breath, I opened my eyes. The ball of light between my palms was slightly larger than the last, more akin to a softball. I grinned, and a rumble of approval sounded from Espen as Øyvin stepped up beside us, his eyes locked on my hands.

"Push forward, not just with your hands but with your mind," Øyvin said, and demonstrated—for the twentieth time in the past few weeks—with his own palms and a ball of water. The liquid sloshed around within the confines of its shape, goading me into playing along.

Slowly pressing my hands forward on an extended exhale, I moved with the breath as Espen had taught me. The ball of light drifted forward and hovered above the snowy field, growing ever so slightly as it went. Øyvin pushed his ball of water further, passing mine and igniting that Martin Family competitive gene.

Oh, you wanna race?

I glanced over at him briefly. His eyebrow quirked high and his lips pressed firmly together in an effort not to smile.

Let's do this.

Rolling my shoulders and returning my focus to our magic orbs, I nudged mine ahead of his, only for his to zip past it two seconds later.

Grimacing, I tried again... The ball shot further across the field, and was quickly surpassed by Øyvin's. A soft chuckle emanated from Espen behind me. Øyvin's lips tilted into a lopsided smile and I faced him, careful to still keep my ball of light within the corner of my eye. He opened his mouth to say something, then stiffened and the ball of water disappeared. Mine followed swiftly thereafter as I dropped my hands, my focus drawn to the Forest Fae at my back turning and staring into the woods behind us.

The snow crunched and compacted, a rustle sounding from between the trees while someone moved among them. Their muffled footfalls audible thanks to the stillness.

The guys repositioned in front of me and turned toward the tree line where Øyvin had been stationed five minutes ago. I peered through the gap between their shoulders, all senses on high alert.

A dark-clad figure moved among the dense trunks, and worry welled inside me, unsure of what to do. Øyvin, on the other hand, with his 237 years of being a fae, knew exactly what he was doing, as did Espen at 225. Both men visibly relaxed as the figure came closer, emerging into our little clear-ing-slash-Lennie-training-center.

"Torsten," Øyvin greeted the Fjell Fae. Torsten nodded, his tawny hair twist-ed into a bun on the back of his head, his outerwear not dissimilar from what the local humans wore in the winter—a thick black jacket with a fur-lined hood and gray snow-pants.

Torsten's eyes slid to me as he tilted his head to one side. "How goes train-ing?"

I shrugged. "Same old—"

"She just maneuvered a light ball across the field, playing chase with Øyvin," Espen interjected.

Torsten smiled, setting his hands on his hips and giving me a nod. "Well done. That's progress and control."

I gave him my best jazz hands and sighed. He was right though, it wasn't nothing. It was progress that I needed to celebrate. I gave him a more vigorous jazz hands gesture again, building up the positivity inside me and receiving low laughs from all three fae.

I brushed a stray hair off my forehead and crossed my arms. "What brings you out here this fine, cold morning?"

"Came to see how your light magic was doing and..." His features pinched together as he winced. "Halvar."

Espen and Øyvin both shuffled on the spot at the mention of the most fearsome Fjell Fae I'd met, further tamping the snow beneath their feet as a shudder ran through my body. A sense of impending doom settled over me. If Halvar had a message for us then shit was about to hit the fan... and that never ended well for me.

"What happened?" Øyvin's voice dropped to his serious tone, the one I'd heard him use around the Fjord soldiers last year when we fought against the now deceased Fjord King who'd gone on a power trip.

"Nothing," Torsten said. He raised his hands as if to say *don't kill the mes-senger*. "I was sent to request your presence in the throne room. Halvar wants a meeting with all three of you immediately."

Yeah, that didn't sound good at all.

Over the past two months, since the last time shit hit the proverbial fan, I'd only seen the big guy in passing. None of us had spent any time with him as he'd been busy with the Fjell Council after Freija's death. And, honestly, I couldn't blame him. Based on the moments I'd witnessed between him and the late Queen, I understood that the man needed time to quietly grieve and handle the political fallout.

"Any clues on what this meeting is about?" Espen piped up and moved to stand beside me. He slipped his hand into mine and gave it a light but reassuring squeeze. The gentle touch was enough to make my cold heart pitter-patter in the most fairytale of ways, and I felt like Snow White in the forest. Were there singing animals in these woods, too? Was this the moment they broke into song before we all walked into a mountain to face our doom? Could they go to this meeting for me?

Torsten shook his head and shrugged. "It's not my place to say. Just know that he's serious."

"I thought that was his resting state. Like Resting Bitch Face, but make it scary Viking Fae."

My guys let out long sighs, which had Torsten chuckling. "Don't worry," he said, a knowing grin forming on his face. "If Halvar wanted you dead, you'd already be six feet under."

"I know," all three of us replied simultaneously.

66
LENNIE

We traipsed up the hill on the north side of Skolvik, striding along the trail between the trees and aiming for the main entrance to the mountain, the home of the Fjell Fae. The snow on the path was downtrodden, but still crunched lightly beneath our boots.

Stepping through the main entrance, the magic washed over me as it granted us passage into the fjell's tunnels. "Any updates on the magic illusions around the entrances?" I asked.

The entrances to the mountain—magically hidden by mirages that would rebuff humans and unwanted guests—had dwindled in number since Freija's death. I didn't fully understand how it worked, but, according to Espen, the former Fjell Queen Freija's magic had been what kept the entrances hidden. When she passed, almost all of them were exposed.

"The guards' quick work on re-doing some of the mirages has been success-ful," Torsten replied from up ahead. His words bounced off the jagged stone walls of the tunnel. "And we don't believe any humans have noticed anything amiss."

"That's good," Espen said beside me, his gloved hand firmly wrapped around my own. "We haven't had any reports at the station."

"It is fortunate, but Halvar and his team didn't have the strength to cover every entrance. Some have been closed off with boulders and cave-ins that seal the passages for good, or at least until we find a way to restore the queen's magic and open them up again safely."

I shook my head. So much had faltered after the demise of Freija and the piece-of-shit former Fjord King, Balder. Both the fjell had weakened and, as Øyvin had mentioned, they'd had to re-erect the wall within the fjord that protected the waters from pollution. It was all a mess, but thankfully things were on the mend.

We reached a crossroads in the tunnel system and Torsten came to a stop. "I'll leave you here," he said with a smile. "Good luck."

"Do we need it?" My gut said we did, but it was worth asking.

"You know Halvar."

My shoulders slumped as the guys chuckled. Because yes, yes we did.

Traipsing through the rocky halls, we wandered into the throne room and found Halvar standing in front of the throne, hands behind his back but his posture as rigid as ever. The space behind him sat empty save for the lingering reminder of the loss that had occurred here a few short months ago. The sky-blue stone of the walls and ceiling shone thanks to the magical lanterns that were built into the wall.

Heat grew around my neck and I unzipped my jacket, pulled off my gloves and hat, and shoved them into my pockets. Even with winter in full swing outside, the temperature within the mountain was subtly warm—some sort of insulation magic keeping the residents protected from the external elements.

Halvar's eyes followed us closely as we came to a halt, the guys flanking me as they had done many times before.

"Thank you for coming." Halvar's silver hair and beard were a stark contrast to the black sweater and pants he wore. His chin tipped up as he looked over us like a general surveying his troops, and I wondered if this was what it felt like to be in the military—decorum and customs constantly on your mind in a superior's presence. How did they know when to salute or not?

I gave Halvar a quick smile, and the guys bowed their heads before straightening up to attention like his soldiers, even though they both carried the same Head Guard title as Halvar, but for their own fae factions. My slouch and shitty posture would have to be enough for Halvar though. I crossed my arms and rested my weight on my hip. "What's up, big guy?"

Halvar huffed at my casualness, taking a deep breath that made me squirm uncomfortably. "I have a task for you. The Fjell Fae Council needs to retrieve an important..." he hesitated for a second, tilting his head from one side to the other. "An individual of great importance to us."

I narrowed my eyes at him. "Have you heard of a cellphone? Fantastic technology that helps you get hold of someone," I said, then muttered under my breath, "when they remember to charge it."

Øyvin stirred beside me, probably tempted to clap his hand over my mouth. But the tension now flowing off both fae at my sides was enough to have me buzzing with curiosity.

"We tried that," Halvar replied, ignoring my sass. "Unfortunately, there was no response. So, the individual will have to be retrieved manually."

"And who is—" Espen started, just as I asked, "Why us?"

Øyvin let out a long sigh, fisting his hands at his side like he was desperate to duct-tape my mouth shut.

Halvar's jaw worked, which considering we'd only been here for a matter of minutes must have been some kind of record. I was exceptionally good at getting under people's skin quickly, and apparently that included this seemingly ancient mountain fae. "You three have been requested by the Council due to your considerable powers, and as a test of your loyalty, Lennie and Øyvin."

My brow furrowed. "Loyalty?"

"Yes, *loyalty*." Halvar focused on me and Øyvin. "Espen and the Forest Fae have proven trustworthy with our alliance over the past few decades. Aside from the assistance we had from Øyvin and some of the Fjord Fae in the battle against Balder last year, you two are untried."

Øyvin opened his mouth, but I beat him to it. "So, that's why you want him as well? You want to strengthen your new alliance with the Fjord?"

Halvar nodded and Øyvin inhaled audibly. "Understood," the Fjord Fae said.

"And I'm just here for shits and giggles?"

Halvar's eyebrows pinched together. "You are a demi-Fjell Fae. This is your opportunity to show you deserve to be one of us. To show you are worthy of the powers you now have. Prove your worth to the Fjell."

"Or else?"

"We return your power to the fjell."

"Which is done, how?"

Halvar's eyes met mine as a grinding noise sounded above our heads. Three crystalline stalactites jutted down from the ceiling. The pointed bits stopped mere inches from our skulls. Air rushed out of my lungs and I hunched over, hoping the massive piece of stone didn't skewer me like a kebab. "Death. Got it. Thanks."

An orb of water appeared above Halvar while Espen grabbed my hand and growled. "Don't you dare, Halvar."

The stalactite above my head dropped an inch lower, and I shuddered.

Halvar's gaze remained fixed on me. "Prove. Your. Worth."

"Nothing like a death threat and a challenge to get the blood pumping," I said.

Both of my guys moved to protest, but Halvar raised his hand, stopping them. "This is Fjell business and part of the Council's plan."

I peered at the men beside me. Both of their jaws were locked, their muscles jumping as they moved into positions like they were about to tackle Halvar. Part of me wanted to let them loose and see what happened. But the other part of me knew that Halvar, with his imposing stature and ability to create axes out of thin air, was the biggest threat in the room.

I reached out and rested my hands on Øyvin and Espen's elbows, drawing their attention. "It'll be fine. We can do this." I really fucking hoped we could. Halvar had thrown down a challenge, and I was going to meet it head-on in hopes he wouldn't take my head *off*.

Øyvin and Espen let out shaky breaths and nodded before refocusing on Halvar. The water ball, which Halvar hadn't even acknowledged, vanished.

Pulling my shoulders back and crossing my arms over my chest, I said, "Fine. I'll prove my trustworthiness and loyalty to the Fjell."

Halvar didn't move, but the stone icicles retreated and disappeared into the sky-blue ceiling as if they'd never existed.

I sucked in a breath and shook off the threat, catching the guys doing the same. "Now, who exactly do you want us to find?"

Halvar's gaze flicked to the side, and he noticeably swallowed a lump in his throat. "We seek to retrieve the heir of the Fjell Fae and return her to the throne."

All three of us flinched. *Heir?*

My jaw dropped, heading for the stone floor. I glanced between my fae, both of whom wore stunned expressions. At least they were as shocked as I was. I may not have known much Fjell Fae history, or fae history in general, but I'd never heard anyone mention a Fjell Fae Heir.

"Obviously you're not going to promote Nora after her betrayal. Long may she rot in the dungeon if you haven't already put one of those fancy icicles through her heart." I pointed to the ceiling where one such crystal stone spear had just been. "But I figured the Council would just make you king, Halvar, and be done with it."

Espen cleared his throat, and Øyvin jabbed his elbow into my side. I tilted away from his movement, the hit not painful but the message received. Time to shut up.

Silence settled over the room.

"Where is the heir?" Øyvin asked once Halvar no longer looked like he was about to drop a stalactite down on me again.

Halvar blinked and looked to Espen. "Alvdalen."

A chuckling noise escaped from Espen's throat and he tilted his head back with a smile. "Of course. *That's* why you need me."

Halvar grunted in the affirmative.

I looked at Espen, my mouth pursed. "Care to explain what this *Alvdalen* is?" I asked, probably butchering the Norwegian. My language skills had significantly improved over the last few months, but my pronunciation could still use some fine-tuning. The main things I struggled with were the throatier words, the rolling Rs and those three extra letters in the Norwegian alphabet—one of which, *æ*, sounded like you were sticking your tongue out at the doctor's office.

Espen faced me, his eyes glittering with excitement. "My hometown."

My eyebrows met my hairline. "Your hometown?"

Espen's head bobbed, his grin growing as he turned back to Halvar. "You want someone who knows the area well."

Halvar nodded.

"I could just call my sister, Turi, and ask her to fetch your heir," Espen continued. "She knows just about everyone in town."

Halvar grimaced, and Espen's bubbly disposition popped. "Won't be that easy."

"And why not?" I asked.

"Because she is only known as the heir by one individual," he responded, but looked around the room as if struggling to find the right words. "That is to say, she's been in the care of an individual who is the only person in the town that knows her secret. The Council has failed to get in contact with her guardian. I'd go myself, but I cannot leave the fjell, not while my magic is tied to the mountain. I also wouldn't want to draw too much attention to them."

"Can I inform the Council of Elders of the heir?" Espen's eyebrows pinched together. "In a closed meeting of course."

Halvar nodded, light bouncing off his silver hair. "But only the Council. We don't want word getting out."

"Agreed. Thank you," Espen replied.

"Can you give us a name?" Øyvin asked, his voice firm and authoritative. "At least for the heir's guardian?"

"Vigdis Johansen is an old friend of the Fjell, and is the heir's guardian." Halvar glanced quickly at the throne behind him before adding, "I know this is asking a lot of you at such a fragile time for the fjord, but I would appreciate your assistance and cooperation. Mark it as a first request in our new alliance."

Øyvin nodded. "It would be my honor to assist you and the Council in this endeavor. I will, of course, have to inform the Fjord Council and receive their blessing, but considering the nature of the request, I don't believe there will be any resistance."

"Thank you," Halvar said with a barely there smile as if he hadn't threatened us all a few minutes ago. He reached into his back pocket and pulled out an envelope. "Please give Vigdis this. It explains why the Council sent you and that you mean the heir no harm."

I stepped forward and took the proffered letter from his extended hand. The beige-colored parchment was rough but lightweight, the envelope sealed with a glob of black wax. Part of me was desperate to peek inside, but Halvar had already explained its contents and it wasn't meant for me. So, I stuffed it into the inner pocket of my jacket and zipped it shut.

"We will make sure Vigdis gets the letter. But what's the heir's name?" I asked. "All this discussion about the heir's guardian is great, but it's the *heir* we need to find, not her."

"Aurora. A distant relative of Freija's." Tension radiated off Halvar, power wavering in the air around him reminding me just how powerful this fearsome fae was. "Give Vigdis the letter. She'll know what to do."

Halvar's sky-blue eyes bore into me and I didn't dare press further. We'd just have to find this Vigdis woman and hope she could fill us in a bit more.

"On behalf of the Forest Fae, we'd be honored to help," Espen said with a nod which Halvar returned in kind.

"How far away is Alvdalen?" I asked, choosing to ignore the threat for now and instead focus on the thrill of a new adventure bubbling up within me.

Espen shrugged. "Roughly a day's drive."

"Quick little road trip?" My voice rose, matching the excitement building in my veins as I looked between my guys.

Espen beamed at me. "Road trip." His hands flexed like he wanted to wrap me in a hug, but then remembered where we were and whose presence we were in. "I know someone we can borrow a car from."

I frowned. "And you didn't think to make such an offer last year when I needed to get back to my cruise ship?"

His smile morphed into a look that was definitely not meant for anyone else to see, and my insides heated at the sight. "I was selfish and wanted you to stay."

Well, if my heart had been pitter-pattering earlier this morning, it was now a full-on conga line with maracas.

With sneaky grins on our faces that promised a whole lot of *yoga* when we got home, the three of us spun for the exit and made it all of two steps before Halvar cleared his throat. Sliding to a halt and hoping the big guy just had a slight cough, I turned back to the Fjell Fae, the guys following suit.

"Lennie, you train with me today."

My mouth fell open and my stomach sank to my feet. *Satan help me.* "Ummm... I already trained today."

"Not with me you didn't," Halvar replied, then nodded to the guys. "You two are free to go. Lennie will be home for dinner."

I spun to Espen and Øyvin, my eyes wide, hands latching on to their jackets, hoping they could save me. Øyvin shrugged out of my hold and wandered off with a cocky grin plastered across his face, while Espen twisted his lips downward. "I'm sorry. You *do* need to train—"

"Not right now, I don't." My pulse ratcheted upward. I'd fully planned on taking a sexy mid-morning nap, and said plan now looked like it was drifting down the fjord.

Espen gave me a wistful smile while prying my fingers off his arm. "I'll make you mac and cheese for dinner."

Groaning, I stepped back and pulled my hair into a ponytail. "Fine, make it extra cheesy please."

"Of course." With a quick glance at Halvar, Espen lurched forward, planted a kiss on my temple, and then departed before he could get conscripted into anything else. *Smart man.*

I spun on my heels and faced Halvar.

He uncrossed his arms and rolled his broad shoulders. His muscles rippled, promising the Fjell Fae equivalent of leg day. "Are you ready?"

I whimpered at the sight, wishing Thor himself would appear and zap me into smithereens instead. "No."

67

ØYVIN

While Lennie was no doubt being destroyed by Halvar's training, I made my way to work beneath the surface of the fjord.

The biting cold water pressed against the air pocket I'd created around myself as I descended deeper. Crossing over abandoned fae homes built into the fjord bed and hidden between boulders—the piles of rocks and former protective shields now gone—I shook my head. Our people had unnecessarily suffered since Balder died, similar to the Fjell Fae. The grim side effects of our selfish and power-hungry former King's actions culminated in a need for those who lived in the deeper waters to relocate to shoreline caves, and a weaker wall against pollution. I grumbled as I zipped past a plastic bag, yet another piece of debris that'd need cleaning up. If I wasn't needed in chambers within the next five minutes, I'd slow to grab it, but as it was... I grit my teeth and pushed on.

The dark waters lightened as I descended toward the Fjord Palace. Glowing lights on either side of the entrance, courtesy of Valdemar, our own light-wielding Fjord Fae, beckoned me. The cavern-like entry with ornate carvings—consisting of aquatic creatures from ancient myth and reality—was guarded by my burliest soldiers, swimming around and scanning for any threats. I didn't expect any dangers in the foreseeable future, but as we'd lost our monarch and the power he'd wielded, we were all a little on edge. Like the Fjell, until our own heir took up the mantle as leader and received more powers from the ancestors, we were a weakened community.

Launching myself through the air pocket around the entrance, I landed with a dull thud against the stone floor, uniformed soldiers on my left and right greeting me with swift nods. My own air pocket dissolved on impact, the magic leaving me completely dry. Without faltering, I miraged my navy Fjord Fae uniform and shoulder-cape over my jacket and jeans, and strode toward the inner arteries of the palace, aiming for the council meeting room.

The council chamber bustled with a low hum of noise when I reached it, wood scraping against the stone floor as people took their seats at the long oak table in the center of the room. Magical light and flame-filled chandeliers lit the space, casting a flickering glow on the aquatic mural that adorned the entire length of the back wall. Mythological creatures, demons of the deep, and a giant sea-serpent with a bright-blue stone for an eye stretched across the stone surface, etched there by ancient hands. I found my chair to the right of the King's former seat, where our new chief advisor, Valdemar, prepared to preside over our meeting.

After Balder's demise, we scrambled to sort out our leadership. Valdemar was no stranger to the Fjord Fae Council, having served as the King's Chief Advisor several centuries ago. Thank the ancestors he'd agreed to take up the position once more.

White robes from a time long since passed draped over Valdemar's hunched form. His thin eyebrows pinched together as he clasped his wrinkled hands on the table in front of him. He turned to me as I sat, light bouncing off the few remaining white hairs on his head. "Do you bring good news or bad?"

I rolled my shoulders and pulled in my chair, before mimicking his hands' position. "Neutral, but politically good for us all, I believe."

A wizened smile spread across his lips. "I like to hear that." He clapped his hands together, the sound echoing around the room and garnering the other members' attention. "Shall we begin?"

Those who were still standing took their seats and all focus turned to Valdemar at the head of the table.

"Thank you all for being here," Valdemar started, his voice shaking slightly with age. "We have several matters to discuss, including an item brought forth by Øyvin. But we shall start, once more, with matters regarding the well-being of the monarchy."

"Have we heard anything else from the children?" I asked the assembled council, wondering if any of Balder's hoard of kids gave a damn about the fjord. It was well known that he'd slept around most of the Norwegian coastline, with his children of all ages now scattered around the world, some ignoring their magic, others living solely beneath the surface. But there was one I was most interested in: his heir, Reuven. Upon Balder's passing, he would've no doubt felt a shift in his magic. He'd need to return to Skolvik to take up the mantle as King and then receive whatever magic the ancestors were willing to re-bestow. Normally, Balder's magic would've been re-gifted to the heir... but, would the ancestors want to do so after everything that happened? Everything he'd stolen?

"All of the children have now been informed," Valdemar replied, regaining my attention. "We just got a message to the youngest, Siri in Scotland. She sends her regards and a few choice words about her late father that do not bear repeating."

I refrained from snorting as several members cleared their throats. Siri's attitude and personality wasn't dissimilar from Lennie's, and, whenever we'd been able to get in contact with her, she'd never minced her words. Clearly, nothing had changed.

Valdemar stirred in his seat. "And, most importantly, Reuven, the eldest, has finally expressed interest to return to the fjord with his wife."

Thank goodness. I'd never met Reuven. He was a century my senior and had been married off to a Fire Fae Princess in Iceland when he was just a boy in an effort by Balder to shore up *alliances.* Those alliances now took on a whole different meaning. In light of what he'd tried to do, and succeeded with in the case of both Queen Ragnhild of the Forest and Queen Freija of the Fjell, the deceased monarch had been amassing power and allegiance for a long time.

"Did Veigar send any messages about the alliance?" I asked, wondering if the Fire Fae King might pose a threat to us. At this rate, we needed to be cautious. And, from what I'd been told, caution was always wise when dealing with Veigar as he had an easily triggered temper. "He isn't concerned about sending his daughter across the North Sea?"

Valdemar shook his head and cupped his hands together on the table. "He sent no word. We shall await their arrival and see if there are any messages sent through Reuven."

I sighed. It was better than nothing. We'd been waiting for a response from Reuven for weeks, needing to know if he was going to take over as King and help maintain the well-being of the fjord and its inhabitants. His return was at least something to be grateful for.

"Does anyone have anything else to share with the Council regarding the monarchy?" Valdemar scanned the weathered faces around the table. When no one else said a word, he added, "Very well, Øyvin?"

All eyes swung to me.

"I have a request from the Fjell."

Valdemar waved his hand for me to proceed. "Go on."

I swallowed and straightened in my seat. "Halvar has requested that myself, the demi-fae, and Espen of the Forest, assist in locating the Fjell heir."

The entire room sucked in a breath, every council members' eyes widening. I couldn't blame them. I too had been shocked to hear that Freija had an heir that wasn't her traitorous sister. "I ask you for permission to take some time away from the fjord to assist with this search."

"Where will you be heading and for how long?" Idar, the fae to my right asked.

"Alvdalen. I don't know exactly how long—a couple of weeks at most."

"Why *you*?" Idar continued. "Or is this an effort to solidify an alliance with us?"

I hummed in agreement. I had no doubt Espen and Lennie could find the heir by themselves, but this was a good faith request after Balder's betrayal. That, and I wasn't entirely certain what would happen if someone denied Halvar what he wanted. From the tales and rumors I'd heard of his past, it would likely end in someone's early demise. His threat to Lennie further solidified those rumors and my resolve to make this happen without her getting hurt.

"It is indeed a request to solidify our alliance. One I think we'd be wise to take," I said.

Valdemar nodded and several other council members muttered their approval.

"If you all agree, I'll take a temporary leave of absence from my post here in the fjord, leaving Captain Sigurd in charge of operations and the wall." I glanced around the room, hoping I had their permission. We needed all the support we could get right now, and if helping Halvar find the Fjell heir would seal our alliance, then I'd do it.

"All those in favor, say aye," Valdemar stated. His sage stare took in every member of the assembled council.

A resounding response of "aye" came through. I relaxed in my seat, tension easing from my muscles.

"Any opposed? Hearing none. We, the Council, agree to this arrangement and wish you well on this endeavor, Øyvin." Valdemar smiled, his lips forming a curved line, no teeth visible. "If there are no further matters to discuss..." he let the sentence hang for a few seconds, but no one spoke up. "Then our meeting is adjourned. Have a good day."

I rose from my seat and pushed the chair back in, leaving it as I'd found it.

That had gone smoothly. Now all I needed to do was tackle the rest of my to-do list, including checking on the wall and temporarily promoting Sigurd. I chuckled to myself as I exited the council chambers and wandered down the smooth, stone hallway toward the main entrance, my cape fluttering around me. He'd find my becoming a Fjell errand boy very amusing.

As I reached the exit, I pressed my right hand to my left shoulder, removed my uniform mirage, and dove through the archway into the fjord.

LENNIE

I strolled behind Halvar into an empty cave, the ceiling of which rose to at least ten feet, the rough-hewn walls glinting in the light cast from the sconces around the space. Aside from those fixtures and the echo of our footsteps, the room sat eerily empty.

"Was this all a ploy to get me alone and kill me?" I asked, half-joking, half-serious, because being alone with Halvar was intimidating, to say the least.

He shook his head as he came to a halt and swept his arms behind his back in a militant pose I'd just seen my guys in—at ease, but most certainly in charge. "I know you've been training with Espen and Øyvin, but you need to finally start testing more of your Fjell powers. We need to know how much of my magic or Freija's magic you have. Plus, it would be useful to ascertain if you have any specialties."

"You mean like Torsten's light magic?" I glanced around the room at the fae in question's handy work, forever amazed at how he kept the lights on around here.

Halvar nodded. "That and any affinity, whether that might be healing, creating, smithing, and so on. Thankfully, you've been able to learn how to hide your ears, so we've got the basics out of the way."

I scoffed. That had been easier said than done and earned me the nickname of *The Streaking American* among the locals who'd witnessed—via their security cameras—one of my failed tests back in December. But, after some more trial and error, I'd eventually been able to shield my fae ears.

Halvar ignored my noise and spread his arms out wide. "This is the youngsters' training cave. One of the first things we Fjell Fae teach our young is how to create rocks and protect ourselves from cave-ins." He clasped his hands behind his back again like a general preparing his troops. I took a deep breath and focused on the lesson as he continued. "We cannot protect the fjell if we cannot protect ourselves. So, we learn how to withstand the pressure of the mountain, seal the cracks that form in the rock, and hold the stone ceilings above us should they start to fall."

He unclasped his hands and swept one in a gentle circle above his head before looking upward. I followed his gaze and startled at the faint trace of magic on the ceiling. Ebbing around and around like a translucent vortex was a circle of magic that pushed against the cavern above us, raising it ever so slightly. A small groan echoed through the chamber.

My mouth opened and closed as I struggled to understand the magnitude of what Halvar was asking of me. "You... You want me to move part of the mountain?"

"It'll be simple to start with, but you need to be able to do it again and again, which is where it becomes more of a challenge."

"Let's just lift a mountain for funsies. What could possibly go wrong?" I muttered then caught the serious expression Halvar wore. "Okie dokie."

"Focus on that well of warmth beneath your ribs, where your energy lies. Then urge it upward into a disk and push."

I did as I was told—which was rather miraculous, but I'd turned a new leaf since last autumn and was now into listening to authority figures... kind of. Channeling my thoughts toward the warm, swirling sensation within my sternum, I took a couple of deep breaths and raised my hands above my head. Pulsing energy swept up my arms toward the ceiling, searing through the lightning-shaped scar on my left arm—a result of obtaining Freija's magic when she died.

Resistance pressed against my power, reminding me I was lifting a damn mountain. I looked up and let out a slow, steady breath. A translucent, swirling mass had formed against the ceiling just like Halvar had done, and I let out a choked cough in surprise. "How was that so easy? Is it because I'm using my powers within the mountain? Or is it your presence?"

Halvar's nose wrinkled. "Now push upward," he said, his voice a soft command as he ignored my string of questions.

I pushed against that invisible opposition, willing my magic to move upward. A grinding noise echoed through the space and where my magic swirled, the cavern ceiling slowly rose.

A short laugh escaped me. "Well, I'll be damned."

I'd done it, and on the first try too. My guys would be so proud of me.

"Do that one hundred times."

My hands flopped back down to my sides. "Seriously?"

He nodded.

With a huff, I rolled my shoulders and bounced on my toes. How hard could it be?

"Again," Halvar commanded, hands gripped behind his back, not bothering to look in my direction where I panted. Exhaustion hung heavy across my limbs and a complaint sat at the end of my tongue, ready to be aimed at the stubborn troll who was accustomed to training soldiers, not demi-fae. Apparently, they were one and the same in Halvar's mind, and I was the lucky one to be stuck with him for a full-day torture session. We'd been at this for hours. He hadn't been kidding about lifting the ceiling a hundred times.

When we were finally done with that, he'd moved on to creating rocks from thin air, steadily getting them to increase in size. All I needed to do was picture a pebble and it would appear, then push my magic into it to make it larger. It was an easy process, willing them into being like my light balls, but at this point I wanted to hurl my little boulder collection at his head. Both my power and muscles were straining to keep up, even with the new demi-fae strength I'd obtained.

"Your bedside manner is shit by the way." I huffed, beads of sweat rolling down my temples. "Don't go into nursing when you decide to retire."

His lips twitched, which I'd learned meant I'd amused or annoyed him. I still wasn't entirely sure on which, but it was as much emotion as Halvar showed most days.

I collapsed to my butt on the cool, cave floor and wiped the perspiration from my forehead. "How the hell do young fae do this? Or are you training me differently than how you normally train youngsters?"

"Slightly different." Halvar rolled up his sleeves, and I gasped at the sight of lightning-shaped scars across both hands and forearms, exactly like mine.

The question that'd been lingering in the back of my mind for months burst forward, and I couldn't stop the words as they tumbled from my mouth. "Halvar, the scars. They're like the ones on the trees, aren't they? Like the ones on Nora's arms? Did Freija illegally transfer *all* her magic to you and me?"

His eyes bore into mine and he let out a slow breath through his nose. "Yes."

How one word could be laced with so much pain and grief was beyond me, but I felt it just the same.

I rested my elbows on top of my knees and hung my head, letting the reality of that confirmation settle over me. For weeks last year we'd been trying to find the culprit who was stealing magic from the mountain and areas around the fjord, illegally transferring it, not using the magic for its intended purpose—to protect the natural environment.

Now, after all we'd been through, Freija's last act had been an act of defiance. Her magic was supposed to go back to the earth, to the ancestors, where it would be handed over to her heir. Instead, she'd illegally transferred it to Halvar and me. *Fuck, he'd basically been a conduit that night.*

But, then again...

What if she hadn't transferred her magic to Halvar? Would he have been able to kill King Balder, the Fjord Fae behind all the chaos? Balder had a vendetta against the humans, and had been trying to amass power to do fuck knew what kind of damage to humankind. Along the way, he'd succeeded in killing not just Freija, but also the Queen of the Forest Fae, Ragnhild.

"Don't think too hard about it." Halvar's statement drew me from my spiraling thoughts and I looked back up at him where he stood as stoic as ever, his arms crossed over his chest.

"Does the Fjell Council know?" Had the Queen's former advisers been informed about what she'd done? Did her own people know what had actually happened in that throne room?

Halvar nodded.

"Well, shit," I mumbled, exhaustion creeping in as I mentally grappled with what that really meant. I'd had my suspicions, but to know for certain that Freija had illegally transferred all of her magic into Halvar, who couldn't take all of it and in turn transferred some to me, turning me into a demi-fae... it was a lot to process. The ramifications were huge. This was royal magic. Power that was to be wielded with great care. It meant I had a new responsibility with this magic that had been forced upon me. A responsibility not just to myself, but to the mountain this power was meant to protect. That pressure was borderline overwhelming, but I never backed down from a challenge. If anything, it filled me with a greater sense of motivation to prove myself to the Fjell and find their heir.

I rose to my feet, my thighs screaming at me and my arms hanging limp at my sides. With every movement, it felt like my muscles were being flayed apart and picked right off the bone. I grit my teeth and whimpered involuntarily, as a stray tear fell across my cheek. I could do this. I could train and use this power for good, for the well-being of the fjell.

I flicked my hands to shake off the pain and realization. Sparks flew away from me followed closely by a light clattering noise.

What the fuck?

Something glinted from across the room, and Halvar narrowed his gaze at the foreign object that hadn't been there a second ago. I lowered my hands as he traipsed over and picked it up.

Inching toward him, my pulse fluttered like a firefly in a corn field. "What is that?"

He threw what looked like an arrowhead into the air and caught it again, studying it closely. Had I made that?

He cast a look at me, his eyes slightly scrunched. "It's a change of plans."

69
LENNIE

Striding down the rocky hallway, glowing sconces along the walls lighting our way, we wound deeper and deeper into the mountain. Every muscle in my body screamed at me, my body begging for a nap, but Halvar had other ideas. My day of training wasn't over yet.

I yawned as my feet shuffled across the uneven ground. Tripping on my own damn foot, I wobbled before catching myself. "Any chance you could slow down? Some of us need time to bounce back and recover after the equivalent of a full-body Viking workout."

Halvar huffed. "You will be fine. Keep moving."

"Where exactly are we going?" I asked as we descended into the bowels of the mountain.

Halvar strode ahead of me, his long strides eating up the distance, and fellow Fjell Fae stepped aside to let him pass with respectful nods. "To my old workshop."

"Old work? You mean you had a job before you became *this*?" I waved my hand at his broad back, referring to his job as Queen Freija's Head Guard, now the Fjell's Head Guard.

"I was chosen for my raw strength and exceptional leadership skills a long time ago," he replied, not slowing down. "But my affinity lies with weapons, and that was where I started."

I snorted. "Let's not be too boastful, hey, big guy."

He didn't roll his eyes at me, but the sentiment was there, clear as day, in the way he shook his head... or clear as an unflappable Fjell Fae who wasn't a fan of my jokes.

A moment later, he turned a corner and headed inside a cavern that was slightly warmer than the rest. The magic within my sternum tingled, but I ignored the sensation as I took in my new surroundings, my eyebrows inching up my forehead.

All around the room, fae hammered and forged stone weapons and tools that looked heavier than a tractor. The cavernous place was filled with iron picks, axes, and a few swords while shields decorated the rocky walls. Orbs of light hung from the ceiling instead of the walls as they did in the rest of the fjell, lending the space a warm glow. It looked like a *ye olde* blacksmiths shop at a renaissance fair, but with one major difference—there wasn't a flaming hot forge. Instead, the fae, most of whom were wearing thick leather aprons over white blouses and black pants, used their magic to slowly carve the stone into weapons and sharpen them, one pass of their hands at a time. The mesmerizing display sent me into a trance-like state, and it wasn't until Halvar cleared his throat beside me that I regained my focus and opened my mouth.

"So, *this* is where you learned how to slice and dice?"

Halvar scrunched his brows and surveyed me like he had no idea what I was talking about.

"You know, I've seen you create an axe out of thin air and then use it to dismember a king. *Slice* and *dice*." I waved my hand in explanation and the air rippled and warmed around my palm.

Halvar's gaze cut to the motion, and the smiths in the room stilled, casting fearful looks in my direction.

I held my hands out in front of me, and didn't dare move in case I accidentally whacked someone with whatever magic I'd disturbed. "What just happened? Maybe bringing a baby fae into a room filled with sharp objects was a bad idea?" I'd never been super accident-prone, but as my time in Norway had shown, *shit* found me.

Narrowing his eyes at my outstretched palms, Halvar reached over and turned them both, examining them. "Hmmm."

"What's the verdict? Will I live or are they about to drop off?"

That one earned me an actual eye roll. Halvar straightened and looked out across the room. "Weapons down."

The smiths instantly set aside their work, several stepping back from their workbenches, their sharp, fear-filled gazes still locked on me.

"Care to explain what happened and why everyone is looking at me like I'm a live grenade?"

Halvar brushed his hand over his silvery beard. "You may have received some of my talents during the magic transfer."

I swallowed hard, and stared down at my hands, turning them over and then palm up again. The lightning scar on the back of my left hand glinted in the glow of the room, as if winking at me to say "bingo."

"You may be able to create weapons," Halvar said, drawing my gaze back up to his.

"So, I'm a demi-fae that can create stone... what, swords?" I peered around the room at the stone blades on the wall, the ones set aside on worktables—their sharp edges shining back at me. "Axes? Shields? Spears?"

Holy shit this was a lot to take in, especially after such an exhausting morning of training. I tightened my ponytail with both hands and every other Fjell Fae in the room, except Halvar, flinched. "Are they going to do that every time I move?"

Halvar tilted his head from one side and then the other, his lips downturned. He reached into his pants pocket and pulled out a stone... which, on closer inspection, as he held it up between his fingers, was the arrowhead I may have accidentally created earlier. "Let's test your magic."

I let out a long breath and rolled my shoulders. At this rate I wasn't sure I'd have any magic left in me to do more training.

"Could I ever deplete my magic?" I blurted. "Is that a thing? Or do I just naturally replenish? Basically, can I run out?"

"No you must stay here and finish training," Halvar replied and motioned for me to move to the corner of the room.

I moved to where he pointed, a secluded corner at the back of the room away from blades that were currently under construction, but beside a display of swords. "I'm not going to leave." At least, that wasn't the plan, and I doubted he'd actually let me run back to the boathouse until we'd finished training. "What I meant is, can my magic run out? Is there a finite amount of it?"

He leaned back, nodding slightly as my question sank in. "Ah, yes and no. As we do not know exactly how much magic you have, I cannot say anything for certain. But full fae can drain themselves and need time to replenish. It would take doing something drastic to warrant such a need though."

"Like..."

He tilted his head, thinking about it for a second. "Razing a battlefield for two days and two nights would do it."

"Do you speak from experience?" I asked, latching onto the word raze, and wondering, not for the first time, if Halvar had fought alongside Vikings. I was desperate to find out how old he was, mostly to sate my own curiosity.

Halvar narrowed his eyes, opening his mouth to say something before swiftly shutting it again. With a twitch of his nose, he mumbled. "You'll have enough magic to see out today's training session."

"How can you—"

"Stand here, hold this." He corralled me into the corner of the room and dropped the arrowhead into my palm. I blinked and stared at the tiny rock shard as Halvar peered over his shoulder. "Brokkr."

"Yes, sir," a stout fae with a thick beard replied, his broad arms covered by a black shirt and pieces of leather that were probably some form of protective garb.

"You and your team may take the rest of the day off."

"Thank you, sir." And with that, the Fjell Fae smiths, who'd all been staring at me in fear and bewilderment, vacated the room, leaving me alone once more with Halvar.

I flipped the arrowhead a few times in my hand. "So, what exactly do you want me to do with this?"

Halvar stepped back, pulled down his shirt sleeves, hiding his forearms, before crossing his arms over his chest. He nodded. "You'll create a blade."

I snorted. "And you don't see any problem with that?" There were a plethora of ways this could go wrong, several of which ended up with me accidentally sawing off my own arm. Or perhaps that was a latent fear after seeing what Halvar had done to King Balder on the battlefield a few months ago?

"I'm here. You will be fine."

"If you say so."

"Focus on the piece of stone. Note its shape and picture it as a short blade. Once you have the image in mind, slide your free hand over your palm with the rock, like so." He did the motion himself, holding his palms so they faced each other, a small gap between them, and dragged the top hand across as if stroking a cat.

I did as requested and imagined a small, stabby blade in the palm of my hand. With a deep breath, I willed my magic to flood through my palms and flow into the shard, doing the same motion that Halvar had just shown me. The warmth of my magic spiraled down my arms and slowly but surely, a blade appeared—stretching from the tip of the arrowhead, forming the stone blade itself, then a small hilt and rounded pommel—just as I'd pictured it.

I let out an awed chuckle, moving the weapon from one hand to the other, testing its weight. My hand flexed around the handle, the stone heavy in my palm. I'd seen some of these weapons during the battle last year with Balder and witnessed Halvar forge an axe out of thin air. But, a couple of hours ago it'd never even dawned on me that I might be able to create and wield a stone sword of my own. "Well, damn."

Halvar nodded and swept his arms behind his back, clasping them there like he so often did. Apparently, I wasn't a threat even with a sharp object in my hand. Which, considering the beast of a man before me, was true.

"The more practice you have, the more blades and weapons you create, the stronger and sharper they will become," Halvar explained.

"How about lighter?" I asked, doing a bicep curl with it. My arm muscles ached, regret and pain washing through my limbs as I gently brought the sword back down to my side.

He shrugged. "Depends what you wield, but you're fae. You have the strength to brandish immensely heavy weapons without damage to your mortal form."

Huffing at his use of the word *mortal*, I cast my gaze around the room. I pointed with my blade at a broadsword hanging on the wall across the room, its knife-edge shining twice as bright as the one in my grasp. "So, one day, maybe even now, I'll be able to create things like that?"

"Yes. Perhaps not as sharp, but yes," Halvar replied. "I think we have ascertained your specialty."

"Safe to say I got some of your magic during the transfer."

Halvar nodded. "Yes, indeed. You have both the power of Fjell Fae royalty with Freija's light magic and my own smithing powers."

I smirked. "You have boy scout badges for those? Or perhaps an achievement pin?"

"We have a hat." His lips twitched slightly at the corners, and my mind whirled back to the baby hat joke I'd made when I'd first become a demi-fae.

"Seriously?"

"No."

"Did you just make a joke, big guy?"

"Also no. Try again."

I'd wear him down one day. I'd bet good money I didn't have that he had a knock-knock joke or a pun locked up somewhere in among all that broody beast-ness. "What do you want me to try now?"

He reached out and motioned toward himself, requesting the short blade I currently held. I passed it over, and he set it aside on the table beside us among the collection being stored there. Blades of all sizes and shapes, some curved like scimitars, others double ended. Brokkr and the smiths had quite the stash down here.

"I want you to make a sword," Halvar said, drawing my attention back to him and my eyebrows to my hairline.

"Are you sure?"

His dead-pan stare didn't falter.

"Okaaay." I focused on that well of energy again and pictured a broadsword like the ones I'd seen in movies: silver, sharp, and hefty. Like something that would've been wielded on battlefields during ancient times. "And I don't need starting material?" I asked, not daring to look at anything other than my own hands.

"No," Halvar replied.

Great. I let out a slow and steady breath as the warm tingling sensation of my magic worked its way down my arms and into my waiting palms. One held over the other, I pulled my hands apart horizontally, and watched in amazement as a piece of rock formed. Suspended mid-air between my palms, the blade in my mind appeared. However, instead of being made of metal, this one was solid stone. A glint of light emitted from the tip as it formed, startling me for a split second, and I grasped the pommel as it took shape in my right hand. The sword dropped slightly upon completion, but I didn't let it clatter to the floor.

"Well done," Halvar said, and I pointed the sword toward the glowing ceiling. Moving it up and down a couple times, the weight was surprisingly bearable.

"Not bad," I replied, assessing my work with a snicker. "But it's a little kinky."

Sure enough about three quarters of the way up the blade it curved slightly to the left. Probably from the light flicker that momentarily distracted me. Perhaps that'd even been some of my light magic trying to come out and play? Either way, my sword had a little bend in it.

Halvar quirked a single brow and shrugged. "Could be worse."

"Anything else I should know about creating swords?" I asked, unsure if this was a one and done lesson or if there was more to know.

"Creating? No. Wielding? Yes," Halvar replied.

I swiveled the sword to my side, pointing it downward so I didn't cause any damage to the room. There were a lot of things in here, especially the collections of shields, blades and daggers that were set aside on countertops to our left and mounted on the wall. I wouldn't earn myself any fans if I accidentally whacked something off the wall with my kinky sword.

"First rule of sword wielding—"

"Don't accidentally stab yourself," I interjected.

"Well, yes that is a good rule. Especially for you."

I laughed and popped my hip to one side. "I see my reputation precedes me."

Halvar let out a long-winded sigh. "It does. The first rule is to never accidentally injure yourself with your own blade. The second rule is to never, under any circumstances, abandon your sword. You do not want it used against you."

Sounded like solid advice to me. "And how exactly do I unwield,"—I waved my free hand at the sword grasped in my right—"a magical stone sword?"

Halvar straightened and rolled his shoulders. He didn't say a word, but instead slowly created a broadsword of his own, the end of the hilt formed into an ancient crown. *Show off.* But I couldn't deny, his ability was impressive. He raised the sword, the light catching on the sharp edges, the tip pointed upward. "To break down the sword, simply pull the magic back inside you. The sword is merely an extension of you and your powers." He brought his free hand down the side of the blade, close but not touching, and my mouth popped open in awe. The sword disintegrated, vanishing into thin air as Halvar drew the magic back inside him. While invisible, I could sense the magic flowing from the blade and into his open hand—returning home. Once the entire blade was gone, Halvar clasped his hands behind his back and nodded to me. "You try."

I pressed my lips together and widened my stance. Pointing the sword upward in front of me, I let my hand hover beside the blade, starting from the top and willing my magic to return to me. As my palm passed the tip, a spark of lightning shot out from the sword and into my left hand, singing up my scarred arm. I flinched and retracted my hand, shaking it out like I'd been stung by static. "What the hell was that?"

Halvar narrowed his eyes but motioned for me to continue.

I tried again. This time there were no sparks, but the air between my palm and the blade heated and pulsed like it was alive. I sucked in a breath, focusing intently on the sharp object. Little grains of stone broke off it, suspended in mid-air, then vanished. I kept my breathing steady as I worked my hand down the side of the sword until nothing remained. *Holy shit.* Had I really done that on the second attempt?

I looked to Halvar to see if I was correct in my assessment, that I'd done good, but the twitch of his nose betrayed nothing. "Not bad?" I asked, hoping for some sort of response.

He nodded slowly and brushed his hand across his silver beard. "Not bad."

Go me! I'd take that as a gold star from the big guy. Heck, that hadn't been as hard as wielding the light magic or as problematic as trying to shield my new fae ears. If I'd had the energy to do a victory dance, I would have. But following a day full of training, I was ready to go home, curl up on the sofa and take a nap.

"Anything else on the lesson plan for today or can I go home and have dinner?" I wasn't quite sure exactly what the time was, but we'd been training for hours and I wanted food—preferably the mac and cheese Espen mentioned earlier.

"That should be all." He motioned to the exit and I strode in that direction, taking one last look around the forge. It really was a spectacular space—the walls glowed orange from the lights in the ceiling, and each bench had a piece of work atop it in various stages of completion.

"You have any homework for me?" I couldn't quite believe the words that came out of my mouth, but seeing as I was a baby demi-fae, I imagined there'd be more training sessions with Halvar in my future. Anything I could do to prepare for those—even if it was just sleep and brace for torture—I'd do it.

"Perfect the process."

"That's it?"

"That's it," he said as we traipsed back up the tunnels toward the Fjell's main entrance. "Now, go find the Fjell heir."

70

LENNIE

My joints creaked, mimicking the sound of snow-heavy boughs around us. The waterproof material of my rain pants and jacket added a swishy percussion as Espen and I traipsed through the forest east of the village. Morning sunlight sprinkled over the hills, lighting our way as we hiked toward the Forest Fae's training location somewhere deep in the woods, away from any humans that might spot them.

"How much further?" I panted, my body sore after my training session with Halvar yesterday. I may have had new powers, but my twenty-eight-year-old body was still growing accustomed to the magic and my ability to endure more.

"Another mile." Espen squeezed my hand, both of us tromping through the snow that reached mid-calf in the deepest spots, the cold air biting at our cheeks. "Don't worry. The terrain will flatten out shortly."

Now there was a statement I longed to hear more of after moving to Norway. Aside from stunning scenery, the one thing this country could deliver on was steep inclines. Apparently on the south coast it was flatter, but here, along the jagged fjords that pierced the country's western flank, peaks and valleys reigned supreme.

I sucked in a breath and continued moving, Espen dutifully keeping pace beside me. "So, your talk with Bente went okay? Any issues with you taking time off?" I asked. I'd been too busy last night stuffing my face with cheesy pasta and then face-planting into bed to ask Espen about his day.

"Bente is the best." Espen nodded, the pom-pom on his green woolly hat wobbling. "She understood that I needed more time to settle family affairs"—our cover story for when he'd been poisoned last year—"and said to take all the time I needed. On one condition..."

"Which was?"

"That I return to work with them."

I couldn't blame Bente for making that request. Espen was great at his job and loved Skolvik. If the police station did an employee of the month thing, he'd probably win every time.

As we crested yet another hill atop a hill, Espen broke out his signature grin. "Almost there. Now, I know you don't like to take orders"—I scoffed because that was the damn truth, even though I'd been doing better lately—"but I'll advise you to stay near or beside me. Don't get drawn into anything. These are young Forest Fae soldiers training today. We don't want a wayward arrow hitting you."

I shuddered at the thought and memory of seeing one such arrow sticking out of King Balder's Chief Advisor-turned-crony Kjetil's head last year during the battle on the mountain. That sight had unfortunately been burned into my brain. I nodded firmly, willing to do anything to avoid a twig speared between my eyeballs. No need to become a plant pot.

"Good," he said. "Can't have you getting into more trouble."

"You're starting to sound like Øyvin."

Espen tugged my hand and pulled me to a stop. With a sneaky twinkle in his amber eyes, he pulled me toward him, spun me around, and dipped me. Pressing his lips to mine, I savored the warmth of his kiss before he righted me again. Standing nose to nose with the fae, my heart thrummed and the smell of moss and leather drifted over me, making me feel like I was home. "We both have a strong desire to protect you."

I bit my bottom lip and tried to hide a smile, but failed monumentally. "You mean to say I'm a naughty princess who likes to rebel and needs saving?"

Espen grinned, his long mop of hair brushing the tops of his eyebrows. "That's exactly what I'm saying... except the princess part." He swatted my behind, and I let out a small yelp, my hands instinctively flying back to protect my ass.

"Well, I promise to be on my best behavior, then," I replied and walked on, exaggerating the sway of my hips a little more and pretending to pick up my "skirts."

Five minutes later, muffled noises, like the sound of someone chopping wood underneath a blanket, met my ears and Espen nudged me with his elbow, nodding toward the tree line. "You go first. I'm shy," he whispered.

I spun on the spot, my arms windmilling from the momentum before I rested my hands on my hips. "Bullshit. You've never been shy a day of your life."

He rested his gloved hand against his chest and fluttered his lashes at me. "I'm shy on the inside."

I snorted, but pressed on. "Come on, Solbakke. I'm not buying your nonsense. Not one bit. You also told me not to leave your side."

"Just testing you," he snickered.

A couple more steps, and we entered a clearing full of Forest Fae in the middle of a massive snowball fight. Balls flew in all directions. One crashed with a splat against a tree trunk two feet from Espen's head. His eyes narrowed, searching the field, trying to ascertain who the launcher was.

"All clear! Back to training!" A feminine voice yelled from among the group and a split second later, Ylva jogged over to us. Her long blonde hair was split into two braids, and her white-and-green snowsuit blended seamlessly with our surroundings. She greeted us, and started saying something to Espen, but I was too enraptured by the Forest Fae soldiers to pay attention to her.

Some were heading back inside a small red-and-white cabin on the far side of the clearing, some were miraging the clothing they were wearing back to fatigues like Ylva's, and others picked up bows and arrows—aiming them at large mounds of snow in the distance.

"So, Lennie," Ylva started, dragging my attention away from her soldiers. "You've come to train with us today? Was Halvar too much for you?"

My brows pinched as I glared at Espen—that most certainly had not been the plan communicated to me this morning. "No to the former. Yes to the latter."

Espen chuckled with a quick shake of his head, and I looked between the two Forest Fae. "She's teasing you. We're just here to discuss what needs to happen while I'm gone and for you to see more of our world."

Well, thank fuck.

Ylva faced Espen and popped her hands on her hips. "So, what's this about you needing to put me in charge?"

"Halvar requested me, Lennie, and Øyvin retrieve an item of importance to the Fjell."

"Using you instead of his own to strengthen alliances."

Espen nodded. "And our destination is Alvdalen."

Ylva hummed like everything was finally clicking together in her head. "What's the motivation?"

"Aside from maintaining a good diplomatic relationship with the Fjell," Espen started and his eyes darkened, "he threatened Lennie."

"Why am I not surprised?"

I shrugged. "I don't even think a threat from Halvar makes me that special anymore. He threatens everyone. My ability to tie cherry stems with my tongue though? *That* is special."

Espen brushed a gloved hand over his mouth, and Ylva stared between the two of us, but I just grinned.

Talk turned to business, and my gaze drifted as Espen and Ylva discussed details and tasks of what needed to be done while he was away. Soldiers continued training. Some sparred with what looked like wooden swords, others appeared to be using tree roots as whips, while the marksmen continued volleying arrows at compacted snow dunes. They were like woodland sprites preparing for battle.

Ylva cleared her throat, drawing my focus back to her and Espen.

"Now, Espen." She crossed her arms and leaned back, quirking a brow in his direction. "How long has it been since you put in some serious training, or even participated in a sparring match?"

"Oh, snap." I laughed, adoring this woman and her combative nature.

Espen ignored me and raised his eyebrows at the woman who stood at least a foot shorter than him, but made up for it in sheer confidence. "Is that a challenge, Colonel?"

Ylva's chin tipped up, a hint of a smirk playing on her lips. "Are you up for the task, General? Or have you grown lax in your loved up haze?"

I blinked and straightened at the titles they used—choosing to ignore her use of the word *love*, too. "General? I've only ever heard people refer to you as Head Guard."

With a dramatic stage-whisper, Ylva said, "We did away with the official titles years ago, but they're fun to trot out from time to time."

I peered at Espen, curious to see how this would play out. My endlessly patient fae grinned, but shook his head as he motioned to the clearing. "Let's go then."

Ylva clenched her fist victoriously and spun. "Clear the field! Espen has agreed to a sparring match! It's high time we teach some of you more hand-to-hand combat strategies." She turned to me, her eyes wide with excitement. "It's been months since I last got him to teach a lesson. Now, we can really have some fun."

I smirked at her exuberance for battle and fighting. It was little wonder she'd been chosen as Espen's second.

"Stay with the class," Espen said. He widened his eyes at me, conveying just how serious he was. "Whatever happens, don't leave the sidelines."

"What do you mean 'whatever happens?'" My voice pitched higher and my heart started to race. The memory of him convulsing on the floor in the mountain last year flashed through my mind. I couldn't bear the thought of him vulnerable or injured.

Espen rested his hands on my shoulders and offered me a reassuring look. "Ylva is the only one who has ever come close to besting me in battle thanks to her shrewd intellect and strategic thinking. Which is why I hired her as my second-in-command. However, I'm still the better of us."

I shook my head at his indefatigable confidence. "Could you actually get hurt, though?"

"Ancestors willing!" Ylva yelled from where she took up position on one side of the oval the fae were forming.

Espen scoffed and dropped his hands to his sides. "Ylva hasn't landed a blow in years."

"Yes, but it *has* happened," she said, stretching her arms where she waited. "It may have been five years ago, but you let down your guard and I got you in the ribs."

"I was drunk! It wasn't a fair fight."

"Well, let's hope you can hold your own today then."

I snickered at their friendly bickering. Espen turned back to me and planted a quick peck on my cheek. "I'll be fine. Just enjoy the show," he said with enough cockiness that my body flushed.

With a smirk on his lips and a flick of his eyebrows, Espen skipped backward onto the compacted snowy field. Murmurs broke out among the gathered Forest Fae soldiers, many of whom had pushed the snow into long mounds and were using them as makeshift benches. I popped a squat at the end of one, wiggling and molding the snow to my butt, and settled in to watch.

The two leaders started pacing at the opposite ends of the clearing, their eyes locked on each other's movements.

"Now, what is the main problem for a fae with destroyer powers in the winter?" Ylva asked the class, sounding more like a teacher using the Socratic Method on her students than someone who was currently in the ring.

"Avalanche," a fae two spots down from me shouted.

"Exactly." Ylva grinned like a cat that had trapped a mouse, and I let out a long-winded sigh. She'd known he would be at a loss during this exercise, which was probably why she'd asked for it in the first place.

Espen didn't look concerned though. In fact, the fae was grinning from ear to ear as if he was enjoying himself. He stretched his arms across him and behind him, like he was preparing for an eighties Jazzercise class. All he needed was the sweatband on his head and a unitard.

Without further preamble, Ylva crossed her arms in front of her before quickly bringing them down to her sides. Energy shimmered around her fists and two lightsaber-length sticks appeared in her hands, the wood polished smooth.

Espen rolled his eyes and several soldiers around me snickered.

"Sword please?" Espen commanded with a quick glance to his left.

A soldier scurried around and a second later, a sharp wooden blade that sparkled as if it had been reinforced with magic flew through the air. Without even looking, Espen caught it and spun it around a few times, assessing its weight.

"Thank you!" he said, never taking his eyes off Ylva. "Are you ready?"

She crouched and knocked her sticks together. "Are you?"

Espen narrowed his eyes at her taunt and launched.

They were a blur of sticks, arms, and swift feet. Espen brought down his blade aiming for Ylva's head, but she blocked its progress, crossing her thick batons and letting them take the hit rather than her. Their weapons had barely touched before they were moving again. Ylva swung for his legs with one stick while aiming upward with the other. Espen pirouetted out of her reach, coming up behind her. She spun on the spot, rising at the same time, and parried another blow from him.

I itched to have my camera, wanting to put it on rapid shutter speed and capture their mesmerizing movements. Especially Espen. I'd never seen him move like this before. For such a tall and built man, he moved like a feather on the wind. A very lethal feather that struck one of Ylva's sticks hard enough to send it flying.

Everyone nearby ducked as it flew over our heads and crashed against a tree with a *thwack*.

Espen chuckled and cocky energy rolled off him in waves, cresting over me and sending warmth down my spine as I watched.

The two in the ring continued their dance. Lunge, lunge, stab, sweep. Lunge, stab, sweep and spin. Dodging each other's blows or parrying them with ease, they kept at it. The sound of their weapons meeting ricocheted across the clearing, echoing off the tree line and the little red-and-white cabin.

I leaned over to the Forest Fae beside me, a short man with a dusting of freckles across his nose who looked too young to be a soldier. "Fifty Kroner says one of them taps out in the next five minutes."

The fae snorted just as Ylva flipped, lost her balance and landed on her back.

"Never mind," I said, refocusing on the clearing.

Espen was there in a heartbeat, sword at her throat, kicking away her remaining stick.

She slammed her fists into the snow beneath her. "Fuck it all."

Espen loomed over her, shook his head, retracted his sword, and extended his hand. She let out a long sigh and took his offer. He pulled her up and dusted the snow off her shoulders.

"Well, I tried," she said as the soldiers around me clapped.

"It was a valiant attempt," Espen said.

Ylva grumbled and huffed as the applause subsided.

With a smile, Espen faced the gathered soldiers. "My recommendation for you all is a minimum of three hours of yoga per week. It not only exercises the mind, but also the lungs and limbs. Improves flexibility too. So, when you need to move swiftly, your body is able to react accordingly." He ended his monologue with a namaste and bowed his head to his hands in prayer position.

I rose from my snowy seat and brushed my hands over my ass, removing any cold remnants as Espen gave the sword to a soldier and walked over.

Espen wiggled his eyebrows. "Did you like my moves?"

"Oh, I thoroughly enjoy your moves," I replied with a cheeky grin I couldn't keep at bay.

Espen slid his hand against my back, steering me toward the tree line and trail we'd taken to get up here.

"Don't get yourself killed while you're gone," Ylva yelled across the clearing, stopping us in our tracks. "I'm interested in a pay raise, not a promotion."

"I promise to bring back *lefse* and a couple extra Kroner for you," Espen replied.

"Deal!" She turned to me with a tiny salute. "Lennie, always a pleasure."

I waved. "Drinks at Fisken when we get back?"

"I'll get the first round." She smiled and bounced toward a group of marksmen lining up with their bows again.

I turned to Espen and shivered. My outerwear was good quality but not thick enough for the season, and I hadn't fully acclimated to Norwegian winters yet. "Can we head back home now? I'm getting cold."

A sneaky grin swept across his face. "Oh, I can think of many ways to warm you up. May take all afternoon to get through the list."

"Well, in that case, lead the way, General."

71

LENNIE

Tiny rays of early-morning sunlight peeked over the horizon and the lack of cloud cover made the air temperature colder than a witch's tit. I stepped out of our boathouse, bundled up in more layers than an ogre, ready for the long drive to Alvdalen. Espen and Øyvin had clearly had the same thought with their chunky sweaters and winter jackets shoved into the backseat of the vehicle.

I threw my duffel bag into the trunk of the dark-gray sedan, tucking it in beside Espen's. "So, whose car is this?"

Øyvin appeared beside me and put his pristine silver wheelie suitcase next to mine. "Oddvar's."

I bit my lip and took a deep breath through my nose, trying to remain calm. "You mean to tell me, that the little old man had a car this whole time? A car he could've used this past autumn to take me down fjord when I originally missed my cruise ship?"

Øyvin nodded and shut the trunk. "Yes, it's his son's—the supply boat captain. Rarely uses it, but he lets friends borrow it on occasion."

I inhaled in through my nose and out through my mouth, steadying my heart rate and mentally talking myself down from the looming expletive explosion that sat at the end of my tongue. It was fine. Oddvar had said most people would laugh at my misfortune and not help, which had certainly proved true. I just didn't realize that meant *him*, too. I hadn't been his friend that first day, but damn it, with all the coffee and sandwiches I bought at the man's café, surely that earned me the title of friend by now?

Øyvin walked away with a slick grin on his face, probably well aware of where my head was currently, and climbed into the front seat. I was about to protest when Espen sidled in front of me and placed his hands on my shoulders.

"One day, probably once you start working at the café this spring, Oddvar will consider you a friend," he said with a gentle smile, his hair in its usual unruly state, desperate to be pushed off his forehead. "And, as for Øyvin claiming the front seat, he's too tall to sit in the back for seven hours."

I sighed. He had a good point about both. Oddvar had graciously offered me a job at the café after my not-so-subtle request back in December, so that was a sign of good favor. But—

Hold up.

"Seven hours?" I shucked his palms off me and grabbed the front of his emerald sweater. "You said it was a long drive, but you failed to mention just *how* long last night."

He wrapped his fingers around mine, warming me, while also untangling my digits from his sweater. "We'll make a few stops along the way, but, because it's winter, we have to weave along the fjords before heading inland and take the long way around the mountains."

A whimper left my lips, and I deflated. Espen swept his arms around me, encasing me in a hug while backing me toward the car. He pressed a quick peck to my forehead. "I promise you a big lunch and some extra coffee at the halfway point."

He opened the door, and I let out an exasperated sigh as I clambered into the backseat. "Fine, but make it a really *big* coffee."

About thirty minutes outside of town, Espen pulled off the main road and started down a smaller side road, wending the car between the thick copse of trees on either side of us. The light dimmed slightly, but up ahead, it appeared a little brighter. He slowed as we reached the opening and drove us into the glade, snow and gravel crunching beneath the tires. My eyes bugged out at the sight before me.

A massive dark-wood church constructed in sections that grew smaller as it rose toward the sky sat in the middle of a snowy clearing filled with weather-worn tombstones. On some of the tallest spires sat rudimentary dragon heads, and on the very top one was a Christian cross. There were no other designs on the building, no runes or Nordic patterns. It looked as if Vikings had torn apart their boats and used the wood to erect a place of worship.

I gawked at the medieval looking building and whispered, "What is this place?"

"It's a Stave Church," Espen replied with a solemn tone as he parked in the little parking lot separated from the burial grounds by a small stone wall. "You can find them around coastal Norway. Some are from the Middle Ages, others are more recent builds."

"By 'more recent' he means the 1500s," Øyvin chimed in from the passenger seat, his shoulders set with tension.

I took a deep breath and let that number, that *age*, sink in. It was mind boggling, to say the least, and I wiped my hand across my face before staring back up at the ancient structure in front of me. "And how old is this one?"

Espen shut off the car and leaned back in his seat with a sigh. "Middle Ages."

"Did you bring me here to pray the trouble out of me, or to take me across the altar?" I wiggled my brows, catching Espen's gaze in the rearview mirror.

He rolled his lips, stifling a smile and the small chuckle that escaped, before shaking his head. "I stop here to leave some flowers every time I head North," he said, then opened the door and clambered out, not giving me further explanation.

I furrowed my brow and unbuckled my seatbelt, leaning forward to Øyvin. "Any idea what this is about?"

He let out a long breath and scratched his stubbled jaw. "This is where the Forest Fae Council used to meet."

I listened intently to Øyvin while Espen opened the trunk and grabbed the flowers he'd stashed in there. Closing it up again, he made his way into the graveyard, walking down a few rows before turning toward two gravestones and coming to a stop.

"Their council meetings were held here for decades," Øyvin continued, both of us watching the Forest Fae with his head bowed. "This is also where Queen Ragnhild and Espen's mentor, Mads, are buried."

My stomach sank, sadness easing through my limbs as I sat back in my seat. Trust me to make a crude joke at such a time, too. You'd think I'd learned my lesson by now, but nope. I reached for the door handle, then hesitated. Did Espen want me out there keeping him company? Would I be intruding?

Øyvin peered over his shoulder and gave me a short nod. "He won't mind."

"You sure?"

He nodded again.

"Okay, then." I opened the door, the smell of snow and pine drifting in the cold air. "Are you staying in here?"

Øyvin turned, facing forward once more, and grunted.

The change in his mood had me worried. But perhaps he didn't like graveyards? I myself wasn't exactly keen on them—the idea of lines of decomposing bodies had always given me the creeps—but this one was ancient and my Forest Fae was standing there looking morose. Maybe cemeteries reminded Øyvin of the brother he lost in the war down south twenty years ago, the battle that we now knew had been spearheaded by the late King Balder and which had led to the demise of the Forest Fae Queen and her Head Guard, too.

"I'll be right back," I muttered, leaving Øyvin in the warm car with his thoughts.

I staggered through the snow toward Espen, and the closer I got to the church, the further my mouth fell open. The doorway was tiny—even at five-foot-eight, I would have to hunch over to enter. The wood sides and tiled roof rose like the masts of a pirate ship. It was practically begging to be photographed, but my camera was in the car and now didn't feel like the right time.

Bracing against the chill, I wandered down the rows of gravestones, each marker more dilapidated than the next, with little tufts of snow adorning the top. Espen stood before two newer, light-gray stones, the bundle of flowers placed at the base of one and a single rose at the other. I stepped up beside him, and he glanced over, giving me a tender smile.

"So, you stop here every time to say hi?" My voice was soft and gentle as I gazed down at the two stones.

Ragnhild Thorleifson.

Mads Robertson.

Espen looked back at the graves. "I do."

The stones were simple, no dates listed, no other markers to reveal who they were or *what* they had been. The only exception was a small sky-blue stone embedded in a crown carved above Ragnhild's name—an indicator of her title and importance in the fae world that blended so seamlessly with our own.

"What was she like?" I asked, not sure if it was appropriate, but lacking anything else to say. Cool air wound around me and I fastened the zipper of my jacket up to my chin.

Espen let out a little scoff-like sound and bit his lower lip, holding back a smile. "She was the fiercest woman I've ever met. Kind and caring, but with a stoic facade that was rarely phased by anything."

I raised my brows, shoving my bare hands into my pockets. "More stoic than Halvar?"

"No one is more stoic than Halvar, but she was certainly a contender for the 'most unyielding' title." He tilted his head to one side, eyes not wavering from her gravestone.

"Sounds like my kinda Queen," I said. I'd always had a bit of a soft spot for the tough eggs. Including the one back in the fjell and the one currently in the car. I inched closer to Espen. "Are you okay?"

He nodded absentmindedly, then straightened up and turned toward me. "Quite all right. I just..." He let out a deep breath, his shoulders falling. "She would've been devastated to lose Queen Freija."

I couldn't blame him for feeling that way. The entire fjell and all the Forest Fae I'd run into at the funeral had been devastated at the loss of the Fjell Queen—her light snuffed out too soon.

"But," Espen continued, "Ranghild would've loved that you got some of Freija's magic. She'd have fun with that, train you till you cried."

I snickered. "She really does sound like Halvar. My poor arms are still sore from his training."

Espen laugh softly and reached for my hand. I pulled one out of my pocket and placed it in his. His palm was warm even in the cold weather, and he moved to leave. We walked side-by-side out of the graveyard toward the parking lot.

"She loved her people," Espen said, continuing his story about Ragnhild. "Always made sure to check in with everyone, knew everyone by name and their life's story. She was an exceptional leader." He tilted his head to the church at our backs. "We held our council meetings here for several decades before things eventually moved further inland and then to Alvdalen. She was able to encourage the nearby town to let a local fae—not that the humans knew what he was—become the caretaker and manager for the property. With him holding the keys, we were able to meet at night when the tourists and humans had gone to sleep and no one dared venture out here in the dark."

I glanced over my shoulder at the looming building and agreed with those humans. I wouldn't want to be wandering around here in the dark either. The church looked like something out of a Gothic or horror movie, all dark and gloomy wood with steeply pitched roofs and no windows. There was an ominous, almost creepy feeling about the place, too. Likely because of how extremely old the church was, and how many dead bodies lay buried around it. I shook off the goosebumps that settled across my skin and climbed back into the car.

Espen jumped back into the driver's seat and started the ignition. "You doing all right?" He asked Øyvin.

The Fjord Fae's eyes were shut tight, his chest rising and falling slowly. "Just taking a quick nap."

"Well, you can nap some more as we've still got six and a half hours to go," Espen replied as I buckled in. "While you do that, I'll listen to my audiobook. Aliens just landed and I need to know what happens next."

Øyvin let out a "mm-hmm" and said nothing more on the matter.

I leaned back in my seat with a groan, letting my head fall against the headrest with a small thump. Over six hours winding around fjords and mountains... part of me wanted to be awake and watch the scenery, the other part wanted to follow Øyvin and sleep.

After about thirty minutes staring out the window as we zigzagged along twisty roads, I decided Øyvin was on to something, and I settled in to sleep for as much of the journey as possible.

72
LENNIE

Around four hours into the drive, we stopped in a minuscule village and grabbed lunch. I'd gone for a reindeer stew which was delicious until Øyvin teased that I was eating Rudolph. Then I'd had to reason my way into finishing the dish. I'd eaten plenty of deer meat before—usually in the form of kielbasa sausages with eggs—but it took a moment for me to shake off the notion of eating a cute and innocent creature.

Øyvin finished his lunch before the rest of us—some sort of veggie sandwich—and ran to the outdoor sports store across the street, claiming he needed to grab something.

Once Espen and I finished eating, I sauntered out of the roadside café, my stomach full and satisfied. Another three hours on the road would be fine. I'd just take another nap, and, voilà, we'd be there.

As I reached the car with Espen, Øyvin ran back across the road, a massive brown paper bag in his hand. I furrowed my eyebrows. What on earth was that? The guys had lived here their entire lives, they were fully prepared for the weather and conditions. I on the other hand... *Oh no... Oh, please no...*

Stepping back and bumping into Espen, my smile vanished and my eyes widened. Øyvin caught the look and grinned as he stepped up by the car and pulled something out of the bag. A neon-orange winter jacket—hunting gear colors in most parts of the world—assaulted my eyeballs. Easily my least favorite color *ever*.

"Who is that for?" I asked, even though, deep down, I knew the answer.

Øyvin wiggled the piece of clothing, the rip-resistant material swishing as he did so. "You."

I shuddered and shook my head rapidly, while Espen desperately tried to contain his laughter behind me and failed miserably. I crossed my arms and pressed my lips together. "There's not a chance in hell I'm wearing that."

"Well, it's your size and will help us make sure you don't get lost," Øyvin countered, that grin still plastered across his annoyingly gorgeous lips.

"Ooooor." I raised my left hand and wiggled my fingers. Light bounced off the sparkling sapphire engagement ring. "You could just put a tracker in the ring?"

"This is cheaper."

Dropping my hand, I narrowed my eyes. "How do you know it's my size?"

That grin slowly turned into something more heated as he angled his head and leisurely ran his gaze down my body and then back up to my face. "Let's just say I'm well acquainted with your curves."

Heat flushed through me and I swayed on the spot under his heady stare, doing my damnedest not to cross my legs.

He stepped closer, leaning down to whisper in my ear. "Trust me, I'll take no pleasure in seeing you wear this." I swallowed hard before he continued. "But I'd rather not lose track of you on this trip."

How could he be such an endearing asshole?

He leaned back and shook the bag. "There's winter trousers in here, too."

I let out an exasperated sigh. "Of course there is."

Espen laughed and swatted my ass. "Get in the car, Lennie."

Øyvin shoved my new outerwear into my hands and gave me a wink before climbing into the passenger seat.

Shaking my head, I shoved the obnoxious jacket back into the paper bag with the matching pants and strode around to the other side of the car. Yanking on the door handle, I stutter-stepped when it failed to open. "For fuck's sake." My mouth curled into a scowl as Espen burst out laughing.

"Sorry." More snickers emanated from inside the vehicle as Espen pressed a button on his door and unlocked the car.

Waking up with an hour to go until we reached Alvdalen, I contented myself with watching the scenery. Trees were bedecked in white, their branches bowing under the weight, and tall orange sticks jutted up out of the snow on the side of the road, indicating where the lane ended. This far inland, the weather had morphed from glorious sunshine to overcast. It felt like the snow and sky were working together to cocoon me in a wintry blanket.

Espen was still behind the wheel, happy as can be, listening to his audiobook, which I hadn't really paid any attention to the entire drive. While I didn't want to stop his story-time, my mind spun with every mile we neared Alvdalen.

"Couple questions before we meet your family, if you have a moment," I said, and Espen quickly switched off the book before peering at me in the rearview mirror.

"Go ahead."

"Please remind me the names of everyone we're about to meet."

"Of course," he said, his bubbly demeanor seeming stronger as we closed in on his hometown. "I have two sisters, Ingrid and Turi. Ingrid is the oldest and she's married to Knut-Arne. They have three children; two girls and one boy. Turi is the middle sibling. She's not married, but does have a few cats that she treats like her children."

"And what are their jobs in the fae world?"

"Ingrid and Knut-Arne are gardeners. But they both work part-time so someone can be home with their youngest. Turi used to work with animals, mostly deer, but she is now the Mayor of Alvdalen."

"So, several members of the Solbakke family are in leadership roles," I said.

"Yes, I guess you're right. And Turi was selected to run our Forest Fae Council meetings when she took up the post as mayor. Always helpful to have someone working on the inside with the humans," he added as almost an afterthought.

"Just like working for the police station back in Skolvik?"

He smiled. "Exactly. Plus, I actually enjoy the work, especially my ranger duties."

He wasn't lying; aside from the chaos that had erupted last autumn, it was easy to see Espen truly enjoyed his job and cared about the people of Skolvik, both fae and human. The number of times he came home buzzing after a day of work was incalculable. It was as if the position gave him energy instead of sapping it from him. Then again, perhaps that was just Espen and his sunny demeanor?

"Anything else I should know about before I meet your family?" I asked, then quickly added, "Do they know about our... erm... impending legal marriage?" I was still mentally coming to terms with the fact that I would be marrying Espen so I could legally stay in Norway and remain close to the other Fjell Fae. I still hadn't told my family and couldn't figure out how to explain that it was for immigration purposes. My mother would be elated that I was getting married, but frustrated that there wouldn't be a ceremony or reception to plan.

"I may have mentioned it," Espen mumbled, and I straightened in my seat.

"Espen..."

"Okay, so I told them over the phone on Christmas Day while you were video calling your parents."

Of course he had.

However fast we were heading toward the inevitable label making—perhaps already had with my moving in with them—the three of us still hadn't said certain words out loud, or made any particular remarks that would be considered *defining the relationship*. Honest to hell, how could you define this? "Your family knows that it's paperwork, right? They know that Øyvin is in this too, even if we haven't made any definitions yet?"

"Yes, they know, and they're excited to meet you."

I glanced over at Øyvin who was still fast asleep, or more likely, pretending to nap while listening in on the conversation. Not much got past him. I doubted this conversation did either.

I also had a feeling we were driving straight toward definitions, and part of me warmed at the thought, while the other part was baffled. I hadn't been in a serious relationship in a long time, and hadn't felt the need for it. I was always traveling, too, which had not lent itself to anything steady. But, then, when I least expected it, this grumbly and bubbly pair came into my life and changed everything. I'd changed too. In so many ways. So, perhaps it was time to let down my guard a bit more and explore exactly where this *entanglement* would take me? I was obviously physically open to this trio. Maybe I was mentally too? Maybe I had been for a while and just hadn't recognized it yet.

"You still with us or did you fall asleep with your eyes open?" Espen said, regaining my attention.

I shook my head. "Yeah, I... Thank you for the run down. Let me know when we get into town."

I settled back in my seat and looked out the window. Maybe, just maybe, this was what people talked about when they said you found love when you least expected it.

73
LENNIE

I straightened as we drove into town, sweeping along snow-plowed roads into a small enclave of about twenty houses nestled at the head of a long lake, but set a ways back from the shoreline proper. Moonlight danced across the ice-covered lake, small snowbanks marking its edges. With a long-exposure and a tripod set-up, I could probably get a few good snaps of it, even in this lighting.

I stretched my arms to the sides and then above my head as best I could in the cramped backseat. "Does the lake have a name?"

"Big Long Lake," Espen replied, turning down another road.

I laughed, but when Espen didn't offer another name, I said, "Wait, you're serious?"

Espen nodded. "And the other lake nearby is Little Long Lake."

"Wow. Some people are not creative."

Espen grinned as we pulled into the short driveway of a dark-red house with white trim and a snow-covered roof. Wooden steps ran up to the front door and a large deck flanked the left side of the house surrounded by drifts of snow. It was a much smaller, simpler home than those in the US, but was well cared for—the driveway plowed, no chipped paint, and a warm glow emanated from the windows.

"We're here," Espen said with a beaming smile. He shut off the car and bounded out of the vehicle like he hadn't just driven for seven hours.

"Finally," Øyvin mumbled, unfurling himself as he got out, then stretching like a swimmer—waving his arms about and slapping himself on his back.

With a pasted on smile, and nerves fluttering like hummingbirds in my stomach, I unbuckled and followed their lead, heading toward the home. This was it. I was going to meet Espen's family. The most important people in his life. We reached the front step and I sucked in a lungful of cold air as Espen gently knocked on the door. Not waiting for a response, he pushed open the door and let us inside.

I was immediately assaulted by shrieks of laughter and tiny growls. Standing in the tiled and cluttered entryway, we removed our shoes and jackets, hanging the latter on crowded hooks full of colorful outerwear. Espen shook his head at the continued cacophony that escaped the living area and peered around the corner. Silence fell, followed swiftly by full on screams of delight.

"Uncle Espen!"

"Uncle Espy!"

Øyvin and I followed Espen through the archway into the living room that looked like something out of an IKEA catalog with toys strewn about the floor. Three small children launched themselves at Espen. Two girls, their brunette ringlets bouncing about their shoulders, wrapped their arms around Espen's, while a little boy who looked like a miniature version of my Forest Fae, locked his arms around Espen's knees.

"Uncle Espy," the boy said, his eyes wide as he beamed up at his uncle. "You can be a dragon with me."

"Nooo," the shorter girl butted in. "Uncle Espen is going to be the knight that kills the troll and saves the princess."

Øyvin scoffed, and I swatted him in the stomach. "Careful or I'll offer you up as the troll. Seems fitting don't you think?"

Øyvin scowled at me as the room fell silent. The trio of kids turned and stared at us like we were aliens straight out of Espen's audiobook. *Ah, I recognize that look.* We were strangers, and young kids weren't always fans of new people. That seemed to be the case with the girls, who hid slightly behind Espen, before starting up playtime again.

"Perhaps Uncle Espen and our guests would like to sit down and have something to drink?" a feminine voice said behind me, and I spun. In the whitewashed archway to a kitchen stood a woman with her brown hair tied up in the messiest of buns, flushed cheeks, and her eyes crinkling at the corners. If you'd put her in a line-up, I'd still know she was related to Espen solely for the clothes she wore: a rainbow striped sweater with a flower and toadstool broach, a yellow-pleated skirt, and black tights. The epitome of a ray of sunshine.

The kids continued playing, too caught up in the surprise arrival of their uncle, but I gave her a gentle smile. "Hi, I'm Lennie. This is Øyvin."

Her lips tilted up at one corner, happiness radiating from every part of her as she clasped her hands together at her chest. "I'm Ingrid. It is nice to finally meet you." Her brown eyes swept to Øyvin and she gave him a reverential nod like she knew exactly who he was. "Welcome to our home. I'm sorry for the ruckus, but when you have three under the age of ten, the volume is always set to high."

"Oh, I bet." I said, laughter lacing my tone, as the two girls tried to help Espen into a knight's costume with a sword and shield.

"May I see the ring?" Ingrid asked, her eyes widening.

I flinched slightly but proffered my left hand.

A gleeful smile spread across her lips as she took my fingers in hers, turning them for a closer look. The tear-shaped sapphire sparkled, light bouncing across its faceted surface.

I was slowly growing accustomed to wearing the silver band of intertwined vines and leaves, but every time someone asked to see the ring, it was a not-so-subtle reminder that I was in fact engaged. Even if it was just to keep me in Norway. Aside from family, the rest of the world couldn't know that though. If we were going to pull this off, I had to fake it and make everyone believe it was true. Operation Fake-Fae-gement was underway!

Ingrid released my hand. "It's beautiful."

Brushing a stray lock of hair behind my ear, I said, "Thank you, but it's just for immigration purposes, you know."

"Uh-huh," she replied, her voice flat and unbelieving as she turned toward the living room.

The little boy jumped off the arm of the sofa flapping his arms and yelling. "*Rawwwwr*! I will burn you alive!"

"Kristoffer, what have I said about jumping off the sofa?" Ingrid asked, her voice terse as she set her hands on her hips. Her lips moved differently from when she'd been talking directly to me. My forehead scrunched as I looked between her and the kids— *Ooooooh*. She'd been speaking English to me, but spoke Norwegian to the little ones.

"But Mamma," Kristoffer said in Norwegian, huffing and panting like she couldn't possibly understand. "I am the dragon. I must do dragon things."

"Well, do dragons like to eat?" Ingrid asked.

Kristoffer's eyes lit up and he gave his mother a look that universally conveyed, "Well duh." He sprinted for the kitchen, slip-sliding on the hardwood floors in his woolly socks.

Giving us a wide berth as he passed, and using his mother's legs as a shield, Kristoffer mumbled a "Hey."

Ingrid steered him toward the kitchen with a nudge. "This is Lennie and Øyvin, Uncle Espen's friends. Now, go wash your hands."

The kid shrugged and ran into the kitchen, swiftly followed by his sisters. Ingrid introduced them as they scuttled past. "Kristoffer, four. Kari, eight," she said, motioning toward the taller of the two girls. "And Katrine, six," she added, nodding toward the second. Both gave us shy waves as they passed, their pink tulle dresses swishing about their ankles.

Espen, meanwhile, groaned and panted, trying to remove a breast-plate that barely covered his left rib cage, without breaking it.

"With how long you've been in the Guard, brother, I'd thought you'd be more adept at removing armor," Ingrid said, a smile curling at her lips.

Espen laughed, finally able to wrangle the Velcro straps off himself and remove the fake armor. He gently threw the costume piece onto the well-worn couch. "They don't make them like they used to."

The remark earned a mumbled "True" from Øyvin.

I shook my head and turned to Ingrid. "You mentioned dinner?"

"Yes." She beamed and headed for the kitchen. "Follow me. Knut-Arne should be done with the steaks on the grill any minute."

"You grill in the winter?" I asked, my voice notching up a few octaves as I stumbled after her.

Ingrid nodded. "Rain, snow, sunshine. We grill whenever we want to here in Norway. If you let the weather dictate what you do, you'll never do anything."

I chuckled. That might be the most Norwegian sentence I'd ever heard.

The kitchen invited us with the warmth of a home-cooked meal. Pale yellow cabinets skirted the length of the room to my right, with white-washed ones running above them. Used cups sat beside the sink, waiting to be washed. We took our seats at a large pine table, the mismatched wood chairs scraping lightly against the tiled floor.

As my butt touched the checkered-cushion, the backdoor beside the fridge swung open, letting in a cold breeze and a large man with light-brown hair and a short beard. Snowflakes dappled his jacket-clad shoulders and a platter of grilled meat balanced on his broad, weathered hand.

"Welcome, welcome. I'm Knut-Arne." The rich timbre of his voice settled over the room as he nodded and turned to his brother-in-law. "Drive okay?"

Espen nodded in return. "Perfectly fine. Only ran into one brief snow shower, clear the rest of the way."

"Good, good, good," Knut-Arne muttered, setting the plate in the middle of the table and shucking off his jacket, hanging it over the back of his chair. The delectable smell of steak drifted through the room, and saliva gathered in my mouth.

"I heard you don't eat fish, Øyvin. So, I made sure we had steak instead," Knut-Arne said. He took a seat between his wife and eldest daughter, across from me, Øyvin and Espen. Kristoffer and Kari were at the ends of the table, with Kristoffer in a Tripp Trapp chair.

"Thank you," Øyvin replied, taking the dish of potatoes from Ingrid and helping himself before offering to help Kristoffer beside him.

Kristoffer quirked a single eyebrow. "You're a Fjord Fae. You don't eat fish because they're your friends?"

I choked on my own spit, covering the cough with my fist. *Damn*. Glad I hadn't taken a sip of water at that moment or it would've rushed out of my nose. Loud squawking aside, for making that remark, I liked the little kid.

"Kristoffer," Ingrid chided the boy who shrank at her admonishment. "We don't say things like that. Just because someone is from the Fjord Fae faction, doesn't mean they automatically don't eat fish. There are many Forest Fae and Fjell Fae that don't eat fish either. Apologize please."

"Sorry," Kristoffer muttered. Before Øyvin had a chance to say "apology accepted" the little guy shoveled a potato into his mouth.

I bit my bottom lip to stop the laughter bubbling up inside me and caught Espen doing the same. Øyvin merely shrugged and continued serving himself.

Dinner proceeded with congenial conversation while we devoured the delicious steak and potatoes with red cabbage and gravy. Ingrid agreed to share her gravy recipe with Øyvin, and Knut-Arne peppered Espen and I with questions about Skolvik.

I looked around the table, a sense of welcome and family washed over me—a feeling of ease and home. My heart fluttered. *This is going well.*

"I am The Darkness," Kristoffer mumbled, trying to get his voice to sound as grumbly as possible. "The Darkness is finished."

"The Darkness can wait until everyone is done with their dinner before he goes on rampaging," Ingrid said with a stern look in her son's direction.

"The Darkness wants freedom."

"You heard your mother," Knut-Arne piped in, and it took every ounce of my less-than-great resolve not to laugh out loud at the kid's antics. "You can wait five more minutes."

Kristoffer huffed and wrapped his little arms around himself, holding onto his shoulders like a bat.

Knut-Arne turned to Espen. "So, what *exactly* brings you to Alvdalen?"

Ingrid bobbed her head beside him as she took another bite of her dinner.

"Well, we need to find someone and this was their last known location," Espen replied.

"A manhunt?" Knut-Arne asked. His eyes widened as he took a sip of water.

"Of a sort." Espen tilted his head from one side then the other before glancing at me and Øyvin, probably wondering how much he should divulge to his sister and brother-in-law. Plus, the kids were present. Little ears had a tendency to repeat things. "We need to find someone for the Fjell. Halvar thought we'd be the best for the job."

Ingrid elbowed her husband's side. "I told you Halvar was involved."

I set down my knife and fork on my plate and folded my hands in my lap. "You know Halvar?"

"Everyone knows *of* Halvar," Ingrid said. A truth that seemed to precede the stoic fae. While I still didn't know exactly how old Halvar was, he had an air of myth and legend around him. Clearly that reputation stretched this far inland, too. "So, you really can't tell us anything else? Not even *who* you're looking for?"

Espen let out a long sigh and rested his forearms against the table edge. "I shouldn't say until I've spoken to the Council. But I'm hoping Turi might be able to help us out. We're meeting her for lunch tomorrow."

"Ah, okay then." Ingrid conceded. "If there's anyone in this town that knows everyone by name, it's Turi. I'd say you fall into that category too, but..."

"Not this again," Espen laughed gently and his chair creaked as he leaned back.

"Don't blame me for wanting you closer."

"I'll consider moving back once enough time has passed. Too many humans are still alive from when I last lived here, even if they are predominantly in nursing homes."

"Fine."

Espen tilted his head toward his sister like he didn't believe she was "fine."

She set down her silverware and clasped her hands together against the edge of the table. "Just promise me this. While you're here, would you please join the kids and I for an afternoon of skating at the lake at the end of the week? I don't want to interrupt your work, but the girls have the day off school and we'd love to spend more time with you while you're in town."

Espen's shoulders slumped and he softened up, a gentle smile tugging at his lips. How could he possibly say no to that? While we needed to focus on our search, a few hours with his family wouldn't hurt.

Espen looked over my shoulder to Øyvin and then at me for confirmation. I nodded.

He turned back to his sister. "We'd love to."

Ingrid smiled from ear to ear, her mom-bun wobbling as she straightened in her seat. "Excellent."

Silence settled over us once more as we finished up our meal until Ingrid said, "Okay, Kristoffer, you may leave—"

Her son flew from his chair and barreled out of the kitchen, his arms spread wide. "The Darkness has been set free! *RAAAWR!*"

"We prepared the little cabin by the lake for you," Ingrid said after dinner, smiling at the three of us as we pulled on our jackets. Knut-Arne furrowed his brow and opened his mouth to say something, but was quickly shut down by his wife with a swat of her hand to his abdomen. She turned to me, adding, "The cabin was in Knut-Arne's family for years. We did some renovations, but it's relatively simple. If there are any problems, please let me know."

"Thank you," I said at the same time as the guys, and Ingrid gave me a toothy grin.

We tugged on our shoes, and said our goodbyes, drifting out the door as Ingrid turned to the living room and said, "Right, children. Time for bed!"

"Mamma, nooo."

"You cannot catch me!"

The door closed behind Øyvin. As we descended the front steps, I was instantly swept away to thoughts of my own nieces and how they never wanted to go to bed. Especially not after I'd visited. I might've had a bad habit of getting them riled up, but my brother Andrew always claimed they slept like logs when they finally got into bed.

The snick of a lock sounded and a door flew open. "The Darkness refuses! He cannot be locked away!" We turned in the driveway just in time to see Kristoffer barrel across the side-deck by the kitchen and launch himself like a flying squirrel into the snow drift, his father chasing after him.

"Do they need help?" I asked, laughing at the kid's hijinks.

Espen waved his hand. "No, Knut's got him."

Øyvin hummed to himself as he climbed into the front seat of Oddvar's sedan. "I like that kid."

Me too. I smiled up at the house. Unsurprisingly, I liked them all.

LENNIE

With the light of the full moon casting a white glow upon the area, we pulled up to the lakeside cabin surrounded by mounds of snow, much of which had been cleared aside to allow room to walk and park. With a little porch by the front door, and a dense woodland of pine trees on the right side of the house, the dark wooden building looked like something out of a wintry movie where the city girl fell for the small-town hero.

I got out of the car and stared at our surroundings, turning to the picturesque lake as the guys began to unload. Just like the big lake near Ingrid's house, this body of water—the Little Long Lake, as they called it—was frozen over, with a dusting of snow across it. Perched in the middle was a small island covered in snow and a variety of hibernating flora, including a few pines and some barren trees with dark bark.

I sighed at the beauty around me, breathing in the crystal clear air, wishing it was brighter so I could get out my new camera. But that could wait until tomorrow. The scenery would likely be even more spectacular in the daylight. I'd just have to sit tight until midday for the best lighting conditions due to Norway's short winter days.

"Are you coming inside?" Espen said.

I nodded and traipsed across the driveway, the snow crunching beneath my boots as I joined him and Øyvin on the porch. Espen pulled out a key and swiftly unlocked the door, pushing it open to let us in.

We stepped inside, and before I could take in the space, Espen instructed me to remove my outerwear. Shucking off our jackets and boots, we hung the former on the hooks by the door, and left the latter in the drip tray beneath them. Beside that was a bizarre contraption attached to the wall. It looked like an air-conditioning unit with four short but wide corrugated hose pipes coming off it.

Øyvin caught me staring at the machine. "It's a boot dryer. You put the hoses into your boots and it pumps hot air into them to dry them out."

"That's amazing."

He gave me a tiny lopsided grin. "Very useful after a long day in the snow."

Espen picked up our bags again and motioned for me to explore the cabin.

The interior of the tiny building was rugged and simple. Along the left wall were three large windows with cream-colored curtains facing the lake. That side of the open living space also boasted a small living room with a gingham-patterned sofa, and two worn and mismatched armchairs. Beyond that was a four person dining set and a minuscule kitchen with the smallest refrigerator I'd ever seen—barely counter height.

To the right of the entry were two more doors. I opened the first and found a small, tiled bathroom with a porthole-sized square window above the toilet. To the right was a slim shower with a glass door that probably wouldn't work for either of the guys as the showerhead was really low. I snickered at the mental visual of Øyvin trying to use the shower, and moved on to the next room.

I strode toward what must've been the bedroom, opened the door, and halted abruptly. There, in the middle of the room, flanked by two tiny nightstands, covered in a green-and-white checkered duvet, was a lone bed covered in rose petals and a white envelope placed in the middle. I let out a snort of laughter. "Espen, your sister's got jokes!"

The Forest Fae sidled up next to me and peered into the room. "Ah, yes, well..." His stumbling words were accompanied by a low grumble emanating from Øyvin's chest as he joined us in the doorway. I couldn't stop the laugh that bubbled out of me.

"Better see what the letter says," I said.

"Agreed." Espen strode into the room, dumped his bag in the corner beside a rickety dresser, and threw himself onto the large bed.

I brushed aside the red petals, snapped up the envelope addressed to: *the three of you*, and settled onto the bed beside the bubbly fae. Espen tucked his hands behind his head, and Øyvin leaned against the doorframe, his arms and ankles crossed. "Any guesses what might be inside?"

"Knowing my sister, it's probably something happy and sappy."

Another soft laugh escaped me. That was the exact vibe I got from Ingrid when we visited this evening. She clearly cared a lot about her brother and shared his bubbly enthusiasm.

I peeled open the envelope and pulled out the little card inside. It was a tourist postcard from Alvdalen with a deer and mountains on it, plus a little Norwegian flag in the shape of a heart. Turning it over, I found beautiful cursive handwriting that I'd never ever achieve no matter how long I lived.

Dear Espen, Øyvin, and Lennie —

Congratulations on your impending nuptials! We hope your time in Alvdalen is full of joy, laughter, and many happy memories. I've stocked the cupboards with some essentials, but you'll need to venture to the shops for bread and milk. If you need anything during your stay, please let us know.

Love,

Ingrid and Knut-Arne

A little note at the bottom in chicken-scratch style writing said, *The petals were your sister's idea. - KA*

Espen chuckled as he read over my shoulder.

Øyvin continued watching from the doorway.

"So..." I set the postcard and envelope on the bedside table to my right. "Any ideas on what we could do for the rest of the evening?" Sure, my back ached from being in the car all day and I was feeling all kinds of warm and cozy after spending time with family, but it wasn't quite bedtime yet.

Øyvin rolled his eyes as a hint of a smirk twisted his lips. "Do you always deviate to sex?"

Leaning back against the headboard, I crossed my arms and lifted my chest slightly. "You know I don't."

"If it isn't *yoga*," Espen said. "It's coffee, photography, what new dish you tried—"

"Or how best to annoy me," Øyvin chimed in. "Like rearranging the spice cabinet by regions or organizing my sheet music by the composer's place of birth."

I snickered. "See, you both know me so well." Pulling off my sweatshirt and throwing it toward Øyvin's face, I added, "So, is that a no on the sex?"

Øyvin caught my sweater and folded it up, setting it neatly atop the dresser. Looking over his shoulder with a heated gaze, he replied, "I never said that." He bent down and unlocked his fancy-schmancy suitcase, withdrawing his wash-bag. "But I'm going to take a shower."

"Boo!"

He didn't even bother to give me the middle finger, let alone say another word before strolling out of the bedroom and into the bathroom, shutting the door behind him. A moment later, the sound of running water met my ears.

Hadn't he showered this morning? I shrugged. Maybe he stank or maybe he just wanted to be close to water. Either way, his absence gave me two-thirds of the bed to spread out on.

"Thank goodness this bed is big enough for all three of us," I said.

Espen rolled onto his side and faced me, propping his head in his hand. "This is the old Mikkelsen cabin. You've seen how broad-shouldered Knut-Arne is. His side of the family are all like that. So, they had this custom-sized bed made. I believe you'd call it a King Size in America."

I nodded. It was definitely big enough to be classified as such.

Doing a full body stretch, I brushed my left hand past Espen. He caught my hand with his and brought it to his lips. Pressing a kiss to each knuckle, he took his time worshiping me as if paying his respects to a medieval queen, and brushed his thumb over the engagement ring.

My pulse sped up and heat washed through me, igniting every part of my body. It was such a simple gesture from Espen. Yet, with each touch of his lips against my skin, it felt like he was giving me unspoken promises or wishing upon a star.

I rolled onto my side and swept my free hand against his cheek.

He drew a breath and sunk his teeth into his bottom lip. His gaze turned molten as he rested his left palm against my waist and skimmed my curves.

A pleasurable shudder ran through me and my eyelashes fluttered.

The way he could draw me into such a comfortable state of bliss was breathtaking. It was as if he understood me and each of my foibles, and knew what I needed and when.

With a choked groan, he flipped us and settled over me, pressing his knee between my thighs. "I'm so glad you're here."

"Because if I wasn't, Halvar would kill me?"

Espen rested his forehead against mine. "Don't remind me. I'm glad you're here *in Alvdalen* so I can show you where I grew up and have you meet my sisters and family. It's been a very long time since I brought someone home... And, well, I'm glad it's you. I'm glad they get to meet you."

I cupped his face with my palms and stared into those gorgeous amber-colored eyes. Seeing him so happy did things to my insides that I couldn't quite comprehend. But I couldn't deny, his joy was infectious. I pressed a kiss to each corner of his mouth and felt his smile bloom.

"I'm glad to be here too," I said, my tone turning sultry. I brushed my palms down his chest, enjoying the pleasure-filled look that swept across his features. "Especially, *here.*"

He leaned in and peppered kisses up my neck, eliciting a throaty moan from me.

Rearing back, he knelt on the bed and raked his hand through his hair. "That's it."

"What?"

"Your moans. They're too much. I have to have you. Right now."

"Right now? While Øyvin is in the shower?"

Espen nodded rapidly.

Who was I to say no? I bit my bottom lip and raised my eyebrows once.

His smile brightened like it had gained wattage from my unspoken agreement.

Without waiting another second, we clambered off the bed and yanked off our clothes. Espen grabbed the bedcover and threw it off, sending it and the remaining rose petals to the floor. He snapped his fingers and pointed at the cleared bed. "Bridge pose. Now."

There was no stopping me from throwing myself back onto the bed and assuming the position, knees bent and my hips hoisted in the air.

Espen was on me a heartbeat later, his head buried between my thighs as his hands palmed my rear while helping me maintain the pose. His tongue lapped at my clit, teasing the bundle of nerves, and sending me into a panting mess. If he kept that up, I was going to combust in seconds.

As if reading my mind, Espen unlatched himself and smoothed his palms down my legs, moving them back onto the bed. I lay back down and straightened out, relishing the sweep of his hands. The care and attention he paid to every inch of my body—from my hips to my chest and everywhere in between—was like a sculptor studying their masterpiece in awe.

He leaned over me and, resting one hand beside my head, lined himself up and gently pushed in. A light moan left my lips and another shudder ran through me.

I wasn't going to last long. Not with the way his eyes melted into liquid caramel, or the way his fingers brushed my every bump and curve like they were made of the smoothest marble. Like I was his to worship and he'd do so forever.

I wouldn't stop him.

Our bodies pressed together and he rested his forehead against mine. "Lennie." His whispered words were like a prayer and secret. I swept my lips over his and breathed in the emotions I couldn't name as we rocked against each other.

Our kisses grew more passionate, and I wanted more of it. Needed more of him.

His thrusts sped up and I hooked my feet against his back, deepening each delicious stroke.

With a stuttered breath, a shock wave of pleasure ran through me, wrenching through every muscle. A deep groan from Espen danced with my euphoria and he fisted the bedsheets as he came.

Fuck, I was one lucky woman.

A smile twisted Espen's lips and his cheeks flushed.

I grinned, feeling the lingering ecstasy from the top of my head to the tips of my toes. Yeah, I was a very lucky woman.

Espen pulled out and settled beside me before brushing an errant hair off my forehead. "I will never tire of that."

I let out a deep breath. "Me neither."

He shuffled off the bed and returned with the duvet, crawling back in and throwing it over us. I snuggled up beside him and—

The shower shut off and I stilled. There wasn't a chance Øyvin would miss the scent of what we'd just done. Nor the clothes on the floor or the naked evidence beneath the covers.

The Fjord Fae vacated the bathroom and appeared in the doorway, his hair perfectly dry but mussed like he'd been caught in a windy field. His gray pajama pants hung low off his hips and the sight of his bare chest was enough to make me feel tingly again.

Espen completely ignored Øyvin, pretending to be fast asleep and like the scent that lingered in the room wasn't his doing.

Øyvin's nostrils flared, but his features didn't betray his thoughts as he climbed into bed, bringing his fresh linen scent with him. He turned away from me with a gentle huff and pulled the covers up to his neck. "I can't believe you two."

I flipped over and sidled up against him with a grin, planted a kiss between his shoulder blades, and fell asleep.

LENNIE

Sparkling in the dim rays of late-morning sunlight, the village of Alvdalen was tucked between rolling hillsides with snow-covered mountains looming in the distance. Similar in size to Skolvik, but hundreds of miles further inland, the small town had the same Nordic charm and bracing temperatures.

"I look like a hazard sign," I said as I zippered my awful neon-orange jacket over my chin, nestling into the puffer jacket for warmth. The whole ensemble clashed violently with my scarlet hat, but Øyvin was adamant that I wear the poofy get-up or I'd be left in the cabin.

"Accurate." Øyvin smirked and I slapped my hand into the middle of his rock-hard abs, likely hurting me more than I had my grumpy fae.

"This is the lovely main street through town." Espen waved both hands, gesturing as he walked backward like a college campus tour guide. We'd spent the morning unpacking and decided to do a quick tour of Alvdalen before meeting up with Espen's middle sister, Turi, during her lunch break. While it meant a slight delay in our search for Aurora, at least Øyvin and I would have a better understanding of the village layout. Plus, I'd never say no to having a look around a new town.

"The street is for pedestrians only," Espen added, pointing at the sign at the start of the road—a car with a slash through it.

We traipsed down the street, the snow shoveled into the middle creating a short divider between both sides of the wide lane. Stores of all types, constructed of vertical planks of wood, ran along what looked like a cobbled road beneath the thin layer of white. We passed several little coffee shops that reminded me of Oddvar's, a real estate office with photos of *eigenboligs* for sale in the area, and several clothing stores with window displays covered in colorful knitwear and boasting the Norwegian wool they used. I could practically smell the fibers and lanolin through the glass panes.

"And this," Espen said, his voice filled with awe. Drawing my attention away from a particularly bright, blue sweater with paw prints across the top third, I turned to where he pointed. "This is Alveskjegget."

Alvin did what? I shook my head. Apparently, my hearing magic didn't work on that word.

"What does... Al-vee-shegget... mean?" I asked, trying my best to pronounce the word that was emblazoned in big white letters above the dark wood exterior and heavy-looking double doors.

"It means," a male voice behind us started and we all spun to find a man with a long, thick red beard, piercing green eyes, and the countenance of a lumberjack... or perhaps it was the flannel-patterned jacket he was wearing that gave him the woodsy vibe. "The Elf Beard."

I stilled. Trying to keep my face from betraying how on the nose that name was.

"And it's my bar." The newcomer smiled before turning to Espen. "Good to see you back in town, Solbakke. You coming in for a drink? Care to share some news with me?"

Espen grinned and reached out a hand, giving the barkeep one of those bro greetings that was half handshake, half hug. "Felix, it's good to see you. We won't be stopping by this morning"—*boo*—"but we'll be at the council meeting."

My shoulders relaxed and I readjusted my stance, letting my hands fall to my sides. So, this guy, Felix, was a fae.

"Ah okay," Felix said. With a quick nod to Øyvin, he turned his attention to me. "Perhaps you could introduce me to your lovely friend here?"

Espen sidled up beside me, placing his palm on my lower back. "This is Lennie Martin. My fiancée."

Show time.

I smiled up at Espen before extending my hand to Felix. "It's nice to meet you."

"Well, damn. The rumors are true." Felix grasped my hand in his, gave it two firm shakes, and let go. "After all these years, Espen Solbakke is getting married. Have you set a date?"

Øyvin cleared his throat.

Espen curled his arm around me and tucked me into his side. Peering down at me with a hooded gaze, his lips kicked into a smirk that sent a tingle down my spine. "We're thinking late summer."

My breath hitched and my heart fluttered as I played along. Resting my gloved hand against his chest like a prom portrait, I stared up into his warm amber eyes. "Good time of year. Easier for family to travel and attend." What were the words coming out of my mouth? And why did they sound rational?

Espen's eyebrows rose as he tilted his head and brushed his free hand across my cheek, pushing aside a stray hair. A wave of comfort washed over me, and I involuntarily leaned into his touch. Why did this feel so good? Like sitting beneath a thick blanket on a cool summer evening by a bonfire.

"How wonderful," Felix said, pulling me out of whatever haze had settled over me.

I tried to blink it away, but it was useless. The cozy and comfortable sensation was glued to me, much like the Forest Fae at my side.

With a contented sound, Espen released me. "It truly is wonderful."

As I stepped back, wobbling at the loss of Espen's hold, a hand landed on my shoulder, steadying me. I glanced up at Øyvin and found a hint of a smile at the corner of his lips. Was he impressed by my acting? Or had he noticed how I practically melted like a popsicle under Espen's touch?

He gave no hint as we turned back to the lumberjack barkeep and my fiancé.

"Any update on our canine friends who paid a visit to the fjord recently?" Espen asked, glancing around at the few passersby that were more concerned with a sale across the street than the four of us.

Felix crossed his arms and shook his head. "Nothing more than what I already passed along."

"Well," Espen sighed and frowned. "Let me know if there are any shifts in power I need to be aware of. Or any more friends deciding to make trips to Skolvik."

"Of course. You have my word." Felix nodded firmly, moving toward the bar's front doors and setting a key in the lock. "But I'm sure your sister knows a thing or two as well."

Espen tilted his lips into a half smile. "Yes, but you have the more informal information that doesn't always reach her ears."

Felix wiggled his brows in a manner that relayed his status as Alvdalen's chief proprietor of Forest Fae gossip. And as owner of a bar named The Elf Beard, that would be fitting. I dared a quick glance at Felix's beard and wondered just how many secrets had passed before it. Based on Espen's use of him as a confidant, I'd wager quite a lot.

Felix gestured over his shoulder to the bar at his back. "Are you sure you don't want to stop in for a quick beer?"

Yes! It was barely noon, but yes!

Espen shook his head. "No, but we'll see you later."

Boo!

"We need to pay a visit to Turi. She's expecting us."

"Welcome, welcome! Come in, come in," a woman with a long brown bob and a wide smile said as she ushered us inside the condo. Freckles brushed across her rosy cheeks and her eyes, the same amber-color as Espen's, beamed at us while we removed our outerwear.

"I'm Turi. It's so nice to finally meet you, Lennie." She swept forward and gave me a firm handshake, formal yet still informal. She instantly made me feel at home and like a long-lost friend, even though I'd barely stepped foot inside the tiled entryway. I could see how she'd won the mayoral election.

"It's nice to meet you, too," I replied, taking a look around as we stepped out of the hallway and into the main living area.

Turi's home was the top floor of a two-story split-house made of white-painted wood and black roof tiles. Where the exterior was a blank canvas, the interior was the polar opposite. Color was splattered across every surface, from the teal walls to the purple and gold furniture, it looked like a peacock had run amok with its feathers and covered everything with the shades of its plumage. Even the balls of yarn in a basket beside the sofa matched the color scheme.

I blinked, helping my eyes adjust to the brightness. A distinct smell of patchouli wafted through the space from a small diffuser on the cramped book-shelf, and a herd of cats, five in total, stalked around us as we wandered into the room. I tried my best not to accidentally step on any of them. "What are their names?"

"The white one is Frigg, the orange one is Thor, the black one is Fenrir, the gray-striped one is Ymir...and that,"—Turi pointed at the biggest one—"is my boy, Loki."

I glanced over at the behemoth of a cat perched like a gargoyle on a cat tree nestled behind a sofa by the window. Loki was the size of a bobcat, his big, black-and-gray fluffy coat sticking out in all directions like he'd just been electrocuted, his ears twitching as if he understood every word we said. "Is he a Maine Coon?" I asked, sitting down on the smaller velvet sofa in the living room as far away from the big cat as possible.

Turi shook her head. "He's a Norwegian Forest Cat. Usually a large breed, but I think Loki is double the average size."

No shit. That thing could probably fell a child or devour a chihuahua whole.

Øyvin sat beside me, while Espen took a spot on the other small sofa near Loki, a knick-knack covered coffee table wedged between us. It was a tight squeeze on the little couch, and Øyvin's knee brushed lightly against mine, sending a trill of warmth through me. I nudged him back, and the corner of his mouth quirked up minutely. Taking a deep breath, I glanced around the room just as the white cat plopped down on my lap and curled into a ball, making herself at home without further fanfare. Loki, though, wouldn't stop staring at me from across the room where he was perched on his cat tree behind Espen, his obnoxiously large tail swishing about below him. Even with Espen and his destroyer powers in the room with us, I got the sense that Loki the cat was the biggest predator. Especially as his gaze never broke from my face.

"Your cat is intimidating."

"Oh, Loki?" Turi said as she took a seat on a little pouf beside the coffee table and opened a tin of cookies. Golden-colored diamond shapes peeked out. *Sirupsnipper*, Espen's favorite. "He hates everyone except me."

"You don't say."

Loki may or may not have quirked an eyebrow at my remark. I couldn't be sure.

"Is he... domesticated?" I asked, wondering if I should be concerned for my well-being in his presence.

Turi tilted her head from one side to the other. "Kind of... he has a really great personality."

I cleared my throat. *Yeah, I'm not taking any chances with that one.*

"So," Turi started with a beaming smile as she extended her arm in my direction. "Let's see the ring."

I placed my fingers in Turi's outstretched hand. She tilted my digits in one direction, then the other, examining the silver branches and gorgeous stone on my finger. I swallowed hard, nervous but sure of the commitment I'd made. I didn't want to get tossed back across the Atlantic by the Norwegian equivalent of Customs and Immigration.

"Very pretty," she mumbled.

"Don't get all excited." Espen tilted his chin toward me. "It's for immigration purposes. So Lennie can stay in the country."

Turi released my fingers and looked between the three of us. "Uh-huh." Her mutter mirrored Ingrid's last night.

I bit my bottom lip to keep from smiling or making any sort of face. With this much attention on me, I didn't trust my facial features. I settled back on the sofa and stroked the cat in my lap.

"Fine. I'm just glad to see you happy." Turi huffed, raising a hand in defeat. She leaned forward. "Now, what exactly brings you home, brother? You weren't forthcoming on the phone."

Espen took a bite of a cookie before answering. "As I mentioned, Halvar sent us to retrieve someone. Her last known location was here in Alvdalen."

"Well, can you give me her name? I might know her." Turi snapped off half a cookie and shoved it in her mouth. I reached forward to grab one myself but the cat in my lap extended its claws into my thigh, hampering any further movement. I grumbled and sat back. The cat retracted her claws. *Little shit.*

Turi, noticing my plight, graciously proffered the cookie tin. I plucked out a *sirupsnippe* and thanked her.

"I know just about everyone in town," Turi continued.

Espen sighed and brushed his hand across his forehead. "I'm aware. Thought we'd meet with you prior to tonight's meeting to see what information you might have. Her name is Aurora. Last known to be living with Vigdis Johansen. Do you know her?"

Turi nodded, her brow furrowed in thought. "Vigdis passed a few years ago and she did have a daughter called Aurora. I, personally, haven't seen Aurora in a long time and don't think she lives here anymore."

That explained why no one at the fjell could get hold of Vigdis or Aurora. A huff escaped me between bites of my cookie. "Do you remember what she looks like?" I asked.

"She had very unique copper and silver hair. Usually wore it in a braid or two. Slight build. Pale skin." Turi nodded at me. "Perhaps a smidgen shorter than you."

"Do you know any of her contacts? Someone who might know where she's gone?" Espen asked gently as if to not fully disturb his sister's thoughts.

Turi bit her bottom lip before letting out a sigh and shaking her head. "For the life of me, I can't remember. The Council might know, especially Gunvor." She narrowed her gaze at her brother. "What exactly does Halvar need her for?"

Now it was Espen's turn to shake his head. "I think it would be better for us to discuss *that* at the Council meeting tonight. I want to share the information with everyone at the same time, avoid any grumbles from some of the council members that aren't exactly happy with my actions of late." Espen glanced at me, before turning back to his sister.

Turi let out a breath letting it create a raspberry noise with her lips. "Fine, you goody-goody, quasi-rule follower."

"*Quasi?*... Oh, yeah, me." I was the exception. He'd told me about the fae. I really was a good influence on people.

Espen chuckled, while Øyvin remained silent, competing in some sort of staring competition with Loki. Had either of them blinked recently?

"You know me, sister. I always follow the rules."

Turi snort laughed. "Uh-huh. Like that time in '89 when you—"

"What about that wolf problem we discussed?" Espen raised his voice, cutting off his sister before she reached the good part of that sentence. I got the feeling he was talking about the wolves that attacked me a few months ago. He'd been less than pleased about that and promised to look into it. By the sounds of it, that hadn't entailed burying anyone alive... yet.

Turi stuck out her bottom lip, equally annoyed that she hadn't been able to throw a barb at her little brother. "Ah, yes, the wolves that came to Skolvik. I have a sneaking suspicion it might have been a few members of the pack. But when I asked Wilhelm, he outright denied any wrong-doing."

"And you believe him?" Espen leaned forward and rested his forearms on his knees.

"I have no other choice at the moment. He's the Alpha and we've..."—she took a deep breath—"we've had a wolf sighting recently among the humans."

All our eyes widened and the room grew silent save for the purring from the cat in my lap.

"What do you mean? Why didn't you inform me?" Espen pried, his usual bubbly persona vanishing and replaced by Head Guard Espen who was a lot more serious and diplomatic.

Turi brushed her hands through her hair, sweeping it back behind her ears—currently in their non-pointy state. "Because it happened two days ago and Town Hall has been on high-alert ever since. I myself went out last night to the location of the sighting to track any markings, but left without any evidence."

"Is it one of the Forest Fae?" I asked, unable to stop the words from slipping out.

Turi faced me and shook her head. "I can't be sure."

"Does this have anything to do with the dissent among the ranks Wilhelm was dealing with a while back? Or did a real wolf wander out of its protected area southeast of here?" Espen asked, and I was lost in the conversation once more, not entirely sure what was going on or what politics I was missing. Øyvin probably didn't know what was going on either, but he listened attentively all while continuing his staring match with Loki. At this rate, and with how tense his shoulders were, I was pretty sure Øyvin was protecting me from the cat.

Turi waved her hand and wobbled slightly on her purple pouf. "Likely the latter. As he mentioned in the council meeting way back when, Wilhelm got those skirmishes under control and we haven't seen any problems."

"Good," Espen answered, sounding like he wasn't a fan of whatever bullshit had happened with the wolves.

"Is there a problem if a wolf leaves its usual habitat?" I asked, still feeling a bit lost, but curious as to why a wolf sighting among the humans was an issue. Couldn't they just leave it be or coax it back home?

Espen turned to me, wrinkles lining his brow. "There's great debate among the Norwegian population and government on how to treat wolves. The Norwegian wolf is near extinction, listed as critically endangered, yet, the government still issues permits to kill and some people shoot them illegally if they are seen as a threat to livestock or towns. There are zones that the wolves are allowed to live in peacefully, but if any stray out of that area, there is a high chance they'll end up shot."

"That's awful," I muttered and stroked the cat in my lap for comfort. "And must make things difficult for the fae shifters."

Espen nodded and Turi chimed in. "A sighting by humans usually stirs the pot and incites violence. Pitchforks and guns style."

"Like in Beauty and the Beast? Where the villagers gather to take down the misunderstood creature?"

Turi pointed at me. "Exactly."

The whole thing sounded ridiculous. Why would anyone want to harm a creature that was trying to fend for itself? Especially an animal that was an endangered species. There had to be a way for farmers to protect their livestock and live peacefully with the apex predator.

"Worth bringing that up at tonight's meeting, too." Espen let out an extended sigh, drawing me from my thoughts.

"That's the plan," Turi replied then tilted her head to one side and clasped her hands over her knee, looking as innocent as her nieces and nephew. "Speaking of council meetings. You really should attend more in person."

Espen groaned and looked at the ceiling. "Not you, too."

"Ingrid's right, you know."

"Yes, but I'm needed in Skolvik for political purposes. We need to maintain strong relationships with the other factions, especially the Fjell. Queen Ragnhild was always adamant about that. So, calling in to our council meetings will have to do for now. You know I'd love to live close to you all, to spend our weekends together with the kids. But I have to take into consideration *all* Forest Fae's well-being."

I bit my lip to stifle a smile as Turi grumbled in reply. It was cute to see how much the Solbakke sisters cared about their brother.

"Fine, but you know Ingrid won't relent any time soon."

Espen sighed. "I know."

Beep, beep. Beep, beep.

Turi rose from her spot and tapped a button on her watch, stopping the beeping noise. All the cats ran over to her and brushed up against her legs. "Unfortunately, that's my alarm to get back to the office."

The three of us moved off the sofas, my lap now thoroughly covered in white cat hair. "We'll let you get back. Thank you for the cookies," Espen said, a smile returning to his face.

"Of course." Turi beamed back at him, looking happy to have her brother around. "I'll see you all at tonight's meeting." She turned to me, her hands clasped in front of her. "I look forward to spending time with you again, Lennie. Perhaps next time can be less work talk and more chats about Espen's most embarrassing stories."

"Oh, I would very much enjoy that," I replied with a grin of my own.

Espen snorted and brushed his hand through his hair.

We strode for the entryway, saying our goodbyes.

As we passed Loki, he hissed at Øyvin, and I let out a quick laugh. "Good kitty."

Øyvin grumbled and kept walking as if the cat were a mere nuisance and not likely to rip his face off. The cat was probably capable of the latter, and I'd pay whatever was left in my bank account to see it try. But I kept walking too, on the off chance Loki thought I would be a tasty snack.

"See you at nine o'clock," Turi said.

"See you then," Espen replied as we zipped up our jackets and finished pulling on our boots.

I shoved my hat onto my head and waved back at the cats. "Bye cats. Bye Loki."

The cat-beast squinted at me like he was a Norse god in hiding, waiting to be set loose and destroy everything. *Wrong move.*

Øyvin muttered, "Evil thing."

I sucked in a breath. I was now ninety percent certain that cat was Loki reincarnate and could fuck us up with a swipe of its claws. "Do you have a death wish?"

Espen laughed and the Fjord Fae grumbled as I pushed him out the door.

76

LENNIE

We strode into Alveskjegget late that night, the doors left unlocked for the meeting of the Forest Fae Council of Elders—the sign on the door marking that a private event was underway. Thick wood tables had been cleared and pushed together to create one large table beside the circular firepit in the middle of the space. The pit was full of smoldering embers that were starting to cool, but still lent a cozy, slightly smoky smell to the space. People—fae with their ears dutifully concealed, like myself—milled around chatting to one another, but silence quickly fell as the door bumped shut behind us.

Turi, who sat at the head of the long table, glanced between the individuals already present and our little trio. With a shrug, she turned to those gathering. "Shall we get started?"

Murmurs of agreement and head bobs came in response, and the fae—some visibly older with gray or white hair, and others with far fewer wrinkles—took up seats at the makeshift table.

Taking a spot near Turi between Espen and Øyvin, I pulled my chair in and rested my hands on my lap. Espen, to my left, brushed his fingers over my hand and started absentmindedly tracing the edge of my engagement ring. Warmth rushed through me at the innocent gesture and my heart did that fluttery thing again. Even as Espen's focus was on the room, with our hands hidden from view by the table, it kind of felt like we were sharing a secret.

"First thing on the agenda," Turi started, her voice resolute and confident, "is Wilhelm's request for more help this spring clearing the river that runs past pack lands." Espen's sister nodded at a lithe man with thick black hair that curled around his temple, eyebrows as dense as Tom Selleck's mustache, and a goatee straight out of the eighties.

Wilhelm gave her a terse nod in reply. "Indeed. We had this problem last year and I'd like to preempt it as much as possible. As soon as the snow melts, that runoff now sweeps closer to the pack cabins thanks to large debris from the woods upstream. We have enough hands to handle a good portion of it, but I could do with a few more on the team. I'm planning a work schedule to avoid too many questions from the locals." He said the last word with an ounce of disdain and I had flashbacks to a Fjord King gone loopy on power.

Several nods around the table drew my attention away from the shifter leader, and another fae—with wispy eyebrows that would give Oddvar's a run for his money—agreed to lend four fae from his stables to assist.

"Excellent. We also need to address the reforesting project northwest of Alvdalen," Turi said, surveying the assembled council. "There are several clearings scheduled for growth and input this spring."

I looked around too. Movement to my left caught my gaze, and I turned toward it. The man beside Wilhelm quickly peeked at me, then glanced away when he caught me staring back at him. His lips turned to a frown as he peered at me out of the corner of his eyes. My brow furrowed. There was something familiar about that slimy scowl.

I narrowed my eyes at Wilhelm and the guy beside him. "Were you the one who sent wolves to Skolvik?" I asked, interrupting whatever Turi was saying and knowing full well I was speaking out of turn. But, the more I looked at him, the more positive I was the man next to Wilhelm had attacked me last autumn.

Wilhelm turned to me slowly and tilted his head, wrinkling his nose as if I smelled like crap. "We have not sent fae to Skolvik."

I flexed my hands at my sides, feeling the attention of every single fae in the room, but ignoring the subsequent tingly warmth that crossed my shoulders. "I recognize that guy." I pointed to the fae at Wilhelm's side. "He and his friend attacked me. Then Halvar snapped one of their necks and told them to leave."

Wilhelm let out a diminutive chortle. "Your eyes must not work very well, *human*. None of my wolves have been anywhere near Halvar and the late Fjell Queen."

Liar, liar, tail on fire!

I leaned forward in my chair, bracing my arms against the table. "You're lying."

"You must've been seeing things," Wilhelm replied. "Humans tend to hallucinate and imagine wild fairytales to assuage their boredom."

I bit my lip. *This gas-lighting motherfucker.*

Øyvin squeezed my forearm as I started to rise from my seat, and Espen let out a shuddered breath like he too was trying to stop himself from ripping Wilhelm a new one.

Turi looked between us and Wilhelm, then clasped her hands in front of her. "Wilhelm, whose funeral pyre were you burning about three months ago? The one you requested a cover story for so the town didn't send out fire trucks."

Wilhelm cast his gaze toward Turi, who, impressively, didn't back down from the malice shot her way. "None of your business," he sneered.

She smiled like she'd won a game of chess. "Why did you send wolves to Skolvik?"

The entire room fell silent and I could almost hear the bubbles at the foamy top of people's beer bursting as I held my breath.

"To eliminate the threat to our existence after our secret was revealed," Wilhelm said, looking straight at me, and an instinctual chill ran down my spine.

Shit.

Øyvin and Espen shot to their feet and chaos ensued. Øyvin yanked me and my chair back. Moving in front of me, he clenched his fists and braced his legs, ready to attack anyone who dared try to touch me. Espen meanwhile, lunged forward grabbing Wilhelm's jacket with his fists, hauled him out of his seat, and glowered at the shifter fae. Snarls rent the air and Wilhelm's second tried to get between the two men, while Turi scrambled to pull Espen off the pack leader. As hard as they tried, the pair barely moved the two guys who looked ready to punch each other in the face.

Uproarious cries filled the air and fists hammered against the table as anger roiled through the gathered group. Shouts of *"We agreed with Espen to keep her close"* and *"She was helping with the investigation"* and *"You fool"* rang around the room, and I started to wonder if the bar was insulated to avoid humans overhearing disagreements if they walked by outside. One look at the unbothered barkeep reassured me that was likely the case, as Felix continued drying beer steins like nothing was amiss, soaking up every word that was uttered by the Council. *Smart man.*

Espen muttered something I couldn't hear through the calamity, and Wilhelm scrunched his face and grimaced. Finally, Espen let go of Wilhelm with a shove. The council members trying to break them apart stepped between them, doing their best to calm the two men. Turi tried to get her brother's attention by waving her hand in his face, but Espen and Wilhelm continued to stare at each other like they were imagining how to tear each other limb from limb.

My body flushed and I wriggled in my seat. I'd never had someone willing to actually fight for me like that before. If I was being completely honest with myself, it was kind of hot. I let out a long sigh turning my focus back to the table of council members.

All of them were either on their feet watching the commotion, or talking wildly, hands gesticulating like this whole thing was a big offense and needed further discussion. The lone council member who looked like she couldn't be bothered by the pissing match to her right was the old lady with long white hair at the end of the table.

With slow and gentle movements, she raised her frail hand to the full beer stein in front of her and gingerly lifted it to her lips. Sloshing only a little over the side, she took three large gulps, downing half the drink, before setting it back on the table with a thunk. My eyes bugged and I closed my mouth with my hand. She spotted me and gave me a gentle smile, her eyes crinkling at the corners, as she rose, leaning her hands against the smoothed out wood before her. "Silence," she muttered, her voice barely audible above the ruckus, but silence fell nonetheless. Everyone stilled, and the woman glanced around the room. "What has already passed cannot be altered. We must move forward with our discussions and"—she shot a glance at Wilhelm—"not act rashly. We are far stronger united than we are operating as lone wolves."

The wolfy remark earned her a sneer from Wilhelm and his friend, but I beamed at her blatant *"you idiot"* sentiment.

"Agreed, Gunvor." Turi extended her arms out wide, palms open. "Let's sit down and discuss matters with reason."

Nods flitted about the room, and once everyone had retaken their seats, Øyvin scooted me and my chair back into the table.

Espen dropped into his chair and clamped his hand down on my thigh, locking me in place. I brushed my palm over his hand, doing my best to calm him down and bring him back to his bubbly, happy self. Not that I didn't mind the guys' protective displays—my insides were still tingling from the rush of seeing them leap into action—but we had a job to do. We needed to find Aurora, and talking to the Council of Elders about our search was at the top of the to-do list.

"Now, what other matters did we have on the agenda for today? Brother, you want to go first?" Turi asked, smiling over at Espen with a look that said *"don't you fucking dare pull that shit again."*

Espen let out a long sigh, his shoulders relaxing as he squeezed my hand beneath the table. "Halvar, Head Guard for the Fjell Fae, asked for our assistance in locating a specific individual who allegedly resides in Alvdalen. We were informed that Aurora lived with the late Vigdis Johansen."

"Why are the Fjell Fae looking for her?" one of the fae elders asked, his thick brows meeting his non-existent hairline. "And why didn't they send one of their own?"

I slowly raised my hand. All eyes turned to me, and I did my best not to shrink back from their gazes. "Part Fjell Fae, right here."

Half the table glared at me, the other half looked at me like I was a science experiment, which wasn't wholly unwarranted all things considered.

"When Freija was dying, she transferred magic to Halvar and Lennie," Øyvin piped up, giving them what I considered a very vague explanation of the events from the night my whole life changed dramatically and I got myself a gnarly lightning tattoo up the length of my left arm. Then again, it was probably best that people didn't know the full details—that Halvar hadn't had the strength to contain all of Freija's magic plus his own and needed a vessel to transfer the excess to. Insert me, the vessel, and voilà: a demi-fae was born.

Wide eyes met Øyvin's remarks, and several of the council elders surveyed me with renewed interest. Wilhelm, on the other hand, scowled.

"As for the why," Espen jumped in, steering the conversation and attention away from me, which I greatly appreciated. "The individual in question is apparently the Heir of the Fjell."

Silence fell across the room. Even Felix the bartender stopped wiping down the bar top, unable to feign that he wasn't eavesdropping on the meeting. They must've paid him off to keep him quiet or something, because the guy had probably witnessed many meetings if they'd been gathering here for long.

Turi pressed her fist to her mouth. "Well, shit. Gunvor, have you heard anything from your cousin Vigdis's daughter?"

The old lady at the other end of the table tilted her head to one side, her long white hair falling over her shoulder. Her eyes narrowed before she let out a short sigh. "Aurora? No."

Damn.

"Do you know where she lives now?" I blurted before either Espen or Øyvin could throw their hands over my mouth. I had a mission after all, and I wanted to get this done without having Halvar split me in two. Failure was not an option.

Gunvor's dainty shoulders curved inward and she shook her head. "I haven't seen her in a couple years. She's about twenty years old by now, an adult. But I'll see what information I can find among Vigdis's things. Perhaps there is a clue as to where she moved."

My heart sank, but she gave the three of us a tentative smile, her lips curling up at one corner.

"Where are you staying? I can stop by with more information and perhaps tell you more about Aurora tomorrow?"

"The old Mikkelsen cabin by the lake," Espen replied.

I gave Gunvor a gentle smile. "That would be great. Thank you."

Gunvor's gaze softened as she took a final swig of her beer. Espen uttered his thanks and Øyvin nodded his head in the elder's direction. It wasn't much to go on, but it wasn't nothing. We needed all the information we could get on the heir.

Wilhelm cleared his throat, probably bored of the conversation.

"Wonderful," Turi piped up again, looking ready to steer the meeting on to the next agenda item. "The final thing we need to discuss this evening is a report from my office. Unfortunately, two days ago we received a call about a wolf sighting."

All eyes turned back to Wilhelm who didn't budge in his seat, but his second squirmed at the attention.

"We need to be cautious that our own wolf shifters aren't caught up in this and aren't the responsible party," Turi continued. "Wilhelm, is there anything we need to be aware of with the pack?"

The shifter sucked on his lips, and I wondered how big his canines were when he snapped into wolf form. Would he look like the saber-tooth tiger in *Ice Age* or a regular dog with a serious overbite?

"It must've been a non-fae wolf." Wilhelm brushed his fingers across his goatee.

"You're certain of that?" a fae elder asked, and Espen glowered at the wolf shifter.

Wilhelm swallowed hard and straightened in his seat. "Positive. My wolves wouldn't step out of line. They know the rules around staying hidden."

The questioning fae leaned against the table and everyone's attention remained locked on the conversation. "So, it's not that same problem you had a while ago? There aren't wolves that have gone rogue?"

Wilhelm snorted and crossed his arms. "You know how the young are these days—all wide-eyed and naive. As I said months ago, the problem was fixed and those wolves were brought to heel." He waved his hand, dismissing the problem.

I glanced at Gunvor, finding her beer stein completely empty and her head minutely shaking. Apparently I wasn't the only one at the table who disliked Wilhelm.

Espen fidgeted beside me, brushing his thumb over my ring again like it was helping him remain calm.

"Okay then," Turi said, her voice growing more stern. "I'll try to quell local fears by stating that it was just a wolf passing through. But, please... Have your wolves be extremely careful for the next few weeks until things die down. We can't have the humans sending out hunting parties again."

Wilhelm nodded, and more agreement peppered around the table with nods and hums.

Turi straightened up and clapped her hands together. "With that, our meeting is adjourned. I'll see you again in two weeks. Same time, same place. Don't forget to return your glasses to Felix at the bar."

We all rose from our seats, chairs scraping across the floorboards as people started saying their goodbyes and leaving.

"Shall we head home?" I glanced between my two fae, my chest warming slightly at the way they monitored our surroundings, like they were protecting me from attack. It was cute, really. I could kind of protect myself, but I'd never say no to someone willing to have my back—especially in a room full of magical beings.

Espen and Øyvin both gave me a nod before Espen waved to his sister. "We're leaving. Have a good night, and please don't tell Ingrid." He motioned to the spot where he'd launched at Wilhelm.

Turi's lips quirked into a grin and she shook her cell phone in the air. "Too late, brother."

Espen let out a low groan, and Øyvin snorted, nudging me in the back toward the door.

As we moved across the room, my eyes caught on Gunvor's long white hair, draping down to her low back. She gave me a quick smile when she spotted me staring.

I pressed up onto my tiptoes and leaned into Espen while prodding him in the ribs. "Who is she, exactly?"

He looked over his shoulder. "Ylva's mother. Her name is Gunvor Nygård."

She bowed her head ever so slightly in my direction, her eyes crinkling at the corners.

I returned the nod, thankful for her support earlier and wholly unsurprised that she was Ylva's mother. With that stoicism and knowing gaze, I should've clocked it as soon as I walked into the room. She was basically an ancient version of Ylva. A take-no-bullshit kind of lady.

"Is she friend or foe?" I asked, unsure of the politics between the council members or what their powers were.

"Definitely friend," Espen replied.

77

LENNIE

We'd just finished breakfast when a gentle knock sounded at the cabin door the next morning. "I'll get it," Espen said, jumping up and sprinting for the door, while Øyvin and I tidied up our bowls. The Fjord Fae set to work on washing them up, as I brushed my hands over my insulated leggings and wandered across the room to greet our visitor.

A gentle and slightly croaky voice sounded from the front door and I stopped mid-stride in the living room.

Gunvor stepped inside, guided by Espen who took a bread bin-sized box from her hands and offered her his elbow for support. She took it with a smile, the weight of time gifting her a collection of laugh lines that swept around the sides of her mouth. Her white hair was pulled back in a low ponytail, as if she'd grown frustrated with it getting in the way, and she wore a thick, emerald-green sweater that swamped her delicate frame.

"Good day to you all," she said as Espen guided her to the sofa and helped her sit.

I pulled up the sleeves of my navy-colored sweater. "Good morning, Gunvor. I'm Lennie—"

"I know, I know," she said with a wave of her hand.

"Did you find anything among Vigdis's things?" Espen asked, getting straight to the point and voicing my own query as he set down the teal box with flowers painted on the sides on the small, wooden coffee table pushing aside a tower of coasters to make room.

Gunvor smiled with her eyes, narrowing them so the skin at the corners crinkled in a knowing look that I'd seen Ylva do before too. "As mentioned last night, I thought I might be of assistance. I rummaged through some Vidgis's items and thought the contents of this box might prove helpful."

We all tilted our heads to take in her words, including Øyvin who'd finished up in the kitchen and leaned against the dining table. Espen and I stood watching her like she was from another world. Which, for me, I guessed she kind of was. Her ears were hidden by her hair, but even if I'd met Gunvor at the grocery store, I'd have thought she was from another planet. There was an ethereal aura when in her presence, and it had me fully ensnared.

"Sit, sit," she said, motioning to the sofa and the armchair around the coffee table. "Let us discuss what I do and don't know about the Fjell heir."

I slid in beside her on the couch, while Espen took the armchair, and Øyvin didn't move from his perch in the dining area.

"What can you tell us about your cousin Vigdis and the girl?" Espen asked, his remarks pointed but still diplomatically kind. This wasn't an interrogation down at the police station. This was a fact-finding mission with an elder as our primary source of information. Therefore, poise—which I'd never had much of—was necessary.

"Vigdis lived on the south coast for years. Three of my four girls moved down there to enjoy the warmer weather and spend time with her. Vigdis then moved back here, oh, about thirty years ago. Then she took in a ward about twenty years ago, saying it was the child of an old Fjell Fae friend from the south coast. The child's name was Aurora."

I sat straighter, hope filling my chest that we might find out more about our mystery girl.

"Vigdis passed a couple of years ago," Gunvor continued, nodding to the box on the table. "These are some of her things, letters, photos, the sort. Perhaps there are some clues in here that will help you locate Aurora."

"You didn't know her?" Øyvin asked, his arms and ankles crossed where he leaned, his cream knit sweater taut across his shoulders.

Gunvor shook her head. "Yes and no. I met Aurora several times, but she was a young girl with a strong sense of self. Aside from Vigdis, she had no interest in spending time with the adults, especially as she grew into her teenage years." She chuckled and patted her thigh. "Vigdis had her hands full with that one after she turned fourteen. Then when Vigdis passed, Aurora disappeared. And I wish,"—she let out a deep sigh, and cast her gaze over her shoulder toward the windows before turning back to us—"I should've stepped in. I should have protected her. But she was eighteen, an adult, and I always raised my girls to be independent by a young age. A woman has enough battles to face in this world and should be given the freedom to choose her own path. All four of my girls were raised as such, and they've all done well for themselves."

I stared at Gunvor as she wrung her hands together and visibly struggled to come to terms with the missing woman. "I should have guessed there was more to her story. That she wasn't merely an orphan as Vigdis once told me."

Growing more curious by the second, I reached out and lifted the lid from the box and set it aside. Inside was a small collection of envelopes secured into bundles with ribbons, a wooden wolf figurine, a few stacks of photographs, and a small green, leather notebook with an oak leaf embossed on the front. I picked that up first, while Espen carefully withdrew a stack of photos. Gunvor and Øyvin watched on in silence.

Inside the notebook were pages of doodles and curly script that I could barely read—in part because it was in Norwegian far more advanced than my current understanding, and also because it was the swirliest cursive I'd ever seen. The intricate drawings were plants, though, that was clear. Each part of the flora perfectly labeled. Near the back of the book, pressed between a tissue, was a bright-pink flower with a slight trumpet shape.

"Ah," Gunvor said softly, pointing at the delicate specimen. "Foxglove, much more common on the coast, and highly poisonous." Espen shuddered. "Vigdis was a botanist and scholar, tasked with researching the plants we Forest Fae are to protect."

After the number of run-ins we'd had with poisonous plants recently, I gently closed the book and set it back in the box. Couldn't be too careful, plus the little notebook clearly wasn't what we were looking for. What we desperately needed was more information about Aurora and where she might possibly have gone.

"Do you think Aurora may have gone south?" I asked Gunvor, while Espen continued thumbing through photos.

Gunvor shrugged. "In all honesty, she could be anywhere."

For fuck's sake. I hung my head and refrained from groaning.

Espen leaned forward and held out a photo toward us. The image was of a woman with vaguely familiar features to those of Gunvor, but the three women beside her would be a match for Gunvor if she had red hair.

"Vigdis and your other daughters?" Espen asked, and Gunvor nodded. I guessed Ylva had never introduced him to them... or perhaps they weren't close siblings.

Gunvor's smile radiated warmth and joy. "Yes, Ylva's older sisters... half-sisters. They inherited their father's, my first husband's, fiery red hair. Ylva, on the other hand, inherited my features and my second husband's penchant for strategy and battle."

Yeah, that tracked. I'd witnessed Ylva in battle against King Balder a few months ago. It was quite the sight to behold. Her recent skirmish with Espen on the training field outside Skolvik had been impressive too.

"And as her boss, I appreciate that skill set very much. She doesn't ever talk about her sisters, though," Espen said, handing the photo to Gunvor. She took the image and brushed her thumb across their faces as if she could magically stroke their cheeks. A pang of love hit my heart at the gesture, and a wave of homesickness and longing for my own family back in Ohio washed over me.

"There's a fifty year age gap between them," Gunvor said, jolting me out of my thoughts. *Fifty years?!* I knew fae had longer child-bearing cycles than humans, but it was still a jarring factoid that I couldn't entirely wrap my head around. With that said, the age gap between Gunvor's girls could explain why Espen didn't know Ylva's sisters.

I glanced at the woman beside me on the couch, trying to discern her age. Was she older than Halvar? Her appearance certainly would allude to that, but if I'd learned one thing while living among the fae, it was that appearances could be deceiving.

"Would they know where Aurora is?" Øyvin asked, drawing our attention back to the task at hand.

Gunvor shook her head and returned the photo to the box, setting it atop the stack that Espen had put back while she spoke. "I doubt they ever met."

"Do you have any other information about the girl?" Espen asked. "Her likes, dislikes. Anything she might've said in passing? Anything we should know about her?"

Gunvor took a deep breath and scooted back on the sofa, relaxing into the cushions and closing her eyes as if to think harder on the subject. The room fell silent as we gave her a second, the only noise coming from the hum of the tiny refrigerator in the kitchen. After another minute where I refrained from bouncing my knee in anticipation, opting instead to hold them in place with my hands, Gunvor spoke. "Aurora enjoyed the outdoors. She was rarely home when I visited Vigdis for coffee and cake. Vigdis always said she was outside in the forest playing with the neighborhood children, running around, building fortresses and the like."

That sounded very Norwegian and a damn sight different than the chalk drawings I'd made on sidewalks and basketball games with the neighbors during my childhood. Forest forts? Really?

"Aurora was never talkative and observed her surroundings with the keen eye of a hawk."

"Did she know she was a Fjell Fae?" I asked.

"I believe so. I don't recall Vigdis mentioning anything about Aurora's powers or affinity, but they did spend a lot of time outdoors together, observing and cataloging nature. Knowing Vigdis, she probably raised Aurora more like a Forest Fae than a Fjell Fae." Gunvor's shoulders rose and fell as she let out an extended sigh. "My first recommendation would be to check the forests around here. Or perhaps the villages to our south."

"Do you think she'd head toward Oslo?" Øyvin asked, arms still crossed over his chest and his eyes narrowed as if he were analyzing every word she said.

I turned back to Gunvor as she replied, "Many twenty-somethings head to the big city to see what's there. Some stay. Some come back. Seems to be the thing these days."

"We will keep that in mind," Espen said with a smile.

"Good. And on that note, I should let you get on with your search." She rose gingerly from her spot beside me and waved away my hand when I offered to help. "Just let me know what you find. I'm curious." She twitched her nose and wandered over to the door.

We agreed to keep her in the loop as she pulled on her boots and jacket, then waved her off as she headed out to her little Mini Cooper. My eyes bugged at the sight of the small car, but on closer inspection it had some beefy studded tires on it that no doubt would stop it from sliding around on the wintry roads.

Espen closed the door and we returned to the living room area. I threw myself back down onto the couch, tucking my feet underneath me for warmth.

"Well, whaddaya think?" I asked the room.

Both fae stood stock still, lost in their thoughts.

"If she's gone to Oslo, we don't stand a chance," Øyvin said.

"Agreed," Espen replied. "But based on what Gunvor said, I don't think Aurora would like Oslo. She preferred being outdoors and in the forests."

I pulled my hair into a ponytail. "What are you thinking?"

Espen brushed his hand across his short beard and let out a sigh. "I think we start canvassing the woods around here and work our way outward."

"As good a plan as any," Øyvin said.

"Agreed," I added.

Espen set his hands on his hips. "Let's get started then."

78

LENNIE

Rays of sun skittered across clear blue skies and a cold breeze wended around the hillsides. My cheeks smarted from the chill, but the sunshine made up for the sting, brightening what was turning into a frustrating day. After spending yesterday afternoon searching the woods around Alvdalen for the elusive Fjell heir, we'd resumed our search this morning.

"You sure you don't want to check the north side again?" I asked after lunch, clambering into the car. The *lefse*—a pastry with cinnamon, butter, and sugar—and a second coffee had been a delicious snack and I was ready to get back out there.

"No, I think we'd better pick up the pace and check the forest south of town," Espen said as he settled into the driver's seat.

Øyvin unzipped his navy jacket and clicked himself into the passenger seat with a deep sigh. The Fjord Fae was extra grumpy today, probably because our hunt was less straightforward than we'd hoped... Or maybe he'd woken up on the wrong side of the bed, so to speak. Either way, food had not improved his mood.

"Where to after the southern forest?" I asked as the engine hummed to life and Espen pulled out of our parking spot.

He took a moment to respond, focusing first on the road and getting us onto the main drag out of town. "Eastern hills. It would be deadly to hide in the western mountains at this time of year."

I twitched my nose. "What if she had a cabin there though?"

Espen shook his head. "Unlikely. Even those who do only venture up there for a long weekend or a week, at most. They're more holiday homes than permanent residences."

"And someone couldn't trespass and squat in one of these houses?"

"They'd be noticed pretty damn quick. The owners may not live in them, but Norwegians tend to visit their cabins regularly and throughout the year, not just seasonally."

"Duly noted," I replied, leaning back in my seat with a huff. Ingrid's statement about doing things no matter the weather conditions rang through my mind. Apparently that applied to cabin visits too.

The world flickered past in staccato images as I stared wistfully out the window. Red- and yellow-painted wood buildings with front steps cleared of snow preceded what I could only describe as fairytale woods. Hundreds of thin tree trunks shot out of the snowy ground, their leaves having abandoned them in the autumn. I wouldn't be surprised if this was where Norway got a lot of their folktales from. Stories of trolls, faeries, and creatures running between the trees, hiding from prying eyes, spreading their magic. I chuckled to myself, thinking of my own pointed ears. Perhaps the old storytellers had actually got that right?

I moved my lower seat belt off my abdomen, the pressure on my bladder growing uncomfortable.

We made a few more turns, the woods growing thicker, more pines blending in with the wispy barren trees. I squirmed in my seat, my bladder staging a protest complete with banners, flags, and chants of *"it's our time to go."* Squeezing my legs together, I tried to think about anything but running water...

Would Ohio beat Michigan this year? Dad would be elated if they did, as would Andrew and Jared.

Maybe my family would go to the game?

Did Norwegian's play American football or was it just soccer?

I still needed to edit the photos I'd taken of Skolvik on New Year's Eve and send a few to Mom. She'd love how the village sparkled under the glow of the fireworks.

We passed a frozen creek and my bladder screamed at me.

"Umm..." I said, interrupting the tranquil silence in the car. "Can we pull over somewhere?"

"We're almost there. You feeling sick?" Espen glanced into the rearview mirror, his eyebrows drawing together. "Staring at those trees is a bit like watching a flickering barcode."

He wasn't wrong, but... "No, it's not that." There wasn't any way to put this delicately, but I was rarely gentle with my words. "I need to pee."

Øyvin chuffed. "You didn't think to go before we left the café?"

"I did!" I exclaimed as Espen snickered and pulled over to the side of the road. "But having two large cups of coffee today may have been a mistake."

I could hear Øyvin's eye roll from the back seat.

Espen shut off the car and turned in his seat with a smile. "Hurry up, then."

"Thank you," I said as I rushed out of the car, accidentally slamming the door shut behind me.

I traipsed through the snowdrifts toward a thicket of snow-laden pine trees, the sound of my neon orange pants swishing together echoing around me. The cold air brushed my face and I was thankful it wasn't snowing today. Just the thought of a snow storm sent a shiver down my spine, and my legs tried to clamp together again. Because snow equals water and water equals...

Circling around briefly, I found a spot that was hidden from the road, beside a line of trees and a slightly larger mound of snow—probably a boulder or something hidden beneath the natural icing. It was as good a spot as any. I pulled down my pants and underwear, popped a squat, and angled my butt so I didn't piss on myself. A sigh of relief passed my lips at the release of pressure in my abdomen, feeling happier by the second. Peeing in the woods certainly wasn't ideal, but I'd left my pride at the café. Two large morning coffees had been a very big mistake.

A rustling sounded to my right, and I rolled my eyes as I let myself drip-dry a bit—the cold nipping at my butt and bits. "I'm not kink shaming, but golden showers are not something I want to experience or experiment with, guys," I said, hoping they weren't about to jump-scare me in such a vulnerable position.

"Disgusting," a female voice said, and my eyes went wide as I quickly yanked up my pants, doing my best not to stumble back into the yellow snow. I spun around, my heart in my throat, panic searing through my veins. A young woman wearing a thick white wool jacket with a deep hood leaned against a tree, her lips set in a firm grimace.

"Kind of rude to sneak up on someone while they're peeing." I scowled, eying up the newcomer. From her gray boots, to the white gloves she wore, her entire outfit was designed to blend in with the terrain, not stand out like my neon get-up.

She scoffed like I was the one in the wrong and shook her head.

A panting noise sounded from behind her, and she stepped aside, revealing a gray wolf with a shock of white across its face sweeping onto its chest and bright gray-blue eyes that bored into me. Perhaps it got a good look at my bare ass and thought I was a tasty snack?

It sneered.

Or not.

"What is this? You two Red Riding Hood and the Big Bad Wolf?" I asked, a mocking tone in my voice.

"No." The woman removed her hood, revealing a thick braid of copper-brown hair with streaks of silver in it, a delicate face fixed with a stern look, and eyes... I sucked in a breath. Her eyes were an unusual blend of gray-and-brown. A coloring I'd only seen on two others in my lifetime—one who was now in a rocky dungeon, the other passed away.

"What are you staring at?" The woman snarled, her attitude similar to someone else I'd come to know in recent months. She crossed her arms, braced her legs, and settled into a stoic posture fit for a queen.

Distant relative my ass, Halvar. I'd bet the limited funds in my bank account that this young woman was Aurora, the late-Fjell Queen's daughter. She looked exactly like Queen Freija—from the eyes, to the set of her lips and her genteel but strong stature. She matched Turi's visual description, too, and that keen look in her eye reminded me of what Gunvor had said: that Aurora observed her surroundings like a hawk.

"Any chance your name is Aurora?"

The woman squinted, her canine companion took a step toward me, and victory thundered in my chest as a smile tilted my lips.

"Nice to finally meet you."

The wolf lunged.

79
ESPEN

"What's taking her so long?" Øyvin ground out, his arms crossed as he leaned back in the passenger seat.

I shrugged and tapped my fingers on the steering wheel. "Perhaps she got more than she bargained for?"

My retort earned me a glare from my friend, and I snickered as I adjusted my wool hat. Lennie had gifted it to me for Christmas, and I really liked the green Nordic pattern and oversized pom-pom. Øyvin, who'd been gifted a navy-blue one, barely ever wore his. But, I saw the way it made Lennie smile every time I put it on, so I wore mine as much as possible. I liked seeing her happy, and I knew—deep, *deep* down—Øyvin did too. He just went about showing it in different ways, like protecting her when she didn't realize she needed protecting.

Sometimes I wondered if she even noticed his behavior. Just the other day he'd lingered behind her, hands loose, ready to pounce at Felix should the barkeep make a wrong move. Felix wasn't a threat to Lennie, but Øyvin hadn't known that at the time. He always put himself between Lennie and anything that might cause her harm—an admirable trait in my book.

"This is taking too long." Øyvin let out a huff of annoyance, his hand resting on the car door. "We should go find her."

I shook my head at him. "And watch her urinate? We don't need to see that."

"We've seen her naked." He yanked on the handle and pushed his door open. "Seeing her relieving herself, while unappealing, wouldn't be the worst thing in the world."

He clambered out of the car, stretched out his arms, and zippered up his jacket.

"Fair enough." I sighed and followed him into the deep snow, even though I'd argue that this was being a tad *too* overprotective.

We'd barely passed through the tree line when Øyvin stilled, then bolted forward, pushing through the snow that reached our calves in some spots. Sensing his panic, I sped up, sticking right behind him.

"Lennie!" Øyvin yelled as we came to a halt around a patch of sunken yellow snow. The only answer was a lump of ice falling off a nearby branch. He called again as I inspected the area.

The drifts around the boulder and tree line she'd stopped at had been trampled, like multiple people had been here. Some of the footprints were Lennie's based on the direction they'd come from—the same as us—but hers weren't the only ones. More worrisome were the paw prints that matched those of a large dog or even a wolf.

"We have a problem," I said, my voice barely a whisper.

Øyvin stomped over to me. "How bad?"

I pointed to the paw prints, and Øyvin's nostrils flared.

Tightening my jaw, I surveyed the traces of a squabble. Prints and downtrodden snow fanned out around the yellow-snow, with the largest grouping heading toward the woods. I moved and squatted around a pair of prints near some trees a few paces away from Lennie's marking. Øyvin followed and passed me, tracking the prints further into the forest, moving swiftly through the snow.

Anger roiled within me, my pulse ticking upward as I clenched my fists. These were definitely wolf prints.

I trailed after Øyvin, taking in every aspect of our surroundings, monitoring for anything that might resemble our girl. Tall trees stood sentry guarding the peace of the land, drifts of snow-covered hibernating flora, and cathedral-like silence reigned.

"There are two sets of paw prints down here, and then the tracks change where they morph from canine to human." Øyvin pointed at markings shaped like large snow boots. They ran beside a smaller pair and the same wolf tracks from where Lennie stopped by the boulder.

Glancing back at the little clearing where all four individuals had met, my gut flipped over. "They took her. And she didn't scream?"

"She was probably too busy mouthing off," Øyvin said, and... Well, he had a point.

Øyvin grumbled and glared at the forest, like he wanted to boil everything within it with just a flick of his wrist. Which, knowing the fae, wasn't entirely out of the realm of possibility. His jaw ticked, hands balled into fists. "We let her out of our sight for five minutes and she lands herself in trouble."

"You have to admit," I said, trying to lighten the mood and hopefully get the Fjord Fae to pivot his focus away from simply killing everything to searching for our missing demi-fae. "It's rather on brand for her."

Øyvin huffed and pressed on through the woods.

Oh well, at least I tried.

We tracked the footprints about a kilometer from our starting point until they vanished, as if they'd been swept away by a phantom wind or tree branches. My head snapped upward, noting the markedly missing snow cover on the trees at the same time Øyvin spotted the oddity. "They've shaken the snow off all the trees from here onward to cover their tracks," I murmured, anger and annoyance skirting up my veins as I ground my teeth together.

Forget lightening the mood. I wanted my fiancée back.

Øyvin nodded and let out a deep sigh. "You think this was the shifter from the Council?"

That destructive power swarmed in my core, heating me from the inside out, begging to be unleashed. I nodded slowly, breathing hard through my nose. "Wilhelm."

80

LENNIE

I slowly opened my eyes, my head pounding from the hit I'd taken from hell knew what before I passed out. The dim light of my surroundings revealed dark wood walls like those in Espen's cabin, buckets and cleaning supplies shoved in one corner, and ratty curtains drawn over a small, square window. I was in a shed and... I shimmied on the seat, rope chafing against my wrists where they were tied to the back of the wooden chair.

Yup, kidnapped.

Thankfully, my clothes were still on and I didn't appear to have any injuries, but honest to hell, could I be more of a trouble magnet? My guys would have a complete conniption when they realized what happened. They'd probably go looking for me when Øyvin inevitably grew impatient and grumbly. And the only trace of me in that clearing was the yellow-stained snow—

The door to the little shed creaked open. Blinding light filtered in and I turned my face away, unable to properly shield my eyes from it. Footsteps pattered against the dusty floorboards and the door eventually swung shut with a gentle thud. I blinked, trying to see who my visitors were.

Aurora stood between two large wolves, both of which assessed me and my bindings from several paces away, careful not to get any closer as if *I* might actually be the threat here... which was ludicrous. Yes, I did have a good deal of power stored within me, but fuck if I knew how to use it all. They, on the other hand, had very large teeth that could definitely do some damage.

"If you're looking for a dentist, you've got the wrong woman. But I'd recommend flossing either way," I said to the brown-and-beige wolf as it stared at me. I didn't expect an answer, but Aurora snorted at my joke and the gray-and-white wolf beside her started to shift. Snapping and cracking noises rent the air and I watched with my stomach in my throat as the wolf transformed from canine to fae. He swiftly pressed his hand to his left shoulder, magically clothing himself before he could expose his family jewels.

Now, instead of one fae and two wolves, I had two fae and one wolf watching me closely. The white-haired male beside Aurora stepped forward, but she gently wrapped her fingers around his wrist. He glanced down at where she touched him, his black wool sweater preventing skin-to-skin contact. Their eyes met and he gave her a gentle nod before she turned her gaze on me again. "Why are you looking for me? Why are you asking around town for me?"

"Reasons," I replied, unsure if I should reveal her status as heir quite yet—did she even know?—or withhold some information in hopes it might buy the guys some more time to find me, or give me a chance to escape... somehow. Turning into puppy chow was not on my to-do list for the day.

I furrowed my brow. "How do you even know I've been looking for you?" That information had only been shared with the Forest Fae Council.

"We have our ways," the man next to Aurora grumbled with enough authority that I mentally marked him as some sort of leader.

"You mean you have an insider on the Council?"

Aurora shook her head, her braid falling off her shoulder and into the deep white hood on her back. "The Council has a traitor in their midst who isn't careful about who they share information with."

Well, fuck... but on the bright side. "That sucks, but either way. I've found you now. We should really get going."

The white-haired man took a step forward, his nose twitching into a snarl, and his eyes flashing silver. The latter happened so fast, I did a double take.

"Your eyes, they shimmered. Is that a normal Forest Fae thing?" I asked, recalling Espen's eyes doing that the day I'd first met—and punched—him.

"They only do that when a Forest Fae is flexing their power, showing off." Aurora turned to the guy, her jaw ticking. "Marius, let me handle this."

His nostrils flared, but he took a step back and straightened up.

"So, you're not like *Twilight* then? Oh no, wait, it was the vampires that sparkled. You're not a vampire too, are you?" Better to be safe than a blood bag. Like always, my tongue ran away from me the moment nerves and adrenaline kicked in and it was anyone's guess what came flying out.

Marius rolled his eyes and leaned against the door, crossing his arms and legs, his snow pants swishing where his ankles rubbed together. Aurora shook her head, while the wolf stared on quietly.

"Are you Team Jacob or Team Edward? Bet you're Team wolf, hey, Aurora?" I wiggled my brows at her suggestively before giving her a wink. "I myself was more of a Jacob fan, but now I think I'm more of a Daddy Charlie Swan fan. The facial hair, the quiet broody protective nature, and the uniform. Ugh, the uniform. Not to mention the wisdom that comes with age." I tilted my head to the side. "Now that I think about it, I guess I do have a thing for older men these days."

"Answer the questions," Aurora said, drawing me out of my thoughts of strolls along misty shores in the Pacific Northwest. "Why do you want me? Why are you looking for me?"

"So, your Council confidant didn't tell you everything? Didn't tell you *why* we were looking for you, just that we were looking?"

Her jaw tightened, and I nodded as I weighed my options. With no visible weapons on them, the trio didn't appear interested in hurting me. Or maybe they were and they wanted me to start talking before their torture session began. Either way, I was in a shitty situation. I could keep vocalizing my inner monologue and nervous thoughts, probably annoying the crap out of them and end up stuck here for days until my guys came to save me after I was beaten to within an inch of my life. Or... I could tell Aurora the truth, encourage her to come with me, see if I could broker an agreement without getting hurt. Neither one was ideal, but the latter might get us back to Skolvik quicker and save my neck from Halvar's axe or the myriad of weapons the Fjell Fae had stashed in the forge.

Oh well, here goes...

"We were sent to find you and bring you back to Skolvik," I said, leaving out some key details.

She huffed and set her hands on her hips in a pretty decent power pose. "I'm not going anywhere."

I admired her staunch tenacity—it would probably help her when she took up the throne— but I'd fucking found her and was *this* close to completing my mission and saving my neck from Halvar's guillotine. Finding and returning Aurora to the Fjell was my ticket to acceptance among the Fjell Fae. And I wasn't going to lose. No chance. Martin Family Rules: Wins only.

I clicked my tongue and tilted my head to one side. "I figured you might not want to, and Alvdalen is a beautiful place to live. But there are very good reasons for you to come with us."

"And those are?" Marius asked, his voice velvety smooth enough to be an audiobook narrator.

I let out a long sigh and tugged on my constraints again. Burning pain swept across the raw skin on my wrists and a wince slipped from my mouth. "You're needed by the Fjell Fae."

Aurora pursed her lips and looked over her shoulder at Marius, who in turn stared daggers at me. The wolf in the corner didn't move. It just watched, calmly monitoring the exchange, its ears twitching ever so often.

"And why is that?" Aurora asked, quirking a single brow.

Well, I could go with the blunt and honest truth… or divulge the information carefully, be respectful of the mountain I was about to dump on her head.

Fuck it.

"Based on your significant resemblance, your mother was the Queen of the Fjell. She died. Regicide by your aunt. Long story. And her Head Guard, Halvar, who I'm sure you've heard of, sent me to fetch you so you could take up the mantle, Little Miss Heir of the Fjell."

The room stilled, and Aurora dropped her arms to her sides.

Okay, maybe I could've offloaded a little better. Too late now.

Aurora's shoulders fell as she took a step backward, spinning to face Marius. He pressed his hand against the small of her back. "Rora," he mumbled, so quietly I could barely hear it. The wolf's brown eyes peered at the duo before swinging back to me and narrowing.

"True story, bro," I said, wholly unable to lighten the mood in the room, but here we were, details out in the open. Now all I needed was for them to untie me, and Aurora to come back to Skolvik. "I even have a letter that was meant for Vigdis, but you should probably have it. It's in my inner jacket pocket."

Aurora turned and stepped over to me. Unzippering my jacket, she pulled the material aside and located the pocket. Her breathing was calm and even as she pulled out the letter. I swallowed audibly as she stepped back and examined the small envelope.

"That should help explain," I said, hoping it was true. I had no idea what was written in there, but now didn't seem like the right time to say that.

Aurora slid her fingers beneath the flap of the envelope and popped the wax seal, withdrew a piece of thin parchment, and unfolded it. Her gaze flitted over the paper, before she huffed and said, "This doesn't explain anything."

I scrunched my eyebrows together. "What do you mean?"

"It says, 'It's time for the flower to come home. Thank you for everything. The trio can be trusted. H.'"

Yeah, I didn't understand the flower part either, but Halvar had meant the letter for Vigdis, and had said the guys and I were trustworthy. "It says you can trust me."

Aurora scoffed, turning her back on me again, and faced Marius.

Nervous energy skittered through me, my knees bouncing in anticipation as I watched them exchange an entire conversation without opening their mouths. A head shake here and a nod there. Yeah, these two were definitely an item. Aside from a couple of ear twitches, the wolf beside them didn't move, his eyes locked on me like he expected me to loosen my own restraints and bolt.

Just as I was about to start whistling the theme song for *Jeopardy*, Aurora glanced over her shoulder at me and shook her head. "You have the wrong person."

My brow furrowed. "I don't think so. You're a Fjell Fae, yes?"

She turned, narrowed her eyes, and gave me a single minute nod.

"You're about twenty years old and you were raised by Vigdis Johansen, right? Who took in her southern friend's daughter?"

Her fists opened and closed while the rest of Aurora's body remained still. I could practically hear the puzzle pieces clicking together in her head.

"Sorry to burst your bubble, sweet pea, but you're the Heir of the Fjell Fae."

"I—" Aurora shook her head and reached for the doorknob, yanking the door open. "You have the wrong person." She waltzed outside and slammed the door behind her.

Marius's nostrils flared and he let out an audible breath.

I quirked my eyebrow. "Something I said?"

Marius scowled and opened the door. "Nils," he said, and the wolf obediently trotted through the doorway.

"We'll be back to deal with you later," Marius grumbled, then swept from the room, locking the shed door behind him. *Fantastic.*

"Bring snacks when you do!" I yelled after them.

Tapping my fingers against the chair legs, I muttered, "Well, that went well."

Hopefully the guys were on their way.

81

ØYVIN

We barreled onto the compound where Wilhelm and his pack lived. The icy gravel road gave way to collections of wood cabins—some tucked away in the trees, others sitting side-by-side like row houses, trails cleared through the snow to each front step. Espen threw the car into park, and I was out of the vehicle before he shut the engine off. A big house, two stories with a sharply pitched roof, loomed over the tract we'd parked in and light streamed onto the shielded deck from two large front windows.

Scanning my surroundings for any threats, a tingling sensation ran up my spine. We were being watched. My pulse quickened, and I loosened my hands at my sides, ready to launch a boiling ball of water at anyone who crossed my path. Trust her to get herself kidnapped by a bunch of wolves. Here we were on a mission to find one woman and we'd lost ours in the process. Ancestors help me, when I got my hands on Trouble, I was tying her to my bed and never letting her out of my sight ever again.

Espen clambered out of the car and strode directly toward the main house. I followed him, uncaring of our stomping against the wooden stoop that further announced our presence. Espen knocked on the front door, but I pushed past him and went straight for the door knob. Unlocked, I strode inside the bright building and was immediately assaulted by the musty smell of wet dog and growls.

"Wilhelm!" Espen stepped in behind me and closed the door. "Wilhelm, we need to talk!"

Espen may have been in the mood for diplomacy, valiantly keeping his destructive powers under control, but I was ready to waterboard the fucker until he gave up Lennie's location.

A sneer sounded from my left and a dour-looking man I didn't recognize appeared from the living room. I grabbed him by the neck, slammed him against the wood-paneled wall, and hoisted him off his feet. A second later, water bubbled out of his mouth, and I growled, "Where is she?"

Saliva and water dripped over his chin, his eyes wide as his fingers clawed at my wrist.

"What the hell is going on here, Espen?" Wilhelm stepped out of the kitchen to our right. He pushed back his dark locks, narrowed his eyes, and raised his chin. Wilhelm's gaze cut to me. "Drop him."

Other men joined us in the hallway, the orange-colored hardwood floors marred by claw marks.

I tightened my grip. The man's pulse faded beneath my fingers.

"Drop him or I'll have my wolves shred you to pieces, Fjord Fae."

"I'll boil you all alive," I snarled, but let go of the blubbering mess in my hand. He dropped to the floor with a thud and crawled away, coughing and spluttering as he disappeared down the hallway.

Espen stepped between me and Wilhelm, blocking me from following through on the threat. "Where is she?" he asked through his teeth.

Wilhelm shook his head. "Who?"

"Lennie, of course." Espen slowly flexed his fingers at his sides. That action alone was a warning shot if I'd ever seen one, and Wilhelm was old enough to know how powerful Espen was. Now, we just had to inform him of how stupid he was for taking our woman.

Wilhelm chuckled and leaned against the staircase that bisected the building, crossing his arms. "You lost your human?"

"My fiancée is part fae," Espen replied.

"And what makes you think I have her?" Wilhelm raised a hand and gestured to the building around us.

"She was ambushed and we found wolf tracks in the snow."

"So? She could've easily been attacked by regular wolves. The locals haven't killed them all off yet."

I shook my head and sucked in a breath. We didn't have time for this. Espen may be playing good-cop and trying to keep his powers under wraps, but I was done being a polite statesman. I'd happily drown the whole house, starting with Wilhelm.

As if sensing my thoughts, Espen threw a brief glare at me over his shoulder, warning me to behave before twisting back to Wilhelm.

I let out a steady breath and relented. For now.

"The kidnappers covered their *boot-shaped* tracks after a while by removing the snowpack from the trees," Espen explained.

"I still don't understand why that means *I'm* suddenly to blame."

"You're the Alpha of the pack, and have previously sent wolves after Lennie," Espen supplied. I sidestepped, positioning myself so I could see both Wilhelm and Espen, and be able to launch myself past the Forest Fae if a fight broke out.

Wilhelm huffed like this was boring him and a waste of his time. Rolling up the sleeves of his shirt, he turned to the fae gathered in the living room to the left of the staircase. "Any of you steal a demi-fae recently?"

Eight fae peered over at us from where they stood against the walls, ready to defend their own. Some shook their heads, some snickered, and others snorted like we were idiots.

"You see." Wilhelm raised his hands in an innocent gesture. "Not mine."

Those weren't all the wolves in his pack, though. I'd bet the amount of fae in here barely scratched the surface of the numbers he had under his care. I jerked my head toward the front door. "What about the others who live on the compound?"

"They wouldn't disobey their Alpha."

"You sure about that?" Espen asked, his voice dropping and sounding like he was ready to tear the place apart. Perhaps he was teetering on the edge of composure, too.

"Positive, but..." Wilhelm let the word linger and sighed, watching us twitch as we waited for him to continue. "You might want to check with the junior pack."

"What?" we said in unison. Espen moved his hands to his hips, resting them there like he did when he wore his police utility belt.

"What happened, Wilhelm?" Espen asked. "You said all was well with the pack. Multiple times. Even when wolves tried to defect, you said you'd brought them in line. Was that a lie?"

Wilhelm grit his teeth and his shoulders dropped incrementally. "In the last year some of the youngsters did defect, claiming they didn't support our ways anymore. They formed their own pack and moved to an old campground near the river. About twenty-five strong, the eldest among them merely 30 years old. This rebellious behavior is just a phase they'll grow out of in time."

I clenched my fists as Espen took a deep breath. "So, you did lie. You lied to the Council repeatedly."

Wilhelm's nose wrinkled. "I did what I had to. The Council would have interfered in pack business if they found out."

"For good reason. We need to maintain harmony, Wilhelm, especially after Queen Ragnhild's demise."

"I have it under control." The Alpha shook his head. "Now, if I were you, I'd head over to the old southern campground and start asking questions there instead of shadowing my doorstep."

"Why should we trust you?" I asked, my voice filled with animosity and betraying the tension riding me.

Wilhelm snorted and glanced at Espen. "Because I'm the Alpha and have no reason to kidnap some silly—"

"Careful," Espen interjected and the building shook minutely, as if he was losing control and disturbing the soil beneath the foundation.

"—half-fae woman. If I were to cross paths with your problematic little thing. I wouldn't steal her. I'd kill her."

My blood boiled over.

I lunged, but Espen spun and caught me, pressing his hand to my chest before I could strangle the wolf leader.

"Don't," Espen said, and I backed down with a grumble. I threw his hand off my chest, but not before I caught the tremble there. He was struggling to contain his power.

Wilhelm straightened up and stepped closer, his pack fidgeting in anticipation. "Now, if you have no further business here, I'd like you to leave us in peace."

Nobody moved except the dust motes that caught in the light drifting out of the kitchen. The wind picked up outside and the wood building creaked, providing the only soundtrack to the tense showdown.

"Thank you for your time," Espen said like the goody-two-shoes that he was. "But if you go after her again, I will destroy you."

I smirked and peered around the room at the gathered shifters, letting them know I'd happily follow through on that threat too. Admittedly, it wasn't good diplomacy, but my patience ran out with this bastard the second he admitted to sending wolves after Lennie in Skolvik last year. Without another word, I grunted and turned for the exit, barely refraining from freezing them all to death.

"Is he lying?" I asked Espen once we were in the car and headed back down the long driveway, gravel and ice clinking against the sides of the vehicle.

He shook his head. "He'd make a bigger show of it if he was hiding her somewhere. No, I think he really wants to pin this on the junior pack."

"Did you know about this rift?" Espen was the Head Guard of the Forest Fae after all; he *should* know about these things.

Espen tilted his head from one side to the other as he steered us back onto the paved road that had been cleared of snow. The studded tires drummed against the ribbon of asphalt. "Yes, I was aware that there was dissent among the ranks, and that a group of fae had defected. But, like he said, and as mentioned in the meeting the other night; those wolves were brought back in and there were *supposedly* no more problems."

I tapped my fingers against my thighs, mimicking a rapid tune I played on the piano when frustrated and I needed to calm my thoughts.

"This will cause more internal instability, won't it?" I asked, my rational Head Guard mind taking over for a split-second, running through all the potential outcomes and scenarios their leadership would face.

Espen nodded with a grim expression.

Hopefully, something like this never happened to the Fjord Fae. We just needed our heir to return to Skolvik soon and we could avoid any potential political fallout.

Shaking off that horrible possibility, I asked, "Do you know where this southern campground is?"

Espen yanked off his hat and threw it over his shoulder into the back seat. "I know exactly where they are."

82
LENNIE

The only thing dustier than the shed I occupied was my wallet. The stiff wooden chair was growing more uncomfortable by the minute, and I was done with waiting around to be saved.

Now that Aurora and the others had left, I focused on picturing the blade I'd created with Halvar in the workshop and flailed my hands toward each other. If I could just bring my palms closer together, I might be able to replicate the magic I'd done so easily within the mountain. Heat flared in my left palm, tingles skipping down my scar, but nothing formed.

Tilting my head back, I let out a groan. Typical Lennie Martin luck. Thankfully, my captors didn't *seem* to want me dead, at least not based on my prior conversation with Marius and Aurora, but damn was I tired of sitting still. I grumbled just as the door to my shed-turned-prison swung open, and a bulb flickered on overhead, the light piercing the shadows.

"What are you doing?" A lightly-accented male voice asked as my eyes readjusted to the brightness and the door bumped shut.

"Flailing unsuccessfully," I muttered, taking him in. The young man had a long face, thick dark brows, and a quiet confidence that made his oversized sweatshirt look more like armor than a cozy piece of clothing. "You here to kill me?" Probably wise to double check in case my hunch was wrong.

He shook his head, but didn't approach. He lifted a paper bag clutched in his fist. "To feed you, actually."

I reared back in surprise. "Really?"

"Really."

"You're not going to poison me?"

"No."

"I thought this was a hostage situation. Isn't this where you give me some serum to make me spill all my secrets? Didn't you talk to Aurora and her beau?"

"I was in here." The newcomer nodded toward the corner by the door. "In wolf form. My name is Nils."

"Oh, so that was *you*! Ever consider wearing collars or something so the rest of us know who's who?"

Nils snorted, setting the brown paper bag on the floor. "That's funny."

"Thank you! I swear no one out here gets my jokes."

A warm and friendly laugh bubbled out of him. "Just don't say things like that around Marius. He's..." He thought for a second before answering. "Particular." He stepped closer, squatted beside my chair, and tapped at my wrist restraints. "Don't run away when I take these off."

"Hypothetically, what would happen if I did?"

"Hypothetically, at least five members of the pack are stationed nearby and would chase you. You wouldn't make it to the woods."

"Fair enough. Cardio isn't my thing anyway... At least not the running kind of cardio."

Nils giggled and blushed as he finished untying my hands and stepped back as I rose to my feet. Blood rushed from my butt to my toes, the same sensation I experienced whenever I got out of my seat after a long flight. I stretched out my fingers and twisted my wrists, enjoying the relief that swept through my limbs.

Nils passed me the bag and I pulled out a small wax-paper wrapped bread roll. Inside the *rundstykke*—as I'd learned they were called—was some cheese, salami, and butter. Not a well-rounded meal, but I wasn't going to complain. I'd been here for several hours and my stomach was starting to protest.

I paced back and forth taking a bite of the round snack. Now was as good a time as any to gather more information about what was going on around here. The Forest Fae may not have been my faction, but they were Espen's. And what was important to Espen, was important to me. Plus, as his fake fiancée I needed to keep up the show of care and affection—even if it was easy to do. I needed to know what was going on and I sure as fuck didn't believe I was held hostage only because I'd been asking around for Aurora. "Nils, my man. While I eat, why don't you tell me what's going on here."

Nils let out a long sigh and leaned against the wall beside a shovel and a rake, rubbing the heel of his palm across his brow. "It's a long story."

"I'm very busy, as you can see. The life of a bargaining chip is exhausting, let me tell you," I said, having had enough time with my thoughts to deduce why having me as a captive might help them get Espen's attention for something. If this was just about me asking around for Aurora, they'd have let me go by now, but as they hadn't... Well, it made sense that they had other reasons to keep me around.

The young shifter hung his head and confirmed my suspicion.

I waved my bread roll at him in a gesture to proceed.

Nils shoved his hands into the front pocket of his hoodie. "A few years ago, there were some problems with wolves again. A lot more sightings, and Wilhelm started to see them as a threat to our well-being as Forest Shifters. As our leader—"

"Your Alpha." I said, pulling on my knowledge from *Twilight*.

"Kind of. He's one of the stronger wolves in the pack, but ultimately, the Forest Fae Council of Elders could strip him of his leadership role. They decide among the candidates who is the better leader for the group, not us."

"That doesn't seem entirely democratic," I said between bites. "Or following any wolfish lore that I've heard of."

"Probably not, but the main goal is to protect nature and the existence of the fae. A leader should be able to do both those things with the faith and support from all members of the Forest Fae, not just the wolves."

"Fair enough."

"Anyway, as our leader, Wilhelm decided that killing the real wolves would help protect our secret and reduce the threat of humans accidentally killing one of our own should a real wolf stray too close to a village or cause a ruckus."

"That's not great," I said, taking another bite, crumbs falling from my lips.

"No, especially when they're almost extinct in this country."

"I heard about that. It sounds awful."

Nils nodded, his mouth turning down at the corners and those thick brows scrunching together. "The Norwegian Wolf has pretty much vanished. There are about 43 wolves remaining in Norway, and constant discussions in government about killing them all off."

My jaw hit the floor. I'd been shocked and saddened when Espen mentioned the wolves being almost extinct, but this was downright insane. "43? In the entire country? Are you serious?"

Nils grimaced again.

"Espen said they were critically endangered. I didn't realize how bad it was."

"A lot of them are inbred, too. So, if a parasite or virus infiltrates the packs, it'll wipe them all out." He snapped his fingers once.

Sadness swept over me as I took the last bite of my roll, brushing my hands off on my neon orange winter pants. How could people be so mean? How could a government actively support the eradication of animals like that? And how could Wilhelm support killing wolves when they were part of the forest he, as a fae, was supposed to protect? My stomach may have been quieted by food, but this new information didn't sit well with me.

"What are the Forest Fae and shifters doing about this? What about the Council?"

Nils's nose twitched and he rubbed a finger across it. "That's where our disagreements lie." He pushed off the wall, grabbing a water bottle from the front pocket of his hoodie, and passing it to me.

I thanked him and took a sip of the cool water as he continued. "The Council don't like the killings and would prefer to help the wolves. Marius challenged Wilhelm's leadership and position on the matter, claiming the need for harmony instead of violence. When Wilhelm laughed in his face and said he'd continue supporting the killing of real wolves, Marius defected, taking a group of us with him. We aren't many, only twenty-five strong at present, and mostly from the youngest generation of Forest Fae, but we all believe that the real wolves deserve to live their lives just as we do—free from harm."

Damn. I loved a good rebellion, and wholly agreed with this younger pack for standing up for their beliefs and sticking to the values of the Forest Fae.

"How many are there in Wilhelm's pack?" I asked.

"143. Most of which live in Alvdalen and the foothills west of town."

He motioned to the chair in the middle of the room, and I let out a long-winded sigh, handing back the water bottle.

"What has the Council said about all of this?" I reluctantly returned to my rickety perch. "Do they even know about your defection?" Based on what Wilhelm had said at the council meeting, I suspected the Council of Elders had no idea what was going on.

Nils's fingers barely brushed against me as he made swift work of retying my wrist bindings. "They don't know about us. We've tried to get messages to Council members, but haven't been successful."

"Do you have anyone on the Council to vouch for you other than Wilhelm? What about this insider that Aurora and Marius mentioned?"

"We have an insider with the senior pack and other local sources, but that's it." Nils stepped in front of me and surveyed his handy work while shaking his head.

"Well, I agree with you that those real wolves shouldn't be killed, and I'd support you, even call my fiancé and his sister, if you hadn't tied me up."

Nils's cheeks flushed with color as he swept his hand through his hair. "A good word with Espen would be helpful. We've tried reaching out to other members of the Council with nothing to show for it. We're hoping Espen might listen."

"I'm gonna be honest with you, buddy, kidnapping me will get his attention, but not in a good way." I tilted my head and raised my eyebrows at him. "In fact, demi-fae-napping me will probably lead to tense words and maybe some waterboarding by Øyvin. Fair warning for when they eventually show up."

Part of me was sad I'd miss it, stuck in here alone when they finally came to save me. Come to think of it, that was probably the horny part of me.

"Yeah, can't say I one hundred percent agreed with Marius and Aurora, but he needs to talk to Espen about some... erm... things. And you were asking around town for her and she was pretty adamant that we needed to find out what you wanted with her."

I scoffed. Could she be more of a pain in the ass? Probably. Best to tread carefully around that one.

"I need to get back." Nils added, heading for the door.

"Thank you for the information. I appreciate it and will talk to Espen." I wiggled my hands and winced, the rope scraping against my wrists once more. "Not too appreciative of the bracelets, though. They're cute and kind of kinky, but I'd have preferred diamonds. Resale value is much higher."

Nils laughed and tugged at the neck of his sweater as he wrapped one hand around the doorknob. "Noted. By the way, that color looks awful on you," he said with a nod toward my puffy getup.

I snickered at his boldness, but damn was he right. "Trust me, I wouldn't be in this if a Fjord Fae hadn't forced me to wear it." This neon orange shit was horrific. Hopefully the guys would rescue me soon so I could get out of it.

83

ØYVIN

The sun brushed beneath the horizon, drenching our surroundings in the pale blue light of dusk as we drove down the winding lane and pulled into a small clearing surrounded by pines and barren birch trees. It wouldn't be long before night settled in, and already too much time had passed since Lennie was taken.

We climbed out of the car, the campsite eerily quiet save for the burbling river nearby. The junior pack campground was located just outside of the village, tucked between two hillsides along a small river. With a copse of seven tiny buildings and some shelters where logs were stacked and stored for winter, the compound was minuscule compared to Wilhelm's.

Wolves appeared from buildings, several shifting into their fae form as they surrounded us.

"Where is Marius?" Espen asked, and I let him take the lead considering I was liable to start drowning people with the anger coursing through my veins like a lethal current. Killing any of these shifters, even Wilhelm's, wouldn't do well for inter-faction relations, especially right now with all we Fjord Fae had been through. I needed to keep a level head, but that was easier said than done when they'd taken what was mine.

A white-haired young man stepped out of a cabin to our right, followed swiftly by a brown-and-beige wolf who shifted beside him, jeans and a large sweater appearing on his lanky limbs.

"Espen, glad you finally made it." The white-haired one descended the front steps with a confident swagger. "Did you get my message?"

"Very clearly, Marius. Has she been harmed?" Espen asked, his voice cool and calm—the polar opposite of my thundering heart rate.

"She's alive and well."

I glanced around at the wolves and Forest Fae encircling us, watching for any tells or signs that they knew where Lennie was being held. Everyone's eyes remained locked on us, hands hung loose at sides, and feet were firmly planted, pointing toward the biggest threats—Espen and I.

"But," Marius added, "I need your help on the council with Wilhelm and for you to stop looking for Aurora. She doesn't want anything to do with Skolvik."

Adrenaline flushed through my body and I tensed. *Wait, Aurora?*

"And you thought kidnapping my fiancée would garner my support?" Espen asked, skipping right over the name of the woman we'd been sent here to find and focusing on the most important woman in our lives.

Marius shrugged. "Desperate times."

I could wring his desperate little neck—

"Well, you certainly got my attention," Espen said. "But I won't discuss any matters with you until she stands beside me."

Marius pulled his shoulders back and lifted his chin, blue eyes catching the last of the day's light. "I'll let her go, if you agree to throw your support behind our values on the Council."

This kid had some serious nerve.

Espen straightened and crossed his arms as he took a deep breath. "If you give me Lennie," he reiterated slowly, his voice dropping lower and lower with each word, "I'll discuss how we might proceed with your pack's concerns. Don't further test my patience, Marius."

Marius flared his nostrils and nodded to a small wooden shed near the forest to our left, a single bulb lighting the muddy front step. "Meet me back in the main house for that chat."

Espen and I moved before anyone said another word.

By the time we stomped onto the shed's front step, I could hear a feminine voice inside.

"That better be a dragon come to whisk me back to Skolvik! I'm done with my puppy playdate!"

I huffed and Espen snorted as I conjured a ball of water around the lock hanging from the door. Making sure the water had penetrated the locking mechanism, I turned my hand, willing the water to freeze and rapidly expand. The padlock shattered, pieces falling to the ground. Espen lurched forward and ripped the mangled metal from the door, tossing the scraps aside.

With a firm nudge from Espen's shoulder, the door creaked open. Inside the dry and dull storage shed was Lennie, tied to a chair.

Thank the ancestors.

"Hey!" She beamed at us, her eyes full of joy. Her hair hung limp around her face and her nose was rosy from the cold—the dusty and cluttered room was little warmer than the outdoors. "Fancy seeing you guys here. I have good news and bad news, which do you want first?"

"You don't want us to untie you first?" Espen asked as he stepped into the room and moved to undo the ropes holding her wrists against the chairback.

"We can multitask," Lennie responded with a half-shrug.

Her voice was like a balm to my frayed nerves and the tension in my muscles eased. I shook my head at her ridiculousness and scanned her for injuries.

Feet. Boots still on.

Legs. Fidgeting and moving without issue.

Wrists. Red and raw. I snarled.

Chest. Bundled in her jacket. Rising and falling normally.

Face. No bruises or marks. Just her damn mouth, pink cheeks, and eyebrows that were slightly more mismatched than normal thanks to a miscalculation with the tweezers last week.

I breathed a sigh of relief.

She was fine. Unharmed. Alive. And her sass hadn't got her torn to shreds.

I leaned my shoulder against the doorframe and crossed my arms, relief washing through me as the adrenaline started to subside. Letting out several steady breaths, I willed my pulse toward a more restful state, and my heart filled with a comforting warmth now that the three of us were reunited.

"Go on," I said, tilting my chin at her. "Good news first."

She smiled as Espen unbound one of her wrists. "I found Aurora!" She twisted her freed hand in circles, splaying and stretching her fingers.

"And the bad news?" I asked, bracing myself.

Espen untied the last rope and Lennie gingerly brushed her wrists where the fastenings had been. "She says we have the wrong person."

A low groan rumbled through my chest.

Espen cupped Lennie's wrists together in his hands. Pressing a gentle kiss to her fingers, he pushed his healing magic into her raw skin. A subtle silver light shone from his hands and, a moment later, the red marks on Lennie's wrists were gone. Thank fuck he was both Healer and Destroyer, because if I had to watch her get those healed by human methods, I'd drag that nearby river through the camp.

Lennie's eyes shot to me like she could hear my thoughts. She extricated herself from Espen's hold and wandered over. Pressing her hand against my chest just above my heart, she let out a long sigh. Her gaze flicked up and met mine. A loving tenderness crinkled the corners of her eyes a split second before a malicious smirk crossed her lips. "Relax your cheeks, Asshole. I'm fine."

This woman.

I pulled her into me and crashed my lips against hers. The shock of losing her, the desperate need to have her back, played over in my mind on a torturous loop. But she was fine, she was here, however troublesome that mouth of hers was. I threaded my hands into her hair, holding on to her as my tongue pressed her lips apart. She granted me passage with a faint whimper, and it took every ounce of the frayed control I had left not to haul her over my shoulder and drag her home. I never wanted to lose her. Never again.

She pulled back and swept her tongue across her bottom lip before straightening. "Oh, I almost forgot. There's a part three to the news."

"Good or bad?" I grumbled, sliding my hold to her sides.

"What else?" Espen asked.

"Aurora is totally Freija's daughter."

84
LENNIE

If there was ever a moment where I could knock down Øyvin and Espen at the same time, this was it. Both stared at me with blank gazes, trying to blink away the shocking news I'd just dumped at their feet.

"Are you sure?" Øyvin asked, uncertainty marring his voice.

"Pretty positive. She looks just like Freija, even has her eyes."

Øyvin grunted and waved his hand in front of his face. "The brown-and-gray ones?"

I nodded.

Espen didn't move, staring at the chair I'd been confined to for the better part of a day. "Espen?" I nudged him with my shoulder.

"Sorry," he said, raking his hand through his hair and brushing it off his temple. "I-I'm... Halvar said she was a distant relative."

"You know I'm not an expert on the man, but lying to protect the mountain and its interests doesn't seem out of the realm of possibility with Halvar."

Øyvin hummed in agreement as Espen nodded lightly. "Freija secretly had a daughter."

"Mind boggling, isn't it?" I said, having had more time to come to terms with the fact and actually met the woman herself.

Espen nodded slowly. "And certainly explains where Freija was twenty years ago when she couldn't come to the south to help Queen Ragnhild."

My eyes widened. I hadn't even thought of that. Freija had probably been giving birth, which was why she hadn't come to her friend's aid. My mind reeled back to something King Balder said while Halvar was interrogating him in the dungeons: *Shame Freija couldn't have been by her dear friend's side during the skirmishes in the south twenty years ago. Where was she anyway?* Had he known? Or did he suspect something? Halvar had certainly been quick to pivot the subject that day. But it did make sense.

"Aurora would've been targeted, wouldn't she?"

Espen straightened and brushed his hand across his short beard. "Yes, Queen Freija probably wanted to keep her hidden due to the unrest in the south and the target she'd have on her back as the heir."

"Is that common practice among the fae royals?" I asked.

"It varies based on the monarch, but it's more common with Fjord Fae and Forest Fae."

"Looks like we still have an heir to locate, though," Øyvin said from the doorway and glanced over his shoulder as voices sounded behind him. "Shall we go *chat* with Marius?"

A groan escaped me. I really didn't want to spend more time with the jerk who'd kidnapped me, but Espen took my hands in his and jumped in before I could complain. "Yes, we need to *discuss* certain matters with the young pup. Like the consequences of stealing what's ours."

Espen pulled me against his chest and sealed his mouth to mine. My knees shook and I melted into his hold, enjoying the possessiveness of his words and actions. He nipped at my lips and pressed himself against my curves, eliciting a subtle moan from me. If I didn't stop this, we'd end up naked on the shed floor.

Coming up for air, I found a satisfied smile on Espen's face. With a wink, he lightly tugged on my hand, coaxing me toward the door. I followed, my steps like those of someone who was drunk on something.

By the time Espen and I stepped out of my shed, Øyvin was halfway across the clearing, hurtling toward the only cabin with lights on.

Øyvin barreled up the front steps and booted the pack cabin door open. Yells sounded from inside as Espen and I passed through the front door and found Øyvin looming over Marius. The black-clad young wolf didn't back down from the monumental glare leveled at him, and if I wasn't annoyed about the kidnapping, I'd have been impressed.

"We need to talk, Marius," Espen growled beside me, squeezing my hand tighter.

Marius's eyes flicked to us as Nils shut the front door behind us. "Told you she hadn't been harmed."

A rumble sounded from Øyvin's chest, as Espen replied, "Which is the only reason I haven't already leveled your compound. Let's talk."

Marius stepped aside and motioned for us to join him in the living room next door.

We took up the three spots on the threadbare couch, the pillows sinking significantly beneath our weight. Marius's cabin was a mix between a frat house and a starter home. The living room furniture was mismatched or cobbled together, and maps of Norway were pinned to the wood walls with little green flags marking different locations on the eastern border with Sweden.

The three of us unzipped our jackets. While the guys left theirs on, I frantically removed my orange marshmallow container and stuffed it behind my back. Like stepping into an air-conditioned room during Ohio's hot summers, it was a relief to finally be out of the damn thing, even if it had kept me warm in the shed.

Espen perched on the edge of the sofa, staring daggers at Marius who took a seat in a lumpy armchair across from us and pushed up the sleeves of his black shirt. The young shifter waved several members of his pack out of the room. The only one who remained was Nils. He took up position by the door like the skinniest club bouncer I'd ever seen, hands clasped together in front of his crotch.

Espen clapped his hands together once, garnering the room's attention. "Let's get one thing clear, right away. If you or your wolves ever lay a hand on my wi—fiancée, ever again, I will bury you all alive. Do you understand?"

My brows scrunched at his almost slip up in title, but my body flushed at the protective display. Why was that hot and why did it make me want to jump him?

Marius blinked back at Espen but didn't move.

Øyvin raised his hand from where it rested on the armrest and a ball of water appeared in front of Nils's face, pressing against his mouth. His eyes widened in panic, his chest rapidly rising and falling.

I swatted Øyvin's rock-hard stomach. "Don't waterboard Nils. He fed me."

The water enveloped Nils's head and the young man swatted at the orb in vain.

"Fed you what?" Øyvin asked.

"*Rundstykke.* Not poison. Now stop. Aim that at the blond one."

The water disappeared and Nils gasped, bending over at his hips. He shook out his hair like a dog, sending water droplets across the wooden floor. A new sphere of water grew above Marius's head.

"Threat received," Marius said. "You can do away with the magic tricks, Håland. We won't touch her ever again."

Øyvin grumbled and lowered his hand. The orb disappeared, but not before letting a single droplet plop directly onto Marius's forehead.

He wiped it off and glared at all of us.

"So," Espen started, graciously pivoting before a fight broke out. "What exactly do you want to discuss? Gaining my support on the Council? Asking to make your pack official and separate from Wilhelm's?"

"More than that," Marius said.

"What do you mean?" Espen asked, his eyes narrowing on the young leader across from us.

"We'd like your backing and support for the harmonious life we've always lived and to refrain from killing the remaining natural wolves, as we Forest Fae are supposed to—"

Espen nodded.

"—But there's additional information you need to be aware of that might change things."

"Get on with it," Øyvin muttered as he leaned back and stretched his arm behind me. Setting his hand on my shoulder, he pulled me into him. Warmth radiated up my right side and I leaned further into the comfort of his unusual public display of affection as we waited for the shifter to respond.

Marius took a deep breath and brushed his thumb across his eyebrow. "Wilhelm is planning to defect from the Forest Fae."

Espen flinched beside me and Øyvin squeezed my shoulder. The room somehow grew quieter as the new information swirled around us in the dim lighting. Wilhelm leaving the Forest Fae couldn't be good, however much of a dick he was.

Espen leaned further forward and rested his elbows on his knees. Swallowing hard, he asked, "Where did you hear that?"

Marius planted his elbows on the armrests of his chair and laced his fingers together. "A rumor started spreading last spring. At first I thought nothing of it, but after a month of watching Wilhelm grow more frustrated with the Council and act outside of not just their guidance, but also our duties as Forest Fae to protect the environment and all creatures, I decided to gather my friends and defect."

"Sighting a disagreement on the wolf treatment as your reason," Espen added, earning a gentle nod from Marius.

"Which was also true. I mean, Wilhelm has been of that opinion for the past two years."

Espen hummed like this was something he was aware of or at least suspected.

"But if I'd started talking to the elders about his plans to defect," Marius continued, his blue eyes scanning Espen, "I'd more than likely end up face down in a shallow river."

Further evidence that Wilhelm thought of himself as and acted like some mafia don.

"Fair enough," Espen said, his amber eyes locked on the Junior Pack leader.

"I thought about calling you or perhaps getting a message to you through Turi, but I couldn't be sure it was safe. Then you came back into town, and... Well, an opportunity presented itself." Marius waved his hand toward me.

"Yes," Espen huffed. "Capturing my fiancée certainly caught my attention."

Marius's gaze latched onto the ring glinting in the low light on my left hand before moving back to Espen. "Like I said, desperate times."

While I was keeping up with most of their conversation, my chest tightened and questions swirled around my mind. The Forest Fae political system seemed democratic, but also not. It had been a monarchy at one point and then reconfigured to a council that had still existed under Queen Ragnhild's rule. It was all so different from how government and leadership worked in the US and other countries.

"I thought the Alpha was chosen by the Council?" I asked, unable to hold in the question any longer.

"They are. For this exact reason." Espen rose to his feet, his boots stomping across the floorboards as he paced. "It stops any one leader from gaining more power than the monarch, even if they too are a leader within the Forest Fae faction."

"Then why the hell was Wilhelm chosen? I think we can all agree the dude is a piece of shit."

Espen crossed his arms. "Because once upon a time, Queen Ragnhild trusted him and the Council agreed he was the strongest leader for the pack. Times have changed though."

"And so has Wilhelm," Marius interjected.

Øyvin listened intently. As Head Guard of the Fjord Fae this must've been a fascinating conversation for multiple reasons, the best of which was serious insight into the bubbling political unrest within the Forest Fae. Thank goodness we were all allies here. Then again, this was probably a prime example of something neither the Fjell Fae nor the Fjord Fae would want to happen to their factions. Øyvin's eyes roved over the Forest Fae in the room, watching their every move and taking in every morsel of information.

"Can you help us with the Council? Support us and alert them before things escalate?" Marius asked outright, looking to Espen for an answer. "They won't listen to me."

Espen brushed his palm across his short beard, his gaze locked in thought as he stared at nothing and everything in the room. I wanted to peer into his thoughts, see and hear what was going on in that mind of his. Espen strongly favored peaceful diplomacy—locking away his destructive powers—but how could he position himself in this situation without triggering backlash? I had an inkling on what side he might favor, and sincerely hoped I was right.

With a deep sigh, Espen halted in front of the sofa and looked over at the Junior Pack leader. "While I don't appreciate how you went about getting the information to me, I'm glad you finally did. Wilhelm defecting would cause immense upheaval and would set a precedent that wouldn't bode well for the Forest Fae, the resources we are meant to protect, and our allies." He glanced back at Øyvin and I, giving us both a gentle nod before turning back to Marius.

"You have my support. I'll need to think about how we should proceed, but keep your phone on you and avoid Wilhelm and his pack unless I say otherwise."

Marius's shoulders slumped and he nodded. "Thank you."

A sense of relief swept through the room and me. Nils rested the back of his head against the door and let out a deep sigh.

It was sometimes hard to remember that Espen was a major leader and revered among the Forest Fae. To me, he was the bubbly ray of sunshine that brightened my days and snuggled me every night. But, I'd also be lying if I said that seeing him in his element wasn't eye-opening... and a huge turn on.

Silence grew and so did my impatience. I'd been sitting for hours today and wanted to get moving. We still had a mission to complete for Halvar.

"Any who." I dragged the word out as I bounced my knees. "Care to share where Aurora is? We could do with talking to her, too."

Marius turned to me and furrowed his brow. "She's not here."

"What do you mean?"

"She left before lunch. After what you said, she had zero interest in sticking around."

Øyvin leaned forward, resting his elbows on his thighs. "Where is she?" he grumbled, a commanding tone lacing his voice.

"She wouldn't tell me."

"Bullshit," I interjected. Those two were definitely an item. I highly doubted she went anywhere without him knowing. He may have been the Junior Pack leader, and only self- or internally-appointed as their Alpha, but this kid had alpha-male energy wrapped around him like a leather biker jacket. His black-on-black attire and confident disposition further solidified my assessment.

Marius tilted his head to one side and looked at me like I was crazy for calling him out. I could practically feel my guys trying to stifle their smiles. They were much more accustomed to my accusatory outbursts.

"I said bullshit," I added, doubling down when Marius didn't respond.

"Oh, I heard you."

"So?" I opened my hands in a serving motion, waiting for him to tell us more. "Where is she?"

Marius leaned back in his chair and wiped his hand over his chin. "She took her camping gear and said she'd be back in a week or so. I doubt she's gone too far, but she wouldn't tell me." A hint of frustration marred his voice, like he was annoyed with her for not telling him *and* us for causing this mess in the first place.

"We'll keep searching," Espen said, leaning his rear on the sofa's armrest, his ankles crossed. "But, I'm warning you now, Marius. We won't be leaving Alvdalen without her."

Marius snorted and smirked. Shaking his head, he replied, "You may have grown up here once upon a time, but Vigdis raised Aurora among these trees. Good luck finding her."

We stepped outside, re-bundled against the darkness and cold. With swift movements, we crossed the clearing to the parked car.

"Øyvin can you drive, please? I need to call Turi." Espen said, tousling his hair and looking more rattled than I'd ever seen him. But, the Fjord Fae nodded and took the keys from him.

We settled in the car, and I spread out in the back, buckling myself in while stretching across all three seats as best as I could. I'd been seated or standing all day long, and it felt like heaven to finally lie down, even if it was in the car.

Øyvin started the vehicle, and Espen had his phone to his ear. A heartbeat later he uttered, "Turi, we have a problem."

85
LENNIE

We lumbered into the cabin, shutting out the cold and dark. I pulled my fingers through my hair and groaned, glad to be back at our little home base. If someone had told me this morning that I'd be kidnapped by wolves, I'd have laughed in their face. What a freaking day.

Arms wrapped around my torso from behind, a soft sigh blowing my hair off my shoulder. I dropped my hands back down and twisted around. Espen's eyelids weighed heavily, his lips set in a soft line, and his hair mussed like he'd vigorously raked his hands through it.

"You okay?" I asked, brushing my palms up his jacketed arms and resting them on his shoulders.

He nodded. "I just... I need to..." His chest rose and fell. "I need to decompress. Eat something. Hold you."

I hugged and nuzzled into him. "You mean you need quiet time to process everything you've learned today?"

A smile slowly unfolded on his face. "You know me so well."

"Good thing I'm your fiancée then, isn't it?"

His smile turned into a beaming grin, like my words had turned it to full volume. "Very, very good." He brushed his thumb across my cheek and I couldn't stop myself from leaning into his touch. The tension from the day unraveled from my muscles and a weightlessness settled over me. I liked it here. In his arms where nothing and no one could get to me.

"It's my turn to cook dinner," he said. "Pasta okay?"

I nodded and tightened my arms around his torso. Pasta was always okay.

"Good." He pressed a gentle peck to my head, and I untangled myself from his hold. "Now go take a shower and I'll have food for you shortly after you're done."

He sauntered across the little living room and rounded into the tiny kitchen, aiming for the wooden cupboard filled with our groceries.

Wasting no more time, I shucked off my boots and hideous jacket and yanked off my snow pants as quickly as possible. Rolling my shoulders, I let out a satisfied sigh, happy to finally be out of my snow gear and inside a building that didn't smell like a garden shed.

"Are you all right?" Øyvin quirked his brow at me as he leaned against the wall by the front door, carefully monitoring my movements.

"Yeah." I grabbed the front collar of my shirt and lifted it to my nose. Bile rose in my throat. I smelled like my brothers' old gym bags when they got home from football practice. Dad had needed a hose to get the stench out of them. I apparently needed the same. "I just really want a hot shower and a ton of soap to remove *eau de puppy shed*."

Øyvin harumphed and tilted his chin toward the bathroom.

I didn't need further coaxing. That hot water and I had a date, and I wasn't even going to ask it to buy me dinner first. I sauntered into the little room with its cream-colored walls and white tiles, and flicked on the light. Nothing was getting between me and the suds this evening.

Øyvin stalked into the bathroom behind me. Without saying a word, he closed the door and settled against the tiny wood-and-stone vanity.

"I know you don't mind watching, but you're intruding on my date with this guy," I said as I turned on the water, grabbed a fresh towel out of the tiny cabinet, and set it atop the vanity beside Øyvin.

His eyes watched my every move. Those perfectly plush lips set in a firm line. "I'm not leaving," he said matter-of-factly.

"You're going to watch me shower?" Something inside me sparked at the thought, and I brushed my palms across my leggings.

"You need protecting," he replied and his gaze drifted to my legs before returning back to my face.

"I'm not going to get jumped while I'm in there." I pointed my thumb over my shoulder at the barely walk-in pantry-sized shower.

"I'm not taking my eyes off you."

"You really are an overprotective asshole." I huffed. "I've been around wet dogs all day. You sure you wanna be this close? I stink."

"Did they touch you?"

"What?" I pulled off my shirt and Øyvin's gaze momentarily dipped to my chest before resettling on my face.

"Did. They. Touch. You?"

Technically speaking I had been touched by a few of them, but not in the way he was asking about. "Only when they nabbed me in the woods. Marius grabbed my wrists and another hauled me by my feet. Don't remember much after that." I rubbed my hand across my temple. "Pretty sure Aurora was the one who clocked me over the head."

Øyvin's jaw tightened and it looked like he was about to break a tooth. *Okay, wrong answer.* This guy did not like losing control of anything in his life. Which extended to me too.

"There were no other touches, no tingly touches," I added, hoping it would calm him down and stop the muscle in his jaw twitching. "You know you and Espen are the only ones allowed to touch me like that."

"Do I?"

The steam in the room thickened, and I rolled my eyes at him. "Of course."

"Prove it."

My heart skipped a beat. "What?"

"Get in the shower, Lennie."

My body shuddered as I sucked in a heated breath. "Fine."

I peeled off my leggings slowly, hooking them over my feet and yanking off my thick woolly socks in the process. Pulling off my sports bra, I flicked it in his direction and, like the impressive ass that he was, he caught it with one hand, his eyes never straying from mine. *Fuck, why was that hot?*

"Keep going." He nodded, and I did as I was told—half caught in my own desire to wash, half swept away by the increasing pulsing between my thighs. I pulled off my underwear and tossed that at his face too. He caught it again, then stuffed it in his back pocket.

"You saving that for later?" I crossed my arms under my boobs, admittedly pushing them up to see if I could get any other reaction out of him.

He rolled his bottom lip between his teeth. "Get in the shower."

I flicked my brows at him and turned, giving him the full view of my ass, then opened the glass shower door, tested the water with my hand, and stepped inside. I let out a low and satisfied groan as hot water sluiced over my shoulders and down my body. Whoever invented showers needed to be knighted *and* made a saint, because this was bliss. Bliss that was made even more satisfying by the heady stare following my movements on the other side of the pane of glass.

I started with my hair, getting it all wet before washing it with both shampoo and conditioner. Then, I grabbed the bottle of soap, doling out a decent amount, and swept it across me. The suds clung to my skin as I moved my hands over my body in languorous strokes, enjoying the heat of the water, room, and Øyvin's gaze.

"Touch yourself," he commanded, and my toes curled, my breath stuttering.

Fog adhered to the shower door, creating a blurry scene of the room beyond and the man watching me like I was his dinner. A shudder ran through me at the thought of bringing myself to climax with him watching and my breaths shallowed.

I dipped my fingers over my stomach and down, reaching the apex of my thighs with a soft moan. Rubbing circles around the bundle of nerves, my eyes fluttered closed, the sensation between my legs building, the room steaming up quicker and quicker.

"Eyes on me, Trouble."

I looked into Øyvin's heated sapphire gaze, wholly aware of his hands gripping the sink so hard his knuckles turned white. I added more pressure from my fingers and let out a little whimper. Øyvin bit his bottom lip, his chest heaving, his breaths coming harder as he watched me. Increasing my pace, I reveled in the sensations fluttering through me and the need on the other side of the glass. The shower door swung open and I jumped back against the tile wall, my fingers stopping. Øyvin's eyes turned molten, his hair askew, the muscles in his arms jumping.

He stepped into the shower, pressing himself against me as the door shut behind him. We barely fit in here together. I was pretty sure his sweatpant-covered ass was plastered against the shower door. But I couldn't focus on that, the only thing registering with me right now was the butterflies in my stomach, the clenching between my thighs, and the man staring down at me like I was his anchor as water cascaded over us.

His hair, usually poking up slightly, fell across his forehead, undone by the water. He pressed his hands against the tiles on either side of my head. "Keep going."

I slipped my fingers back to my clit and slowly started massaging the sensitive mound. Sparks shuddered up and down my spine, as his breath brushed against my cheek.

My head dropped momentarily, but Øyvin pressed his thumb and forefinger against my chin, tilting it back up to look at him. "Once again, eyes on me, Trouble. And don't you dare stop." He rested his forehead against mine. "Fall apart for me."

My whole body shuddered at his words, the feeling of being protected yet vulnerable washing over me. The sensation of having this man, this creature, practically begging for my release invaded every nook of my mind. He'd lost control today. He'd lost me. And now he was reclaiming what was lost.

The tenderness between my thighs sparked like lightning, my fingers moving in faster and tighter circles as I chased my climax. Water swept across us, heating me from the outside in while the feeling of having him watch such an intimate moment warmed me from the inside out. It was all too much. I panted, desperate. Hungry. Wanting him to touch me, but knowing, if I asked, he'd refuse.

I fell apart with a cry and his lips were on mine, swallowing my moans, holding me upright with his own body. The brush of his wet cotton shirt against my nipples, the press of his length against me, plus the trembles of my orgasm—I never wanted this to end.

He pulled his lips from mine and nuzzled against my hair. "Don't ever run off again."

"I was kidnapped," I breathed and splayed my hands against his firm chest.

"Sentiment stands."

"You're such a demanding asshole."

He shut off the water and hitched my leg over his hip, rolling himself against me. "And you're rage-inducing trouble."

"We established that a while ago. Search your memory banks for a boat thief."

He grumbled and nipped at my ear. "Just be glad I'm feeling merciful and that lake outside is frozen over."

"You can't just throw me in the fjord or a body of water every time I annoy you."

"It's worked thus far."

"And yet"—I rolled my core against his erection—"I don't think you're annoyed with me right now."

His head tilted back and a low groan escaped his lips. A satisfied smirk grew on my face as he slowly released me and stepped out of the shower. Leaving the door open, he tossed my towel at me, and I caught it before it could land at the bottom of the shower stall. "Dry off, and come to bed."

The stubborn part of me wanted to counter him, but my head wasn't in charge at the moment. So, I followed him into the bedroom and settled for a sultry, "Yes, sir."

After watching him change and return his wet clothes to the bathroom—no doubt hanging them up to dry—I pulled on a clean pair of leggings and an oversized t-shirt from my bag, and crawled onto the bed beside Øyvin where he sat, propped up against the headboard. I snuggled in beside him and settled my leg over his. With a contented grumble, he pulled me into his side and held on like I might disappear.

"I'm okay," I whispered.

He squeezed me tighter and his eyes fluttered closed.

"I'm alive. Unharmed. And only made seventeen thousand wolf jokes while cooped up in that shed."

Øyvin's lips twisted into a smirk before straightening out as he sighed. "I don't ever want that to happen again."

I pressed my hand to his chest, and his heart thrummed beneath my palm. "Neither do I. That chair was as comfortable as a front row church pew."

Øyvin laughed softly as Espen's voice sounded through the cabin. "Dinner's ready!"

86

LENNIE

The next morning I found myself in an empty parking lot with Espen and Øyvin, ready to search for Aurora. The sun hid behind a thick layer of clouds as it rose above the horizon, lending a dull glow to our snowy surroundings. The cold air nipped at my cheeks and snot threatened to run from my nose.

Espen grabbed our borrowed skis and poles from the back of the car where we'd stuck them through the trunk and into the backseat to make room. He handed a set to Øyvin, then rested another pair against the back of the car, before turning to me with his signature smile plastered across his face. "You got your ski boots on?"

I lifted one foot and then the other, showing him the short-shafted white-and-blue boots I'd put on in the car when we first pulled in. They were a lot different from the downhill skiing boots I'd worn before, but we weren't doing downhill. Today we were cross-country skiing. The skis were thin and long compared to their curvier downhill counterparts, and the boots were shorter, narrower, and much lighter.

"Excellent. Cross-country skiing is a lot of fun. I promise," Espen said. He handed me the poles for balance, setting the skis in his hands down beside my feet, and kneeling before me. Not an unwelcome sight. I clenched my gloved fingers around the poles, wanting to brush them through the floppy hair that poked out of Espen's hat.

He stalled and peered up at me through his lashes, his amber gaze warming like he could hear my thoughts. His lips curved up at one side, those soft cushions begging—

I cleared my throat and mentally shook off the tingling sensation. "So, do you think Aurora might have tucked herself away at the ranger cabin along this mountain trail?" I asked, confirming today's search activities and distracting myself from the handsome fae on his knees in front of me.

"Yes," Espen replied. "She might be camping as Marius suggested, but in these temperatures she'd need to be careful. Plus, the ranger cabin is rarely occupied and frequently used by skiers and hikers who need to seek shelter for whatever reason."

That seemed as good a hiding spot as any and worth looking into. Espen tapped my left foot with his hand. "Step forward and point your toe so I can click you into your ski." I curved my foot like a ballerina. He clutched my boot in his hand and pressed the toe of the shoe, which had some form of locking mechanism on it, to the boot-mount on the ski. The front of my shoe locked into place with a click.

He moved to the next foot and I repositioned some of my weight onto the poles. While Espen worked on the second boot, I glanced over at Øyvin with narrowed eyes as he clicked himself into his skis. He moved with ease in his navy-colored winter gear like he'd done this a thousand times.

"Let me guess, you're a professional skier because the snow is technically frozen flakes of water?"

He gave me a tiny smirk, his eyes glistening with humor. "No."

"No?" My voice rose several octaves, shocked by his confession.

"I'm a good skier because we live in Norway."

There it was. My lips fell into a firm line. I really should've heeded the phrase, "Norwegian's are born with skis on their feet," because it was apparently true for both fae and humans. Øyvin glided forward in swift movements, warming up and testing out the waxed underside of the skis.

Click.

"You're ready to go." Espen launched to his feet and planted a delicate kiss to the end of my cold nose. I slid one ski forward and then the other, hesitantly lifting my poles. The sensation was new, but not wholly unfamiliar after skiing trips in New England. These boots were like highly-engineered soccer cleats and only fastened at the front, letting the heel lift off the back instead of having the whole foot locked in. It was going to take some time to get used to. I rolled my shoulders, my orange jacket rustling with the motion and adding a soundtrack to my tingling nerves.

This was fine. We'd be venturing across mostly flat terrain, not hurtling down a hill at twenty miles-per-hour. The odds of falling on my face were low. Really, what could go wrong?

Click. Click.

I looked up at the sound and found Espen fastened into his skis, shimmying and ready to go. "Follow me!"

Trees weighed by snow lined the wide trail, some boughs so heavy they met the tops of the snow dunes. A peaceful calm wrapped around the three of us, only broken by our panted breaths and creaking branches.

It didn't take long for me to get the hang of cross-country skiing, but the first ten minutes of our journey were spent in my head thinking hard about the movements.

Slide one foot forward, move pole.

Slide other foot forward, move other pole.

Slide again.

Stay in Espen's tracks.

Don't hold up Øyvin—even if it would annoy him and bring a smile to my face.

After a little while, I grew confident enough in my coordination to strike up conversation.

"Okay, fill me in on some of the Forest Fae politics. I feel like I should probably know this stuff as the future wife-for-immigration-purposes of the Head Guard. How did the wolves come to be? Have the Forest Fae always had wolf shifters?"

"Good questions," Espen said with a quick grin over his shoulder, the pom-pom on his knit hat wobbling. "No, there haven't always been wolves among the Forest Fae. No one knows the full story—those who were there have all passed and when they were alive, none spoke of what happened."

"Sounds interesting," I mumbled, sliding one foot in front of the other. Øyvin let out a low grumble of agreement from behind me.

"It is," Espen replied. "It was about a thousand years ago. The King of the Forest Fae, Olaf, was concerned about deforestation, pelt hunting, and increasing population after the Viking era. He journeyed from the east where he resided at the time, back to Skolvik. Rumor has it he met with the Royals of the Fjell and Fjord. No one knows what was discussed or how it happened, but the soldiers who ventured west with King Olaf returned as wolf shifters."

"Well shit," I said. "That must have been a helluva pivot for those soldiers and probably their families. *Hey honey, I'm home and now I have a tail!* It's almost as wild as me becoming a demi-fae."

"Indeed." Espen nodded. "The men and women returned to their village, established their own settlement, and worked on their powers, learning how to shift and running around in their wolf forms protecting wildlife and defending the forests."

"And the rest is history?" I came to a stop at a split in the road and rested my hands on top of my ski poles. Espen stepped back beside me and pulled out a bottle of water, passing it to me for a swig—which I gladly took—before taking a sip of his own.

He set the bottle back in his pack and continued, "Wolves have been with us ever since. They've always had a seat on the council. They've always deferred to the monarch... Well, they did until we moved to a council-led governing system twenty years ago." Espen's voice faltered slightly at the reminder of the loss of his Queen and mentor in the southern battle. "Since then, Wilhelm has always been in concert with the Council of Elders."

"Until now," Øyvin said from where he stood on my other side.

"Until now," Espen reiterated.

"And no one knows exactly how the wolves were created? Was there a magic witch that cast a spell on them? Was it Heidi? No, never mind, she wouldn't be old enough. Not that I wouldn't put it past the Forest Fae Healer to pull some sort of witchy brouhaha. If there's any one fae that gives off crazy-witch-hidden-in-the-woods vibes, it's our dear friend Heidi."

Espen sighed, and rested his wrists atop his ski poles, matching my stance, his cheeks flushed from exercising in the cold. "The wolves never spoke of it. Stories over the years said they were sworn to secrecy by King Olaf. Other tales said their new magic tied their tongues and didn't allow them to speak on the matter. At this point it's become more myth than history. But they're part of us: even with their shifter magic, they're fae. Never, at any point in time, have they been treated as lesser or unwelcome."

I liked that about the Forest Fae. I was slightly biased as Espen was the first to trust me, bringing me into their inner circle by telling me their secret, but it also seemed to be a trait that all Forest Fae shared; they were welcoming and caring. So, it was unsurprising that they'd accepted their own with open arms.

"Shall we continue on?" Espen said, pivoting the subject and drawing me out of my thoughts. "It's not far to the Ranger's cabin."

"Yeah, let's go." I readjusted the pole straps around my gloved wrists and slid toward the fork in the road. With a deep breath, I aimed for the road on the left that went downhill slightly and ignored the incline on the right.

"Um, Lennie." Espen cleared his throat. "Other road."

I glanced back over my shoulder and found him pointing to the hill on the right that wove into the trees.

I tilted my head and pouted. "Are you sure?"

Espen chuckled and skied up beside me. "Positive."

A groan befitting a toddler rumbled in my throat. I was totally going to end up on my ass... or face plant. Or both.

"Come on. It's only a slight incline." Espen nudged me with his elbow and gave me a salacious wink. "You can handle it with your new fae stamina."

I smirked and rolled my shoulders, feeling the pop of my joints and a spike of adrenaline. Both him and Øyvin really knew how to activate my competitive side. *Challenge accepted.*

The trees on either side of our narrow trail hung heavy with snow, some even leaning over the path and creating a quasi-tunnel, guiding us toward our destination. The cold air and lack of breeze gave the entire scenery a sense of stillness like that of a church. The quiet punctuated by my sharp breaths and the swish of our skis through the snow.

My hand-eye coordination was not cut out for cross-country skiing *up* a hillside. While I could physically handle the strain on my muscles thanks to an active lifestyle and whatever new fae juju I possessed, my ability to slide one ski forward in a vee shape, then the other, and use my poles to keep myself upright was a challenge. My skis wanted to go downhill, and, to be honest, so would I once we reached the cabin.

Thank goodness I'd left my camera back at the cabin, because odds were I was about to end up falling ass over tits at some point on these slippery skis. As if to prove my point, my left ski slipped backward and I wobbled. Plonking my ski pole hard enough into the snow to stop me from sliding downhill, I regained my balance.

"How much further?" I asked with a huff and set off again.

"Just over that hilltop," Espen replied from up ahead. I glanced toward where he pointed, a curve in the horizon maybe a couple hundred feet away, and relief washed through me. Not far to go at all.

A few moments later, I hauled myself over the final stretch and the trail flattened out, opening into a clearing. Surrounded by dense forest and mounds of snow was a weather-worn wood cabin. The roof was covered in snow, and icicles the length of my arm hung from the eaves. A tiny path was cleared in front of the cabin, but we all sank slightly as we neared the door, the snow here still deep and relatively untouched. Darkness seeped from the small windows and the only sign that anyone had been here recently was the distinct break in the icicles—someone had broken away the ones by the front door and tossed them into the snow.

Espen and Øyvin clicked out of their skis, using their poles to press the button on the housing mechanism. I followed suit, popped my boots off the skis, and leaned the equipment against the cabin wall beside Espen and Øyvin's.

Espen went for the door and stepped inside, Øyvin ushering me to follow as he took up the rear again.

Inside was... basic. An ancient wood-burning stove sat in the middle of the single room against the back wall. To my left was a thick wood table and chairs, plus a bookshelf with old Norwegian map books and novels with dusty, curled covers. On the right was the most uncomfortable looking sofa I'd ever seen and two chairs that looked like they could collapse if someone breathed wrong. I wasn't going to complain though—it was shelter and I had somewhere to sit down for a minute. I aimed for the wood couch that looked more like a bench and took a seat. The thin padding was practically non-existent as the hard surface pressed against my bright orange snow pants. Espen plopped down beside me and pulled my water bottle out of his backpack, handing it over to me. While I took several swigs, Øyvin perused the cabin for any recent signs of life.

"Anything?" I asked, as he opened the stove door and peered into the ash-covered fireplace.

He shook his head and shut the door, crossing to the other side of the room. "There are some footprints on the floorboards disturbing the dust, but they're all different sizes, which doesn't help us." Picking a random book from the shelf, he browsed the front and back cover. From my vantage point I could just make out a naked chest and a big, poofy skirt.

"To each their own," Øyvin muttered.

"Historical Romance not your thing?" I asked with a smirk. "Or does it feel weird to read about eras that you lived in that people now call *historical*?"

Espen laughed beside me, and Øyvin set the book firmly back on the shelf. "I prefer action and adventure books."

"And Espen, which of those books would you read?"

"Sci-fi and the maps," he said before taking a sip from his water bottle. "I've always enjoyed looking at maps."

Could he be more of a cute little park ranger nerd? Honest to hell, it was adorable. I nudged my knee against his and he nudged right back, giving me another smile. My heart pattered in a happy rhythm. He was so cute, caring, and outdoorsy. It was little wonder I was so attracted to him. The way he—

"Here," Øyvin said, and my gaze snapped back to him.

"What did you find?" I asked.

He pointed to the bookshelf. "There's one missing."

Espen and I returned our bottles to his backpack and crossed the room. Øyvin pointed to the empty spot on the shelf. Sure enough, a book had recently been removed. The tiny spot was dust free compared to the books and space around it.

I looked over the disheveled shelf. "And they can't have set aside the book elsewhere?"

"Mm-mm," Øyvin hummed. "There's a layer of dust on everything else except the floor and the sofa. The book has been taken."

Espen crossed his arms. "It could be anyone."

"True," I added, straightening and setting my hands on my hips. "But..."

"But..." Øyvin said.

"Grab your things and let's double check outside," Espen said. "It's only been twenty-four-ish hours since she left, and it didn't snow much last night. There's a chance it might've been her and there might still be some tracks outside." He hoisted his bag onto his back and buckled it at the waist.

I grabbed my gloves from the couch and followed the guys.

87

LENNIE

Stepping outside the cold air assaulted me once more, the chill grazing my cheeks as the snow crunched beneath our footfalls. I pulled the door shut behind me, double-checking that the old wood and metal had latched properly before turning to the task at hand: searching for signs of recent life.

Øyvin circled the perimeter while Espen kneeled in seemingly random spots. "What are you doing?" I asked as I tromped through the snow and stepped up beside the Forest Fae. He glanced back the way I came and then peered left into the pristine white clearing.

"Checking the height of the snow," he replied absentmindedly.

"Nothing around back," Øyvin muttered, and I flinched at his sudden reappearance.

"That's because they went this way." Espen gently swept his arm across the top of the snow in front of us, his thick, winter jacket rustling and removing a layer of powder. Beneath the newly fallen snow were indents the perfect shape and size of a human's stride and footwear.

I let out an impressed huff. "Note to self: if I ever misplace something, I'm asking you to find it. How'd you know what to look for?"

He set his hands on his hips and tilted his chin up slightly, then pointed to the tracks that aimed toward the tree line. "When the snow is compacted in these temperatures, it freezes in spots."

Øyvin crossed his arms and assessed the scene. "Remove the new layer that hasn't had time to melt in the sun and fuse with the tracks below. You're left with dips and can find a myriad of things beneath."

"So this is what they teach you in school in Norway. Snow 101. Or is it a fae thing?" Either way, their knowledge was impressive.

Neither deigned my genuine question and comedic brilliance with a response.

"Follow me." Espen strode in the direction of the tracks. Øyvin and I followed quietly, with our feet and shins traipsing and pushing through the snow that was knee-height in some spots.

My feet felt like they'd been introduced to a freezer and I mentally thanked Espen for talking me into wearing two pairs of socks this morning. Not only were the outer wool ones doing some serious work, but having the extra, thick cotton layer underneath was a blessing in disguise. Had it originally made the boots a tight fit? Yes. But the fact that my feet were only now getting cold, after hours outdoors... Yeah, I'd be adding more thick wool socks to my collection as soon as we got home.

We reached the edge of the forest, the thick pines and spindly, black-and-white birch trees standing sentry to the silent depths. Coming to a stop, Espen set his hands on his hips and shook his head. "They disappear." He motioned to the tracks. I peered further into the forest, hoping for something to leap out at me, but nothing snagged my attention. The dull gray day darkened the forest and the snow appeared untouched.

"Dead end," I muttered.

Espen nodded beside me, then sucked in a breath through his nose. His eyes widened, and both him and Øyvin spun on the spot, turning back toward the cabin.

I pivoted to see what had them tightening up like a wedgie and stilled at the sight before me.

Between us and the cabin stood a large wolf, its sharp eyes focused on us. Its brown-and-beige coat rippled on a phantom breeze, like it had just stopped moving but the fur hadn't got the memo. Muscled legs were entrenched in the snow, the white stuff brushing the underside of its belly. It tilted its head and assessed us, narrowing its eyes at me.

A pang of familiarity washed through me. "Hang on," I whispered. Brown-and-beige coat. Was this Nils, the guy who'd brought me lunch? Honestly, I wouldn't be surprised if Marius had sent someone to follow us. Who better than the guy who was clearly his second-in-command? "Nils?"

The canine tilted its head the other way like a curious puppy. I took a step toward it.

It didn't move.

Definitely was Nils.

I sauntered a little closer, a non-toothy smile blooming on my face to show that I wasn't going to hurt him. If he was going to follow us, he could do so in fae form. He didn't need to be all wolfy and hide from us. "Can you sniff Aurora around here? Do you think we're on the right track?"

Nils lifted his tail straight and up, like a dog spotting a friend.

"Lennie." Espen's voice wavered. I furrowed my brow and turned half-way, keeping one eye on the wolf and one on the Forest Fae. Espen's throat bobbed. "That isn't Nils."

"Yes, it is."

"No." He shook his head slowly. "It's not."

I set my hands on my hips and tilted my head. "And how do you know that? You barely met the guy... wolf."

Espen's gaze was securely on the canine close to me, and Øyvin didn't move a muscle, his limbs locked in place, hands hanging loose at his sides—his battle ready stance.

"Forest Fae shifters keep their eye color," Espen replied. "Only normal wolves have yellow eyes."

I glanced at the wolf and flinched. Shiny yellow eyes blinked back at me.

Shit.

The wolf took a tentative step forward, and I shrunk back, eyes wide and my stomach in my throat.

"Don't turn your back on it," Espen said, his voice calm and low. "Don't run."

Him and Øyvin appeared on either side of me, Espen to my right, Øyvin to my left, their arms spread out wide. The wolf slunk backward, its ears and lips twitching.

My chest rose and fell as I tried my best to remain calm and not spin around and high-tail it out of here. Just my luck to land myself in another shitty situation.

"Fuck," Øyvin grumbled and my head snapped toward movement to my left.

Another, smaller wolf, with a reddish-tinged beige coat appeared from behind the cabin, blood smeared around its mouth, blocking our path to warmth and safety.

"A female," Espen said. "Less to worry about, but still as dangerous as Not-Nils here. Based on the blood, there must be a kill site nearby, which is going to make them more aggressive than normal."

"Fuck," Øyvin said again, his voice rumbling softly. "Another one."

Espen and I followed his gaze to the right and another wolf with a beige-and-gray coat appeared from the tree line.

"What do we do?" I asked as my body started to tremble. To the wolves I probably looked like a shaking orange marshmallow. "Espen?"

If there was any one of us who'd know what to do in this situation, it would be him. As part-police officer, part-ranger, and 100 percent Forest Fae, he'd know.

"Here's the plan. Act aggressively, use your magic to scare them. They're currently trying to protect their kill, but if we present ourselves as the biggest predator, they'll start to back down. Whatever you do, don't hurt them."

I nodded, entirely on board with the plan and uninterested in causing the creatures harm. "Got it."

Espen reached over slowly and brushed his hand down my arm. "Øyvin, flank me and take on these two males. Lennie, go for the female. Whatever you do, don't turn your back on them."

Swallowing hard, I nodded once more. I was well aware that I was completely out of my element here. The wolves continued staring at us, snarling as their tails barely wavered.

"Ready?" Espen asked.

Øyvin settled into a fighting stance and called forth a ball of water in each hand. The liquid magic swished around and looked like tiny waves curving in on each other. "Ready."

"On the count of three," Espen muttered, and I nodded minutely as I swallowed the large lump that had formed in my throat. My heart pounded in my chest, hopefully not loud enough for the wolf to hear, and I pulled on my power. The magic prickled and tickled as it swept down my arms and appeared in my hands in the form of two shiny balls of light.

"Three..." Espen started.

"Two..."

"One..."

The guys veered away from me and Øyvin volleyed orbs of water at the wolves' feet. I raised my arms above my head, making myself look as big and scary as possible—light shimmering in my palms.

The largest wolf, Not-Nils, followed Espen, pivoting away from me. My guys focused on their targets, using their fae magic to scare the animals.

The smaller wolf approached me, pulling her lips back and showing off a row of sharp, red-tipped teeth. Gloria Gaynor's *I Will Survive* started playing in my head and I belted out the lyrics as I launched my first ball of light to the right of the wolf. She dodged to the side away from the light and shook, her fur bristling. I threw the other ball, still singing at the top of my lungs. The sound was atrocious, but if it got the wolf back into the woods and me safely home, then these hills would be alive with my cringe-worthy singing voice.

My wolf darted back and forth to the left of the cabin, carving a trench in the snow between the building and the tree line. I twisted my body, following her movements like some form of dance, careful not to show her my back.

"She's herding you!" Espen yelled and I stopped singing.

"Stun her, Lennie," Øyvin commanded. "Don't kill."

I shook my head. "I'm not going to hurt her."

"Use your royal light magic and spook her!" Øyvin roared. "Now!"

Stun only. I pulled on my power once more, willing that swirling mass in my sternum forward. Tendrils of magic swept through me, sparking down my arms.

I could do this. Careful to keep the wolf in front of me, I inhaled deeply, curved my hands toward each other, and formed a large magic ball of light that sparked gently.

The wolf stopped her strategic pacing and stared at the crackling light.

Mimicking Øyvin, I launched the light toward the snow around the wolf's paws. It crashed into the cold powder, snowy spray flying all over the canine and the magic disintegrated. The wolf shuffled backward, spun around, and loped into the forest.

I let out a shuddered breath and shook out my hands as my pulse pounded in my ears.

Øyvin and Espen continued dancing around the other two wolves. Espen's yells were incoherent as he waved a barren branch around him, corralling Not-Nils toward the tree line. Oversized snowballs littered the clearing between Øyvin and the other snarling wolf.

A howl sounded from the woods, echoing through the valley and snow fell from boughs of surrounding trees. The two remaining wolves' ears twitched, and a second later they ran toward the forest and the noise. Whichever wolf had made that howl had called back their pack.

Thank fuck.

Espen tossed aside his big stick and both he and Øyvin came running over, their steps muffled by the snow.

I hunched over and rested my hands on my knees, my panted breaths fogging in front of me. "You know... There have been way too many traumatic incidents on this vacation."

Øyvin crossed his arms and snorted. "You're no longer on vacation, Trouble. This is just your life."

An erratic laugh escaped me as Espen brushed his hand over my back like he needed to reassure himself that I was there and in one piece. "Why do you have to be right?" I smiled and straightened.

Espen wrapped his arms around me, pulling me into his warmth, and Øyvin quirked his lips. "You're getting better though."

"Huh?"

"Your light magic," Øyvin said. "That last ball wasn't merely light. I saw it sparking. You could've stunned the wolf with that."

I'd certainly felt the slight difference when creating that bit of magic compared to the normal magic I used to form light balls. I'd put the stun intention behind it too. But still... My brow creased. "How do you know? How is that even possible?"

"I've seen Balder use it in the past. Don't ask why or how."

I got the distinct feeling he was referring to battles best left to history.

"Me too," Espen said, taking a step back and dropping his hands to his hips. "But with Queen Ragnhild, not Balder."

I let out a high-pitched humph. "Well, look at me leveling up. Torsten and Halvar are going to be so proud."

The guys snickered as I raised my hand, extending my pointer finger toward the sky. "And I'll concede. That wasn't Nils."

"No, shit," Espen replied with a laugh.

Collapsing onto my butt, the snow catching my fall, I rested my arms on my knees and stared up at the guys. Adrenaline rushed out of my system, leaving me buzzing but exhausted.

Another day, another gratefully missed opportunity to become puppy kibble. *I should start keeping track at this rate.*

I looked out toward where the wolves had disappeared into the forest and then to the trails we'd first followed across the clearing, now scuffed up by our canine encounter. "Any chance those wolves were coaxed over here by Aurora? Could she have used them as a distraction?"

Espen shook his head and followed my gaze. "Highly unlikely. If—as seems to be the case—she is truly affiliated with Marius's new pack, which wants to protect the wolves, I doubt she'd plant a kill site this close to humans."

"You're probably right. But if she were a wolf, could she voodoo communicate with the real wolves and encourage them in this direction?"

Espen shrugged. "I mean, we don't know who her father is. He might've been a shifter. But even Forest Fae wolves can't mind-speak like they do in movies or books. Aside from howling and barking, their communication is instinctual and non-verbal, which doesn't exactly lend itself to messages of 'go exactly here and antagonize these people.'"

"Fair enough."

"We're all okay, though," Espen said, rolling his shoulders and brushing his hands across his arms as if to remove invisible lint or anxiety from his limbs. "That's the most important thing."

Øyvin inhaled audibly and nodded.

I had a bad track record with hikes now. Almost dying when I fell through the bridge last year, getting ganged up on by Forest Fae shifters and then saved by Halvar, and being herded by real wolves this year. I really was a walking target.

It hadn't always been like this. Growing up and post-college, I was always careful when setting out on a hike. I always wore the proper attire and shoes, and never went hiking without a substantial first-aid kit and huge bottle of water. But after several months in Norway, all that preparation was useless. At this point, it felt like the wilderness was out to get me. "Perhaps, in the future, we should teach me more about Norwegian wildlife before hiking."

"I'm going to agree with that," Espen conceded.

Øyvin huffed. "But who steps *toward* a wolf?"

I pointed to myself. "Apparently this dumbass."

He rolled his eyes.

"You can't entirely blame me though. It made sense for Marius to send a wolf to follow us, and that wolf looked exactly like Nils."

Øyvin shook his head like I was being ridiculous. "At least you're cute."

My skin warmed at his backhanded compliment. "I have my moments," I countered, my voice coming out more sultry than planned. Cold nipped at my butt through my neon snow pants, and I rose to my feet with a helping hand from Espen. Planting my hands on my hips, I started a heated staring competition with Øyvin. His sapphire gaze darkened and he didn't blink.

"Unless you two wish to give snow sex a go"—my eyes widened at Espen's statement—"I suggest we head home for the day and take a break from the search."

While I wouldn't mind some adventurous yoga, hypothermia was a thing, and I couldn't have their dicks freezing. I liked that part of their bodies too much to lose. Plus, I was exhausted and could do with a nap. "Let's table that idea for spring. I'm thinking a rainy day instead of snow." Why just kiss in the rain when you could go all the way?

"Deal," they both muttered.

Espen looped his arm through mine and steered us back toward the cabin where our skis rested against the wall beside the front door. "I'll call Turi when we get back to the car. The Mayor's Office should know there's been another wolf sighting this close to town."

"You think the locals will make a ruckus about it?"

He shook his head. "As long as Turi makes sure the information gets out correctly, the right departments are informed, and the news outlets don't make a huge deal out of it, we should be fine. It was only a sighting"—I scoffed at his belittlement of the canines and the magical Argentinian tango I'd just performed in an effort to protect my back—"and no one was injured or bit. The humans get worked up when livestock or people are hurt."

Understandable. For the Forest Fae's sake and the wolves, I hoped things didn't get chaotic. Hopefully, Turi could keep the town calm.

"Come on." Espen grabbed my skis and handed them to me. "Let's go home and have some coffee. Then we can have a fun family day tomorrow before refocusing on our search for Aurora."

"Family day?" Øyvin said from my other side, voicing the same question that rang through my head. I didn't remember scheduling a family day. But perhaps I was too caught up in the whole hounded-by-wolves thing that my memory was failing me.

Espen beamed from ear to ear. "Family day. We promised Ingrid that we'd join her and the kids for an afternoon."

Oh, yeah. She'd mentioned that at dinner the other night. While it wasn't exactly staying on mission to find Aurora, I wouldn't say no to spending more time with Espen's family.

"But first," Espen said. "We need to ski back down that hill."

I whimpered. "What could possibly go wrong?"

Espen brushed his gloved hand over my cold cheek and stared into my eyes with both joy and laughter. "Just point your toes together and sit on your butt if you start to go too fast."

I'd give it a go, but I'd probably end up scooting down the hillside. "Can do, but it's on you if I hurt my butt."

Øyvin grabbed his skis and turned to me. "We'll kiss it and make it better if you do."

I smiled. "Well, in that case."

88
LENNIE

Our morning was spent searching the western forests for Aurora, and this time the guys didn't let me out of their sight. We searched high and low, peered through windows of vacated cabins, and considered going door to door asking villagers if they'd seen the woman. But our efforts were frustratingly fruitless. There was no sign of the heir anywhere. It was like she'd donned an invisibility cloak or camouflaged herself as a rock in the endless scenery of white and gray.

By mid-day we abandoned our search and headed for the lake to spend the afternoon with Ingrid and the kids. Our agenda: ice skating.

The sun's rays glittered across the frozen lake framed by white snow drifts from where the local residents had cleared it. The aptly named "Big Long Lake" was exactly that—surrounded on three sides by dense forest and hills, the body of water stretched for at least a mile and was longer than it was wide. We pulled into the small parking lot that abutted a beach and boat landing area, finding Ingrid and the kids already setting up camp at a wooden picnic table by the shore.

Shrieks of laughter met my ears as I clambered out of the car, my borrowed skates firmly in hand. All three kids were donning their ice-skates, even four-year-old Kristoffer.

"Glad you could join us!" Ingrid smiled and propped her hands on her hips, letting out a quick breath like she'd been busy all morning and hadn't taken a break. Which, considering she was a mother of three under ten, I didn't doubt was the case. Her hair was piled on top of her head again and she was bundled up in bright yellow outerwear paired with a knit headband that shielded her ears from the cold.

"Are you hungry?" she asked. "I brought lunch, too."

"Oooo," Espen and I muttered at the same time, while Øyvin nodded and politely thanked Ingrid.

Øyvin took a seat at the picnic table, hoisting his legs over and under the wooden structure with ease. I perched on the edge of the same bench and Espen stood by his sister, his legs spread into a triangle and his arms crossed over his chest as he surveyed the lake and watched the kids.

"The kids are so excited to have you here today," Ingrid said as she pulled a thermos from her backpack and a square paper bag.

"Pretty sure that excitement is solely for Espen," I replied. All three kids tried to coax Espen out onto the ice, appealing to him with pirouettes and, in Kristoffer's case, *fast* movements and karate chops.

"That may be true, but it's still nice to have all three of you here." She retrieved a napkin from her backpack and then pulled a small tortilla from the paper bag on the table, setting the latter atop the former.

Espen laughed at his nieces and nephew, the sound warming something within me and settling somewhere near my heart. I glanced over my shoulder and found Øyvin quirking his lips into a gentle lopsided smile that didn't quite meet his eyes. He caught me looking and his mouth dipped back into a line as he clasped his hands on the table and looked back over the lake.

I hoped he was okay. He hadn't been his usual grumbly self this morning. Ever since we crawled out of bed, he'd shut down a bit. It wasn't too alarming, but... I needed to keep an eye on him. Something was up.

Out of the corner of my eye I caught Ingrid spearing something in the thermos with a fork and—

"Did you just put a hot dog in a tortilla?" I asked and turned my attention back to the Solbakke sibling. I'd seen some interesting dishes on my past travels, but this was a new one.

Ingrid chuckled, her eyes creasing at the corners, but continued preparing the "meal."

"It's not a tortilla," she said, a beaming smile sweeping across her lips as she squirted ketchup onto the hot dog and rolled it up. She wandered over to her eldest daughter and handed the hot-dog-burrito she'd just put together to Katrine, who took a huge bite and skated off with it. "It's called sausage in *lompe*."

I shook my head at that last word and pressed at my ear, hoping the tap-tap would get my magical translation juju to work. Ingrid noticed the movement, and Espen must've told her what Nora had done to my hearing, because she added, "Ah, there isn't a good direct translation for the word. But the tortilla"—she retrieved another from the paper bag on the table and waved it about gently—"is actually a soft potato flatbread. The humans, and we, commonly have them as snacks or part of meals. Some people even have eating competitions on Norway's National Day to see how many they can eat with sausages."

Kristoffer appeared next to me as if out of thin air, still somehow wearing his skates—which couldn't have been good for them or safe for him. "I eat five thousand."

"Five whole thousand?" I asked and Ingrid translated for me since the kid didn't know English and my Norwegian wasn't great yet.

Kristoffer nodded, pursing his lips and narrowing his eyes like an old man. "It is serious business. Big competition."

"I bet. And did you win this competition recently?" Ingrid translated for me once more.

"The Darkness always wins."

I snorted and clapped my hand over my mouth to stop from laughing in the kid's face.

Espen stepped up beside me, placing his hand on my shoulder. "The Darkness had four hot dogs in *lompe* last *Seventeenth of May* and proceeded to vomit on his uncle an hour later."

Kristoffer stuck his tongue out at Espen, plucked a hot dog and *lompe* out of Ingrid's hand, and scampered off. Ingrid scolded him in Norwegian as he swept back onto the ice.

She turned back to me with a smile and a wobble of the mom-bun on her head. "Would you like one?"

"Yes, please." It was a little unusual, but I wasn't going to say no to warm food when we were outside in the cold. Storing cooked hot dogs in a thermos for a picnic or a hike was a genius idea I would be implementing in future.

Ingrid handed me my lunch and I took a bite, pleasantly surprised by the taste. And hey, I'd also found another food made of potatoes. That was definitely a win.

The guys practically inhaled theirs and a few minutes later Espen was shucking on his borrowed skates and encouraging me and Øyvin to put ours on. I yanked the white skates on and laced them up over my ankles, glad that Knut-Arne's family cabin came fully stocked with every kind of outdoor equipment a Norwegian might ever need.

"You ready to head out onto the ice, Trouble?" Øyvin asked.

It'd been a long time since I'd skated and that had been at a pop-up rink in my hometown for the holiday season eons ago before I moved to Massachusetts for college. "As long as you help me not fall on my ah—" I stopped myself before I swore around kids. "Butt. Fall on my butt."

Øyvin flicked his brows. "That can be arranged."

I narrowed my gaze. "Why do I get the feeling you mean me on my butt can be *arranged*?"

He smirked and pulled me to my feet, helping me over to the lake's edge. Meanwhile, Espen had bolted after the kiddos, a complete natural on skates.

Because, of course, my Forest Fae was good at skating. Was there anything outdoorsy he wasn't good at? Or indoors for that matter?

I peered back to Ingrid before stepping onto the ice. "Aren't you joining us?"

She shook her head and waved her hand before crossing her arms, her yellow jacket scrunching with the motion. "Oh no. I've fallen one too many times and I bruise far more easily at my age."

I raised my hand. "Fair enough." I wasn't going to counter her 200-plus years of knowledge and experience.

Øyvin tugged lightly on my wrist. "Come on. Stop stalling."

"Don't be an Ass—"

"Uh-uh," he tutted.

I pursed my lips and let him lead me onto the crystal clear ice scarred with crisscrossing lines where people had already carved it up with their skates.

Øyvin dropped my hands and I slid one foot outward then the other, forming a tiny vee with my movements. My steps stuttered and I held my arms out to maintain some semblance of balance. Turning in a wide circle, pride bubbled within me as I completed an ungraceful yet princessy pirouette. Flailing but upright was better than ass down on the ice. So, slow and steady was the way to go.

Øyvin glided up beside me and caught my hands in his. I grasped his fingers, holding on tightly as he steered me across the lake, his strides smooth and even, like he'd been doing this his entire life.

He skated like he was water personified and I couldn't look away. Øyvin near his natural element really was a sight to see. His hair fluttered in the wind, sunlight caught on the stubble across his jaw, and his legs moved in a steady rhythm. He gave me a lopsided grin that turned evil as he sped up and let go of my hands, launching me back toward the shore where the girls were twirling around Espen, their mother watching on from land. An undignified squeak left my lips as I flapped across the ice.

"Look at you!" Espen beamed, holding his arms out wide.

I mimicked his movement but wobbled and thought better of it—which earned me a few giggles from shore.

I rounded back toward the middle of the lake, then drifted closer to shore, enjoying the freedom and feel of gliding across the frozen water. The cool air whipped against my cheeks and the sun shone down on the ice, making every inch sparkle like a blue, crystal vase. More families joined us on the lake. Fae or human, I couldn't tell the difference, but within minutes, Ingrid was striking up conversation with some other moms and the girls were chatting away with other kids.

Spinning around, a smile on my face, I searched for Øyvin. He stood further from the shoreline, barely moving, watching the goings-on with a solemn face.

Hmmm. Something wasn't right with my grumpy fae. He'd been in this funk ever since we arrived in Alvdalen, and it was worse today.

Maybe he was worried about being so far from the fjord? His actions and comments when I first met him would certainly allude to that, but... that didn't feel right. He'd willingly agreed to this trip. Accepted the mission from Halvar to find the Fjell Heir. So, it had to be something else.

I skated over to him, finally feeling like I was getting into a rhythm that wasn't going to earn me a bruised butt by the evening.

"You okay?" I asked as I bumped into Øyvin. He wrapped his arms around me, letting my momentum move us back slightly.

His hooded gaze met mine. "Yes."

"Mm-hmm." I didn't believe him for a second. Here I'd given him ample opportunity to laugh at me today and make grumbly little remarks that I'd come to find endearing, and he hadn't taken the chance at all. "I call bullshit."

He shook his head and brushed his hands down my back, peering over me. I followed his line of sight and landed on the families having fun... *oh*. It dawned on me like being doused in cold water. Family. Øyvin was missing his family. The loves and lives he'd lost over the years. And here we were gallivanting around with such a young family with their lives ahead of them, centuries if they were lucky.

"You miss your family," I said, not a question but airing what was written across his face.

Øyvin nodded. "My brother and I used to skate together when we were young boys. He was exceptionally fast and I could never keep up."

A tiny smile twisted my lips as I imagined a small and frustrated blond-haired boy trying to chase after another, their skates cutting up the ice. "Even as the older brother?" I asked, and his pensive gaze dropped to mine.

Mired in thought, he replied with a nod. "Peder, like many Fjord Fae, loved being on the water. Whenever the lakes froze over, he was the first on the ice. We'd make courses out of branches and race each other for hours."

My heart clenched on Øyvin's behalf. Of course being out here today would stir up memories. Memories he was clearly caught up in as he stared off into the distance, lost in a trance.

I slid in closer and brushed my hands up his arms. His sapphire eyes locked on mine, and he let out a heavy breath. "Lennie."

I pressed my palms to his chest and pushed lightly. "Skate with me."

He needed a distraction. A happy memory to pull him from the mental spiral he was winding down.

With a hint of warmth in his eyes and a twitch of his lips, he placed his hands atop mine on his chest and drifted backward. Controlling our movements, Øyvin turned us around in a wide circle. The wind curled around my cheeks, chilling my flushed skin, and the sun shone over us as we glided across the frozen lake.

We passed Espen and the girls, all three of whom smiled at us as they spun in ever faster pirouettes. The girls' brown curls flew around their faces, their scarves whipping in the breeze as they giggled and laughed with their uncle. Before we drifted away, Espen gave me a quick wink, and I gave him a gentle smile in return.

Øyvin moved his hands, placing them on the small of my back, and my lips parted into a wider smile as I returned my gaze to him. Unwavering, we swirled around and around, carving large circles and infinity symbols into the ice. After a few moments, he drew me closer into his embrace, holding me against his broad chest. I let out a satisfied hum and wrapped my arms around his back, still never breaking eye contact. It was the most intimate moment we'd had out in public. And yet, it felt like we were locked away in our own little cocoon where nothing and no one could touch us. In his arms, I felt protected and at home. Nothing could break us as long as we held on to each other. I pressed my head against his chest. His heart beat in a rapid but steady rhythm.

He swept his hand up my back, neck, and cupped my head. "This," he muttered so quietly I could barely hear him. "I like this."

"I like this, too," I whispered back and squeezed him a little tighter. I was acutely aware of every spot where our bodies touched, warmth radiating through me. I didn't want to let go. In fact, realization settled over me like a warm blanket on a cold day: I would never want to let go of this, of what we had together. I'd always been a bit of an ostrich with my emotions, dunking my head into the sand when things got uncomfortable or I didn't know how to respond. But with the swell of feelings coursing through me, the pitter-patter of my heartbeat, and the strength of the man holding me as we glided across the ice, I wanted to respond. To tell him just how much I liked this.

"Ø-Øyvin," I faltered, my throat thick with emotion.

"Hmmm." He tilted my head up until our eyes met again. His pupils were dilated, his lips slightly parted.

"I-I..." My voice trembled and I took a deep breath.

Bubbles of laughter emitted from the girls near the shore and a cracking sound rent the air.

I turned toward the noise, looking past Øyvin's shoulder, and stilled, my stomach flipping into my throat. Kristoffer was out in the middle of the lake. The cracking grew louder, and before anyone could move, Kristoffer's eyes went wide and he dropped through the ice.

89
LENNIE

I screamed, people on shore screamed, and the cry of despair that could only ever be emitted by a mother losing a child struck through the air like lightning.

Øyvin pushed me back toward the edge of the lake, yelled at Espen to get everyone off the ice, and barreled toward the spot where Kristoffer had disappeared.

Shaking and sucking in sharp breaths, I slid toward land, all the while casting glances over my shoulder.

Øyvin dove into the water, crashing through the broken shards of ice like they were butter and he was a hot knife.

My lungs stopped working and time stood still as I reached the shore and wobbled to the picnic table. Maybe an hour passed, or maybe it was just seconds, but time stopped as we all watched the jagged ice and waited for them to appear.

Two heads breached the surface, and the gathered crowd let out a collective sigh of relief. Ingrid whimpered and her daughters cried, tears streaming down their faces.

Øyvin slid Kristoffer onto the ice and gingerly pulled himself out of the frigid water, his hair plastered to his forehead, his jaw locked.

Espen made a move to head back onto the ice, but even at that distance, Øyvin caught his movement and raised his hand. Espen stopped immediately and let out a shuddered breath. I slipped my hand into his and squeezed. He squeezed back, keeping his eyes locked on the duo that slowly crossed the lake.

Øyvin cradled the young boy in his arms. Kristoffer's shaking subsided the closer they got to shore.

My stomach was in my throat, adrenaline coursing through my system. I wobbled and remembered I still had my skates on. Stepping briskly over to the picnic table, I exchanged them for my boots. Espen did the same, but never took his eyes off his nephew.

As Øyvin and Kristoffer crossed onto land, Ingrid bolted to them and brushed her hand over her son's cheek.

Kristoffer's lips were blue, his skin as pale as a starched sheet, but he was alive and moving.

"Help him," Ingrid said, her voice thick with worry.

Droplets ran down Øyvin's face and clung to his outerwear, some appearing to freeze. "I am," he replied, glancing around us.

I followed his gaze. *Shit.* Humans. They'd gathered around in their worry, and Øyvin couldn't use the full strength of his magic to wick the water off the boy. He must have subtly used some already as Kristoffer wasn't shivering.

Espen nudged his sister. "To the car. Now."

Øyvin moved straight past the gawking crowd and headed for the parking lot. Ingrid and the girls followed swiftly behind him, mentioning which car was hers. All the while, Øyvin never loosened his hold on the whimpering boy.

"Can you do anything?" I asked Espen as we rushed behind the others.

"Not fully. Not until we get home," he said, his brows drawn together and his focus never wavering from Kristoffer.

Ingrid yanked open the back door to the mini-van, and the girls shuffled inside without being asked, having already removed their skates while Øyvin crossed the lake.

We all came to a stop outside the vehicle.

"I've wicked away as much water as I could," Øyvin said. "Get him in the car and I can get the rest." He looked around at the people behind us who'd gathered along the shoreline, several of which were parents stopping their kids from returning to the ice or holding their hands over their mouths in terror.

Tears streamed down Ingrid's reddened cheeks as she gulped down controlled breaths and stepped aside for him. Øyvin deposited the shell-shocked boy into his car seat and stepped back. Espen immediately swooped in. We needed his healer fae skills to check the boy for any injuries.

"It's okay," Espen said, his voice calm and soft as his hands hovered over Kristoffer, moving from his little legs upward. "Øyvin, a moment?"

Øyvin and I moved in a heartbeat, our backs to the rest of the world, shielding Kristoffer from onlookers. Øyvin reached over and rested his hand on Kristoffer's shaking shoulder. A moment later his clothes were completely dry and his hair had lightened to its normal brown color instead of the inky drenched state.

"Thank you," Ingrid muttered, her hand clutched to her chest.

"No injuries, but he's not out of the woods yet. He's still too cold." Espen turned to his sister. "Drive out of here swiftly, pretend you're rushing to the hospital, but head home instead. We'll meet you there and I can heal any other lingering effects."

She nodded and didn't hesitate. We stepped out of her way and she slid the mini-van door shut and bolted around to the driver's seat. We ran back to the picnic table and grabbed our things, throwing them into Ingrid's forgotten backpack. By the time we got back to the car, Ingrid was long gone.

We pulled up at Ingrid's house, launched ourselves out of the car, and barreled through the front door.

"In here." Ingrid's voice drifted into the hallway from the living room and we rapidly shucked off our boots. Espen moved so fast he practically floated, his focus locked on helping his nephew, and he was beside him in a heartbeat.

Boots and outerwear deposited in the hallway, Øyvin and I joined the gathered fae in the living room. Kristoffer lay on the sofa with a blanket thrown over his lower half, his head nestled against a plump pillow in Ingrid's lap. The girls were on the other side of the room next to their overflowing toy baskets playing with some dolls while pretending not to pay attention to the grown-ups. Espen kneeled beside the boy and rested his hands over him, assessing Kristoffer with his magic.

"No external injuries," he muttered. Rubbing his hands together he did another pass of the kid's head. His fingers splayed as he used his healing powers. "Stay still for me."

The little boy nodded.

I glanced over my shoulder and found Øyvin still in the archway to the living room, surveying the scene, his lips in a firm line. He crossed his arms, shoulders curved inwards.

Taking a step backward, I leaned into him and whispered, "You doing okay?"

He let out a low hum, but made no other reply.

"Are you hurt?" I asked, unsure if he'd even admit it if he was.

He shook his head.

Footsteps thundered outside and a moment later the front door swung open and closed. "Where is my boy?" Knut-Arne yelled, his voice shaking. He didn't bother removing his shoes, and dollops of snow followed him into the living room. Øyvin discreetly waved his right hand, and the little puddles disappeared behind the distressed father.

Espen peered up at his brother-in-law. "He's going to be all right," he said as he brushed his hands through Kristoffer's hair and rose to his feet. "I've eased some of the aches in his legs from the ice and a couple bruises, but he will be fine once the shock subsides."

Knut-Arne brushed his light-brown beard with one hand and patted Espen on the back with the other. "Thank you, brother."

"Of course," Espen replied. "But it's Øyvin who deserves the thanks. He dove in."

Øyvin clenched his jaw as the entire room turned to look at him.

"Thank you," Knut-Arne said. "Thank you for saving my boy."

Øyvin nodded once, tension strung through his brow and limbs.

Knut-Arne and Ingrid switched spots on the couch, and she strode over to us with Espen at her side. "I think we need coffee. Follow me." She strode into the kitchen and none of us disagreed.

The kitchen counters were covered with thermoses, lunch bags, and dishes that had been left out to dry on tea-towels. Light streamed through the bank of windows on the opposite side of the room, dappling the centralized pine table in a soft glow. The three of us pulled out a chair each and sat down while Ingrid rolled up the sleeves of her striped sweater and busied herself making a pot of coffee. Part of me wanted to ask if she needed any help, but the other part recognized a woman who needed to distract herself from the chaos and shock of the day.

At the head of the table, with Øyvin and I on either side of him, Espen set his elbows down and leaned forward, brushing his hands across his face and through his hair. Øyvin stared at the table, tracing the lines and knots in the wood with his finger.

My heart clenched seeing them like this. But the way they'd both handled the near-tragedy, how they'd sprung into action, had pride welling inside me. My breath stuttered as I looked between the two of them. One so kind and caring, never wanting harm to come to anyone yet capable of immense amounts of destruction. The other calm and reserved, but ferociously protective of the fjord and... me.

I leaned back in my chair, the wood biting against my shoulder blades, and pushed up my sleeves as my mouth fell open into an *o* shape. All I wanted to do was hold onto these two men, squeeze them with every fiber of my being, protect them in turn and never let go. *Shit.* I brushed my hands across my cheeks. I was totally, irrevocably, falling in love with them. Probably had been for some time.

Staring down at the shimmering ring on my left hand, I let out a long winded, but contented, sigh. This thing between us had been brewing for a while. Well before they got me the highly personalized ring for our *immigration purposes* engagement. While that had been fake, nothing about our actions around each other or how we went about our lives together was fake. It was like a pot of coffee, slowly percolating into the perfect brew.

I wrung my hands together before crossing my legs and shoving them between my thighs. Turning my gaze back to the guys, I found them both deep in thought, their heads hanging heavy. I looked between the two of them. Øyvin had always challenged me, put me in my place or egged me on. Not out of spite—well, at least once we got to know each other beyond names and snide remarks—but out of a desire to broaden my perspective. Espen, on the other hand, had always made me smile, made me feel young and giddy. But, at the core of both relationships and what all three of us had together was a prevailing sentiment that I couldn't ignore anymore: love.

Fuck me sideways, I'd totally fallen in love with two fae men.

Ingrid brought over a steaming pot of coffee and three small white mugs, setting them on the table between the three of us. "Drink up. I'll be in the other room."

We nodded and thanked her before she swept back into the living room.

Espen poured out three servings and passed out the cups. I took mine with a murmured thank you and pressed the rim to my lips, my hand shaking as I did so.

"You all right, Lennie?" Espen asked, and Øyvin's gaze shot from the table to mine, his brow momentarily furrowing. I wanted to smooth those lines off his forehead with my fingers, and cup Espen's jaw. Ease their troubles...

Yeah, I had it bad.

"I'm okay."

LENNIE

We drove home in silence, all three of us emotionally exhausted and lost in our own thoughts. Espen pulled into the driveway and as Øyvin and I climbed out, he moved slower, trailing behind us as we climbed the stairs to the porch and front door.

"Are you coming?" I tilted my head to one side as keys jingled and Øyvin unlocked the door and stepped inside.

Espen rolled his shoulders, stared at me, then shook his head.

"Is everything all right?"

He pressed his lips together and straightened. "No, but it will be."

I started at his remark. "What do you mean?"

"I have something to take care of." He gingerly lifted his hand and pointed at me. "You head inside, keep Øyvin company. I'll be back in a couple of hours." He took three long strides and was on the step in front of me before I could blink. Grabbing my hand, he squeezed it lightly and pulled it against his chest.

"You promise?"

His eyes crinkled at the corners and a gentle smile crossed his lips before he pressed them to mine. "I promise."

After shedding my outer layers and boots, I leaned against the bedroom door-frame, my arms crossed over my chest. Øyvin sat on the edge of the bed, his hair rumpled, shoulders curved, and his head hung heavy as if a depressive cloud had settled over him.

He looked through the doorway and into the entryway behind me. "Where's Espen?"

"He said he had something to deal with."

"Did he elaborate?"

I shook my head.

Øyvin nodded solemnly, turning his gaze back to his hands as he wrung them, leaning his forearms against his thighs. I'd never seen him so encumbered and wracked with emotions. Even in the mountain after I'd been attacked by the wolves, he hadn't shown this level of emotion.

"Are you doing okay?" I asked.

He sighed and didn't reply.

"Kristoffer is all right. You saved him."

Øyvin ran his hand through his hair and took a deep breath. "I keep seeing his little face drop through the ice. It's running on repeat."

"And you saved him. Øyvin, look at me." His head rose slowly and his eyes met mine. Pain and fear and torment filled his dark-blue gaze like a never-ending ocean. "You saved that little boy today. You saved Katrine and Kari's brother."

I knew I'd hit the nail on the head while we were out on the ice before Kristoffer had fallen through. All this happy family stuff was a reminder to Øyvin of the family he once had that no longer existed. Long years and a life well-lived had taken his parents, but his brother was killed in the battle twenty years ago, the same battle that took the lives of Queen Ragnhild and Espen's mentor, Mads. So, it came as no surprise that the events of the day were taking a toll on Øyvin. It was little wonder he needed some time to grieve again.

"You saved him," I reiterated.

"And Espen healed him."

"He did. Do you need some healing, too?" I shuffled across the room to stand in front of him. It sounded silly, but I wanted to help him in any way I could.

He gave me a deadpanned look.

"Yeah, I know I don't have healing magic like the all-powerful and mighty ball of sunshine that's probably perusing the cheese aisle right now trying to decide between a Gouda and a blue—"

"Whoever eats that moldy stuff is mad."

"Another thing we can agree on."

"Is he actually at the grocery store?"

I shook my head. "I have no idea, but see how that distracted you? And... is that a smile?"

It most definitely was not and he emphasized that fact by scowling even further.

I put my hands on my hips and settled into a confident power pose. "Look, I'm not the sunshine in this sandwich situation we have going on here."

"You're the pain in the ass that sits in the middle."

"Exactly. But I can bring a smile to your face or make you feel a bit better." Without giving him a warning, I moved forward and straddled him, doing my best to distract him from his fidgeting. Perhaps my tits in his face would help divert his attention.

He stared up at me, and I swallowed a breath. He looked so fragile, so hurt. An urge to protect him swelled within me, the same feeling I'd had sitting at Ingrid's kitchen table.

"Am I about to get Serious-Lennie?" he asked.

"That you are." I wrapped my hands behind his neck, resting my forearms on his broad shoulders. "Brace yourself, honey."

He settled his hands against my waist, gently squeezing my curves, and I took a deep breath before diving in.

"You did everything you could today and succeeded in saving the life of a little boy. None of us could've done what you did. Not even Espen. He may have been able to break through that ice, but who knows how much damage he would have done and there is a good chance that he could have accidentally hurt Kristoffer in his panic to get to him. *You*, on the other hand, knew exactly what to do. And the Mikkelsens are going to be forever grateful for you. I know I am."

I cupped his cheeks and brought his attention back up to my face, lest he decide to burrow and hide in my boobs. He could do that later. "You can't save and protect everyone."

He bristled, but I didn't stop. I didn't let go.

"You may not even be able to save me some day."

"Don't say that."

I warmed at his words, but didn't let them stop me. He needed to hear this. He needed to be reminded before his mind spiraled even further. "You may not have been able to save your brother all those years ago"—he flinched, and I sank deeper into him, bringing my hands to his shoulders and holding him tight—"but in the past few months you've saved countless lives, helped save the fjord from a dick of a king, and saved a little boy. You do so much for this world, and your *family*."

"I don't—"

I pressed my finger to his lips. "Yes, you do have a family. The Fjord Fae look to you as a leader and care about you, members of the Forest and Fjell Fae care about you, and most importantly, I care about you. We are your family. Especially, Espen and I."

It was true. Every word, every syllable. This man was cared for, whether he realized it or not. He was a protector of the Fjord, and I didn't doubt for one second that its inhabitants wouldn't protect him in turn. They'd rise from the waters and come to his aid, not because he was their Head Guard, but because they valued him and the work he did for them.

Øyvin took a deep breath. "You're right." Before I could do a victory dance and bask in the sound of those words, he spun and flipped me onto my back, laying me on the bed with his hands on either side of my head, his hips between my thighs. "And I care about you, too."

I pulled my hands down the expanse of his chest, enjoying the way his abdomen tensed under my touch. "Look at us."

His gaze bored into mine, the weight of the moment settling in the room, and that smell of clean linen washed off him, even though he hadn't showered since this morning. The thought of showering pulled my focus to a couple of days ago when he'd watched me shower. The way he'd made me feel then and the way he made me feel now, looking down at me like I was breakable or might run away, had my throat tightening and my adrenaline running a million miles per hour.

He leaned over me and settled us further back onto the bed before skimming his nose up the side of my neck. Goosebumps skittered down my arms in response, but my newfound emotions, feelings, and truths needed to be released.

"Not to break the moment," I said, hoping to hell this was going to come out the way I wanted. This was brand new territory for me, but it felt right. It felt like home. He had to know. "But I was thinking..."

He tilted his head to one side and huffed. "Always dangerous."

"Maybe," I muttered, but highly doubted it. "But you should know..."

His eyes roved over my face, taking in every detail.

"However much of an asshole you are," I said, garnering a faint smirk, "I'm pretty damn sure I've fallen in love with you."

He pressed his forehead to mine and breathed us in. The world around us fell away and in that moment there was only me and Øyvin, the steady thrum of our heartbeats, and the truth. He brushed his thumb across my bottom lip and let out a sigh. "I didn't stand a chance."

I swallowed the lump in my throat and my heart skipped two beats.

"More than that," he whispered. "You've ruined me."

I let out a shuddered gasp, my lips brushing over his. He pulled back ever so slightly, not giving in to the kiss I desperately wanted to share with him.

"I've never been good with this sort of thing, but I've fallen so hard, I couldn't ever possibly love another," he admitted and then crashed his lips against mine. I melted into his hold, my hands raking into his hair, desperate to have our bodies closer, to say how I felt with actions alone. Because, and I couldn't quite believe it had happened. I'd fallen for him. This grumpy, dedicated, and protective Asshole had stolen part of my heart.

A second later, clothes flew to the floor and Øyvin guided me back onto the bed. I lay down on the soft sheets and he settled on his knees between my legs. A delicious shudder ran through me as he brushed his palms over my breasts and continued down. He caressed my curves like a god worshiping his own creation, marveling at every peak and valley.

I clutched at the bedlinen, my toes curling.

He took his time exploring me, like this was the first chance he'd had to see me naked and at his mercy. His eyes hooded and the warmth of his body enveloped mine like an invisible embrace.

How did I get so lucky? He was beautiful. Utterly stunning. Photographs could never do him justice.

That usual push and pull between us was momentarily gone, and in its place was something solid, something intangible yet clearly defined. A mutual respect, care, and love.

He notched himself at my entrance and planted his hands on either side of my head.

I reached out and wrapped my fingers around his forearms, feeling the taught muscles there.

With a sweet smile on his face, Øyvin slowly sank into me, and I let out a soft moan.

He leaned forward and nuzzled underneath my ear. "I love that, too."

"What?"

"Those little noises you make. The sounds that escape when we're together."

All I could do was nod as we explored each other with our hands and Øyvin pushed inside me with languorous and passionate strokes. My body quivered and my lungs expanded, desperate for more of everything. For more of him.

"*Fuck*, Øyvin."

"You can take it," he said, keeping a gentle but steady pace that would unravel me.

As if he could tell I was already on the precipice, he thrust deeper, harder. His breaths mingled with my own as my focus narrowed in on us. Just us. The press of our bodies together, the heat flaring in his eyes, and my fingers digging into his shoulder muscles—holding on to what I could have for a lifetime. Sparks shot through me and Øyvin's breath stuttered as we fell apart together.

We came down from our high and Øyvin pulled out, rolled off me, and tucked me into his side. I felt like the most precious thing in the world, more valuable than his fjord... I felt like his.

"I never want this feeling to end," I said, unable to stop the words from tumbling out of my mouth as I rested my palm against his bare chest.

Øyvin squeezed me tighter and brushed his hand through my rumpled hair. "It won't. I'll make sure of it."

My heart pulsed hard. He didn't mean the post-orgasm bliss. He meant us. The challenging, supportive, and protective love we shared. I'd do everything I could to safeguard this too. Forever.

"I love you, Lennie."

I tilted my head to meet his gaze. "Are you getting emotional on me?"

A smile grew on his face. "Are you?"

With a chuckle, I pressed my lips to his in a tender kiss and lost myself in the comforting joy that hummed through my entire body.

91
ESPEN

After sending a quick text to Turi and Gunvor asking them to meet me at Turi's apartment, I hopped in the car and left Lennie and Øyvin at the cabin to rest and talk through their feelings. No one had missed the moment they'd shared on the ice today, least of all me. While they annoyed and challenged each other, deep down they truly cared for each other.

I was happy for them. I'd always be happy when she was happy. And I liked the dynamic between the three of us. I may have been the one engaged to her for immigration purposes, but we were a trio. Even though Lennie still hadn't put any definitions on us, I could feel our connection in my bones and see it in her actions. Those emotional barriers she'd erected were slowly but surely crumbling, and I was confident she'd realize soon enough how deeply Øyvin and I both cared for her. She was it for me—for Øyvin too.

Smiling to myself, I turned down the road toward Turi's house and refocused my thoughts to the matter at hand. The Forest Fae had an internal threat and today was a reminder that time was precious. This wolf problem needed fixing immediately. Wilhelm defecting would cause major upheaval in the delicate balance we'd established with the Council after the demise of Queen Ragnhild. I'd sworn an oath to serve and protect the Forest Fae, and that included trouble from within.

I pulled into my sister's driveway, Gunvor's little Mini Cooper already parked up.

Without bothering to ring the doorbell, I knocked once and let myself in. I was instantly assaulted by the smell of cats and whatever herbaceous thing Turi was burning somewhere.

"We're in here!" my sister's voice called from the depths of her living room. I pulled off my boots and hung up my jacket, stuffing my hat into the pocket, and headed toward the chattering noise of two women.

"How's Kristoffer?" Turi asked when I was barely two steps into the eclectic candle-lit room. "Ingrid called me and told me what happened."

I threw myself down on the vacant velvet sofa, narrowly avoiding Loki the cat, who hissed at me and sauntered to the kitchen. "He'll be fine. Still a little shell-shocked, but physically all right."

"Thank the ancestors Øyvin was there." Turi leaned forward and poured steaming hot coffee into an emerald-colored mug and passed it to me.

Nodding in agreement, I accepted the drink and took a gulp before setting it on the coffee table. If not for Øyvin, the outcome would've been monumentally different.

Gunvor sat forward, her black-and-white poncho a stark contrast to the bright mug in her hand, and tapped Turi's thigh. "The little ones bounce back quickly, and he's young enough that the memory will ease and fade with time."

I certainly hoped that was the case for him, because the memory of him disappearing under the ice was burned into my brain. No doubt it would play on repeat for years to come.

I shook my head, ready to pivot the topic as Turi's white cat walked into my lap, kneaded my thigh, and curled into a ball. "I have news about Wilhelm and the pack."

"What is it that was so urgent?" Gunvor asked, and Turi took a sip of her drink, already aware of what had transpired as I'd called her after finding Lennie the other day.

I let out a long breath, the weight of the problem in front of me making my shoulders sag. "According to Marius, Wilhelm has plans to defect from the Forest Fae."

Gunvor blinked twice and took another sip of her coffee before gently setting it on the table between us. "Well…" She folded her delicate hands in her lap. "The man has always been a challenge. Even when he was a boy, he tried to bend rules to fit his purpose."

I brushed my hand across my mouth, stifling a laugh, but coming away with a smile nonetheless. Sometimes it was easy to forget just how old Gunvor was. While her outward appearance portrayed her as a sprightly, albeit petite, octogenarian, she was actually several centuries my senior.

"How do we go forward with the Council now that we know this?" Turi asked. "Can we call a vote of no confidence in his position as Alpha? Do we even have grounds for removal?"

"He sent wolves after your fiancée. I'd call that grounds enough." Gunvor nodded to me, and I wholeheartedly agreed. I knew there'd be consequences for me telling Lennie about the fae, but I never in my wildest dreams thought she'd be attacked by wolves because of me.

"I agree," I said. "The Council was angry with me after I told Lennie about the fae, but agreed that keeping her close during the investigation into illegal magic transfers was important. Wilhelm should never have acted alone and sent his wolves after her. Knowing him, he probably meant to come for me too, but I just so happened to be poisoned at the time, unconscious at Heidi's place in the woods."

Turi pursed her lips, her usual tell when she was thinking hard about some kind of puzzle. "There's never been a vote of no confidence for the Alpha position."

Gunvor shook her head, her long, white ponytail sliding across her shoulder.

"If we call a vote of no confidence, it has to be swift," I said.

"Agreed," Gunvor added.

Turi straightened. "And we need the votes lined up beforehand—"

"Plus security measures in place," I interrupted Turi, and both women nodded. "We can't have Wilhelm lashing out. I need to call in some of the local soldiers to hang out at Alveskjegget during the vote, and perhaps send a couple to stake out the pack compound, just in case."

Gunvor sucked in a long breath, before slowly letting it out and relaxing her shoulders. "The votes shouldn't be too difficult to obtain, but I fear we may have some convincing to do."

With twelve people on the council, including myself and the two women in the room, we'd need to convince another four council members to support the motion if we wanted it to pass.

Turi leaned back against the sofa and brushed her hands through her hair, the brown locks matching the color of my own. "Jan has never been a fan of Wilhelm's. We shouldn't have any trouble there."

"Hanne dislikes conflict, but I think I can bring her around to vote in favor of removal." Gunvor stared off toward the fireplace where embers smoldered, keeping the entire room cocooned in a cozy warmth. "And Frøydis should support us too, especially after the debacle a couple of years ago."

Turi nodded, but I couldn't remember what happened at the event they were referring to. Either way, we had a couple more votes easily secured, and only needed one or two more.

"Can you talk to some of the others?" I asked Gunvor. She was the eldest member of the Council, and a majority of the members looked to her as a bellwether on things. If she could sway more council members, we'd have enough votes to remove Wilhelm from his post.

She nodded. "I'll see what I can do."

"Thank you," I replied with a solemn smile. "Let's see if we can get this done as swiftly as possible. I don't want him to get suspicious, nor enact whatever plans he might have in the next few days."

Turi poured herself another cup of coffee. "In the meantime, do we need to discuss his replacement?"

"Good point. We need someone the council can trust and who has all the wolves' best interest at heart, fae or otherwise." I stroked the cat in my lap and its purrs hummed against my thigh. Biting my bottom lip, I grimaced and glanced over at my sister. "I have a suggestion, but you might not like it."

She narrowed her eyes. "What are you thinking?"

92

LENNIE

"Looks like I missed something," a low voice said.

Shucking off the covers from my post-coital nap, I blinked away dregs of sleep to find Espen leaning against the bedroom doorframe, his arms crossed and a smirk on his lips.

"Good times befell the kingdom." I yawned and stretched my hands over my head.

Øyvin grumbled and buried his face in his pillow where he lay beside me.

"Glad to hear it." Espen smiled, his eyes crinkling. "Would the kingdom like to go get something to eat? It's already past dinner time."

Øyvin shook his head and threw the duvet over himself, cocooning his entire body under the warm covers.

I, on the other hand, was starving. "Are you thinking take-out or grabbing something from the store?" I asked as I slipped from the bed and searched my duffel bag for a pair of clean underwear.

Espen cleared his throat. "Let's visit the shops and pick up something we could cook here. Wear layers, we're walking."

"Sounds good to me." I put my bra on and grabbed a clean, long-sleeved shirt. "You figure out the thing that needed sorting?"

He nodded, pursing his lips. "Yes, everything's good. A plan is in place."

"Hmmm," I mumbled and grabbed a pair of jeans from my bag. "Do I want to know?"

"It's to do with Wilhelm."

I bristled and grimaced as I buttoned my pants. "Just get rid of the slimy fuck."

"That's the goal."

Pulling on my white-and-blue Nordic knit sweater, I flipped my hair out of its confines and set my hands on my hips. "Great. Now, food?"

"Let's go."

We walked about two miles through the snow to the nearest grocery store that, when compared to American supermarkets, was more the size of a convenience store. But it had everything we needed, from potatoes and green beans, to some frozen meatballs that'd be easy to throw together when we got home. With our bags in hand, we made the short trek back to the cabin under the dull glow of the moon that tried to pierce the cloud cover.

Tall street lamps cast golden rays onto the snowy road and the air hinted at the chilly night to come as we strolled home. Barely a single person was out on the roads, and those that had ventured out for the evening, were securely ensconced in the warmth of their cars. The exhausted part of me wished we'd taken the car into the village, the other part of me—the part of me that was slowly melting and had developed serious feelings for the Forest Fae holding my hand in his—didn't mind at all.

I glanced over at Espen carrying our bag of groceries, taking in his dark locks that poked out from beneath his green bobble hat, and I couldn't hold back the smile that swept across my lips.

"What?" he asked, grinning back at me. "Do I have something on my face?"

I shook my head and looked forward again, my body warming under his gaze. Damn, I had it bad. Every time I looked at him a wave of contentment settled over me. Not in a *"I need him to survive"* kind of way—although, with my track record, that might be true. But in a *"I want him by my side"* manner. This perfect ray of sunshine, with his caring heart, his beaming smile, and hugs that could melt a snowman, had broken my defenses completely.

Snow crunched beneath my boots and Espen tugged on my hand, spinning me in a perfect pirouette and wrapping me into his arms. "Out with it, Lennie. What has you thinking and smiling like that?"

I let out a strangled breath and pressed my back against his front as we continued walking. If he ever gained the ability to read my mind, I'd be in serious trouble... Then again, that look he'd had in his eyes told me he probably already knew exactly what was going on in my head. Or at the very least assumed it was something dirty, and seven times out of ten that would be correct.

"I'm thinking about you."

He nuzzled against my neck. "Are you, now?" he whispered, and his warm breath sent a shiver down my spine.

"Mm-hmm."

"Dirty things?" There it was.

I snickered. "More like happy things."

"Care to elaborate?" He tightened his hold on me as we turned down the road that would lead us out of town and toward the little cabin.

Spinning in his arms, I walked backwards, fully trusting that Espen wouldn't let me fall on my butt. I could do this. I could be vulnerable with him. Today was the most openly emotional I'd been in a long time. Even with my old exes and dalliances, I'd never been so forthright with my emotions—which was in part why some of those relationships hadn't lasted very long. Or perhaps those relationships weren't *meant to be*? I took a deep breath, the cold air tickling my throat. "I was thinking about how we met, and how you've somehow broken down my defenses, and wormed your sunny little ass into my heart."

Espen bit his bottom lip as if that could stop his beaming smile. The corners of his eyes crinkled as the Forest Fae moved us closer to the edge of the road and stopped. Creating a small divot in the snow with his gloved hand, he put down the groceries in the waist-high snowbank. The lamp above us lit our surroundings, from the pine trees behind it to the little driveways on the other side of the road. But all I could focus on was the man in front of me.

"Well, that's excellent," Espen said. "I'm glad to hear my plan worked."

My eyes bugged. "Your what?!"

He snickered and flicked his eyebrows. "Once upon a hill in Skolvik, I met a woman—"

"Who better have been me." *Hello Jealousy, welcome to the party.*

"—who *bewitched* me with every fiber of her being." He held one hand against my back keeping my trembling body upright, while pressing the other to his chest as if he were about to recite Shakespeare. "That day I vowed to myself that I would win her heart."

Yeah, this was definitely veering Bard-like.

"Even if she was to leave my fair kingdom in a week's time."

Houston, we have Full Bard.

Smiling at his ridiculousness, I said, "Long story short: you saw something you wanted?"

"Yes, I did. And I did everything I could, even revealed my fae secret, to entice her without forcing her hand."

I narrowed my eyes. "*Everything* you could? Like getting me alone in your cabin on a Friday night for a game of cards? Seducing me with forest yoga? Or making a bridge a little rickety to engineer a hero moment?"

Espen sucked in a breath and shuddered. "Definitely not that. Seeing you fall through that bridge took ten years off my life."

I chuckled. Almost falling into that ravine had given me a few more gray hairs.

"So, what was it then? What caught your attention?" I pried, stepping into his embrace once more. He wrapped his arms around me completely and pressed our bodies firmly together.

"It was love at first punch."

My heart stuttered. "Seriously?" That was novel. I hadn't meant to punch him, it was a knee-jerk defensive reaction to having him appear so close behind me.

"I *bullshit* you not," he replied with a sly grin. "It's not every day that a Forest Fae is punched by a human. I dare say you were the first."

A tiny snowflake settled on the edge of his woolly hat, its spokes caught in the wisps of yarn. Another alighted on my cheek and Espen swept it off with his thumb. The rays from the moon had disappeared behind the clouds, the street lamp above us now our main light source. We stood there in the silence, our eyes locked on each other, our breaths intermingling, as more snowflakes drifted down around us. It was like we were stuck in our own little snow globe where nothing could touch us, and if shaken, we'd weather the blizzard together. My heart hammered in my chest, a rhythm that had started up a long time ago, but that I'd only deigned to fully recognize this afternoon while we sat in his sister's kitchen.

Espen swallowed audibly and cradled my head in his hands. "You're the best thing that has ever happened to me."

My heart officially melted and I couldn't stop myself, I pressed my lips against his, wrapping my arms around his neck. A warmth that felt like home swept through me. There would be no more denying this. No more ignoring my own feelings. No more bottling them up or hiding in the proverbial sand. I was in love with Øyvin *and* Espen, and I felt more alive today than any before.

Espen pulled back, his eyes blown wide. "You're pure chaos, Lennie Martin, but I love every part of your storm."

I bit my bottom lip, letting his words sink in, before admitting, "I love you too, Sunshine."

If I thought I'd seen Espen's biggest smile, I was wrong. The grin that swept across his lips in that moment was the broadest and happiest smile I'd ever witnessed from my bubbly fae, and I was glad to be the one to put it there. He kissed me once more and dipped me for good measure. If anyone drove past us right now, they'd think we were some love-sick teenagers... and they'd only be partially wrong.

"Love at first punch, hey?" I said as Espen righted me.

He nodded as snowflakes flitted around us. "Love at first punch."

93

LENNIE

After dinner that night, I sauntered into our bedroom and started pulling off my clothes. It'd been a long, eventful day and I was ready for bed, even if my brain wouldn't shut off. Thoughts of the day ran rampant.

The bedside lamp emitted a soft glow that danced across the wood-paneled room, and the rumpled bed invited me toward its warmth. Wearing nothing more than my underwear, my bra abandoned on top of the dresser, I scrambled into the king-sized bed and pulled the fluffy duvet up to my chin.

Caught up in my own thoughts and the soft sheets, I barely noticed Espen and Øyvin coming into the room. The men I'd exchanged *I love you*s with today. I shook my head at the surprise of my own actions.

Taking a deep breath and letting it out slowly, I let my shoulders drop. They both loved me.

We'd reached the point of no return.

It was label making time.

Scrambling from beneath the covers, I sat up and looked at the fae crawling into bed on either side of me. Was it rude to stop them going to sleep? Yes, but if I didn't get this off my chest now, I'd never actually do it. *No time like the present.*

I slipped from beneath the duvet and crept to the end of the bed where I turned to face the two of them. "We need to have *the* talk."

Øyvin's eyes were already locked on me, and Espen stretched his arms above his head as a cheeky grin settled across his face. The cold air in the room brushed against my skin, and I shivered. Only wearing underwear to bed was fine when you were sandwiched between two guys, but outside of that little cocoon of warmth... Well, my nipples were putting on a full Broadway show.

"Now, Lennie," Espen said, his voice husky as he leaned back onto the plump pillows. "When two people care about each other very much—"

I waved my hand at him just as Øyvin snorted, propped himself against the headboard, and crossed his arms. I motioned between the three of us. "We're not only two people. We're three... and fae. That doesn't exactly make things simple."

"How isn't it simple?" Espen asked and Øyvin tilted his head in a way that said the exact same thing.

"Cover your tits or neither of us will be able to focus," Øyvin grumbled, pointedly staring at my eyes.

I crossed my arms over my boobs, and continued. "There's three of us. Do you..." I tried to form the words, but it was like my entire vocabulary had drifted out the window looking for a more hospitable location. "You both like me, yes?"

They both nodded, while Espen mumbled something that sounded like "and more."

"Do you like each other?" My voice lifted at the end of the question. We hadn't ever fully discussed *their* relationship. We'd just sort of started cohabitating and orbiting around each other.

Øyvin shook his head, and Espen scrunched his face together before responding. "We both love *you*, and are okay with sharing you, and spending more time around each other isn't necessarily a negative."

My shoulders relaxed again, and I looked to Øyvin. "And you agree with this?"

"Not in as many words, but yes. He isn't wholly annoying to be around and I trust he'll protect you."

"So, you'd be okay with me calling you both my partners, but you won't use that term for each other?"

They shared a look and returned their focus to me. "Exactly," Espen replied with a gentle smile.

"And are you all right with me using those terms in public?" My eyes landed on Øyvin knowing full well that Espen wouldn't have a problem with it.

He took a deep breath before nodding, and I let out a sigh of relief.

"And let's not forget," Espen added. "You're technically my fiancée."

I hadn't forgotten. Not at all. In fact, that gorgeous silver ring with the blue tear-shaped sapphire sparkled on my hand every day—a constant reminder of what I'd agreed to. And, ironically, where things were truly heading for us. I think, in that moment at Christmas when they'd given me the ring, deep in the recesses of my refuse-to-acknowledge-or-rock-the-boat mind, I'd known this would develop into something more. Into something I didn't want to let go of. Truth be told, I was obsessed with both of them and the thought of spending however many years I had on this earth without them rattled me.

"You are my fiancé," I responded to Espen, who adjusted the duvet around his waist with a gentle smile on his lips. "You both are." Espen's grin widened, and I turned to Øyvin. What did he think of all this? What thoughts were swimming through that mind of his?

He crossed his arms over his bare pecks, rolled his bottom lip between his teeth, and gave me a single nod.

"Thank fuck," I said on an exasperated sigh. Adrenaline coursed through my veins and my hands shook as I raked my fingers through my hair, pushing it away from my forehead. That went better than expected, but there was one more thing I wanted to address.

I took another quick breath. "And... So... We're getting married not just for immigration purposes. This isn't fake. We're doing it because we love each other?"

Espen bit his bottom lip. "Yes. Now how about you remove your underwear, assume bridge pose, and let Øyvin and I have our way with you?"

"You are exceptionally good at pivoting a conversation."

Espen beamed. "Is that a yes to sex?"

"Always."

"Fantastic," Espen said and jumped out of bed.

Øyvin raised his hand and gave me a come-hither motion with my two favorite fingers of his.

Crawling across the bed to him, my body lit up from head to toe under his heady stare. Butterflies swept through me at the prospect of having them both, especially after everything we'd said today.

Øyvin made a turn motion and I spun, settling back against his bare chest where he leaned against the headboard.

Espen swept his hand through his hair, and a wave of heat brushed across my bare skin under his gaze. "Pull those off and touch her," he commanded.

Øyvin obliged, and with a little maneuvering, we got my underwear off. He nipped at my ear and pressed his hand down my stomach before reaching the apex of my thighs. My clit ached to be touched and my breasts hung heavy, my nipples erect and begging for attention. As if hearing my own thoughts, Øyvin moved his free hand to my boob and cupped it, taking the weight of it in his broad palm. I whimpered and let out a moan at the sensation plus the pleasure he wrung from me with his fingers drawing circles around my clit.

My skin tingled and my mind cleared of all thoughts under his ministrations and the heady stare from Espen who stood at the end of the bed watching. A plea sat at the edge of my lips, desperate for Espen to join in. "Please," I whimpered. "More."

Espen gave me a sly grin, removed his boxers, and sidled onto the bed. He was already hard, and watching him fist himself drew me closer to the precipice of my orgasm. Øyvin must've sensed the roaring inferno that threatened to overwhelm me. He cupped his palm against my bundle of nerves and pushed two fingers inside. I gasped and rocked my hips forward as Espen settled between them, pressing our legs into a wider vee with his hands. "Fuck you're wet," he growled.

I couldn't do anything but whimper and writhe, needing more from both of them.

Øyvin removed his fingers and returned them to my clit, painting lazy circles around the tender bundle. Espen settled in closer and grasped my legs, holding them just above the knee and opening me up completely to him. He licked his bottom lip, his gaze locked on my core. Releasing me for a split second, he notched himself at my entrance, planted his hands on the bed, and slowly slid inside. Tiny sparks zipped up and down my spine and Øyvin let out a low rumble behind me, his warm chest rising and falling with the motion. My skin heated and Espen pulled back before pushing in again. Back and forth he went while Øyvin continued touching me, the two of them eliciting whimpers and moans from me as I climbed toward my undoing. My breaths came harder, Øyvin squeezed my breast and nibbled at my ear, and Espen pumped in a steady rhythm that a few moments later had me cascading through waves of pleasure. My body convulsed and Espen pulled out, his chest heaving.

"Switch," Øyvin said, his voice husky and teetering on the limit of control. Something he clung to so valiantly, but I was desperate to watch him lose in the bedroom.

We were a tangle of limbs as the guys moved around, repositioning but somehow still keeping me between them. I had no idea what they wanted to do with me next, but I honestly didn't care. I was a trembling mess, blissed out on pleasure and ready for more if they wanted it. Based on the hungry looks in their eyes that was a solid yes.

I settled on my hands and knees, my rear toward Øyvin as Espen rested his head on the pillows at the top of the bed.

Øyvin trailed his fingertips down the line of my spine then smacked his hand across my ass. "I think I'll take this now."

Fucking finally.

His hand cracked across my rear again and I couldn't help myself. I wiggled my ass in his face, taunting him. It earned me yet another smack, but I relished in the heat that bloomed across my skin.

"You think you can take both of us, Trouble?"

The thought of having both of them inside me sent shivers through my body, and I let out a throaty and strained, "Yes."

Øyvin leaned over me, warmth washing across my back, as he tangled his fingers in my hair and pulled my head gently to one side. "Slide forward and take him first," he commanded, his breath skittering across my cheek. I glanced up at the heat-filled amber eyes before me and swallowed hard. Øyvin lifted his weight off me and released his grasp on my hair. I shuffled forward over the sheets and straddled Espen, pressing my palms against his firm chest.

"You ready?" I asked.

Espen nodded and pressed his dick against my entrance. "There's a bottle of lube in the bedside table," he announced to the room and slid home with a groan. "Not that I need it for this part of you."

He really didn't. I was soaking wet and desperate for what was to come. I rocked forward and back, taking every inch of him and savoring every brush of my clit against his pelvis. Espen's fingers dug into my hips, urging me to slow our pace, and I obliged with a reluctant huff.

The bed dipped and I peered over my shoulder. Øyvin squirted a heavy amount of lube into his hand and tossed aside the bottle, letting it land on the floor with a dull thud.

Øyvin's free hand was on my back once more, this time coaxing me forward and bending me over, pressing my chest against Espen's. He quirked his dark brows and gave me a salacious grin before sweeping his mouth across mine. His tongue slid between my lips and possessed me, taking my breath away.

At the same moment, Øyvin swept the lube in his hand down between my cheeks, spreading it around in preparation. It was cold against my heated skin and I shuddered at the sensation, which only seemed to make them happier as satisfied noises filled the room.

I barely moved against Espen when Øyvin pressed his fingertip to my asshole. "You ready?" he asked.

My lips broke away from Espen's and I let out a breathy response. "Yes. Please."

Øyvin gently pushed through that first tight ring. *Damn.* I moaned as he stretched me wider, adding another lube-slicked finger to prepare me for his cock. The slow way he toyed with me, driving in and out, had sweat beading across every inch of my skin, my nipples rubbing against Espen's hard chest beneath me. I needed more. I needed everything.

"Øyvin, please," I begged.

His free hand grasped my ass cheek, sending sumptuous pain through my rear as he pulled his knuckles out of me.

He nudged his tip inside me and let out the sexiest groan I'd ever heard. "Fuck."

I relaxed my body against Espen, letting Øyvin control our movements. He took the invitation and pressed another inch of his thick length into my ass. My legs shook and my heart pounded. I wouldn't last long like this. Øyvin moved and pushed in further, dragging an incoherent noise from my mouth. I definitely wasn't going to last long.

The fullness of having them both inside me was insane. Something I'd dreamed about. *Why the hell hadn't we done this sooner?*

Espen wrapped his arms over my back and Øyvin grasped my hips, steadying me, as he slowly began thrusting back and forth. Espen moved beneath me, demanding more from my soaking core, and it was all I could do to maintain my own sanity. I wanted this bliss to last forever.

Tension spiraled within me, building with each thrust from below and behind. In and out. In and out. Deeper, and deeper, and deeper. Espen's ragged breaths brushed over my ear as Øyvin dug his fingers into my curves. His shallow thrusts drove me wild and I bucked against them. A minute later, a heady symphony rocked me with a toe curling crescendo as my orgasm tore through every nerve.

Fuck indeed.

I pressed my forehead against Espen's and watched him come undone beneath me. His cock twitched inside me as he let out a sexy groan.

Øyvin was right behind him with sharp exhales punctuating the room. He pushed forward one final time and shuddered, his thighs slick against the backs of mine.

Spent and blissed out, I collapsed forward onto Espen, letting Øyvin fall out of me.

He flipped over onto the bed beside us, lying on his back with his arm bent behind his head. "Fuck," Øyvin muttered again.

With the little breath that remained in my lungs, I had the audacity to say, "I told you I'd never had any complaints."

He shook his head and lightly smacked my ass again.

I jolted at the searing sensation, my skin raw and sensitive. My core pulsed, happy and sated.

Espen wriggled slightly and slipped out of me, but didn't move me from where I rested against his chest. He delivered a gentle kiss to the bridge of my nose, then another against my lips. "That was..." he drifted off.

"Sensational. Fan-fucking-tastic—"

"Definitely happening again," Øyvin finished for us.

He was right. There was no way in hell I wasn't doing that again.

And we had a lifetime and then some to do it. Together.

94

ESPEN

Late the next morning, well after the sun had risen above the horizon, I donned my winter gear and slipped out of the cabin as quietly as possible, trying not to wake up Lennie and Øyvin.

The three of us would continue our search for Aurora this afternoon, but first I needed to have a chat with Wilhelm about his behavior. As Head Guard of the Forest Fae, he was my problem to deal with. Wilhelm's actions—disregarding the wishes of his junior members, attempting to kill the love of my life, planning to defect, and causing chaos with his beliefs on the wild wolves—were a problem. A problem that would explode in our faces if something wasn't done about it.

I climbed into the car and texted Turi that our plan was in motion, then left a voicemail with Gunvor, asking her to stop by the cabin in half an hour so we could follow up on the number of votes we had to remove Wilhelm as pack Alpha. She quickly replied, saying was waiting to hear from one last council member.

With those messages sent, and a quick "go" message to my local soldiers on stand-by, I started the car and set off for the senior wolf pack compound on the north side of town.

I parked in the middle of the compound, the headlight beams bouncing across the front porch of the rugged main house where Wilhelm resided and held court. I didn't need to honk the horn or alert them to my presence—they had guards half a kilometer back, all of which were hidden in the trees and had, no doubt, called ahead to warn Wilhelm of my arrival.

Wolves appeared from behind buildings and Forest Fae alighted their doorsteps as I got out of the car, stepping toward the main house. Their hooded stares were like an ice storm, frosty and unforgiving, filled with animosity I'd never experienced from them before.

I stopped halfway between my car and the house, careful not to get too close. I was ten times more powerful than Wilhelm and the other wolves here, but I didn't want to hurt anyone. Plus, the winter months put me at a disadvantage—avalanches and ice fall were a serious consequence should I decide to tap into my destroyer powers.

The front door opened and my gaze snapped to it. Wilhem stepped out of the main lodge, his heavy boots thudding against the wooden porch that wrapped around the building, brown eyes focused on me. He reached the top step of the deck and crossed his arms, standing his ground.

"To what do we owe the pleasure, General Solbakke?" Wilhelm's lips curled around the words as if they left a sour taste in his mouth. The use of my rarely used title told me he'd been alerted to my Forest Fae soldiers at the end of the driveway, and maybe even the ones I'd asked to stand watch at the north end of his compound in the woods.

I crossed my arms too and braced my feet in the snow. "I'm here on official business."

"Out with it kid," he huffed, and several chuffs from the other wolves present echoed around the clearing. Lennie was right, this guy had become a piece of shit.

"Concerns about your leadership have been brought to my attention and—"

His brows met his hairline. "With *my* leadership? Who was it that told a human of our existence?"

I ignored the jab, refusing to let him get a rise out of me. "We have a duty to uphold, Wilhelm, and you've been reneging on your oath to protect the Forest Fae and all wolves."

He sneered, but I didn't back down. Energy coursed through my limbs, pushing at me, begging me to be released against this would-be tyrant. "Are you planning to defect from the Forest Fae?"

His lips quirked to one side. "Planning? We've already started."

Shit. "When?"

He raised his hands in a motion that said *look around*. My eyes flicked over the scene—snow, ice, wolves at attention. Their gazes locked on me, paws steeled in the snow. *His* wolves.

I shook my head slightly. He'd already rallied his forces and turned them against the rest of the Forest Fae. And at this time of year...

"The timing of it all. You did this during the autumn and winter, knowing full well I couldn't retaliate, didn't you?" I asked, aware of exactly how much Wilhelm disliked me, as so many others did for the destructive powers I held. It was why Queen Ragnhild had kept me close when she found out about my powers. I was cognizant of her intentions, but, as like-minded individuals, we established a good friendship and bond that lasted until her final day.

Wilhelm's shoulders and head bristled. "Everything is always about you, isn't it Espen?" he spat. "I did it because the Council has never prioritized the wolves." A lie—they were an important part of our faction and always treated as such. "I sent those wolves to Skolvik because you were incapable of protecting us the moment you revealed our secret to a human. Exposing our world—"

"I was protecting our world, both fae *and* humans! You don't think I know what would've happened to Lennie if she spoke of what she saw, what she photographed?" Some bastard would've killed her. Probably Halvar, but even members of my own faction weren't fans of our secret getting out.

Wilhelm clenched his fists at his sides, the knobbly knuckles paling. "You were a love sick fool."

"That may be the case, but I would never do anything to jeopardize the well-being of my people. By telling her and keeping her close, I've been protecting her ever since. Protecting her from idiots like you who follow the old ways and simply kill the problem, the same way you are with the natural wolves."

Wilhelm tutted. "Even in your two-hundreds, you're still so young and naive."

"And at your age, you still cannot fathom another way of living." I shook my head. This was going off the rails. "We have a duty to protect the forest and the creatures that reside within them, Wilhelm. Human, fae, and all others. Or have you forgotten that?"

"I take care of my pack."

I scoffed, sounding a bit like Lennie. "By foregoing your sworn purpose in this world? By ostracizing those who disagree with you?"

"They don't know what it's—"

I raised my hand for him to stop and miraculously he did. "Spare me." I'd heard this before and understood that the shifters had their own struggles to contend with. We'd eased their burdens countless times over the years, helped each other where we could. But we needed to keep working together, be one cohesive unit of Forest Fae. His actions threatened that precious harmony. "I'm already on my last thread of patience with you for what you tried to do to Lennie."

"Would've got away with it too if it hadn't been for that oaf from the mountain."

Ancestors, I wish he'd said that in Halvar's presence, then I'd no longer have to deal with him.

My power swirled in my sternum as I took another deep yogic breath, letting it fill every part of my lungs and chest. "Here's what's going to happen."

"No." Wilhelm descended the porch steps to the snowy, circular driveway. "Here's what *my* pack will—"

"You're no king."

His eyes widened and nostrils flared. "And neither are you."

He strode forward, raising his hand toward my throat. I stepped back and something zinged past Wilhelm's head, stopping him in his tracks. A stony blade impaled the doorframe behind Wilhelm with a dull twang, and a firm and unforgiving feminine voice behind me said, "Back away from my fiancé."

95

LENNIE

Well, that knife hadn't gone exactly where I wanted, but hey, I'd successfully created and thrown a stone weapon. Halvar would be so proud.

Wilhelm snarled, his dark, beady eyes narrowing.

"Try me puppy dog, and we'll see who ends up with severed balls." I stepped up beside Espen. He looked down at me, his eyes wide and a tiny smile lingering on his lips. Shocked or turned on, I couldn't tell.

The second Gunvor and I had pulled up and spotted the two arguing, I'd been on high alert. When Wilhelm lunged toward Espen, looking ready to transform into his wolf, I fucking lost it. No way in hell was he laying a hand on my man.

Wilhelm took three steps back and the wolves and fae around us relaxed. The pack leader raised his chin and exposed his throat. "What's going on?"

Espen opened his mouth to speak, but Gunvor appeared on his other side and rested her hand against his shoulder. "I can take it from here."

Espen nodded, and I looked on in bewilderment at the elder fae. Gunvor clued me in on what their plan was on the drive over, and while I was slightly disappointed that Espen hadn't shared all the information with me, I also understood. He wanted to get this sorted as quickly as possible without putting me or any innocent bystanders in harm's way.

Gunvor strolled toward Wilhelm, her tiny lithe frame practically floating over the snow, coming to a stop a few paces before him.

"Wilhelm." She clasped her gloved hands in front of her, reminding me of some kind of ancient pixie as she stared down the pack leader. Espen was quiet, his gaze flicking between Wilhelm and the wolves around us, same as mine. "Your presence has been requested at an emergency council meeting tomorrow."

Wilhelm tilted his head to the side, scrunching his nose. "To discuss what, exactly?"

Wolves on our left stepped forward, and the magic in my sternum swirled, wanting to protect Gunvor.

Lightning fast, she waved her hand over her head and roots erupted up from the ground. Reaching high above our heads, some taller than the buildings, the roots clunked against each other and wove themselves together into an impenetrable lattice that encircled the three of us, plus Wilhelm. Wolves howled and paced outside, their eyes focused on us. One wolf prepared to lunge but Wilhelm barked a no at him and the canine slunk away into the trees surrounding the clearing.

My eyes widened as I took in our confines. Gunvor definitely didn't need protecting.

She held her hands together at her waist, her puffy jacket swishing with the movement. "We need to discuss the matter that was brought up at the last council meeting regarding the wolves you sent to Skolvik and—"

"You mean the pack member who didn't return because he was *murdered*?" Wilhelm's voice rose at the end of the sentence, more anger seeping into his tone.

Gunvor didn't rise to his bait. "We are greatly concerned with the leadership you've shown and will be holding a vote of no confidence. Consider yourself summoned."

"And if I refuse to attend?"

She shrugged. "Then you'll be unable to argue your case and the odds of your replacement increase significantly."

"You can't do that." He took a step toward Gunvor, and Espen and I took a half-step forward. Fae crept out of the large cabin behind Wilhelm, providing him some sort of macho back up. But still, Gunvor, the Galadriel of the Forest Fae, creator of root-cages, and consummate badass, didn't so much as flinch. She reminded me of a willow tree, with broad vine-like branches that moved with the wind like nature's wind-chime. Whenever I'd photographed one, I'd always marveled at how you could see through the branches to the thick and wizened trunk at the center—wholly unyielding.

"The Council has the authority to appoint and remove all Forest Fae Alphas," Gunvor said. "You know the rules."

I really wanted to learn more about these rules and more about the inner-workings of the pack. They didn't operate like the ones I'd seen in movies, where the strongest was the Alpha and that usually ran in a family. No, no. These puppies did things differently. Fascinating shit. Perhaps I could attend tomorrow's meeting and bring popcorn?

"We meet at Alveskjegget tomorrow at nine o'clock. Attend, don't attend. It's up to you. You have been summoned." Gunvor peered over her shoulder and looked directly at us. "I think we're done here. Unless there is something else that needs to be conveyed?" She raised a single eyebrow at Espen.

Espen straightened and his voice took on a firmer tone as he looked to Wilhelm. "As you're no doubt already aware, Forest Fae soldiers have been stationed around the compound."

Wilhelm brushed a hand across his wrinkled and rugged cheeks, wiping down his chin.

"They'll remain there for a few days," Espen continued. "You and your pack aren't prisoners—"

Wilhelm scoffed.

"—but we have put measures in place to stop you from leaving the area until the meeting. And safeguards to protect the wolves and villagers from any retaliation."

"Do you really think me so callous and cruel?"

"Previously? No. Now? Yes," Espen replied without hesitation.

"You're kind of a dick," I added.

The root barriers around us slowly receded back into the disturbed snow and earth. My jaw hung open in awe of Gunvor and her powers. What exactly was her job with the Forest Fae? Or had once been? I highly doubted she was a botanist like her cousin Vigdis. Maybe she was a bit more like Ylva, a warrior defending her people? Either way, I was developing a girl crush on the woman.

Once the tendrils returned to their winter slumber beneath the snowy driveway, the three of us headed back to our cars.

Espen opened Gunvor's car door for her. "The votes?" he asked, his voice barely a whisper.

Gunvor nodded. "We have them. More than enough."

Espen's shoulders slumped. "Thank you."

She patted his arm and climbed into her car.

"Thanks for the ride over," I said before she departed.

"Of course. I'll see you both tomorrow at the meeting."

I was silent in the car with Espen until we'd passed the last snow-laden trees of the compound driveway and reached the main road. I twisted in my seat to face him.

"So, this is what you've been planning?"

Espen looked at me briefly before turning his gaze back to the windshield and nodded. "I wanted to take care of this myself. Keep as many people from harm as possible. Including you. Wilhelm's already had wolves nipping at you, I didn't want that to happen again."

"Fair enough. I suspected as much, but I'm not wholly human anymore. I have balls of light and stone knives at my disposal now."

He nodded. "I know you're stronger than you were last year, but I don't trust him around you. Please believe me when I say, keeping this from you was more about protecting you from his hatred than purposefully leaving you out. But, I'm sorry if you felt excluded. That was not my intent."

I melted in my seat, my heart pattering happily. "It's okay, I get it. I would probably do the same. For the record, Øyvin would've come too if he could've folded himself into Gunvor's Mini-Cooper." I really wished he'd tried. It would've been hilarious. Instead he took one look at the vehicle that was primarily meant for two people, huffed, and sauntered back inside. I'd even offered to strap him to the roof, but he'd grumbled and slammed the door, leaving us ladies to head over to the compound by ourselves.

Espen laughed softly.

I set my hand on his thigh, and he placed his atop it, brushing small circles over my knuckles with his thumb.

"I have to say though... Super impressed by your throwing knife," he said, pivoting the conversation with a sly smile in my direction. "I like that you swooped in to protect me."

My cheeks flushed. "It was pretty hot, wasn't it?"

"You have no idea. I very much appreciated the fiancé line, too." He lifted my hand to his lips and pressed a soft kiss to the back of it. My whole body warmed at his simple touch and I slumped in my seat.

Here he was, my ray of sunshine. My fiancé who could level battlefields and heal flora and creatures. A man that had me worried one minute and proud the next. Someone I'd defend at all costs.

"Please know that if we weren't in Oddvar's car right now, I'd ask you to pull over and show me just how much you enjoyed my heroics."

His grin turned wicked. "Oh, I already considered it." He flicked his gaze to mine. "But, fucking you in your future boss's car might not be wise. I'd never be able to keep a straight face and order coffee from him again."

A snort bubbled out of me. "Same."

"Let's get home and have a snack instead," Espen said. "Then we can continue searching for Aurora."

He was right. We needed to focus on our mission. "Deal."

LENNIE

After an eventful morning handling the wolf situation, Espen, Øyvin and I spent the remaining daylight hours searching the neighboring village for any sign of Aurora. From snow laden parks, to a World War Two-era bomb shelter dug into the hillside, the thick metal door covered in bright graffiti. No matter where we looked, there was no sign of the Fjell heir. So, we returned to the cozy cabin, started a fire in the fireplace, and made a plan for tomorrow's search over dinner—a trip to the town of Lillehammer, home of the 1994 Olympics and, according to Espen, a decent number of campgrounds.

As we washed and put our clean plates away, my phone rang. I glanced at the caller ID and smiled, heading into the living room area and taking up position by the window to accept the call.

"Torsten! Hey, buddy! How's the mountain?"

"Not good," a gruff voice that definitely wasn't Torsten's replied, and my whole body tensed at the words.

Shit.

"Who is it?" Espen whispered behind me.

I twisted and mouthed, "Halvar."

His eyes widened. "You need—"

I shook my head. I could handle a phone call with the big guy... probably. Espen took the hint and sauntered toward the bathroom, just as Øyvin wandered into the bedroom, the sound of the bed groaning under his weight meeting my ears.

"Are you there?" Halvar grumbled.

"Yes, here." I spun back to the window, a narrow slip of glass visible between the pair of cream-colored curtains. "What's wrong?"

"Find Aurora and get back as quickly as possible," Halvar said, his voice tense and laced with an ounce of panic.

"Forgive the bluntness"—he scoffed—"but are you aware that Aurora is not a *distant relative* and possibly Freija's daughter?" It hadn't been fully confirmed, but the young woman was a match for the late-Queen. "She even has her unique, gray-and-brown eyes."

Silence hung heavy across the line, like the world was holding its breath to hear what the beast from the mountain had to say.

A deep and long sigh met my ear. "She is Freija's." A statement, not a question.

"Why didn't you tell us?" I pushed the curtain further aside before peering across the lake. Something on the island moved, but I refocused my attention on the phone call. Probably just the wind.

"Because the fewer people that know the better," Halvar replied. "Her safety and the fjell's safety are at stake here, and I won't have either jeopardized."

My stomach lurched at the underlying threat, and I sucked in a breath between my teeth—which was a grave mistake.

"Tell me what happened," Halvar ground out, and part of me, the part that had never done well with orders or authority figures, wanted to hang up on the guy.

"About the whole *safety* thing..."

"Tell me. Now."

"We may have lost her." A rumble of anger started up, so I quickly pulled the pin on the proverbial grenade. "She kind of ran away after I pulled the *who's your mommy* card."

Heavy breathing thrummed against my ear and I scrunched up my face, bracing for impact. "Find her and get back before the end of the week. Or else..."

"Or else, what?" *I really should have duct tape on standby for my mouth.* No wonder Øyvin was always slapping his palm across my loose lips.

Halvar sucked in a breath. "The fjell needs her and *you* back here immediately."

I reared back. "Me?"

"We have cave-ins, mirages, and entrances crumbling around us. There is only so much my magic can do. What I have of Freija's magic—the main source for keeping those entrances shielded but open—clearly isn't enough."

"Isn't enough? Espen said you and the guards had closed some of the entrances to hide them. That you'd used your magic to create those cave-ins."

"Some, not all. The royal fjell magic was never meant to stray too far from the mountain. I didn't realize that would extend to *you* having her magic, too."

I pressed my fingers to my temple. "What *exactly* do you mean, big guy?"

"Majority of those cave-ins weren't controlled. Parts of the mountain are growing weak. A fissure we have been monitoring grows by the day. We need both you and I here to protect the fjell."

"But I went back to the US for Thanksgiving and nothing happened. I was gone for a week and thousands of miles away. A literal ocean and some cornfields away."

He sighed. "There were cave-ins while you were away. The Council and I attributed those to Freija's demise. It would appear that we were wrong."

I swallowed hard. "Well shit."

"Get back as fast as you can." He hung up, and I let my hand and the phone fall away from my ear, unease creeping across my limbs.

My thoughts ran a mile a minute, flitting between everything he'd said and back again. If what Halvar said was true—and I wasn't going to question the likely-ancient being's logic—then he needed me and my new magic back at the fjell ASAP. Plus Aurora, of course.

I huffed and brushed my palm across my mouth and chin. Trust me to land myself in yet another chaotic situation and have the well-being of an entire hidden community resting upon my shoulders.

Something moved on the island across the lake again and my head snapped to attention. Narrowing my eyes, I tried to discern what it was, but it was a bit too far away to distinguish whether it was an animal, human, or just a tree swaying in the wind. My gut yelled at me and my curiosity peaked, so I sprinted across the room and grabbed my new DSLR camera from its bag. Turning it on, I ran back to the window and lined up a couple quick shots.

The lens clicked twice, and I peered at the screen. Nothing unusual. Just a snow-covered island, with rocks and trees dotting the slightly mounded surface. The glow from the moon reflected off the snow, providing a decent, but not ideal, light source.

Popping my hip and settling my weight to one side, I zoomed in on the image and scanned it for any other sign of life. I could've sworn I saw something moving out—

I sucked in a breath. In the middle of the second picture, slightly obscured by a thin birch tree, was a white-and-gray figure—too tall to be a rock and too curvy to be a tree. A line of copper peeked out of a white hood-like shape...

"Have you been hiding right under our noses?" I whispered to myself.

It couldn't be her. Could it? No, it was probably just a trick of the light. At this hour and with only the delicate blue glow of moonlight for clarity, my mind was likely playing tricks on me. It wouldn't be wise to head outdoors in the dark and cold right now. I'd wait until sunrise to have a better look.

LENNIE

I opened my eyes. What if it *was* Aurora?

There was zero fucking chance I was waiting any longer. With my eyes having adjusted to the dark bedroom, I gently removed Espen's hand from my abdomen, nudged Øyvin's foot aside, and wiggled to the end of the bed like a worm. Slipping from beneath the covers, I crossed the room and grabbed my clothes. I was much less likely to bump into something in the hallway while pulling them on. So, I tiptoed across the floorboards, hoping they wouldn't creak, and snuck toward the door.

With a quick look over my shoulder to make sure my guys were still sleeping, I let out a soft sigh of relief and slunk into the hallway.

Once dressed, I peeked at my phone. *Six in the freaking morning?* It was way too early to be up, and yet, I'd barely slept. Thoughts of my island photo and the potential Fjell heir had haunted me every minute. If that was her and she moved before dawn, I'd be kicking myself... and dead as soon as Halvar found out.

I had to take charge and be a little secretive this morning. I had to check on this hunch by myself. How embarrassing would it be if it wasn't her and instead was a weird branch? No, I couldn't tell my guys. If I was wrong, they'd never let it go. Especially Øyvin.

Whatever I found on that island, there wasn't a chance in hell I was making the long drive back to Skolvik empty-handed. I had to prove myself to the Fjell Fae Council. And, while I usually wasn't one for obeying orders or any sort of authority figure, Halvar, admittedly, scared me enough to spur me into action. That and with Fjell Fae magic now coursing through me, I felt an obligation to the place and its people.

I moved to close the bedroom door completely and Espen stirred. He peeped out from beneath the covers, narrowing his sleepy eyes at me.

"Can't sleep. Going outside for some fresh air," I whispered.

He nodded and yawned before turning and hitching the covers back over his face.

I didn't like partially lying to him, but I had a hunch, and I wanted to follow it through. The guys would yell at me for it, but the mountain was struggling and needed me back, so we didn't have time for dilly-dallying.

I pulled on my jacket, snow pants, boots and gloves. Stepping outside into the chilly morning air, the sun's rays barely peeked over the horizon, and the snow twinkled in the soft glow from the porch light.

I needed to find Aurora... today.

If yesterday's photo was anything to go by, I knew where to look.

In the middle of the frozen lake, the little island sat peacefully, covered in a thin blanket of snow. There had been no signs of life over there last night, not even a puff of smoke from a fire, but I could've sworn I saw movement among the skinny trees during my call with Halvar.

I took a deep breath and assessed my options, which were, rather unfortunately, limited to one. I had to cross the frozen lake.

A shudder ran across my skin at the thought. It was stupid. Extremely stupid. But, today I was getting shit done. Curiosity may have killed cats, but I was a demi-fae. Huge difference... I hoped.

I traipsed around the edge of the lake, moving further and further away from the cabin and honed in on a spot that looked like the shortest distance from shore to isle. The entire time I cast looks over my shoulder, making sure I wasn't being followed. Øyvin would lose his ever loving mind if he saw what I was about to do... and would probably mutter something about me constantly finding trouble. Which wasn't wrong, but wasn't helpful. I was taking initiative, being a leader. Had I failed to loop in my team? Yes. Had all our other ventures proved unsuccessful? Also, yes. This was more of a potentially embarrassing, ask for forgiveness later kind of thing. I should know, I was well versed in those.

I reached the edge of the lake where I would cross and knelt down in the snow to inspect the ice. It appeared thick from multiple angles, but as we'd seen on the other lake, the ice could be deceptive. With that in mind, I straightened up and took a deep breath, checking in on my powers. Warmth swirled in my sternum—present and awake. If things went awry, I couldn't use water magic, but I could at least blast my way back through the ice with rocks.

Sending a prayer down to the devil in hopes I wouldn't be meeting him today, I crept slowly onto the ice, sliding one foot forward and then the other, the frozen water holding my weight. *Thank fuck.* I shimmied further along, one step at a time, listening carefully for any creaks from the ice. Hearing none, I kept moving. If the guys looked out of the cabin window right now... Well, I'd probably get my ass handed to me and not in the pleasurable way I'd prefer.

Crack.

My heart jumped into my throat and my gaze snapped to my feet. The ice had splintered like a spider-web with sharp tendrils, but only under my left foot.

"*Fuck.*"

I swallowed hard and gently scooted my right foot forward. The ice creaked like an old wooden door, but didn't crack further. Sliding my left foot again, I let out a sigh of relief. That was too close and probably too much weight on one spot.

"Maybe I should distribute my weight more?" I crouched and moved onto my hands and knees. The ice beneath me remained silent, my blurry reflection staring back at me. "Yeah, that feels safer."

With a deep breath, I started to shuffle across the frozen lake.

About halfway across, my arms began to tremble. The tension in my body put pressure on my muscles, but I didn't dare relax. "Nicely done, Martin," I muttered to myself, voicing my thoughts in hopes that my mind wouldn't drift to images of falling through. "What would your mother say? *Evelyn Martin, how dare you put your life at risk... again! I taught you better than that.* Yes, I know, Mom. You did. I'm sorry. Can I introduce you to my two partners?"

My mind drifted back to her meeting them last year at her house. The look on her face when she'd seen Espen and Øyvin looming over me was priceless. And most definitely had her internally doing a happy dance in hopes that I might marry one of them. "Well, Mom, I am marrying them... or at least one of them."

Had I told her yet? If not, note to self.

I scooted forward, getting closer to my destination, my gloved hands splayed over the glassy surface.

"But there's more too." This part I could never tell her. "I'm actually part fae now, and in order to keep me safe and the magic close to the mountain, I need to become a permanent resident of Norway. Marrying Espen is the easiest way to do that."

Saying it out loud sounded as crazy as it was.

I peered toward the shore, and my lips twitched into a quick smile. I had roughly a quarter of the distance remaining as my mind drifted back to my fake conversation with my mom.

"*Do you even love him?* Yes, I do love him. No, it's not just for immigration purposes... At least, not anymore." I shook my head and chuckled, willing myself to keep moving over the ice. "Look at me, talking to myself to distract from the fact I'm a few inches away from death. What a way to start the day."

With a soft breeze and the stillness of a church keeping me company, it took another ten minutes, but I eventually made it to the other side and threw myself onto the snowy shore. Flopping onto my back, I stared up at the sky and took a moment to catch my breath. The sun peeked over the horizon, casting my surroundings in a light-blue glow.

My heart beat hard and fast, like a camera stuck on rapid shutter speed, as I took several steadying breaths. "That was stupid."

"Agreed," a feminine voice said.

98

LENNIE

I scrambled to my knees, finding Aurora leaning against a tree, arms crossed and her braided hair resting over her shoulder. Her lips were pursed and her eyes watched me closely, like an owl visually dissecting their prey.

"We need to talk," I wheezed. Had I tried holding my breath across parts of the lake?

"There's a land bridge on the other side of the island by the way."

My shoulders slumped and I hung my head in defeat. "Fucking hell."

"I was hoping you'd fall through."

"Rude!"

Aurora shrugged and walked off, muttering, "Entertainment."

I clambered to my feet and shot after the fae as quickly as I could, lifting my feet extra high to step through the calf-deep snow. Aurora's white jacket and pants blended seamlessly with the natural surroundings. If she put her hood up, I could easily lose her again. I couldn't have that. Halvar would probably sacrifice me to some Fjell Fae gods that I'd yet to learn about or their ancestors that bestowed magic. Or maybe he'd present me on some sort of rocky platter saying, "Apologies but this one is faulty. You should probably take her powers back and redistribute them elsewhere. In fact, please do." I shook off the thought and pushed aside a snow-covered branch, refocusing on the task at hand.

"I know you don't want to come back with us, Aurora, but the Fjell needs you."

She scoffed and pressed deeper onto the little island.

"The car is that way." I pointed behind us, doing my best to follow her. Boulders the size of tiny houses inhabited the middle of the isle along with a dense copse of tree trunks, their branches empty for the winter, save for the pines. Everything was covered in a layer of snow and the entire scene looked like a beignet doused in icing sugar.

"I never said I was going back with you."

"Did you not hear the part about the Fjell needing you?"

Reaching a clearing in the middle of the island where the mainland and our cabin wasn't visible, Aurora spun on me. Her eyes flared, full of rage and annoyance. "No one has ever asked if I care. *I* do not need the fjell now, and I never have before."

"Are you sure?" I turned around, pointing at her little campsite. A small gas camping stove, the size of a coffee-press, sat outside a pale gray one-man tent that looked like an oversized butterfly cocoon, and a few logs were scattered around the tamped down snow, likely used as little chairs. "This setup is great and all, but looks kind of cold."

My breath caught in my throat as it dawned on me. *Oh, shit.* "Do you have a home? Have you been homeless since Vigdis died? I thought you lived with Marius and the young wolves?"

She sneered and crossed her arms, popping her hip. Damn, the sass on this one. She was giving me a run for my money with that attitude. "I have a home. But someone has been hunting me, so my home is no longer safe until they leave." She waved her hand as if to *shoo* me. "Please do."

I matched her stance. "I'm not leaving here without you."

"Then you'll be here a while, because I'm not going anywhere."

Was this what it was like to try and reason with me? Damn. I felt bad for everyone who'd ever tried to make me do anything.

"Look here," I started. "All I'm saying is, you are needed by people who you may not know, nor even care about."

She squinted and tilted her head. *Good, she's listening.*

"When your mother died she illegally transferred her magic to Halvar and, by extension, me. I don't know the ins and outs of the Fjell Fae magic or royals or, shit, even the full extent of whatever magic I have in here." I tapped my chest.

"Sounds like a *you* problem."

I took a deep breath and tried to quell the frustration that arose within me. "It is. But *you* are the heir, not me. Your presence is needed by the Fjell Fae Council and the residents of the mountain, to accept or reject whatever their proposal is. From the brief history I know, there's some form of ceremony for the heir, and the royal power will be recycled by the ancestors and bestowed upon the new monarch. But since Freija didn't die with her magic, things might have changed a bit, so who the fuck knows now. My point is, Halvar and the Council need you. I have to bring you back with me."

"You have the wrong person," Aurora said.

"Why do you think that?"

"Heirs are powerful. I'm not."

I let out a sigh, my breath fogging in front of me. "Heirs are granted more power when they ascend to the throne." Fuck, I hoped Nora hadn't been lying about that history lesson.

Aurora held out her palm and let out a steady breath. Slowly but surely a gray pebble formed in her hand. "See?"

"That just reinforces that you're a Fjell Fae, chickadee."

Aurora grimaced and threw the rock aside. "That's the extent of it."

"Size isn't everything," I said, glad that my guys couldn't hear those words coming from my mouth.

"Really?" Aurora tilted her head to one side, her voice filled with sarcasm. "Royals have decent power and skills from what I've been told—"

"And you're without *any* impressive skills?"

She took a step back and shrugged. "You have the wrong person. I'm not who you think I am."

I readjusted my hat. This was like arguing with a tree. No, not a tree, a stump. "Look, if you don't come back with me, I may very well be killed and the mountain is already falling apart."

She blinked and a flicker of concern washed over her face. "Falling apart?"

"I don't know the full extent, but there have been cave-ins, cracks, and the like. The fjell is home to hundreds of fae and it's crumbling without the royal magic to keep it intact."

She opened her mouth and paused, her eyebrows drawing together. "People are losing their homes?

"Like I said, I don't know everything, but I do know they need their heir." Hope bubbled within me. "Please, come back with us. We have cookies."

Aurora shook her head and took another step backward. "Don't ever become a diplomat."

My bubble of hope popped, and I grumbled like Øyvin as I paced a few steps before turning to her. "Just come back to Skolvik. Talk to the Council. Hear them out. That's all I ask."

She set her hands on her hips.

"Please."

Those brown-and-gray eyes, the same as her mother's, studied me intently as she tilted her head to one side. Did she think like her mother? Was she considerate and kind in nature? Hopefully she at least had some of the late Queen's traits. That she might see reason and come to the fjell and speak to the Council.

Aurora's lips hooked into a grimace, and panic welled inside me. This wasn't working. I needed to do something. I peered around frantically, coming up empty handed. *Wait a second...* My gaze flicked to my hands. My magic! I could show her.

"I'm pretty sure this shit"—I formed a ball of light in my palms and motioned it forward, letting the glowing and swirling orb float between us—"was meant for you."

"Don't use that magic on me." Aurora stepped forward and swatted it away. The ball disintegrated at her touch, the magic fizzling out. "I'm not going to Skolvik."

My shoulders slumped, but an idea popped into my head. I cursed myself for my own brilliant, but troublesome, thinking. If this went wrong, I'd end up with my head on a stone tableau. Or my ass. Or both.

Please work.

"Go long," I said and backed up, preparing a sparking ball of light in my hand. Specifically, an orb that could stun, like the one I'd shot toward the wolf. I pushed the intention into the ball that formed, hoping it would work. My stance matched that of a quarterback, my arms bent, hands hiked up as if I was preparing to launch a football into the end-zone. Aurora stepped backward, her eyes wide like I was crazy—which wasn't untrue.

Taking a deep breath, I pulled my arm back. "Ready?"

She shook her head, brows pinching together.

I launched the ball toward her face. She dipped left, narrowly avoiding it, which I was expecting. I swung my tingling left arm and sent a second curved shot that came at her from the side. Before she could figure out what I was up to, the new orb hit her smack-dab across the face and sent her to the ground with a thud.

Yes!

She didn't move.

Shit.

I ran over and bent down in the snow beside her. The light ball hadn't burned her, but her cheek and temple were both red, like a big ol' shiner was going to form in the next few hours. I winced at the sight, then stuck my palm in front of her nose and mouth.

"Please don't be dead."

Warm air brushed across my fingers, and I tilted my head back in relief.

Was this whole plan utterly ludicrous? Yes.

Had it worked though? Also, yes.

I didn't like taking away Aurora's choice—she really should be able to have her decisions respected—but right now the fjell was falling apart, I needed to prove myself, and I'd seen what Halvar could do when he was angry. So, she was coming back to Skolvik, no matter what. All I had to do was figure out how to get her off the island.

I surveyed my surroundings: trees, snow, Aurora's small camp with tent and—

My eyes widened. *Her tent!*

Stepping over her prone form, I raced to the small tent. I tugged the zipper and pushed aside the fabric. There, on the floor, was a gray-and-navy sleeping bag and thin camping mattress. *Jackpot.* I grabbed both and ran back over to Aurora. She still lay in the snow, which probably wasn't good for her health, but that was the least of my worries right now.

I sized up both the mattress and the sleeping bag. Which would be easier to slide her back to the cabin in? The mattress was lightweight, but there weren't any straps to hold her in place. The sleeping bag though... That could contain her and I could scrunch the material in my hands more easily than the flimsy mattress. I flung the latter aside and stepped up beside Aurora.

Grabbing her by the feet, I shoved them into the bag first then pulled it underneath her, sheathing her in it. She didn't make a noise, but her chest still rose and fell. Hopefully she hadn't hit her head, but Espen could heal her, surely. Problem for future Lennie.

With Aurora securely inside the sleeping bag, I hooked the top end around my fists and started dragging the bag toward the land bridge she'd mentioned that was indeed right behind us. Snow covered the thin spit of earth, trampled and frozen enough to let me easily walk on the surface.

Aurora didn't stir, her face poking out of the hole at the top of the bag near my hands, the "foot" end sliding along in the snow. She wasn't extremely heavy, but I'd be in trouble without the bag.

I heaved the Fjell Fae heir across the little bridge and set out for the cabin, hoping she didn't wake up until I could enact part two of my plan: shove her into the car and drive.

I looked over my shoulder at her and chuckled, recalling how she'd kidnapped me recently. "Payback's a bitch in orange."

99

ESPEN

Subtle rays of golden sunlight kissed the window in the bedroom, alighting on my features and bringing a smile to my face. Today was the day we'd remove Wilhelm as pack Alpha and the three of us could continue our search for Aurora in peace.

"She bolted!" a grumbly voice yelled in my ear. I snorted and rolled onto my back. "Lennie's gone missing."

With a sigh, I opened my eyes. Øyvin hovered above me, his gaze wide and blond hair a mess. "She woke up early and went for a walk," I replied, my voice hoarse with sleep.

"I know. I was half-awake, too." He waved his hand toward the window. "She's not out there though."

My pulse quickened and I pulled the covers away from my face. "What?"

"I can't see her anywhere."

Shit.

I jumped out of bed, swaying slightly on my feet as I grabbed my socks and a pair of winter trousers. Øyvin threw a t-shirt at me. He was already fully dressed, jacket on and boots fastened, ready to go. I tugged on my clothes and grabbed my sweater off the floor before moving out into the living room. Øyvin ripped open the curtains, and the wintry lake vista came into view.

"See. Nowhere!" he exclaimed, panic lacing his tone. Panic that slowly infected me too.

I pulled my sweater on and stepped up to the window, scanning the scenery. White on white on white with specks of green and the light-blue of the frozen lake was all I could see. I let out a long breath and put my hands on my hips, assessing the situation—

Orange. A dot of orange came into view on the far side of the lake, and I pointed toward it.

Øyvin stepped up beside me and narrowed his eyes. "That troublesome little..."

"I told you she went on a walk." I turned away from the window and aimed for the kitchen. She'd want coffee this early in the morning, and so did I. "Coffee?"

Øyvin grunted and took up a vigil by the window, his boots still on and his jacket securely fastened at his neck. I took his grunt as a yes and set to work on preparing the coffee, making sure I added some creamer stuff into Lennie's and a huge heap of sugar.

"Espen," the Fjord Fae said after a few minutes, that panicked tone still stuck in his throat. "What is she doing?"

"Walking," I replied, not bothering to look up from my coffee making.

"Espen, she's dragging something."

The spoon fell out of my hand and clattered on the countertop. "What?" I abandoned the drinks in the kitchen and waltzed back to the window to see what he was talking about. Sure enough, just over halfway around the lake, Lennie dragged some sort of bag behind her, straining a little with the weight and the snow. I squinted. "What is that?"

Øyvin inhaled sharply. "It's a fucking sleeping bag." He spun on his heels and stormed out the front door.

My eyes widened. He was right. I shot for the cabin entrance, throwing on my jacket and boots, rushing outside into the cold.

Øyvin stilled by the lake edge, watching Lennie in awe, his eyes about to pop out of his head. I stepped up beside him and took in the frenzy headed toward us.

"Get in the car!" Lennie yelled as she tromped closer. "Get in the car!" She started sprinting—running as best she could with the heavy sleeping bag and the snow boots she wore, making surprising progress.

"What have you done?" Øyvin growled as she ran straight past us toward the car.

"Go get our shit, and get in the car," she bit out, hauling— *Oh, no.*

"Lennie, is that Aurora?" I asked, shock weighing down my limbs and inhibiting any movement. *Halvar is going to kill us.* There would be no more forest hikes, no more morning coffee dates at Oddvar's, and, most sadly, no more *yoga.* We were doomed.

Lennie panted as she set down the sleeping bag with the person in it, the latter's eyes firmly shut, her chest moving lightly.

Lennie gave us a shaky two thumbs up. "Yes. I got shit done."

I brushed my hand across my beard while Øyvin stewed beside me, his eyes no doubt boring a hole into Lennie's chest. "Sometimes I think you're more trouble than you're worth," he ground out.

"Your cock believes otherwise," she replied, then clapped her hands together. "Chop chop. Let's go." And with that she disappeared inside, probably going to grab her stuff and the keys.

Øyvin stomped after her, crossing the threshold with a growl, just as a rustling sounded from the sleeping bag. Aurora groaned and lifted her head. Our eyes met and her gaze widened. I sucked in a sharp breath, and, before she could extract herself from her cocoon, I called forth my power and pulled the roots that lined the gravel driveway toward us. The tendrils shook off their snow cover, snapped in places, and swiftly wrapped around her from shoulders to feet. I wasn't a tree-speaker like Gunvor—able to command trees—but I had some control over the roots thanks to my destroyer powers. Unfortunately, the roots would probably need healing after I was done with them.

"You piece of shit," Aurora spat and wriggled to no avail—the thick tendrils tightening around her upper body.

This was definitely Aurora. Lennie was right, she shared quite a few of her mother's traits, including those marble-like eyes.

I sighed and crossed my arms, my shoulders still tense beneath my jacket. "This goes against a lot of my personal rules and code of ethics."

"Then why are you helping?" Aurora seethed, giving me a familiar glare that I couldn't quite place. I shook off the eerie sensation that rippled across my body at the sight. "Let me guess, you love her, would do anything for her."

I shrugged. "Yes, yes I would."

"Pussy." Aurora kicked her legs like a puppy trying to get out of being held.

I tightened her bindings and frowned. "Behave."

Aurora's responding grimace was the equivalent of a middle finger. I opened my mouth to speak, but Lennie and Øyvin stepped out of the cabin with our bags, the latter with his shiny silver suitcase in one hand and my duffel in the other. He pointed the keys toward the car and unlocked it, the lights on the little passenger car blinking.

Lennie yanked the front door shut and made it all of two steps before a ringing noise filled the morning silence. We all stopped, glancing at each other. Lennie grumbled and dropped her bag on the front deck, unzipping her jacket and grabbing her phone out of the internal breast pocket.

"Andrew," she said, answering the call. "Is someone dying? Mom and Dad okay? Kind of early to be calling."

I let out a breath and turned my focus to the angry heir still stuck in her sleeping bag. Øyvin shoved our belongings into the boot and came over to help me with our other cargo.

Coaxing the roots off her, I let them fall into the snow. Aurora growled and wriggled incessantly as I grabbed her feet and Øyvin opened the door to the backseat before lifting her at the shoulders. While we worked on loading the unhappy Fjell Fae into the car, Lennie scurried and loaded her duffel bag into the boot while trying to get her eldest brother off the phone.

"This really isn't a good time," she muttered, slightly out of breath. "Yeah, yeah, sure." She pulled the phone away from her ear and covered the end. "Shotgun," she said and put the phone back to her ear.

Øyvin grumbled and closed the door to the backseat. I shut my side and clambered in behind the wheel. I was definitely going to miss today's council meeting, which was unfortunate, but even without my vote, we had a majority of the council members to support our motion to remove Wilhelm as Alpha. Part of me—the vengeful Lennie's fiancé part—wished I could've been there to witness his downfall though.

Øyvin made an attempt to get into the front passenger seat, but Lennie grabbed his arm and yanked him back. Shaking her head, she mouthed, "Calling shotgun means I get the front seat. She will kill me. You get in there." She pointed at the back, before returning to her call. "No, no, I'm fine. Sorry, Andrew. Yeah, totally, but I really need to go. I'll talk to you soon."

She hung up and swung herself into the seat that Øyvin had tried to claim. His jaw tightened, but he relented and climbed into the back, moving the sleeping bag bound Fjell Fae to a seated position so he could fit.

"Right," I said, trying to pierce the tension in the car with some positivity. "Are we ready to go?"

A single yes sounded among a low hum of displeasure.

Øyvin leaned between the two front seats, grabbed the handle between Lennie's legs and yanked her seat forward, giving himself more leg room. He slumped back in his spot, all scrunched up still, and threw on his seatbelt. "Now, I'm ready."

"Is the child-lock on?" Lennie asked, her cheeks slightly flushed as she turned to check on the two in the back.

They both grumbled, sounding wholly unamused.

She beamed. "Great. Let's go home."

100

LENNIE

I sat at the small, circular dining table in the boathouse finishing up my oatmeal with cinnamon and sugar. Øyvin sat across from me drinking his coffee, his shoulders relaxed as he gazed toward the kitchen window. We arrived back in Skolvik late last night and chose to wait until this morning to return Aurora to the fjell. To make sleeping arrangements easier and protect our precious cargo from bolting, we'd split up, sending Espen and Aurora to his cabin for the night.

So, it was just me, Øyvin, and the water lapping against the building's stilted foundation this morning. The curtains were drawn to keep in the warmth, and my duffel bag was still downstairs beside the piano, much to Øyvin's annoyance.

"Are you going to join us at the mountain or do you need to head below the surface?" I asked before eating another spoonful of my breakfast.

Øyvin set his coffee on the table between us and leaned back in his chair, brushing a hand through his hair. "Thought I'd see this through before—"

Ring, ring, ring.

We both straightened, and Øyvin pulled his phone out of his pocket.

Ring, ring, ring.

His eyes narrowed momentarily as he read the name, then answered the call and brought the device to his ear. "Yes?"

Muffled words breached our contented silence. I started to mouth "who is it" as Øyvin rose to his feet, the chair scraping across the hardwood floor. His brow furrowed and he marched toward the sofa, resting his free hand on the back of it. His grasp tightened, knuckles paling, and I gulped down the last mouthful of my meal. I gingerly returned my spoon to the now empty bowl, careful not to disturb his call. What on earth had him tensing like the roof was about to cave in?

"How long?" he asked. Whatever the answer was had him pivoting toward the front door. He pressed his phone between his ear and shoulder, holding it in place while he pulled on his boots. "Have they been informed?" He didn't even give me a backward glance as he grabbed his jacket and strode out the door.

I leaned back in my chair and crossed my arms. *What the hell is going on?*

Not wanting to be kept out of the loop, I stood, placed my bowl in the dishwasher, and headed over to the entryway. While it wasn't my responsibility to know everything as a non-member of the Fjord Fae, a nervous energy rode me hard today, low-grade adrenaline coursing through my limbs. And color me curious, but early morning tense phone calls never bode well.

I pressed my side against the front door and sporadic words met my ears. "Fjord... Ceremony... Heir..."

Heir?

My brow furrowed as silence grew again, Øyvin no doubt listening intently to the call. Jittery interest and concern rushed through me. I needed to know what was happening.

Without waiting another second, I yanked on my boots and grabbed my jacket off the hook. Øyvin's voice subsided, footfalls tapping against the dock that wrapped around one side of the boathouse. He was moving to the fjord side of the building.

Purposefully avoiding wearing my orange snow pants and opting for only insulated leggings instead today, I pulled on my jacket and gloves, threw my hat on, and headed out into the cool morning.

Øyvin stood with his back against the red boathouse beside the boat garage door, his phone nowhere to be seen as he stared across the fjord. The tall, snowy pines and gray waters sat dormant beneath a dull glow, the sun not bothering to grace us with her presence today. Øyvin watched the scene closely with his hands in his front pockets, like something was about to breach the surface. The picture of him and the fjord in front of us sent a shiver of anxiety down my spine.

"What's wrong?"

Øyvin pursed his lips and shook his head.

I rolled my eyes. *Love it when he's verbose.*

Stepping beside him, I settled against the wall and pulled my hat down over my ears to hide from the cold breeze that swept across the fjord. "Is there a Fjord heir?" I asked. Based on what I'd overheard, it sounded like a spawn of Balder was about to rise from the depths and wreak havoc on our little village.

Øyvin nodded, and I drew in a sharp breath. "His name is Reuven."

Well, shit. "Anything like his dad?"

Øyvin shrugged. "I've never met him in person, but from what I gather, he's a shade of his father—has some of his temper but not the entire brutish personality."

"This Reuven doesn't live around here, then?"

He shook his head and glanced down at me. "He lives in Iceland. Has for quite some time after a betrothal that now has more meaning than we first thought."

"Sounds dramatic."

Øyvin looked back across the fjord and sighed. "Story for another time, but let's just say Reuven didn't have a choice in the matter."

Another heir with their choices taken from them. My chest tightened and I toed the planks beneath me. I was to blame for taking away Aurora's choice, bringing her to Skolvik against her wishes. My stomach churned at the thought. Yeah, I'd made a mistake—one that would likely save me from a beheading, but it still didn't sit right with me. I'd apologize at some point, but first we needed to head up the mountain and introduce her to the Council.

As if thinking of them magically produced them, light footfalls thumped against the dock and Espen and Aurora waltzed around the corner of the boathouse.

"Good morning." Espen beamed and hopped over to me, planting a kiss on my cold cheek. He was in his thick green winter jacket, with the hat I'd given him for Christmas firmly on his head, wisps of his unruly brown hair peeking out across his forehead. "You sleep all right?"

I nodded toward Øyvin. "Yeah. He didn't bite."

"I was too tired," the Fjord Fae groused and honed in on Aurora. She locked eyes with him and didn't blink, didn't move. She stood there, tendrils of her silver-and-brown braided hair whipping around her, the white jacket tightened around her chin shielding her from the chilly air drifting down the fjord. I sucked in a breath between my teeth—her right cheek was still a little pink from where my stunning magic had smacked her yesterday. Yeah, I really had a lot to apologize for.

"Did *you* sleep okay?" I asked Espen. Hopefully he hadn't had any problems with Aurora.

"Yes, but..."

My eyes widened at his remark. "But what?" Why was there never a dull moment in life? Could a woman never have five minutes of peace?

"Wilhelm was removed from the Forest Fae Council of Elders last night."

"That's great news!"

"Agreed, but that's not all."

Nope, apparently there wasn't any peace for an almost twenty-nine-year-old demi-fae. I let out a long sigh and wiped my fingers across my brow. "What now?"

"Wilhelm disappeared. Ran off with a bunch of his pack according to Turi. Evaded my soldiers."

Of course he did. "That can't be a good sign. But at least he's out of everyone's hair."

Espen shrugged while Øyvin let out a low grumble of agreement.

"Who's pack Alpha?" Aurora piped up, reminding us that she was still here and hadn't bolted herself.

Espen turned to face her. "Marius. Gunvor sponsored him and the Council agreed to test his skills and appoint him Alpha."

Aurora let out a long-winded sigh, shoulders relaxing. "Well, good. Now, can we get this over with?"

"Do you promise not to run off while we walk over to the mountain?" I asked. "Are you being agreeable today?"

Aurora shrugged. "I'm already here. You have the wrong person, and I'd like to get through this without being tied up again or threatened."

Espen cleared his throat. "I also promised to drive her back to Alvdalen if she decides not to stay."

I swatted his arm. "Why'd you do that? She's the heir."

His face creased and he raised his hands above his head. "I'm trying to keep the peace here."

Øyvin let out a single grunt, and I couldn't argue with my bubbly fiancé. While I may disagree with offering her passage, Aurora was mellower today and didn't look like she wanted to rip my face off.

"Fine," I muttered and set my hands on my hips. "Want to get going then?"

All three fae nodded.

We traipsed through the snow-laden village. Frost painted the corners of the windows we passed and our breath fogged before us. I waved to Oddvar through the window of the café as we passed, the elder villager preparing for the day's customers, some of whom already graced the tables within the establishment.

The trail on the north side of the village rose into the dense forest, the snow cushioning our steps as we strode out of town toward the nearest entrance to the fjell—one of the side entrances I'd learned about over Christmas. We passed snow-covered rocks, treetops dusted with a layer of powder, and frozen brooks, the ice undulating where it had been locked in place by the cold. It wasn't long before we reached our destination and my mouth fell open.

"Well, shit," I muttered as we stilled at the entrance to the mountain. This was what Halvar had been talking about on our phone call a couple of days ago.

A mound of stones covered in a light layer of snow blocked the magical entry to the fjell.

Espen brushed snow off the nearest boulder. "We'll have to try the main entrance further down."

"Use your magic," Øyvin said to me with a raised brow.

"What?"

He rolled his eyes. "Press your magic into that."

I looked around, my eyes wide. "It's the middle of the day, and we're not that far from town. Now doesn't seem like the best time to be testing my demi-fae powers."

Espen stepped aside and Øyvin crowded me, forcing me to take a couple of steps backward until my butt bumped against the rockfall. "Try."

Damn did he know how to activate that Martin family competitiveness within me. I rolled my shoulders and grumbled before turning to face my adversary. The magic in my sternum swirled, like it could tell it was home and where it was needed.

I pressed my gloved hand against the nearest boulder. Magic zipped down my left arm, winding its way down the lightning-shaped scar and through my palm. I willed the stone to budge, pictured it rolling aside like the ones they used as doors in the dungeons. The rock grumbled and groaned as it moved minutely to the left, setting off a ripple effect. The stones around it shuddered, and I immediately removed my hand, withdrawing my power. "Maybe not," I muttered as I shuffled back toward the others.

Øyvin pressed his thumb and forefinger against my lower back, steadying me. "At least we know you can move a couple tons of stone."

"Uh-huh." While I'd almost caused another rock slide that could've injured us, he was right. I had moved the stones with ease. Was it enough to get us inside? No. But it was *something*. A bubble of pride grew within me, warming me from the inside out.

"Good attempt." Espen's eyes crinkled at the corner as he extended his hand to me. "Shall we head for the main entrance? See if that one is open?"

"Yes, but first"—I looked at Aurora and nodded over my shoulder—"give it a go."

"You've already seen the extent of my Fjell powers," she replied.

"Sure, but now you're right next to the mountain. It might help."

Aurora grumbled and shook her head.

She pressed her hand against the rock closest to her and a second later it budged... by a quarter of an inch and settled back into its position like it couldn't be bothered to get out of its comfortable spot.

My eyes widened and I glanced at Espen and Øyvin. The former pinched his lips together, while the latter wore an unreadable blank face. Their gazes met mine though, and their eyes betrayed them—uncertainty.

"Well..." Espen straightened and gave Aurora a smile. "Not every fae perfects their skills early in life. I'm sure with a bit of time you'll be moving mountains!"

If there was ever a time to appreciate Espen's ability to pivot a conversation or lighten the mood, now was it.

Aurora stuffed her hands in her jacket pockets and stepped back. "Told you."

"It'll be fine," I said, sounding more like I was trying to convince myself than her.

She rolled her eyes and strode away, Espen following and then pulling up beside her as they headed back down the trail. "Come along, this way to the main entrance," the bubbly fae said.

I peered after them, my steps faltering as I followed Øyvin along the snowy trail. This wasn't good. What if she was right and I'd nabbed the wrong person? Everything I'd been told and seen had led me to believe she was the heir, but... My stomach churned and visions of the guys calling my parents to inform them of my untimely demise filled my mind.

As Espen and Aurora traipsed ahead, I pulled on Øyvin's sleeve and brought him to a stop. "How common is the name Aurora in Norway?"

His forehead creased. "Not uncommon."

"Shit."

"What are you thinking?"

"Maybe we *do* have the wrong person."

Øyvin shook his head. "She does look like Queen Freija, but..."

"But?"

"There's only one way to find out, and Espen and I won't let Halvar kill you." I squeezed his forearm. "Promise?"

He smiled. "Promise."

Thankfully, the main entrance was miraged like a cliff-face with no rock slide in sight. When we pressed against the rocky facade, the magic granted us entry and let us slip behind the illusion.

The temperature inside the rugged mountain tunnel was slightly warmer than that outside, so I pulled off my hat and gloves, shoving them into my jacket pocket. Espen did the same, while Aurora lowered the oversized hood of her white jacket, and Øyvin ran his hand through his blond hair.

"Where's Halvar?" I asked the two soldiers guarding the entry.

Their short capes, attached at one shoulder, fluttered around their waists and both nodded to Espen and Øyvin. The one to my right turned his gaze on me. "Council chambers. He's in their daily meeting."

"Excellent." I strode forward, Espen on my heels and Aurora between him and Øyvin. Without discussing it, we fell into a protective formation, our treasure secured between us. While I still owed her an apology, that would have to wait until after we spoke to Halvar.

We wound our way through the rough stone tunnels dotted with magical sconces every few yards, passing fae who nodded in greeting before staring at Aurora. It had only been a handful of months since I first stepped inside these meandering passages, but I now recognized them and knew where I was going... or maybe that was my new magic guiding me? Either way, it wasn't long before the four of us stepped through the blue quartz-like stone archway into the throne room.

Guards spun to attention, their gazes honing in on us—the only other beings in the room. A pang of emotion ripped through me at the sight of the empty throne and I glanced over my shoulder at Aurora. She scanned the space, taking in the glassy sky-blue walls and the crystal facets around the seat of power. Who knew what was going through her head right now, but the time had come to deliver her to Halvar and the Council as requested.

I aimed for the door to the left of the throne. I'd never been through it, but I'd witnessed Halvar and Queen Freija use it countless times.

A guard stood vigil outside the arched door that was fastened to the mountain. I strode toward it and he stammered, moving to block me from the doorway. Raising my hand to knock, he reached for my wrist. One grumble from Øyvin had the soldier rethinking his priorities and he stepped back.

"We were sent on a mission by the Council," I said, hoping I could calm down the soldier. "They're expecting us." *Kind of.*

He narrowed his eyes, then shrugged as if to say it was my funeral. Which it might honestly be, but I was also doing as requested. So, the Council couldn't be too annoyed by my interrupting their meeting.

I knocked, and instead of waiting for a reply, pushed open the wooden door.

The walls inside were slate-gray but veins of the sky-blue stone in the throne room cleaved through them like a mangled spiderweb. Light orbs hung from the ceiling and flickered from sconces on either side of the doors—of which there were two more on the other side of the room. Eleven council members, including the light-wielding Fjell Fae, Torsten, sat around a large stone slab in the center of the room.

All eyes spun to me, and I felt Halvar's annoyance from the head of the table before I caught his tightened glare.

Clasping my hands together in front of me and rocking on the balls of my feet, I announced, "Delivery."

101

LENNIE

"You found her in one piece, I presume?" Halvar said as he rose from his chair and strode across the room.

"That I did. Vigdis has unfortunately passed, but Aurora is alive and breathing steadily," I reassured the big guy towering over me in his black shirt, equally dark pants with a bajillion pockets, and a stone sword hanging from a belt cinched at his hips.

"Good." He peered over his shoulder. "Shall we move this to the throne room?"

Nods flitted around behind him and chairs scraped across the floor.

He motioned for me to return to the throne room and I did as requested, backing up a few steps before turning to the trio I'd arrived with. Aurora stood between Espen and Øyvin. Her eyes widened and she swallowed hard as she took in the beast of a man behind me.

Øyvin nudged her and all four of us moved into the middle of the room. It felt like I was about to give a PowerPoint presentation, but instead of a slide show, I was presenting the heir to the Fjell Fae Council. No pressure. Maybe the guys and I should've set up a safeword if something went wrong? A cue that it was time to run. Like papaya or tripod or sexy trolls. I bit my lip. Too late now.

The council members filed out behind Halvar with Torsten bringing up the rear and closing the door behind him with a dull thud. The group fanned out on the left side of the room, some taking a seat on the bench carved into the blue stone wall, while others remained standing. All of them had their eyes locked on the four of us.

Halvar took up position in front of the throne, like a de facto king. But having spent some quality time with the fae in recent weeks, I knew he hadn't claimed that seat. He'd protect it until his dying day, though. His sky-blue eyes honed in on me, Espen, and Øyvin, stopping on each of us in turn. "Thank you for your work. I speak for the Council when I say we are most grateful for your assistance in the retrieval of the heir. Should your factions ever need anything from the Fjell, know that we are amenable." The council members nodded in agreement.

"If you'd please." Halvar raised his hand and motioned to the right side of the room. The three of us slipped to the side, and Aurora made a move to join us—

"Aurora Johansen," Halvar said, his voice echoing around the chamber, and Aurora stopped in her tracks. "My name is Halvar. Welcome to Skolvik."

She turned back to the center of the room and let out a long sigh. Anxiety zipped through me, wondering how this was going to unfold. I shook my hands out hoping to dispel some of the jitters, but there was no use. We were all about to witness a conversation that was unlikely to end well considering her prior thoughts on returning to the fjell.

I looked between Aurora and Halvar. Halvar and Aurora. Then again. *Wait a second.*

My head whipped from one Fjell Fae to the other. Their shoulders were set back like soldiers, their sharp chins slightly raised, their noses a smidgen crooked, and silver hair...

My eyes widened and my pulse thrashed.

"Oh, Halvar..." I let out a long, quiet whistle. "You naughty, naughty boy."

The man himself didn't hear me or chose not to acknowledge me. Nor did he make any remarks about the tittering that rose from the council members and soldiers, their heads flitting between Halvar and the heir. I wasn't the only one who'd noticed.

Espen let out a chuckle while Øyvin quietly mumbled, "Shit."

Now there was no doubt in my mind that we had the right person. Her magic may not have been strong—likely untrained as Espen had touched on during our trek here—but *this* Aurora was a thousand percent the woman we'd been sent to find.

She was a perfect combination of Queen Freija and Halvar.

I didn't know why I hadn't noticed it until now. But seeing them in the same room, facing each other, there was zero doubt in my mind. Aurora was Halvar's daughter, too.

Halvar's gaze washed slowly across the room, bringing the murmuring to a close. He turned back to Aurora and clasped his hands behind him. "You've been made aware of your status as the heir of the Fjell?"

Aurora looked at me before turning her gaze to Halvar. "Yes, I was *bluntly* informed."

"Way to throw me under the bus," I whisper-yelled. I'd done what I needed to do. With minor regrets, but still. We'd found her and she was here. Mission accomplished.

Halvar let that information sink in, his body language betraying none of his thoughts before he continued. "Did Vigdis Johansen ever inform you who your mother was?"

My body tensed and I swallowed hard as my heart clenched at the use of the past tense. I reached out to Espen and Øyvin on either side of me for comfort. Espen gave my hand a gentle squeeze while Øyvin brushed the back of his hand against mine in a reassuring gesture.

"She did not," Aurora answered, regaining my full attention.

Halvar blinked at the response and several council members tilted their heads in surprise.

"What did she tell you of your parents?" Halvar asked.

Aurora crossed her arms, her expression pinched with tension, her tone flat and succinct. "That she didn't know who my father was, but that my mother was an old friend of hers. The two women met centuries ago while she lived on the south coast. Vigdis mentioned that the woman asked for help and requested her guardianship. She never said anything else."

"Did you ever ask about your mother?"

"A couple of times when I was very young."

"And what do you recall of those conversations?" Halvar leaned into the questioning, digging for information from the young woman.

"Not much. She said I looked just like her and that my mother was a Fjell Fae."

"She never mentioned anything else?"

Aurora shook her head.

"Did she ever teach you any specific magic uses?" In other words, what powers did Aurora have? Damn, Halvar really was a good soldier and inquirer.

"Vigdis was a botanist. While she taught me some basics, they were limited to Forest Fae magic which I cannot wield and what little understanding she had of the Fjell."

"So no affinities were cultivated?"

"None of note."

"Expand upon that... please?" Halvar asked with a nod.

"I whittle and I'm good with knives, but aside from being fast and able to call forth tiny pebbles, there isn't much important."

A line formed between Halvar's eyebrows and several members of the Council brushed their hands across their chins. Sounded to me like she hadn't had the right people to train her fjell powers. No doubt Halvar and the others were thinking the same.

Halvar lowered his head slightly. "Thank you for sharing."

The room fell still, tiny dust motes swirling around in the white-and-blue glow reflecting off the walls. Halvar turned his face to the Council and appeared to have a non-verbal conversation with them all. Nods flitted between several members before Halvar straightened again and faced Aurora who still stood alone in the center of the room.

"Aurora Johansen, daughter of the Fjell, heir of Freija, child of mine."

A collective gasp zipped around the room, and Aurora's eyebrows hit her hairline.

The cat was definitely out of the bag now.

"Based on your story and the evidence presented, the Fjell Fae Council recognizes you as the heir and formally requests your ascent to the throne." Halvar's voice never wavered. "While we don't know what magic the ancestors may grant you considering Queen Freija's actions during her last moments, you are the heir of the Fjell. Do you accept your position as monarch?"

This was it, the moment we'd been waiting for. The moment we'd been working toward. Would she opt to stay, deal with whatever magic nonsense needed to happen for her to become Queen? Would the ancestors bestow royal magic to her? Did she already have some? Or...

"No," Aurora said, her voice echoing through the chamber.

Several strangled breaths emitted from the council members, and I winced.

Halvar didn't budge.

"I have a family in Alvdalen." Aurora straightened and unfurled her arms, setting her hands on her hips. "That is where I belong."

I wanted to argue for her to stay, wanted to convince her to change her mind, but Gunvor's voice popped into my head—a reminder of her parenting strategy and choices. *A woman should be given the freedom to choose her own path.* Regardless of who her parents were, Aurora deserved the right to make her own choices in life. Part of me felt guilty for bringing her here under duress—I'd forced her hand and I shouldn't have. The other part of me was glad to help the Fjell Fae, even if it hadn't gone according to plan.

The beast of the mountain watched his daughter with emotionless features, his eyes locked on her, betraying none of the thoughts likely running through his mind. This probably wasn't the family reunion he was expecting. But I'd seen the way he broke when he held the dying Freija in his arms. To see their child before him must be difficult, and to hear her rejection of his request, even more so.

He swallowed, rolled his shoulders, and clasped his hands behind his back again. "If that is your choice—"

"It is," Aurora said firmly, not backing down from the pressure.

"—then we shall honor your decision."

Aurora brushed her braid off her shoulder and muttered a "thank you" as Torsten stepped up beside Halvar, his eyes wide with panic.

"What does this mean for the Fjell? We can't go on like this. We need a royal and their power to maintain the integrity of our home."

"I'm well aware of the consequences," Halvar replied, swiping his hand across his short beard before casting his gaze toward me.

I flinched at the attention and squirmed on the spot when Torsten looked over, too.

Halvar narrowed his eyes. "Perhaps our future lies elsewhere."

Ah, fuck.

"We must consider our other options," a Fjell Fae council member announced from the other side of the room. His wizened stare locked on me before flitting back to Halvar.

Double fuck.

I clenched my fists together and Espen nudged my shoulder with his. "It'll be okay."

I wasn't so sure about that, but the gnawing anxiety in my stomach didn't last long. Heavy footfalls sounded from the hallway, growing louder and louder by the second. All eyes turned to the entry, and Halvar brought his whispered conversation with Torsten to a close.

Øyvin went ramrod straight beside me and muttered, "He's here."

"He, who?" I peered toward the entrance and took a few steps away from my guys to get a better look.

Aurora spun on the spot, turning her back to the throne, and stumbled backward three paces.

A pair of Fjell Fae soldiers strode into the room, blue-caped Fjord Fae soldiers hot on their heels. A contingent of Fjord Fae breached the archway and broke aside, revealing the two individuals they were guarding, just as Øyvin replied, "Reuven."

102

LENNIE

Air left my lungs as I took in the newcomers, and, more specifically the man in the middle. His dirty blond hair was buzzed short, a scar cleaved his right eyebrow ending at the top of his cheek, and a smattering of stubble graced his chin. If you'd put him in a line-up and asked me to pick out King Balder's son, I'd pick this guy. And it wasn't because of the light-blue eyes or the oval face shape he'd inherited, but the cunning gaze and countenance. This man looked like he'd weathered centuries and could withstand several more.

"Seems like I'm not the only heir to return to Skolvik today," Reuven said as he strolled further into the room, his gaze briefly lingering on Aurora.

I peered over my shoulder and looked up at my Fjord Fae. Øyvin bowed and Reuven returned the gesture with a nod and slanted smile.

Soldiers around the room followed Øyvin's lead, bowing to the Fjord Fae heir. Torsten stepped back among the other council members, all of whom watched on with rapt attention.

"Reuven," Halvar said, his voice like rolling rocks as he nodded toward the royal.

The Fjord Fae heir's short blue cape fluttered around his waist, the underside covered in intricate silver swirls and aquatic creatures, some of which I didn't recognize, including a snake-like animal.

"Halvar. It's been some time." A shrewd note laced Reuven's every word, like he was picking each with care.

"Indeed. Might I welcome you both to the fjell. I don't believe your wife has ever had the fortune of a visit."

Reuven shook his head and motioned to the woman at the back of the room. "May I introduce my wife, Salka Veigarsdóttir."

A tall woman hung back by the entrance. She wore a long beige tunic-style dress with a swirling Nordic pattern down the front, and her onyx hair was bound into a crown braid that wrapped around her head, small tendrils floating down around her pointed ears. Definitely fae, and that notion was hammered home when our eyes met across the room and I flinched. They were pitch black. Completely and utterly black with no whites. It was as if she only had pupils. My body and instincts screamed at me to be wary, my magic swirling faster within my sternum like a warning.

"The Council and I weren't sure you'd be taking up your position as heir."

"You killed my father, Halvar," Reuven said with a single mocking laugh. "You don't expect me to come home after that?"

"I'd expect you not to take several months."

I tilted my head toward Øyvin and mouthed, "New boss?" He nodded once and turned his eyes warily back to the woman, his hands open at his sides in what to some might look like a relaxed state, but I'd seen Øyvin in battle and been around him for long enough to recognize that as one of his ready positions. He didn't think Reuven was a threat, but *she* was. Why?

"As you know, my wife cannot travel via aircraft or among humans as freely as the rest of us," Reuven drawled, his deep voice resonating throughout the chamber.

I looked to Espen and mouthed, "why?"

His eyes were wide and he swallowed hard before mouthing back. "Fire."

Every ounce of oxygen in my lungs disappeared and my stomach sank to my feet. *Fire Fae?*

I needed to hit pause on this show, turn to my guys, and immediately ask for a full fae history lesson. Classes 101, 202, 300. Hell, throw me into the deep end and give me PhD level classes on the fae, because I was seriously lacking in knowledge. Fire fae? We're they kidding? What'd they do, control lava or some shit? Wield balls of fire?

One look at the woman standing at the back of the room would say so. She was, for lack of a better term, other-worldly.

"What brings you here today, Reuven?" Halvar asked, sounding very much like the leader he was.

Reuven opened his mouth to speak as howls sounded down the hall, followed by yells from men and women.

Time slowed and everyone stilled, myself included, like air had been sucked out of the room and replaced by terror.

A moment later a wolf appeared in the archway, the azure-hued light of the room catching the blood stains on his fur. His brown eyes locked on me and his lips pulled back from his teeth. Tremors ran through my body and I gulped down air. Before the creature could move, the Fjell soldiers guarding the entrance had rocks levitating over his head, waiting for orders to crush the invader.

Reuven swept to one side, taking Salka's hand, his own soldiers crowding around him with orbs of water swirling in their grasp. Øyvin did the same, while Espen...

Anger rolled off the Forest Fae in waves as he moved closer, positioning himself between me and the wolf.

Swallowing my fear, I slid in front of Halvar and Aurora, drawing on the magic within me, the need to protect coursing through my veins. The lights in the room flickered, matching the rhythm of my hammering heart as if the fjell and I were one. I placed my forearms against each other, holding them diagonally, and pulled my hands apart. By the time my right arm was fully extended, magic shooting and prickling across the scar on my left, a short stone sword appeared in my hand, light-magic bouncing off the tip of the blade. A shearing noise sounded behind me, and I chanced a quick glance over my shoulder. Halvar had drawn his sword and pressed his daughter behind him.

"Do not threaten the Fjell," Halvar grumbled.

The wolf snarled and launched toward Espen.

Fjell Fae rocks crushed its head and cracked its spine, the snapping noise ricocheting off the walls. Water balls washed over its thick brown fur, drenching it from nose to tail as it collapsed to the floor and froze.

This wasn't good. My chest heaved and my magic swirled in my sternum, begging to be released.

"What have you brought to our door, Espen Solbakke?" Halvar growled, sheathing his sword.

I stepped toward Espen as he turned around, his eyes wide with shock and anger.

"I never imagined he'd bring his fight and animosity to Skolvik. Run away to lick his wounds, certainly, but Wilhelm has never had a death wish."

I looked between Espen and the dead animal. Was that wolf Wilhelm? Or one of his cronies?

"That's exactly what'll happen if I get my hands on him," Halvar bit out.

I shivered at the threat, glinting sparks shooting from the tip of my blade where it hung in my hand at my side.

"I'm sorry for any injuries that may have occurred to Fjell Fae," Espen said. He shouldn't have been the one apologizing, but I understood where his mind was. Wilhelm's removal from the Council of Elders was spurred on by his actions, and he was feeling the guilt of its result. "But I don't think he's after your heir."

"The timing is suspicious," Halvar groused and several council members nodded in agreement.

"It's unfortunate. But I think they're after me and Lennie."

"And what of you?" One of the council members asked, pointing to Reuven, their wispy brows reaching their salt-and-pepper hairline.

"Don't worry." Reuven moved his focus from the council member to Halvar. "I'm not here to kill your heir or your friends. Quite the opposite." He squeezed his wife's hand.

"How can we be assured of that?" Halvar asked, nodding to Salka. "You're aligned with Veigar's house."

Reuven's eyes crinkled, his scar twitching with the movement. "I will always prioritize the well-being of the fjord."

Howls rent the air once more and fae around us stiffened. My heart hammered against my ribs. There were more of them?

"Fjord Fae, time to go!" Reuven announced, heading toward the exit. "Øyvin, you're with me."

I stared at Øyvin, my eyes wide. He hesitated for a second, looking between his new monarch and me, his brow creased. "Permission to stay and assist our new alliance, sir?"

Air caught in my throat. He'd always prioritized the fjord. And while this was, in a way, helping the fjord, I got the distinct feeling he'd just put me first.

Reuven narrowed his gaze at Øyvin and tilted his head to one side. With a nod, he said, "Report to my chambers when the threat is eliminated." With another nod to Halvar and the Fjell Council, the incoming Fjord king and his fiery queen swept from the room in a crowd of billowing blue capes.

Fjell soldiers entered the room after them and bolted toward us, or more specifically, Halvar. I stepped out of their way, but still somehow ended up on the fringes of the group of twenty-plus in their gray Fjell Fae uniforms. "Orders, sir."

Halvar raised his chin and his nostrils flared. "Find the weakened entrance and seal it. No one out. No one in."

"Yes, sir!" They shouted in unison.

"They harm one of us, they harm all of us." Halvar's gaze swept across the gathered soldiers and he raised his stone sword above his head. "Hunt them down."

103

LENNIE

Chaos erupted in the throne room. Soldiers running to and fro, growls echoing down hallways. The tunnels and entrances must've been severely troubled if the wolves could sneak into the mountain unnoticed.

I used my magic to collapse my stone sword, amazingly getting it to disappear on the first try.

"Espen, I want you here with me," Halvar announced through the bustling noise of soldiers and commanders growing around us as more people barreled into the room.

Espen tightened his jaw and shoulders, readying to protest.

"You know these creatures better than anyone else here," Halvar said with an unyielding tone. "You stay with me."

Espen let out a long breath. "Of course."

There was more to it than just Espen knowing the wolves. It was no doubt wise to keep him nearby should he get angered, lose control, and let loose his destructive powers within the mountain. The consequences of which would be disastrous. If he could level a battlefield, he could probably bring down the mountain.

"Torsten," Halvar turned to the light magic wielding Fjell Fae. "Take Aurora, Lennie, and Øyvin into the tunnels. Keep moving, head for you-know-where."

"Of course." Torsten nodded, already turning for the council chamber door. "Follow me."

Espen caught me by the arm before I could take a step and pulled me into his embrace. The smell of leather and moss settled over me as Espen scanned every inch of my face, like he was committing it to memory. He pressed a gentle kiss to my temple before muttering, "Stay safe. Come back to me in one piece."

I brushed my palms across his chest, feeling the steady thrum of his heartbeat beneath my fingers. This wasn't a goodbye. I wouldn't let it be. Yet, my heart clenched and a lump formed in my throat. "I'll be okay," I said, unwelcome anxiety trembling through my words.

"Come on, Trouble." Øyvin placed his hand on my shoulder. "We need to move."

I stepped out of Espen's arms, already missing the warmth and comfort I'd always found there.

"Keep her safe," Espen said.

"Always," Øyvin replied, tugging me by the elbow. I acquiesced and sucked in a breath, pulling on all my courage to get through this new shitstorm. After taking one final glance at Espen, who strode over to Halvar and other fae who appeared to be commanders or some sort of leaders, I walked away with Øyvin.

"Let's get one thing straight," I muttered as we hurried after Torsten and Aurora who were already at the large wooden door. "I can take care of myself."

Øyvin's lips quirked into a tiny smirk. "That's usually the problem."

I swatted his ass.

His eyes flared.

"Come on, then." I wiggled my brows, mentally distracting myself from the chaos unfurling around us.

Torsten opened the door to the council chamber and ushered us through. The stone slab table rested like a dragon in the middle of the room, chairs strewn around it, and dust motes dancing in the glow from the magical lights.

"This way." Torsten circled the table to one of the doors on the other side of the space. He pressed against the exit, the wood groaning on its black iron hinges, and cool air blew across my cheeks. "We need to head down. Keep you two safe."

"You two?" I asked, my voice notched with confusion. "There are three of us."

Torsten turned to me, his thick brows pinching together. "I have no doubt Øyvin can defend himself. Probably drown the wolves with a snap of his fingers."

Øyvin's lips tipped down at the corners and he bobbed his head.

"But our priority," Torsten continued. "The Fjell's priority is you two." He pointed to me and Aurora.

Aurora waved her hand as if to say "can we get this over with?" She no doubt just wanted to go home, and I couldn't blame her.

"Fine," I replied and brushed my hand across my forehead. "Let's keep moving."

All four of us strode through the doorway—Torsten taking the lead, accompanied by Aurora, me, and then Øyvin who closed the door behind us.

We followed Torsten down winding tunnels I'd never seen before. They looked similar to all the others I'd been through—gray stone walls and magically lit sconces every few feet—but this one was slightly different, darker. Or maybe it was the fact that as soon as Øyvin passed a light, Torsten twisted his right hand and snuffed it. The darkness at our backs sent a shiver down my spine and the anxiety that'd been riding me earlier, poked at me once more.

We descended deeper and deeper, passing intersections and divergences, never slowing, but always turning out the lights behind us. Fjell Fae scurried into their apartments, several motioning for us to join them, but Torsten waved them off with a grateful nod.

"Where exactly are you taking us?" I asked, careful not to trip over my own feet.

"Somewhere safe," Torsten replied.

"That isn't exactly reassuring," I said as Øyvin grumbled, "More details, Torsten."

A sigh sounded from up ahead. "This is one way to the tombs."

"Dead people? Really? That better not be a sign of things to come."

Aurora snorted, sounding like she agreed.

Torsten cast a look over his uniformed shoulder, his tawny man bun bobbing with the movement. "There's a safe room of sorts down there. Very few individuals have ever been granted access."

"And it's defended?" Øyvin asked, hot on my tail.

"Near impenetrable," Torsten replied as we swept left, into another tunnel.

I was about to open my mouth and ask about the defenses when a howl sounded up ahead. Tiny shards of stone sprinkled across mine and Aurora's heads and we all sucked in an audible breath.

Øyvin pushed past Aurora and I as we brushed the debris off our jackets.

The guys slowly moved forward, balls of light and water forming in their respective hands.

A cracking noise reverberated around us and unwelcome flashbacks from the frozen lake flitted through my mind. Kristoffer's little face as he fell—

Before I could grasp what was happening, Aurora yanked my arm, pulling me back five steps.

The horrific noise grew louder and a table-sized rock came crashing down. Then another. Separating us from the guys.

The next second my vision swam with Øyvin's fear-stricken face disappearing behind boulders and chunks of the mountain. "Len—" His roar was cut short and my heart felt like it exploded into a million pieces.

Where Torsten and Øyvin had stood was a wall of boulders, the largest of which were tall enough to reach my waist.

No. No no no no no no no...

"Øyvin!" My scream ripped through my lungs and echoed through the tunnel. I sucked in a lungful of dusty air and coughed it all back up. "*Øyvin!*"

I couldn't lose him. We'd only just defined our relationship, shared I Love Yous. When I pictured the rest of my life, he was in it, standing beside me. Challenging me. Calling me Trouble with that irresistible tiny smirk curling his lips. Holding me in the quiet moments when we needed each other.

My heart clenched and my hands trembled as I brushed them through my hair, tangling them in the debris-covered strands.

I stepped back and back and back. This couldn't be happening. I blinked once, twice, three times... but the rockfall remained. I'd lost him. At the start of our story, our picture coming into focus, it had come to a crashing halt and blurred. A tear fell across my cheek and I swatted it away as I swallowed the need to cry. To mourn. The three of us, together, had formed not just a bond, but a family. A unit I'd believed to be unstoppable, with men I never wanted to lose.

I can't lose him.

Something touched my shoulder and I flinched, throwing my hand up to bat—

"It's just me," Aurora said. "Breathe."

I nodded and pulled in air through my nose, then sputtered. "Are you okay?"

"Mm-hmm."

The lump in my throat swelled and I looked back at the mound of rock that blocked the tunnel ahead. "We—"

"Lennie!"

My eyes widened and I whimpered at the sound. "Did you hear that?"

"Yes, I did," Aurora replied.

"LENNIE!"

Holy fuck. He was alive.

I scrambled toward the rocks, moving toward the sound of his voice.

"Lennie, up here!"

Following the noise, I pinpointed what he was talking about. In the top right corner of the rockfall was a tiny opening, no larger than a coffee mug. Light streamed through it, sending a subtle ray into the dim and dusty tunnel.

I clambered up onto the bottom boulders, careful with my foot placement. "Øyvin, I'm here." Pressing up onto my tiptoes, my fingers clawing for purchase... I couldn't see. My heart burst. I couldn't reach.

"Are you all right?" Øyvin asked, his voice clearer now that I was close to the gap.

"Yeah. You?"

"Dusty, but fine."

I snorted as another tear fell down my face. "There's an age joke in there somewhere, but I think I'll save it for later."

A chortle sounded from the other side and I wasn't sure if it was from Torsten or Øyvin. "Is Torsten dead?"

"No, he's fine," Øyvin replied. "But I need you to focus. Torsten doesn't have usual Fjell powers. So, he can't move the rocks. We need you to carefully start dismantling the blockade. Can you do that?"

His voice was like a balm to my frayed nerves, slowly easing the shock out of my system. He was fine. He was alive. We were okay.

"Lennie, we need you."

I nodded vigorously. "Yeah, yeah, I can do it."

I would do it. To save him. To save us. To get us to the hiding place Torsten had mentioned.

"Lennie... Trouble. I believe in you."

A scoff shook free from my throat as I climbed down to the dust-ridden floor. "I never thought I'd hear those words from your mouth."

"Enjoy the moment," he replied.

"Will do. Now, please step as far back as possible. I don't want to crush anyone."

"Do it."

I stepped away from the mound of rocks and twisted to Aurora. "You may want to scoot back."

She shuffled backward without any complaint.

Raising my hands, I focused on the top rocks in the barricade. I inhaled deeply and focused on the power in my chest, willing it forward and down my arms as I raised my hands. Aiming my palms at that top rock, I gently pushed my magic toward it and pulled it back. The power latched onto the stone with ease, like a hand reaching out and plucking it. A satisfied squeak left me as the stone moved through the air and I set it down to one side.

I was fucking doing this.

Repeating the movement like a Tai Chi practice, pushing and pulling, picking up one rock after another and moving them aside. Slowly but surely, the opening at the top widened and—

A howl brought my magic to a stop and I dropped my hands. The rock in mid-air came crashing down.

I rushed toward the right side of the barricade and yelled up at the gap, "Øyvin! What's happening over there?"

Please don't be a wolf. Please don't be a wolf. Please don't be a wolf.

"We've got company," he replied.

Fuck.

"Stay there. We'll get through these and come to you..." A beat of silence broke his sentence. "Torsten says it'll take at least ten minutes to get there. Don't move!"

All I wanted to do was rip down this wall. But if they were busy fighting wolves and not focusing on potentially tumbling rocks, then I could get someone hurt. And I couldn't have that. So, for the gazillionth time since moving to Norway, I did as requested. "Don't die!"

The only reply was growls and grunts.

I shuffled back and turned to Aurora.

"We stay here and wait," I said, sounding like Halvar commanding a soldier. Which was some character growth I had not been expecting when I crawled out of bed that morning.

Aurora nodded and brushed her hands over her arms, removing more dust from her now less-than-white jacket.

I glanced around the dim tunnel-turned-cavern we were in. Rock walls surrounded us on all but one side and the single orb-filled sconce flickered like a candle. "Let's get some more light in here."

Holding my trembling hands out in front of me, I called upon my magic, picturing the light we needed. Faster than I'd ever done before, power prickled through me and flooded between my palms, forming a ball of light that crackled and swirled like lightning. All I needed to do was place it into one of the sconces along the wall and keep—

A skittering noise sounded from deeper within the tunnel and my head whipped in its direction.

A light padding of footsteps met my ears.

We weren't alone.

Aurora moved into a defensive position, hands loose at her sides. I followed suit, switching the orb of light to my right hand. My jaw tightened, my knees locked, and my pulse raced. A moment later, the shadows at the end of the tunnel shifted, revealing a big, black wolf.

Dust and detritus skittered around us, and the wall of boulders loomed at our backs. My breathing hitched and my stomach filled my throat again. Aurora panted beside me as neither of us dared to move—unable to escape the figure blocking our path.

The shadow shifted off its haunches and a cracking noise sounded as it transformed, straightened, and stepped into the last vestiges of light.

My heart stopped.

"No one will save you this time, human," Wilhelm said in his human form, his top lip curled into a snarl.

He wasn't wrong. Halvar couldn't save me now, neither could Espen or Øyvin. Aurora and I were quite literally stuck between rocks and an angry puppy with very big teeth. But... unlike the last time I'd been cornered by two of his goons, this time I had my own tricks up my sleeve. And dammit, I wasn't going down without a fight.

I raised my ball of light to the ceiling, swept my leg behind me and braced for impact as I called forth my power and formed it into a short sword. "Here's the thing," I started, willing my light magic to skitter across the stone sword in my hands and pointing the tip in his direction. "I don't need saving." Totally did, but now was *not* the time to dwell on my never-ending unfortunate circumstances.

"Neither do I." Aurora crouched and pulled twin knives from her boots.

Sisterly pride swelled within me as I added, "We can take care of ourselves."

Wilhelm huffed. "That's the problem with you youngsters. You're too naive, too gullible."

What a dick.

"Says the fallen Alpha who couldn't unite his own pack, who wants to stand against his own kind and defect. Tell me, Assface, what kind of leader refuses to listen to his people? His family?" Aurora sucked in a breath, but I didn't hold back. The proverbial gloves were off. "Why the power trip? Mommy drop you on your head when you were a baby? Or no, let me guess, your wife got tired of sucking your cock and you now retaliate by belittling others?"

A low growl ricocheted off the stone walls around us. I tightened my hold on my sword. Yeah, that last one may have taken it too far. Wilhelm apparently agreed as he snapped and crackled back into a wolf. Those wolves last year had scared me, but Wilhelm in his wolf form was straight-up terrifying. Broad paws stomped against the floor, large canines protruded from his jaw, and his thick black coat danced with the shadows.

With a gut-clenching snarl, he lunged.

Wilhelm's maw opened wide as he launched himself through the air, aiming toward my legs. Aurora moved out of the way and I twisted to the right, bringing down my sword to act as a shield and parry away his sharp teeth. He dodged at the last second, narrowly avoiding my blade.

I stepped back, readjusted my position, and braced for his next move.

He spun on us, a low grumble emanating from his chest.

This wasn't good. We couldn't outrun him. Those tunnels wouldn't save us. We had to fight him.

Aurora moved to stab him, but was swatted aside by his large head. Wilhelm growled, saliva dripping from his lips, and refocused his attention on me. He leaned back on his haunches again and I raised my sword, instinctively angling it at his head. I could do this. I had to do this or he'd kill me and probably Aurora too. I winced as he neared, closing my eyes for a millisecond. Which was a grave mistake...

Agonizing pain ripped through my left leg and all the air in my lungs escaped as I dropped my sword and let out an almighty scream. Fire seared my calf as I collapsed onto the cold stone floor, dust and debris clouding around me. I cast my gaze across the tunnel. Wilhelm stood between me and Aurora. His lips pulled back from his teeth and he spat out blood and bits of—

My stomach roiled and I glanced down at my leg, or what remained of it behind the flesh that had been torn to pieces and the blood pooling around me. That was another mistake. Bile rose in my throat but I swallowed it down. I couldn't puke now.

My power swirled within my chest, buffeting against my insides like it could tell I'd been wounded and was panicking on my behalf. I twisted onto my side and leaned on my forearms, panting and groaning through the agony. My vision faded in and out like an old TV turning on and off.

Wilhelm turned slowly, his paw pads featherlight on the floor. This fae wasn't just a shifter, he was some sort of phantom wolf—even if he wasn't spectral. As he set his sights on Aurora, my nerves sparked and the top of my head tingled.

"Come on, Wilhelm," Aurora goaded, settling into a crouched stance, a knife in each hand. In her dusty white coat, she was the light to his dark. "Try your best."

The wolf responded by hurtling toward her, tilting his head and stretching his jaw wide. But Aurora was fucking fast. She dipped and rolled beneath him as he soared over her head. She extended her arms, the twin knives in her clutches sliced into Wilhelm's hind legs and came away scarlet. They both spun and faced each other once more, Wilhelm stuttering his steps. I, on the other hand, couldn't move, I couldn't do a damn thing but watch—my sight growing hazier by the second.

Beads of sweat dappled my forehead as I panted and balled my hands into fists. My magic swirled within me once more, reminding me of its presence, but what the hell could I do? The pain in my leg... Fuck, it hurt. Would I bleed out? Could I? What if— No, don't go there. Would they— *Goddamn, this mind-numbing pain.*

Wilhelm lunged again and Aurora spun in a pirouette befitting a ballerina. She let out a wince as his sharp claw nicked her arm, but she was still standing, participating in this battle that could only end in death or severe injury. I couldn't let that happen though. My breaths grew harder, in and out through my nose, and I ignored the smell of copper in the air.

With his back to me, Wilhelm howled, the noise bouncing and echoing off the stone tunnel around us. Even the magic light I'd created flickered at the sound. He lunged again, and, in a split second, he had her on her back, landing with a thud and groan. Her knives flew from her hands, skittering across the floor and out of reach.

He raised his head and bayed like a beast that had caught its prey.

My heart stopped. Power burned through me and I aimed my trembling hand toward them.

He opened his jaw and went for her neck.

Not today, Satan. Lightning power surged through me, arching my spine as it flew from my palm. The ball of crackling light crashed against his back and wrapped around him like a vice. Wilhelm yowled and collapsed on top of Aurora.

Aurora's screams echoed around us.

My screams joined hers as the power flowed out of me, burning and searing, wholly uncontrolled, but protecting. Doing what it was sworn to do, what I needed to do: protect the fae of the fjell.

My vision blurred and my head throbbed as I dropped my hand to the stone floor. The magic vanished, my eyes shut, and everything went dark. *Please be okay...*

I couldn't feel my left calf anymore. There was only pain as exhaustion took over and delirium set in. All I wanted was my guys. I wanted to curl up in bed with Espen and Øyvin, their arms around me, holding me together. Maybe even a hot cup of coffee from Oddvar's on the bedside table for me to sip on. Yeah, that sounded... That sounded... Fantastic...

105

ØYVIN

After dispatching a trio of wolves, we careened through the tunnels. Blood and dust stained our clothes as Torsten launched orbs of light ahead of us, illuminating our path.

"Down here." Torsten pointed left and I followed his instruction.

Eerie silence rang through the tunnel and the smell of copper singed my nostrils, panic filling my veins. If someone had hurt her, I'd boil them alive and then hand them over to Espen for a brutal burial.

We rounded the corner and my footsteps faltered at the sight before me, my world shattering.

No.

Lennie lay on the floor, her eyes shut, hair splayed around her like a halo, and blood pooling around the lower half of her body.

"Lennie!" I stumbled forward and crashed to my knees, ignoring the sting of pain.

"Shit," Torsten said, scrambling past me. I peered over my shoulder and found Aurora lying by the cave-in, trapped by a large black wolf splayed over her. Torsten's muscles strained as he hauled the singed, dead animal off Aurora. She appeared unharmed, but Lennie...

I looked down at her and my breath stuttered.

Head. Fine.

Chest. Rising and falling in shallow but consistent movements.

Legs... I grit my teeth together and pulled in air through my nose. Her left leg was mangled, torn apart.

"Lennie," I said. "Lennie. Wake up."

She groaned, and I leaned in, brushing my hand across her cheek. I couldn't lose her. She was everything I'd never dared to dream of. Mine. My family.

"Lennie."

"Nibbled," she mumbled.

I huffed. Of course she'd try to make a joke while barely conscious.

Drawing on my magic, I formed a swirling orb of water between my palms. "This will sting."

I didn't want to cause her more pain, but I had to do it. If I didn't, she'd bleed out or get infected.

She hummed. Her eyes still shut. "Bumble bee…"

Shaking my head at her delirious muttering, I tensed and moved the ball of water over her leg. Settling it around—

Lennie's eyes flew open and her fingers scraped against the rocky ground. "HOLY MOTHER FUCKING SHIT BALLS!"

"I need to keep it clean until we get you to a healer." The water would act as a bandage of sorts. It wouldn't stop the bleeding, but would slow it and keep the gnarly wound clean until we could get help. I wasn't a healer by any means, but I'd seen injured soldiers and knew the signs. With how pale she was, we didn't have much time.

"I'm going to pick you up now."

She moved her head in a motion that was neither nod nor shake, but somewhere in between.

"This might hurt too, but we need to get you upstairs."

A sly smile twisted her lips, eyes fluttering closed, and her body went limp. Unconsciousness wasn't a good sign either.

I hoisted her into my arms, carrying her like a princess—her legs hanging over the side. She was going to destroy me if we didn't get to a healer strong enough to save her.

I glanced over my shoulder. The black wolf lay at Aurora and Torsten's feet, their jackets covered in dust and blood. Red stains marred Aurora's wrists as she wiped two bloody knives on her thighs before returning them to hidden holsters in her tall boots. Torsten's bun had come undone, his blondish hair hanging around his clavicles in stark contrast to his gray Fjell Fae uniform. He looked like he'd seen a ghost.

With a nod to the dead wolf, I asked, "Who was that?"

Aurora swallowed. "Wilhelm."

I should've known. Anger roiled within me like a tidal wave ready to destroy everything in its path. At least the mongrel was dead.

"You grab the wolf. I've got Lennie," I commanded.

Torsten nodded. "Of course."

I strode behind the others as they carried the wolf back through the re-lit tunnels. Aurora held onto the rear legs, while Torsten carried the wolf's front legs. The canine dangled between them like a pig on a spit roast. After a minute of walking as quickly as possible, Aurora said, "We're lucky he didn't rip off her leg."

I grunted. "Thank you for stopping him."

She peered over her shoulder. "That wasn't me. She's the one who killed Wilhelm."

What?

Lennie's lips were lightly parted, drawing faint breaths. Her eyes shut, lashes brushing the tops of her cheeks. She looked so harmless like this. Incapable of killing, but... I didn't doubt for a second that she'd tear anyone apart if they threatened something she cared about. It was one of the many things I loved about her.

"How?" I asked.

Aurora kept her focus forward again. "Royal fae magic. Don't know how it works, but it looked like he was being electrocuted from the inside out."

Torsten stutter-stepped and jostled the wolf. "Say that again."

"Zapped from the inside out."

"Wow," he replied and kept moving.

Wow, indeed. I furrowed my brow. I'd only ever heard of monarchs using that type of power. The fact that she'd used it was unfathomable.

"Almost there," Torsten said, interrupting my thoughts.

We rounded yet another corner and the pale blue stone of the throne room entrance came into view, the jagged pieces glinting in the light from the wall sconces. Voices echoed out of the chamber as we darted closer and closer, Wilhelm probably leaving a bloody Hansel and Gretel style trail all the way behind us.

Stepping into the throne room, the space quieted immediately, all eyes trained on us.

106

LENNIE

As I came to again, chatter around us stopped along with the jostling. The crystalline blue of the throne room ceiling blinked down at me and I sucked in a deep breath as my vision blurred at the edges.

A strangled whimper sounded from my left and drew my attention. Espen stumbled over from the dais, his eyes wide, face pale, and the corners of his lips turned down.

"She needs you. Now," Øyvin said, his voice thick with emotion.

Espen nodded as a thump and gasps sounded elsewhere in the room, but my eyes were locked with my fiancé's. He brushed his hand through my hair. "Lay her down over here. Quickly."

The room spun as Øyvin turned, and I clamped my eyes shut until I felt the stone floor against my back.

Hands settled around my knee and I chanced a quick look down. Øyvin removed the layer of water with a grimace, the deep red liquid slowly vanishing into thin air.

"Hold her still," a blurry Espen commanded from where he crouched, and Øyvin knelt beside me, grabbing my wrists. He moved my arms upward and positioned them like football goalposts, elbows bent at a ninety-degree angle.

"I'm sorry, Lennie," Espen said. "This is going to hurt."

Everything felt numb. Whatever Espen was about to do couldn't possibly be that bad, so I mumbled a "mm-hmm" in reply. He'd just magic it better like Heidi did with that Forest Fae soldier last year. I furrowed my brows, trying to remember how that'd gone. There'd been lots of blood... and did two fae hold the man down?

Øyvin tightened his hold on my wrists. "Eyes on me, Trouble."

"That was so much hotter when we were in the shower."

He smirked.

With a feather light touch, Espen assessed the wound and took a deep breath. A soft glow appeared near Espen and fiery pain shot down my calf, a scream ripping from my lips as I bucked. It was like flames themselves wrapped around my leg, burning and knitting the wound shut.

Øyvin leaned down and pressed his forehead to mine. "Keep still." His words were a balm but that was the last thing I wanted to do right now. I wanted to wriggle free of the searing sensation weaving across my leg. I wanted to kick Espen's hands off me, remove them from my knee and ankle—stop the fire incinerating my leg.

Espen gulped like it pained him to see me like this. "A little bit longer."

A tear fell across my right cheek, shortly followed by another on the left. The only thing visible through my watery gaze was an anguished Fjord Fae—his lips locked in a grimace, brow creased.

The burning sensation spiked and I whimpered in response, but didn't move. I wanted this to be over. I wanted to curl up in a ball with my guys on either side of me in a world where a wolf hadn't taken a bite out of my leg and ruined my favorite fuzzy leggings.

"Almost there," Espen panted.

I wanted to go home to the boathouse. I wanted five fucking minutes of peace where trouble wasn't breaking down the door. I wanted the pain to go away and leave me alone.

Øyvin nudged my nose with his, the motion sending another stream of tears to the stone floor. He glanced over his shoulder and a moment later, released my wrists, his lips curving into a gentle smile and the corner of his eyes crinkling. "Well done," he mouthed, sitting back on his haunches.

I wrapped my arms around my torso, giving myself a hug.

Espen appeared on my left and brushed his hand over my head. He swallowed hard and cleared his throat. "Don't ever get injured like that again."

With panted breath and my vision clearing of the dizzying haze and unshed tears, I nodded. There wasn't a chance in hell I'd ever go toe to toe with a wolf again. Suffering one gnarly bite was more than enough, thank you very much.

The throbbing pain slowly eased to an uncomfortable pulse that matched the exhaustion weighing down the rest of my body. "How bad was it?" I asked, my voice raspy.

"Let's just say I'm glad you got here when you did."

I grimaced.

Espen extended his bloodied hands in Øyvin's direction and he swiftly wrapped water around them. A split second later, the pinkish liquid vanished, leaving Espen's hands clean. The Forest Fae looked to Øyvin and asked, "How'd it happen anyway?"

"Tunnel caved in between us. Wolves found us. Took Torsten and I ten minutes of running through other routes to get to Lennie and Aurora."

"Thank fuck you did." Espen brushed hairs off my forehead with his fingertips.

I leaned into his touch and chanced a look at my leg. The skin was red raw and warped in places as if Espen's magic had wrapped and twisted it shut. Several red lines puckered together, overlapping in multiple locations like a diamond-patterned tapestry. "That's going to leave a scar, isn't it?"

Espen sighed. "Yeah..."

Fantastic.

"My entire left side is getting scarred," I huffed. "What, with the lightning one on my arm and now my leg being used as a chew toy."

"Well..." Espen nodded. "That seems to be the—"

"Oh my god," I gasped and smacked their arms. "I could be like Phantom, but instead of the opera, I'd be the phantom of the fjell. With shields for my scars and a mask. Do either of you have a mask kink?"

Snorts sounded around me.

"I think she's gone into shock," Øyvin said.

"I think she's coming out of it actually." Espen tried to hold back a smile, but failed spectacularly. "Will you sing opera, too?"

"I could try."

"Please don't," Øyvin grunted and crossed his arms.

Movement by my feet caught my attention and Trygve—the head Fjell Fae healer—came running over, his apron flapping around his knees, his white blouse sleeves shoddily rolled up above his elbows. "Miss Lennie," he gasped, taking in my scarred leg.

"Another day, another injury, Trygve. You know me."

"Indeed." He cleared his throat. "But you are in good hands."

"I am. Any chance you have some of that fancy scar salve lying around?" The stuff he'd given me for my arm was bottled bliss and had cooled the skin nicely. Hopefully it would work for my leg too.

"I'll see if I can find some once I'm done tending to the others."

"Thank you."

Espen smiled. "We might need a bucket, Trygve."

"I will see to it and have someone bring it to you. Now, I must check on my other patients. I'm glad to see you're doing well." He nodded to all of us and departed in a swirl of herbaceous smells.

As Trygve left, he was replaced by a set of crossed arms, pursed lips, and a braid on the verge of giving up. Aurora glanced at my leg. "You'll live?"

"Looks like it."

She hummed and made to move away—

"Aurora, wait." Now was as good a time as any to apologize. She wouldn't have been put in harm's way if I hadn't ignored her wishes and brought her to Skolvik.

She stopped and blinked at me.

"I owe you an apology." I'd done wrong and needed to own up to that shit... even if it had saved me from being beheaded by Halvar. "I shouldn't have kidnapped you and brought you here without your consent. I regret it, and I'm sorry."

Aurora sucked in a breath and stared at the ceiling. Sweat settled at the nape of my neck. I'd never wanted her to get hurt or put her life at risk. I'd never meant for her to get caught in the crossfire of Wilhelm's anger and wrath. All I'd wanted was to bring the heir home and facilitate a peaceful conversation between her and the Fjell Council.

"I don't forgive you," she replied. "This isn't my home, nor will it ever be. But... I can see why you did it. Halvar looks like he might have a temper-tantrum if things don't go according to plan."

I snorted and bit my bottom lip. That was something we could definitely agree on.

"But, I'm not faultless," she added. "I'm sorry I kidnapped you first."

"I guess we're even then?"

"Let's call it a truce."

"I can work with that."

"Are your boyfriends going to agree?" She raised a single brow and looked between the two fae who were doing their best to pretend they weren't listening to the conversation.

"They'll do as they're told," I laughed in reply.

She wandered off with a chuckle, and I leaned onto my elbows as the guys rose to their feet on either side of me. While she hadn't forgiven me, that interaction went better than expected.

I scanned the room. On the far side of the space, triage stations had been set up with healers flitting between three stations where injured soldiers and Fjell Fae lay on the ground. Trygve flapped between them all, doling out bottles to healers and pressing magic into patients. By the archway—

My breath hitched. To the left of the entryway was a lump of black fur, unmoving but guarded by three soldiers.

Wilhelm.

I swallowed hard and my pulse thrummed. I'd done that.

Staring up at the stubble coating Øyvin's jaw, I whispered, "Is he... dead?"

The guys crouched beside me again, and Espen rested his hand against my upper back, holding me upright.

Øyvin took a deep breath and nodded.

My chest tightened, my lungs constricting as if they'd been bound by barbed wire. "Shit. I didn't mean... I don't know how..."

All I'd wanted was to protect Aurora, protect the fjell.

Øyvin's gaze met mine. "You did what you needed to do to protect yourself and Aurora."

"He's right," Espen added.

"Yeah, but I hadn't meant to kill him." It was an instinctual reaction. I barely felt in control—blinded by pain and the need to protect.

"Whatever magic you used, you did the right thing," Øyvin said.

Espen brushed circles with his hand between my shoulder blades, easing the tension in my muscles. "He wasn't going to stop until he'd removed you from the board in payback for me telling you about us and for having him removed from the Forest Fae Council of Elders."

I sighed and accepted the reality. I'd killed a creature, and while it would take some time to come to terms with, Espen was right. Wilhelm wouldn't have stopped until he got his revenge.

"We all know you're Espen's weakness," Øyvin said, and my gaze flitted between my two guys. "Hurting you, hurts him."

"And you," I mumbled.

Øyvin nodded, his elbows resting on his knees and his hands clasped together. "And me."

He was right. By falling in love with each other we'd forged not only a loving bond, but something that others could target. We'd become each other's weakness, but I wouldn't change that. We were stronger together. The three of us were one unstoppable unit—a trio forged of three fae factions.

They were mine and I was theirs.

The room fell silent and we all looked toward the throne where Halvar took up position in front of the glacial looking chair.

"The wolves have been routed and run out of the mountain. My thanks to you all," Halvar said, his voice booming through the room, grabbing the attention of injured and healers alike. "If you are able, please make your way to the Great Room. The Council has some announcements to make."

That sounded ominous.

Halvar's gaze flicked to me. I gave him a quick salute which earned me a sharp nod in return before he strode from the room with a cadre of soldiers at his back and members of the Council following suit.

I looked to Espen as he brushed his hand through his beard. He'd been with the council and Halvar during all of this. "Do you know anything about this?"

He shook his head, dashing my hopes. "No idea." He looked down at me with a creased brow. "Do you think you can stand and walk to the other room?"

I shrugged. "Worth a try."

I was exhausted and in need of a nap, but I wanted to know what these announcements were.

Rolling onto my right side, I pushed my hands against the floor, lifting myself into an upright position. The room didn't spin and the pain in my leg had subsided to a dull burn, the movement not making anything worse. So, I pivoted my right leg underneath me and rose, keeping most of my weight on my right foot. Espen and Øyvin remained on either side of me, their hands out in front of them ready to catch me should I wobble and fall.

With a deep breath, I settled more weight onto my left leg and the twisting, burning sensation grew worse, but it was more like a bad leg cramp than the absolute agony I'd been in while Espen healed it.

"I've got this," I said, mentally cheering myself on. "Let's go."

Espen looped my arm through his. "Are you sure?"

"Yeah. What's the worst thing that could happen? I've already been bitten by a wolf today."

107

LENNIE

We wandered into the great room, the same ballroom where Freija's birthday party had been held last fall. Fae in all manner of attire, from the gray Fjell Fae uniform, to the traditional looking dresses, to shirts and jeans, were assembled around the cavernous, pale gray room, all looking toward the little platform at the far end where the band had once played.

Sconces lit the curved stone walls, and several orbs of light hung high above our heads as Torsten conjured and launched a few more from near the dais. A low hum of chatter echoed through the chamber, buzzing in anticipation of whatever the Council had to announce.

Halvar stepped up to the edge of the platform, the council members assembled behind him. "Espen Solbakke, Head Guard of the Forest Fae, Lennie Martin and Aurora Johansen, will you step forward please?"

Ah, fuck.

The crowd parted and let us through, forming a large circle around us.

Halvar stared at the fae on my right. "Espen. Members of your faction were killed in our tunnels today, including the pack Alpha. We have an alliance, but I must know, in front of our council and residents of the mountain, was this an official attack?"

Espen sighed, his hands clasped behind his back in a diplomatic posture. "It was not. Wilhem was removed from his post as pack Alpha yesterday by the Forest Fae Council and acted alone."

Murmurs swept through the room as Halvar gave Espen a quick nod.

"Speaking on behalf of the Council, our alliance remains," Espen added. "Wilhelm's actions were neither condoned nor sanctioned by our Council of Elders. You have our sincere apologies for the havoc he has wreaked upon your families."

My heart fractured hearing his words. Of course Wilhelm was wholly to blame for this shit show, but Espen in his role as Head Guard had to make reassurances to his friends.

A Fjell council member shuffled forward a few steps, their frame so much shorter than Halvar. "The wolves have been removed to an anti-chamber of the throne room."

"What *exactly* happened to Wilhelm?" Espen asked with a quick glance to me and Aurora who twitched minutely on the spot. "I was preoccupied when Torsten and Aurora brought him in."

Yeah, stitching me up. We hadn't exactly had time to mention all the details of our run in with the snappy puppy.

"That is why the two of you were called forward too," Halvar said with a nod to me and Aurora. "Perhaps you would care to enlighten us all on what happened?"

I peered over at Aurora. Quirking a single eyebrow, she waved her hand in a motion that said *go ahead.*

I rolled my eyes and took a deep breath. Best to give everyone the Cliff Notes version of today's events. "We were cornered by Wilhelm in his wolf form after a cave in. He attacked, and we retaliated in self-defense, me with my powers and Aurora with her knives. She, like someone else I know"—I gave Halvar a pointed look—"sliced and diced our assailant, and I launched... erm... lightning or royal magic at him when he lunged for her."

Halvar's beard twitched and, in a blink-and-you-miss-it moment, I could've sworn I saw a hint of a smile.

He turned to his daughter. "You were the one who cut his thighs, thereby slowing his movements?"

"Aurora here is apparently good with knives," I chimed in.

She shrugged. "I whittle."

A snort escaped me. "That was a damn sight more than whittling. You carved up the guy's junk."

Another shrug from Aurora was met by winces from the assembled crowd.

"Lennie was compromised. She needed help."

"Thank you," Espen whispered from my other side, and Aurora's lips twisted into a wry smile from my left. "As an act of self-defense," he added, his voice carrying through the large space so everyone could hear, "these actions will not be held against them by the Council of Elders."

"Thank you," Halvar replied.

"The bodies may be claimed and removed from the fjell," a dark-haired council member to Halvar's right said. "We ask that you do so as swiftly as possible."

Espen nodded. "I'll have them removed today."

"Good." Halvar turned his gaze to me. "Aurora, thank you for helping protect the mountain. You and Espen are dismissed."

What? No, they couldn't leave me up here. My heart raced as I stared at the hundreds of people watching. I'd done as requested and brought the heir home to the mountain, but I'd inadvertently brought back some stray dogs too. Dogs with big teeth that had—based on the injuries I'd seen in the throne room and the words spoken by Halvar and Espen—severely injured and killed Fjell Fae. Their families and Halvar were no doubt upset about that turn of events, even if it wasn't my fault that people got injured.

I reached for Espen's arm and he gave my hand a quick squeeze. "It's all right," he said with a soft smile. "He won't harm you. I won't let him."

The former was debatable.

Espen lifted my fingers off his forearm and kissed my hand before retreating back into the surrounding circle, joining Øyvin and Aurora.

I swallowed the massive lump in my throat and looked back at the dais, taking in the figures standing there. This did not bode well for me.

Halvar straightened, his voice projecting across the cavernous room. "As Freija's royal magic is now split between both of us"—gasps broke out in the crowd—"and you're a demi-fae with both Fjell Fae magic and that of a royal, the Council has deemed you of great importance. Indeed, the mountain itself was unwell with you away." My heart beat faster than a camera on sport mode and I caught people nodding out of the corner of my eye.

"With the heir having respectfully declined to take the throne," Halvar continued, "it is the Council's opinion that another leadership system be put in place. One that will be council led, should the Fjell Fae deem it so. Council members have been discussing this option with residents for the past few weeks. So, Fjell Fae, how do you vote?"

The room rumbled with movement and murmurs, and the gathered masses settled onto one knee, bowing their heads.

My jaw fell open and I looked around at their version of democracy. Nobody objected. Several hundred fae took a knee, choosing this new governing system. The only people who remained standing were Øyvin, Espen, and Aurora.

"The people have spoken," Halvar boomed and raised his arms.

The crowd rose to their feet once more, their gazes flitting between me and the folks on the dais.

"Now that's settled..." Halvar locked his gaze with mine and raised a single eyebrow.

My heart hammered in my chest and I sucked in a breath. *Oh shit, oh shit, oh shit...*

"Lennie Martin, demi-fae, resident of Skolvik, we offer you the position of Deputy Head Guard, a role that has not been filled for centuries, but is befitting of your powers and importance to the Fjell."

Fuck me. This was their plan B? Create a council-led government and add me to their roster? Had they met me? Chaos-incarnate over here.

Crossing my arms, I narrowed my eyes at Halvar. "What exactly does that entail?"

"You have now proved your worth and willingness to protect us. So, you will be an official member of the Fjell Fae Council, serve as a commander, and swear an oath to protect all Fjell Fae."

My eyes widened at the gargantuan weight of those tasks. That was a lot of responsibility. Hundreds of fae watched me like a deer caught in the proverbial headlights as I looked around, the *Jeopardy* theme song playing in my head. *No pressure.* Rolling my shoulders, I took a deep breath in an attempt to calm my pounding heart.

Here I was, standing before a community of fae, having been asked to take up a position of authority. How ironic. I'd never done well with authority figures and now they were asking me to be one. How did that Shakespeare quote go? Something about thrusting greatness?

I looked between Halvar and the assembled council members. "Are you sure about this?"

They all nodded.

Halvar tilted his head but withheld any sign of emotion from his facial features. "Are you rejecting the position?"

Was I rejecting their offer? With everything that had happened recently I knew they needed Freija's power—now my power—near the mountain to keep things stable and protected. That degree of tying me down to something was new and novel, definitely forcing me to remain in Skolvik. Then again...

I peered over my shoulder to my guys at the edge of the circle around me. One a grumpy and protective asshole. The other a bubbly ray of sunshine that cared deeply for everyone around him. I'd already committed to them. I'd even committed to a part-time job at Oddvar's this summer. In so many ways, I was already part of this community. Already swept up in the magic of this world. And I loved those two fae... would be marrying them, not just for immigration purposes.

I had no intention of going anywhere else. I'd traveled all over the world, from the dizzying tops of Machu Picchu, to the crystal waters of Croatia. I'd seen so much... And, yet, this right here, being tied to this place was so much more important than the freedom to see the world.

This was my new home. And it needed protecting.

Using these powers for good, to help the people of the fjell and the surrounding fjord region felt right. I may have started by taking photos of the landscape, but now I had the ability to protect it from harm. To protect these people and their secret. To protect my new family.

I wrung my hands and rubbed my right thumb over my engagement ring.

It wasn't a hard decision.

"Do I get a badge?"

The council scrunched their faces in confusion and Halvar rolled his eyes.

"No, but I'll get you a hat," Halvar replied.

I smiled at our inside joke. "Deal."

108

LENNIE

A few weeks later, the house was quiet, with both Espen and Øyvin called in to work—the former back at his job with the local police station, and the latter beneath the surface of the fjord. With the boathouse to myself, I'd planned a quiet evening with the TV. Grabbing a hot mug of cocoa and wearing my comfiest sweatpants and sweater, I settled on the couch beneath a blanket.

While flicking through the movie options for the third time, my phone dinged, signaling the arrival of a text. Setting aside my drink with a huff, I swiped my phone off the coffee table, unlocked it, and checked to see who it was from. The guys and I didn't usually text much while they were working—I was trying to be respectful of their time and work—but every so often I'd get cute little messages from Espen telling me that he missed me. Those always sent my heart fluttering and sometimes devolved into something akin to sexting. So, my pulse was racing when I opened the text and found...

Andrew: Incoming!

I shook my head and furrowed my brow at the odd message in the group chat with my three older brothers. What the fuck was he talking about?

Lennie: Incoming, what?

Ryan: Funny! That wasn't a knock-knock joke.

Jared: lol

What the hell was going on? And what sort of inside joke were they sharing? Had I missed something? I started typing out a reply when a knock sounded at the front door, followed by a peeling ring from a doorbell I didn't know we had.

Wrenching the warm blanket off my legs, I flung my phone onto the sofa. I'd deal with my brothers once I'd dealt with whoever had stopped by.

Wandering across to the little foyer, I narrowly avoided tripping over the pile of shoes. They annoyed the shit out of Øyvin, but at least the snow boots were in a tray so they didn't leave puddles on the wood floors.

I opened the door and my stomach fell to the floor, my eyes bugging out of my head. There, on the doorstep, beaming from ear to ear, were all three of my older brothers with duffel bags slung over their shoulders.

"What the fuck?" The words slipped from my mouth on a long exhale as my two worlds collided.

"Language, Lennie," Andrew said, his blond hair in complete disarray compared to his usual coif.

"You gonna let us in or what?" Jared asked, his dark brown hair half-hidden by a wool beanie.

"H-how did... How did you get out here?" None of them answered my question as they pushed in, not interested in waiting in the cold a moment longer, and dumped their stuff beside the shoes. I shut the door behind them, then spun and fell against it. All feeling in my knees started to disappear as two of them failed to remove their boots, leaving gritty blobs of water in their wake. Øyvin was going to have a conniption. "*Why* are you here?"

Jared scoffed and headed straight for the refrigerator, hunting for snacks like this was our parents' house.

Andrew pulled off his shoes and set them neatly beside his bag, while Ryan popped a squat on the piano bench, stretching his arms as if he was preparing for a workout.

"What are you talking about, Lennie? I called you weeks ago and you agreed to a sibling ski vacation," Andrew explained, before surveying the living quarters with his hands on his hips.

"No, you didn't," I countered. When had I'd last spoken to my brother? Surely, I would've remembered if I'd spoken to him.

"You did sound busy, may have even said as much given how you practically rushed through the call, but you agreed to the last-minute trip."

"I don't..." I trailed off as a tiny light bulb went off, shattering inside my brain as I recalled when we'd last spoken. I'd been trying to bundle Aurora into the car in Alvdalen and attempting to make a hasty getaway before she could escape. I pressed my palm across my forehead and groaned. I *had* agreed to the trip.

"Well, no take-backs as we're here how," Andrew said, his voice as warm as his brotherly smiles.

I pushed my hair behind my ears and straightened up. He was right. They were here now. In my house. In Norway. Where I lived with two fae. What could possibly go wrong?

Jared wandered past me and took a bite out of an apple before throwing himself onto the sofa, his long arms and legs spreading out in exhaustion. "Nice ears by the way, didn't realize it was Halloween."

My heart stopped beating and I gingerly brushed my hand over my right ear. Fuck me sideways, my ears were out!

"It's... uh... it's..." I swallowed hard, desperately trying to come up with an excuse. I flipped my hair back over my ears and blurted, "Øyvin has a fairy kink."

"Gross!"

"Evelyn!"

"Wow." Jared waved his apple in the air, the core already visible on one side. "I did *not* need to hear that."

"You three are the ones who just showed up unannounced! What if I was in a compromising position?" I set my hands on my hips, my breathing steadying even though my heart was racing a mile a minute. *Sorry, Øyvin. Hope that bus didn't hurt too much after I threw you under it. Beep, beep.*

Andrew shook his head and pinched the bridge of his nose. "Technically not unannounced. We spoke about this weeks ago. How could you forget?"

"More importantly," Ryan piped up, narrowing his eyes at me. "Where are your Vikings? We better *not* have interrupted something."

"They're at work for a little while longer," I explained.

"Can you please take those off, then?" Jared pointed his apple at my head. "We don't need a reminder that our baby sister has—"

Ryan made a gagging noise, cutting him off. "Don't say it."

"Fine." I lifted my hands in the air. "Just... nobody move."

I scurried past the kitchen to the bathroom and slammed the door shut behind me. I'd have to make this quick, pretend I was removing prosthetics. Focusing on the magic swirling in my core, I pulled on some of it and pictured a magical hat being placed over my head, hiding away the pointy bits. My reflection in the bathroom mirror morphed as the power hid the evidence of my new demi-fae-ness. I was glad for all the ear training we'd done over Christmas and the time since then that I'd had to perfect the magic. While it was by no means easy, it came to me a lot quicker than it used to. And right now, I was grateful for that.

Ears hidden, I yanked open the bathroom door and strode through the kitchen area, finding my brothers where I'd left them. Miraculously, they'd all listened when I'd asked them not to move.

"Okay," I said, coming to a stop between the kitchen space and the sofa that marked the start of the living room area. Time to triage. "Let's figure this out, shall we?"

"By the way, Jennifer's pregnant. You're going to be an aunt again," Jared announced nonchalantly before taking another bite of his apple.

"That's wonder— Hang on. You left your *pregnant* wife at home alone?!" My emotions swung from elated to WTF in under two seconds. Jared was the most introverted of all the Martin siblings, and as kind and caring as Andrew was, but sometimes I wondered what went on in that head of his.

"It's only for a week." He waved the apple core. "She'll be fine."

My brain caught on his words, my heart careening to a stop. "You're here for a week?"

"Yes," Andrew said. He glanced around the room with his brow furrowed like he was analyzing the space for safety concerns. Typical father of two behavior. "Although, when you agreed to let us stay, I thought you actually had room. This looks like a one-bedroom. We can find a hotel," he added, clearly not having done his usual degree of research before booking this trip.

"Not possible. The main lodge is closed for the season," I countered.

Andrew furrowed his brow and brushed his hand across his chin. "Really?"

"Yes, really. Skolvik isn't a skiing town. Except for this one guy that skis through the village every day wearing a tight bodysuit that hugs all the wrong places. We cater to summer cruises and hikers out here."

"Any rentals then?" Andrew asked.

I nodded. "A friend might have room for you."

"Great."

I hung my head and ran my palms across my temples. Damn me for not paying attention on the phone. Now I'd have to call in another favor with Solveig and hope she had room at her house.

I let out a long sigh and straightened up. "You've all gone mad. You've become a dunce who leaves his *pregnant* wife for a week-long vacation." I pointed to Jared before motioning to Andrew. "And you've suddenly gone lax on your planning and follow-up."

Andrew beamed. "I'm trying to be spontaneous."

I ignored him with a shake of my head and turned to Ryan who was smirking by the piano. "And, let me guess, you're here for the booze?"

His smug grin widened. "I've heard Aquavit is amazing."

"Trust me." I huffed, stroking my hand across my neck, memories of fire-breathing invading my mind. "It's not."

"Don't worry, Lennie," Andrew started, his usual calm voice easing my nerves. "We'll figure out a place to crash and have a great week together."

I was about to remark on how there was too much testosterone in the house, when the front door opened.

Øyvin stepped in—thankfully wearing his usual jeans and cream-knit sweater and not his uniform—his eyes wide and a bewildered look plastered across his features. My brothers, on the other hand, were being childish little kink-shamers who needed to keep their damn mouths shut. Which was wishful thinking, especially with Ryan present, but still, a woman could hope. All three looked like they were struggling to keep it together—with Andrew pursing his lips, Ryan investigating the music sheet on the piano, and Jared snickering into a throw pillow.

"What's going on?" Øyvin asked, his voice straining to not vault into a higher volume as he turned to me. "Why are your brothers here?"

"Hi..." I said with a smile, clasping my hands behind my back. "Welcome home. Here's the deal—"

"She fucked up," Ryan interjected, and I gave him the middle finger in response just as the front door swung open again.

"Ah, hello guys. A family reunion I see," Espen said as he walked into the boathouse and shucked off his shoes and police jacket. He looked at me, his amber-colored eyes full of warmth and joy. "Why didn't you tell us they were coming?"

I shook my hands above my head. "I didn't know!"

"Well, this does provide the perfect opportunity to go out to dinner and properly celebrate with your family." Espen pointed to the engagement ring on my finger and hell broke loose.

All three brothers gasped, their eyes bugging out of their heads.

"Evelyn, are you engaged?"

"Are you pregnant, too?" Jared asked just as Ryan said, "Who's the daddy?"

I gave them both a deadpanned look and rolled my eyes. "I'm *not* pregnant," I retorted, withholding the fact that I was currently on my period.

"Why didn't you tell us you were engaged? Or is this recent?" Andrew crossed his arms before sucking in a breath. "Have you told Mom and Dad?"

Espen bit his bottom lip and did his best not to laugh, while Øyvin tilted his head and narrowed his eyes at me.

I wiped my hands across my cheeks, wishing I could turn back the clock by thirty minutes and hide underneath the blanket on the sofa. I'd spent the past few weeks since the attack on the mountain trying to figure out how to tell my family about the engagement. This was decidedly *not* the family video call I'd had in mind.

"I can explain."

EPILOGUE

HALVAR

She had her eyes.

I never thought I'd see them again.

Never thought I'd see our daughter after delivering her to Alvdalen all those years ago.

It was a safety measure, a way to ensure no one tried to take her or kill her. She was our weakness. The one thing that truly spoke of our bond, our love, our union, and it broke our hearts that she was safer away from us. Aside from Lennie's magic, this young lady was the only piece of Freija that remained on earth.

She had her mother's eyes, and I couldn't look away. "Thank you for joining me. I have something I'd like to show you before you leave."

"Sure." Aurora shrugged, peering around the council chambers like this wasn't a burden on her time.

After the debacle with the wolves, she'd agreed to stay for a week to learn more about her own powers. So far, she spent her days training with my soldiers and her nights at Espen's cabin, which he'd kindly offered to her for the duration of her stay. While I knew she didn't want to stay with us in the fjell, I was glad she wanted to take some time to train with us. If anything, it would keep her safe over in Alvdalen.

I nodded and motioned her to follow me into the tunnels skirting past the Royal chambers, residences, and deeper into the mountain.

"There is something you need to see as a royal—"

"I don't want—"

"I know," I said, interrupting her by raising my hand, too. She'd made her choice, and just because we were related by blood didn't mean I was her family. If she wanted a relationship with me, she was welcome to it, but I had no illusions on who her true family was. She belonged with the pack of Forest Fae, if that's where she was happiest. I wouldn't come between her and them. "But, as a Fjell Fae of royal lineage you have a right to know this information."

"Sounds ominous," she muttered, strolling beside me.

I tried not to roll my eyes.

"Where are we going exactly?"

"The royal tombs."

She screeched to a halt. "I don't want to visit my mother." Her voice was flat and the look in her eyes was one of caution.

"We will walk past her." The words stung in my mouth, and I lowered my voice. "What I need to show you lies beyond the tombs."

"All right." She shrugged again, looking more like she wanted to get this over with and back to her friends and family. I couldn't blame her, but she had a right to know, and I wasn't going to be the one to withhold this from her. I'd withheld enough from her already in her twenty years. And, most importantly, Freija would've wanted to share this with her one day.

We continued further into the mountain. The temperature dropped the deeper we went, the rugged stone walls turning from light-gray to dark. Sconces dotted the tunnel walls every few meters, lighting our way. Fjell Fae of all kinds passed us, nodding to me and staring at Aurora with confusion and curiosity. No doubt talking about her resemblance to her mother. If only Aurora had had a chance to know her mother. But Freija had been right to hide the pregnancy with a magical mirage gifted from the ancestors, and then keep our child hidden away. After the battle during her birth, we both knew it was safer to do so.

"What do you know of the fjell and fae history?" I asked, hoping her guardian had at least taught her something about us even if it was generalizations.

"The basics. Fjell Fae protect the mountains, hold them upright, can create rocks," she rattled off, having done the latter all week with my soldiers.

"And fae history?"

"Is this a lesson or is there a reason for all the questions?"

Ancestors help me, she was definitely mine.

I clasped my hands behind my back and ignored her remark. "You likely know that Skolvik is considered the birthplace of the Fae."

She huffed and nodded, the light catching on her shiny hair. "Yeah, that old rumor."

I let out a long sigh as we turned into the cool and dry anti-chamber to the tombs. Swallowing hard, I continued. "It's not a rumor. It is a fact."

Her eyes widened and she let out a surprised little noise.

At that moment two guards stepped forward, their gray Fjell Fae uniform capes fluttering around their elbows. "Sir," they both said with a nod, resting their hands on the stone swords slung from the belts at their hips.

"At ease."

They did as they were commanded, adjusting their feet slightly and taking up the triangular position, hands behind their backs. Aurora, meanwhile, remained quiet and observant, her gaze flitting over everything.

We passed the soldiers and entered the royal tomb, separated from the other tombs that lay on the other side of the hallway, through the stone mirage sealing it off. Twenty past monarchs, and their family members that had been deemed worthy of such a burial, lay in neat rows. Each stone tomb had an effigy atop it with the fae's likeness. As we wandered through, I kept my eyes off the most recent addition to my right. Hands clenched behind my back, I aimed for the rear of the cavern-like room, where thick pillars of stone had been carved out of the mountain, seemingly holding it aloft.

Reaching the back of the space, we drew to a stop before a wall covered in a carving of a large mountain, its peak dusted with snow, and stars all around it. At the base were swirls of water and on either side was a large tree with branches so long they reached out onto the adjoining walls like vines snaking around the room. Beside the roots of the tree on the right was a carving of a wolf, baying at the starry sky. The canine was added to the mural about a thousand years ago when the Forest Fae King Olaf had paid a visit and asked for help.

With Aurora off to the side behind me, I placed my palm against the center of the mountain, pressing my power into it and requesting entrance. Silvery light spread through the carving, bringing it to life, waking it up.

A small gasp sounded behind me, but I didn't turn nor move my hand until the magic had filled every single line and crevice of the picture. When every part of the mural glowed, a grinding noise filled the cool air and the mountain part of the etching pivoted inward like a door.

I stepped through first and Aurora hesitantly followed, her footsteps light against the quartz-stone floor.

"What is this place?" Her eyes widened as she peered around the room in awe.

The space glowed like the inside of an iceberg, the blues and whites shimmering as if lights moved within the walls. Glossy pillars held the ceiling, while the walls looked similar to the history cave we had elsewhere in the mountain. Unlike that room, though, the carvings in here were far older and of a time that hadn't existed for eons on this earth.

"While the Fjord Fae and Forest Fae have the waters and forests to protect from pollution and harm," I explained, "we, the Fjell Fae, have yet another obligation. We are sworn not only to protect the mountain and its inhabitants, but to protect this, The Temple of the Fae. The birthplace of our kind." Only those with royal magic or head guards had access to the temple. While select soldiers and the Council knew of its existence, it was purposefully a small number of people in order to protect the space from threats.

Aurora's eyebrows rose to meet her hairline. "And you're sharing this with me?"

I took a deep breath and swallowed the lump in my throat. "Because your mother would've wanted you to know." It was true. While Freija hadn't spoken of her much, she longed for the day when she could share the mountain's secrets with our daughter. "And I'm curious to see how the ancestors will react to you declining your title."

She stilled, but didn't flinch at my words. "What do you mean by that?"

"I mean, this is where you would have come to receive your powers once you accepted your place as Queen of the Fjell." That time she flinched. "I do not recall ever having an heir decline, so I'm curious to see what will happen."

I nodded to the plinth at the back of the room. Aurora's gaze drifted to it warily. The sky-blue quartz pedestal rose from the matching stone at our feet reaching the height of a tall table. Nothing sat atop the small square surface which was chipped at three corners, but the glossy piece was carved with intricate swirls and designs that were far older than I. It was a language that hadn't been spoken in over a millennium, maybe even two.

"When an heir..." My throat tightened. I couldn't say the words, couldn't mention the loss of the monarch. "When a Fjell heir takes the throne, part of the private ceremony is to come here and receive the magic of the prior monarch, bestowed from the ancestors. From what I've been told by those I've served, in what information they have told me"—her mother told me everything—"the heir comes here and receives all the magic that their predecessor had, plus anything that might be required at the time."

Aurora huffed and crossed her arms. "And this only applies to the Fjell, not Fjord, Fire, or Forest monarchs?"

I shook my head. "We do not know for sure. I assume there is a similar process... unless there's something they're not telling me." It wouldn't be surprising if the past monarchs had kept information to themselves. Those three corner chunks of the pedestal had been missing from the fjell forever, and it was long suspected that the other factions each had a piece. "What I do know is that this cave and the magic contained herein was our birthplace and a location monarchs have visited in the past for greater assistance from the ancestors."

"So, you want to use me as a test subject?" Aurora asked.

"There have been a lot of firsts in this mountain recently. My hope is that it hasn't thrown off the delicate balance of magic."

"And how exactly are we supposed to find out?"

I nodded at the pedestal. "You place your palm on that."

She snorted and shook her head like I'd lost my mind.

"It won't hurt you…" I hoped.

"Put *your* hand on it then."

I grit my teeth and crossed my arms, taking a step back from the whole situation. "I'm not the heir."

She blinked twice. "You've done it before, haven't you?"

Pursing my lips, I let out a huff through my nose. She was right. I had. Freija had snuck me down here one night, testing my patience and teasing me. Then she challenged me to do it. I'd argued, she'd rolled her eyes, next thing I knew I'd smacked my hand atop the podium. The thing zapped me and I'd pulled back my palm only to find a red mark in the middle of it, as if the ancestors were scolding me for touching something I was merely sworn to protect, not interact with.

"You did, didn't you?" Aurora's lips curled into a smile and my heart clenched. She had her mother's smile, too. One that looked like she was hiding a secret and wouldn't dare share it with you unless you could guess it correctly.

"I did," I conceded. "It merely zapped me."

"And you think shoving your daughter's hand on there is going to do something different?"

"You're Freija's daughter, too. I doubt the ancestors will harm you."

"Are you sure about that?"

No. But I'd destroy anything that harmed this girl. "Try it and see."

She rolled her eyes once more, but stepped up to the plinth. The lights within the walls swirled, as if the magic within them watched us. Taking a deep breath, she stretched her hand over the pedestal and gingerly set it down.

All the oxygen in my lungs stopped moving, waiting to see what would happen. The shimmering lights in the wall picked up speed, like glitter running in circles around us. Silence grew, her eyes narrowed, and my heart beat like I was on a damn battlefield, ready to strike at a moment's notice.

Aurora slowly removed her hand from the top and flexed her fingers.

"Anything?" I asked.

She furrowed her brow and shook her head. "Nothing. Absolutely nothing at all."

I sighed and brushed my hand over my beard. I was worried that might happen. It further solidified mine and the Fjell Council's theory.

"Great. So, the ancestors are okay with me staying in Alvdalen." It was both a question and a statement.

"It would seem so. But it certainly matches my theory."

She gave me a look as if to say, *"which is?"*

"Freija illegally transferred *all* her magic into me"—I tilted my head briefly to one side—"some of which went to Lennie. Which means, there is none of her magic to be gifted on to you. Not until Lennie and I die, and the magic returns to the ancestors for redistribution." Which I had no plans to do any time soon. There was only one fae remaining on this planet that could potentially overpower me, and thankfully, he lived on an island over a thousand kilometers away.

"Okay." Aurora gave me a blank look, and I shook my head. She was as verbose as I was at her age.

"Thank you for coming down here and trying, though," I replied.

"Sure."

"Let me escort you back to the entrance. I'm sure your pack is anxious for your return to Alvdalen." I motioned toward the exit and she followed without any hesitation. "Promise me you will never tell anyone about what you have seen today."

She nodded. "I promise. And yeah, Marius doesn't like me being away from the pack for too long," she replied as we walked past Kings and Queens, ancestors that she'd never learned about and probably never would.

"And this... Marius..." I couldn't believe the words about to come out of my mouth, but I couldn't stop them either. "Is he your... partner?"

She grew quiet, but her breathing stuttered as we passed the tomb guards. "It's... complicated."

I sighed. It always was.

"Halvar..." she muttered and I reduced my pace as we wound further into the tunnels.

"Yes?"

She stopped and turned, her eyebrows drawn together. "Why exactly did she hide me?"

"To keep you from harm."

"I guessed as much."

"Heirs are born with targets on their heads," I said. "You were born during a tumultuous time. War had been brewing in the south and Freija's best friend, Queen Ragnhild, died in the ensuing battle. Freija feared that unrest would come to Skolvik. With everything that has occurred over the past two decades, I'm glad you were safe in Alvdalen."

"Now that I and more people know about"—she waved at herself and then me—"will that target increase?"

I certainly hoped not, but we would always need to be careful. "Word will no doubt spread, but if you keep a low profile and continue practicing your magic, you should remain unharmed."

Her head bobbed and she pursed her lips.

As we were on the subject matter of future plans, I cleared my throat and motioned between us. "How do you wish to proceed?"

She shrugged and twitched her nose. "I appreciate knowing who you are and who she was. But my life isn't here."

"Agreed."

"So, I'm going to head home to Alvdalen."

I straightened. "I accept that. But, if you ever need anything—whether it be a safe haven or a legion to route your enemies—you may always call on us."

A snort escaped from her and her lips quivered into a momentary smile. "Thank you."

With a nod, I took two more steps down the tunnel.

"One more question," Aurora said. I came to a stop once more and faced her. "Lennie stunned me when she kidnapped me and blasted Wilhelm to death."

I grimaced at the tidbit Lennie had no doubt purposefully left out of her tales of searching for Aurora.

"How much Royal Fjell Fae power does she have?" Aurora asked.

My jaw tensed. I was hoping nobody else had noticed. Torsten had spotted it the first day they'd trained together. It wasn't surprising that Lennie's magic was strong since it came from Freija, but it had shocked the light-wielding fae. I'd noticed it when she'd drawn that sword in the forge and again in the throne room, power sparking and dancing across the blade. Then there was the death blow she'd delivered to the wolf—a tactic I'd only ever seen monarchs use in war. I doubted Lennie fully understood what was happening or what she was doing.

My lungs expanded and I exhaled the truth. "More than she knows."

The Fae of the Fjell

110

LENNIE

That damn cruise ship was back. A year after it had abandoned me, the last ship of the season loomed large in the harbor as some of its guests sauntered past me in their tour group.

I leaned against the side of Oddvar's café, the white-painted wood siding biting into my bare shoulders that lay exposed thanks to the tank top weather that graced us today. Taking a long sip of my morning coffee, I tilted my face to the sun, enjoying the last rays of summer.

August in Norway was absolute perfection. The village was decorated with a myriad of colorful flowers spilling out of window boxes outside the main street storefronts. Signboards littered the roads and walkways, welcoming everyone to the different establishments. Wispy white clouds dotted the bright blue sky, the verdant greens on the mountainsides practically sang with euphoria, and the water—Øyvin's blessed fjord—reflected all of it like a shiny plate of glass.

"Skolvik fjord is one of the deepest fjords in the country," a little thing with an English accent said as she walked backward at the front of the passing tour group. She waved a triangular red flag, the white cruise logo emblazoned on it mocking me. "The fjord is 1308 meters deep. Or, as the locals say"—she giggled to herself—"fifty-seven trolls deep!"

I snorted. "More like fifty-seven sexy trolls."

An entire population of fae creatures called this place home, my demi-fae-self included. These tourists had no idea that two worlds collided here, living *mostly* in harmony side by side.

The group meandered on, and a bell tinkled behind me.

"Lennie?" Oddvar's gravelly voice sounded from the doorway. I spun and found the septuagenarian leaning out the door, his bushy gray eyebrows waving at me. "I need you back inside."

I gulped down the remainder of my delicious bean nectar. "On my way."

Oddvar popped back into the café, and I followed his cardigan-clad, short frame. No matter the weather, Oddvar was always in some form of knitwear—like a hardy fisherman who would never give up the lifestyle and was perpetually ready for a stormy day.

The bell above the door rang as I entered the building. Contented customers' chatter filled the air as they munched away on their lunches, and the sweet, sweet smell of coffee permeated the brightly lit room. Summer was almost over in the little village of Skolvik, but the tables at Oddvar's Café teemed with the last of the cruise ship tourists visiting the fjords like I'd done a year ago. Except now I worked here and was a demi-fae with magical powers, instead of a human tourist who missed her cruise ship.

We strolled behind the counter, and I put my used mug in the industrial dishwasher, shutting the door with a metallic clunk. Smiling softly, I donned my khaki apron and set to work.

I stroked a finger over one of the chrome knobs on the fancy Italian espresso machine. "Hello, Robertina, you gorgeous, sexy bea—"

"Stop talking to the machines," Oddvar groused from behind me.

I ignored his grumbles and winked at the machine. "Are you going to be good for me today?" I whispered, keeping my back to the surly Norwegian who was busy preparing a customer's hot tea. Robertina didn't reply, but then again, she never did. Was I crazy for talking to inanimate objects? Probably. But over the past few months working here I'd found the nicer I was to the machine, the better she performed for me. Same theory as talking to plants—keep them happy and they'll respond in kind with excellent growth and performance.

With everything on my plate this week, including my family in town, I really needed her to be kind. Said plate happened to be full of my wedding to one dapper and bubbly Forest Fae by the name of Espen Solbakke, with our partner and third member of our relationship, Øyvin Håland, set to officiate.

"One cappuccino," Oddvar said in Norwegian. My hearing juju still worked great, but this one I'd understood without the magical tinkering. Ever since Oddvar had offered me the part-time summer job at the café, I'd been voraciously studying the Norwegian language, picking up as much as I could before my employment began. There'd been a slight dip in studies while searching for the Fjell Fae heir last winter, but I'd resumed as soon as that debacle was over with. Now, I could understand most of the words spoken in and around the café, including people's orders. It was as if the more Norwegian I learned and could comprehend, the less my hearing magic stepped in.

"*En cappuccino,*" I replied in Norwegian, and set to work making the hot drink. Tamping down the grinds, flicking the knobs on the machine, the steady movements of making coffees had become a rhythmic dance routine that I thoroughly enjoyed. And seeing the looks on customers faces when they sighed with contentment at that first sip made it all worthwhile.

I set the completed drink at the counter, grinning at the woman with short strawberry-blonde hair who picked it up. Her T-shirt said "I Heart Trolls" across the front, no doubt from the gift shop down the road.

"Lennie," an older feminine voice yoo-hooed from across the room. I wiped my hands on the tea towel tied in the waist belt of my apron and peered around.

Solveig waved at me from a four-person table by the front windows, two of the other seats occupied by her friends, Jorunn and Dagny.

Sauntering around the counter, I approached the white-haired trio by the sun-kissed window. "Can I get you anything else ladies? The sandwiches okay?"

"Oh, yes, my dear. Lunch was wonderful as always." Solveig smiled brightly, her short hair perfectly styled. The other two nodded in agreement, their empty plates sprinkled with crumbs. "But we were wondering why you're working today?"

"Shouldn't you be taking the day off to get ready?" Dagny pulled up the sleeves on her lightweight striped pink cardigan, the color matching the lipstick stain on Jorunn's cup.

"My mother and Espen's sister, Ingrid, have been handling all the arrangements," I replied. "I was told to get out of their way." I'd taken that wish and scampered out of Espen's cabin as swiftly as possible earlier this week. The two of them were like Pinterest on steroids. They'd even had video calls this spring to discuss wedding details. While I'd helped out here and there, and made decisions between suggested color palettes, this whole thing was down to them. And I didn't really mind.

"Well, we look forward to tomorrow," Jorunn said. She must have visited the hairdresser's yesterday as her bob was sharper than usual. "We've had our dresses picked out for months."

"Awww." I placed my hand on my heart. These three really were some of my favorite villagers. While they gossiped to no end, they'd always shown me kindness. "You're all wearing big fluffy ball gowns, yes?"

The trio snickered, leaning back in their chairs, as the bell above the front door rang.

"Solveig was considering stripper heels," Jorunn said.

Solveig's mouth fell open and her eyes widened. "I was not!"

Jorunn cackled at her own joke, wiping a tear from the corner of her eye.

"That would be dangerous considering the ceremony is outside my cabin," a familiar male voice said and a hand settled against my lower back.

My shoulders relaxed, and I leaned into the pressure, welcoming the warmth at my side.

"You know I wouldn't wear those things, Espen. I'd roll an ankle going up that hill," Solveig said.

Espen rested his free hand on the police utility belt around his waist, his usual rain jacket replaced for the season with a black T-shirt with *politi* written across the left breast in bold silver letters. "I know, I know."

Dagny pulled her glasses half-way down her nose and peered over the rim. "Would you consider carrying her if she did, though?"

Espen smiled. "For you three, anything."

The trio swooned.

"Now, if you don't mind, I need a word with the bride."

They shooed us away with little grins, lapping up the loved-up haze that'd settled over the village in the run-up to our nuptials... or maybe that was the blur of activity that was happening all around me that I could barely keep up with.

Espen planted a kiss on my cheek and steered me back behind the counter, not daring to step a foot over the bright, white line on the floor and incur Oddvar's wrath.

"I just came to check on you," the Forest Fae said. He brushed his hand through his hair that he'd recently had trimmed in preparation for the wedding. It still hung long on top and was shorter along the sides, but he'd taken enough off the front that it wasn't constantly in his eyes.

I set my hands on my hips. "I'm fine."

He quirked a brow. "When a woman says those two words, it usually means the opposite. And when that woman also happens to be you, it usually means you're thinking hard about something or preparing a prank against Øyvin."

Shaking my head at him, I reached out and brushed my palm across his neatly trimmed beard. "I'm doing exceptionally well and having a decent day at work."

"Only decent?"

I rolled my eyes. "It got better when you walked in."

He gave me a beaming smile, and something fluttered in my stomach at the sight.

"Now, is there something I can get for you or were you actually just visiting to see my pretty face?" I rested my chin on the backs of my fingers and winked.

Espen chuckled and raked his gaze across me. "No coffee order for me today." His eyes sparkled and his lips curved into another one of his signature grins. I couldn't help myself. I leaned in and pressed my lips to his. Warmth swept over me, lingering in my bones and turning them to jelly. *A hundred plus years of this? Yes, please. I do. Sign me up.*

Someone cleared their throat behind me. Reluctantly, I unlatched myself from Espen and glanced over my shoulder. Oddvar stood there in his apron, arms crossed, mouth pinched together, and a single eyebrow raised toward his thin, gray hairline.

"Sorry, Oddvar," Espen said, well aware of *why* Oddvar had painted a line on the floor by the counter this summer.

Before I could add my apologies to my boss for canoodling on the job, clinking sounded across the room. I looked for the source of the noise and found Solveig, Jorunn, and Dagny tapping their spoons against their coffee cups.

"Again!" Solveig yelled.

"Kiss!" Her two friends chimed in at the same time.

I glanced at Oddvar. He leveled a deadpan stare at me, wholly unamused about his café turning into "lunch and a show." Other customers chimed in, tapping their spoons against their cups and clapping. Jorunn and Dagny did their best to explain to the patrons around them that Espen and I were getting married tomorrow. Within seconds, the entire café was cheering for us.

I tried to hold back the smile twisting at my lips. "Got to give the people what they want, Oddvar."

He sighed, rolled his eyes, and raised a single finger.

Espen didn't wait a second.

He grabbed me from behind the counter, spun me into the open space between tables, and dipped me. His lips crashed into mine, passion and need bubbling beneath the surface, wanting to take things much further but holding back... just. I squeezed his arms for purchase. A tingling sensation flowed through me like a cool breeze on a hot summer's day and my heart clenched with joy. Forget about one-hundred years of this, I'd gladly take a thousand.

Happiness and applause swept through the room as Espen righted me but didn't let go.

His eyes sparkled as our gazes met. It'd been an interesting—some might argue unconventional—journey to get here. But the thought of being this man's wife, committing to a life with him and Øyvin, didn't scare me away like it would've done a year ago. In fact, there was now no place I'd rather be than here in Skolvik with them.

Espen let me go and I took two shaky steps back and bumped against the counter, heat flushing across my cheeks as the applause died down.

"I'll see you at home," Espen said with a wink, stepping backward toward the front door. "Then, tomorrow..."

"Tomorrow." I grinned.

111

LENNIE

Afternoon light shone through the bedroom window of Espen's cabin, brushing across the wood-paneled walls and rustic furniture. My white dress with long lace sleeves practically glowed in the happiness and light that flooded the room. The garment was simple and refined. A lace top with some floaty tulle material on the skirt that was perfect for the warm end-of-summer day.

I reached for the crown of white flowers and greenery on the dresser and set the delicate piece atop my curled hair. It wasn't entirely my style, but I appreciated including nature, which was so important to us, in our wedding. Turning to face the full-length mirror by the closet, I fastened the circlet with a couple of pins Ingrid had set aside for me. I looked like me, but perhaps a touch more feminine than usual.

"I wouldn't be caught dead in white," Ylva muttered, her reflection appearing in the mirror as she pulled lint off the black lapel of her body-hugging suit which matched her black Converse. I expected nothing less of Espen's fearsome best friend and second-in-command.

"I'll be sure to tell Gunvor that the next time I see her."

"Please do." She patted her hair which had been braided, twisted, and pinned to the back of her head. "Mother sends her regards and regrets by the way."

Gunvor was as much of a badass as her Forest Fae daughter, and while I'd have liked to have the elder stateswoman in attendance, Alvdalen was a decent drive away and she wasn't the youngest fae in the forest.

"That's sweet. Thanks." I spun to face Ylva, the skirt of my dress swishing around the comfy hiking boots on my feet. "Is he ready?"

"He's bouncing around as happy as a dog, greeting every single person in attendance... twice." She cleared her throat. "Are you ready?"

Good question. One with an easy answer.

"Yeah," I replied. "Yeah, I am."

"Good, but also debatable." She wandered over and motioned for me to squat. I acquiesced to her request, bending at the knees. She reached over and adjusted the flower crown on my head, fussing and straightening it. A second later, a bobby pin was retrieved from her own braid and used to re-fasten the circle.

Pulling back, she examined me and gave me a nod. "Excellent. Now put on your best smile and look all bride-like. I have a sizable bet with some of my soldiers on how long it'll take before Espen tears up."

I chuckled and rose back to standing position.

She clapped her hands together in a prayer position. "I'm down for sub ten seconds. So, if you could help me out…"

"How much is the bet?"

"Two thousand five hundred *kroner*."

"I knew I liked you."

"Same here. You give that man more hell than I ever could." She grinned. "Now, let's go find the little ones and get you married to those lovesick guys."

"Guy," I corrected. "It's only Espen."

She snorted. "Don't lie. The entire village knows the three of you are an item and that this was originally for immigration purposes."

My shoulders dropped and my mouth popped open. "How'd they find that out?" It technically was still for immigration purposes. At least, the speed in which we were pulling this off. But the main reason for this marriage was because we loved each other.

"Please." She raised her brows at me and set her hands on her hips. "You three are practically glued together. Plus, do you really think Solveig, Dagny, and Jorunn would let that gossip go?"

"Yeah, there wasn't a chance of that was there?"

"Not at all. As soon as that ring hit your finger last Christmas, the whole town knew what was going on."

Small towns. What was a woman to do? Grin and bear it, really.

"Shall we find the children? Pretty sure one of your brothers gave them sweets to make today a little harder on everyone."

I rolled my eyes. As my brother Jared and his wife Jennifer had just had their own little girl and couldn't travel, and Andrew or Amanda sure as hell wouldn't give their kids candy, there was only one viable candidate. Ten out of ten chance Ryan was the guilty party. He was constantly going for the Favorite Uncle title and had always been the most gregarious of the Martin siblings.

Ylva opened the bedroom door and we strode through the tiny kitchen area into the cabin's living room.

Peals of laughter met my ears. Four young girls in white dresses with pale-green sashes around their waists sat on the small chestnut-colored sofa, two with dirty blonde hair, the other two light brown. Their locks were braided into a matching half-up, half-down hairstyle with ringlets brushing their shoulders. All four of them looked like tiny princesses.

Andrew's daughters, Abigail and Amelia had made fast friends with Ingrid's girls, Kari and Katrine, even if neither could speak the same language. Over the past week of them staying in Skolvik, they'd been inseparable. And then there was Kristoffer...

The young kid, now five years old and calling himself a big boy, stood atop the coffee table in his Norwegian *Bunad*—the traditional attire. Cream socks and a pair of black pants that cinched under his knees were paired with a red-and-green tartan vest over a white shirt. The ensemble was adorable, especially with the pieces of family silver at his cuffs and a broach comprised of two silver balls connected by a chain at his collar—the latter of which had once belonged to Espen.

"What are you doing?" Ylva's commander voice boomed across the room.

Kristoffer spun, his eyes wide as he stumbled off the table, sending the girls into fits of laughter. He righted himself and dusted off his pants, mumbling something I couldn't hear.

"We need all of you to behave today," I said in English before turning to Ingrid's kids and asking the same of them in Norwegian.

They all nodded.

"You look pretty, Auntie Lennie," Amelia said, twirling a lock of her hair around her finger.

"Thank you, cutie."

This was probably the prettiest I'd ever dressed. As the only daughter, Mom had certainly dolled me up over the years but this was a whole new level of girliness. Definitely not my everyday wear, but I didn't mind it.

A knock sounded and the front door creaked open. My parents walked in and closed the door behind them. Mom wore a lavender, beaded dress with small flowers on it, while Dad was in a black suit with a lavender-and-pale-green tie that matched Mom's dress.

"Now, now, kiddos." Mom swept into the room with her arms open wide, her dark eyes full of warmth, and her dark hair perfectly blown out and full of volume.

"Grammy!" Amelia said.

"Hello, sweetie. Don't y'all look great." The girls hugged Mom before turning their attention to Dad who gave them a massive hug each. Mom's watery gaze met mine. "And so do you."

"Did you bring tissues?" I asked.

"I have a pack in each pocket," Dad replied for her.

She glided over and set her hands on my shoulders, her lips already quivering with emotion. "I never thought I'd see you in a wedding dress."

I let out a long sigh and drew her in for a hug, squeezing her tight. "Miracles do happen."

She squeezed me back. "They most certainly do." Pulling away, she took two steps back and tilted her head to the ceiling while dabbing her pinky finger underneath her eye. "Ugh, I don't want to ruin my make-up."

"Need a tissue already, Deb?" Dad asked from under a pile of kids on the sofa.

Mom waved her hand at him before glancing at her watch. "We came to tell you it's time." She turned to the kids. "Are you ready?"

All five of them understood her and bounced off the sofa, leaving my dad behind. In quick movements, they lined up by the door per my mother's verbal and hand-motion instructions.

A hand landed on my shoulder and Ylva swept past whispering, "Less than ten seconds."

I chuckled as she crossed the room. "I'll do my best."

"I am the ring bear," Kristoffer said in Norwegian and let out a growl while taking up position by the front door.

"Now, Kristoffer," Ylva said, setting the rings in the boy's hand. "Don't drop these."

He gave her a quick salute. "I shall guard them with my life, Commander."

I grinned. Thankful that the young boy who'd crashed through the ice earlier this year was happy and healthy. Even if he was obnoxiously loud.

"Thank you, soldier." Ylva played along, and part of me wondered if Kristoffer might one day serve as a Forest Fae soldier. With the way he looked up to his uncle, I wouldn't be surprised.

One by one, each of the kids followed my mom and Ylva out the door, starting the processional. A guitar strummed a happy tune, the notes matching the children's boundless energy.

"Ope, don't want to step on your dress," Dad said, doing a little sidestep to avoid the flowing tulle hem. He smiled down at me, his eyes wrinkling at the corners, his white hair swept to one side. Daniel Martin, father of four, Ohio born and raised, friend to all, was the biggest softy—and Ohio State Football fan—anyone would ever have the fortune of meeting.

He looped his arm through mine and I picked up the tiny bouquet of lavender and white wildflowers that waited for me by the door. "I'm so proud of you, Lennie. It's wonderful to see you so happy."

"Aww." I swallowed hard, gripping the bouquet. "Thanks, Dad."

"I mean it." He patted my arm with his free hand. "While your mom and I would've loved to have you closer to home, I always knew you'd find your own place in the world, likely a little farther afield."

"Was Norway on that list?"

He tilted his head from one side to the other. "Western Europe was," he chuckled. "And you've found very nice *gentlemen*."

I sucked in a breath, my eyes going wider than I would've liked.

He chuckled again. "Of course we know. It's a little unconventional, but like I said. It's great to see you so happy. That's all I've ever wanted for my little girl. When you brought them home for Thanksgiving and stood there in the hallway with them looming behind you, that grin on your face..." He shook his head. "We'd seen that look countless times when you were growing up. There was never any arguing with that power pose and staunch resolve. Those two were yours and no one would be taking them away from you."

My throat tightened and I took two trembling breaths. Trust my dad to get me all emotional.

"There she is, poking her head out of the sand for once."

I snort-laughed and nodded. He'd always likened me to an ostrich with my emotions, dunking my head in the sand any time things got too much. But he was right. I didn't hide from my emotions anymore. I didn't shy away from how I felt, especially regarding the two men waiting for me outside.

A lone violin began to play, the lilting tune like something from a Norwegian folk tale, rising and falling in notes that promised magic and adventure. My breath hitched as I recognized the melody, one I'd heard played countless times, but not on violin. It was Øyvin's song, the one he played on his piano when he was deep in thought. I closed my eyes, letting the music wash over me, and the tension in my shoulders eased.

"You ready, pumpkin?" Dad asked, tugging lightly on my arm as he opened the front door.

We took two steps outside, rays of sunlight dancing across the field beside the cabin, and my heart stuttered.

There, in the flat part of the field where I'd *yoga*'d with Espen for the first time underneath the Aurora Borealis, was the entire wedding congregation. As one, they rose to their feet and looked down the aisle between the mismatched chairs. And at the end, with the forest behind them, under an arch of lilac and white flowers with boughs of greenery and ribbon, wearing crisp gray suits, stood my two guys.

I smiled. "Yeah, I'm ready."

112

LENNIE

Sighs and smiles mixed with the violin's melody as Dad and I meandered down the grassy aisle. The spectacular view to my right was otherworldly, like mother nature was putting on a show and winking at us. The trees appeared greener, the sky the brightest blue I'd ever seen, and the fjord... The fjord twinkled like starlight.

At least a quarter of the village was in attendance, from Espen's boss and Oddvar to some of Øyvin's soldiers. The kids were all up front, Ylva beside the arch in her role as Best Woman. But I only had eyes for the two fae underneath the arch. Everything else seemed to fade away as we got closer.

A lone tear fell across Espen's cheek, and I caught movement out of the corner of my eye. Probably Ylva celebrating her victory.

My heart galloped in my chest and my body tingled from all the people staring at me. This was it. I was getting married. I was marrying a Forest Fae and secretly a Fjord Fae too, even though Øyvin wouldn't be calling himself my husband. This was a commitment ceremony for all three of us—today we were officially becoming husband, wife, and partners. Holy shit.

We stopped in front of the guys and my dad let go of my arm, giving it a double pat before finding his seat next to Mom.

Espen reached out taking my hands in his with a broad smile and all felt right in the world.

Øyvin's commanding voice welcomed everyone and moved on to a speech about life and the values of a partner. With a shaky breath, my focus shifted to the gathered crowd.

Smiling friends and family peered back at me. From my parents and brothers upfront in their snazziest suits, to Solveig and the ladies in beautiful traditional dresses. Leif and Torsten held hands, the former giving me a toothy grin. Even

Oddvar was in attendance, wearing a dark gray suit and an expression that was far brighter than his usual surely state.

My gaze drifted back, finding townsfolk I'd come to know through work, and settled on the last row. Heidi sat beside none other than the big guy himself—Halvar had actually deigned to leave the mountain. And he was wearing a fucking suit. Black shirt with black suit and black tie—more ready for a human funeral than a wedding—but the man had dressed up.

Halvar straightened in his seat and inhaled sharply as a latecomer sat in the final chair beside him. I didn't recognize the man, but he wore a double-breasted navy suit and black sunglasses, his salt-and-pepper hair slicked back off his wrinkled brow. He looked like a more refined version of Halvar, one who perhaps lived in a gorgeous apartment in Paris and not a rugged mountain cave.

Øyvin cleared his throat. "And now the two have selected to exchange their own vows—"

My eyes widened and I whipped my attention back to Espen.

Shit. I knew there was something I'd forgotten. Vows. I was supposed to write my own vows.

Kristoffer appeared beside us, right on cue, and opened his little hands, proffering the silver wedding bands to us. We plucked the rings from his clammy palms, and Espen gave him a little wink. The young boy beamed and scampered back to his spot beside Ylva.

My gaze drifted to Espen, panic welling inside me. How the hell had I forgotten to write my own vows? Too late now. "You go first," I mumbled.

Espen smiled, gripping my hands a little tighter—having probably deduced my current predicament.

"Evelyn—Lennie—Martin," he started. "I've searched for a love like this for what feels like centuries." My heart clenched, and he squeezed my fingers. "A love that makes me dream of waking up. A love that adds buoyancy to my days, bolstering me in the moments when I feel lost. And, most importantly, a love that challenges me."

The crowd snickered and one of my brothers outwardly laughed while I lost myself in Espen's honey-colored eyes and the blanketing warmth of his words.

"Never in my most wayward dreams could I have imagined meeting a woman like you," he continued. "Someone so passionate about life, steadfast in her beliefs, and unwavering in her loyalty to family. Lennie..." He took a deep breath as if trying to quell the tears that lingered along his lashes. It felt like my heart, my entire chest was about to burst in half. "I will love you till the end of my days. And, until that end, I vow to protect your peace and bury your enemies." He scrunched his nose like it was a joke, but I knew, and so did all the fae present, that he meant every word exactly as they'd been spoken. He'd vanquish anything that crossed my path. "You have my word, my heart, my everything."

He gently pushed the silver wedding band onto my finger then raised my hand and tipped it to his lips. His kiss sent sparks of joy and comfort through my body, lighting it up from the inside. Leaving absolutely no doubt just how much he loved me.

Øyvin tilted his head in an almost imperceptible nod. His sapphire eyes met mine and extolled his agreement with everything Espen had just said. The combination of the look and the spoken words was enough to have my throat close up.

How the hell was I supposed to follow that?

Fuck, I was gonna have to wing it.

I turned my gaze fully to Espen and swallowed the gargantuan lump in my throat, desperate for a breath that wouldn't result in waterworks. "I-I... I'm sorry I punched you the first day we met."

Half the crowd laughed, half snorted, and I was pretty sure the shocked guffaw was from my mother. Before I could forget, I slipped Espen's wedding band onto his finger where it belonged.

"I don't doubt for a second that *we* were meant for one another," I added, making sure to include Øyvin in this even though the event was billed as mine and Espen's wedding. "I can vow to be a pain in the ah—butt, to make you laugh every day, and to cherish every single one of your smiles. You've brought so much light to my world." I looked between both of them and then back at Espen. "A light I never want to let go of, even if I was hesitant at first."

My guys snickered.

I straightened as the gentle summer breeze brushed tendrils of my hair across my cheeks. "I promise to love you for a thousand years and I can't wait to see what this life and world has in store for us."

I meant every word, for both of them. Based on the way their eyes hooded, they understood.

A collective awe wound its way around the gathering, and Espen practically melted on the spot as he brushed his thumbs over my fingers.

"Espen Solbakke," Øyvin started. "Do you take Lennie Martin to be your wife?"

A burst of sunshine radiated from the Forest Fae. "I do."

"Lennie Martin. Do you take Espen Solbakke to be your husband?"

I gave his fingers two quick squeezes. "*Ja.*"

Espen beamed at my Norwegian reply and took a step forward. His head tilted toward me, lips puckering, and Øyvin cleared his throat, stopping the bubbly fae in his tracks.

The crowd and I chuckled at his eagerness, and Espen pulled back, a flush of pink filling his cheeks.

"By the power vested in me," Øyvin said with a pointed look to Espen, "I pronounce you husband and wife. You may *now* kiss the bride."

Espen's lips were against mine in an instant and I entwined my arms around his neck, relishing in the steadfast promise of his kiss. Yeah, I'd gladly take a lifetime or five with these two guys.

The violin music started up again. A tune that sounded vaguely like *The* Ohio State Fight Song, *Buckeye Battle Cry*. I furrowed my brow but shook it off as Øyvin announced, "May I present, Mr. and Mrs. Solbakke Martin."

The crowd applauded and cheered as Espen led me back down the aisle. Smiles and congratulations matched the timing of my footfalls and the notes of what was either my dad's contribution to the wedding or a prank from my brothers.

As we reached the end of the aisle, Espen tugged my hand and pulled me into him. I stumbled into his embrace. "I love you," he whispered and dipped me, pressing his lips to mine.

ØYVIN

I grinned as Espen dipped Lennie at the end of the aisle. Seeing her happy was always a joy, and Espen brought that out in her as much as I did. Her smile only added to her beauty today. A day that was turning into a memory I'd forever cherish.

My gaze slid to their right, taking in the crowd. Everyone stood, clapping and beaming at the newlyweds. The wedding couldn't be going any—

I stilled, fist clenching around the speech in my hand.

What the fuck was the Veigar doing here?

The well-dressed man applauded like every other guest wishing the couple well, his dark sunglasses covering the black eyes hidden beneath. Despite his pleasant smile, I knew better, knew the man's fiery history and what he was capable of. Everything he touched turned to ashes. Rumor had it the last time he'd shown up to a village unannounced the place was burned to the ground by him and his minions.

Nothing good could come of him being in Skolvik.

"Are you joining us?" Andrew Martin asked with a quick pat on my shoulder.

I shook off my shock and refocused.

This was the plan. I was supposed to follow the family down the aisle and then be present for family photos. Which sounded awful, but I'd do whatever was necessary to keep my partner and her family happy.

"I'll be right there," I said, not moving from my spot.

"Okay."

Andrew wandered down the aisle with his wife and girls and I looked back at the wedding crasher.

Halvar stood beside Veigar, seeming ready to wrap his arms around the man's throat and choke him. I'd certainly jump in and help if needed. Despite my building concern, we couldn't do anything with this many humans around, or fae, for that matter.

I scanned the sunny field, looking for options as the guests started moving. My gaze locked on an onyx-haired woman walking among the crowd. I didn't recognize her from the back, but the way she moved in that blue dress looked familiar. With each step she got closer to where Veigar—

The spot where he'd been was empty, and the muscles in my jaw twitched.

Where the fuck had he gone?

Striding into the crowd, I continued surveying the scene, avoiding bumping into too many people in the throng.

Lennie and Espen were back in the cabin waiting for photos.

The family were heading that way too.

Halvar stood outside the cabin.

Oddvar was helping Heidi across the uneven terrain.

Dresses and suits mixed with *bunad* of all different colors.

But Veigar was gone.

Fuck.

The woman in the blue dress turned, her gaze landing on mine, and my stomach bottomed out. What was Salka doing here too? She hadn't been invited either. The Fire Fae Princess, now Fjord Queen should be in the Fjord Palace.

"Øyvin!" A feminine voice yoo-hooed and I spun toward the noise. Deb Martin waved from the cabin's front door. "Øyvin, we need you for photographs!"

"I'll be right there!"

As I twisted back, the crowd thinned around me, and Salka was nowhere to be found.

Shit, this couldn't be good.

LENNIE

Chatter flooded the sun-lit room and crested into rounds of applause as Espen and I entered Fisken, the local restaurant and bar where we'd had our first date. Øyvin and our families strolled in behind us after we'd taken the obligatory group portraits by the harbor. A tiny dance area had been cleared to my left near the bar and several long tables displayed a myriad of American and Norwegian dishes, set up buffet-style. The rest of the space was filled with the restaurant's usual dark wood tables and leather booths.

Everywhere I looked, I could tell Ingrid and Mom had put in some serious work. Each table was covered in white linen with hollowed birch tree tea-light candle holders. Tiny lilac and white flowers decorated the base of each adding a burst of color. It was simple, elegant, and absolutely perfect.

My ever present smile continued as we pressed into the throngs of people. Espen was practically buzzing, our fingers tangled in their own embrace as he gently tugged on my hand. I thought I'd seen him at his happiest when we'd exchanged *I love you*s, but this was something else. Something more. He radiated joy and wasn't hiding it from anyone.

My heart clenched at the sight, warmth spreading across my sore cheeks. I'd done that. I was the one making him this happy.

"Congratulations! What a wonderful ceremony," Solveig said as she stepped into our path, brushing her hands over the blue skirt of her *bunad* with a bright floral pattern along the edges.

"Thank you, Solveig," Espen said, and I matched his gratitude.

Dagny slid in beside Solveig and peered over my shoulder. "Fantastic officiating, too."

I looked behind me and found Øyvin caught in the old woman's gaze. He nodded once, let out a strained cough, and headed for the bar. Dagny, wearing her emerald green *bunad* with white blouse, eyed him the entire way and I shook my head at her antics. She really was obsessed and I couldn't blame her. For all his grumpy asshole behavior, Øyvin was a great guy.

Solveig smacked her friend's shoulder, drawing my attention back to the two older ladies. "Can we get you anything to eat or drink before you make your rounds?"

"I'm fine, but thank you," I replied and nudged Espen. "We really should go say hello to everyone."

Solveig gave us a grandmotherly grin, filled with warmth and care, and stepped aside so we could delve deeper into the crowd of guests.

From Espen's sisters and friends from Alvdalen, to my brothers chatting away with Torsten and Leif, it was amazing to see our lives gathered in one space. Peace and harmony met us with every greeting and I felt like I'd finally found the composition I'd been searching for my whole life: a home where family and friends were filled with happiness and joy, laughter and light.

The only scene that gave me pause was Heidi and the kids. All five children—both human and fae—sat at a table with her, their eyes wide, fully enraptured in whatever tale she was spinning. Knowing the Forest Fae healer, it was probably something she shouldn't be talking about to children, something that would scare the shit out of them, or that coffee was the devil's juice and should never be consumed.

After more handshakes, hugs, and smiles, my stomach grumbled, and I excused myself from Espen's side. While Espen continued being the groom and acting like a politician up for re-election, I aimed for the food.

My dress swished around my feet as I strode over to the buffet table. It hosted dishes ranging from tiny sandwiches and Buckeyes, to *Sirupsnipper* and a tower of almond-paste rings with white icing piped on it known as *Kransekake*. I found a small plate and started gathering a collection of treats for myself.

A bead of sweat trickled down the back of my neck as I grabbed a Buckeye. Someone really needed to crack a window. With this many people in the restaurant, it was going to get hot fast.

"He's a lucky man," a low voice rumbled and the salt-and-pepper-haired man in a bespoke suit and black sunglasses stepped up beside me.

"You have no idea," I quipped, turning and giving him my best smile. Was it a slightly crude answer? Yes, but I was the bride so what was anyone going to do?

The older man's face wrinkled, and he gave me a tight-lipped grin. Who was this guy again? No one had mentioned inviting their fancy-dressing great uncle to the wedding. This man looked like he belonged in Paris, sipping an espresso along the Seine, not in a tiny Norwegian village.

"Might you know what these *Buckeyes* are?" He plucked one of the little chocolate-covered treats off the platter and eyed it closely. "An American delicacy, no?"

"Ohio's finest candies. They're peanut butter balls dipped in chocolate and made to resemble the tree nut that's prevalent in my home state." Not to mention the mascot of my parents' and brothers' alma mater, *The* Ohio State University.

The man smiled and popped one in his mouth. His sharp jaw worked overtime as he chewed, his eyes widening more and more by the second. He swallowed. "My wife would've loved them. Delicious."

"Agreed." I picked one off the plate in my hand and took a small bite. The sweet and salty combo danced across my tongue. Delicious indeed.

Halvar appeared beside me, his black suit straining at the shoulder seams and his eyes locked on the man in front of me. "A little far from home, Veigar."

The man brushed his hands as if removing crumbs and pressed his fingertips together, casually pointing them away from his torso. "Always a pleasure, Halvar."

Muscles jumped in Halvar's neck as Espen and Øyvin joined our little conversation. They both sidled up next to me, angling inward like I needed protecting. I scrunched my brow at the behavior. The old man was harmless and asking about peanut butter treats not bombs.

"What brings you to Skolvik?" Espen asked, his gaze welcoming despite his tense posture.

"Visiting my daughter, of course." Veigar panned and looked at each of us. Or at least, I thought he was surveying us. I couldn't be sure as he was still wearing sunglasses... inside. Weird, but to each their own.

Halvar crossed his arms and grumbled like he didn't believe the answer. "Don't you have some volcanoes to attend to? Katla? Eyjafjallajökull? How is the town of Grindavik these days?"

Volcanoes?

Veigar's lips spread into a sinister smirk, like a barn cat that had been caught inside the farmhouse and didn't give a damn. "Now, now, Halvar." I flinched at the informal way he spoke to the beast of the mountain. "Now is neither the time nor place." Veigar peered over his shoulders. No one was around us and everyone else was busy chatting and eating—except Ylva. The Forest Fae's knuckles had gone white as she clutched her drink and blatantly stared in our direction from a booth.

"*Here* most definitely is not the place, Your Majesty," Espen stepped in.

My brow furrowed. Your Majest— Lead filled my stomach, and my eyes widened to the size of a camera lens. *Oh shit.*

That's what had them all freaking out. That's why Halvar had bristled when Veigar sat down next to him during the ceremony. That's why my guys were ready to launch like rockets. This wasn't just some random wedding crasher. Veigar was the goddamn King of the Fire Fae!

"I wouldn't dare interrupt such an auspicious day."

And yet here he was... in Skolvik. At my wedding.

I set my plate down behind me and took a deep breath. Everything was going to be fine. Everything was going to be abso-fucking-lutely fine.

"What do you want?" Halvar asked, his voice laden with more malice than I'd ever heard from the big guy.

Veigar tapped his fingertips together. "A diplomatic solution to our mutual problems."

"Diplomatic?" Espen tilted his head to one side, eyes narrowing at the monarch.

"That is the..." he thought on it for a second. "*Preferred* course of action."

I swallowed hard as all three local fae straightened and leaned back.

"Is that a threat?" Øyvin asked through gritted teeth.

"Gentlemen!" My Dad appeared between Halvar and Veigar, and all the air in my lungs vanished. He turned to Veigar. "I don't believe we've met." He extended his hand to the Fire Fae. "Dan Martin, Father of the Bride."

Veigar took his hand, gave it a shake, and returned my dad's beaming smile. "Veigar Eldjotnarson. Pleasure to meet you Mr. Martin."

"That's quite the last name you've got there. Where are you from, son?"

"Iceland."

"How wonderful," Dad said, sounding like the kind Midwest man my grandma had raised him to be.

"Indeed," Veigar replied. "We were just discussing what great fortune it was that Lennie missed her ship and met such a splendid partner. Life altering, one might even say."

Bile churned in my stomach, threatening to bring back up my Buckeye. This guy had done his homework. We hadn't mentioned anything about the cruise ship or how I'd met everyone. Yet with his careful choice of words, he'd not only shown what he knew, but that he'd happily start pulling the pins on the grenades in our lives.

My dad retracted his hand and turned to me, his smile never faltering. "We're so happy for her."

Heart beating faster than a camera stuck on sports-mode, I swallowed the lump in my throat. "Did you need something, Dad?" Hopefully the tone of my voice didn't betray the panic swelling inside me.

"Your mom and Ingrid said to get ready. I'm sure you know what they're talking about." He straightened his tie and lowered his voice. "I might not have paid attention last night when your mother was going over things. So, I can't give you any *exact* details."

I pushed past my guys and nudged my father away from the four fae. "No worries, Dad. I've got it." I totally didn't *got it*. In fact, the only thing I had right now was a higher risk for a heart attack and an overwhelming amount of testosterone at my back.

Sending my dad toward the throngs of guests, I turned back to the situation brewing by the buffet.

"I'm going to leave you guys to chat. Please don't break anything." I gave them a gentle jazz hands motion and skedaddled. Hopefully they could keep their cool and, in one case, not burn down the restaurant full of people—most of which were humans who had no idea what milled around them drinking beer and laughing at their jokes.

My eyes scanned the room and landed on Ylva. Perched at the end of a booth bench, she gave me a quick upward nod and I scurried toward her like she was air conditioning on a hot summer's day.

"You catch all of that?" I asked, stopping in front of her. I doubted she could hear what was being said across the busy room, but if anyone could read lips, it'd be Ylva. Espen's second-in-command was like a hawk—nothing got past her.

Ylva nodded and proffered an open flask.

"Is this what I think it is?"

"If you're thinking aquavit, then yes." She set the metallic container on the table. "Drink up. You're going to need it for what's about to unfold."

Was she talking about the wedding or the chaos that had crashed the party? With the adrenaline currently coursing through my veins, my magic rattling around inside me in a panic, and my past experiences with the fiery liquor, I doubted it would help. I shook my head and plopped down on the other bench in the booth, the supple, leather seat sinking slightly beneath me.

Were weddings always this eventful and blurry? It felt like I'd just pulled on my dress, but based on the clock above the kitchen entrance, that was hours ago.

Glassy tinkling noises started up and I peered toward the dancing area. My Mom and Ingrid stood in the center of the space, looking like pastel statues in their dresses. Mom's lilac number complemented her dark hair color, and Ingrid's pale-yellow ensemble draped across her like a Greek goddess. Their smiles radiated across the room and their eyes glittered with a mutual plan that likely included me in some way.

"It's time for speeches," Mom said in English and Ingrid translated the announcement into Norwegian.

My eyes widened. I really should have paid more attention to them when we were discussing the schedule this morning over breakfast.

"On second thought." I reached across the table, grabbed the flask of aquavit, and tilted it to my lips.

115

LENNIE

The village bobbed around behind me like a fishing boat on the fjord—up and down, up and down, up and down. The streetlights threw gentle rays across the road but were almost unnecessary. Even at this hour... whichever hour it was... the sun still graced us with her happy presence, like an operatic soprano I could sing along with.

"Silver balls—" A hiccup escaped my lips, and I wriggled in Øyvin's hold, grinding my lower abdomen against his shoulder. His grip on my legs tightened and his broad hand moved up my dress and cupped my ass. "Silver balls. It's sleepy time, in the Skolvik."

Øyvin snorted. "Those aren't the lyrics, Trouble."

Espen chuckled beside us, his tie missing, the top buttons of his shirt undone, revealing a hint of the muscles that lay beneath, and his hair rumpled. His entire being was practically begging for me to fuck him. And damn did I want to. Nay! Need to. If only the world weren't so wobbly, I could reach out and drag my hands through—

"Would you stop moving?" Øyvin groused.

I stuck out my bottom lip.

The Fjord Fae wasn't as disheveled unfortunately. He'd held off on the alcohol once Veigar made his presence known. I, on the other hand—

Another hiccup bubbled up and out.

Espen looked over and our gazes caught. His eyes were full of something... sultry, happy, thirsty. Or maybe I was projecting? "I'm so merry."

"Your merry ass is going to feel like shit tomorrow." Øyvin's words were laced with laughter as we reached the boathouse and one of them opened the front door.

"That's a problem for future Lennie. Current Lennie is merry and being carried across the threshold. Silver baaaaaalls!"

"Ancestors save me," Øyvin muttered.

The door clicked shut and the room swam as Øyvin trudged upstairs with me still draped over his shoulder. Which I wasn't going to complain about. Not at all. It'd been a long day. Who knew getting married was so exhausting? So much chatting. Lots of eating. Many, many drinking with Ylvas, and Torstens, and Leifs, and brothers. Not to mention the dancing and the speeching. Ugh, the speeching. Note to self, always include the *al* in *aldri* or it sounds like you're saying *shit*.

Øyvin grunted, the room spun, and a wayward squeak left my lips before my back landed on our cozy bed. My feet hung off the edge and the white sheets cocooned me like Princess Peach on a cloud.

"Ugh, bed, yes. Great thinking." We needed to consummate the marriage. Now.

I stuck my boots in the air, one pointed at each of my fae husbands. Partners. My fae-sbands?

They both rolled their eyes and acquiesced to my request, untying my hiking boots. Their fingers drifted to my ankles and the simple brushes of skin against skin sent goosebumps up my legs. They gently yanked off the cumbersome shoes and dropped them to the floor. A groan of pleasure rumbled through my chest as I flexed my toes. Blessed freedom.

Reaching down, I grabbed the dirtied silky hem of my dress with both hands and flipped it up over my stomach, letting it fall under my chin. "Do me!"

Espen buckled over and laughed, gasping for breath between each bout while Øyvin bit his bottom lip and brushed his hand across his forehead.

"We can't..." The blurry brown-haired blob that was my dearly beloved straightened up and put its hands on its hips. "We can't fuck you when you're this drunk."

Whaaat? My sexy turned sad as I covered a yawn. "I'm not that drunk."

"Trust me," Espen said. "I'd love to fuck you right now. I want you on all fours, screaming my name around Øyvin's cock. But you're intoxicated, Lennie."

"Now, see that's a great plan. We should do that. I want that." I really really did. I could picture it now. Me being fucked in my wedding dress. The guys so turned on and desperate to get me out of it that they ripped the bodice piece apart before claiming my tits with their mouths.

"Lennie?" Espen said, drawing me from my erotic thoughts. "How many drinks did you have?"

"Many, many drinking," I slurred.

Øyvin turned to Espen. "Silver balls, remember?"

Ugh, they were being no fun. And right now, all I wanted was fun *yoga*. The kind that lit my body on fire and had me aching the next morning.

I scrambled to the top of the bed and flipped over to face them. "I'm so glad you're my f-usbands," I mumbled through another yawn and raised my arms above my head. "I love you both, soooooooo much. Now, please fuck me."

"Trouble." Øyvin's voice was like rumbly velvet. So smooth, so yummy, so sexy. If only he could put that mouth to good use.

I rolled onto my stomach, nuzzled my face into the pillow that smelled like leather and moss, stuck my ass in the air and promptly fell asleep.

116

LENNIE

Yesterday I was the bride, today I was the Deputy Head Guard of the Fjell Fae attending an emergency council meeting with a gnarly headache. Drunk Lennie was a horny dumbass that should've known better than to do shots of aquavit. Thankfully, the only council members that'd been at the reception were Torsten and Halvar. Neither of whom were currently paying attention to me.

I leaned forward in my chair, resting my forearms on the gigantic rock slab that hosted the weary Council. Imposing stone walls arched high above us, and rugged pillars jutted from the floors in the corners of the room, seemingly holding the mountain aloft. Magical light flickered over the heads of the twelve other council members, including Halvar, who stood at the head of the table, palms flat on the surface, arms locked.

"As all of you have no doubt heard, King Veigar is in Skolvik."

Shudders ran through those gathered as the meeting began in earnest.

"He made the journey from Iceland?" One council member asked as another muttered, "We're doomed." A third, Johann, who sat across from me, clenched his fists on the table. "I heard his anger caused the Holuhraun fissure eruption in 2014. The lava flow lasted for months and by the time it ended, the lava field covered eighty-five square kilometers."

My eyes widened at the stat. I had no idea how big a kilometer was compared to a mile, but based on the weight behind the council member's words, it must be huge.

"And let us not forget the Askja eruption," Halvar said, and people around the table nodded.

A council member to my right—Bodil, if I remembered correctly—straightened in his seat. "The 1875 eruption was rumored to be caused by Veigar's immense anger and despair at losing his wife." He shook his head. "The ash poisoned the land, killed creatures, and even drifted over to our shores."

Well, fuck. If Veigar was powerful enough to cause monumental volcanic eruptions, what the hell did he want here in Norway?

Halvar stared around at the panicked chatter that arose and cleared his throat. Silence fell and everyone's eyes flicked back to the stoic fae at the head of the table.

"Did he say what he wanted?" I asked, breaking the silence. I couldn't help myself. The panic rising within me and my goddamn curiosity couldn't stop the words tumbling from my mouth. "Yesterday, at the wedding. Did he say anything else to you? Explain why he decided to show up to my wedding uninvited?"

Halvar's gaze turned to me. "He wanted more stability in the region and among the fae. As for the timing, he mentioned it was a good opportunity to get our attention."

Well, it certainly had.

Grumbles wove around the table like a crowd doing the wave at a football stadium.

"I think we can all agree that Veigar is not to be trusted," Halvar said. "With his volatile behavior once tempered by the presence of his late wife, and his history of killing anyone who disagrees with him, we must fortify our defenses and notify the fjell residents. I hope nothing escalates, but I will not be caught unprepared."

The Council nodded.

"In the meantime," Halvar continued. "We shall monitor his movements and find out what *exactly* his intentions are."

Part of me wanted to believe Veigar was just on his summer vacation, visiting family and taking in the sights of the majestic fjord. The other part of me, perhaps the demi-fae part or the Fjell Fae magic continuously warming my sternum, knew better. There was more to this than *regional stability*. Why would a powerful creature care about Skolvik's regional stability when he's not in the area?

"Why doesn't Veigar live in Skolvik, or Norway, like the other fae monarchs? Why is he in Iceland?"

All eyes around the table flitted to Halvar again who inhaled sharply.

"Well over a thousand years ago, the Fire Fae powers were no longer needed in the north, but scouts found a small island in the North Atlantic that could use their help and expertise with volcanoes and tectonic plate movement."

"So, they were sent over there?"

Halvar nodded. "They went willingly, and, as the human population on earth grew, it became a safer place for the Fire Fae to hide while still being able to train their army."

Interesting, and yet another chapter of fae history that hadn't been included in the user manual when I got pointy ears. Someone really should put together a book about that shit.

"Thank you." I leaned back in my chair, letting the meeting continue.

"Any idea where he's staying?" Johann wiped at his chin in a phantom motion that alluded to a beard having once been there.

"I sent soldiers to scour the village under nightfall," Halvar replied. "They found no easy trace, but suspect the hotel at the back of town. If anyone has a chance to find out what he's up to, take it. But be warned... The man cannot be trusted."

Another question bubbled to the front of my mind, and I cleared my throat. "Forgive me if this is already common knowledge, but why? Why can't he be trusted?"

The entire council spun on me, and I straightened in my seat, refusing to cower under their wizened gazes.

"He has a dictator-esque leadership style with a history of subterfuge and killing," Halvar explained. "Back during the Viking raids in England, Veigar installed fae among their forces. When anyone dared challenge or question an order, they ended up burned with villagers. Their heads were so disfigured you couldn't tell if their ears had been pointed or not. One of the only tells was the weapons they bore."

I swallowed hard. It sounded like he spoke from experience.

"Plus, his element is extremely dangerous and destructive." Halvar explained. "It would wreak havoc and devastation on this country if unleashed."

"Which is why he still lives in Iceland?"

"Part of the reason, yes. Tectonic plates merge there, and a Fire Fae's purpose is to protect and control the volcanoes."

A sharp inhale expanded my lungs. "That's never not going to be weird. How the hell does someone live near a volcano?"

"Beneath it," Halvar said.

"Underneath it?" I blinked twice. "Are they insane!"

"Their eyes are as black as midnight skies." Johann widened his own eyes and drew attention to them with his hands. "Said to be so to help them see in the dark beneath the volcanoes. It's why they all wear sunglasses when above the surface."

I shuddered at his use of the word *surface* as it was regarding the *earth's* surface not that of water.

Bodil piped up. "You all saw Salka's eyes when she returned to the fjord with King Reuven this winter."

Murmurs of agreement filled the room.

"I mean... I'm not going to immediately think of them as bad because their eyesight differs from my own," I said. "Seems kind of rude."

Halvar shook his head and waved his hand, dismissing the line of discussion. "Their eyesight does not matter. They're a threat when angered or provoked into attack. Veigar especially. And if he is aligned with King Reuven, then we have two powerful factions that could stand against us."

Yeah, that didn't seem ideal.

"Do you think Reuven is fully aligned with Veigar?" I asked.

"I wouldn't doubt it," Halvar replied. "Especially considering the Fjord King's marriage to Veigar's daughter."

The group nodded again, and my shoulders slumped. Fire and water aligned didn't bode well. Especially for the woods which would be susceptible to Veigar's powers. I hoped Espen and the Forest Fae Council of Elders had a plan or defensive measures they could put in place in case shit hit the fan.

"Our plan moving forward," Halvar started, his commanding tone drawing me from my fear-filled thoughts. "Garner information on his movements and true purpose here in Skolvik."

The group rumbled in agreement once more, and this time I joined them. We needed to know exactly what the Fire Fae leader was up to and prepare accordingly. If subterfuge was his usual game plan, then I needed to be vigilant.

"I'll keep my ears open for any gossip or chatter at the café. Maybe even ask Dagny, Solveig, or Jorunn if they've seen anything unusual or run into Veigar. If there's anyone in town who knows everyone's business, it's that trio." I could trust them to know the movements of a debonair newcomer.

Halvar tilted his head to me in thanks, and pride welled within me. I was doing this—a part of something bigger than me. Part of a community that took care of its natural surroundings, and a leader in my own right. I just had to see that through to the best of my ability... even if I didn't really have leadership skills.

"Meanwhile, I think we should send some soldiers to the fissure west of here and have them monitor it," Johann chimed in. The break in the mountain had been a frequent discussion point this winter and spring, with fears that snowmelt and subsequent runoff would exacerbate the fissure's size and threaten a monumental landslide. If more stuff got into that rift, it could shear the land off the mountain.

"Agreed." Halvar leaned forward again, resting his hands on the table and peering around the room, capturing everyone's gazes with his own. "I will order three soldiers to take up position there and rotate them on twelve-hour intervals. I don't want that crack growing or being manipulated by outside agitators. Now, let us all do what we can to protect our mountain."

The council members thumped their fists against the table three times, and I joined them in their usual signal for the end of a meeting. We all rose from our seats and departed, heading off to assigned duties, jobs, and lives. As my hangover headache resurged and the fleshy side of my hand smarted from being pounded against the table, I hoped I could meet the Fjell Fae's expectations. Either way, I was going to try.

ESPEN

Stillness ebbed through the open living space and a gentle light dappled the floorboards of the boathouse. Sat in the dining area with Ylva, I rested my elbows on the kitchen table and placed my head in my hands. In the past twenty-four hours I'd gone from positively elated to apocalyptically terrified. Because that's what Veigar was: a walking apocalypse. We Forest Fae may have been strong—hell I was the most powerful of us all, capable of snuffing out life with a flick of my wrist—but against fire, against him… I let out a long and jagged sigh.

"How dry is the terrain?" Turi's voice asked down the phone lying on the table. She was driving home and had looped the rest of the Forest Fae Council on the call too.

I swallowed hard. "Extremely. Just like the rest of the country, this summer was hotter than the last. The forest brush is kindling. It's a miracle we haven't already had a forest fire."

Grumbles of fear and agreement echoed down the line. Ylva inspected the end of her braid.

I leaned back in the dining chair and stared at the ceiling. What could I do? How could I protect my people, the village, my wife? Even if a fire did break out and I used my destructive powers to bury it under the soil, the ground lacked enough water to help smother the flames. My damn powers that I tried to keep locked away after all the damage they'd caused these past two centuries, would be almost useless in the dehydrated woods surrounding Skolvik. But I was the only thing that stood between a Fire Fae and the Forest Fae. The only one who could stand against him and protect the Forest Fae from being eradicated like pests.

Perhaps Øyvin and his soldiers could help? Maybe we could work together—

"Espen?" My sister's voice drew me out of my thoughts. "Espen are you still there?"

"Yes, I'm here."

"What else did Veigar say to you?" Gunvor asked. The elder-stateswoman was probably fearful of the damage to the trees and the well-being of her daughter, Ylva. Yet, her voice didn't waver. "Did he say why he's in the area?"

I crossed my arms and ankles, leaning onto the table once more. "He made no direct threats but wants greater peace and stability in the region."

Turi scoffed, Ylva snorted, and I agreed with the sentiment. Veigar couldn't be trusted. Based on all the stories I'd heard from my late mentor, Mads, and even Queen Ragnhild herself, the King of the Fire Fae was much like the volcanoes he lived under: explosive and unpredictable. Not to mention, incredibly old.

"His remarks were cut short by wedding speeches," I continued. "But his main intention was to see more stability here and among the fae overall."

Several people huffed and grunted.

"I'll believe that when he's dead," Turi muttered and received more muffled agreements.

"I'd like to arrange that funeral," Ylva added, leaning so far back in her chair that it tilted onto its back legs.

I wouldn't disagree with either of them. Though Veigar had a point about the fae needing more stability after the loss of not just one, but *three* monarchs in the past twenty years—two in the last year alone—I highly doubted his altruism. I rubbed my palms across my face.

"Do you need extra patrols?" Marius asked, and I appreciated the consideration and forethought. He was an astute addition to the Forest Fae Council. The youngest by a century, but his protective instinct was as finely honed as Øyvin's.

"Not yet," I replied. We might need the wolves at some point, but it was best to keep them in Alvdalen and the mountains. I didn't need hysteria around wolf sightings on my plate too. "A small contingent of soldiers should be moved from the northern reaches of the country. I'll coordinate the movement with Ylva, but I think it's wise for us to have a larger cadre on standby, and perhaps a few extra healers." Just in case everything went to hell.

Ylva gave me a thumbs up, having received and understood the order. Shifting forward and bringing the front legs of her chair back to the floor with a smack, she pulled out her own phone and started tapping away on it.

Anxiety gnawed at my insides like a bear mauling its prey.

"I'll circle back with news, but if anyone hears anything, please let me know," I said.

Agreement flitted across the line, and we ended the call at that.

I rested my chin in my hands again and turned to Ylva.

"We're not entirely fucked," she said without looking away from her phone.

"I'm not too sure about that."

The texting stopped and she looked up at me. "I'm trying to be optimistic here."

A low and short chuckled slipped out of me. "You've never been very good at that. You're far better at getting my wife supremely drunk though."

"Well, I should get points for the attempt." She pocketed her phone and rose from her chair. "Now, I've got one of our top teams of archers heading our way, just in case Herja shows up too, but it's going to take a couple of days for them to get here. Do you think we have that kind of time?"

I nodded, but didn't feel certain. We shouldn't bring more Forest Fae into harm's way, but if there was a chance they could help in any sort of attack, even one from the menace that was Herja, then we needed them here, however long it may take for them to arrive. "I will start informing nearby Forest enclaves, tell people they need to be vigilant, and increase our scouts around the town's perimeter."

"Good, and about what Marius said..."

Scratching at my beard, I motioned for her to continue.

"We should keep it in mind. The wolves are fast, vicious when needed, and could move between lines of fighters much quicker than we can. They would be useful messengers, and more helpful than trying to call each other during a fight."

She was right. I loved that strategic mind of hers.

"I'll think it over," I replied with a sigh.

She patted my shoulder and slipped out the front door as I shoved my face back into my hands.

Hopefully the others were having a better morning than me. Especially Øyvin. With King Reuven married to Veigar's daughter, there was probably some tension beneath the fjord.

ØYVIN

I strode through the tunnels of the Fjord Fae palace. Cool air drifted across my face, the dampness magically removed by powerful filters at the entrances to the residence. The monstrous polished cavern system swept into the lower regions of the mountain and beneath the fjord itself—an impenetrable fortress.

With aquatic creatures carved into the smooth stone walls and magical lights guiding my path, it wasn't long before I made it to the royal wing. Guards milled about, standing at attention beside large wooden doors leading to rooms and chambers where the monarch and their family lived and entertained.

A door swung open seven paces down the hall, and I slowed to a stop. Salka, newly anointed Queen of the Fjord Fae and Princess of the Fire Fae, strode out wearing a boxy, bronze tunic with intricate embroidery around the neck. As she glanced down the hall, her black eyes locked with mine.

I dipped into a shallow bow. "Your Majesty."

She bobbed her head in thanks for the deferential display, tendrils of black hair flitting around her regal, pale face. "General."

General? I hadn't been called that in a while. Everyone referred to me by my first or last name. My title was Head Guard unless we were at war. I schooled my features. "Forgive me, ma'am. I don't often hear that title used."

A gentle smile tugged at her lips, and she clutched her hands together at her waist. "The error is mine, Øyvin. My father has always referred to his Head Guard as General."

Had he now? I'd heard nothing but horror stories of Veigar's Head Guard, Herja—laying waste to tundra, scorching villages alongside the King during long ago battles. Hearing that he referred to her as General was unsurprising. Yet, worrying considering his current location.

"Did his General join him on his visit to Norway?"

She tensed and shook her head. "Not that I'm aware of."

Potential lie. Why would he travel without a guard? Or maybe he left his General behind in Iceland to watch over his heir? I could dig deeper, but the odds seemed high that she would report any questioning to Reuven. Best to keep things congenial.

"And are you enjoying his visit?"

"It's always nice to see family."

I forced a smile. "Indeed."

Her jaw tensed and she eyed me warily. I drew a sharp breath through my nose, refraining from any sudden movements. Silence wrapped around me like a blanket smothering a fire as we continued to watch each other. I wanted to wriggle free of the scrutiny. Escape the uncomfortable tension flitting between us.

This wasn't going well.

"How's your day going?" I asked, pivoting the conversation like Espen.

"Busy." She motioned to the room she'd just left. "There's a lot more to learn about the fjord and how things have been run by the late king."

"Making any changes?"

She stared at me, not blinking at the lighthearted but pointed remark. "Some."

She was just like her husband. Quiet, demure, secretive.

Motion behind Salka drew my attention. A member of the royal household staff wearing a long skirt shuffled out of the door. Her eyes widened when she saw me, but shot back to her boss. "Ma'am, the historian is ready for you down the hall."

"Thank you," Salka replied before turning her gaze back to me. "Have a good day, Øyvin."

"You too, ma'am."

She swept down the hall and I bowed my head as she passed.

An uneasy feeling settled in my stomach. While neither of the new monarchs had done anything wrong or unusual, my gut didn't fully trust them. They'd lived in Iceland with or near Veigar for years. The odds of them being loyal to him was high.

Shaking off that horrific thought, I walked deeper into the royal wing of the palace, aiming for the corner where my office sat, along with the Council chambers and the king's office.

A few moments later, I arrived at my destination. I straightened the sleeves of my uniform and knocked on Reuven's office door.

"Come in!"

Shoving open the heavy wooden door, I entered the room. Dark wood shelves surrounded the space, each one laden with trinkets that looked like they belonged on a ship. Long gone were Balder's books and chess set. Even the desk had been cleared of erroneous papers. Instead, orderly stacks of documents lined one edge, while the rest of the surface remained clear save for a green library lamp.

Reuven sat at his desk leaning back in the large leather chair, the sleeves of his white shirt casually rolled up to his elbows. It was a marked difference from the way his predecessor dressed and acted within this room. Where Balder ruled with immense confidence and shows of power, Reuven's presence was far more understated. He was casual and quiet with a cunning look in his eye that was more fitting with a well-traveled sailor than a power-hungry commodore. But appearances were often deceptive.

I straightened my spine, standing to attention. "Good morning, sir, may I have a word?"

"Of course." Reuven rose from his seat. "What do you wish to discuss?"

I needed to find out what he knew of Veigar's visit, figure out how concerned we should be. He had most recently been in contact with the fae and was married to his youngest daughter too. If anyone knew what the Fire Fae King was planning, it should be Reuven. My lungs expanded with my deep inhale. "Your father-in-law's arrival in Skolvik."

Reuven's light-blue eyes narrowed, the scar through his right eyebrow crinkling. "What about it?"

"Did you know of his visit?"

"I'm not my father-in-law's keeper. I dare say no one is," he said, his tone firm and considerate. He picked his words with care, noticeably not answering the question. I had to proceed with caution.

"Are you aware of his intentions with this visit?"

Reuven raised his hand to his shoulder. His shirt and beige trousers disappeared, replaced by the navy Fjord Fae uniform and the decadently detailed cape that fastened at both shoulders. "Why don't you join me at the wall? I was planning a visit today. We can check on the new fortifications and continue this discussion."

I bowed my head. "Of course, sir."

Reuven may not have been monarch for long, but I was duty bound to the fjord and would treat the man with the respect he deserved.

The sights, smells, and sounds of the human world above were gone at these depths, as was any ray of sunlight. Murky darkness owned these parts of the fjord as we swam toward the wall. Using our Fjord Fae powers, we'd both crafted air bubbles around ourselves and propelled downward to the fjordbed. Fjord Fae inhabitants nodded as we passed. Several schools of fish ignored us as we navigated around them, doing our best not to disturb the creatures. After ten minutes of swimming in silence side-by-side, we landed on the silty bottom with a dull thump. Sediment billowed around our feet as we took in the massive magical barrier.

The shimmering shield sat a third of the way down the fjord, not far from the village, and protected the inner waters from anything deemed a pollutant. Once torn apart by Balder, the two-kilometer-wide sheer structure now stretched from the fjordbed to the surface again, bolstered by Reuven's magic and power from the guards I'd mobilized down here.

"Everything looks in order, at first glance." Reuven strolled past one of the soldiers and I followed at his side, our air bubbles and special fae abilities allowing us to communicate at these depths.

"We haven't had any issues of note since your return to the fjord," I said. "But there are always threats."

"We must always remain vigilant."

I couldn't agree more.

"How is the Queen settling into life beneath the surface? It's been a few months now."

"It's not overly different from our residence on the island," he replied as we reached an unguarded stretch of the wall.

I squinted at him. What kind of housing did they have in Iceland? Did they live with Veigar or separately? He glanced over at me, and I looked away quickly.

"Do you have concerns about my wife, Øyvin?"

"I have concerns about her father."

Reuven's scar wrinkled and his lips quirked as he crossed his arms. "Like I said, I am not his keeper."

"But you are his son-in-law." I was skirting close to disrespect. I knew it. Could feel it in the way Reuven studied my every move.

"That I am. Is there a problem?"

"What *exactly* is he doing here?"

"Visiting Salka."

"I don't believe it. What do you know?"

Reuven pursed his lips. "Tread lightly, Head Guard."

Fuck the line in the sand. I was stepping over it. I needed to protect my home, my family, my everything. "Veigar crashed the wedding and started talking about more stability in the region and among the fae. Did he share his plans with you?"

Reuven raised a single brow. "I should think those are things we would all want."

They were, but we were already heading in that direction before the Fire Fae had arrived. "The fjord has already been subjected to terror this past year. I don't want more of it."

Reuven looked down the fjord, his gaze mired in thought.

Was he considering sharing what he knew with me? Or had I landed myself in trouble for speaking so boldly? Balder had always appreciated a level of candor, but I still wasn't sure where that limit was with Reuven.

With his arms crossed over his chest, he snapped his attention back to me, his brow furrowed. "Trust me. The fjord will always be protected."

My gut twisted at his non-answer.

Limit found.

"I have a few requests for you as my Head Guard."

"Okay."

"First, keep an eye on the oil refinery down the way. I heard mumblings of oil slicks near the fjord opening and don't want them coming in this direction."

That was news to me. "I'll increase our surveillance. Have soldiers swim past daily."

"Good. I also want you to report to me on all Forest and Fjell happenings."

My lungs tightened as if my Fjord Fae magic had stopped working and the water was set on squeezing every last bubble of oxygen from my chest. The message beneath his words hung over me like an anchor. He wanted me to spy on my partner and friend. He wanted me to put the Fjord first.

I swallowed hard and turned my gaze to the protective wall. I'd always put the fjord and its residents first. It was my job, my purpose. But that had all changed when a tourist breezed through town and stole my heart one troublesome act after another.

Reuven's request directly challenged me to pick a side: the fjord—which I'd valiantly served for a century—or my family. *Ancestors help me.* What would happen if I said no? What would happen if I said yes? Who was the biggest threat here? Who was most vulnerable? More importantly, what was most important to me?

"Well, will you honor my order?" Reuven asked, drawing me from my tumultuous thoughts.

Could I? Could I put my loved ones at risk? After all these years alone, would I dare to?

Images of my woman flitted through my mind. Her mischievous brown eyes always plotting and scheming. The way her hair got in her way or drifted onto her cheeks and how she flicked it aside as if it had offended her. The sound of her laughter that ignited a joy inside me that I hadn't felt in years.

"Øyvin?"

"Yes," I lied and turned to continue our walk along the wall.

119

LENNIE

The scent of herbal spices and sound of happy chatter permeated the air in Fisken as I pulled out my chair and took a seat at the large dark-wood table. Our remaining family members gathered for a final meal together. Smiles alighted everyone's faces, jokes flying between Andrew and Knut-Arne, while Ingrid and Mom corralled the young girls to their own table. My four nieces had spent every day together and were now best friends. When my side of the family departed tomorrow morning, there'd be some tears shed and frowns.

"So, Lennie, what on here do you recommend?" Dad asked from across the table as he peered down at the menu. I could now read the whole thing thanks to practicing my Norwegian and having tried everything.

"You'll like the stew, Dad."

"I do like a good stew."

Espen settled on the chair to my left, Øyvin on my right. Kristoffer sat at the end of the table between the Fjord Fae and my dad—who had earned himself a five-year-old shadow since arriving in Norway.

The waiter came and took our drink orders, swiftly returning with a tray of water, beer, and wine. As he departed to leave us more time with the menu, heat washed across my neck and I pulled my hair up into a ponytail to cool off a bit. The poor air conditioning unit in here must've been on strike after our reception yesterday.

Dad straightened and waved across the room. "Veigar! Nice to see you."

My eyes widened and my stomach clenched. This was not happening. This could *not* be happening. I twisted in my seat and found the sophisticated looking monarch ambling toward an empty table.

Mom leaned toward Dad, whispering, "Oh, Dan, is he alone?"

"I think so."

She readjusted in her seat like that simply would not do and let loose her most welcoming smile. "Why don't you join us, Veigar? We have a spot open!"

Fuck. This was happening.

For once in their lives, I needed my parents to be less of the Midwest Super Nice Neighborly Happy People that they were, and a helluva lot more like my Asshole, Øyvin. If ever there were a moment for them to sample the unwelcoming smorgasbord that was being a dick, now would be the time.

I leaned across the table to my mom. "We don't need—"

"Hush, now Lennie." Mom scolded me under her breath and beamed again two seconds later. "Everyone is welcome here."

"If you don't mind the intrusion, Mrs. Martin."

I looked up and found Veigar giving my mother a suave smile. For that alone I wanted to lunge past Øyvin and swat his face.

"Of course not. We'd love to hear about life in Iceland."

Veigar pulled out the vacant chair beside Dad and Kristoffer. "Fire away."

Øyvin cleared his throat while Espen rested his hand on my thigh. I took a deep breath and squeezed Espen's fingers. This was actually happening.

Kristoffer tilted his head and pointed at Veigar's sunglasses. "Are you blind?"

"Kristoffer Mikkelsen!" Ingrid erupted from the other end of the table, her face as white as snow, and started scolding the boy in Norwegian. "Apologize at once."

The young boy's shoulders curved as he slunk back in his seat and stared at the table. His lower lip wobbled. "Sorry."

Veigar lightly tapped the table space between him and Kristoffer. "Thank you for the apology. I have light sensitivity," he explained, and half the table bristled knowing full well that was not the whole story. "My eyes don't like a lot of light, it hurts them. So, I wear these to avoid some horrible headaches."

A tiny tear streaked down Kristoffer's face as he tilted his head up. "So, the sun is not your friend?"

Veigar smiled. "The sun is needed for all forms of life to flourish, but unfortunately, my eyes don't think so. Both of my daughters have the same thing. It's a family trait of sorts. We just learn to live with it."

Kristoffer sniffled and bobbed his head. Øyvin passed the young boy his napkin, which he took with a whimper.

"Have any of you tried *lutefisk* while you're here?" Espen piped up, mercifully pivoting the conversation.

"That's the gelatinous, fish stuff that's brined, right?" Ryan asked.

Andrew leaned back in his chair. "No, I thought it was cured in lye?"

My brothers turned their full attention to my partner. "Yes, it's usually a white fish soaked in water, then cured in lye, and soaked once more. Which does give it a gelatinous texture."

"I'm always down to try anything," Ryan piped up, exhibiting that Martin Family competitiveness that all of us siblings had inherited. From which parent, I was never quite sure, but my bet was secretly Mom.

"Are you enjoying your time in Skolvik?" my dad asked Veigar. I decided to focus on their conversation and not the other one further down that table discussing the different types of fish in Norway.

"I am. It's a magical place and my daughter just moved here. She recommended a few shops to visit, so I spent my day looking for souvenirs to take home."

"Ah yes!" My dad straightened. "We spent some time at the gift shop earlier today and the jewelers on Friday. Deb found some beautiful silverware."

"Were you able to find anything nice to take home to Iceland?" I chimed in.

Veigar turned to me with an overly congenial smile. "Not yet. But there's still time."

"You plan on staying for a while?"

"Ever since my wife passed, I've tried to spend as much time with my daughters as possible. So, we shall see what the family wants. At this time, my trip has an indeterminate end."

"Oh, our Lennie knows how that goes." Dad chuckled. "One second you're missing your ship, the next you're moving in."

A strained laugh left me and I brought my beer to my mouth and gulped down half of it.

The waiter returned and took our orders—plenty of stew, fish, and reindeer meatballs—and the rest of our dinner remained cordial and uneventful. Mom and Dad carried on conversation with me, Øyvin, and Veigar, while the other end of the table was in a riotous debate about sports—Andrew, ever the quarterback, steadfast in his belief that American Football was better than football.

Mom finished her stew and reached her hand across the table. "Lennie, you seem a bit quiet this evening? You doing okay?"

My final bite of meatball slid down my throat and I set aside my knife and fork. I had been quieter than usual. Mostly because I was listening to Dad and Veigar's conversation. My guys had been less verbose too, likely doing the same thing.

"You know, it's okay to be sad we're leaving. It means you've had a good time," Mom said, her tone full of warmth and love I wanted to wrap myself in.

I was a bit sad. While I usually handled my mom best in small doses, and this trip had been no different, having everyone gathered together, smiling and laughing, was a joy I didn't want to end.

"It's been great having you all here."

She smiled back. "I'm so glad we could be here for you. We're so happy for you."

My heart swelled and threatened to burst with the outpouring of love I'd experienced this weekend. "Thanks, Mom."

The cool night air brushed across the back of my neck as we stepped outside of the restaurant and started saying our goodbyes.

Mom took my hands in hers. "Now, I know we've just had a trip to see each other, but I want to know your holiday travel plans as soon as possible."

My stomach nosedived and pulled back up again, threatening to return my meatballs with it. I couldn't leave Skolvik. Couldn't leave the mountain. The last time I'd done that, the fjell had experienced cave ins and cracks. Damage that had taken weeks to repair.

I had a responsibility with this new magic, and to my new home, but I loved my family with every fiber of my being.

This was too hard. Pitting my two worlds against each other.

But at the end of the day, I couldn't hurt a society of fae just because I wanted to go to Ohio for turkey and Christmas morning.

"Well, Mom." I cleared my throat. "Since we were back for Thanksgiving last year, we'd been thinking we would spend the holiday here in Norway and share it with our Norwegian family."

Was it an American holiday? Sure. Had we discussed such plans? No, but we could. What was most important here was keeping the fae secret safe and the mountain protected. Especially considering a recent tourist's arrival in town.

Mom's shoulders deflated before she donned her hostess smile and squeezed my hands once more. "I'm sure you'll have a great time."

"We can set up a video call and maybe even a computer board game night too."

"Your brothers would love that."

Hugs, well wishes, and promises of phone calls filled the air as both sides of our family said their goodbyes. The young girls sobbed, tears streaming down little Amelia's sun-kissed cheeks as she clung to Andrew. I squeezed Ingrid and Knut-Arne and promised Kristoffer we'd call him in a few weeks for a catch up. Finally, I hugged my parents goodbye.

Dad sighed as he let go of me. "Well, Lennie, you survived the weekend."

"That I did, Dad," I said with a smile. "Are you ever going to tell me who was responsible for the Ohio State Fight Song being played as I walked back down the aisle?"

"Only the guy in charge of the speakers knows the truth."

I tilted my head to one side, giving him a look that said I wasn't buying a word of that.

Dad checked his empty wrist. "Oh, would you look at the time? Bye, pumpkin."

With a snort, I let them go. I'd bet good money he was behind the little stunt.

Half the group walked back to their hotel, the other climbed into waiting cars. We waved them all off and my heart cracked in one corner. It'd been so nice to have everyone in one location, to see tables filled with our loved ones. I swallowed the lump in my throat and wiped the corners of my eyes. My fingertips came back damp. *Don't cry, don't cry, don't cry.*

As I fought against the welling emotions, Espen wrapped me into a hug and Øyvin pressed his hand against my lower back.

"Your mother was right, you know," Espen said. "Sadness means you had a good time."

Øyvin grumbled in agreement.

I sniffled. "However much I hate you saying my mother is right, she does have a good point."

Snickering, Espen brushed his hand across my head where it rested against his chest.

They were right. I'd had a wonderful time. And all wasn't lost. I had a family here in Skolvik too. My guys, my friends, the villagers that seemed to have taken a reluctant liking to me and welcomed me into the fold. This was my home, and while I didn't have my immediate family with me, it was still brimming with love and care.

"Family is so important," a somber male voice said from behind us, and we spun to find Veigar near the doorway to Fisken. "Don't you agree?"

Emotionally spent and tired, I pulled out of Espen's hold. "What do you want, Veigar?"

A slick grin crossed his lips. "What's best for *us*: unity and regional stability."

"Yeah, yeah, yeah, you're Mr. Peace and Love. We get it." But I sure as hell didn't believe it, not with all the rumors and stories I'd heard about the guy.

"Believe what you want, Mrs. Solbakke Martin." He straightened his cuff links and turned down the road into the main part of town. "But I think you'll come round to my way of thinking quite swiftly."

"Doubt it."

My guys huffed in agreement, both stood with their arms crossed over their chests.

"You will."

"And if we don't?"

A wisp of a flame curled around the man's hand and disappeared. My stomach flip-flopped. "Family is such a precious thing to lose." Veigar's eyebrows rose above the top edge of his sunglasses, and he strolled around the corner, out of sight.

All three of us deflated, and I bent over, resting my hands on my knees. My heart beat so hard it threatened to jump through my ribs.

"Did he just threaten our families?" I asked.

"Mm-hmm," Øyvin replied as Espen nodded, his eyes locked on where Veigar had disappeared.

"What the hell do we do? Can he reach my side of the family? Would he go all the way to Ohio to do… whatever that threat just was?"

"I don't think so," Espen said. "But we should warn those *like us* in Norway to keep an eye out for anything suspicious, and we should prepare."

"Prepare for things to escalate? For a fight?" That's what Halvar had been saying at the Council meeting this morning. *I wonder if Espen and Øyvin had similar conversations with their factions?*

Espen hummed in the affirmative as I straightened.

"Exactly," Øyvin said. "He wants something. I'd guess more power, more control of the fae."

Espen slid his hand into mine as if he needed to reassure himself that I was still by his side. "I agree, but until we know for sure, we have to remain vigilant. He's already powerful and I don't think Skolvik would survive any further surprises from him."

I stared back at the place where Veigar had vanished. "Fuck."

The next evening, magical lights flickered against the barren, gray cavern walls and Halvar, dressed in all black, paced at the back of the youngster's training room. I hadn't seen any others training in here before, but that might have more to do with Halvar and the prior uncertainty about my powers.

"You summoned me." I raised my arms in the air like I was in a Miss America pageant. Luckily, I wore leggings and a light sweater, not some slinky little gown. Training in heels and a dress sounded like cruel and unusual punishment—then, again, this was Halvar.

"Thank you for coming." Halvar's silver hair caught in the beams of light. "As Torsten's text said, we need to increase your training immediately." An ominous tone laced his words and my gut twisted in on itself.

I set my water bottle down by the entrance and looked over at him. "Does this have to do with the town's latest visitor?"

He nodded once.

"Pretty sure he threatened my family last night." Maybe I shouldn't have been so feisty with him after dinner with the family.

"He is *the* threat."

I took an involuntary step back. I knew Halvar was worried. Hell, he'd been practically shrouded in concern at the emergency council meeting. But hearing those words from him sent an uneasy wave of fear through every inch of my body. I definitely shouldn't have been testy with Veigar.

"What kind of training are we talking about?" I asked, pivoting back to his previous comment.

"Crack sealing, weapon forming, strength training, and making sure you *fully* understand your royal magic. What it can achieve for you on the field of battle."

"Hold up, big guy." I raised my hand and popped my hip to the side. "Did you just say, field of battle? You want *me* on a battlefield? Like the one on top of the mountain where you fought Balder?"

He nodded again.

Fuck me sideways. A woman really couldn't get a moment of uninterrupted peace around here. I rubbed my fingers across my forehead. With these powers and my new role, I didn't have a choice. I had to step up. I needed to do everything I could to protect my new home and not screw it up. "Where do we start?"

Halvar's lips twitched in what might have been the blossoming of a smile but quickly sank back into a firm line. "Seal the crack." He waved his arm over his head and brought it back down in the blink of an eye. An explosive snapping noise echoed around the room and a sharp divide formed to my left where the ceiling and wall curved together. "Stop the wall from caving in."

I gasped and bolted for the rugged gash, adrenaline shooting through me. The wall groaned and threatened to fall. Instinctively, my arms shot above my head and I pressed my hands into the highest point of the cave I could reach, right beside the yawning crack.

My magic swirled within me, desperate to be released and help. I listened to it and pulled forward that swell of warmth, pushing it down my arms and into the rock. An invisible wave of power burst from my palms and rippled toward the fissure.

The break stopped growing.

I was doing it.

Just like Halvar had done during our first training session where he'd pushed the ceiling above his head and shifted the stone, now the magic ebbing from me put the stone back into place. It wove over the crevice and stitched it together like I wielded a thread and needle—the jagged edges clicking back into place.

When the grating noise stopped, I remained in my outstretched position and slowly willed my magic to return to me. It did so gladly, like a puppy that'd been a good boy.

"Nicely done," a male voice said, and I spun around.

Torsten leaned against the back wall of the training cave. His hair was swept up into his signature man bun and the cape of his gray uniform draped over one shoulder. I shouldn't have been surprised to see him. The busy, teddy bear of a man with a wicked sense of humor and delightful life partner, was a staple by Halvar's side.

"How long have you been there?"

"Long enough to applaud your natural instincts."

"Awww, thanks," I said, and did my best not to preen. "I thought you were with Leif this evening. He said you were having a movie night when he stopped by the café this morning."

"He's been called in for emergency training with the local Forest archers." He twisted to Halvar. "Here to help with her other training as requested."

Halvar gave him a nod in thanks and turned his eyes back to me. "I have one more thing I want to test before we move to your royal and light magic."

I quirked a single eyebrow. "What's that?"

"Shield." Halvar waved his hands. A blast of light flared toward me and crashed against my chest, sending me onto my ass with a thud.

"What the fuck was that?" I yelled and rubbed my fist against the spot where I'd taken the hit.

"I rescind my comments about natural instincts," Torsten said.

An agreeing rumble sounded from Halvar's chest. "You have more to learn."

I pushed off the ground, rose to my feet, and brushed off my leggings. "Warn a woman next time—"

"Veigar will not give you a warning," Halvar interjected.

"Fair enough." He had a good point. Any man who threw around threats against someone's family wasn't the kind of guy to announce his actions. "So, you gonna teach me how to shield?"

He grunted and our training began in earnest.

We started with shielding for both Fjell and royal powers. The former consisted of creating a piece of stone as flat as slate that I could bury in the ground like a surfboard in sand or fasten to my wrist. The royal magic was a bit more complicated, but Torsten took his time explaining the movement and the intentions—a waving motion and *shield*. It took me several tries to get both to work even half decently, but by the fifth attempt of both, I was getting the hang of it and shielding faster.

Next, we moved on to forms of stunning magic with my royal powers. Balls of light zipped across the room as I practiced the easiest part, before we pivoted to equipping it to a sword.

"I've done this before," I muttered, feeling the stone sword hum with power in my hand as royal magic crackled at the end like lightning.

Torsten nodded. "In the throne room earlier this year. But did you know what you were doing?"

I shook my head. When the wolf barged into the throne room, I'd acted on instinct—a need to protect flaring within me. Drawing the sword had been second nature in that moment, but I would always remember how it felt. It was as if the mountain and my heart beat as one.

"We didn't think so," Torsten continued. "Being able to use both concurrently is imperative for you to protect yourself and utilize the magic to its full potential."

Halvar grunted in agreement where he leaned against the wall, his arms crossed over his chest.

My training continued with Torsten giving me orders on how to push and pull the royal magic in and out of me, guiding it down the sword. That was followed by basic sword handling and jousting from Halvar.

The way he moved with a blade was like an artist knowing exactly what brush strokes were needed for the perfect composition. But one thing was certain, Halvar wasn't used to painting with oils or watercolors. No, the beast from the mountain, with his assured actions and immense strength, had a history of painting with blood.

I mimicked his movements, and my arms slowly started to ache in protest. We'd been at this for hours, and in true Halvar fashion, he'd saved the most difficult task for last. While holding the sword wasn't hard, the repetitive motions and unrelenting orders from the sidelines turned me into a panting mess.

After what felt like another painful hour, we finally had a break. I took a gulp of water from the bottle I'd set by the entrance and relished the feeling of cool liquid sluicing down my throat. Sweat ran down the side of my face and pooled beneath my boobs, gluing my sports bra to my chest.

"You are a weakness." Halvar swept around the front of the room, his hands balled into white-knuckled fists as I set down my water bottle.

"That's kind of rude, don't you think?"

He narrowed his eyes at me. "You're a target. One Veigar will take advantage of at the first hint of an opportunity."

I let out a sigh. *That* kind of weakness.

"You mean he'll use me as bait? Try to kidnap me and make the boys heel like dogs?" *Been there, done that already.* Although getting kidnapped by Aurora and her merry band of wolf-shifters hadn't been a calamitous plight. They'd ultimately just wanted to question me and use me to get Espen's attention. They'd even fed me while I was holed up in their garden shed.

I doubted Veigar would be so kind.

No, that fae would probably dangle me over a ravine of fire. Maybe even a volcano.

Halvar strode straight at me. I took two steps back before stopping, forcing him to crash into me or halt. He brought us toe-to-toe and hit the brakes.

"He will hold your life over a precipice and force everyone's hand."

While I didn't like the thought of dying, especially at the hands of a Fire Fae, I was surprised that I was somehow The Chosen One in this scenario.

"He'll force Espen to bow to him or use his destructor powers," I started, breaking down the problem that Halvar was struggling to verbalize. The big guy had never been very verbose. "Which we all know Espen only whips out as a last resort. Veigar, through his son-in-law, Reuven, now King of the Fjord, will force Øyvin to submit. Hell, maybe even try to use him to get to me. Which won't work unless I've pissed him off that morning."

Halvar snorted and Torsten stifled a chuckle with his hand.

"But you." I pointed to Halvar. "You're the one I'm like, magically. And my magic is tied to the mountain. I'm the Fjell's Deputy Head Guard. A leader and council member. But only a demi-fae. I don't have full fae powers."

Halvar and Torsten's eyes met for a brief second and I stilled.

The air in the room felt like it had evaporated.

"What aren't you telling me?" I tilted my chin down and glared at them. My heart rate picked up speed, galloping faster and faster, as neither of them met my gaze. They'd been keeping secrets. "What other target do I have on my back?"

"Not informing her makes her weaker," Torsten said, pointedly not telling Halvar what to do. Smart, all things considered.

Halvar rolled his shoulders and straightened, looking every bit the role of Head Guard and protector of the mountain. "Our theory is that Freija had more magic than we realized when she died. A gift we believe was bestowed from the ancestors."

I tilted my head to one side like that was supposed to make sense.

"We think you got *all* the extra magic. It appears to have passed through me."

My eyebrows hit my glistening hairline. "You mean to tell me, I'm like the Energizer Bunny of the Fjell but with a whole extra battery?"

Lines formed on Halvar's forehead as his eyebrows pinched together.

"I'm..." I continued, hoping to clarify. "I have extra power that you don't have?"

"That is our working theory, but I do not know for certain as Freija never confirmed nor denied what powers, if any, were given to her."

Air whooshed out of my lungs. *Holy shit.* "But even with extra powers, I'm still partially human, right? Still classified as demi-fae?"

Halvar nodded. "Trygve doesn't believe you will have the full life span of a fae, but thinks it may be longer than your average human."

Well, that was a positive.

"When did you realize I'd been given more powers?"

"Earlier this year when you killed Wilhelm by slamming a light ball into his back," Torsten replied.

"And when you apparently stunned Aurora," Halvar said.

I winced. "She told you about that?"

He grunted.

"That killing light isn't normal, then?" I asked, looking to Torsten.

He shook his head. "I can't do it."

"Only monarchs are known to have that power," Halvar said.

"Do you have it?" I asked. "Or was it just me that got that bit during the transfer?"

Halvar's shoulders relaxed minutely, and he let out a long breath. "I haven't been successful, no."

Shit on a stick. I stared at the slate-colored wall and took in the ramifications of that. I had power that only fae monarchs had. Power that could kill—*had* killed someone on the spot. It'd hurt to use, burning and searing down my arms and arching my back, but was that because I didn't know what I was doing? Or was that a burden of using and inflicting that power on someone else?

"We aren't a hundred percent certain how that power is used or if it can be channeled into anything else," Torsten said, drawing my focus from my spiraling thoughts. "But our guess is the intention, just like the stunning magic."

I brushed stray baby-hairs off my forehead with both hands. An unwelcome shudder ran through me as the memories of that day resurfaced. The gaping maw of the wolf. The agony as he ripped through my leg. And the anger and desperation that settled into my bones when he moved on Aurora. "I was thinking about death and stopping Wilhelm when he launched toward Aurora. It would have to be that thought and a burning desire to protect someone."

Torsten murmured like that made sense to him, while Halvar didn't move a muscle, quietly taking everything in.

Silence settled over the room once more as the weight of that fact washed over us. I, a demi-fae, who was human only a year ago, had the power of a monarch. Enough power that I could kill someone on the spot. Magic that had once belonged to the Queen of the Fjell Fae.

"Why do you think Freija got extra powers from the ancestors?" I asked. "What did she need it for?"

The two men looked at each other once more before they turned back to me with thoughtful gazes. Torsten clapped Halvar on the shoulder. "I'll leave this one to you," he said and meandered out of the room, tossing a "well done, today, baby fae" over his shoulder.

I returned my gaze to Halvar. Curiosity bubbling within me. "What else have you been keeping from me?"

He cleared his throat. "There's something you need to see."

LENNIE

"Where exactly are you taking me?" I asked as Halvar and I wound through tunnel after tunnel, deeper into the mountain.

His long strides ate up the rocky corridors, steps neither slowing nor faltering. "A location you must swear to protect."

"What do you mean by that?" Scurrying beside him, I did my best not to trip over my own feet. "I'll always protect the mountain."

He ground to a stop and narrowed his eyes at me. "Will you? Without question?"

The weight of his words settled across my shoulders, but I'd already agreed to it this past winter when I took up the role as Deputy Head Guard. I'd proven myself worthy of the title and sworn to take care of the Fjell. If I set my mind to doing something, I was damn well doing it. I'd also grown to know and like the fae of the fjell, and the village below the mountain was my home, my new family. "I'd do anything to protect those I care about, including this mountain. Except, perhaps, anything that would hurt Espen or Øyvin."

Halvar straightened and an emotion I could only describe as pride filled his gaze. He nodded once and set off down the tunnel again.

I shrugged. "I'll take that as an *okay great,* then."

We continued our downward trek, and I pushed away the memories of the last time I'd been this deep in the mountain's tunnels and the canine that had tried to kill me there. My lungs tightened, my breaths came faster, and I pinched my nails into the fleshy part of my hands.

I'm safe. Wilhelm is dead and gone.

I took a deep breath through my nose and pivoted to happier memories.

I'm safe. Wilhelm is dead and gone.

Øyvin baking me cookies and plying me with tea when I had a head cold this spring.

I'm safe. Wilhelm is dead.

Espen playing dress up with his nieces and nephew in Alvdalen this winter.

I'm safe.

The look on my guys' faces when I walked down the aisle to them.

The thoughts and mantra eventually drifted away as we stopped in front of a stone wall protected by two Fjell Fae guards.

Halvar gave them a nod and passed through the stone wall.

I snorted. "Those mirage walls will never cease to surprise me." Honest to hell, who knew where they were? How did anyone find them? There was probably some sign that I'd yet to learn about, and if I went testing walls, I'd probably end up bruised and with a gnarly concussion.

Following Halvar through the mirage, the magic washed over me like walking into an air-conditioned building on a hot summer's day. What I found on the other side, though, drew me to a stop and my eyes bulged to the size of camera lenses.

Rows of stone caskets with prone statues spread across the large room and rocky pillars the size of redwoods held the vaulted ceiling.

"You want me to protect the dead as well as the living?" My day was taking some seriously interesting turns. First training and the magic revelations, now a visit to the tombs. What was next? Were they secretly harboring the Norse Gods in the basement of this place?

Halvar huffed. "Herein lies a place only those with royal magic and Head Guards have access to. You shall be included in those numbers."

"You mean one of these"—I motioned to the tombs around me—"is a secret passage to a sacred place? Like in an Indiana Jones movie? Should I have brought a hat and whip?"

Halvar's throat bobbed. "This is the royal tomb."

Emotions barbed his words and scraped over my buoyant bubble of humor, bursting it. My smile dropped.

Freija was in here. One of these stone statues was the image of her representing the place where she'd been laid to rest. I peered around the room, but didn't see her likeness in my immediate vicinity.

While I'd been to her funeral, I didn't know exactly where they'd buried her. I assumed there was a royal tomb. I just never expected to find myself *in* it.

"I'm sorry." I cleared my throat and straightened up. "You said there was somewhere I needed to see?"

Halvar spun on the spot and strode to the back of the room.

I followed, my footsteps echoing off the walls of the silent chamber.

We reached the end of the walkway through the sarcophagi and stopped in front of a mural etched into the stone surface. The image encompassed the entire facade.

A pointy mountain sat in the middle of the wall with two large trees on either side. Their branches stretched onto the adjoining walls as if wrapping the room in a hug and the tiny leaves looked like flames. Swirls of water lapped at the base of the picture and in the bottom right corner was a wolf, baying to the sky.

"It's beautiful," I muttered. Photographs would never do it justice.

"This is a sacred space for the Fae," Halvar said. He placed his hand in the middle of the mountain, his chest rising and falling as he took a deep breath and pressed his magic into the stone. Silvery light flowed into the lines of the image, slowly filling every nook and crevice, until the entire mural shone. The back of the room illuminated with a soft glow and a gentle breath passed my lips in awe.

"Wow."

Halvar pushed against the center of the mountain once more. A grinding noise, like that of a large mortar and pestle, echoed through the chamber as the mountain swung inward on a set of hinges.

"Follow me," he said.

I picked my jaw off the floor and followed him through the triangular opening.

Inside was a small room, no bigger than a classroom, with walls made of the same light-blue quartz as the Fjell Fae throne. In the center of the space, atop the slate-gray floor, sat what could only be described as a pedestal or place of offering. From the rugged base to the cylindrical leg that held up a square-shaped platter, the small table-like structure looked like it belonged in a church.

As Halvar shut the door behind us and paced around to the other side of the room, I took a closer look at the sole object in the chamber.

On second thought, the top wasn't a complete square. Three corners were missing—shorn off as if someone had hacked them off with a pickaxe.

Straightening, I shoved my hands behind my back, stopping myself from reaching out and brushing my fingers across the glassy surface. My gaze drifted to my surroundings once more. There were no light sconces in here. Only a blue glow, as if the walls themselves were the light source.

Magic.

Definitely, magic.

"What is this place?"

Halvar stopped on the other side of the pedestal, his eyes locked on me. "This is the Temple of the Fae. The birthplace of our kind."

Air stilled in my lungs and my eyebrows hit my sweat-covered hairline. "What?"

"I do not know what your partners have told you regarding the history of the fae, but Skolvik has always been rumored to be where we first came from. That rumor is true."

"Well, shit," I muttered.

"The Fjord Fae protect the waters and creatures from threats like pollution. The Forest Fae protect and care for the flora and fauna. Fire Fae protect volcanoes and tectonic plate movement. And we, the Fae of the Fjell, are sworn to protect the mountain. That protection also extends to the Temple of the Fae."

My mind whirled with the new information and the existence of a sacred place for the fae—hidden away within the mountain. It was beautiful. Magical. A glittering shrine of history. "Why are you showing me this?"

"Because as Deputy Head Guard and holder of royal power, you have a right to know."

"Do all the Fjell Fae know about this place?"

He shook his head. "Only those on the Council and the few select soldiers charged with guarding the tomb entry."

"And they can get in here too?"

"No, only those with royal magic and a monarch's Head Guard have access." He raised his arm and tapped a spot on his wrist. A small white dot, a little larger than the one I had from Nora's hearing juju, marred his skin. A royal must've used their magic and granted him entry.

"And I have both title and power."

Halvar made a noise in agreement.

I looked around once more. It was a stunning place. The walls were like facets of a diamond, bouncing blue-toned light across the room as if it was twilight. No objects adorned the sides of the room, no carvings marred their flanks. The only other *thing* in here aside from me and Halvar was the fractured pedestal fit for a museum display.

I tilted my chin toward it. "What's that for?"

"This is why we are here," Halvar replied. "This is how Fae monarchs communicate with the ancestors."

It did look like a place of worship. A chamber where offerings could be made to gods and deities, or where prayers might be heard. The absolute silence in the room would allude to such a sacred space, too.

"How'd it break?" I motioned to the pedestal again.

Halvar eyed the broken corners. "I don't know for certain. But we believe that each of the other factions have a corner of the plinth and use it for their ceremonies."

"Oh. Is this where the new queen or king comes after their coronation to receive the recycled magic?"

Halvar squinted like he was surprised I knew about that process.

"Nora mentioned something about it."

Halvar's features relaxed. "Yes, this is where the Fjell heir comes and receives all the magic their predecessor had, plus anything that might be required at the time."

"Does that apply to monarchs of the other factions?"

"I'm not sure. I assume there is a similar process with their own shards from the Temple, unless they've been withholding information—"

"Which is plausible, all things considered." Like Balder being an ass and Veigar being a dick.

"Exactly."

My fingers itched to touch the pedestal and brush across the smooth blue walls, but I kept them clenched together behind my back.

"What we do know," Halvar continued, "is this cave has been a place monarchs have turned to for greater assistance from the ancestors."

If this was where King Olaf of the Forest Fae had come all those years ago and had his soldiers changed into wolf shifters, then the other royal lines must know of this place. No doubt told their trusted advisers too. "So, the other kings probably know of its existence?"

"Considering Veigar's arrival in Skolvik, I would believe so. I also think one of Freija's last visits here may have been to request additional power, but she never confirmed. Never got the chance."

"Hence your suspicion that I have more power than I know what to do with."

Halvar nodded and crossed his arms.

"Is this why Veigar is in town? You think he wants access?"

"We can only make assumptions at this time. Which is why I asked everyone at the emergency council meeting to find out as much as they could regarding Veigar's presence in the village."

"Yeah, I don't buy his 'unity and regional stability' bullshit either. I get the feeling he wants something more." He'd also crashed my wedding and threatened my family last night. I wasn't a fan.

"Agreed. Now, place your hand on it." Halvar motioned to the pedestal.

I reared back. "Erm... come again? You *want* me to touch it?"

"Put your palm on the pedestal."

The podium's glossy facets winked back at me.

"Will it kill me?"

"Probably not."

"That's not reassuring, big guy."

"I'll bury you with the kings and queens if it does."

I cocked my head to one side. "Really?"

"No."

"Are you making jokes again?"

"Also no."

He totally was. This was Halvar humor. He delighted in confusing me. One day I'd get the man to admit to making a joke. Or, at the very least, laughing at one of my own.

"What do I do?"

"Just put your hand on it."

"No incantation? No spell? No, *hear ye hear ye oh great and wonderful being from the beyond*?"

His jaw muscles tightened. "Put. Your. Hand. On. The. Pedestal."

"Have *you* ever tried it? Maybe it would respond to your royal—"

"Do it now," he grumbled and lurched toward me, malice shining in his eyes.

Fear shot through my body and I slapped my hand atop the pedestal. Lights swirled in the walls around us, lightning zipped down my arm, and my vision blurred before the world faded to black.

122

LENNIE

Someone had turned the lights back on... But why were they blue?

Why were they flashing?

Had I been teleported to a rave? That would be fun, but kind of inconvenient. The Norwegians knew how to party, but now probably wasn't the best time.

Or was it?

I peeled open my eyes and pulled my hand off the glowing pedestal beside me. Definitely not a rave, but...

Magic twinkled in the walls as if someone had set an entire Christmas display of dancing white lights within the shiny blue stone. I looked around and my breath hitched.

Halvar had disappeared.

Fuck.

Where'd he go?

Did he get left behind?

Or had he teleported somewhere else? If this even was a teleport... which wouldn't surprise me at this point. With magic being real and me turning into a demi-fae, why wouldn't teleportation be real too?

I shook away the thoughts and refocused.

Halvar had mentioned the Temple being the place where monarchs spoke with the ancestors. But the room was empty. There was only me, the pedestal, and an eerie silence.

A strange sensation rippled across my shoulders and down my spine. My fight or flight instinct kicked in, raising the hairs on my arms.

I was being watched.

Not just by one person, but hundreds, maybe *thousands*.

It was as if I stood in the middle of a football stadium, the only player on the field, with a packed crowd watching my every move.

"Anybody there?" I asked, my voice echoing around the chamber.

The silence cheered back at me.

"Did I die?"

My body tingled and I pinched my arm. A sharp sting burst where I'd marked my own skin. "Okay, probably alive."

I tapped my palm against my clenched fist and brought it to my mouth like a microphone. "Testing, testing. One, two. One, two. Do we have any sexy trolls in the house tonight?"

The little light dots within the wall swished from the right side of the room to the left.

I stilled and cocked my head. No *body* responded, but the magic in the walls certainly had.

Weird.

Maybe the ancestors were these tiny blobs of light magic?

"Halvar didn't tell me what to do or what would happen. So... um... Hi, I'm Lennie Solbakke Martin. Wife of Espen Solbakke Martin and partner of Øyvin Håland. Some may call me a pain in the ass, but I'd argue I have a *great* personality. No, really. Ten out of ten, would recommend. I can party with the best of them, make you look fantastic in photos, and, as of this spring, make the second-best cappuccino in Skolvik."

Was I rambling? Sure. But what the fuck else was I supposed to do? Ask for guidance? Pray for my soul? If you asked my brothers, that ship sailed decades ago.

The walls shimmered, saying nothing.

I let out a huff and wiped my hands across my leggings. This whole experiment was proving fruitless, and I didn't want to get stuck wherever this was.

"While I appreciate the quiet types, this date isn't going great. It's not me, it's you. And with that said, I think it's my time to leave."

The lights in the wall zipped from left to right, congregating like a pack of fireflies on one side of the room.

"Glad you agree. Next time, maybe we can have some face-to-face action."

The lights brightened momentarily before dimming and spreading out again.

"Bye to you too." I placed my hand on the pedestal once more and pushed an ounce of my royal magic into it. "Take me home, please."

A tingling sensation started tickling my skin and grew into zapping, lightning crackling up my arm. Darkness clouded my vision again and when the world faded back into view, Halvar appeared in my periphery. He stood right where I'd left him, arms crossed and features as stoic as usual. Relief and joy swelled between my ribs. I'd never been so happy to see the guy.

"Where'd I go?" I asked.

"You didn't leave."

"What?"

He tilted his chin toward my feet. "You've stood there for a couple of minutes staring at the wall without blinking."

That would explain why my eyes felt dry. I rubbed at them with the backs of my thumb knuckles. "So, you didn't hear or see anything?"

Halvar shook his head.

"The lights didn't flash in the walls?"

"They did when you put your hand on the pedestal but stopped shortly after."

"And I didn't move at all? Didn't touch myself?"

His eyebrows furrowed. "Touch yourself?"

Ugh, on second thought, that sounded inappropriate. "I mean pinch myself. Did I pinch my own arm?"

"No."

I let out a harumph and set my hands on my hips. So, I hadn't been here. I'd been on, what? Some ancestral plane? Was that who had been watching me? The dead fae? Or maybe I was in my own head? "Did Freija ever tell you what happened when she spoke to the ancestors?"

"Not in detail," he replied. "Just that they responded."

"Well, they don't seem to be a talkative bunch. At least not to me."

He narrowed his eyes, brows pinching. "Care to explain?"

"The lights were on, but no one was home. It felt like I was being watched, though, but no one"—I waved my hands in front of me—"appeared."

Halvar let out a quizzical noise.

"Maybe they just weren't in the mood for a chat."

"Maybe," he mumbled.

"Or maybe they were offended that you sent a demi-fae?"

"Unlikely."

"Why?"

"Because in our entire history, and as far as I am aware, there has never been a fae like you."

"Say that again." I stifled a yawn with the back of my hand. "My ego liked it."

He rolled his eyes. "Go home. Rest. You train with my soldiers tomorrow night."

"More training?"

"Every night." Halvar's gaze cut to me. "There are two groups of people in this world: those who always prepare for battle and those who don't worry about it until it's too late. Only one of those groups survives when war comes calling."

Fuck. He had a point, and I wanted to be on the right side of history and not in that second group. I raised my hands and backed away. "I'll see you tomorrow after work, boss."

LENNIE

"Sleepy Lennie?" Someone shook my shoulder, and I groaned into my pillow. My thighs burned, my arms felt like spaghetti, and my eyes refused to open.

"Lennie." The soft voice brushed over my cheek again and someone swept my curtain of hair behind my ear. Sunlight beat against my eyelids.

Morning.

It was morning.

Yet, I felt like I'd flopped into bed an hour ago. "Five more minutes," I mumbled.

"You need to eat breakfast," Espen said. "Then get your cute behind to work."

Why did he have to be right? Why did I have to go to work? Did no one understand that training with Halvar all evening meant I needed a vacation day?

A palm smacked against my ass, and I flinched. "Wake up, Trouble!"

There's the other one.

I rolled over and peeled open my eyes. My two handsome men stared down at me. Espen perched on the edge of the mattress beaming like a happy puppy while Øyvin stood beside the bed, his muscled arms crossed, and an impatient frown plastered on his face.

"Øyvin made you bread rolls for breakfast."

I perked up. "Fresh bread?"

Øyvin grunted in the affirmative.

"What are you stress baking? Is it bread week? Is Paul Hollywood downstairs waiting to taste test your bake?"

"She's awake," Øyvin grumbled and strolled out of the room.

Espen snickered and pressed a kiss to my forehead. My eyes fluttered at the loving touch. We'd been so busy the past few days, I'd barely had a moment with them. Even last night, I'd come home from training after midnight and face-planted between the two of them in bed where they laid, fast asleep. My limbs could do nothing but flop on top of the covers and pass out. How I'd made it underneath the thin, summer duvet overnight was anyone's guess.

I reached out and grabbed my husband's shoulders, bringing him down to me. Pressing my lips to his, I swept my hands into his unruly hair and relished in the pleasure that settled through my body. He traced his tongue across my bottom lip, and I opened my mouth to him. He deepened the kiss further and warmth unfurled low in my abdomen.

I didn't want him to stop.

The things he did with that mouth of his could bring a smile to my face or a moan to my lips. One such low moan slipped from me, and he pulled back, panting, his eyes brimming with desire.

He brushed his thumb across my cheek. "You have no idea how much I want you right now, but you really do need to eat and get to work." He cleared his throat and adjusted his pants with his free hand. "We both do."

However much I disliked it, he was right. We both had duties to fulfill—me at the coffee shop and him at the police station. Thankfully, business was slowing with the impending departure of the final cruise ship of the season, but until then, our days would remain busy.

Once Espen left, I hauled myself out of bed, ran through the shower, and threw on a clean black T-shirt and jean shorts. Downstairs Espen sat at the circular dining table, sipping on a mug of coffee while Øyvin stood at the kitchen sink washing dishes. Golden light streamed through the windows, casting a warm glow over the spotless room—from the leather sofa to the light-wood table. It was like someone had set up professional-grade softboxes around the place, diffusing the light and making the space worthy of a magazine cover.

A plate with a stuffed bread roll waited for me at my spot. I plopped into my chair and settled on the checkered cushion. Lifting the top piece of the bun, I found cucumber, butter, and orange-pinkish goodness perched between the two lumps of golden bread.

"Who brought smoked salmon into the house?"

"Øyvin let me add it to the shopping list." Espen raised his coffee mug. "Saves you eating it only at Oddvar's during lunch."

My heart grew two sizes. I'd been obsessed with the smoky delicacy ever since I started working at the café, but never brought it into the house—Øyvin didn't eat fish and I didn't want to make him uncomfortable. Not that I thought he'd mind, but still.

"Thank you," I said and looked between the two of them.

Øyvin waved a hand over his shoulder, dismissing it like it was nothing.

I took a bite and choked down a moan at the salty, smoky, and soft morsel. Swallowing, I extended my hand to Øyvin and cleared my throat. He turned to face me, suds-covered hands braced over the edge of the sink. "This definitely deserves a handshake."

His brow furrowed. "What do you mean?"

My eyes rolled as hard as Halvar's did when I made a joke. "You really need to stop falling asleep on Sunday nights while I'm watching the *Great British Baking Show*."

"I listen," he replied and spun back to his washing up.

Espen chuckled, watching the entire exchange with a subtle grin.

It felt good to have a moment of normalcy amid the chaos that had invaded our lives. Not just the arrival of the Fire Fae King, but the wedding had been a lot. Then there were the threats flying around, the training session with Halvar, and the big guy revealing the Fjell Fae's secret temple deep within the mountain. Fuck, after this week alone, I needed a year-long vacation.

I took another bite of my breakfast as I thought back over last night. "Have either of you heard about the Temple of the Fae?"

Espen choked and spluttered on his coffee as Øyvin dropped a bowl into the kitchen sink, porcelain clattering against stainless steel.

Setting my roll back on its plate, I looked between the two men. "Don't lie to me guys. Tell me what you know, and I'll tell you what I know. Sharing is caring, remember?"

Øyvin peered over his shoulder and squinted at me—the depths of those blue eyes deepening. "What have you learned, Trouble?"

"You two go first. I'm pretty sure I'm not supposed—"

"Then you shouldn't," Øyvin said.

"But, this is important. I know it is."

Espen rubbed his fist against his sternum and cleared his throat. "I'm aware the Temple exists."

My head spun to him. "You are?"

"I am." He nodded. "It's the rumored birthplace of our kind. A sacred space somewhere in the mountain."

"Who told you about it?" I asked.

"Queen Ragnhild. Back when I first became her head guard. It's usually information only shared with royals and their inner circles for security reasons."

"But you've never been?"

He shook his head and brushed his hair off his forehead. "How do *you* know about it?"

"Halvar showed me where it is. Since I'm Deputy Head Guard and have some royal powers, he took me inside too."

Espen's eyes widened. "He did?"

"Stop!" Øyvin interjected, spinning to face us. He grabbed a dish towel and wrung his hands in it. "We shouldn't be discussing this."

I narrowed my eyes at his fidgeting. He rarely fidgeted, and when something was upsetting him, he took it out on the piano keys. "Why? What's wrong?" I asked.

"What happened, Øyvin?" Espen added.

Øyvin's throat bobbed and he set aside the towel, noticeably *not* folding it or hanging it up on the rail in front of the oven. Something really was bugging him.

He shoved his hands into his jean pockets and glanced between the two of us. His brows drew together, and my pulse kicked up at the sight.

"Reuven asked me to report on Fjell and Forest movements."

I froze, yet the house bobbed as if it had been set adrift down the fjord. "What?" I said, my voice shaking.

"Those were his words?" The chair creaked as Espen leaned back. "He wanted you to spy on us?"

Øyvin let out a breath and nodded.

He wouldn't do that. I couldn't believe for a single second that Øyvin would do anything to hurt us or the delicate alliances he'd fought so hard to forge. I trusted this man. I loved him. He wouldn't betray our secrets. Sure, he would challenge me any chance he got, but actively deceive and report on our movements to others? Not a fucking chance.

"What did you say?" I asked.

"I said I would. But it was a lie."

I knew it.

Øyvin would always be loyal to the Fjord Fae and the waters he'd sworn to protect, but I'd seen him pick me earlier this year. When Wilhelm and his hoard of wayward wolves descended upon the mountain, Øyvin had chosen to stay behind and protect me instead of going back to the fjord with his king. A king, it now appeared, who was trying to use our relationship to get information on the other factions' movements and thoughts.

With my elbows braced on the table and my hands clasped at my chin, a sigh slipped through my lips. "We can't trust Reuven, can we?"

Øyvin shook his head.

"It would appear not," Espen replied. "When did this happen? When did he ask you?"

"Day after the wedding."

So only a few days ago. We'd barely seen each other in that time, so it made sense that he was telling us now. That would also explain why he'd appeared on edge and the stress baking.

I shoved the last bit of my breakfast into my mouth, scurried across the kitchen, and wrapped my arms around Øyvin's torso. His heart thundered against my ear where I pressed my head to his chest.

"I love you," I said.

He cradled my head in his hand and pressed his lips against my hair. "I love you too, Trouble," he whispered. "Now, tomorrow, and forever. You can trust me."

"I know," I replied, my voice barely audible.

He squeezed me tighter against him like he heard the weight of that truth.

I trusted him. Both of them. End of story.

A jazzy song sounded from Espen's pocket, the noise breaking the silence that hung in the room. It was the ringtone he'd assigned to the front desk of the police station. He pulled the device to his ear. "Good morning!"

I spun in Øyvin's hold. He refused to let go, looping his arms around my waist and pressing my curves against his body. The warmth radiating off him locked me in place. Forget work, I wanted to stay right here all day. Please and thank you.

Espen's brow furrowed and he gulped down the rest of his coffee. "I'll be there in a minute," he said and hung up.

"What's going on?" I asked.

"One of the security cameras outside the jewelry store *and* the webcam filming the town square were burned."

"Burned?" Øyvin and I exclaimed simultaneously.

Espen shoved his coffee mug into the tiny dishwasher and sprinted to the entry area. As he pulled on his work boots, I asked, "Did they see who did it?"

"No." He clipped on his utility belt. "No suspect. No witnesses. Just torched cameras."

"I bet Veigar is behind it."

Øyvin's chest rumbled against my back in agreement.

"We won't know for sure until we get this investigation underway," Espen said. "But I think you might be right."

124

LENNIE

Spending the day peering out the window between coffee orders, I looked for any sign of what had happened to the village security cameras. Nothing stood out to me, and there were no sightings of Veigar down main street, but that didn't lessen the worry that had taken hold.

After filling the last of the seasonal tourists' orders, I ate a quick dinner alone at home, before I bolted up to the mountain in my workout gear and ponytail for an evening training session with some of Halvar's soldiers.

I sauntered into the training cavern and was met by the clattering of swords, the crashing of stones, and grunts worthy of a college football gym. Fjell Fae soldiers in gray and black attire filled the gymnasium-sized hall, as far as the eye could see. A stone platform rose from the floor at the end of the space like a boxing ring without ropes, while a throng of people to my left worked on hand-to-hand combat, their fists raised in protective stances. To my right were strength trainers using rocks the size of microwaves and ovens as weights. It was like a prehistoric caveman had created his own gym in the mountain.

A pair of sparring soldiers charged past me, and I leaped out of the way before I could meet the pointy end of their swords.

That was too close.

"Evening," Torsten said as he stepped up beside me. "Ready for another night of training?"

"I don't really have a choice," I replied with a chuckle. Halvar had ordered the daily training sessions, and since he'd already threatened my life once this year, I wasn't in the mood to test his patience.

Torsten snorted and crossed his arms. "Don't you want to continue practicing how to protect yourself and the mountain?"

I did. Fear of Halvar aside, it was what had ultimately dragged me up the hillside the past few evenings. Learning how to use my powers to their fullest had taken on a new sense of urgency. One Halvar had been adamant about. And, while my muscles screamed in disagreement, he was right. I needed to be at full strength and competency if I was going to have a chance at protecting the mountain and my home.

"Where do we start today?"

Torsten motioned toward the sparring mats. "Over here."

I followed him across the room, and people parted before loitering around us in a large circle.

"You've mastered all the basics." Torsten removed his uniform cape and chucked it aside, letting it fall in a heap at the feet of the surrounding soldiers. "So, tonight, we're focusing on your death magic."

Air caught in my chest and my heartbeat tripped over itself. "Death magic? Did I miss something? Is there more you haven't told me about my demi-fae-ness?"

A trill of gentle snickers sounded around me.

"The killing light you used against Wilhelm."

My shoulders slumped. "Oh. *That* magic."

I wasn't a huge fan of that power. It still haunted me from time to time when I trekked through the mountain's tunnels. The burning and searing magic had wrapped around Wilhelm and killed him before he got a chance to rip out Aurora's throat, but it had left a mark on me too. It was going to take time to mentally recover from killing someone, but as Øyvin and Espen had reminded me: I'd done the right thing.

Wilhelm wouldn't have stopped.

He would have gone on seeking revenge, leaving a trail of bodies in his wake.

"Are you ready?" Torsten asked, drawing me from my thoughts.

I shook my head and arms, ridding myself of the strained emotions within me. "Yeah. How do you want to do this without me accidentally hurting someone?"

"We'll stop you."

"Who's *we*?"

He pointed to the watchful eyes around us.

I raised my hands. "Okay, if you think you can stop it."

"Everyone here is aware of the dangers."

"Are you, really?" I made a slow turn, catching the resolute faces of the men and women standing at the edge of the sparring zone. "You know I could accidentally kill you?"

Nods and murmurs of agreement sounded from the soldiers.

"Fine," I said. "Tell me how this is going to work, Torsten."

The stout man stepped forward with a soldier by his side. "Pretend this is Øyvin."

I tilted my chin at the guy. "He has brown hair. Let's call him Fake-Espen." The man looked nothing like my husband aside from the hair color. He had slim shoulders, gangly limbs, and a lack of facial hair that alluded to youth, *not* a clean shave.

"Okay, then. Espen it is," Torsten conceded. "Pretend this Espen is your husband and when one of the soldiers tries to attack him, you kill them."

My eyes widened. "That's your big plan? Seriously? And what if—"

Torsten stepped back just as another soldier lunged from my left toward Fake-Espen. I instinctively drew on my Fjell power and extended a stone sword toward the woman's abdomen. She dodged and sucked in her stomach, narrowly avoiding the shiny double-edged blade. Ragged breaths left my lungs, and I swallowed hard.

Okay, so, they weren't going to go easy on me. This was a proper fight.

Cool.

Great.

Awesome.

I could do this.

The woman circled me like a lioness corralling her prey. Keeping Fake-Espen at my back, I matched her movements and monitored her gaze for any tells. She fluttered her fingers and a stone sword extended from her grasp as a wicked smile crept across her lips.

Smithing magic like me and Halvar. Nice.

I tightened my grasp on the hilt of my blade. She launched, but I parried away her advances until we circled each other again. Her eyes flicked to my right. I didn't fall for it. A second later a roar sounded from that direction, and I spun, yanking Fake-Espen by the wrist and shoving him back. A broad male soldier lumbered across the space where I'd been standing.

Stun. I raised my sword and arced it from where the female soldier loomed and toward the incoming threat. Tingles ran down my arm, and sparks crackled across the blade. Forks of lightning shot from the top, zapping toward both assailants, and—

The ring of soldiers shifted, and a barrier of stone fell from the ceiling, caging me and my magic. My assault bounced off the stone and dissipated.

My sword arm dropped along with my shoulders. "What the fuck?"

Chest heaving, my blood raced through my veins. Fake-Espen was still behind me, but the guy seemed to be under orders not to help himself. This entire exercise was down to me.

The stone barriers rose, revealing the soldiers and Torsten.

"That wasn't the death magic, was it?" he asked, his eyes narrowed.

I shook my head.

"Let's try again, then."

"Fine." I had to do better, but that instinctive response had still been effective. Now, I just needed to focus on calling on more of the magic—going a level above the stunning magic to the power that could only be wielded by monarchs... and me.

Another soldier launched toward me, and I crossed my sword, meeting his blow with a grunt. He withdrew and slashed toward me once more. I lifted my blade in front of me and the two weapons met with a mighty crash. The energy behind the blow rattled my teeth and ignited that tell-tale burning sensation in my sternum. This guy, with muscles the size of boulders, was far stronger than the woman had been, but he was slower than her. I could use that to my advantage.

I took hit after hit, but my steps swept across the stone floor like that of a hummingbird—light and always moving, never yielding.

Don't let him near Espen.

Hit number eight cracked against my sword, and I pushed him back with all my strength, throwing my weight behind it too. The man stumbled back, giving me enough time for the roiling power in my sternum to sear through me. It was either him dying at my hand or Fake-Espen dying at his. There was only one option I'd accept. *Kill him.*

I thrust out my left arm and the lightning power seared down my scar. A crackling orb of blinding light flew from my palm—

A single panel of stone descended from the ceiling and pierced the floor. My magic burst against the wall like a firework, and I raised an arm over my face to shield from the sparks.

I did it.

With uneven breaths, I dropped my arm and found the surrounding soldiers' eyes as wide as telescope lenses—like they hadn't believed the rumors they'd been told. Torsten popped his face around the troll-sized stone surfboard in the middle of the circle. His man bun wobbled and a smile split his lips. "Much better."

My shoulders slumped and the adrenaline that had taken up residence in my limbs melted. I brushed the back of my hand across my forehead, bringing away beads of sweat. "Thanks, Professor."

"How about a quick water break after all that, hmmm?"

"Gosh, yes." My throat was as dry as the sands of the Sahara.

Fake-Espen gave me a quick nod and "well done" as he strode back to the group of dispersing soldiers.

Torsten and I wandered across the room, back near the entrance, where a fancy water-fountain with paper cups perched within a nook in the wall. The water station looked like something out of ancient Rome, although far more rugged. An arched shelf had been carved out of the slate wall, and a stream of water flowed from the top into a sink-like basin with a drain at the bottom. It was as if they'd installed their own self-watering dog bowl in the mountain's gym.

I grabbed a paper cup, stuck it under the water, and brought it to my lips.

The ice-cold liquid sluiced down my throat, and I bit my lip to hold back a moan.

"That feeling you just felt." Torsten grabbed a drink of his own. "That raw magic. How would you describe it? How is it different from normal light magic or Fjell magic?"

"A burning desire to protect. Then searing pain as it shoots out of me." It was the best way I could describe the sensation. It filled every pore of my being and begged to be let loose, to protect what was most important to me and kill the threat.

"Draw from that. That is where the death magic sits. That is what will help you, should you find yourself in a situation where you need it."

I nodded and took another sip of my drink, enjoying the momentary training reprieve.

Torsten turned his attention to the room, and my thoughts drifted to pressing information that the Council needed to be aware of. While I had him here...

"By the way, the big gossip at the police station and among the café customers is that someone's burning security cameras around the village. My first guess is Veigar, but why do you think he'd do that?" The town had been buzzing with the news of a potential arsonist in our midst. I had zero doubt that the lead purveyors of said information were three little octogenarian ladies who enjoyed their morning coffees by the window at Oddvar's. But how they'd found out about it so quickly was anyone's guess.

Torsten shuffled on the spot. "All the cameras?"

I shrugged. "Quite a lot, apparently. They got the ones on the jewelry store, the toy store, town webcam, even the library if Jorunn is to be believed."

"Hmmm. I don't see what he would stand to gain from that, but I wouldn't put it past him to stir up trouble."

"Can you let the Council know?"

He nodded as a voice rumbled, "Let them know what?"

I flinched. Twisting and peering around Torsten, my gaze met a pair of sky-blue eyes and black fatigues, a bundle of gray material clutched in one hand. Halvar cocked his head to one side, awaiting a response.

"Tell them what, Lennie?"

"Veigar's been burning security cameras around town. Maybe. Possibly. Probably."

His silver brows furrowed, and that mountain of a chest rumbled.

"Any idea what he'd stand to gain from that?" I asked. "Torsten and I can't think of anything."

Lines marred Halvar's forehead and his lips pinched together, that mind of his appearing to sprint through options and viable answers. He let out a long sigh. "Whatever it is, I would wager he's setting the stage for something or pushing up timelines. I have never known him to be patient."

"So, bad news bears, then?"

Halvar grunted and Torsten let out a minuscule groan, like he too wasn't a fan of the Fire Fae King's antics.

"Training successful?" Halvar asked, turning to Torsten.

"She did it. Called on the killing magic."

"Nobody hurt?" Halvar continued.

"No Fjell Fae were harmed during the demi-fae's training session," I deadpanned.

"Good." Halvar huffed. "Follow me."

I tossed my cup in the recycling bin beside the water station and hurried after the tall brute, Torsten right on my tail.

Halvar aimed for the back of the room and hopped onto the stone-slab-come-boxing ring at the back of the cavernous training gym.

"Everyone gather!" Halvar's voice boomed through the room, his words echoing against the rough-hewn walls. Men and women scurried across the space and assembled in front of the platform. I stood in their midst, arms aching but mind curious as to what Halvar had to say to the group.

A calm silence settled over the crowd. Halvar's eyes scanned the masses like a general inspecting his troops.

"It has been some time since we have altered our leadership within our forces, but things *have* changed." His gaze cut to me.

Shit.

"Lennie, our new Deputy Head Guard, please join me up here."

Double shit.

I'd always hated being called on in meetings, and now Halvar was dragging me in front of a host of soldiers. Fan-fucking-tastic.

I hoisted myself onto the platform. "You know, if you wanted to remove me from my post, you could do so without an audience." I straightened and brushed my hands across my thighs. "Or is this a public execution for something I've done wrong? Something I've said? Bad leadership potential?"

He grumbled and shoved the bundle of gray material into my hands. "Lennie Solbakke Martin, welcome to the Fjell Fae Army. Here is your official uniform."

My jaw crashed to the stone floor as a round of applause wrapped around us and I accepted the clothing. What the fuck was happening? What had my life become? Me... in uniform?

Finely woven wool with tiny silver threads at the seams stared back at me. I unfolded the material, and a pair of pants fell to the floor. "Sorry," I muttered, my eyes locked on the other two items, one in each of my hands. A jacket, like the ones I'd seen soldiers wearing around the mountain, and a waist-length cape that would fasten at the shoulder with the help of a black leather strap.

"How'd you know my size?" I said in a daze, unable to tear my eyes from the gift.

"I asked Øyvin and Espen," Halvar replied.

I chuckled. Yeah, Øyvin was, in his own words, "well acquainted with my curves" and had already bought me winter gear in the correct size.

But that wasn't what shocked me the most. Yes, I'd been bestowed with the title of Deputy Head Guard when I became a demi-fae with royal magic and successfully proved my worth to the Fjell Fae by retrieving their heir last winter. This, the uniform, was different, though. More meaningful. This was them welcoming me into the fold as one of their own.

A lump formed in my throat, and I swallowed it. "Thank you," I mumbled, unable to conjure up any other words to express the well of emotion bubbling up inside me.

"You're welcome."

Brushing my hand across the soft wool, a smirk tilted my lips. I glanced up at Halvar. "Still no hat, though?"

He crossed his arms and rolled his eyes.

"One day." I pointed the cape at him. "One day I'll get that hat from you."

"Only when you earn it."

I smiled. "Oh, I'll earn it."

"Good. Now, fight me."

My smile vanished. "You can't be serious."

"Very," he said, his voice unwavering. "Torsten, can you take her uniform for her?"

"Of course," my friend replied. He tugged the clothing from my grip and retrieved the pants from the floor before disappearing from the periphery of my vision and blending with the crowd.

"Here?" I squeaked. "You want to spar with me up here?"

Halvar nodded, his features unyielding.

I peered around the space. Wide, excited eyes stared up at me as if seeing Halvar spar with someone was a rarity and popcorn-worthy entertainment. So much for being welcomed into the Fjell Fae army family. The other major problem was a lack of sparring mats. There were none up here. If Halvar pulled my feet out from underneath me, I'd crack my skull open on the slab of rock.

Shifting my weight from one foot to the other, I wrung my hands together. "Are you sure about this?"

"Yes."

Halvar rolled up his sleeves, revealing thickly corded muscles that looked like they could choke a man in a headlock.

I swept my palm down the column of my throat and swallowed hard. Fingers crossed that wouldn't be how I met my demise. In fact, now would be a great time for Odin to shepherd me to Valhalla. Save me from the pain of death by the hands of one Fjell Fae Head Guard. I may not be a warrior or amazing leader, but if the Allfather could open the gates, that would be appreciated.

Then again, if I snuck out now...

While Halvar conjured a sword worthy of a beheading, I turned and slunk toward the edge of the platform.

"Lennie." His voice rumbled through the room.

"I, uh... Forgot something back at the water fountain. Won't take a moment."

Something whistled past my ear and air thundered against my eardrum. The people in front of me ducked as Halvar's sword sailed over their heads and smashed against the far wall.

My breath caught and my eyes threatened to pop out of their sockets. "What the fuck!"

I pressed my hand against the side of my head and pulled it away. No blood, but damn did that pressure hurt. I spun, my ponytail whipping through the air. "What was that for?"

"Fight me."

"Counter to a lot of my actions, I don't actually have a death wish."

Halvar crossed his arms and quirked a single brow. "You have had plenty of training, and, as the only other fae with both royal and Fjell Fae magic, let us see what you can do with a matched opponent."

He pointedly excluded Nora who resided in the dungeon. But she was a bitch who'd killed her sister and the love of his life. I couldn't fault him for leaving her out of the equation. "So, this is a science experiment?"

He shrugged.

"Fine." I set my hands on my hips. "But when I die, I promise to come back as a ghost and haunt these tunnels, wreaking more havoc than I did while alive."

Halvar ignored my threats and motioned with his hand for me to step further into the center of the platform.

I shuffled forward and sent a silent message down to the devil, warning him of my impending arrival.

"We duel with whatever weaponry we can conjure." He said. "Do you agree to the terms?"

"Terms? What is this ancient warfare? A Renaissance joust? Is this where you tell me you're actually Thor and have a *really* big hammer that can zap me with all kinds of lightning—"

"Lennie..."

I huffed. There was no getting out of this. I had to spar with Halvar. Be his science experiment and try not to land myself in a stony casket. "Sure," I muttered.

"Don't hold back," he said as a stone broadsword slowly emerged in his hand.

I shuddered at the sight and summoned my own blade—a warm flow of energy pouring from my sternum as I called on the Fjell Fae magic. "If you say so."

His reply came in the form of him settling into a fighting stance: legs bent slightly, elbows angled just-so, and his gaze locked on me.

I felt like an actual deer in the headlights of an oncoming truck. A really, really, big semi-truck that would barrel right through me.

Bending gently at the hips, I set one foot out in front of the other into what Espen would liken to a high-lunge position. My grip tightened around my stone sword, and I steeled myself for the onslaught of a fight, my mind flying as fast as a camera stuck on sport-mode shutter speed.

What would Espen say about this? Would he be angry? Would he cheer me on from the sidelines like he did during our winter training sessions?

And what would Øyvin say? *No*, I shook my head. I knew exactly what Øyvin would say. He'd remind me it was a challenge—something I could either win or lose.

The mere thought of winning kicked that Martin Family competitive gene into the *on* position. There wasn't a chance I was losing. Even if it was to the beast of the mountain. Martin Family Rules: Wins Only.

I narrowed my eyes and glared back at Halvar.

Challenge accepted.

He swung, and I met his attack with my own blade. The force of the blow reverberated through my body, threating to dislodge the sword and take my arm. I pulled back and struck again, careful to avoid the pointy bit.

Halvar was certainly stronger and faster than the other two I'd dueled with today, but I still got the feeling he was holding back. His steps lacked an urgency that the others had.

I thrust the tip toward his stomach. He knocked aside my advance. I twisted and spun, only giving him my back for a split second before we started circling each other again.

The push and pull continued. Both of us launched volleys of royal magic at each other, too. The audience watched on with rapt attention—their eyes wide, focus locked on us as we danced across the proverbial mat. My muscles screamed, begging me to sit on the edge of the stone platform and take a break. But I knew what Halvar was like. Knew from whispered tales and rumors that he was a battle-hardened warrior. If I showed any sign of weakness, he'd exploit it.

I had to keep moving.

Yet, the blows didn't stop coming.

"Are... you trying... to kill me?" I asked.

"No." Halvar launched again, gripping his sword with two hands, the blade slashing through the air toward me. I pushed out a volley of stunning magic. He teetered and twisted out of the way, narrowly avoiding the balls of light.

Rounding back, he prowled and studied me, his chest as still as if he were meditating along sandy shores.

Meanwhile, my breaths came in short bursts, matching the staccato clashes of our swords.

With blade in one hand and magic in the other, I charged.

"Have you."

Block, push, zap.

"Ever."

I twisted and countered another strike.

"Wanted to?"

Our swords crossed, and we stared into each other's eyes.

"Yes."

"What!" I pushed off him and hobbled back to my side of the boxing ring, letting my sword arm droop. "When?"

"Arm up!"

I did as I was ordered, my shoulder muscles screaming in reply.

"After our first meeting in the throne room," he answered.

The first day we'd ever met. When Espen had brought me to a meeting with him and Øyvin at Queen Freija's request. About a year ago. I narrowed my eyes at Halvar. "What stopped you? My charm and sharp wit?"

Silence responded as Halvar bowed his head and turned away slightly. My stomach dropped to my toes and my shoulders sagged.

Fuck. No, it wasn't me who'd stopped my own untimely death at his hands. It was Freija.

Apparently, I had a lot to thank the late Queen for.

Unable to do so in person, perhaps the best way to honor her protection and power was to protect the one thing she cared for the most: the mountain.

That certainly had been my intention with everything that had happened this year, but now that knowledge offered me even greater motivation to do just that. Protect the mountain. Protect these people. Use this magic I'd been given for good.

A muscle feathered in Halvar's jaw as he straightened. The light magic in his palm evaporated and was slowly replaced by an axe that looked like something out of a Viking movie. Two sharp stone blades protruded from a thick gray handle. He peered down at the runic design on the cheeks of the weapon. Untold pain flooded his gaze, and my stomach flip-flopped at the thought of causing him such emotional turmoil.

I needed to pull an Espen. I needed to pivot.

"Hypothetically speaking. If a Fjell Fae wanted to make the world's largest rock, how big would that rock have to be?"

Halvar rolled his eyes, and the crowd chuckled at my remarks.

Bingo.

"Hey, some people around here finally found my jokes funny."

Halvar didn't give me time to bask in the joy from my audience. He barreled forward once more, aiming both weapons at my sword.

He crossed his weapons, and my sword struck at the apex. Pulling upward, he started to dislodge it from my hands. I jerked a hand free and blasted a plain ball of light at his face. With a grunt of alarm, he threw his head back and narrowly avoided the royal magic before scurrying to his side of the platform. The light flew across the room and evaporated over the crowd.

Magic! I needed to keep using my magic. It would keep me on my feet longer, especially considering he'd put his away and gone back to what I could only assume were old habits. Magic would help me win this thing. And if there was one thing I really wanted right now, aside from a long-ass bath and foot massage, it was to win this sparring match.

We lunged toward each other once again.

Stun. His axe descended, and I shot my stunning magic at his arm. It wrapped around his wrist, and he splayed his hand dropping the medieval weapon. His eyes widened, leaving me an opening. My blade sparked with power, and I swung it at his with all my strength, throwing my weight behind it. The stone edges crashed against each other, and my magic zipped down the opposing weapon.

Halvar grunted, and his sword flew across the ring, clattering to the floor.

Silence so quiet I could hear my own pounding heartbeat settled across the room.

"Holy shit," I mumbled.

Gasps and murmurs swelled and echoed off the rugged ceiling and walls. Magical sconces flickered, casting random shadows across Halvar's body.

Holy fuck. I'd just disarmed Halvar. My arms burned, my stomach was in knots, and it felt as if I stood on the edge of death's abyss where Satan himself waited for me with open arms. But I'd fucking *disarmed* the beast of the mountain. I'd won!

Halvar turned to me slowly. Light and shadow danced across his features. "Well done," he said, with a nod of approval and his lips tipped into a smile.

125

LENNIE

I ran through the village, dodging locals on their morning walks, zipping past stores, and narrowly avoiding the goddamn summer skier in his skintight suit. He really needed to get a cup. I'd have stopped to tell him, but... I was late.

Beyond late.

Sparring with Halvar a few nights ago and daily evening training sessions with the Fjell Fae this week were taking a toll on my mental and physical resolve. My strength and skill were improving, but damn was it exhausting. So much so that I'd slept through my alarm.

I scurried through the front door of Oddvar's Café wearing Espen's black T-shirt and a random pair of jeans, my ponytail flailing behind me, and ran straight into someone.

"Ope!" Hot coffee sloshed over my forearms as I reached out to steady myself. I hissed at the scalding liquid on my skin. Today really wasn't my day. "I'm so sorry," I said and stared up into a pair of mirrored-sunglasses.

Shit.

With her wavy black hair, porcelain skin, and coffee dripping from her hands, Salka, was *almost* the last person I wanted to run into. I'd seen her from a distance, wandering around town every so often, but I'd never spoken to her since she moved to Skolvik this past winter.

"Here, let me get that." I took the half-empty cup of coffee from her hands and shuffled over to the counter. Oddvar narrowed his eyes at me but continued serving another customer. Setting aside the mug, I rinsed and dried my hands and turned to find Salka waiting by the counter. I grabbed some paper napkins from our stash and passed them to her. "Again, I'm so sorry. Are you hurt?"

"I'm fine," she replied, taking the napkins and wiping down her hands. I gave her a quick once over to check for coffee on her clothes but her rust-colored linen dress that cinched into a bow on one side of her waist was stain-free.

There wasn't even any on the floor where we'd collided, thank goodness. We couldn't have people slipping and falling.

"I'll make you a new cup. On the house. Again, I'm so sorry."

"It's all right. No one was hurt." She gave me a gentle smile. She was right, thank fuck. Although my wrists had turned red from the hot liquid, hers appeared unmarred.

"What was your order?" I threw on my apron.

"Macchiato, please. To go."

Interesting. Someone around here who liked having some milk or foam in their coffee. It was a rarity here—most Norwegian's liked their coffee dark with minimal accoutrement. The tourists were always different, though.

I set to work creating the drink, noting that she'd changed her order from a café mug to a to-go cup. Oddvar always wanted customers to stay in the café as the chances of them ordering a second drink or food increased. I'd just brought those chances with Salka crashing down. This Friday really was turning into a sucky Monday.

"So, are you enjoying living in Skolvik?" I asked, hoping to break the tension between us and assuage any ill will thanks to my clumsiness.

"It's a nice town. Not too much different than Iceland, but a lot more trees."

"You don't have trees?" I'd never been myself, but most places had trees, didn't they?

She chuckled, the sound warm and inviting. "We have some trees, but not nearly as many as Norway. Our terrain is more... arctic tundra. Brush, basalt, and even some glaciers."

I nodded, having seen photos online. My heart longed to photograph Iceland's black sandy beaches, the crystalline glaciers, and the otherworldly waterfalls. Not to mention...

I returned to the counter with her drink, gently setting it down. "And volcanoes."

She bit her bottom lip. "Yes, we have those too."

The air heated, and my palms started to sweat as I stared at her sunglasses. My own wide eyes stared back at me in the mirrored glass, and I shook my head, breaking away. I grabbed a rag and wiped down the clean counter as she picked up her cup.

"Thank you for the new drink."

I tucked the useless cleaning towel into my apron, and rocked back and forth on my feet. "Of course. Again, I'm sorry."

She gave me a closed-lip smile and headed for the door with her Macchiato.

"Well, that was awkward," Oddvar said, his arms crossed and lips pinching at one corner. "Thank you for making her another coffee."

I wiped the back of my hand across my forehead. "Uh-huh." I knew next to nothing about the woman other than she was Reuven's wife, Veigar's daughter, and liked to go on long walks around the village. Aside from that, she was an anomaly and a question mark. I didn't want to assume the worst and perceive her as a threat to the fae here in Skolvik, but part of me couldn't help but panic at her presence. A Fire Fae near this many trees? It couldn't be safe. Unless she was super kind and had absolute control over her fiery powers. Satan help us, I hoped she did.

I took a deep breath and spun around, setting to work on some sandwiches and getting on with my workday. Customers came and went, brown goat cheese was sliced, and drinks were brewed to perfection. Local gossip about burned cameras drifted around the room, and when the crowds thinned in the late afternoon, I sent a slowing Oddvar home. I could wipe down tables and close up shop. He obliged with a weary nod, hanging up his apron and buttoning his cardigan to the top button. His departure left me in the stillness of the café. Just me, the machines, the lingering smell of coffee grinds, and a caddy of cleaning supplies.

I reached for the spray bottle as the bell above the door rang.

"Did you forget something?" I turned and all the breath inside my lungs evaporated.

The person I most definitely *did not* want to run into walked through the door.

Yeah, today was not my day.

I set aside the caddy and assessed the man for weapons and threats. His hair was perfectly coiffed, his linen shirt tastefully rumpled, and his pants looked like they'd been hand sewn in Italy. Not a single weapon graced his hands or his hips. But that didn't mean he wasn't a threat. He'd already made that known. Plus, based on the Fjell Fae Council's tales, Veigar didn't need weapons—he *was* the weapon.

"We're about to close." I swallowed the lump in my throat. "Can I get you something to-go?"

Veigar peered around the space, his sunglasses shielding his dark eyes. "I'm here to see if you might deliver a message for me."

My eyebrows met my hairline. "You want me to pass something along?"

"Yes, please."

"Look, if you have something to say, you should—"

"You're the Deputy Head Guard, are you not?"

Who the hell told him that?

I nodded.

"Then you are a leader among your people and a sufficient point of contact."

I crossed my arms over my chest and popped my hip. Hearing someone of his standing call me a leader was some serious whiplash, but he wasn't wrong. This was my new role. I had the uniform now too. So, I needed to own it, especially when other powerful beings crossed my path.

"I'm the Deputy Head Guard, but I believe you may want to talk to Halvar, my boss." Wasn't delegating part of being a leader? Couldn't I toss this to the big guy and avoid being in the same room as this walking, talking bomb?

"Diplomacy isn't the man's strong suit."

I pinched my lips together to refrain from snorting or laughing.

Veigar sighed, his shoulders dropping. "Perhaps I should find someone else." He bowed his head and turned to the door.

Halvar's comments about getting information from Veigar rang through my mind as my opportunity to find out exactly what the man wanted sauntered out of the building. If I wanted to know, I had to act. Fuck it, I had to be brave. Not just for me, but for the mountain, for my new home.

I ran across the café and threw open the door. "Wait!" This was stupid. Beyond stupid. It was signing my own fucking death record. "Let's hear it then."

Veigar's lips tilted up at one corner. I strode back behind the counter with my heart in my throat and made the King of the Fire Fae a cup of coffee.

126
LENNIE

Coffee sloshed over the rims of the mugs as I set them on the table by the window where *His Majesty* had taken up residence. Ironically, it was the same table I'd sat at the day I'd missed the cruise ship. Though, this time, *I* was the one asking the out-of-towner questions and wishing them on their merry way.

"So." My voice wavered, but hopefully not enough that he'd notice. "Tell me a bit about yourself, and why you're *really* here."

Veigar slowly reached up to his face and removed his sunglasses. *Damn.* I swallowed hard under the assessment of his pitch-black eyes as he folded the glasses and tucked them into the front of his button-down shirt.

Silence hung heavy in the café, sweat beading at the nape of my neck as I waited for his reply.

"I'm here to help."

My eyes narrowed at him. "With what?"

"Stability and the endurance of the fae. We've been around for a long time. I want that to continue without internal or external threats."

External threats? Was that a dig at me being brought into the fold? Or were there other things besides human knowledge of our existence that could cause harm to the fae? Or maybe he was just trying to throw me off?

His smile twisted at one corner like he could hear my anxious thoughts.

If this was his attempt at trying to unnerve me, it wasn't working... entirely. "What do you want in Skolvik, Veigar?"

"My hope is, with your connections to each fae faction, you might pass along a message for me. Specifically, the fae need unity and new leadership, and I'm here to offer my services."

It was just as we suspected. "They're doing fine without a hegemonic douche-canoe in charge."

"Says the woman who killed an Alpha wolf."

My eyebrows betrayed me and drifted toward my hairline. "How do you know about that?"

"A king has his ways."

Or a daughter who'd found out and passed along information.

I let out a long sigh. "Okay, so you're the Fire Fae equivalent of Miss America and you want world peace. Tell me why *you* should get the crown."

Veigar furrowed his brow like he had no idea what I was talking about. "I'm the leader of an entire faction of fae that lives harmoniously on an isle in the North Atlantic where life flourishes, secrets remain secret, and our way of being is not under threat from ill-equipped leaders, like promoted Head Guards after the failure of keeping royal lines alive."

Well, that definitely felt like a dig at both Espen and Halvar, all in one sentence. *What a dick.*

I took a sip of my coffee and set the warm mug back on the table to one side. "And why do you think that qualifies you to lead the other three factions?" There better only be four types of Fae or I'd skewer my husband and partner for not giving me the full Fae-101.

"All three remain leaderless."

"I doubt King Reuven sees it that way."

"My son-in-law is brand new to the throne. He's already committed to defer to my advice and leadership."

Fuck. Øyvin's suspicions were right. We couldn't trust Reuven. My first impression of Reuven wasn't of a man who buckled to others, and, based on the stories from the Council meeting, it sounded like Veigar's temper was fiery in every sense of the word. But then again, what did I know about being a ruler? I clasped my hands together and rested them on the table. "So, you want to be everyone's leader."

"I think I'm the most qualified candidate for the position."

"I'm not sure Halvar would agree with that."

A suave grin swept across Veigar's face. "Halvar and I have never quite seen eye-to-eye."

"I sensed that at my wedding reception."

"A lovely occasion."

"One I don't recall inviting you to."

He smiled, and a bead of sweat ran down the underside of my arm. Either I was nervous or someone had turned on the heating in here.

Veigar tilted his head to one side. "Haven't you noticed all the problems the local factions have with their leaders and how the natural world has suffered from it? Polluted waters, rock falls, I'm sure the forest has had some struggles too."

I pinched my lips between my teeth. Hot weather and drought conditions aside, there had been a lot of issues across the board this past year.

"You know I'm right."

He was. No matter how much I disliked the guy for his history of violence and threats to my family, he was correct in his assessment.

"You are." I sighed.

"And balance and harmony would benefit us all. With me at the front, leading, we could mitigate the troubles we currently face and prepare for future eventualities... together."

This entire conversation felt well outside my area of expertise, but I had to get as much information out of him as possible. Especially considering his chatty mood. "What happens if we don't agree to your terms?"

"I *escalate* matters."

There he went again with the lack of clarity and threats.

"How?" I asked. "How would you 'escalate matters?'"

His lips twisted into a sly smile, onyx eyes twinkling with mad delight. "Have you ever seen a village on fire?"

Fuck. This guy was a wild card.

Tapping my foot on the floor, I narrowed my eyes at the man. "I think we can both agree that I'm not your biggest fan. You crashed my wedding, threatened my family, and appear to be threatening my home. Not to mention burning down security cameras all over the village. Quit the bullshit, Your Majesty, and tell me what you really want."

"I don't know what this accusation is regarding security cameras—"

"Bull-mother-fucking-shit."

He let out a low hum of annoyance and cocked his head to one side. "You do have a way with words."

"I'm a walking, talking dictionary of profanity."

"It would appear so." He reached for something in his pocket, and panic flared within me. I pulled on my magic. It whooshed down my arm, and I crafted a sharp stone knife. The tip glinted in the light from the window.

Veigar's eyes widened, but he didn't stop moving. "Now, now. No need for violence."

There was a missing *yet* at the end of his sentence that I felt in my bones. "I'll be the one to decide that."

"Will you now?"

"Yes."

"All right," he said and plopped a triangular lump of sky-blue stone onto the table between us.

My breath hitched, and I cleared my throat to cover my own shock. If that was what I thought it was...

My shoulders slumped and I slid my hands back into my lap but gripped the knife just in case Fire Grandpa decided to go ten rounds.

He leaned back in his chair, arms crossed. "Do you know what this is?"

I shrugged. "A rock."

"More specifically?"

"A blue one."

He shook his head and bit his bottom lip. "You have quite the sense of humor, too, Deputy Guard."

"You should come to one of my stand-up shows."

"Perhaps I shall."

"I'll leave tickets for you at will-call under the name, Dolly Parton."

He let out a huff. "Enough of this coy behavior."

Here we go. I'd finally got under his skin and irked the man into truth. A dangerous game, but hopefully it would give us more information and have him play his cards right into my open and waiting hands.

"Pretend all you like that you don't know what this stone is, Lennie. I know, you know. You didn't school your features fast enough to hide your shock."

Okay, the fucker had me there. Unless he was lying to me, this was a piece from the Temple's pedestal. A piece that likely granted him some sort of access to the ancestors who could bestow powers. I swallowed hard and straightened in my seat. "Let's say I know what that is. What meaning does it have regarding your purposes here in Skolvik and request to be leader of all the fae?"

"We must find the missing pieces of the Temple and bring them back together, as they once were. For only then can we be truly united, truly one fae with the power we need to succeed."

What a load of—

"Over a thousand years ago," he started, "back when the fae factions started wandering further afield from this region, a Fjord Fae king grew restless and more powerful than the other three monarchs. After much arguing, the four factions decided to split the Temple plinth, sharing a piece with each group and leaving the Fjell Fae to protect the Temple."

Holy shit! Did Halvar even know this? I didn't dare move, not even to take another sip of coffee, and let Veigar keep talking.

"With a shard, each monarch may commune with the ancestors and ask for help in the form of greater power or skills that match their element."

Yeah, Halvar had not been this descriptive in the Temple the other day.

"It is believed," Veigar continued, "that if you can combine all the pieces in the Temple, the ancestors can grant even more magic—power previously unseen that could help our natural world and resources avoid devastation from pollution, destruction, et cetera."

Hmmm. Øyvin had once said that if monarchs died the region would fall into ruin, with animals and plants dying, rockslides becoming the norm, and pollution tainting the waters. That had certainly proven to be the case when Freija and Balder died. We'd seen an uptick in cave-ins and from what Øyvin had said, the wall beneath the fjord's surface hadn't been as strong until Reuven returned and took up the mantle as King of the Fjord.

Maybe Veigar was on to something.

I wiggled in my seat. "Why are you telling me this?"

"Because you asked, and I'm tired of your games."

Fair enough, but one thing still nagged at me. "If we brought together the pieces and you had a little chat with the ancestors, would the enhanced dosage of power help *you* in any way personally?"

He shrugged.

Nevermind. Fuck this guy. He's just another power-hungry man.

A low chuckle escaped from my chest. "Let's get your words right, shall we?" I stabbed my knife into the wooden table and the blade twanged in reply. Veigar didn't flinch. "You want to unite the fae under your rule and bring all the missing pieces of the Temple back together so *you* can obtain more power?"

He sneered. "So *we* can all gain more power to protect our natural world, protect the Nordic Fae."

"Bullshit." Smelled like it. Sounded like it. Didn't believe it for a second.

"You may not believe me—"

"You've yet to give me reason to, Your Majesty." Sweat dripped down my spine and an eerie smile crept across his lips. "What exactly would you do to make the lives of the Fjord, Forest, and Fjell Fae better? How would you lead? Would you sit on your throne of lava and command from your island in the Atlantic? Threaten people and their families if they stepped out of line?"

The muscles in his jaw clenched, but the rest of his body relaxed—that cool and calm veneer remaining firmly intact.

"Would you use the power you get from that rock and the place it may or may not belong to—"

"You know exactly where this is from," he interjected, pointing at the shard.

"I'm not done talking. Wait your turn." Heat flushed through my body like the hot Midwest winds in the middle of August. "Will you use the newfound power to help the factions in Norway and Scandinavia? Or will the only recipients be those in Iceland?"

He took a deep breath and crossed his arms. "I will help all fae. Protect us from harm. Ensure our duties to nature are upheld."

My gut twisted and bells went off in my mind. That sounded like a lot of pretty words. Partially truthful words. And yet, my gut screamed at me that we wouldn't like the consequences of this bologna sandwich. The ancient fae had split up the temple pedestal for a reason.

Maybe it was because of everything that happened over the past year to the fae in Skolvik, or maybe it was my royal magic warning me not to trust him. Either way, I didn't believe a single word.

"By doing what exactly?" I asked. "How will you uphold your responsibilities to nature?"

"By uniting the factions to help one another. Work together."

"They already do."

"We could add the Fire Fae to that mix," he replied. "Use the fire powers to assist."

"I don't know how safe that would be. Aren't you in Iceland to work with the tectonic plates and volcanoes? Won't those be a hazard out here in Norway?"

I could picture it perfectly: volcanoes erupting from the snow-capped peaks of central Norway, lava flowing down hillsides into the fjord, and forests set ablaze.

"It will be perfectly safe," Veigar said, his tone firm and confident. "I'll make sure of it."

"What about these nasty little eruptions I keep hearing tales about?" There was nothing *little* about them at all. Eyjafjallajökull erupted years ago and stopped all air travel over northern Europe for days. And that apparently wasn't the first time this man's temper or actions had caused such an explosive reaction.

Veigar brushed his finger across the table and then rubbed it against his thumb as if inspecting for dust. "Minor disruption; that won't happen here."

"They didn't sound like *minor disruptions* to me."

"Do you always believe everything you hear?"

"No, but over the past year I learned that this thing called magic is real. So, I've decided to continue doing life with more of an open mindset."

"And that doesn't apply in this situation?"

I shrugged one shoulder. "I've always questioned leaders. Hard habit to kick."

"Wise woman."

"Thank you. Now, let's get back to the main point here." I leaned forward, putting my hands on the table. "What happens when I deliver this *unifying* message and Halvar tells you to get fucked? What then?"

He mimicked my previous movement, shrugging a single shoulder. "Like I said earlier, I'll resort to other methods of persuasion that you and yours won't be able to counter."

Another day, another threat. What had my life become? One second, I was a human tourist who had missed her cruise ship, the next I was a demi-fae promoted to Deputy Head Guard within a secret society of fae in the fjords of Norway.

"Oh, I wouldn't underestimate us, Your Majesty." I slowly pressed my palm down over the hilt of my blade, magically crushing it and pulling the power back inside me.

Veigar's soulless eyes watched closely, and a single salty eyebrow quirked toward his hairline. "Such violence."

My palm slammed against the wooden table. "Judge me and move on."

He chuckled, pocketed the shard, and rose from his seat, the chair scraping against the floorboards. "That I have. And yet, I don't think I'll be going anywhere." He returned his sunglasses to his face, pushing them up the bridge of his nose.

I stood from my own seat, my shirt glued to my back. "Shame."

"Please share my offer of becoming the fae leader and requesting the stones be united with your counterparts. And keep me informed of how the Fjell Fae and others wish to proceed." He sauntered to the door and rested his fingers on the knob. "I hope to hear back from you within twenty-four hours."

I swallowed hard. "Will do." I plastered on my most bitchy smile. "And before they close for the day, I'd recommend stopping by the town's gift store. They have a miniature troll that looks just like you."

A low rumble sounded from his chest.

"Too far?" I asked, my tone chipper and hiding my own worry. That might have actually been too far. I'd never been good with lines. Always felt a need to cross them. Even to my own detriment. Definitely something I could work on. "I thought you said you liked my jokes?"

Veigar yanked open the door, the bell chiming above him. "Twenty-four hours."

With that, he strode outside and clicked the door shut behind him.

As he sauntered down the street and out of view from the window, all my bravado vanished like a balloon fart-exhaling air. I crumpled to the table, resting my forehead on my arms.

"What the fuck just happened?" I yelled to the café's empty chairs.

I may have put a big ol' target on my back, but at least I now knew for certain what Veigar wanted: To unite the fae factions and pull together all the pieces of the Temple.

With all those parts in place, and no doubt a fiery army that looked like a legion from hell itself, the Fire Fae King would be unstoppable. A shudder ran through my bones. I couldn't let that happen. Even if I got myself hurt in the process, I wouldn't let him take over.

127

LENNIE

I put away my cleaning supplies and apron, locked the café from the inside, and barreled through the streets of Skolvik. I needed to get home. I needed to tell the guys what had just happened. I needed to tell the mountain too.

Yanking my phone out of my pocket, I dialed Torsten and brought the device to my ear. The dial tone beeped twice before he picked up.

"Hello? Lennie?"

"Get me Halvar."

"What happened?"

My chest heaved, my words coming out in a jumbled, panted mess. "Veigar... Stopped by... Café."

"Hang on. Here he is."

"Speak," Halvar's gruff voice thrummed down the phone.

"I spoke to Skolvik's latest wayward tourist. He doesn't want world peace."

"Obviously."

Through erratic breaths and *ope, sorry*s as I dodged villagers out enjoying an evening stroll, I told them everything the Fire Fae King had just said, plus the fae history he'd slipped into our impromptu story time.

"Thank you for letting us know," Halvar said when I finally finished. "We will take this to the Council immediately. Can you inform Espen and Øyvin?"

I skidded to a stop outside the boat house. "About to do so."

"Good," he replied and hung up.

I tucked my phone away in my pocket and pushed open the front door.

A trill of somber music drifted past me and the smell of chocolate chip cookies and something syrupy filled the air. I cast my gaze around the room and found Øyvin at his piano and Espen on the couch reading.

"Where are the shards?" I asked, breaking the peaceful ambiance.

Both men stilled at my question, the music cutting off with a clank.

I slammed the front door behind me. "Where are the Forest and Fjord shards?"

Øyvin turned back to the piano and continued playing. "I don't know what you're talking about."

"We had this discussion the other day. I know there's a Temple of the Fae. I also now know that each fae faction has a piece from the temple that their monarchs probably use at their anointing ceremonies and to *commune* with the ancestors." Not that I'd had much success with that endeavor myself.

The music stopped again, and Øyvin's shoulders rose and fell like a marionette given slack.

Espen set aside his book, resting it on the coffee table as he took a deep breath and turned his gaze to me. "What happened, Lennie?"

"Veigar just showed me his own shard, stone, thingy. We had a chat about his five-year plan for the region."

"He did what?" Espen's voice was the lowest I'd ever heard it.

"The King of the Fire Fae decided he wanted to chat, and I took my new leadership role to heart and had a *tête-à-tête,* as the French say. He proceeded to inform me why he's in town and threw down a motherfucking gauntlet!"

Øyvin turned on the piano bench, his eyes locked on me. "What *exactly* did he say?"

"That we could bow to him as our new leader or face his almighty wrath."

"And about the shards?"

"That he wants all of them and access to the Temple. *For only then can we all be truly united, truly one fae,*" I mimicked. "Oh, and that we have twenty-four hours to get back to him."

The temperature in the room dropped, the bubble of domestic bliss bursting. I leaned back against the door and took a deep breath, willing my heart rate to stop running wild.

"The Forest Fae shard is hidden and safe," Espen said. "No one aside from the Council of Elders knows where it is."

I tilted my chin at Øyvin. "What about the Fjord piece?"

He squared his shoulders. "The Fjord shard cannot be accessed by any non-Fjord Fae without assistance from someone with the correct credentials and ability to breathe under water."

Well that certainly protected it from outsiders. But what of the threat beneath the water and within the Fjord Fae palace?

"And what about King Reuven?" I asked. "Would he offer it up to Veigar? Would his wife? Because Veigar just told me Reuven is, and I quote, 'committed to defer to my advice and leadership.'"

Øyvin stilled and a muscle in his jaw feathered.

I pressed on. "You've already aired your concerns about Reuven and his loyalties. Do you think he's going to give it to Veigar?"

Øyvin sighed. "He might."

Yeah, we were well and truly fucked.

I told them everything else Veigar had told me, then slunk across the room and plopped onto the sofa beside Espen. "Please tell me the Forest Fae shard is a thousand miles from here."

Espen pursed his lips and blinked twice. My stomach dropped to my toes.

"It's in Skolvik, isn't it?"

He shook his head.

"Within driving distance?"

He looked to the floor and his brow furrowed as if trying to decide how much information to reveal. He brushed his hair off his forehead and sighed. "It's thirty minutes away."

"So, close but not easy to find."

That was great. Perfect even. If there was an emergency, we could probably go get it and if not, it was hidden away—

"You've kind of already seen it," Espen added.

My shoulders fell. "What?"

"You've already seen it."

Ice washed through my veins, and I slumped further into the couch cushions. Grabbing a throw pillow, I pressed it against my stomach like some squishy shield that might protect me from the direction of this conversation. "I don't remember you ever showing me a piece of blue stone."

"In the graveyard." Espen's eyes met mine and a serious tone laced his words. "At the old stave church. Where Queen Ragnhild is buried alongside Mads."

"Holy shit." I had seen it. Earlier this year when we stopped at the ancient church on our way to Alvdalen. It had been right in front of me, embedded in Ragnhild's gravestone. Above her name and beneath the engraved crown was a sky-blue stone that matched the one Veigar had just shown me. The same type of crystalline structure of the plinth in the Temple. But instead of protected within a mountain, the Forest Fae shard was out in the open for anyone, myself included, to see.

I covered my mouth with my hand. The Forest Fae stone was hidden, but also wholly unguarded. "Are you positive no one else knows its whereabouts?"

"People may have guessed, but the truth remains with the Council." He twisted to Øyvin. "You will say nothing of this."

Øyvin bowed his head. "You have my word."

Espen reached out and held my hands in his. "I ask that you don't tell Halvar either, Lennie."

"I promise." I squeezed his fingers, then swiveled and peered over my shoulder to the piano. "What about the Fjord shard, Øyvin?"

He took a deep breath and let it out through his nose.

Would he relinquish the details, or would he keep this secret, even though neither Espen nor I would ever be able to descend into the depths of the fjord like he could?

"You promise this information doesn't leave this room?" Øyvin asked, pursing his lips and giving us a serious look.

"You have my word," Espen replied.

"Me too."

He nodded like our promises would suffice. "The eye of Jörmungandr beholds the monarch's key," he said, sounding like he was extolling a prophecy not a hiding spot.

I scrunched my nose. "The what now?"

"The sea serpent, the monarch's pet, is carved into the Fjord Council chamber walls. His eye contains the stone."

Damn.

I brushed my hair behind my ears and stared at the ceiling. "So, they're basically all in Skolvik."

I didn't need to look at them to know what they were thinking, the fear that ran through their minds. I could feel it in the silence. The well-being of the fjord region and the fae in it rested in a precarious position. We were teetering on the brink of battle—one that could have devastating consequences for everything I'd grown to love and call mine over the past year.

Espen's phone beeped and he pulled it out of his pocket, swiping a finger across the screen. "Fuck."

My stomach twisted in on itself again, bile churning like a tornado. "What happened?"

"Ylva just texted. Apparently, there is a new wildfire in the skiing town, Geilo, about halfway between here and Alvdalen."

"Any fatalities?" Øyvin asked.

"Unknown. But this seems like too much of a coincidence."

"How come?" I asked.

He typed out a quick reply before setting aside his phone and refocusing on me. "Because the town is very similar to Skolvik as far as its position. It's nestled in a valley, surrounded by forested slopes, and has limited road access."

Øyvin grumbled.

"So you think, what, that Veigar is doing a test run before moving on Skolvik?" He wouldn't do that right? After we'd just chatted. Or maybe our conversation was a distraction while someone else ran tests for him further inland?

"Maybe. I've instructed Ylva and some other soldiers to scour the region and keep watch over different zones. They will alert us of any suspicious movements or fires nearby."

"What information does Ylva have on Geilo?" Øyvin leaned forward and resting his elbows on his knees.

"Authorities aren't certain of starting location nor cause, but the ground is almost as dry as it is out here."

Fuck. I'd never witnessed a wildfire in person, but based on the photos I'd seen online and the dehydrated woods, it was little wonder fear had engulfed the room.

"Okay, so we have wildfires in Norway that might be started by a Fire Fae and Temple shards to deal with in addition to a walking volcano living among us," I said, hating each and every word as they came out.

Øyvin grumbled again, his gaze locked on something on the floor.

Espen straightened, a determined look washing over his features. "Veigar can't get hold of the shards." He turned to me. "He can't get access to the Temple."

"I doubt he's going anywhere near the Fjell considering him and Halvar aren't exactly besties."

"Halvar is in danger." Øyvin's ominous words settled over me like a joke.

I scoffed. "No one is a threat to Halvar."

The guys looked at one another, and my heart skipped a beat.

"That may be true," Espen replied. "But if there ever was anyone to truly match him in battle..."

My stomach twisted itself into a knot and I squeezed the pillow in my lap a little tighter. "I thought you were the almighty *Destroyer*? In fact, I've heard words from Halvar's own mouth, that you would always be a threat."

Espen straightened up like I'd just given him a second-hand compliment, his eyes wide with excitement, floppy hair bouncing. "Really?"

"Yes, really. Back when you were poisoned, he warned me that you might be behind the shit going down with the fjell, the landslides, etcetera."

Øyvin's lips turned down at the corners. "He had a point."

"You don't believe that, do you?" Espen's voice notched higher, his eyes widening. "You both know I would never purposefully cause harm with those powers. Not here. Never here. Not unless it was my last option."

"I do know," I said and took his hands in mine. "Very well. Which is why I defended you. Told Halvar he was full of shit."

"Did you use those exact words?" Øyvin's voice rumbled.

"I... Erm... He got the gist." I highly doubted I'd ever tell the big guy he was full of shit, at least not to his face. I didn't have a death wish. "Either way. You're all mighty and powerful."

Espen beamed and brushed his thumbs over my knuckles. "I am. But both Veigar and Halvar have more experience, more life led than I do."

Note to self, find out exactly how old Halvar is.

"So, that's why they're a threat to each other?"

Espen half-nodded, half-shook his head. "Yes and no. They have battlefield experience and are both immensely powerful beings. They can raze swaths of soldiers in a single attack, pierce through attackers with fire or stone, and sever heads with their bare hands."

A shiver ran through me as the echo of Balder's head being ripped off by Halvar flashed through my mind.

Øyvin cleared his throat. "They are god-like tacticians that should not be underestimated under any circumstances."

"Ruthless," Espen added.

I wiped my hands across my face. We couldn't have them starting an all-out brawl in the streets of Skolvik. The picturesque wooden buildings wouldn't withstand Halvar's wrath, let alone Veigar's fire.

"What can we do?" I looked between the two men, hoping they might have an answer that didn't include a deadly dance between the fae factions.

Their eyes narrowed, both of them mired in thought.

A moment later Espen rolled his shoulders and puffed his chest. "We prepare as best we can and do our best to keep Veigar away from the other shards and Temple."

"Agreed," Øyvin said. "And we find ways to remove him from Skolvik."

It wasn't ideal, but it wasn't nothing. Perhaps fluid plans were best in these kinds of situations? Maybe we needed to be willing and able to pivot at a moment's notice? I certainly had enough experience of shit hitting the fan—even in the last year alone—that I knew how to triage a problem. Whatever happened, we'd face it together.

"What a fucking mess," I muttered and stifled a yawn. "And what a day."

Espen's hooded gaze flicked to mine and he tilted his chin up. "Come here, wife."

A wave of warmth washed over me, prickling against my skin. The things that man said and did could melt me into a puddle of love in seconds—and I never wanted that feeling to end. I set aside the throw pillow and scooted across the couch. Espen opened his arms, and I snuggled into his embrace with a sigh. Adrenaline ebbed from my system like a draining battery.

This.

This right here was what life was meant for.

The little moments of love and peace that punctuated the wild and crazy days.

And I loved this life. The village I'd been abandoned in, the secret magical world I'd stumbled across, and the men I now called mine. No matter the damage it did to my body, my mind, or my precious sleep schedule, I'd defend it until my last breath. Protect them at all costs.

I peered over at Øyvin, whose eyes snapped to mine like he could hear my thoughts as loud and clear as his own. The look alone sent goosebumps across my arms. "Get over here," I whispered.

Without saying a word, nor breaking eye contact, he strode over to the sofa and settled beside us. He traced a finger up the side of my thigh, and I squirmed in Espen's arms. Øyvin's hand skirted up my side and swept between my breasts before coming up to cup my cheek. A tiny smile curved the corner of his lips, and I melted all over again.

"Arms up, Trouble."

I leaned away from Espen, lifted my arms over head, and let out another yawn. Øyvin gently gripped the hem of my shirt and, in one fluid move, had it off me. Folding it into a neat square, he set the material on the coffee table.

I nestled back into Espen's hold, and he kissed the top of my head. The warmth of his body pressed against my curves, and I inhaled the scent that always lingered on him, the leather and moss smell that I now associated with home. It was like the forest he'd sworn to protect clung to him no matter where he went.

A clicking noise sounded, and my breasts dropped down. Espen peeled my bra off with a moan of a hungry man.

Øyvin palmed one boob and nuzzled into my neck, inhaling like he needed my air to live. Espen cupped my other breast, and heat welled between my thighs at the sensation of them worshiping and caressing my curves. The way they pleasured my body was like musicians composing a symphony. They knew which strings to pluck, which parts of my body would elicit notes of pure satisfaction.

Øyvin's fingers slipped from my breast down under my jeans and between my thighs, finding my center ready and wanting. He stroked that mound of need and tender sparks hummed through my body. Eyes fluttering shut, a moan slipped from me and Espen caught it with his lips.

This was the perfect Friday night. The best way to end a chaotic week. And there was one way to make it even better. "Come upstairs with me," I mumbled.

Both men rose to their feet, and Espen pulled me up off the sofa.

His smile reached the corners of his eyes. "Gladly."

128

LENNIE

My eyes peeled open, goop filling the corners as late-summer rays streamed through the gap in the curtains. Lying on my side, I stretched and arched my back, brushing my fingers and stomach against two other bodies. "What happened?" I asked, my voice raspy.

The last thing I remembered from the night before was snuggling up with my guys and kissing them. Had I fallen asleep during sex? Would they actually continue without me? No, that couldn't be right. Espen would never. Øyvin on the other hand... No, he wouldn't either. He'd spout something about ethics too. And, honestly, if they had sex with me while I was asleep it'd be both weird and rude.

I peered over my shoulder and found the Fjord Fae watching me, his blue eyes twinkling like the tops of water ripples in morning light. "Good morning, Trouble."

Turning beneath the soft duvet, I faced Øyvin and brushed my hands across his bare chest. A low rumble hummed against my palms.

"What happened last night?" I asked again.

"You fell asleep," he replied.

"Really?"

"As soon as your head hit the pillow."

I groaned. Fuck Halvar and his coitus interrupting workouts. I needed to give the man a new nickname. No longer would he be *Big Guy*. Oh no no. He was now *Cockblocker*.

A palm brushed over my ass, and I let out a sigh.

"You did seem rather tired during our chat yesterday," Espen said and nuzzled into my neck while wrapping his arm around my stomach.

"Yeah, but who falls asleep with two guys pawing at them?"

"You," Øyvin deadpanned.

I groaned again. "Can we make up for lost time?"

Espen's lips spread into a smile and trailed up the side of my neck. Øyvin brought his palm against my chest again, kneading one of my boobs. My nipple rose to attention, and he rewarded it by circling his thumb around it. A moan slipped from me and morphed into a yawn. I did my best to swallow and hide it.

"Don't fall asleep again," Øyvin said and stopped his ministrations.

"We can't have sex if you're going to doze off," Espen added.

Fuck. They were right. I couldn't fall asleep on them. Not again.

I shimmied free of their grasps and shuffled to the end of the bed before falling off with a thump. Scrambling to my feet, I set my hands on my hips and flipped my hair over my shoulder.

"Let me go make us coffee. That'll for sure keep me awake," I said. "It's been like a week since we've done the deed, and I don't want to miss another *yoga* session because I'm either drunk or asleep."

Two restrained grins peered over the white duvets.

"I'll take that as a yes, then."

Espen nodded vigorously.

Without further preamble, I yanked on a pair of leggings and a random T-shirt from the dresser, which from the clean linen smell and white color, was probably Øyvin's. The wooden steps creaked beneath my feet as I loped downstairs, the smell of brine and a cool morning dew brushing across my exposed skin. Water lapped against the underside of the house and golden light seeped through the windows of the main living space.

I aimed for the kitchen and set to work on making some coffees. Two black and one with plenty of sugar and creamer. If I was going to stay awake all day, I needed the caffeine and sugar-high.

As the sugar landed in my mug with a plop, sending a drop of coffee over the rim, the doorbell rang.

I stilled.

Who the hell would be visiting us at this time of day? And on a Saturday? All our friends were usually fast asleep or, in Ylva's case, patrolling the forest to get over the self-inflicted hangover from a heavy Friday night at Fisken.

The peeling ring of the doorbell echoed through the house again, and I tossed the tablespoon I'd been using into the sink. Metal on metal clattered, matching the incessant ringing.

"All right, all right. I'm coming."

I padded across the room and yanked open the front door.

A shock of spiky white hair, a wrinkled face free of makeup, and a pressed button-down uniform greeted me.

"Bente," I choked out.

What the hell was Espen's boss doing here? "Espen is upstairs. Let me go get him."

She cleared her throat. "Evelyn Solbakke Martin"—my eyes widened and my heart stopped beating—"you're under arrest for arson. Please come with me."

LENNIE

Well, I'd done it. I'd officially landed myself at the police station. After a year of avoiding Espen's place of employment, I'd been perp-walked here sans-bra by an official summons from the Chief of Police herself. The consequences of my actions were biting my ass and not in the pleasurable way I'd prefer.

I glanced around the interrogation room I'd been bundled into. It was cozier than expected. The white-washed walls were bland, but there was a slight yellow tint to them that made the room feel sun-drenched, even without any windows. A two-way mirror adorned the wall behind Bente and a clock ticked away over the door to the hallway. It wasn't as austere and intimidating as the one's I'd seen in movies and on TV shows. But happily basic would be a good description.

Bente settled into the wooden chair across from me and set down a pile of folders on the table. Her collar cinched around her throat, pressing against her neck, while the silver threads of the town's police department emblem on her breast-pocket sparkled at me in greeting. "Mrs. Solbakke Martin—"

"Call me Lennie, please."

"Lennie. Can you please explain what you did last year on the night of December 23rd?"

Well, fuck. I sucked in a breath. I was challenged by my now partners to raise my own ear magic and walk across the village while holding the ear-mirage in place. That went to shit when I accidentally magicked myself naked. Fuck out of luck, I decided to bolt. Miraculously my night ended with me getting plowed by the aforementioned gentlemen. It'd been a lose-win situation, but that was almost a year ago.

"Well..." Bente prodded, her brows raised toward her gel-infused hairline.

I clasped my hands together on the table. "I lost a bet."

"Really? That's how you want to explain what happened?" She nudged a manila folder across the table with my name on it.

I didn't need to open it to know what was inside. Images and screenshots of my naked ass barreling through town, hoping I wouldn't get picked up by anyone's security cameras. Unluckily for me, the town had been riddled with them, including a goddamn webcam that live broadcast the harbor to the town's website. By New Year's Eve I was the proud owner of a new nickname: The Streaking American.

"Look, I made a grave mistake. Had my cheeks caught on camera and have to live with the embarrassment of that for the rest of my life." Which was probably a damn sight longer than her own now that I was a demi-fae. "The footage captured of me is unfortunate, but I did not burn those cameras."

"So, you *do* know where my questions are heading?"

I nodded. The burned cameras had been the main topic of discussion at the café this week. Who knew how long it had actually been going on for. But I had my suspicions.

"As the woman at the center of our investigation, I have some questions for you. Please answer them honestly and we will get this over with."

Would I need a lawyer present for this? Did Skolvik have any lawyers? I didn't recall ever seeing a legal office, but maybe there were some who worked remotely and might be able to stop me putting my foot in my mouth. I pinched my lips together and motioned for Bente to proceed.

"Where were you yesterday morning?" she asked.

"Working at the..." Oh, wait a second. "I was running a bit late, but working at Oddvar's Café."

"Why were you late?"

Exhausted from relentless training with Halvar and Fjell Fae soldiers. "Overslept. Accidentally turned off my alarm instead of hitting snooze."

"Can anyone vouch for your time of departure from home? Did anyone see when you left the house?"

Fuck. No, nobody could. Espen and Øyvin had both left for work by the time I scrambled out of bed in a panic.

I wrung my hands in my lap and shifted in my seat, the chair squeaking beneath me.

"Where were you three nights ago? Around eleven o'clock?"

With Halvar. I'd been training with Halvar, but she couldn't know that. I swallowed hard. "In bed."

Her eyes narrowed. "Can anyone vouch for that who doesn't live in your household?"

"No."

"I see. What about four nights ago around midnight?"

Same. Training.

At my lack of reply, Bente pulled her phone out of her pocket and tapped on the screen before turning it to me. A video clip from the town's webcam, pointed toward town square and the harbor. A blonde figure lumbered across the frame, stopped in the middle to catch their breath, then kept going.

I winced. "Evening stroll?" Even I didn't buy the wavered answer.

Bente shook her head then picked up another folder and scooted my cheery Christmas moon-shots to the other edge of the table. Opening the new folder, she pulled out some large photos and positioned them in front of me.

"Do you recognize these buildings?"

The top left of the jewelry store stared back at me. The white swirly lettering marked the front windows and in the center of the frame was a singed spot, blackening the white wood siding. I turned my focus to the other photo. The red-painted library was well cared for, window boxes blooming with multi-colored flowers, a signboard outside promoting the children's reading hour on Saturday mornings, and windows filled with drawings by local school kids of their favorite characters. All that joy was marred by a charred patch, the black mark spreading like an explosion had hit the right corner of the building.

"Those are the *Gullsmed* and *Biblioteket,*" I said. Hopefully my use of the local tongue would buy me some favor in this situation. Because right now, things weren't looking good for me.

"Can you tell me how those cameras were burned?"

I leaned back and furrowed my eyebrows. "Umm, no. But I could make some guesses."

"What would those guesses be?"

I couldn't tell her the truth. Studying the photos again and keeping my eyes firmly on the images, I started spitballing ideas. "Blow torch. Lighter. One of those fire stick thingys you guys handed out on Christmas Eve at the caroling event—"

"A *fakkel*?"

I snapped my fingers and pointed at her. "Yeah, that."

Her head shook like she didn't believe me.

"A firework," I continued, grasping at invisible straws of hope. "A flare. Matches? Oh no wait, what about a flamethrower? That could reach the eaves of the buildings where the cameras are."

"Have you ever seen a flamethrower here in Skolvik?"

My knees bounced and I pressed my clammy hands together. "No, I haven't."

"Where would you consider buying one?"

"Well, first of all, Chief— Can I call you Chief?" She shrugged like she didn't really give a damn. "Well, Chief, I'd consider purchasing any of the aforementioned items from the camping and hiking store."

"Really?" Her brow's pinched together. "Why there?"

I shrugged. "Because I've seen a lot of random stuff in that store that doesn't exactly fit the bill for hiking or camping. Like, who needs a four-burner grill on their hiking trip? Or a unicorn shower curtain? Or allergy-friendly laundry detergent?"

"I wouldn't take that large of a grill on a hiking trip, but one of the small charcoal ones are wonderful for day hikes."

"Really?"

She nodded and then tapped the photo of the library. "Did you burn down the cameras, Lennie? Was it to erase the photographs? To seek revenge for—"

"Revenge for what?"

Bente brought back the Little Christmas Eve Lunar Event folder and pushed it toward me. I flipped it open and found picture after picture of my buns and boobs sprinting through the village. I knew it had been bad—the locals were still laughing at it months later—but seeing them all spread out like this... It was little wonder that Bente thought I was on a revenge spree.

Shutting the incriminating folder, I shoved it back across the table. "It wasn't me, and you have no proof."

"We have very strong motive and unaligned accounts of your whereabouts during the arsons."

I wiped my hands across my face. Was this happening or was I still asleep? Please, Satan and whatever deities were watching, let this be a nightmare I could wake up from and laugh about later.

Bente stared at me, eyes narrowed, surveying me like my silence might hold the answers to her questions.

"Look, it wasn't me." My mouth went dry, and my legs wouldn't stop bouncing of their own accord. It was like my own muscles were nervous of the woman, wanting to abandon me in my time of need. "Where is Espen?"

She hadn't let him talk to me on our walk over here. But if Espen could chat with Bente, he could tell her I was innocent. If anyone could vouch for me being a somewhat-kind-of-good-slash-improving citizen of Skolvik, it was my husband.

"He and Øyvin are in the hallway waiting," she replied.

"Can I see them? Just for a second?"

"No. Did you burn all of the cameras in the village?"

Nausea roiled through my stomach. Maybe I did need a lawyer?

130

ESPEN

A buzz of energy ran through the entire station, from the glossy front desk to the white-washed hallway outside our two interrogation rooms. My shoes squeaked against the floor as I paced back and forth in front of the three gray chairs that sat opposite the rooms, dodging Øyvin's outstretched legs as he pretended to nap in one of the rigid armchairs.

"You knew this would happen eventually," he mumbled, not bothering to open his eyes.

I huffed. He wasn't wrong, but I thought I could protect her from her own antics. Stop this inevitability from happening.

Pranks and jokes? Sure.

But arson? She would never.

She cared about the village and her neighbors. That wasn't the Lennie I knew and loved. She didn't have some secret vendetta against anyone here in Skolvik.

"It wasn't her and you know it."

A low grumble emanated from the Fjord Fae.

"She wouldn't. She must've been framed."

"Yes, but those security camera photos of her aren't great, and the fact that she hasn't already been charged with public indecency for her actions on Little Christmas Eve is a miracle."

I pushed my hands through my hair, pulling it off my forehead. "This is really bad."

"Uh-huh."

"But they don't have any evidence for this, though. For the burned cameras. We didn't find any link or footage of the culprit earlier this week."

"No images of a perpetrator at all?" Øyvin sat up properly in the chair and rested his elbows on his knees.

"None. The footage cuts out as flames wrap around the device. It's as if someone is standing behind the camera or at a distance, purposefully avoiding the field of view."

Øyvin grumbled. "I think that tells us all we need to know."

"It does, but it can't be proved to the... erm... locals." No, the humans couldn't know that a Fire Fae walked among them, torching their precious security devices. They had to find a culprit, and the only viable option right now appeared to be my wife, even if the evidence was circumstantial and reaching.

"They shouldn't be arresting her," I muttered. Sure, they could bring her in for questioning as she was guilty of public indecency, but still... I plopped into the chair beside Øyvin and raked my hands through my hair again sending the already messy strands into a bird's nest of disarray. "I just want them to let me in."

"You're her husband. You know that's a conflict of interest."

I was, and I did. But that didn't stop the swell of emotions growing within me like uncontrollable weeds. I wanted to rip them out and replace them with the bubble of happiness I'd woken up to: the feel of Lennie next to me, the warm duvet cocooning us as the morning sunlight doused us in a gentle glow. She was always beautiful, but there was something ethereal about her in the morning, however grouchy she may be. It was as if the sun radiated from *her*, illuminating her in a halo worthy of an angel.

Øyvin cleared his throat, drawing me from my thoughts, and peered over at me. "We also don't know *exactly* what evidence they have or don't have. They might have kept something from you."

He was right...

But that didn't mean I couldn't find out. I jumped from the chair and strode down the hallway to the front desk. Jens, the station manager, perched in a tall office chair behind the high white-and-gray desk, his glasses sliding down his nose as he peered at his computer screen.

"Jens!"

The man startled.

"Sorry to disturb you." I rested my forearm against the tabletop and gave him a smile. "Was there any new evidence brought in on the camera investigation?"

The lump in his throat bobbed. "Um... I... Erm... I really can't say, Officer Solbakke Martin."

"Don't worry. I'm one of the investigators on the case."

He dropped his chin to his chest and stared at his hands, wringing them in his lap. "Y-you were removed."

I reared back but kept my tone calm and friendly. "When?"

"T-this morning. The Chief made the request before bringing in your wife."

My smile fell, and I took a deep breath to steady my thoughts. This would be fine. We could still handle this. It was protocol to remove an officer from a case if one of their family members was involved, and I didn't want to break the Station's rules. However much I didn't like them right now, they were in place for good reason. We couldn't have conflicts of interest.

Lennie would be fine. I had to trust her. She may have had an uncanny ability to land herself in trouble, but she was kind, determined, and smart—traits I truly admired in her. She would explain the mix up to Bente and set the record as straight as possible without revealing the Fae secret.

A colossal boom sounded outside, and I gripped the edge of the desk as the walls and floor trembled. Dust rained from the ceiling, showering us all in a thin layer of debris. The plant pots flanking the front door crashed to the floor, cracking and spilling soil over the polished tiles.

What was that?

"Earthquake?" Jen muttered from where he'd half-ducked beneath the desk.

I shook my head and peered around the space, assessing for any damage. Smooth walls sans cracks stared back at me, the floors equally unmarred.

Jens sneezed, his eyes watering.

"Bless you," I muttered.

No, it wasn't an earthquake. Something, or *someone,* had happened outside. And I'd wager it was the start of another grueling chapter in my life.

Adrenaline flooded my system, and my thoughts calmed, focusing on the most important things.

I rushed down the hallway toward my wife and friend.

The door to the interrogation room flew open, and Bente popped her head out into the hallway. "Everybody all right?"

I skidded to a stop and nodded, but my brow remained furrowed. Whatever just happened outside was bad. Part of me wanted to run and check, see exactly what had caused the explosion. The other part didn't want to leave Lennie. Either way, I took the opportunity presented to me and strode for the open door. "Lennie! Are you okay?"

Bente's arm shot out, bracing against the frame and blocking my path.

"It wasn't me. The arson or that boom!" Lennie yelled back, probably hoping people would start to catch on that not all calamities in the village stemmed from her. And, for the most part, that was true.

A low rumble emanated from behind me, and I peered over my shoulder. Øyvin stood a few feet away, glaring at Bente. She pursed her lips and didn't waver in her stance.

The sound of ringing phones and yelling echoed down the hallway, matching the harried rhythm of my heartbeats.

"Bente, let me in to check on Lennie, please."

She opened her mouth to speak, but smacking footsteps drew our attention away.

Jens came running down the corridor, eyes wide, panic engraved in the lines on his face. "We have a massive problem," he said between panted breaths.

"What was it?" Bente and I asked at the same time.

"The oil plant down the fjord exploded."

Øyvin stepped into the man's path, towering over him. "What!"

Poor Jens looked like he was about to wet his trousers but nodded.

"Okay," Bente said and exited the interrogation room. "We need to gather all officers. Jens, put out the call including members off duty. I also want a direct line open to the village fire station in case we need to contact them. Our response will follow the protocol laid out in the disaster plan. Jens, please have that PDF sent to all officers as a reminder too."

"Yes, ma'am." The man spun on the spot, sprinting down the hallway.

"Now, you three."

I turned to Bente, awaiting orders, and found Lennie had snuck into the open doorway. She wiggled her brows at me, and I bit my lip to hide my growing smile.

"I'm going to let the questioning go for now, Mrs. Solbakke Martin," Bente said, facing Lennie. "You're not *off-the-hook* as you Americans say, but I may ask you to return to the station at a later date for more information."

"Yes, ma'am," Lennie replied with a salute.

Bente pivoted on her heels and looked up at Øyvin. "As we have you here. I'll have the police boat take a few officers down fjord, but might we borrow your boat to assess the situation too?"

"Of course. I was planning a trip down the fjord to check on the waters myself." Though knowing what I did about him, the Fjord Fae probably hadn't planned on taking his boat. Swimming over there was likely faster, but... We needed to keep up appearances. However annoying that might be under current circumstances.

"Excellent. Thank you." Bente strode down the hallway and we all followed after her. "I want as many eyes on this as possible."

I couldn't agree more.

131

ØYVIN

After a quick stop at the boathouse for Lennie to put on a bra and "I Heart Skolvik" sweater, all four of us climbed aboard my boat and set off down the fjord. Wind lashed at our faces as the shiny, white vessel skipped across the water at full speed, keeping pace with the silver-and-black police boat, its blue light whirring above the skipper's alcove.

I stood behind the wheel with Espen between me and Bente, while Lennie bounced up and down on the uncushioned seat on the prow. My stomach twisted in on itself, adrenaline coursing through my veins.

Who did this?

How bad was it?

How many creatures had already been impacted beneath the waterline?

Bente had her phone to her ear, talking to someone about the cause behind the explosion. Unfortunately, I could only hear what she said and not the other person on the line.

"No casualties?" she asked, and I held my breath. "Good."

I let out a sigh of relief and caught Espen doing the same as he peered ahead at the scenery, his face marred with lines. Emerald pines shot into the sky along the fjord's flanks while water sloshed against the rugged shoreline. Jagged peaks and cliffs loomed above, casting shadows over parts of the water. Spray splashed my face as we hurtled along, and I was glad I'd put on my long-sleeved shirt this morning. It may have been late Summer, but the wind was unforgiving as it raked across my cheeks and promised cooler days to come.

As we rounded the bend in the fjord, chaos unfolded before us, and I slowed the purring engines.

My fingers clenched around the wheel as I sucked in a smoky breath.

On the fjord's left embankment sat the oil refinery. Copper and gray silos the size of three-story buildings and thick pipes sprawled along the water's edge.

Flames licked every inch of the property, and a tower of black smoke billowed into the clear blue sky, blocking out the sun. Wailing sirens and the smell of burned metal and fuel filled the air like an invisible, toxic cloud. Firetrucks dotted the scene, with specialized tanks and foam aimed at the main part of the blaze. Even a fireboat floated along nearby, its water jet set on the foliage surrounding the massive inferno.

I cut the engines and let us drift, as the intense swell of heat buffeted our faces. "Shit."

Bente hung up with a clipped goodbye, shoved her phone into her jacket's breast pocket, and sighed.

"Cause?" I asked.

"They suspect a pipe leak, but won't know more until the flames are out and the site can be safely accessed. All employees have been evacuated and accounted for, though."

That was good. But my thoughts swam back to Reuven's request. He'd asked to monitor the waters around the oil refinery only a few days ago. Had he known something was about to happen? He wouldn't have been behind this, would he? Or was he warning me about his wife? His father-in-law?

My gaze landed on Lennie, and she mouthed, "Why?"

I shrugged. Until I could get closer, get into the water, I couldn't be sure. I scanned the fjord, searching for oil and pollutants in the waterway.

Bente cleared her throat. "They're concerned about the chemicals used to put out the fire spilling back into the fjord."

"As they should," I mumbled. Tension gripped my shoulders. If Bente weren't here, I'd jump in and start cleaning up.

Fuck, I had to do something.

I glanced to Espen and found his gaze locked on the terrifying scene. He brushed his hand across his beard, his chest rising and falling in jagged motions like he was trying to contain an outburst or a panic attack.

"You all right, Espen?" Lennie asked, having also noticed the unusual behavior.

He flicked his attention to her, those amber eyes filled with fear and something I couldn't quite name, but reminded me of when he'd shied away from discussing the southern war that happened twenty years ago. He quivered minutely and straightened up. "I'm glad no one is hurt."

"Me too," Lennie muttered.

Bente waved over the police boat and ordered them to move toward shore and take a closer look. The officers did as requested, cruising closer to the scene.

"You stay here," Bente said with a nod to me.

"Yes, ma'am."

I looked back out across the water. This was all too suspicious. An explosion at the local oil refinery in the weeks following the Fire Fae King's arrival and coffee shop proclamations? There was a good chance this wasn't just an errant pipe failure. My money was on the Fire Fae King or his daughter. We couldn't trust either of them, or anyone affiliated with them. Who knew how long it would take for someone to come forward and claim responsibility or for us to investigate?

For now, though, I needed to do my job.

"Lennie? Trouble?" I whispered and Lennie twisted in her seat to face me. I cocked my head toward Bente behind her back and mouthed, "Distract her for ten seconds."

I needed to assess the water. Feel it. Check it.

Lennie rose from her seat and wobbled slightly as the boat bobbed. Shifting closer to Espen, she bumped into him as the vessel swayed. He wrapped an arm around her, steadying and pressing her against his chest. Those big brown eyes peered up at him taking on a doe-like look that some would confuse for innocence, but I knew better. That was a tell-tale sign she was up to no good.

She pointed to the blackest part of the refinery. "That looks like it might be where the fire started."

Bente's gaze followed her finger, while Espen furrowed his eyebrows and peered at me, searching for clarity. I leaned over the edge of the boat, one hand centimeters above the waterline. I tilted my head and widened my eyes.

Distract her. Now.

He nodded to my non-verbal request, and spun, giving me his back and blocking me from view.

I dipped my hand into the water and pushed some of my magic into it. A trill of warmth skittered down my arm and burst into the water. It sung back to me, but not its usual harmonious tune. No, this felt grim, darker, like something had cut the strings to the keys. I raised my hand, dragging some of the liquid upward for a closer look. Rainbow swirls slid over the curve of water. I inhaled sharply and pursed my lips.

Fuck.

Slicks of oil had made it into the fjord.

I needed to get down there fast. Send soldiers out to clean up before it could spread and start killing the local wildlife. And it wasn't just creatures that lived within the water that would be threatened by this. Birds that used this waterway for nourishment could mar their feathers with this mess, and humans could get it on their skin if they weren't careful.

I plopped the crest of water back where it belonged and caught Lennie watching out of the corner of her eye, her brows rising in question.

"There's already oil in the water."

She spun, Espen's arm still wrapped around her middle like he was worried she might fall in even though she was nowhere near the railing.

"What can you see?" she asked.

"Can you see a slick?" Bente chimed in, peering around Espen. "I can't see any signs."

"It's just beneath the surface." I returned to my spot behind the driver's console. "I wouldn't be surprised if it gets worse within the next few minutes."

Espen let out a frustrated hum and Lennie sagged in his hold.

This was bad. Really, really, bad. Not only was there a massive fire emitting who knew what kind of pollutants into the air, but oil had seeped into my fjord. If the Fjord Fae didn't clear it up quickly and inconspicuously, lives dependent on it would be harmed.

"We should go back to town," Bente said. "We've got work to do at the station."

Lennie turned to face her again. "And you're sure you don't need me to come back in for questioning?"

The evidence didn't look good, but they couldn't hold her unless they had something concrete.

Bente scanned Lennie once from toe to head. "Not today."

Thank fuck.

Lennie slumped against Espen. "Thank you."

"I agree, let's head inland," I announced, starting the engines again. "I'd like to see how far this oil might stretch."

"Agreed," Bente replied.

"Start her up, Captain," Lennie said and wobbled back to her perch at the front of the boat.

The engines roared to life, matching the fear igniting inside me. Whoever was behind the explosion, it felt like they'd just set off a cannon marking the start of a war.

132

LENNIE

We wound our way back down the fjord at a significantly slower pace. While the others focused on the water, looking for rainbow-colored sheens and lumps of black detritus, I focused on our surroundings. I'd never been this far down the fjord, at least not from this vantage point. The first and last time I'd been down here had been with Øyvin *beneath* the water.

The mountain peaks were harsher here, more dramatic, like they were cast in a production and doing their damnedest to live up to the expectation set for them. Skolvik harbor was a dot down the way, surrounded by trees and steep hills. My gaze drifted to the left mountainside, and a reminder of something the Fjell Fae Council had said danced through my thoughts. "Do you think there may have been any other impacts from the explosion?"

"There is a crack up there." Bente pointed to where I'd just been looking.

"Yeah, would that be impacted? Could the blast have widened it?" And what would the culprits stand to gain from that? My money was on Veigar or Salka being behind this. Or perhaps it was whoever had been starting wildfires in other parts of the country.

Bente narrowed her eyes. "You know about the fissure?"

"Ummm." I swallowed hard and pulled my hair into a ponytail. "Yeah, I saw it on a hike. Some folks have been talking about it in the café too."

Bente nodded like that made sense—it had been a common discussion topic in Skolvik since before I'd arrived. "It's a significant concern for the village. If that part of the mountain fully dislodges and falls into the fjord, not only will it take all that forest with it, it'll cause a massive tsunami-style wave that would wash out the entire town."

Blood rushed from my head, and I clenched my fists at the horrific image Bente painted with her words.

"Is there anything you can do?" I asked.

"We have an evacuation protocol in place." Bente sighed. "I don't ever want to use it. But if that piece weakens, I'll have to ask villagers to leave their homes." She stared back down the fjord. The refinery was gone from view, hidden by the bends in the waterway, yet the black plume of smoke in the sky marked the problem. "But we may already have one such issue on our hands."

My eyebrows pinched together. "What do you mean?"

Øyvin cleared his throat. "She means, the water may be severely polluted by that explosion. Many people rely on these waters for their livelihood."

Shit. I hadn't thought about that. Of course, it would impact the people who relied on the fjord for a living and not just the wildlife and fae that called it home.

"But that crack," Bente said, drawing my attention back to her. "That crack is our biggest threat. These waters are known to be almost self-healing. The pollutants evaporate like magic. So, with help from our crews and some government resources, we can have the oil slick cleared in no time."

I refrained from looking at Øyvin, lest my face reveal any of my thoughts surrounding *why* exactly the fjord had a reputation among the locals. Instead, I peered back up at the mountain in question. The one I was all too aware of thanks to my connection to the Fjell Fae within it.

An idea sprung to mind.

"Bente," I started, my tone cautious and calm. "Why don't Espen and I hike up to the fissure and make sure the explosion didn't cause any further ruptures? I can bring my camera and take some photos for you."

My beautiful camera hadn't had an outing in a while, and this would be a useful way to get it outdoors while also helping the town.

"That would be wonderful," she said. "Thank you, Lennie. We have laser systems up there to warn of any shifts, but I'd like updated images. I can share them with the geologists in Oslo too."

I smiled. "Happy to help."

A few minutes later we docked the boat alongside the boathouse and climbed ashore.

"I'll head back to the station, please report your findings to me as soon as you return from your hike."

"Of course, boss," Espen said, and I nodded in agreement, glad to lend a hand.

We rounded the corner to the front of the building, our footfalls tapping against the wood planks before muffling against the asphalt of the road.

As we said our goodbyes, Bente tilted her chin toward the house. "There's a note on your door."

The three of us spun on the spot.

A small, white envelope was taped to the front door with *Lennie* scrawled across it.

Who's handwriting was that?

LENNIE

We said goodbye to Bente and watched her disappear down the road before scrambling to the front door. I yanked the envelope off and ripped it open. Inside was a *Greetings from Skolvik* postcard with an aerial shot of the village and fjord. I turned it over and my stomach flipped into my throat.

I grow weary of waiting. Your deliberation time has concluded. I gave you ample warning.

- V

"Fuck, he really did mean twenty-four hours," I muttered and handed the card to the guys who'd been reading over my shoulders. "And I haven't heard shit from Halvar. Not that I was expecting to. This non-reply is probably the big guy's way of saying 'go fuck yourself.'"

"Well, I think it's safe to assume the explosion was Veigar's calling card too," Espen said.

"Yes, to both." Øyvin grunted and peered at the water lapping along the dock. "I'm going to head below. Start clearing up his mess."

I rose to my tiptoes and pressed a kiss to Øyvin's lips, drawing his attention to me. He cupped my head with his hand and deepened the kiss like he needed to reassure himself of my well-being. If I could, I'd stay here with both of my guys, kissing and cuddling—finally having sex with them—as the world collapsed around us. But I wouldn't. Couldn't. I had a responsibility to them, the mountain, and my home. With a whimper, I extracted myself from Øyvin's hold. "Stay safe."

"Whatever you do, stay out of the water until I say so," he said.

Espen and I both nodded.

A moment later we entered the house as a gentle splash sounded from outside.

After I quickly changed into hiking gear and Espen slipped into his police uniform, we trudged up the slope on the north side of the fjord and headed for the fissure in the mountain. My camera dangled against my chest while sweat beaded beneath my T-shirt and behind my ears. The cool breeze was a balm as it washed over my heated skin and wound through the forest. Thick trees rose all around us, their needles and leaves weaving a dense tapestry that let through peeks of blue sky.

I peered to my right and found a gentle grin on Espen's lips. The sight warmed my heart and reminded me of the first time we'd hiked together on the trails up here. That day he'd told me all about the Forest Fae and shown me his healing magic by coaxing a sapling into growth. Now look how far we'd come.

I slid my hand into his. His amber eyes found mine, those damn luscious lashes of his framing the warm gaze like it was in a museum.

"What?" he asked.

A sigh drifted from my chest as my shoulders rose and fell. "Just thinking about how much has happened in the past year."

"I was thinking the same."

"Really?"

"Mm-hmm. How we went from you punching me to going on a dinner date. Then hiking around here to marrying you. We may have faced a lot of challenges in that time, but it's been the best year of my life." His thumb brushed across the back of my hand. "I'm so glad you stayed."

Every nerve ending in my body tingled in reply and I squeezed his hand. "I'm glad I stayed too."

I really was. These men and their secret magical society had changed my life for the better. I'd once been searching for a place to call home, a place where I belonged that filled me with excitement. Skolvik, the fae, and my partners were exactly that. I'd found love in the most unexpected of places and wouldn't change it for the world.

From days at the coffee shop, to the hikes through the forest, to *yoga* sessions with my partners, my life was full and complete. However...

"I'll admit, though, this isn't how I wanted to spend my Saturday afternoon and evening. But, explosion and interrogation aside, I don't mind the turn of events."

"What were your plans for tonight?" Espen asked, swinging our joined hands back and forth between us as the sun dappled across our faces.

"Honest to hell, I just wanted to get laid by my husband and partner."

Espen chuckled and tugged me against his chest, bringing us to a stop. With his thumb and finger, he tilted my chin up. "I'll never tire of hearing you saying that."

"That I want sex?"

"No, that I'm your husband."

A smile swept across my lips and those conga-line dancing butterflies returned to my stomach. Everything about this man made me happy. His gregarious personality, general excitement for life, and the way he cared for the world around him. He loved his people, loved his family, loved me. I leaned in to kiss—

"Well, isn't this sweet," a male voice drawled up ahead and my attention snapped toward the terrifying sound. Veigar emerged on the trail in all-black hiking attire, his sunglasses perched on his nose. "Husband and wife out for an evening hike. Do enjoy the view."

My stomach fell so far out of my body it prepared to tumble down the hillside and into the fjord.

Espen's hold on my hand tightened. "Veigar."

"Espen," the Fire Fae king replied as Salka came up behind him in her hiking gear. They sauntered past us, heat radiating off them like a furnace in winter. With a knowing grin, Veigar looked like a barn cat that had made a kill and proudly lain it on the front steps of the house. Salka meanwhile didn't move her face at all. It was as if she was giving a blank sheet of paper a run for its money, keeping her secrets to herself.

"What are you doing out here?" Espen's voice was clipped and firm.

"The forests in Norway truly are spectacular," Veigar replied. "So lush and full of... life."

Espen tightened his jaw, and his left foot slid forward, putting himself between me and them.

"We got your note," I said, hoping I could diffuse the tension swarming around us.

Veigar tilted his head like a man doffing his top hat. "Wonderful, and yet, I've had no reply from the mountain."

"I don't think you're going to get what you want."

"What a shame."

"Leave us," Espen bit out. "Leave Norway."

Veigar's lips twisted into yet another stomach-churning smile. "I don't think I will."

"He has decided to stay a little longer," Salka added, and my shoulders tensed.

"Do enjoy the view," Veigar said. "The mountain is so... majestic."

What did he do?

I didn't say a word, didn't need to. I spun and my legs moved of their own accord, needing to run, needing to get to the site as swiftly as possible. Espen did the same, sprinting along behind me. Letting me take the lead and leaving the two Fire Fae in our dust.

I bolted through the trees, leaped over logs, and carved up the rugged trail beneath my feet. My lungs heaved, sweat spreading across my back, as I pressed on.

The flora along the path appeared unharmed as I hurried past it, but up ahead... What would I find? What could they have done with their fire powers? What had he done to my mountain?

Øyvin was correct. We couldn't trust Reuven and I really didn't trust Salka. Especially right now.

Sunlight shone through the thinning trees as the two of us rushed out into the opening, wild heather and rock-filled brush spreading before us.

I sucked in a lungful of air and set my hands on my hips, scanning the scene.

The hillside appeared free from harm—bees flitted from clusters of pink heather and purple blooms peeking through rocky outcroppings. A gentle breeze danced through the plants making them wave at us in greeting and swept through the loosened strands of my hair that had fallen from my ponytail. I looked to my right, toward the pointy mountain top. The jagged gray edge carved a line through the darkening blue sky, remnants of sunlight bouncing off specks of quartz embedded in the stone.

Espen wandered further up the clearing while I got out my camera. Pulling off the lens cap and securing it in my legging's pocket, I turned on the device and aimed at the darkest spot of the craggy mountain.

The stone edge opened like a monster's maw, the serrated edges looking more like teeth than pieces of rock. The gap between the top and the bottom edge of the fissure was large enough to fit a man length wise.

Shit. Even from this vantage point and without the camera's zoom, the fissure had shifted since I'd been here this spring with Torsten. Widened like it'd been pried apart by Thor himself.

I snapped a few pictures for Bente. While her handy laser contraption had probably noted the movement of the mountain, seeing it was another thing. Hopefully, these pictures would help her and the other decision makers in the village.

With pictures taken at all zoom levels, I returned the lens cap to its rightful home and turned off the camera.

Espen still surveyed the edges of the clearing, sticking close to the tree line, searching for any clues of malpractice. What exactly had Veigar done here? Was he the one who'd widened the crack or was that a result of the explosion down the fjord? Or maybe Salka was behind it? There was no doubt in my mind that he'd touched something he wasn't supposed to. We'd angered him enough and he didn't seem like the kind of man that was told *no*. Nor took kindly to hearing the words when they were thrown at him. But what could he have done?

I knelt on the ground and pressed my hand into the soil, pushing some of my magic out, acting on natural instinct and need to check on the rocky facade beneath. A warm flow of energy washed down my right arm and spread into the dry yet hardy vegetation.

An oscillating sensation ebbed back to me, like a heart beating beneath my palm. My eyes fluttered shut, and I focused on that pulsing.

Thump.

Thump.

Thump.

It was like I'd reached into the mountain's chest and asked permission to see what had hurt it. Threads of power wove across the entire mountain, and I could... I sucked in a breath.

I could *feel* them.

All of them.

Each thread had its own distinct pattern. A clear and beautiful picture, in its own right.

I swallowed the lump in my throat. These were the Fjell Fae residents. The people of the mountain. I'd heard mutterings of the royals being tied to the mountain itself. Hell, since I'd inherited some of Freija's magic there had been cave-ins when I went to Ohio and Alvdalen. Halvar himself said those were caused by my absence and that his presence alone wasn't enough to stop them.

But this was more than that. This was an undeniable connection to the fjell and its residents.

I'd felt this before, but only briefly, when the wolf had stormed into the throne room this past winter. I'd slid in front of Halvar and Aurora, drawing a sword that had sparked with royal magic. In that same moment, the lights within the room had beat in tandem with my own heart. It was like the mountain and I had been one and the same. A part of a greater whole.

Placing my other hand to the ground, I pushed more of my power into the earth and let it flow up the hillside toward the fissure. It glided and danced up the stone beneath the soil, reaching and reaching and—

Black.

My shoulders curved inward, and a shudder ran down my spine.

Where the fissure lay was a pit of darkness. A gaping wound with fractured strands of magic around its edges where countless soldiers and Halvar... Halvar had tried to heal this too. But he'd failed. The massive, splintered piece of rock hung off its rightful home, threatening to fall at a moment's notice. And there, among the other pieces of Fjell Fae magic, was a glob that didn't belong. The magic was dark, hot, and angry as it clawed its way into the rock, shearing it further. Melting the fragile bindings that kept it in place.

My eyes flew open.

This was going to come down. This hundred-yard-wide piece of land was going to fall into the fjord and wash out any and all life in its path before the ensuing tsunami throttled the town.

"Fuck," Espen muttered, drawing my attention.

My gaze found his—fear filling his eyes—and my gut lurched again.

I ran up the hillside to where he stood beside a copse of birch trees. "What's wrong?"

He pointed to a lump of ash by his feet.

"That's odd," I said. "Why would Veigar light a fire up here? We didn't see any smoke and there are no smoldering embers, so it can't be fresh. Maybe some other idiot started a bonfire up here even though the Station and you rangers put a ban on them for the summer?"

Espen lips downturned and he shook his head. "How many soldiers did the Fjell Fae send up here to monitor the fissure?"

"What?"

He pointed around us. "How many soldiers did Halvar send up here?"

Three lumps of ash dotted the landscape. Scorch marks in the terrain beneath them. My lungs contracted, my hand flying to my mouth. "Fuck."

They'd burned the soldiers alive!

They'd killed them and messed with my mountain.

My lips trembled. How dare they!

A groaning noise sounded from the top of the hillside and our gazes snapped to the source. Tiny pebbles of soil and stone skittered down the mountainside, but the land, mercifully, didn't move. That didn't mean it wouldn't in the near future, though.

Bile churned in my stomach, images of terror and devastation flashing through my mind. Veigar was meddling with the town and putting everyone—fae and human alike—in his crosshairs.

"That part of the mountain is unstable." I sucked in a breath to hold back the rage and tears. "I felt what I can only describe as Fire Fae magic in there, weakening it."

"How long do you think we have before it falls?"

This was way above my pay grade, but I had to trust my gut. "Days, if we're lucky."

"We need to warn the village."

"And the fjord," I added. "We have to warn those living underneath the water before this comes down on top of their heads and crushes their homes."

"I'll text Øyvin," Espen replied and pulled out his phone.

While he focused on that, I took a moment for myself and the lives we'd just lost. I plucked three wildflowers from a nearby mound of rock. The delicate purple blooms fluttered in the breeze as I set each atop the three lumps of ash.

"Thank you for your service," I whispered to each. I may not have known those soldiers by name, but they deserved better than this ending.

They deserved to live long lives with their loved ones. They deserved to be honored for their sacrifice. They deserved so much more than what had no doubt been a horrific and painful death.

I swallowed hard.

"Lennie," Espen yelled from the trailhead. "Let's go!"

I nodded and bolted after him. We needed to get back to town. We needed to warn everyone. If Veigar wasn't going to get what he wanted, then no one would have it or their lives.

We careened down the hillside, moving as fast as we could without tumbling over our own feet or fallen trees. I yanked my phone out of my pocket, miraculously not falling on my face in the process. Scrolling through my contact list, I found the name I needed and clicked call. The line rang twice before the recipient picked up.

"Torsten." I didn't give him a chance to say hi. We didn't have time for that. "Get Halvar on the phone, now."

Whatever the man heard in my voice, spurred him into action. His breaths panted down the line and muffled footfalls sounded as if he were running through the tunnels to get to the big guy. A few seconds later I got who I wanted.

"What's wrong?" Halvar's rumbling voice echoed through the call.

"Veigar has fucked with the crack. Left behind three piles of ash too."

My words were met with silence, then, "I'll prepare the soldiers. Clear the town."

"On it."

I hung up just as Espen brought his own phone to his ear. A second later he said, "Bente, evacuate the village."

I bolted into the station and aimed for my office near the back of the building. Passing Jens at the front desk and the abandoned interrogation rooms, I hurtled down the hallway and barreled through the door to my room. I didn't spend much time here and had left the place in disarray. My hiking pack was thrown in the corner, boxes of papers sat untouched beside the metal desk, and several pointy snake plants perched on the windowsill. But the one thing I was looking for waited for me on top of my dusty filing cabinet.

Grabbing my rolled-up copy of the town map, I strode back down the hall to the main conference room. Voices grew louder the closer I got.

"We need to canvas each street."

"Boat owners need to be alerted too."

"Do we have extra vans for the elderly? Those unable to drive themselves?"

The cacophony continued as I stepped into the brightly lit room. The entire Police force had squeezed into the space, some sitting around the sleek conference table, others standing against the wall, taking everything in. Bente stood in front of the white board at the head of the room.

Her wizened gaze shot to me and the voices died down. "Do you have the map I asked for?"

I held it aloft, then unfurled the large map of Skolvik across the table. Colleagues further down the table set their coasters and mugs on the corners to stop the paper from curling in on itself. Stepping back, I settled in an open spot against the wall between two fellow officers who also happened to be Forest Fae.

"Now, then," Bente started, her voice filling the room. "I agree we go road by road as outlined in the emergency plan. I want teams of two attacking each street, one person on the left side, the other on the right."

Quiet murmurs of understanding flitted around the table.

"As for the boats." She braced her fists on the table and leaned forward. "Espen, can you talk to Øyvin? He's the de facto harbor master around here. Have him alert the other boat owners."

"Of course." I held back a wince. Øyvin had enough on his to-do list beneath the fjord; adding this could slow down the Fjord Fae evacuation efforts. But we had to keep up appearances. "I will let him know. I'm sure he has everyone's phone numbers and one word to the local fishermen will have them all coordinating among themselves to get their boats out of here."

Bente gave me a single nod. "Good. They'll need to get the vessels all the way out to the Atlantic to keep them safe, should a tsunami happen."

Rumbles of agreement sounded, and I couldn't have agreed more. A tidal wave would be devastating in the narrow passages of Skolvik Fjord. The water would likely ricochet from one side to the other, sloshing back and forth until the ferocious force eventually dissipated.

I listened in as discussions continued, all while mulling through what I'd need to do for the Forest Fae. Ylva was already working on alerting residents in the region that could be impacted, while a text to Turi had informed the Council of Elders what was happening. I hadn't had time to respond to her expletive laden text in my rush to get here.

"Now, the disaster plan includes a few officers remaining to watch over the village and a few to block the roads in and out of town. I'm okay keeping the blockades but I've decided I won't have any officers remaining in the village. Your lives—"

"I volunteer." The words were out of my mouth in an instant.

"No," Bente said. "I can't allow it."

"You can. You will."

"Espen."

I pointed to the map. "Boss, my cabin sits high up on the hillside. Probably out of reach of any tsunami that might crash through town."

"That *potential* is what I'm concerned about."

"I appreciate that, but someone needs to stay behind. It was in the plan for a reason. The cameras are gone. We need eyes on the town to protect it from theft and stop individuals from entering."

"You're newly married. I won't—"

"My wife agrees with me."

We hadn't talked about it, but I knew she would. If she were here, Lennie would have interrupted Bente and volunteered long before I piped up.

Bente let out a long-winded sigh. "I'm not going to win this argument, am I?"

I shook my head. While I couldn't elaborate further on *why* I was the best person to stay behind, I had to make her agree. I had to protect the forest and the village.

"Your bravery is commendable... and stupid."

I smiled. "Is that your way of saying you love me like a son?"

She snorted and waved her hand with a smile. Chuckles and chortles rose from the other officers.

She really did treat all her officers as an extension of her own family. It was one of the many reasons why I respected and liked her.

I found her gaze again. "I'll be fine. I will call you every few hours or if there are any updates or concerns."

The room fell silent again, everyone looking between me and Bente as the Chief considered my stance and proposal. She shuffled her feet and clicked the cap on her whiteboard pen on and off as her eyes turned glossy with thought. With a shake of her head she said, "You'll obey any order I give you from afar?"

"Always."

Another sigh left her, and she deflated a bit. "Fine. But only you and Lennie stay."

"Only me and Lennie," I repeated with a nod.

With her spiky head bobbing and a determined look plastered across her face, Bente turned her attention to the rest of the room and the map spread out before her.

"All right! Split into pairs. I want the village cleared of all people by tomorrow night at eight o'clock." She clapped her hands together. "Let's get to work!"

I wiped the sweat from my forehead, another street canvassed and cleared, a full evening of work almost complete. As the sun neared the jagged horizon, something moved out of the corner of my eye.

Ylva waved from where she leaned against the last house on the street, the eaves of the white-wood building casting her in shadow. "Get over here."

Scurrying toward her, I asked, "What have you got for me?"

She crossed her arms as I stopped in front of her. "Bad news, I'm afraid."

"Shit. We have enough going on already."

"You wanted to know if there were any changes or unusual events."

"What happened?"

She peered around, making sure none of the other officers or villagers were close enough to hear us. "Another wildfire started up about an hour east of here."

Fuck. I pulled my fingers through my hair, pushing it off my forehead. "Do they have a cause yet?"

She shook her head. "The locals think it might be summer tourists not putting out a camping fire correctly, but most of the tourists are gone for the season. So..."

Yeah, it was well past peak camping season. Only expert adventurers traversed the mountain woods at this time of year, and they all knew the rules, especially after another hot summer had left the country looking more like tinder than a verdant oasis.

Ylva's phone beeped, and she pulled it out of her pocket. "Ah, I don't want to say this is perfect timing, but I had those incoming archers check out the scene—without getting too close to alert suspicion among the humans—and they suspect Fire Fae based on the burn pattern. It's not natural and they think they've found multiple starting points."

That sounded like classic Fire Fae techniques. "Did they find any of Veigar's soldiers?"

"No."

"Are our archers still in the area?"

"They're awaiting next orders."

I tapped my foot against the asphalt. Veigar really was done waiting and seemed to be spreading us out. Or, at the very least, flexing his strength elsewhere in the hopes we would relent our opposition. Which we Forest Fae, and our friends, did *not* plan on doing any time soon.

"What do you want me to do?" Ylva asked, pulling me out of my head.

I had enough going on right now trying to clear the village. Until that was done, I needed to keep my focus locally. "Let me get the humans out of town while you focus on our people. I trust you to do what's best."

She nodded, gave me a tiny salute, and strode away with her phone pressed to her ear.

I turned back to the street I'd just cleared and found several families loading up their cars with their most prized possessions. The sight was like a punch to the gut. I texted Lennie and Øyvin, letting them know the news and got expletives in response.

As I stared down the street, families locking up their homes wondering if they would ever be able to return, I couldn't have agreed with my partners more.

"Fuck."

135

LENNIE

Øyvin didn't come home that night, neither did Espen. Both were busy with their respective jobs—alerting residents of the impending danger—and I'd been tasked with packing go-bags to take to Espen's cabin. I spent the next morning shoving spare clothes into our duffel bags and Øyvin's fancy-schmancy silver suitcase, and hauled them up the southern hill to the cabin before running back into town.

I sprinted past people loading up their cars and store owners boxing up window displays—saving as many of their precious wares as possible. Flower pots sat abandoned, curtains had been drawn, and keys clinked in locks as residents said goodbye to their homes and businesses.

I stumbled into Oddvar's Café, my chest heaving as sweat beaded along my hairline and beneath my white T-shirt. Chairs were stacked on tables, their wooden legs pointing toward the ceiling, the bread case sat empty, and rootling behind the counter was Oddvar.

The octogenarian's wispy eyebrows saluted me as I shut the front door.

"You heard the news?" Oddvar grumbled.

I nodded and crossed the room. "I was the one who reported it to the Station."

Oddvar's nose twitched, and he shrugged before motioning wildly around himself. "Help me with all this stuff, will you?"

"Of course." That's why I'd come here. I knew the man would need help packing up the café and loading his car. I wouldn't let him do that by himself. "Where should I start?"

He waved at the commercial-grade coffee pots and Robertina, my favorite espresso machine. "These will be covered by insurance."

"They cover potential tsunamis out here?"

"They cover landslides," he said with a nod to the back of the building. "This way."

He retreated into the storeroom, and I followed in the wake of his flapping, emerald cardigan. The storage room, that was barely larger than a pantry but could somehow fit a few people inside it, smelled like coffee and cleaning supplies. A smell I'd affectionately come to associate with Oddvar and his café.

Basic wooden shelves lined two of the three walls, with the final one housing the little kitchen set up with a fridge and freezer for our sandwich making. He turned his attention to the shelves, stacked with mugs, bags of beans, and boxes of teabags, among a whole host of other things.

Crouching down and eliciting several creaking noises, Oddvar pushed aside three large bags of sugar and retrieved a wooden box I'd never seen before. The size of a bread-bin, it reminded me of the one Gunvor had kept her cousin Vigdis's things in. However, this one was dark blue with traditional hand-painted white and yellow flowers.

I crossed my arms. "What have you got in there?"

Oddvar peered up at me, the lines around his eyes tightening as if he wasn't sure he should tell me.

"Have you been pilfering cash from the store, Oddvar?" I asked, a joking note in my tone.

He scoffed. "Never. Take this for me."

I reached out and took the box from his grasp, shocked by the surprising weight. As he rose, I assessed the box. "No really? What have you stashed in here? Gold? Your favorite mug? A mug made of gold?"

He tapped the box and motioned for me to exit.

I spun and sauntered back out into the bright light of the café, setting the lidded container on the counter beside a cardboard box that had been labeled *café*.

"Can I look inside? Or is it a secret?"

Oddvar tugged on the sleeves of his cardigan. "It's coffee."

My shoulders dropped. "What? Seriously? That's it?"

"They're special beans."

"You have a secret stash of beans?"

He pulled the box from the counter and gingerly set it in a cardboard one. "They're mine."

"You mean to tell me you've been making your own coffee with these beans and not the ones you sell to patrons?"

He nodded once.

"And you never thought to offer any to me?" I set my hands on my hips. "I thought you loved me, Oddvar."

He scoffed again and wagged a finger at me. "If you tell anyone, I will fire you when they deem it safe to return."

A laugh ripped from me. "Deal."

We set to work packing up his box and filling another with bits and pieces he deemed necessary for survival or worth taking with him. From a portable coffee pot and recyclable cups to napkins and teaspoons. Wherever he was staying, he could run his own rustic coffee shop from these items alone. As long as the patrons only wanted black bean juice.

"Lennie?" he said, breaking the companionable silence between us.

"What's up?"

"You'll take care of my café while I'm gone?" Oddvar asked, his thick accent adding another emotional layer to his words.

I swallowed a lump in my throat and my heart clenched like someone had wrapped their fist around it. "Of course. I won't let anything happen to the café nor our precious Robertina." I stroked a finger across the top of the fancy espresso machine as Oddvar failed to hide his eye roll. "Embrace the name, Oddvar."

He grumbled and stacked his pour-over container into the box in front of him.

"Thank you," he muttered, and a tiny smile tilted his lips before vanishing like it would be offensive to be caught.

"No, Oddvar. Thank *you*. I don't think I've ever said it properly. Thanks for taking a chance on me. For hiring me."

I'd needed a job when I moved here and wanted one I'd be good at and passionate about—which was hard in this economy. Sometimes you needed to find a job that would put bread and butter on the table. And I had with this one, but it had also become a place I enjoyed working and had taught me so much. Working here had fully entrenched me in the community. And Oddvar, along with my own plucky courage, was to thank for that.

His mouth twitched and he waved his hand at me. "No crying. Back to work."

I smiled. "Yes, boss."

We continued packing things up, wrapping favored mugs in towels and discussing where Oddvar would be seeking shelter. Apparently, he'd be staying with his youngest son in Bergen on the coast. They'd already made plans to visit a few good restaurants together and go on a fishing trip. Just the thought of Oddvar out on a boat with his family brought another smile to my face.

As I taped up the box I'd been working on, the bells above the door chimed. In walked Solveig, Dagny, and Jorunn in a wild assortment of T-shirts and unshapely pants, their silver and white hairdos in more disarray than I'd ever seen before.

I shuffled past Oddvar and around the counter to see the trio.

"We came to say goodbye," Solveig said and swept me into her arms. I hugged her tightly, before bracing my hands on her shoulders and holding her at arm's length.

"Where are you going for shelter?" I asked, my tone firm.

She patted my hand with her own. "Over the mountain to Vanheim. There are several hotels over there that have opened their doors to us."

"That's good to hear." I squeezed her shoulders and turned to the others. "What about you two?"

"Trondheim." Jorunn leaned against the counter and wiped the back of her hand across her forehead. "To see my daughter and grandchildren. The youngest just started walking."

"That'll be nice. And what about you Dagny?"

She doffed her hair in an attempt to tame the wayward curls. "My niece is coming to pick me up and take me to Oslo."

"Sounds like you're all going to have a nice time with family. It'll be a good distraction from everything happening here."

Solveig's eyebrows pinched together. "Where are you going, Lennie?"

Hadn't she already heard? Or was this part of their gossip-slash-factfinding mission?

"Espen and I are staying to watch over the village. Chief of Police approved it."

Gasps sprung from each of them while Oddvar grumbled behind the counter.

"You're staying?" Solveig exclaimed.

Jorunn shook her head. "You shouldn't be staying."

"Agreed, what a horrific honeymoon," Dagny added.

I choked out a laugh. "Would it surprise you to know that we never had any honeymoon plans?"

All three gasped in unison again while Oddvar grumbled something else inaudible.

"Unacceptable!"

"Foolish!"

"Do we need to have a word with you husbands?"

"Now, now, Ladies," a male voice said and I turned to find Espen in the doorway. "Who says I won't take my wife on a honeymoon at a later date?"

The elder trio swooned, but my eyes worked their way from his boots to the ends of his floppy strands, scanning for anything amiss. His black cargo pants and matching police T-shirt clung to his muscles. His utility belt hitched around his hips. The only sign that anything was wrong was the exhaustion weighing his movements and the bags under his eyes.

Like a lost puppy, I drifted toward him, wanting to be in his orbit and as close as possible.

A warmth filled his gaze as he took me in and smiled.

"Where would you take her?" Solveig asked.

I turned in Espen's hold and he wrapped his arms around my middle. His thumb tucked beneath my shirt, and he brushed tiny circles on my skin, sending a trill of tingles across my entire body.

"Yes, where *would* you take her, Espen?" Jorunn added.

"Spain?"

"Croatia?"

"Greece?"

"Bali?"

"Wales?"

"Wales? Why on earth would he take her to Wales?"

"It's where they filmed a lot of *Game of Thrones*."

"No," Jorunn said. "They filmed in Northern Ireland."

"Are you sure?"

My head shot back and forth. When the three of them got going, it was like watching Olympic-level table tennis.

"Besides, Wales is damp and wet!"

"Fine. Scotland, then."

"That's not much better."

"They have castles." Dagny turned to me. "Do you like castles?"

"Ummm, sure," I replied. "I guess castles are—"

"See," Dagny interjected and flapped her hands. "She likes castles. They should go to Scotland."

Espen set his chin on my shoulder, his beard brushing against the sensitive skin of my neck. "Should we stop them?" he whispered.

I shook my head. "They'll run out of steam soon."

"Would you die for her? Take a sword for her? Protect her life with your own?" Dagny asked.

Or not.

"Don't listen to her, Espen." Solveig waved her hand at her friend. "She's been watching *Game of Thrones* again and wants to marry Jon Snow."

Dagny harumphed, dipped around Solveig's hand, and shoved her finger toward Espen. "Answer the questions."

The band of Espen's arms around my stomach tightened. "Always."

His answer hooked on something in my chest and tugged. How had I gotten so lucky to find him? I twisted, rose on my tiptoes, and leaned in for—

"No kissing!" A gruff voice said.

I bit my bottom lip and stared into the merriment in Espen's eyes. "There aren't any customers here, Oddvar. And he's not behind the line."

"Rules are rules," he replied. "Now, help me with these boxes. I'm ready to go."

Espen winked at me, and I brushed the tip of my nose against his, promising that kiss later.

Espen and I each grabbed a box, letting Oddvar lead us to his gray sedan parked outside the café. It was odd seeing cars on the pedestrian-only walkway, like a final sign this town was in a panicked frenzy. The ladies offered moral support before saying a final goodbye and scurrying down the road out of sight.

Oddvar locked up the café and turned to me. He shoved a big ring of keys toward my chest, a troll keyring dangling off them. "Take these."

"You're trusting me with your keys?" I asked, accepting the bulky collection he'd amassed over the years.

"Take care of the café and the village."

"I will." I nodded and shoved the wad of metal into my leggings pocket. The keys poked against my upper thigh.

"Good." He climbed into his car. Rolling down the window, he added, "Don't die."

Espen and I chuckled as my boss drove down the street.

I leaned into Espen's embrace, enveloping myself in that welcoming smell of leather and moss. Letting out a sigh, I relaxed in his hold. So much had happened in the past few weeks. My parents had been in town, I got *married*, and then had been interrogated for arson. Who the fuck got married and dragged down to the local police station in the space of a week?

Movement down the street drew my attention. Veigar sauntered around the corner, his sunglasses trained on us. His lips curled up slowly at one corner, and a ball of dread settled in my stomach. What the fuck was he up to now? Hadn't he done enough?

He continued walking across the street, slowly clapping his palms together, and disappeared behind another building. My gut twisted at the sight and fear took hold.

"Where's Øyvin?" I whispered.

Espen squeezed me tighter. "Still in the fjord."

ØYVIN

We started on the north side of the fjord, escorting eighty-nine fae from their homes and sending them toward the coast or into the depths of the palace. Standing on the silty fjordbed, I stretched my arms above my head and then behind my back, watching fae and creatures coming and going. Soldiers zipped by, swimming through the murkiest depths of the watery inlet. I let out an extended breath as another family swept past me, their bags hitched over their shoulders, heading toward the fjord's southern slope.

This was just the start of our evacuation efforts. We still needed to put in magical buffers around the palace and clear more of the cave homes down fjord, not to mention help anyone above water who might need the extra assistance.

An elderly fae in a long, green dress and gray cloak drifted past, her large military-style duffel bag swamping her fragile frame and slowing her movements. She looked ready to collapse in a few meters.

"Let me carry that." I lifted the bag from her back, the air pockets around us allowing communication underwater.

"I'm doing quite well. Thank you," her voice croaked.

I grumbled and hoisted the oversized, canvas bag over my shoulder as she squeaked in a minor protest. The uneven weight settled against my back, bending my knees slightly. She shouldn't have been carrying this. It must've been twice her weight.

"Did no soldier offer help?" I asked.

"Several did," she replied through heaved breaths. "But I refused."

Lennie should meet this woman; they'd get along well. Perhaps *too* well. I shook off the thought of my partner corrupting more little, old ladies with her wry sense of humor and chaotic personality and refocused on the task ahead of me.

"Are you heading to the palace or down fjord, ma'am?"

"The palace, please," the woman said and gently set her hand at the crook of my free arm. The touch was so delicate, her body so frail. *Should I carry her too?*

Her long gray hair waved around her in her air pocket and a determined look hardened her fragile features.

A minute smile tugged at my mouth, but I locked it away before she could see. No, I wouldn't be carrying her. But I'd be making sure this resolute elder got to safety under her own steam.

"Are you prepared to swim, ma'am?"

She nodded and set her shoulders.

I pushed off the fjordbed and used the lightest amount of my power to propel us forward. Her air pocket brushed against my own as her jaw tightened and her brow furrowed. She was fully committed to making it, a trait that reminded me of Lennie and sent a wave of warmth through my heart.

We took our time swimming through the chilled waters of the deepest part of the fjord, moving through the darkness and aiming for the lights of the palace that glowed in the distance. Thank the ancestors I'd requested additional light magic be used around the entrance and Valdemar had granted my wish without question. He understood we needed to do everything in our power to make sure people got to safety without trouble.

I swam at a pace she seemed comfortable with, and it wasn't long before we arrived at the palace entry, the aquatic creatures carved around the arched passage shrouded in beaming light.

Sweeping into the entry, we removed our air pockets and she released her hold on my arm. Her body slumped to the floor with a thump.

"Shit."

I dropped her bag and hoisted her back onto her feet. "You did it. You made it."

"I did," she whispered.

A bubble of pride built within me as I scanned her for injuries.

Pale skin.

Heaving chest.

Spindly fingers.

Nothing appeared amiss, her cloak concealing and protecting her body well, but the way she swayed in my hold alluded to exhaustion.

Her feet wobbled beneath her, and I tightened my grip on her elbows as another soldier shot over to us.

"Take her bag," I ordered.

The soldier nodded and lifted the canvas sack over his own shoulder.

"You've made it this far," I said to my charge. "But let me carry you the rest of the way."

A low rumble sounded from her and her jaw tightened.

I bit back a smile. "Ma'am."

"Oh, fine."

It wasn't like she had much choice. If she tried to take another step, she'd probably hit the floor again. I hooked my arms under her knees and against her back and hoisted her up. She was as light as a seashell tumbling across the shoreline. Her body trembled in my hold as we continued our journey, but she refrained from any more grumbles or obstinate commentary.

I strode through the shiny, gray hallways and turned into the palace's ballroom. The grand space had been turned into a makeshift shelter, with dividers separating gathering spaces and cots with wool blankets neatly folded at the ends. It looked like something out of a war scene; something that hadn't happened here in a long time, and certainly not in the century I'd been Head Guard.

The vaulted, polished ceilings glimmered, their fish scale pattern appearing to ripple thanks to the magical balls of light that dotted the space. Beneath them, Fjord Fae milled, children playing in the back corner with dolls and cars, while adults watched over their young, chatting animatedly with each other.

I found a free cot in a quiet corner and set down the woman.

She shimmied onto the bed and pulled the thick blanket across her legs, her dress peeking out from beneath the wiry weave.

I motioned to the soldier with her things to set her stuff beside the cot. He gingerly rested it on the floor before returning to his post.

"You'll be safe here," I said with a curt nod to the woman. "What is your name, ma'am?"

The lines around her eyes creased. "Ingeborg."

"Well, Ingeborg, the soldiers here will be available should you need any assistance."

She waved me down and I bent at my waist, bringing my face closer to hers. Frail fingers pressed against my stubbled cheek. "Thank you, Øyvin."

I tilted my head to the side. "You know my name?"

"I know who you are, Head Guard." Her lips pulled into a slim smile. "I also knew your mother."

A bolt of pain shot through my chest, ripping it apart. I straightened and took a step back. Ingeborg's hand fell back into her lap.

"She'd be proud of you."

A lump settled in my throat, and I swallowed it down. "You knew my mother?"

"Unni was a dear friend. Helped me when my husband passed, and I moved beneath the surface permanently."

That sounded like something my mother would do, but must've happened a long time ago as I couldn't remember ever having met the woman in front of me. "How long have you lived in the fjord?"

A dreamy look crossed Ingeborg's face, her eyes glossing over as if lost to a memory. "The day I moved, a man rode into the village heralding the mysterious creation that had arrived on Norwegian shores. It was a carriage that didn't need a horse."

She was talking about cars. The first car in Norway had arrived in the 1890's. I wiped my chin and tried to avoid widening my eyes. She'd been beneath the water for over a hundred years. That would explain her pale complexion and frail figure. We Fjord Fae may have been capable of living and breathing underwater, but that didn't mean there weren't adverse effects to long term submersion.

"That was a while ago," I said. "Haven't you been above at all since then?"

She shook her head and fussed with the edge of the blanket. "Time passes and we move along. I belong down here."

I gave her a nod. I understood that draw to the water. It was why I lived right above it.

"Let any of the soldiers know if you need help," I said and moved to step away.

"I am grateful for your assistance." She smiled. "Please do stop by for conversation when you have a moment to spare. The company would be appreciated."

My chest spasmed again. This woman, that I couldn't recall meeting before, cared about me. "I will."

With that, I moved back to the entrance of the ballroom and took stock of the scene. The space had been completely transformed from the last event here. Reuven and Salka's coronation celebrations and ball had been full of fancy food, traditional trinkets, and magical displays of light and power. Silvery fish made of light had swum around the ceiling, tables along the room's flank had been laden with delicacies from chocolate to fruits from far off places, and in the center of it all was a crowd of dancers, twirling around in their finery and uniforms. Today, though, all that remained was a beautiful room filled with austere furnishings and people who feared they might never return to their homes.

But, there were no injuries.

No casualties.

No harm had been done to our residents... yet.

"They seem to be doing well," a male voice said, and my second-in-command, Sigurd, stepped up beside me. His black hair was held back by a piece of leather, the sleeves of his uniform rolled up to his elbows, like he was ready for an impromptu sparring match or cleaning session. Either wouldn't have been a surprise.

"Have you seen the King?" I asked.

He turned his gaze to the room. "Uh, no I have not."

He's probably in his office.

"I'll go find him," I said. I needed to give him a brief update and see if he wanted us to expand our shelter into the soldier training rooms or open up empty barracks. "You'll stay and guard the guests?"

Sigurd nodded. "Yes, sir."

Winding through the hallways, I gave short nods to the soldiers I passed and made my way to the royal quarters. If there were anywhere in the palace that I'd surely find King Reuven, it was in his office. I strode through the hallways and past artwork of the creatures we'd sworn to protect, until I reached the thick wooden door to Reuven's office. I lifted my hand to knock and—

Muffled voices sounded from the nearby Council chamber.

My hand fell back down.

More voices. Different voices.

Odd. Very odd.

There wasn't a meeting scheduled until tonight. I was supposed to give an update on the evacuation efforts to the full Council at eight o'clock. Who was in there?

I crossed the hall, strode into the Council chambers, and was met by ten sets of eyes. I ground to a halt and my breath caught in my throat. "What's going on?"

All the chairs around the Council's meeting table were filled, except mine. Reuven sat in his larger chair, peering at me sidelong, his hands clasped in front of him and resting on the table. Tension flooded the room as an awkward silence unfolded.

"Has something happened?" I asked.

"We could ask the same of you. This is an emergency meeting," Reuven said. "Aren't you supposed to be evacuating residences?"

Had they been meeting without me? How long had this been going on for?

"I was looking for you. The residences on the northern fjordbed have been evacuated. Your Majesty," I said, careful to make sure my voice didn't waver. "Is there something we need to discuss?"

"Is there enough space for everyone in the ballroom?" he asked, his gaze locked on the table.

"We may need to open up other rooms depending on the number of people who evacuate their homes further down the fjord."

"Any places in mind?"

"The empty barracks."

His head snapped to the side. "You mean the rooms that sit empty because you didn't notice that soldiers were derelict in their duties and supporting my wayward father? The soldiers he corrupted on your watch and put up for slaughter?"

I tightened my jaw and clenched my fists. "Yes. Those." I'd never forgive myself for not noticing the soldiers acting oddly sooner. But now wasn't the time to wallow in that shame. We had greater worries on our doorstep. "Do you have other concerns I should be aware of?"

Council members' eyes drifted toward the table, heads hanging low as they all shifted in their seats.

"I have revoked our alliance with the Fjell Fae. We are moving forward with a new Fire Fae alliance."

I knew it. I knew this was coming. My chest rumbled. "Why?"

"Because it is what's best for the Fjord."

"That's a fucking lie and you know it." The words were out of my mouth before I could stop them. "We are stronger when allied with the Fjell and Forest."

Reuven's seat scraped across the stone floor as he rose to his feet. Straightening to his full height, his gaze locked with my own. "Øyvin Håland, as your loyalties no longer remain with the Fjord, you're hereby relieved of your duties. Effective immediately. You'll be stripped of all titles and rank, but not banished from the palace. However, please remove your belongings from your office."

My heart stopped beating.

137
LENNIE

The sun was setting across the fjord, the curtains drawn for the night as I curled up on the sofa. My limbs ached and waves of worry washed through my mind like someone had turned on the spin cycle in the laundry machine. But even with the chaos and threats hanging over my little family and the town, I was proud of the work I'd done today. We'd successfully evacuated Skolvik. And now, me, Espen, and Øyvin were the only ones who remained.

The back door to the boat garage swung open and Øyvin stepped into the house. His hair was disheveled and his T-shirt and jeans clung to him as a puddle trailed in his wake. If the sight of Øyvin soaking wet wasn't enough of a warning, those tantalizing lips of his sat in a firm grimace that had alarm bells ringing.

I kneeled on the couch. "What's wrong?"

Eyes distant oceans of shock and anguish, he swayed on the spot.

My heart skipped several beats, and I gripped the arm of the sofa. "Øyvin, say something."

He shook his head.

Launching from the couch, I crossed the room in three swift strides and pressed my hands to his wet chest. Heat radiated from him, yet the water droplets remained cold as ice.

"Øyvin."

His gaze drifted to mine and he ran his hand up my arm. "I was fired."

My breath stilled in my throat and my eyes widened. "What?"

He nodded slowly.

That wasn't possible. I couldn't believe it. He was the Head Guard of the Fjord Fae. End of story.

"You're perfect at your job, though," I said, and his mouth tilted up at one corner before dropping back down. "They can't fire you."

"He can and he did."

This was wrong on so many levels. Øyvin had done nothing wrong. He'd always protected the Fjord Fae, unlike Reuven and his ass of a father-in-law. What a piece of shit. I pulled out of Øyvin's hold and moved to step around him. "Fuck Reuven."

Øyvin's hand shot out and he grabbed my wrist. His eyes met mine, his expression marred with shock. "Don't. You'll get yourself killed."

"Not the first time I've gone toe-to-toe with a monarch in the last few weeks—"

"I won't have it be your last," he said, and his unyielding tone sent a shiver down my spine.

"Last what?" A male voice said behind me, and I spun to find Espen closing the front door, done with his shift at the police station. His gaze raked over us, as if looking for injuries or problems, before pivoting to the puddle on the floor beneath the Fjord Fae. "Tell me what happened."

Øyvin pulled me into his side like he needed a life ring to keep him afloat. "Reuven fired me."

Espen pushed both hands through his hair, his eyes as wide as camera lenses. "He can't have."

"He did."

"What about this?" I brushed my hand over his wet T-shirt. "Did your magic disappear?"

"I broke my air bubble halfway home and swam normally the rest of the way."

My breath caught again, calculating just how far that was. Half distance from here to the Fjord palace was over a mile. "You swam all that way?"

He nodded.

My heart broke in two and I pulled him in for a hug. He grunted as my arms squeezed his torso. What was happening? Why the hell would anyone fire someone as dedicated to the fjord as Øyvin? They'd have to be insane to do so... Then again, maybe Reuven was crazy like his father?

Heat radiated across my back and Espen's hand settled on Øyvin's shoulder. "I'm sorry, my friend."

Øyvin's head bobbed once, his eyes narrowing with warmth and appreciation.

While I didn't like the circumstances, it was always nice to see my two guys supporting each other.

"You get in here too," I said over my shoulder to Espen.

He chuckled and pressed his front to my back, wrapping his long arms around both of us. I settled the side of my face against Øyvin's chest, listening to the steady thrumming of his heartbeat. Here, between the two of them, was my happy place. My body relaxed into their holds, and I relished the feel of being sandwiched between them. This right here was my home, my everything, and fuck did I hate that it had been hurt today.

I stepped back from Øyvin, pushing Espen with my butt. Motioning to Øyvin's state of dress, I said, "Dry off."

Staying in those wet clothes wouldn't help his mental state.

His grimace had disappeared, replaced by a gentle line, but his eyes shone with more ease. Like our group hug had temporarily settled the storm that'd been raging there.

He moved his hands to his sides and splayed his fingers. The puddle on the floor slowly receded and evaporated before he lifted his magic to his clothes. His jeans and shirt lightened as the powers swept up his body. The Fjord Fae magic ended at his hair, sending it into a tangled disarray that reminded me of wheat fields on a windy summer's day.

"Better?" he asked as his magic washed over my dampened front too.

"Much better," I replied. "Now, do you want to tell us *why* Reuven fired you?"

Øyvin inhaled and motioned to the sofa.

I followed his request and Espen did too. He kicked off his work boots and threw his police utility belt over the back of the couch. The little radio and gadgets landed with a thud against the supple brown leather. The two of us curled up next to each other and focused our attention on our partner.

Øyvin dropped onto the piano bench and wiped his palm across his face. "Reuven said my loyalties no longer remained with the fjord."

I scoffed. "Has he not met you?"

Øyvin's eyebrows flicked upward once. "I was worried about *his* loyalty to the fjord. But when he asked me recently if I would keep information from the two of you... I hesitated."

My heartbeats collided with each other and I clutched one of the throw pillows to my stomach.

"Why?" The words slipped from my lips, but I already knew the answer.

Øyvin's intense gaze met mine and heat washed through my body. "You know why."

Ever since I'd met him, Øyvin had prioritized the fjord and the fae that lived there. From clearing it of pollution, to leading the soldiers, he'd dedicated his life to the well-being of the waters. He loved the fjord. However, on several recent occasions, he'd put his love for *me* above the Fjord Fae.

"He sees you as a weak link that can't be trusted anymore."

"Mm-hmm."

"He doesn't want you reporting back to us," I muttered.

The air in the room thickened, filling with unspoken truths that we knew in our bones and our hearts.

We were a unit.

A family.

A powerful trio formed of three different factions and forged by love.

While I would always uphold my duty to protect the Fjell Fae, I wouldn't let anything come between me and these two men. They were the loves of my life and I'd protect them at all costs.

My magic swirled within my sternum as if it understood my allegiance and accepted it.

Espen took a deep breath behind me. "On that note, the village has been cleared, and the remaining officers have driven over the mountain to Vanheim."

I raked my fingers against my scalp. "They shouldn't have been forced from their homes."

Øyvin grit his teeth and Espen muttered, "Agreed."

Nobody should ever be forced from the place they called home. Asked to pack up their most cherished belongings and flee from a foe. In this case, it wasn't just an environmental disaster that loomed above them like an anvil; it was a living, breathing menace that could scorch the earth beneath their feet in a single heartbeat.

The tension in the room reached boiling point, and frustration whistled in my ears like a screeching kettle. "I hate how everything is falling apart around us."

"It may get worse before it gets better," Espen said.

"Don't say that."

"He's right, Trouble."

Rising from my spot, I threw the pillow back onto the couch and started waving my hands about as I stomped back and forth in front of the sofa. "First Balder steals magic and Nora kills Freija, resulting in the battle on the mountain top. Then the wolves attack us, and Wilhelm uses my leg as a chew toy. Now this?"

It was too much.

"Our lives may be facing a challenging chapter right now," Espen said, "but we'll get through this. Together."

We could. No, we *would*. But that thought didn't quell the frustrated energy trying to burst out of me.

"I hate this bullshit! I hate that there's a threat to this town and its people. I hate this feeling like I can't do anything about it. And I hate that I haven't fucked my partners in over a week! We haven't even consummated the marriage!"

I set my hands on my hips and panted. That last bit may have been too far, but dammit, it was true.

The room stilled and dust motes danced in the light from the kitchen.

My pulse beat in my ears and water lapped against the boat hull in the garage. The sound always seeped through the walls and cast the entire house under its lulling spell.

Espen stood and extended his hand to me. "Come along then, wife."

My toes curled at the title and my body flushed, cheeks probably pink from the emotions humming through me and the heated look in Espen's eyes. I placed my fingers in his and let him lead me to bed.

Once upstairs, Øyvin splintered off to one side of the bedroom while Espen corralled me toward the mattress.

Warmth swept around me, swaddling me in a loving haze. "Everything will be fine in the end," Espen whispered. He brushed his hand across my cheek and tucked my hair behind my ear.

My heart thrummed in my chest, and I hoped he was right as I leaned into his touch.

A low rumble sounded from Øyvin, and Espen bit his bottom lip as he swept to my side, his hands gliding over my hips.

Espen had always been more touchy-feely with me than Øyvin. Always needing to be physically connected to me in some way. Øyvin, on the other hand, always needed to have me in eyesight, where he could watch my movements and protect me from trouble. I didn't mind either, really. They were the same in the bedroom too.

Øyvin leaned against the dresser and crossed his ankles. A heady look of lust washed across his face. His gaze rose lazily from my toes to the top of my head, visually caressing every inch of my curves like he was seeing them for the first time.

My breaths faltered.

He shook his head.

"Are you seriously going to deny me sex after more than a week of celibacy?"

His lips quirked at one corner, and he cast a look at Espen. His voice was thick with passion as he said, "Undress her."

Espen smiled. "Gladly."

The Forest Fae stepped between me and Øyvin, blocking him from view. Espen's long lashes skimmed the tops of his cheeks as a satisfied grin settled across his face. With deft, yet slow movements, Espen skimmed his hands down my torso before flipping underneath the hem of my tank top. He gently pulled the material up and over my head, tossing it aside. Where it landed, I didn't know. Nor did I care. All I could focus on was the swelling warmth within my body and the molten look in Espen's eyes.

He grasped my shoulders and spun me around so Øyvin could see what he was doing to me. Then he slid his hands across my stomach, and I sucked in a breath as he popped open the button on my denim shorts.

Øyvin's eyes flared.

A whimper slipped through my lips.

Espen hitched his thumbs beneath the waistband of my shorts and pulled them down, dragging my lacy black thong with them. They pooled at my feet, and, without breaking eye-contact with Øyvin, I stepped out of them. Espen kicked them away as those blue oceans watched me from across the room. It was like he could drown me, and I would love every second of it.

Nuzzling against my neck and eliciting a shudder from me, Espen unfastened the clasp on my bra and removed it, throwing it between us and Øyvin. Before I could say a word, he pressed his body against my back and palmed my breasts, taking one firmly in each hand.

I groaned at the attention, and my eyes fluttered shut from the bliss that seeped through my body. As he toyed with one nipple, he smoothed his hand down my stomach once more and pressed two fingers against my clit.

A satisfied moan slipped from my lips. It'd been too long since I'd been touched like this. Sparks zipped in the most desirable places as Espen circled that tender bundle of nerves while gently kneading my breast. That pleasurable sensation swelled within my core, begging for more attention, and my legs wobbled. Espen moved his ministrations to my other breast and my nipple peaked against his rough palm.

An unintelligible sound emanated from me.

"Come for us, Lennie," Øyvin said.

I stared him down, wanting to be defiant, but my body wouldn't let me. Stars twinkled at the corners of my vision and my core pulsed.

Espen increased his pressure and pulled on my nipple so hard I saw galaxies. The two of them, working me into my undoing, was enough to drive me straight toward that precipice that promised release. I ground my ass against Espen's thighs as he nipped the hollow behind my ear.

"Now, Trouble."

Øyvin's words sent me careening over the edge and I let out a strangled moan as my body convulsed with bliss in Espen's arms. He tightened his hold on me, not letting me fall to the floor.

"Fuck," I whimpered.

Espen tilted my head to his and pressed his lips to mine. The kiss promised more passion and was laced with a love so consuming, it couldn't be defined, nor captured.

Øyvin growled. "Get on the bed. Now."

I did as requested, too dazed to counter.

The cool cotton duvets brushed against my hot skin as I climbed onto the bed. I turned and faced my guys, both of whom watched me like hawks waiting to dive onto their prey. Those looks were enough to have me panting again—my soaking core already needing more from both of them.

I stared directly into Øyvin's eyes. "How do you want me, partner?"

His tongue swept across his bottom lip. "Get on your back."

Fuck, yes. I did, relishing in the sensation of having them watch my every move.

Being worshiped like this by the two of them was a high I never wanted to come down from.

Øyvin reached over his shoulder and pulled off his shirt in one swift move, the fabric sweeping across his muscular form. In what felt like slow motion, he removed his pants, neatly setting them atop the dresser behind him. Without even touching me, it was as if he was all over my body.

Another shiver of pleasure ran through me. Fuck, I wanted them both so much.

Reaching the edge of the bed, Øyvin climbed up and pulled me by the ankles, hitching me closer to him.

He traced his fingers up my thighs and avoided the place where I wanted him the most. My core fluttered with need. I wriggled and he clamped his hands over my thighs, holding me in place.

"Øyvin, please," I said, my voice barely a whisper.

He hooked my legs over his arms, letting them hang in the crook of his elbow, and baring me for him.

A low rumble sounded from his chest. "I will never tire of this view."

He slowly pushed his cock inside me, gliding through the wetness that pooled between my thighs, and wringing a moan from me. The fullness was everything all at once. Based on the quirk of his eyebrow, he knew it too. Øyvin pressed his hand right above my clit and moved his thumb to the bundle of nerves while holding the top of my thigh with his other hand.

I fisted the duvet beneath me.

Having removed his clothes, Espen joined us on the bed and leaned over me. He pressed his mouth to mine with a desperate passion, kissing me like I was the air he needed to breathe, the only thing that might keep him alive. Our lips brushed against each other, tongues lapping, souls intertwining. He bit down on my lip, and I responded in kind by sucking on the tip of his tongue. He groaned and pressed himself against my side. His cock rubbed against me, and I wrapped my free hand around it, pumping once.

"Lennie," he ground out.

Øyvin continued slowly pushing in and out of me.

I swirled my thumb across Espen's tip.

"Fuck." His head fell back.

If I had enough oxygen in my lungs I would've agreed. These men knew how to handle me. Knew how to wring every last drop of tension and passion from my cells and weave them together into a photograph of pure ecstasy.

Øyvin picked up the pace, slamming against me. Each hit sent a zap through my core, building up that precious release once more.

The air in the room sizzled with need. I wanted to run my fingers through Øyvin's hair, wanted to hear Espen's stuttered breath as he finished, wanted both of them—

Øyvin pumped into me again and I unraveled alongside him with a loud moan.

My hand around Espen's cock stopped as I rode out my release. It was a promise, an undoing, a possession. It was everything and then some.

Espen pulled my hand off him frantically. "Let me..." he panted. "Let me finish inside you."

I nodded. Unable to form words.

As Øyvin shifted and pulled out, I sighed at the empty feeling he left behind.

He flopped onto the bed beside me and brushed his knuckles across my heated cheek. "Beautiful."

My entire body flushed at the word.

Espen nudged me onto my side and curled against my back. Sweeping his hands over my curves, he worshiped them like a delicate masterpiece. The feel of skin against skin was an irresistible vice, and I arched against him as he pressed his cock against my ass.

I'd gladly take a lifetime or three of lying between the two of them, letting them touch me wherever they wanted.

"I love you," I whispered. "Both of you."

"We love you too," Espen breathed against my neck.

"Forever and always, Trouble."

Our breaths intertwined and I pressed my lips to Øyvin's. He pushed his fingers into my hair and squeezed, tangling himself in the locks. Espen splayed a hand across my thigh, guiding my leg to rest over Øyvin's hip. The movement opened me up for him, which he took full advantage of—brushing his fingers slowly around my thigh and back through my soaking core. A low grumble emitted from both men, their chests vibrating against my front and back.

My body numbed, tingling in the best way. Heat wrapped around us like a hedonistic vice, unrelenting in its hold.

"Espen." The name was a prayer and a plea.

He murmured against my neck, and the sound sent a shiver down my spine. Without further preamble, he slid inside me from behind. A groan escaped me and Øyvin caught it with his mouth. Together the three of us morphed into a tangle of moans, gentle thrusts, and loving touches. Our hands were all over each other. Sliding and holding. Feeling and kneading. Gripping and kissing, as we ebbed toward that precipice once more.

My orgasm pulsed through me in a heady haze I could only describe with one word: love.

138

LENNIE

I awoke to gentle caresses, sandwiched between the loves of my life with the duvet covers draped over our lower bodies. Øyvin cradled my head against his chest, while Espen lightly pressed my fingertips to his lips. Early morning sunlight seeped between the curtains, the only sounds gracing the dawn were delicate breezes from our breaths and the steady hum of Øyvin's heart.

It was one of the most peaceful moments I'd had since moving to Norway. Like a perfect photograph, where the light hit just right, the depth of the scenery was luscious and layered, and the entire composition evoked a sense of calm.

I could lay here for days. Listening to the gentle rhythms of the two men at my sides. Cocooned in a safe blanket of warmth. Their arms wrapped around me like impenetrable walls of a fort or castle.

The thought of forts drew my mind to the threat facing the village and fae.

"What do we do?" My voice was barely a whisper, yet broke the silence like an axe cleaving a log. The question was meant to be rhetorical, a slip from my mind, but I must not have been the only one thinking it as the sun rose.

"We're going to need help," Espen said. "And we'll need each other."

He meant the factions. The alliances we'd forged. But what good could the Fjell and Forest do against the Fjord and Fire Fae? We needed more than each other. We'd need a fucking miracle. It wasn't like they had secret forces or weapons that could save them... Or did they?

I looked to Espen. He was a weapon of sorts. His destructive powers balanced with healing magic. Yet, what could he do against Veigar? Against the Fjord?

"Where do the fae go for help?" I asked.

Espen pulled my hand against his chest. "The ancestors."

My eyebrows furrowed. "Like Forest Fae King Olaf did with the wolves?"

He nodded.

"But we don't have any monarchs. At least none that are on our side."

A low rumble escaped Øyvin.

"But we have access to the Forest Fae shard," Espen said.

"What could we do with it? Ask for help? Would the ancestors even listen to you?" The questions spilled from me as my groggy mind slowly woke up. I needed coffee if we were going to talk strategy at this hour.

Espen's shoulder rose and fell.

"Only those with royal blood or royal magic have been known to successfully commune with the ancestors," Øyvin supplied.

My mind flew to one such royal heir in Alvdalen. Maybe Aurora could help us out? Though, with what we'd put her through earlier this year, I highly doubted she'd be charitable. In fact, the more I thought about it, she'd probably cackle down the phone and hang up on me if I asked. We'd need to find another. I hadn't exactly been successful reaching out to the ancestors when Halvar had me slap my hand on the pedestal in the temple. Maybe Torsten would have better luck?

"We could get Torsten," I said. "Or maybe even Halvar?"

Espen released his hand from my grasp and brushed a stray hair behind my ear. "We also have you..."

Øyvin clutched me tighter to his chest, his broad palm pressing against my back.

"Yeah, because that went so well last time I was in the Temple," I said with a scoff. "I'd grade that first date a solid 5.5. Awkward, but not awful considering they weren't exactly a talkative bunch."

"Doesn't mean you can't try again," Espen countered, ever the bubbly ray of optimistic sunshine.

I guessed I could try. Maybe without Halvar in the room... Or... Wait a second...

The most stupid, hypocritical and bat-shit idea drifted through my mind, but I latched onto it with both hands like it was a life-raft in the middle of the tumultuous North Atlantic: what if I went to the Temple and brought the Forest Fae shard with me and asked for help?

Would the ancestors talk to me then? What was the worst thing that could happen? I'd get smoted for trying? Sent to hell a little earlier than expected? I'm sure the devil would welcome me with open arms after all the chaos I'd been responsible for over the past year alone.

I bit my lower lip. "I have an idea."

Espen bolted to a sitting position, and Øyvin tilted my head to meet his.

"What are you thinking?" Øyvin asked.

"It's crazy. Would make me the shittiest leader in Fjell Fae history. Halvar would probably decapitate me, slice and dice me into a million pieces and distribute them to the fae as a warning of his—"

"Lennie, focus," Espen said.

I swallowed hard. "What if we unite the Forest Fae piece with the pedestal in the Temple of the Fae? What would happen? Would that increase our odds of favor with the ancestors? Or would I just be doing the same exact thing Veigar is trying to do?"

Looking between the two of them, I found their eyes wide, their expressions stuck in a state of shock and thought.

It was *exactly* what Veigar wanted to do. But maybe, if we did it... If *we* were the ones to unite the Forest Fae shard with the pedestal, we might be able to gain more powers to defeat Veigar and whatever army he had. It was pure lunacy, but I'd never been one to shy away from crazy ideas.

I wriggled from Øyvin's hold and sat in the middle of the bed, my legs crossed. Draping one of the white duvets over my shoulders like a shawl, I took a deep breath.

"It's not the worst idea," Espen said. "For starters, you wouldn't do what Veigar wants with those stone, would you?"

I shook my head. "I don't want to be an almighty ruler of all."

"Which is why that stone is safer in your hands than they are in his. Didn't he mention that a Fjord King was once getting corrupted by power? Getting too powerful?"

"He did."

"History has a tendency to repeat itself if we don't pay attention to it. Giving you the stone to use for good *is* a good thing compared to what Veigar would do."

Tension rolled from my shoulders as I sagged on the spot. All I wanted was to do good by the mountain, my home, and my guys. I wouldn't use whatever powers those stones might bestow for my own gains.

"Do it." Øyvin's gaze shot to mine. "We should do it."

"Are you sure?"

"We don't stand a chance against Veigar without help. Especially with Reuven and my— *his* forces standing against us."

If there was anyone who knew how the Fjord fought, it was Øyvin. And with his mind for military matters, he'd also have a good handle on what the gameboard looked like.

"What are we facing?" I asked. "What does each faction have in their arsenal that we need to account for?"

"The Fjord has several hundred fae soldiers beneath the surface that can muster at a moment's notice. The Fjell probably the same."

True. I'd seen a lot of them during my training sessions.

"The Fire Fae legion is small but mighty. I wouldn't be surprised if Veigar had brought across fifty to a hundred soldiers even if only half that could emaciate a regiment."

Images of black-eyed Fire Fae burning down human corpses flooded my mind and a shudder ran through me.

"As for the Forest,"—Øyvin looked to Espen—"their greatest weakness is fire."

Espen shifted and propped himself against the pillows. He dragged both hands through his hair, tangling the tendrils. "He's right. Veigar's forces, no matter how large or small, are hard for us to combat. They only have me as their biggest weapon. And I'm not sure I can save us. Reuniting the shards and asking for aid could help us monumentally."

I'd long suspected Espen was the Forest's fail-safe. A dangerous gift bestowed by the ancestors to *literally* level the playing field. But even Halvar feared Veigar. And, if I was completely honest, that scared me.

"Would you consider getting the Forest shard for us?" I asked.

Espen looked to me, his gaze filled with emotion. He nodded. "We'll take the police car and drive to Queen Ragnhild's grave."

"Thank you." That was going to be hard for him. But the more I thought about it, the more I believed in this insane idea. There was only one thing that might upend it. "We get the Forest Fae shard, bring it to the Temple of the Fae, and ask the ancestors for help with Veigar. Do we tell Halvar?"

"You've always just asked for forgiveness." Øyvin arched an eyebrow. "Why stop now?"

I snapped my fingers and pointed to him. "Very true, but I'm trying to be a good leader here."

So far, as Deputy Head Guard, I'd give myself a solid C grade. Not the worst, not the best, could do with refining and a better understanding of what it meant to be a leader. But if there was one thing I was sure of, it was that I'd do whatever it took to protect my family and new home. Fae and humans alike.

Espen's gaze flicked to Øyvin. "You're not going to like my response."

Øyvin's eyebrow inched higher.

"We don't tell Halvar until after we've accessed the Temple," Espen said.

Yup, this was as bonkers as my dad wearing University of Michigan colors.

"So, I sneak into the mountain with the Forest shard, slap my hand on the pedestal, and beg the ancestors for help."

"It seems like our only option," Espen said with a sigh.

"It's not," Øyvin piped up.

I squinted at him. "What do you mean?"

He swallowed hard. "I'll get the other one."

What?

"Come again for the demi-fae?" I stared at the blond-haired man leaning against the headboard. "What do you mean, you'll 'get the other one?'"

"I'll steal the Fjord Fae shard for us too."

139

LENNIE

"You can't be serious." My voice rose as I jumped off the bed and dropped the duvet on the floor.

Øyvin's gaze followed the material like it was a greater sin to let it fall to the ground than steal something from the Fjord Fae King who had fired him yesterday.

"Are you sick?" I rushed over, bare tits jostling, and placed my wrist against Øyvin's forehead. Not clammy, just his usual warm self. "Did the sex last night mess with your head?"

It had been a pretty epic love-making session. Not just carnal, but an emotional joining of... Yeah, I had it bad.

Øyvin nudged aside my arm. Brushing his fingers down it, he took my hand in his. "We might have access to both stones. And I won't let it get into Veigar's hands."

Espen cleared his throat. "Not that I condone theft, because I don't. But how do you propose stealing it?" He scooted off the bed and headed toward the new dresser that housed his clothes. The light-colored wood scraped as he opened the top left drawer and pulled out a clean pair of boxer briefs.

"I'll need Lennie's help," Øyvin said.

I flinched.

Espen shook out his underwear with a *flap*. "I don't want her anywhere near—"

"Don't worry," Øyvin cut him off. "I'm going below alone. But I need her help first."

Espen bobbed his head like he could work with that, while I crossed my arms and narrowed my eyes at the Fjord Fae.

"Don't look like that," Øyvin said.

"Like what?"

"Like you aren't powerful enough to help me."

"I mean, tell me what you want, Asshole, and I'll see what I can do."

He smirked at the pointed moniker.

"You are powerful," Espen said as he settled on the bed, wearing a black police T-shirt and cargo-pants, both of which clung to his toned muscles. I did a double-take. How had he gotten dressed so fast?

"Sure," I conceded and looked back at Øyvin. "But what exactly can I do to help you steal a shard from the Fjord Fae? If I remember correctly, you said it was in the Council chambers in the Palace."

Øyvin nodded.

"So?"

"I need you to make me a blade or weapon that can cleave through the ancient granite bedrock that houses the shard."

Arms falling to my sides, a chortle bubbled out of me. "A rock sword that can hack at other rock? Without breaking the pretty piece of rock we want? How hard could that possibly be?"

Øyvin's gaze didn't break from mine. "You tell me, Trouble."

I wiped the back of my hand across my forehead. I *could* make stone swords, decently sharp ones. But what Øyvin wanted sounded more like a chisel than a blade. I'd never made one of those. Fuck, I didn't even think I'd actually seen one in person. Only ever in movies. But... I did have Halvar's smithing powers. So, in theory, I should be able to smith a bunch of different weapons out of stone.

Setting my hands on my hips, I let out a sigh. "I'll give it a try."

After a quick shower and some breakfast, we reconvened our planning session in the living room. Øyvin perched on his usual spot on the piano bench while Espen sat on the sofa, his arms spread across the back. I pushed aside the coffee table and stood in the middle of the room, sunlight angling through the windows and casting the entire space in a strong orange glow. At this time of year, even nine o'clock in the morning was as bright as midday—the land of the midnight sun living up to its name with over sixteen hours of daylight in late summer.

I took a deep breath and focused on my magic. I'd grown accustomed to its swirling presence. It wasn't an extension of me, it was part of the mountain that lived in me, connected me to the fae world. Or at least, that's what it felt like.

A swell of warmth built in my sternum and the memory of a short sword filled my mind. I drew my hands over each other and pushed the magic out of me. A slate-gray dagger took shape, the point shimmering in the morning light, the weighty hilt and grip cooling in my palm.

"What's that for?" Øyvin asked, his voice still rumbly and husky.

"Practice sword," I replied. "Got to get the juices flowing before I start on your piece."

Øyvin huffed.

"You're doing great," Espen said from his spot on the sofa with a beaming smile.

He was right. I was doing great. Crafting swords came naturally to me now—like an instinctual reaction. Within seconds I could draw on my magic and give it form.

I set the smooth, stone blade on the coffee table. "We can use that as decor. Maybe a paperweight."

Both men snorted a laugh.

I turned to Øyvin. "What kind of pick or axe do you need?"

He pulled out his phone and tapped the screen a few times before typing something in. A moment later he turned the device to face me. "Something like this."

Leaning in, I took a few steps closer to get a better look.

A short, thick chisel stared back at me—the butt rounded for impact from a hammer, the blade section sharpened to a wide point. That shouldn't be too difficult to make. I'd need to pay particular attention to the blade section, but it was small and would be easily concealed underneath Øyvin's clothes.

"I'll try," I said and retook my spot in the middle of the living room.

Closing my eyes, I focused on the image Øyvin had just shown me and placed my palms over one another while leaving a small gap between them. I pushed my magic out of me, willing it to take the desired shape. An effortless swell of warm energy pulsed between my palms. Opening my eyes, I found the chisel forming with near invisible ripples flowing around it. The mottled black-and-gray piece of stone dropped into my hand as it finished up—the tendrils of magic vanishing.

"Well done," Espen said.

I let out a breath and rolled my shoulders. I'd done it. But would it be strong enough to hack through rock?

Something in my gut twisted. A sensation I felt the need to listen to.

I quickly called forward a plain rock into my palm and knelt beside the coffee table. Placing the chisel at an angle against the blade, I raised the stone above my head and aimed.

"What are—"

"Not on the ta—"

I slammed the rock down on the chisel. The pointy tool crumbled. The stone in my hand smashed against the dagger, clattering together and sending reverberations up through my arm. My teeth juddered against each other, and my body quivered. I lifted the stone and assessed the underside. Tiny hairline fractures webbed from the point of impact, but the two pieces remained intact.

Frustration rumbled through my chest as I stared down at the broken chisel and plopped the stone onto the table beside the blade. "It's not strong enough."

There wasn't a chance in hell that thing was going to cleave through rock successfully. We needed something weightier, something sharper, something that wouldn't potentially crumble in Øyvin's hands.

We needed...

A smile tilted my lips. "I have another idea."

"You seem to be full of those today," Øyvin said with a pointed look at his dust-covered coffee table.

"Quit the sass." I snickered. "This one will help you too."

He smirked and raised his hands as if to say *fine, go on.*

I turned to Espen. "You know how you said you don't condone theft."

Espen's eyes went as wide as the satellite domes on the cruise ships that visited the village. "What are you about to do?"

Ten minutes later we stood outside the camping and hiking store staring at the floor to ceiling window of my cheesing face holding up a pair of hiking boots.

"I mean, at least it's kind of classy," I muttered even though the only thing *classy* about it was my nice Norwegian jumper and traditionally patterned red hat.

"Really?" Espen's voice cracked. "I mean... It's something."

"And you." I turned to Øyvin. "What do you think of this artwork before us?"

He glanced down at me with hooded eyes, those luscious lips pressed together in a firm line, and shoulders set back. "I want to know why you did it," Øyvin said. "Why did you agree to do an advert with the store?"

"I wanted to make sure I was earning my keep and they approached me about the opportunity, saying I'd be the perfect fit as I was a former tourist." I tilted my head to the ad with *Lost in the woods? Get your gear here!* arched over my head. "This is how I'm paying for your Christmas presents this year."

Espen squeezed my shoulder. "You didn't have to do that."

"We take care of you now," Øyvin said.

My vocal cords failed me as those conga-line dancing butterflies were back in my chest, jiving to the rhythm of my partners' words. If we hadn't been out on the streets of Skolvik on a mission, I'd have started kissing them right here. But, we had a robbery to complete. One where the livelihood and safety of countless humans and fae rested on our shoulders. And, somewhere around here, a Fire Fae king lurked. So, we needed to keep moving.

I looked back at the store and rubbed my hands together.

"How do you plan on sneaking in?" Espen asked.

"Oh, we're not sneaking." There was nothing sneaky about my plan. "We're robbing the place in broad daylight."

Espen squeaked.

"We're going to smash this window, storm inside, and grab what we need."

Espen let out a strangled whimper and started pacing in a circle. "That's not just stealing. That's vandalism. Breaking and entering. Theft. Destruction of property. We can't do that."

I bit my lip and stifled a smile.

"Trouble…"

"Ugh, okay we're not breaking in." I pulled Oddvar's overflowing keyring from my pants pocket and jingled it. "We've got the key."

Espen pressed his hand to his chest. "Now is not the time for joking. I don't think I can handle it."

"Oh, you handle me quite fine, husband."

His eyes lit up before he pulled on his collar and cleared his throat. "So, the keys."

"Explain," Øyvin added.

"Oddvar's has been around for eons, and over the years other businesses have come to trust the man. Many of them have given him back up keys to their stores in case of emergencies."

"And he gave them to you?" Øyvin asked.

"Apparently, now is an emergency." I'd been surprised by it myself. But Oddvar had trusted me enough to hire me and was now entrusting me to watch over his business while he fled to safety.

I stepped forward and started testing keys on the lock. While he may have had a whole bunch of them, none were labeled. The eleventh key slid home and allowed me to turn it. The front door clicked, and I pressed down on the handle. Hinges squawked as the door swung open.

Turning to the guys, I motioned for them to go first. "Lost in the woods?" I said, mimicking the slogan on the window. "Get your gear here!"

Espen chuckled and swept inside while Øyvin rolled his eyes and followed.

The store's interior looked like something out of a horror movie. Shadows blanketed the racks and shelves, the only light coming from the windows at our backs. The wood beams holding the ceiling aloft seemed more like gnarled trees looming over us, while the shelves felt like they were concealing haunted corn-maze actors, ready to leap out and scare you with their chainsaws and gory makeup.

A shiver ran down my spine as I followed the guys past the cash register and into the depths of the store.

Espen came to a stop in front of an aisle of yoga gear and exercise equipment. "What exactly are we looking for, Lennie?"

I pulled up beside him and Øyvin. "Ice picks."

"Clever girl," Øyvin said, and a bubble of pride swelled inside me.

If we couldn't make our own chisel, then finding any sort of climbing gear or ice hacking equipment was our best bet. Bonus points for tools that were made of steel.

"And if they don't have any?" Espen asked, his amber gaze filled with light and his cheeks flushed.

I shrugged. "Then we head over to the hardware store and *break in* there too. But I'd prefer something that is more portable. Swimming into the palace with a chisel and hammer, or even a sledge hammer, isn't exactly inconspicuous."

Øyvin grunted.

"You raise a good point," Espen said, peering through the store. "Let's split up and take an aisle each."

We divided the store into sections. Espen would tackle the middle while I took the left and Øyvin took the right. I doubted ice climbing equipment would be near the swimming and hiking section, but I couldn't be sure. This place had a wild array of items. Where the middle part was pretty normal with clothes, the rest of the space was littered with objects that couldn't possibly be considered nor needed for camping or hiking.

They really needed to re-brand themselves as a general store.

I set off to the left and scanned the head-height shelves for anything that looked remotely pokey.

An orange rubber ducky glared at me from beside a display of hiking boots. Five boxes of unicorn floaties begged for new homes, while the heavy bags of intricately folded tents weighed down the shelves below them. Nothing along here looked helpful.

I spun to the wall at my back. Covered in backpacks of all shapes and sizes, the display was a colorful rainbow of variety that outclassed Øyvin's vast collection of spices. From cute little pink ones that my nieces would love, to monstrous green ones that could only be wielded by someone Halvar's size. The store had every backpack one could ever need. But none of them had axes attached to them.

I peered up at the top shelves. Maybe they'd stashed the winter stuff away for the season like we'd done with our heaviest wool sweaters?

Labeled boxes lined the uppermost shelves. *Jul, påske, halloween.* Those must've been seasonal decorations. *Båt, truger, is.*

Is.

"Bingo," I said.

But how the hell was I going to get the ice-labeled box down from up there? I needed to find a ladder. Scurrying around the store, I eventually found what I needed and dragged the a-frame ladder to the left-side wall.

I set it beneath the shelf, clambered up, and grabbed the box.

"Let me get that," Espen said, appearing beneath me. He reached up and I heaved the large cardboard box into his waiting hands.

"Thank you," I said as I climbed back down.

He set the box on the floor, and I opened the flaps. Inside was a mound of carabiners, rope, two helmets, and half a dozen pick axes for scaling ice and glaciers.

I gave myself a round of applause, the claps echoing around the silent store. "Double bingo."

"Well done." Espen picked up something from beside the other shelving unit. "All I found was this."

My eyes widened as I rose and took in the long stick in his hand. "What the hell is that?"

He beamed. "Fishing spear."

"You Norwegians and your outdoor activities will never cease to amaze me. Do they teach you how to spear-fish in school too?"

"No," Øyvin grumbled as he stepped into the aisle. "But most of them know how to fish by the time they're five."

Figures.

"Well, I got lucky." I plucked an axe from the box and gently waved it for him to see. "But did you find anything that might be useful?"

"Unless Espen wants a new shower curtain for the cabin, I found nothing." I chuckled.

"That won't be necessary," Espen said and stashed the spear on the shelf beside him.

Movement by the front window caught my eye. A sliver of silver glinting in the light. "Get down."

Both men dropped into perfect push-ups while I splooted on my stomach like a puppy. My heart hammered against the floor, my breaths coming out in short pants.

Out on the road, Veigar wandered past with his hands behind his back, like he was out for a stroll along the French Riviera. I could just make out his profile, his mouth opening and closing. Was he talking to someone? He paused and peered at my advertisement. Tilting his head to one side, he mumbled something else. *Shit.*

Had he seen us? Would he attack us in here? My initial instinct to hide would say yes. He'd killed those soldiers on the mountain without any other warning than his note. And, while unconfirmed, he'd been the one to set fire to the oil refinery down fjord. Halvar and the Fjell Fae Council were right. Veigar was ruthless when he didn't get what he wanted.

The Fire Fae King shook his head and continued his walk down the street, vanishing from my view on the floor.

A shiver ran down my spine and I pulled my knees underneath me—

Espen pressed his hand against my back. "Wait. He might circle back."

Staying on my stomach, adrenaline coursed through me like a live wire begging to be tripped. Espen brushed his hand in circles against my lower back, while Øyvin peered over his shoulder.

After another few minutes on the floor that felt more like a lifetime, Espen said, "Okay. We should be all right, now."

Both men flipped onto their haunches and slowly rose, their gazes locked on the large windows at the front of the building.

I scrambled to my feet with as much grace as an antelope on ice. I grabbed the ice pick that was a little longer than my forearm and featured a jagged axe point. Øyvin plucked it from my grasp and tested its weight before measuring it against different parts of his body. The handle was a bit long, but against his torso, it should work.

"Yes?" I said, my voice sounding more hopeful than I felt.

He nodded and grabbed one of the ropes from the box. As quickly as a sailor, he fashioned a few knots and tied the neon-pink string around his middle, holding the thin, metal axe against his T-shirt-covered stomach. "I may need to use a layer of magic, pretend to be in my uniform, to help conceal it."

A whoosh of air left my chest, and I braced my hands on my knees. One of my crazy plans had worked... but we still had more plans to see through.

"Let's get this tidied up and get out of here," I said. "The quicker we get the two you-know-whats, the quicker we might get rid of Veigar."

We strode back through the village, peering around corners before continuing in case the Fire Fae King was still on his midday stroll.

The red, wooden walls of the boathouse waved in welcome as we approached home. What had once been a place I'd stomped toward with anger, was now a place I'd run toward if in danger. I peered up at Øyvin as our footsteps tapped against the dock by the front door. "When are you heading below?"

"Now," Øyvin replied.

"Already?" I squeaked. "We haven't discussed exactly what happens next. We need more time."

"I have everything I need."

Espen brushed his hand down my arm, offering an ounce of reassurance.

"I've already been planning," Øyvin continued. "You've done your part. I just need you to wait here and have your phones on in case something goes wrong or if I need to abort."

That competitive gene kicked on and I straightened. "Nothing will go wrong."

Øyvin pressed in on me, and my head tilted back to look at him. Those blue eyes shone with a determination that could power through defensive lines on a football field. A sense of need and pride tugged low in my belly at the sight.

"If something does go wrong"—he swallowed hard—"promise me you'll get the Forest shard and run to the mountain with it anyway."

I shook my head. Nothing was going to go wrong. We'd get that damn rock and the one at the graveyard and kick Veigar out of town. Together.

"Lennie..." Øyvin said my name like an order and a promise.

"If something goes wrong, I'm coming after you."

"Don't."

"I will."

Øyvin let out a long-winded sigh and backed us toward the edge of the dock, the water lapping at the pylons beneath us. "I love you. Your courage. Your dedication to the people you call family. But I won't let you get yourself killed for me."

I narrowed my eyes at him while my heart fluttered like a million fireflies had taken up residence. "Fine," I conceded. "But since when do you decide who I can and cannot die for?"

"Since you married us."

My limbs felt as if they would melt into the fjord and I spread my hands against his broad chest.

He smirked and tipped my chin up with his finger and thumb. "Would you cry for me, Trouble?"

I chuckled. "Don't get your hopes up, Asshole."

Yeah, I probably would.

A wicked grin swept across his face, and he pressed his lips to mine in an all-consuming kiss before spinning and diving into the fjord without me.

140

ØYVIN

As soon as my head submerged, I pulled on my magic and created a bubble of air around me. I pressed my hand to my shoulder and pictured my Fjord Fae uniform. The magical illusion rippled into place. Hopefully, this would help conceal the weapon tied to my stomach and people wouldn't take a closer look at a soldier walking through the palace in their uniform. The only problem would be if word had spread of my termination... I'd deal with that problem if it arose.

I pushed forward through the cool, dark waters, aiming for the Fjord Fae palace. Schools of fish flitted past, their beady eyes watching me with equal amounts of uncertainty and curiosity. The colors of their scales shifted beneath the diffused rays of light, reminding me of how I'd changed in the past year and what I was setting out to do.

In Reuven and Veigar's hands, the Fjord Fae shard was a weapon—something they could use against other fae and against my partners. I couldn't let that happen. It would destroy the peace among the fae and my new family. I didn't like stealing from my people, but I had to. Had no other choice.

The betrayal burned a hole in my chest, but I ignored the singe.

My heart thumped heavily against my ribs as I approached the palace entry that loomed ahead like the maw of a whale. Two soldiers swam around the entrance—the same number I'd usually station there. Inside, two more stood sentry with fishing spears in their grasps. I removed my bubble and kept my head down.

Keeping my breaths and steps even, I continued on as if nothing were different. I was Øyvin Håland, come to work for the Fjord Fae. Not to steal their most prized possession.

The soldiers gave me brief glances, but didn't question my presence.

I let out a quiet sigh of relief.

Assessing the scene as I strode through the pristine corridors, I took an indirect route to the Council chambers that wove through the living quarters and not the busier tunnels.

Muffled sounds of daily life crept out of vestibules and apartments.

Lights flickered against the polished stone.

Fjord Fae went about their business.

Life in the Palace continued as if nothing was amiss.

Exactly as I needed it to be.

As I approached the long hall that led to the King's quarters and Council chambers, a door opened up ahead and I spun back around the corner. Sigurd stepped out of my old office.

I bit back a grumble.

It had been less than twenty-four fucking hours and they'd already reassigned my office space.

So much for loyalty.

At least, by the looks of the silver-threaded cape that hung from Sigurd's shoulders, they'd picked a decent successor. Sigurd was a good man. A bit of a sycophant it would seem, but good nonetheless. I'd trained him myself. If only I'd trained him to stand up against shit leadership. Then again, how good had I been at standing up against Balder and his authoritarian ways?

I shook off the thought and turned my back as Sigurd and a small group of soldiers headed past me down the main hallway.

Don't move and they won't have reason to look at you twice.

Taking five steady breaths, I waited until the sound of their steps abated, then peered back into the main thoroughfare.

Soft sconces and marble-smooth walls shimmered back at me.

Empty.

Perfect.

I strode down the hallway as fast as possible, listening for any signs of movement or life. Everything was quiet, and I sent a quick thank you to the ancestors I was about to betray. I had good reasons for doing this, but I wasn't sure the ancestors would agree.

They can yell at me when I'm dead.

Pressing my shoulder against the thick Council chamber door, I nudged it open and held my breath.

Unlike yesterday, the chairs sat vacant, the table free of forearms and tales of tyranny. At the back of the room, its sky-blue eye blinking at me in the low light, was Jörmungandr.

I shut the door behind me with a gentle thud and crossed the room to the sea serpent carved into the back wall. The carving itself was a marvel—stretching the length of the room and wrapping toward the monarch's seat at the head of the table. Only the Monarch, Head Guard, and select council members knew what the stone really was. Everyone else was led to believe it was decor. Whenever anyone walked through the—

My breath caught again.

The door.

I'd almost forgotten.

It wouldn't lock. Never had.

But I needed to slow anyone who might enter and dampen any sound that might flow through its slats.

Focusing on the warm well of magic in my chest, I pulled on a thread of it and crafted a wall of water. The thick, aqueous barrier would muffle any noise and buy me a little time. I settled the boiling translucent rectangle over the door where it sloshed around in its confines like a liquid bandage.

Pressing my hand to my shoulder again, I dropped my miraged uniform and turned back to the stone wall. The rope around my middle came undone with two easy tugs, and the ice pick Lennie had so cleverly suggested I use, fell into my waiting hand.

I planted my feet, grasped the axe with both hands, and focused on a point beside the shard.

Ancestors forgive me.

I swung.

The axe chipped at the rock, reverberations skittering up my forearms. A tiny fracture sprang from the serpent's socket like the lines around an old sailor's eyes. I could press some water into the crack, forcing the stone to separate from the shard, but it likely wasn't deep enough. Not yet.

According to Lennie, that shard was most likely a triangle. Like the icebergs that floated past the island of Svalbard, there was more beneath the surface. Only one corner of blue sprung from the snake's eye—there was more underneath that I had to be careful of.

I aimed at the other side of the eyeball and swung again.

The pick impaled the rock with a sharp crack. Bits of stone splintered and sprinkled across my feet.

Prying at a loose piece, I popped it off the wall and let it thump to the floor. A larger chunk of the shard stared back at me. How long had it been ensconced here? Hundreds of years, at least.

I set down the axe and pushed a bubble of water into the cracks around the stone. Drawing on more magic, I willed the bubble to swell and push against the stone around it. Creaking filled the empty chamber, and the cracks splintered further, more dust falling across my shoes. I brushed aside rock with my hands and water magic until a large enough hole formed over the shard.

Putting my hand into the gap, I pulled out the shard.

The bright stone shone in my hand. Cool against my palm, it reminded me of a lump of ice. Almost translucent, yet filled with a blue that was similar to both the sky and the floating cathedrals that passed the northernmost shores of Norway. "Fuck."

A piece of Jörmungandr's cheek fell from the wall and crashed against the floor, drawing me from my stupor.

Whipping around, I faced the door. The water barrier remained intact, no movement of the door handle either. But that didn't mean there wouldn't be.

I needed to get back home. Get back to Lennie.

I grabbed the rope and tied the shard against my stomach.

Setting the now dilapidated axe on the table, I put my hand to my shoulder and pulled another illusion over my clothes. This time, instead of my uniform, I settled for a long-sleeved white shirt and dark jeans. Plain and unassuming. If anyone asked what I was doing down here, I'd tell them I'd forgotten something in my office but hadn't been able to find it.

Waving my hand, the protective wall of water disintegrated.

With adrenaline humming through my veins, I gently opened the door and peered out into the hall. No movement. No noise. Reuven must've been in the living quarters and Sigurd headed for the wall. It was about time for daily checks—at least this was when I'd always gone to the wall.

Feeling confident there was no one lurking, I swept into the hallway and strode for the exit like I belonged here and the Fjord Fae shard wasn't strapped to my front.

A wave of guilt washed through me as I passed doorways, Fjord Fae going about their day, and the turn toward the ballroom where displaced fae were sheltering.

I'm doing the right thing. Stealing the shard would help all three factions, including Fjord Fae. This was protecting them from someone who didn't have their best interest at heart. Someone who had aligned with a being who would rule us like a dictator, bringing fire and brimstone to our precious waters.

There was zero doubt in my mind that Veigar would harm the creatures in the fjord. He'd already lit the oil refinery on fire for merely ignoring his wishes and not considering falling in line. Men like that were volatile and unworthy of trust.

"Øyvin," a frail, feminine voice croaked, and I ground to a stop as Ingeborg stepped out of a nook in front of me.

Small eyes peered up at me from her hunched form.

I cleared my throat and gave her a toothless grin. "Ingeborg. Are you well?"

"I'm quite well," she replied. "Thank you for asking."

"Good."

She touched her hand to my elbow. "But I'm concerned about you. I heard a rumor that you'd been dismissed?"

Fuck.

"I... Yes. I was."

"That's such a shame. They'd better have a good reason other than this ridiculous notion that you could no longer be trusted with our fae secret."

So that's what they'd been telling people. Not that I couldn't be trusted by Reuven, but that the Fae in general couldn't trust me to not keep our society's existence a secret from humans.

"The King and I no longer see eye-to-eye," I said. "You must excuse me, I need to head home. My partner is waiting for me."

She let me pass with a hum I couldn't place. Did she not believe me? Even if it was taken as a lie, I didn't have time to wait. If I hung around, I could get caught.

I twisted and looked over my shoulder. "Have a good day, Ingeborg."

She raised her hand in goodbye.

I spun and ran directly into someone. Heat washed over me like a bonfire and I steadied the person who tumbled into my arms, holding them away from my body.

Black eyes stared up at me and all the oxygen in my lungs evaporated.

"Your Majesty," I coughed out. "I didn't see you there."

Salka's brows furrowed as she regained her footing and brushed her hands over her plain black dress.

"What are you doing down here?" she asked, her voice tinged with suspicion. The sound reminded me of smoke drifting off a fire, of flames curling around logs and making the moisture in them pop.

"Forgot something in my office."

I kept my gaze locked with hers, holding my ground.

"Did you find it?"

I shook my head. "Must've already been thrown away."

"Shame."

"Indeed."

Her tongue swept across her top teeth, and I took a step back, bowing my head. "Apologies for crashing into you. Have a good day."

I didn't wait for her reply. I strode as fast as I could for the next turn in the hallway before sprinting for the exit.

If she went to Reuven and told him she'd seen me, he'd send soldiers after me for questioning. I didn't have much time. I needed to get back home, to Lennie, above the water where the two of them could defend me if needed. Not that I wanted them to have to, but I knew, deep down, that they'd do whatever it took to protect me. Lennie had said as much before I dove into the fjord today. And

Espen... the man had become a close friend and partner. Did I love him like I did Lennie? No. That was impossible. But another bond had formed between the two of us over the past year. One built on camaraderie and care, and sealed by the love we shared for the same woman.

The main entrance to the palace came into view and I ran for it, ignoring the confused looks on the guards' faces. I dove through the large hole in the wall and into the cold waters of the fjord.

The weight of the fjord pressed down on me as I built an air pocket around myself. Using every ounce of magic within me, I propelled myself through the water.

Fish darted out of my way.

Ripples and bubbles crashed together in my wake.

Up.

Up.

Up.

The murky waters grew lighter and clearer the closer I got to the surface.

Something large moved beneath me, rippling through the depths and disturbing the currents. I clenched my jaw and swiftly scanned the darkness. Inky water and a distant, rocky fjordbed stared back at me. Nothing was down there. But that didn't mean I wasn't being followed.

I swam.

Harder.

Faster.

Using more magic than I ever had.

A jet of water blasted past on my left and I flinched.

Rip current. Dangerous. Lethal even.

A quick glance behind me didn't calm my fears. Three figures gave chase.

I turned back and pushed my magic to its limit.

Move.

Move.

Move.

A moment later the pylons of our house came into view, ripples of the red-and-white building painted across the surface.

Two shapes moved up there. One blonde, the other dark.

My chest ached and my arms trembled as I untied the shard from my stomach.

"Put it down, Håland!" A firm, male voice echoed through the water. Pressure wrapped around my ankles pulling me back. I opened my free palm and aimed it backward, shooting a pulse of power and freeing myself.

"Stop!"

I didn't listen.

A tickle ran down my spine and the water around me rippled. *Shit.* I dodged to the right, narrowly avoiding another jet that could haul me back into their arms.

Too close. They were too close.

With a final push of magic, I breached the surface and burst my air pocket.

Cool air whipped across my cheeks and through my hair.

I slammed the stone onto the dock, peered into Lennie's beautiful wide brown eyes, and said, "Run."

141

LENNIE

Øyvin was yanked beneath the surface.

"No!" I clawed my way to the edge of the dock and leaned out over the water, stretching my hand toward the circular ripples where he'd just been.

"Lennie, no!" Espen hauled me back and pulled me across the weather-worn planks.

My body trembled and my breaths caught in my chest, screaming for release. "What just happened? What the fuck just happened?"

Espen held the Fjord shard in one hand and his free arm banded around my torso.

"We have to go after him. We have to save him." I scrambled against Espen's ironclad hold, my shoes scraping and screeching across the dock. "We have to help him!"

This couldn't be happening. Nothing was supposed to go wrong. I needed to get him out of the water. *Now.*

My breaths grew ragged as I fought against Espen, scratching at his police jacket.

Water rippled out on the fjord, not far from the boathouse, and an arc of translucent scales breached the surface like the Loch Ness Monster.

Every ounce of oxygen inside me disappeared and my limbs went limp.

"Run!" Espen yelled against my ear and spun me toward the road.

I didn't have to be told twice. Sprinting across the dock and onto the street, I ran as fast as I could toward the village.

"Police station," Espen said, coming up beside me.

I nodded. My breaths sawing in and out of my lungs. "Wh-what the fuck w-was that?"

"I don't want to stick around to find out."

Agreed.

Tears streaked across my cheeks as we bolted for Espen's workplace. My legs pistoned as I pumped my arms at my sides, pushing my body to move faster.

The austere walls of the station came into view, the lights in the windows turned off, save for the one above the front door. Parked against the right side of the building sat a lone police cruiser, blue lights above white-and-neon-yellow lines. Espen pointed toward it and we both aimed that direction, slowing as we reached it.

I came to a stop and bent over, pressing my palms against my thighs as I sucked in lungfuls of air. "What do we do? What do we do? What do we do?"

"There's nothing we can do. We made a promise to him." Espen corralled me against the side of the station and gripped my chin, forcing me to look at him. "There is nothing we can do to save him, Lennie. Neither of us are strong enough, can't breathe under water like they can. We'd be signing our own death certificates by diving into those waters right now."

"We could try."

He shook his head. "While I love your strength and resolve, you know I'm right."

My chest rose and fell like an animal caught in battle—fight or flight instinct kicking in. I loved Øyvin. Would do anything for him. Even take on yet another monarch whose powers probably far outweighed my own. My rational mind recognized the stupidity of that insurmountable task, but my heart felt differently.

"We'd die trying to get to wherever he's been taken," Espen said.

"So, you think he's been captured?"

"I think it's a distinct possibility. But I can't be sure."

There it was. The *what if*. What if they hadn't spared him, hadn't sent him to a watery prison, and instead just killed him on the spot. My shoulders slumped as the thought ran through me, my muscles giving up on me as the grief settled in. Espen caught me and pulled me into his embrace.

"We need to leave now," he whispered into my hair.

"We can't..." My throat tightened. "We can't just abandon Øyvin."

"There is nothing we can do."

"I can't just leave him to die," I said, my words soft and without force. Like they recognized the reality of our situation. "It's my fault."

"Lennie." Espen brushed his free hand through my hair, tucking it behind one ear and pulling my focus back to his grief-stricken gaze. His voice dipped into a stern tone. "We promised him to get the job done even if something bad happened. We're in that scenario, so we need to get to the stave church. I need you to focus."

He dropped the sky-blue stone into my palm. It was triangular and rounded at one corner with a jagged main edge. But it looked just like the material the Temple was made of.

"It's my fault," I muttered again, staring down at the lump of rock.

"None of this is your fault."

"This was my idea. My plan. And it fucking failed. Some kind of leader I am."

He tilted my chin to face him. "You haven't failed."

"Not yet."

"Leaders make plans. Sometimes they work. Sometimes they don't. And while it's admirable that you're trying to take responsibility—which is a valuable trait in a leader—Øyvin volunteered to do this. In fact, Øyvin was the one who suggested stealing the Fjord Fae shard."

"He wouldn't have thought of it had I not suggested—"

"You don't know that."

He was right. I didn't. But guilt and fear still sat on my chest like a boulder, pressing down and cracking my ribs.

"We haven't failed yet." Espen moved his hands and held my head in his palms. "We follow through with what we need to do, and we trust that Øyvin is far stronger than you're giving him credit for. We get the other shard. We stop Veigar. We save the fae. Can you do that with me, Lennie?"

However much Espen's words rang true, it didn't feel like it. Not right now. This whole thing had been my crazy plan and, like most of my ideas, it had jettisoned off the rollercoaster rails and plummeted to the ground with an almighty crash.

"Yes," I replied with a gentle nod.

"Good." He pressed his lips against my forehead and my eyes fluttered shut for a brief moment.

He was right. I'd made a promise, and we had a mission to complete.

We peeled out of the police station parking lot, blue lights swirling above the car as Espen zipped out of town. I clutched the Fjord shard in my hand, letting the rough edge bite into my palm while rubbing my other hand across my thigh. Focusing on the contrast in the material—cool stone versus soft denim—helped me lower my heart rate and drew my attention away from my tumultuous thoughts.

Ten minutes outside of town, we slowed. A police barricade—several wood-en barriers and another cruiser—blocked our path.

"Don't worry," Espen said. "He's with us."

"By *with us*, you mean Fae?"

Espen nodded. "Forest Fae."

"How many of your soldiers do you have on the roster down at the police station?"

"Only a couple."

"Handy."

One of his shoulders lifted. "They're part of the volunteer force of rangers. So, yes, it's convenient. But they don't report to the office that often. They primarily work in the field and report to me."

It was like they'd thought this all through. Then again, most of the fae I'd met were several hundred years old, so I guessed they'd had time to plan for all eventualities.

Espen shut off the car and opened the door. "Stay here."

With the shock and adrenaline draining from my system and emotions welling inside me, I wasn't going anywhere.

He strode over to the other cruiser and exchanged a few words with someone through the car's window. A moment later he removed the blue-and-white wooden barrier from in front of our car, opening the road for us.

As Espen got back in and started the engine, I said, "Bente really did mean *nobody in or out*."

"Can't be too careful. Every entry into town is blocked. And a ten-mile minimum radius has been cleared of all residents."

I stared ahead once more and hoped the roads would stay barricaded. We couldn't have any innocent humans stumbling into town. Not with Veigar on the loose and a mountain threatening to crumble. Hopefully, the severity of the potential natural disaster would have folks thinking twice before heading for Skolvik.

The thought of innocents being hurt or killed opened the floodgates to my emotions. I swallowed a hard lump in my throat and tilted my head back against the headrest. What if someone like Solveig or Dagny came back to get something and got caught by Veigar before we could get to her? What if Veigar burned down the village? What if Øyvin never resurfaced?

A tear welled at the inner corner of my eye, and I wiped it away with a finger.

Espen flicked his gaze to me. "He'll be all right."

I fidgeted in my seat and turned the shard in my hand as another tear slipped down my face. "You can't know that for sure."

Silence responded.

We all understood the risks. We all understood what might happen. But like a fool, I'd let hope swell inside me, let it unpack the throw pillows, set its toothbrush in the jar beside the sink, and flop onto the couch.

Another tear streaked down my cheek, and I closed my eyes. Grief settled over me. That unwelcome beast gnawing at my insides. I couldn't calculate the odds of Øyvin's survival. Fuck, I didn't even know what had been strong enough to pull him under like that. But Reuven was a king and must've had more power than Øyvin. He'd have some royal power like me and Halvar too. But how much and how he would use it was anyone's guess.

A hand rested on my thigh, and I opened my eyes. Another tear fell into my lap.

"We keep moving," Espen said, his voice thick with emotion. "We keep moving and do what we need to do to save the Fae from Veigar and protect Skolvik."

I sniffled and set my hand atop his.

He moved his fingers and squeezed my hand. That melancholy monster inside me backed down slightly, bowing away from the brightness that was my husband.

With a glance over at Espen, I nodded.

It was all we could do. I wouldn't let the villagers down, nor the Fjell Fae, and most of all, Øyvin's sacrifice.

I sucked in a lungful of air, held it for four seconds, before controlling its exit. I just hoped it hadn't actually been a sacrifice, that he was still alive, still with us and hadn't been sent to the ancestors he constantly begged for patience from.

Twenty minutes later, Espen pulled down a narrow road, gravel crunching beneath the tires. The last time we'd been down here the entire place had been covered in a thick layer of snow. Now, luscious green leaves waved as we passed, moss crawled over boulders within the forest, and the dense canopy opened into a clearing where the stave church loomed like a gargoyle.

The building looked as if it had been hammered together with nails and planks from a Viking ship. Thick wood beams stacked on top of each other formed the walls, while black, weather-worn shingles covered the different tiers of the roof. At the top of each high point of the roof were dragons whose long snouts aimed toward the sky, projecting their doom and gloom on all those who dared come close.

The car came to a stop in front of the stone fence, and Espen shut off the engine.

Silence filled the vehicle as a mournful aura seemed to float off the building and through the ancient graveyard.

"Are you ready to do this?" I asked.

Espen lifted my hand to his lips and kissed my knuckles, then sighed and nodded.

142

ESPEN

I climbed out of the police car, my heart in my throat, but my world at my side. If this went wrong, not only would her life potentially be at risk, but the Council of Elders would never forgive me. The Forest Fae shard had been with us for centuries and used to transfer magic from the ancestors to the monarch. But, when Queen Ragnhild died with neither heir nor successor, we'd chosen to hide the sky-blue stone with her and her Head Guard. Never to be used again.

Until now.

The time had come. I knew it in my bones. In my soul. We needed the power in this stone to stop Veigar. His igniting of the oil refinery and murdering Fjell soldiers was tame, child's play for him. Whatever he planned to do next would be much, much worse. And we had to do whatever we could to counter that. Including stealing the Forest Fae shard.

Lennie and I strode across the parking lot, gravel grinding together beneath our shoes. The ancient dark-wood stave church rose out of the grassy clearing, its tall steeples defying gravity. Dragon heads from Viking ships glared at us from the roof beams, and the Christian cross on the top spire pointed toward the clear sky. The surrounding forest was as still as the occupants of the graveyard, and the wind barely rustled the verdant foliage.

Passing lines of gravestones, we made our way toward the site's newer additions.

I brushed my hand over Mads' gravestone first, letting the stone scrape across the pads of my fingers. If he were here, if he were put in this situation, would he do the same? I'd like to think so. He'd always advised me not to fear my destroyer powers and let them find balance with my healer side. But I had never given in to that. Didn't dare to. Not until that day twenty-one years ago when I'd unleashed terror upon the battlefield that had claimed his life and Queen Ragnhild's.

My gaze shifted to her marker, and I took two steps back.

Something pressed against my lower back, and I glanced over my shoulder. Lennie stared up at me, and my muscles relaxed properly for the first time since leaving Skolvik.

She'd seen my powers unleashed too—just not quite to the same extent. I'd still been weak thanks to the poison last autumn, but had buried a large swath of Balder's forces on that mountaintop. Whether those soldiers had deserved such a burial or not was another matter. The most important thing that day had been the need to protect the Forest Fae, and her. Always her.

Reaching out, I nudged us in front of Mads' grave and positioned Lennie behind me. "Stay here."

Her brow furrowed and she glanced between the two graves. She pointed to the blue stone peeking out of the front of Ragnhild's gravestone. "Isn't that it?"

I shook my head. "Decoy."

"Smart."

"Now, stay behind me, please." I lifted my hands in front of me and pulled on the mass of dark energy that sat like a knot in my sternum ready to unleash hell at a moment's notice. Like it could hear my thoughts and feel my intent on using it, the power sat up and begged to be set free. I rolled my shoulders, let a sliver of it past the gates, and down my arms. Pushing it outward, I aimed my hands at the top of the gravestone and launched the magic.

Power crashed against stone and a sharp crack shot through the air.

Lennie flinched and sucked in a breath.

Shit. No.

I clenched my hands into fists and spun. I shouldn't be doing this with her so close. "You shouldn't be here. You should be in the car. Out of harm's way."

She tilted her head to one side, and her gaze flicked to my balled-up hands.

Fear lanced up my spine. I should have been more careful. Should have known better.

Lennie took my right hand in hers and peeled open my fingers. "Stop your worrying right this second, husband."

My heart stilled at the title.

She entwined her fingers with mine and stared up at me. Those large brown eyes held me ensnared—they always did. The sight of them, the sneaky smile perpetually crinkling the corners, the light shining out of her. Everything that she was—it was intoxicating in the best way.

And something that needed protecting from the destructive force that resided within me.

"You won't harm me," she said, drawing me from my thoughts.

"You don't know that."

That signature smirk appeared, though, far less joyful than usual. "Yes. I. Do."

And there was that challenging nature that Øyvin loved so much.

I let out an extended sigh, and she pressed her free palm to my chest.

"I trust that the power in here"—she tapped against my sternum—"won't dare hurt me."

"And how can you be sure of that?"

"Because you love me too much to ever cause me harm."

I freed my hands and cradled her head. "I do—"

"See?"

"—but we can't trust that destroyer part of me."

"Yes, we can."

There was her obstinate side. The part that always got her into trouble, but I loved it, nonetheless.

"Espen Solbakke Martin, you know, deep down, that you'd never hurt me. Your power knows that too. Try."

I shook my head.

"Try it. Quickly."

I could barely handle this woman, and I wouldn't have it any other way. She was an unyielding storm that swept in and crushed any other thoughts of continuing this life without her in it. And she did have a valid point. It didn't feel like my power wanted to hurt her. Quite the opposite. I closed my eyes and reached inside myself, focusing on that churning constant of magic. I gingerly willed the tiniest amount toward her and... the power bristled and retracted.

Fascinating.

I tried again. This time the power pushed back, begging to go in the other direction.

Very fascinating.

The dark mass wanted to be unleashed but pointed away from her. Like it wanted to defend and protect *her*.

She was right.

Opening my eyes, I found my world staring back at me. That awe-filled and righteous look was enough to shake the fears from my mind.

I was using these destructive powers for good. For the good of my people and the rest of the fae in our region. I glanced over my shoulder at the two graves—one now slightly cracked, the other unharmed. What *would* they think about this?

I scoffed at myself. Mads would've told me to trust the powers and find that balance. While Queen Ragnhild would've told me to do whatever I could to protect our people. *No fear, no relenting, no remorse.* Those words rang through my mind like an echo from the past, and a shiver ran down my spine. Lennie was right, and so was Queen Ragnhild's old motto.

"Aaaaaand?"

I turned back to Lennie and sucked in a breath. "I don't think these powers want to hurt you."

"See. Told you." She gave me a wobbly smile and pointed to the gravestone behind me. "Now, let's get that magical little rock out of the grave and get back home."

Brushing my hand across her cheek, I said, "Thank you."

"I love you too."

"And yet, you couldn't possibly love me more than I love you."

"Oh, that we can debate at length another time."

And there was that unrelenting competitive side her entire family had.

"I look forward to it."

"Now..." She grabbed my shoulders, turned me around, and smacked my bottom. "Let 'er rip."

"You really do know how to break the moment."

"Oh, I learned how to pivot a conversation from my darling husband. You should meet him sometime. Great guy, stellar ass."

I snorted. "He must do yoga."

"So much yoga."

As a warm breeze drifted across the graveyard and our words settled, I focused on the cracked stone in front of me. A sharp fissure cleaved vertically from the top of the grave and down toward Mads' name. I raised my hands once more and pulled on my magic. It flowed down my arms and shot out toward the grave. With another *crack*, more fissures appeared. I blasted it again, and splinters cut through *Mads Robertson*.

Another shot of power. *I'm sorry.*

Another crack. *I'm sorry.*

A final push to knock the lumps aside. *I'm so sorry.*

A blue shard tumbled onto the grassy mound with a thump.

It was done.

Stepping forward, I retrieved the stone. The sky-blue lump of rock shone in the sunlight, its glassy surface smooth and cool to the touch.

Lennie wrapped her arms around my torso. "Well done."

I pulled her tighter to me, brushing my hand over her back as I pressed a kiss to the top of her head. "Thank you for believing in me."

"Always," she whispered.

"Here." I handed her the shard. She took it and watched as I knelt and picked up the pieces of Mads' gravestone. I precariously rearranged the lumps, doing my best to set them back where they belonged. But... I let out a frustrated sigh. The pieces were too many, and the grooves too damaged—

"Let me." Lennie dropped to her knees beside me and shoved the Forest Fae shard back into my hands.

With deft movements, she twisted and adjusted the stones like large puzzle pieces. Then, with a deep breath, she closed her eyes and pressed her palms against the gravestone.

My eyes widened and my heart sputtered as the fissures on the rocky facade healed and the broken chunks melded back together once more. I'd never witnessed her use this form of Fjell Fae magic before. Those training sessions at the mountain were working. She was learning and... she was good.

With another deep exhale, Lennie pulled back her hands and opened her eyes, studying her work. The cracks were gone, the gravestone had reformed, the only sign that anything had changed were the faint scars where the fissures had been.

"You're incredible." The words tumbled from my lips on a whisper.

Lennie turned and looked up at me, her eyes full of pride and sadness. "Make sure Øyvin hears you say that when we get him back."

An invisible knife twisted through my heart. Denial. Pain. The oncoming onslaught of grief. I hoped to the ancestors he hadn't been killed in the fjord. But we had no way of knowing. If he'd been taken, they'd have confiscated his phone. And if he'd been killed...

I swallowed hard and Lennie's eyes locked on the movement.

Damn.

I had to stay strong. Had to maintain composure, because if Lennie saw how worried I really was, she'd fall apart.

"I'll tell him," I said. "Loud and proud."

A wistful smile twisted her lips. "Good."

We rose to our feet and wandered out of the graveyard, the stave church looming behind us as we went. I slipped my hand into Lennie's and gently squeezed as a tangle of emotions settled onto my shoulders. Worry, sadness, and fear retook their seats, but a bubble of joy settled in beside them.

We'd done it. We had two of the shards in our possession. Now all we needed to do was return to Skolvik and rush them to the Temple in the mountain without getting caught by Veigar... or anyone else for that matter.

As we reached the car, a warm gust of air washed across the parking lot, and I stilled. "Did you feel that?"

Lennie spun and faced me, her brow furrowed. "Feel what?"

Where had that wind come from? Hadn't it been still since we got here? An unseasonably warm gust didn't just come out of nowhere... unless a storm was rolling in. I shrugged. "Probably nothing."

"Come on," she said, her voice breathy and laced with weariness and grief. "We've got a world to save."

LENNIE

Holding a shard in each hand, I examined the pieces in a daze as we sped back toward town. Each lump of quartz-like stone was unique but shared the same triangular shape with one jagged edge. If anyone else found them they might think they were two halves of a whole, but I knew exactly where they belonged. They were a perfect match for the pedestal that sat in the middle of the Temple of the Fae.

I stared out the window, brush and leafy birch trees whizzing past as Espen drove what I could only assume was *exactly* the speed limit. Øyvin would probably grumble and roll his eyes at that.

My heart fractured further.

Øyvin.

Memories of him playing the piano flooded my mind. The smell of him baking chocolate chip cookies for me feeling as real as if we had a batch stashed in the car.

I didn't want to believe he was gone. Couldn't stomach the idea. He had to be alive. He had to come back to me. Because if he wasn't and he didn't—

A lump clogged my throat, and I swallowed it down.

I couldn't think like that.

And yet... It felt like this was just the beginning. This was the first quarter, and we were down fourteen points already with three whole quarters to go. Football games may be won in the fourth and final quarter, but, even with both the Forest and Fjord shards in our possession, we were already down a man. Our team was missing a key player, and an awful feeling took up residence in my stomach.

"People are going to die, aren't they?" I said, breaking the silence in the car.

Espen nodded. "It's inevitable."

I sighed.

"We will win this, Lennie. We're going to be all right."

I glanced over at the ray of sunshine behind the wheel. "I really admire your optimism."

"I know you can be optimistic too."

"I don't feel it right now."

"Then get that frown upturned or however the saying goes, because we're going to do this," he said, his voice filling with urgency like a rally cry. "We're already doing this. We're getting those stones to the Temple, asking the ancestors for help, and kicking Veigar's ass right out of town." A gentle smile played on his lips. "I believe in us, Lennie."

The way his gaze warmed as he briefly glanced across the center console had me melting into a puddle of hope. Hope that we would do this. Hope that we could save the fae from a dick-tator. Together. The three—

My brain stalled on the number, and I faced the window again.

There wasn't three of us right now.

Espen cleared his throat. "Are you really going to let some ancient asshole take the mountain away from you? Let him tell *you* what to do?"

I rolled my neck and breathed through my nose. He was right. If I could barely take orders from Halvar, there wasn't a chance in hell I'd be kneeling to a man as volatile as Veigar. A man who didn't have the best interest of the fae at heart.

The only men I'd be getting on my knees for were my partners.

Martin Family Competitiveness: Activated.

"You really do know how to get me going, don't you?"

He snickered and a flush pinked his cheeks. "In more ways than one."

My responding chuckle was drowned out by a whooshing roar from behind us.

"What kind of backfire was that? This thing have turbo boosters or something?" I twisted in my seat, peering over my shoulder at the road behind us. My eyes widened and my entire body flooded with adrenaline.

Flames shot up on one side of the road, quickly jumping the asphalt and igniting the trees on the other side—a wall of orange and red chasing us.

"Espen, we have a problem."

He peered into the rearview mirror. "Shit!"

The fire swelled behind us, licking its way up the trees and devouring them whole. They were like kindling, oversized matches that ignited in the blink of an eye. A burst of flames shot toward us, and I clutched my seatbelt. "Drive, drive, drive!"

Espen slammed his foot against the pedal and the car shot forward, pushing me back against my seat. I swallowed hard as he gripped the steering wheel, his knuckles turning white.

The flames barreled around the bends—the roads up here twisting back and forth along the mountains that shielded the fjord on both the north and south sides. I clung to the "oh shit" handle as we sped down the hillside, the blaze barely twenty yards behind.

"What the hell is happening? Is that a forest fire?"

"Yes..."

"But? I sense a but."

"He brought his best backup." Espen slammed his palm against the top of the steering wheel. "Fuck."

We'd already surmised that Veigar wasn't alone—those wildfires further inland were way too suspicious—but, we hadn't exactly had time to discuss his forces in extreme detail. "What else does he have in his arsenal?"

"Herja."

"And that is?"

"She's Veigar's Head Guard."

My eyebrows hit my hairline, and I swallowed hard. Of course he had his own Head Guard. Why wouldn't he? And one whose name sounded like she ate Norse Gods for breakfast to bulk up. "Omen of death and devastation by chance?"

Espen nodded.

"Fuck."

"This must be her handy work. She must've snuck past our scouting parties."

I peered over my shoulder again. Flames swept across the road, chasing us like a lion desperate for food. Was Herja standing in those flames? Or was she behind them, pushing them toward us?

"You've fought her before?" I asked as the car veered around another precarious switchback, my shoulder bumping against the window.

"No, I don't remember a time when she's been back on the mainland. But if there's anyone as volatile as Veigar, it's her."

"Can we just set Halvar on her? Watch the big guy slice and dice her into bite-size pieces?"

"We can ask, but if Herja is here and not at the mountain then I'd imagine Halvar might have his hands full with Veigar himself."

I blanched. "They're dividing us. Spreading us out."

Espen sighed, and I didn't like the sound. Not one bit. It sent my stomach plummeting.

"We're going to have to split up," he said.

"Nope, don't want to do that." I shook my head. "I've already lost one of you today, I'm not losing both."

Espen sighed again, this time sounding like he agreed. "The stones, remember."

I looked down in my lap to the two Temple shards and swore. He was right. Dammit, we *did* have to split up.

"I have to get out down here and stop it," Espen said between gritted teeth.

"What are you going to do, bury the fire?"

"No." Espen pulled the steering wheel to the right, drifting us around another sharp bend. "Can't do that."

"Huh?"

"There's still oxygen in the soil. The roots will catch. It won't put out the fire."

"Then how the hell are you going to take on that?" I pointed over my shoulder.

"Magic."

"And a helluva lot of luck."

"Yes, that too."

"Espen!"

"Lennie!"

I huffed.

"I can bend it away from the town, tear down parts of the woods and create fire corridors," he explained. "It's not easy but it can be done."

"Like trenches and barriers to funnel the fire in a different direction? Stop it from encroaching further?"

"Exactly." Espen yanked on the wheel and pulled to a hard stop beside the other police car, still parked where we'd passed him earlier.

He shut off the vehicle and rushed out. I unbuckled my seatbelt, dropped the shards onto my seat, and followed him to the other officer. The poor guy's eyes blew wide as the raging inferno curved around the bend behind us—a decent distance away thanks to Espen's rally-style driving.

Espen gave orders of what they were going to do and what calls needed to be made to Ylva and the fire station.

Before I had a chance to absorb what was being said, Espen spun to me and held me by my shoulders. His features were locked in Head Guard, leader-mode: brows drawn, eyes alert, lips pursed.

"You're going to have to drive back to Skolvik yourself," he said.

"You want me to drive the police car? Government property?"

"You have to get those shards back to the Temple."

"Doesn't mean I like leaving you by yourself out here to take on *that*."

I didn't like it at all. But I also had a duty to the Fjell and a responsibility to get those shards to the Temple. I'd made that promise to Øyvin too. And no matter what had happened to him, I needed to follow through.

"I know," Espen said, his voice thick with raw emotions. "I don't want to let you out of my sight, but we have to split up." He shoved the keys into my hands. "Take the car and drive as fast as you can."

The fire loomed and crackled, felling trees with cacophonous thuds. We didn't have time for lengthy farewells.

I lunged at him, wrapping my arms around his neck and pressing my lips against his. He tasted of peppermint and coffee, his signature smell of leather and moss washing over me. I pulled back and whispered, "Don't die. I can't lose you too."

"You won't." He brushed my hair off my forehead, fingers trailing down my jaw before letting go. "I promise. Now drive."

I nodded and spun before I could let the emotions bubbling to the surface boil over onto the road. There was a mission to complete.

Sprinting to the police cruiser, I climbed into the driver's seat and pulled the chair forward so I could reach the pedals.

Three. Why are there...

I glanced at the footwell and then at the center console, the gearshift pointing toward the roof. "Oh my fuck, it's a manual!"

We were doomed. There wasn't a chance I was getting this thing back to Skolvik. This hatchback would be my coffin. Of all the places for me to die, of course it would be in a police cruiser on fire. I could picture my brothers' reactions perfectly: once they got over their grief, they'd cackle themselves to death.

"For fuck's sake." I stomped my feet on the clutch and brake pedal, put the car into neutral, and turned the ignition. "Trust me not to notice the type of transmission until now."

The car sputtered to life, and I cautiously released the handbrake. Easing pressure off the pedals, I squeezed my foot on the gas. The car juddered and groaned, and I let out a wince. Hopefully Espen was too busy with the fire to notice that I was about to break his boss's car.

With another flustered attempt at getting the car moving, I crunched it into first gear and got it rolling forward. "Thank Odin and all his sons this is mostly downhill."

The fact that the rest of the journey into town was a winding ribbon of asphalt that snaked back-and-forth down the mountain was a saving grace for both me and the car's gearbox.

I let it remain in first gear, which, based on the shudders and scratchy noises, it didn't like. But dammit, I wasn't going to ruin my chances of getting back to town, nor accidentally jettison myself of the road's steep embankments—most of which terminated at the fjord's shoreline, hundreds of yards below.

After five minutes of rolling and picking up some speed, I peered into the rearview mirror and found it empty of flames, but filling with smoke. Gray tendrils reached between the trees, curling around branches and pulling their way through the brush.

"Don't you dare die on me, Espen," I whispered.

I'd lose my mind if I lost them both. Even as I rolled toward town, I wasn't sure if I hadn't already lost a piece of myself to the darkest depths of the fjord.

As I finally entered the village, I blew through stop signs and barreled around corners. The car careened into the vacant lot beside the police station, tires screeching. Through some quick trial and error, I shut off the vehicle and breathed a sigh of relief, resting my head against the steering wheel. I'd made it. The car's gears and transmission may be in worse condition than this morning, but I'd done it.

An eerie quiet hung over the town as I grabbed the two stones from the passenger seat and clambered out of the car. The stillness sent a shiver down my spine. Lights were off in all the buildings, streets sat completely empty, and a smoky haze inched down the southern mountainside. It was like the place was waiting for something awful to happen, like it knew what lurked on its streets.

Shaking off the thought of Veigar sneaking around town, I popped open the trunk and searched for something to hide the stones in. Collapsable traffic cones, clear evidence bags, and a first aid kit stared back at me. Opting for the aid kit, I dumped its contents into the trunk and shoved the two shards inside, zipping it up tight. It was the most conspicuous of my choices—a first aid kit on the eve of battle might even be smart.

Slamming the trunk shut, I turned my attention to the village. It was time to get these back to their original home.

ESPEN

Watching Lennie drive away had terror seeping into my bones. But it wasn't nearly as terrifying as the scene behind me.

The fire was otherworldly. An inferno as tall as the pines that blanketed our hillsides.

In quick movements, I made a meter-wide trench near the bend, then watched it jump the barrier like it was nothing. Flames wrapped around branches and ate the forest floor as the asphalt cracked and leaked oil. Heat blasted against my face like I'd opened an oven, and I narrowed my eyes against the intensity, sprinting back to the police barrier before it could catch me.

"Stand back," I said to Morten Olsen, the police officer and Forest Fae who'd been stationed here.

"Yes, sir!"

Once we reached a safe distance back from the fire, I pulled on that ball of power lurking within me, waiting to be unleashed. With a deep breath, I stretched my arms out and curled my hands into fists. The trees in the flames' path folded over one another, snapping noises joining the popping fire as their roots strained and broke. I pushed the power away from me and moved the fallen trees back from the fire line, setting them closer to the cruiser where we stood. We didn't need to add fuel to the fire, but I needed these trees out of the way.

Embracing the overwhelming roar through my muscles, I pulled on all my strength, ignoring that need to be careful, and let loose again. Magic flowed from me and widened the trench before the flames, throwing the upended soil and ash back into the oncoming disaster.

Seeing the forest in so much pain boiled the blood in my veins.

I grit my teeth and eyed the destroyed road. No one would be entering town now. Hopefully, the firebreak would slow the advancing flames, but if it didn't... "Ancestors help us."

Siren noises pierced the echoing cacophony, and I turned to find the fire truck pulling up beside the police car.

Thank goodness. We needed water up here.

Ylva hopped out with a wild light in her eyes, her blond braids bouncing over her shoulders, and a fireman's jacket wrapped around her frame.

I smiled. Glad to see our long-held emergency plans among the Forest Fae had been successfully put into motion. Infiltrate local ranks. Take ownership of leading the efforts. Use our powers to help the humans when we could.

"I think Fire Chief suits me, don't you?" Ylva said with a cocky grin as she modeled the oversized jacket.

"Take that thing off before you break it."

"Buzzkill."

"Buzzkill?" That was a Lennie word if I'd ever heard one. "You've been spending too much time with my wife."

Ylva shrugged out of the jacket and threw it back into the truck's cab. "You were invited to Tequila Tuesdays at Fisken. Not my fault you can't *hang with the kids these days.*"

I wiped my hand across my forehead, about to launch into my plans, when a wall of skirts descended from the back of the truck's cabin. Narrowing my eyes, I tilted my head to one side as Heidi hopped out and landed beside Ylva. The other truck door swung open and out jumped Anders Langholm.

What on earth?

I schooled my features, hoping he hadn't seen my reaction. He shouldn't have been here. Neither should Heidi, but she was Forest Fae and he was human.

A few others piled out of the firetruck, all of whom I recognized as members of Ylva's elite cadre, the most powerful soldiers in our regiment. They went about getting the hoses off the truck and my attention flicked to Ylva as she strode up beside me, her own gaze locked on the stalled inferno.

"Ylva," I said, keeping my lips as still as possible. "Care to explain why Anders Langholm is here?"

She waved her hand, not taking her eyes of the fire. "Minor inconvenience. Apparently, he decided to shelter in the fire station's attic. Said someone should be here in case of emergency."

Good grief.

"So, you brought him with you?"

"He wasn't exactly amenable to staying put when he saw the fire break out."

"And he didn't call in for back up?"

"No, I stopped him." She set her hands on her hips as the man in question started unfurling a hose off the truck. "Told him I'd already done it."

I brushed my hand over my beard. "What are we going to do with him?"

"Like I said, minor inconvenience."

Heidi jabbed something against the man's throat. His eyes went wide, and he dropped to the road like a puppet with broken strings. The other Forest Fae caught him before he could hit his head and then picked him up and loaded him back into the truck.

Today was getting worse by the second.

I strode over to Heidi. "What did you just give him?"

"A delicate little concoction that packs quite the punch. Personal favorite." She snickered as she adjusted her hair into a bun on the back of her head.

"What does it do? Will he remember seeing us?"

"No, it'll render him unconscious for roughly forty-eight hours and scramble his thoughts. He won't know dream from reality."

A sigh slipped from my lips. I knew Heidi's potions and tinctures were effective and potent, but... Ah, I shouldn't be complaining. It had come in handy.

"You're welcome, by the way," Heidi said as if reading my mind. "You know my work is effective. Didn't your wife enjoy that tea I gave her for Christmas?"

I shook my head. Yes, Lennie had very much enjoyed that brew. So had Øyvin and I. It had left Lennie a hyper-sensitive, moaning and writhing mess. And we'd wrung seven orgasms from her that night. It was a very merry Christmas.

"Okay, let's focus," I said, an order for them and myself. I couldn't be thinking about Lennie right now. If I did, I'd end up sprinting to the mountain on the other side of the fjord and whisking her somewhere safe.

The group that arrived in the truck and Officer Olsen gathered around, their gazes falling to me.

"While some of you shoot water at that, I need to keep building these trenches." I motioned to the ones currently holding back some of the blaze. "But we need to work up and down the mountainside, clearing any debris and trees along this line." I continued giving orders. The fae nodded, accepting their tasks.

Ylva motioned between her and Heidi. "We will stay here."

"Good." I didn't want the healer walking the woods alone. We might need her, and keeping her here at our makeshift base was best.

"All right, everyone! You have your tasks!"

"Yes, sir!"

As one of the Forest Fae finished preparing the firetruck hose, Ylva pulled a large sack out of the vehicle's back seat and gingerly set it on the road. Heidi scurried over, hitched her skirts, rolled up her sleeves and bent down, opening the bag. She extracted what looked like a poultice at this distance—a ball of gauze-like material held shut with twine. The two women conferred and mumbled, heads nodding as they assessed more of the little bundles.

"Ladies, what are those?"

Ylva set aside one of the balls and smiled. "A side project I've had Heidi working on."

I didn't like the sound of that. With a quick look over my shoulder to make sure the fire hadn't jumped the line—*it hadn't*—I set my hands on my hips and asked, "What exactly does this little *project* entail?"

Heidi's eyes went wide. "Kaboom!"

"Bombs?" My voice peaked and cracked. "Heidi!"

"I'm highly adept at potion-making, young man."

"Yeah." Ylva smiled, the overly gleeful look filling every corner of her face. "Let the woman work."

I rolled my eyes and checked on the fire again. The hose, and the Forest Fae manning it, started launching water at the flames behind the ditch. At least someone was following orders.

Heavy metal music sounded from my pocket and my stomach sank. I pulled my phone out and didn't bother looking at the caller ID. The plume of gray and black above me had probably been spotted over the mountains and set off alarms.

"Bente," I said, answering the call while Ylva and Heidi whispered about their *project*.

"Where's the fire?"

My boss didn't even hesitate. She never did.

"Forest south of the Fjord. Ten minutes outside the village center."

"Contained?"

"Almost—"

"I'll call in the Coast Guard plane and the authorities in Oslo for—"

"No need." My stomach twisted in on itself. I hated lying to Bente. But I had to protect our secret, the fae, and the humans. "I've already reached out. We have support coming in on the other side and the Meteorological Institute says rain is on the way."

Bente cleared her throat. "Good. And you're following protocol with the local firefighters?"

"Yes, ma'am."

Both the human plan and the fae plan. The only hitch was the Fire Fae King and his Head Guard roaming around that I couldn't account for.

"Good. Call me if you need anything or if the weather report shifts."

"Will do." I hung up before the conversation could take a turn.

Leaving the two women to their explosives, I rolled up the sleeves on my police jacket and set to work clearing the forest behind the trench. Branches creaked, needles and pine cones fell to the ground, and roots snapped like pops of ancient gunpowder. Ripping apart the woodland cut at something inside me. These trees had stood for hundreds of years and could've weathered hundreds more. They were home to fae and countless creatures.

Rabbits, deer, and birds fled past me, seeking shelter. A massive elk with a scorch mark on its hindquarters rumbled down the hill toward the water, trampling over the plants in its path.

These innocent flora and fauna were the true victims here. But ripping the roots up and clearing the landscape would prevent an equal fate for the rest of the forest behind us.

With sweat clinging to my brow and heat battering me, I continued my work, grateful for the efforts of Ylva's cadre doing what they could. Heidi stepped in too, desperately attempting to heal some of the plants I'd ripped up.

"Any luck?" I asked her over my shoulder.

Her hands waved over a scorched sapling. "Yes, but it will take time."

A whistling noise that didn't belong drew my attention back to the fire line, and a shiver ran down my sweat-soaked spine. A figure emerged from the inferno, long hair blending with the oranges and reds, broad shoulders draped in leather, palms filled with flames.

Herja.

Lennie was right calling her an omen of death and destruction. The woman was as tall as Halvar and somehow twice as menacing. Those black eyes darker than the clothes she wore and the coals burning at her feet. Herja was a powerful Head Guard who protected the island of Iceland like a hawk protecting its nest. Rumor had it, even without the royal magic, she was almost as powerful as Veigar's daughters. It was little wonder Veigar had appointed her as his General.

I rolled my shoulders and stepped closer, careful of the imposing heat that could incinerate me in seconds.

"I don't think we've had the fortune of an introduction," I yelled across the expanse as she stopped on the other side of the road trench. "My name is Espen Solbakke Martin."

"Oh, I know who you are, little destroyer," she said, her voice a rumbling bellow. "The legend of you and your power has crossed the North Atlantic."

"Then you know what'll happen to you if you don't turn back and leave Skolvik."

Her mouth lifted into a lopsided grin. "We look forward to the challenge, Forest Fae."

We?

Shit.

I took a quick step back. "Heidi, grab your special project!"

A second later more figures appeared among the flames. This time, humanoid creatures made of fire. Four in total.

"What the hell are those?" Ylva yelled over the roaring wildfire.

I lifted my hands and settled into a defensive position, ready to unleash my power.

Words didn't exist for the creatures that prowled on the other side of the wide ditch between us and the flames. Their entire body, from head to toe, was formed of fire. Where a face should be was orange, white, and yellow—no eyes, mouth, or any other discernible features. They were fire incarnate, walking from tree to tree and setting them ablaze.

I shot my power toward the closest one, churning the soil beneath its feet. As Herja scrambled away, her minion stumbled into the ravine. If I buried it, would it keep living? Flames could smolder under the ground if they had the material to continue burning, and the soil here beneath the road didn't have as much life or roots calling it home. The being clawed against the edge of the trench, and I didn't wait another second, sending a mound of dirt and asphalt down upon it.

One down. Three remaining.

My focus turned back to where Ylva launched a bomb at Herja and one of the creatures. The Fire Fae neatly dodged the blow and explosion, but the humanoid wasn't quick enough. A green plume engulfed it.

"Cover your mouth!" Ylva yelled, and I shoved my face into the crook of my elbow and held my breath. The updraft from the fire swept the ominous cloud over and up, stinging the corner of my eyes.

A split second later it dissipated, and I inhaled a smoky breath. "Any chance that was poison?"

"Of course." Heidi handed Ylva another bomb, then scuttled back toward the fire truck.

The impacted creature disappeared among the flames at Herja's back. She twisted her fingers, and her lips curved into a gut-wrenching grin. A fire-being stepped out of the flames like a phoenix reborn and another materialized at its side. Hair rose off my arms and my scalp prickled as if it were being poked by hundreds of tiny needles.

"She's been toying with us," Ylva yelled.

I grit my teeth together and nodded in agreement. While I now led a simpler life, I was far from useless, and Queen Ragnhild had hired me for a reason. I had the skill and experience to lead an army, and the power to end a war. Herja, a warrior in her own right, was tempting us to play our hands, lose our ammunition in a game of folly, but I had every intention of outlasting this game of cat and mouse.

"Hold fire!" I roared. "Regroup!"

The nearby cadre ran to join us, and Ylva backed up with me, assembling at the firetruck, its flashing lights still on, blue beams bouncing against the smoky air.

Herja launched a ball of flame over our heads and my gut lurched. Time was up and I hadn't even been able to hand out new orders.

Another fireball arced over our heads and crashed against brush further down the road, igniting the kindling and sending a wave of heat against our backs.

Shit.

We didn't have time to spare.

"All-out assault on them all, especially Herja." I looked between the group and my commander, Heidi watching on with the blank stoicism of a nurse in an emergency room. "Arrows to the head. Bombs. Throw everything at them."

"Yes, sir."

I cast a quick glance back at our enemy and squinted through the smoke. Herja watched her creatures closely but didn't let them stray too far. As if they were only allowed as far as her arms could reach.

Realization dawned, and I let out a panted breath.

"They're tied to her. She has to maintain control to keep them sustained." Which meant we had to kill her to kill them.

My gaze met Ylva's, and she nodded in understanding.

"All-out assault," I repeated. "Attack her."

"Yes, sir!"

The group dispersed, Heidi wisely staying back behind the truck and out of harm's way.

Our soldiers called forward their powers, crafting sharp bows and arrows, notching them and letting them sail. Herja dodged one and launched a wisp of fire at the other, letting it crumble to ash in the air.

I launched another volley of destruction, aiming at her feet.

She tumbled and scrambled back toward the flame. Regrouping with her own team.

Pulling on another string of destructive power, I threw even more soil and debris at them.

"Everything we've got," Ylva yelled, clutching something to her chest.

I turned my face to her.

She gave me a single nod.

The next second she was running. She launched into the air over the trench and threw the bomb in her hand at Herja.

The green explosion clouded everything. The biggest bomb we'd thrown yet.

And Ylva flew straight into it.

My heart stopped, and I stilled.

As the cloud of poison cleared, a figure with blonde braids and a wild grin appeared... alone.

She did it!

I raised my hands above my head in victory. "You brilliant woman! I knew I chose well when I picked you as my second!"

She stuck out her tongue and winked.

Flames moved behind her, and a smoky breath lodged in my throat.

Herja lunged from the inferno and wrapped her arms around Ylva's torso and throat. My friend's eyes blew wide, a silent scream ripping from her lips as Herja squeezed. The next second Ylva went up in flames.

ESPEN

"NO!"

I crashed to my knees. Smoke coated my lungs and the heat from the fire stung my eyes as I stared at the pile of ash that had been my best friend two seconds ago.

Herja's lips split into a crazed grin, and she laughed. The nauseating sound echoed through the crackling flames and that black swirling mass of power in my chest unraveled and broke free.

I was death.

I was pain.

I was destruction.

Rising to my feet, I pulled tree after fiery tree from the ground and launched them toward the Fire Fae. She ducked and dodged but wasn't fast enough to escape scrapes from branches before they too turned to ash.

The soldiers on my side all retreated.

The flame creatures vanished.

It was just me and Herja.

Locked in a battle of death.

I roared and raised the road before me into the air, launching the ribbon of asphalt at her. She scurried out of the way, but not without getting hit by small chunks of tarmac. A volley of fire balls responded, and I sidestepped them.

That destructive, invisible power flowed from me, widening the trench, tearing apart the soil, and throwing trees out of its way. The opening ground chased her like a wolf hunting its prey, snapping at her heels. Another snap and she tripped. Crashing to her knees, she scrambled for purchase, before falling into the pit with a scream. A whip of fire lashed against the tall sides of the ravine.

But it was useless.

Useless against me.

Useless against the destruction that I'd become.

I slid down the muddy side and faced her.

"How dare you take my friend," I growled. "*How dare you threaten my home!*"

As she tried to regain her footing, blood seeped from her split lip and her eyes lacked any remorse. "Veigar always gets his way in the end."

"Not this time."

Power erupted from me like a shaken bottle exploding after being capped for over twenty years. Green, sinewy power crept from my hands and wrapped around her like a vice, twisting and contorting, pulling at her very being and soul.

Death filled my thoughts, my vision, the commands for my magic.

She didn't stand a chance. One second she was standing, the next she was in the dry dirt at my feet, writhing in pain.

"You're undeserving of final words." I twisted my hands, ordering my magic to kill, to destroy.

Herja jerked then curled in on herself like the worm she was. Her eyes widened, lids extending so far it looked like they were pushing the balls out of their sockets. With a cough and shudder, the skin around her throat tightened, and she took her final breath. A second later her body bloated, her skin pushing outward before it started to dry and disintegrate. The pungent odor of decay mixed with the smoke in the air, but I ignored it and continued pushing my darkest magic into her. Her body blended with the bloody dirt beneath her, and a moment later all that remained was her skeleton.

The sight drew some sick satisfaction through my chest as my heartbeats collided with each other. She deserved worse. Deserved torture. But my patience had blown away with the ashes of my best friend.

Ylva was gone.

Her smile was gone. Her laugh was gone.

She would never command an army again.

Would never tease me.

Would never smile and laugh and make crude jokes with my wife, the two of them forming a blossoming bond of friendship and camaraderie.

The one who tried to beat me at everything like a younger sibling. The friend who had been my valued confidant for centuries. The one person I trusted as my second-in-command. She made me laugh, called me out on my teasing, and bolstered my confidence whenever I worried about using too much power.

She's gone.

With an agonized roar, I pulled on another dreg of my power and ripped Herja's bones apart. They flew in all directions. Some into the flames she'd been born of, some into the woods she'd yet to harm. Let her rotten form feed and rejuvenate the forest she'd destroyed.

As my ears rang, a single tear ran down my cheek. My chest rose and fell rapidly, my panted breaths dancing with particles of ash.

The demon was destroyed, but the wildfire still raged.

I fell to my knees again and tilted my head back. Smoke blanketed the sky, turning the sun red, while flames continued eating away at the remaining tree tops. There was too much kindling around. Too much food for the fire. We needed more water.

We needed a Fjord Fae. I needed my partner. I needed Øyvin.

146

LENNIE

Racing through town and up the hillside toward the main fjell entrance, my hair whipped around my face as my legs propelled me forward. Gripping the first aid kit containing the shards, I didn't dare look over my shoulder at the fire crackling on the southern side of the fjord. Didn't dare stop in case Veigar decided I was an easy target. Didn't dare think about the threats looming over my home.

We had to... No, we *would* survive this.

At least the two of us that remained.

My stomach twisted at the thought of Øyvin and the shocked look that crossed his face milliseconds before he was sucked into the fjord and taken from me.

Shaking off those encroaching thoughts, I plowed through the rocky mirage concealing the mountain's main entrance and raced through the rugged hallways. Down and down and down I went. Deeper and deeper within the tunnels I now recognized and called home. Light sconces lit my path every six feet, the magic within them flickering as I passed. The rocky walls bounced and absorbed light in its cracks and bumps and uneven facades. The temperature remained steady, neither hot nor cold, and kept me comfortable, even in a T-shirt and jeans. It was as if the mountain could self-regulate its body temperature and protect its denizens from inclement weather or hazards.

A stone door ground shut somewhere behind me, pebbles skittered at my feet, and an image of a large black wolf flooded my mind.

Vicious teeth.

Gut-wrenching howls.

Pain searing through my leg.

Power wrapping around Wilhelm and killing him on the spot.

My breath caught in my throat and my steps faltered. Coming to a stop, I leaned against the cool rock wall and clenched my eyes shut, hoping to rid myself of the unwanted flashback.

I did the right thing. I did the right thing. I did the right thing. If I hadn't killed Wilhelm, he would've killed Aurora and then turned back to finish me off. Yet, killing him still didn't fully sit right with me. I'd never wanted to be a killer. Never thought I was capable of it.

My lungs constricted. *I did the right thing.* "I'm safe. Wilhelm is gone," I muttered and slowly reopened my eyes.

Wilhelm had been on a warpath, intent on hurting me to hurt Espen. Members of his pack had injured and killed Fjell Fae. The former Alpha had been out for blood, and I'd stopped more of it from flowing. I needed to keep reminding myself that.

I took a deep breath and tapped the toe of my shoe against the hard ground.

No, it would never feel right, but I'd protected my home, and I was going to do so now too.

With another long inhale, I straightened and hurried through the tunnels, aiming for the Royal Tombs.

Nobody look too close.

Scuttling past a confused fae, I gave them a broad grin as if nothing were amiss.

Don't look at me.

I bolted around another corner before slowing to a walk.

Nothing to see here.

My grip on the first aid kit tightened as I passed a couple groups of soldiers. Several bowed their heads or muttered a polite "ma'am" as they went by. I returned the nods, feeling a little out of place and unworthy of the deference, especially considering the cargo I carried and my intentions with it.

Hoping none of them noticed my sense of urgency, I kept moving until I reached the miraged entrance to the royal tombs. The rocky facade was a strong illusion, and anyone would walk right past it if two uniformed soldiers with sharp looking swords weren't guarding the entrance.

They stood with their feet braced, hands resting on the weapons hitched to their belts.

I slowed to a stop and swallowed hard, pulling forward as much courage as I could muster considering the anxiety riding my every move, hoping my crazy scheme wasn't about to fall apart. With a nod and a tiny salute, I said, "At ease, soldiers."

The two men furrowed their brows, but bowed their heads and twisted out of the way, granting me passage into the tomb.

Holy shit, that worked! Even without a badge or a hat, they knew who I was.

Sucking in a tiny breath, I strode past them with purpose, like I was meant to be there. I didn't dare breathe again until I was three rows deep into the lifeless chamber, the mirage hiding me from view.

Stillness wrapped around me, the smell of dust and granite lingering in the air. Heart racing, I rushed past the prone statues staring blankly upward, and headed for the back wall.

My magic pulsed as I closed in on the dormant mural. The jagged mountain loomed beside two large trees with flaming leaves, swirls of water curved at its base, and a wolf bayed in the bottom corner. A starry sky glittered above the entire scene.

"Let's do this," I muttered and pressed my hand to the middle of the stone mountain.

Open. Silvery light spread through the carving, rousing it from its slumber. The light filled every nook, crack, and crevice, until the whole thing cast a glow over me and the kings and queens of centuries past.

"Okay, I'll concede." I huffed, staring at the illuminated stone. "Magic is cool."

I pushed my shoulder against the mountain and the rocky door groaned open, granting me entry into the Temple.

Glossy sky-blue walls and plinth stared back at me as I stepped inside. "Yeah, this will never get old."

Using my butt and my fists, I leaned against the door and pressed it shut—just in case someone who wasn't allowed to be in here decided to show up.

I set down the first aid kit and retrieved the stones, then moved over to the center of the room where the pedestal sat waiting to be repaired. Setting one shard on the floor, I focused on attaching one at a time.

Distinct jagged lines and grooves graced three corners of the pedestal. I brushed my fingers across the southeast corner, the cool stone and sharp edges grazed my fingertips. It reminded me of the harsh peaks that dotted Norway.

I adjusted the shard in my hand, trying to get it to fit like a puzzle piece—turning and re-angling. When it didn't work on the first corner, I moved to the southwest. The shard slid into place like the final piece of a puzzle. All that was missing was that perfect click that sounded like my camera's shutter button.

"I wonder..." Could my magic fasten this back on? Would it be the royal magic or the Fjell magic at work?

Fasten. Pressing my magic into the corner, I willed the piece back into its spot, asking it to reattach to its home. A grating noise was followed by a drawn out click, and I opened my eyes. The shard had reconnected itself to the pedestal, sharp lines fused back together. The blue chamber light glowed brighter, washing across my face as I stared around in awe.

"One down. One to go. Call me Bob the Builder because I'm fixing this thing!"

Grabbing the second shard, I ran my hand across its jagged edge, feeling the bumps and ridges. I tried it against the left most corner before shifting back to the front right. It slotted in perfectly on the second try. A match.

"Your turn. *Fasten*."

I pushed my magic outward once more and fused the second shard to the plinth. It shifted into place, a faint silvery line forming between the addition and its base. Lights in the wall swirled and my hair lifted on a phantom breeze. I took a step back. "Woah, there."

My heart hammered against my ribs, my lungs tightened, and my eyes widened.

"What's happening?"

No one replied, but the wind shifted direction, coming at me from the left.

I turned toward it, looking for a gap in the cave, but found none. I was completely sealed in. No other beings, no other objects. It was just me, the pedestal, and the empty first aid kit, abandoned on the floor.

I scanned the plinth-like structure like it might jump and attack me. Halvar hadn't mentioned exactly how it worked, other than to put one's hand on it. And the last time I had, I'd been on the world's most one-sided date, with only twinkly blue lights to laugh at my jokes. What would happen with the shards returned to their spots? Would it zap me harder when I touched it? Would it kill me?

I shook my head. I'd come this far. There was only one thing left to do.

"Fuck it."

I stepped up to the pedestal, took a deep breath, and slapped my hand onto the top.

Lightning shot through my right hand and up my arm, ripping a scream from my lips. The magical lights in the cave walls swirled wildly, flashing on and off, as the errant wind kicked up and spun my hair around me. It was like being caught in a mini tornado I couldn't escape.

Warm voices echoed against my mind in a language I couldn't understand. *Striith. Steinabarn. Timi.* It was all a jumbled mess. But someone, or many somethings, tried to talk to me.

"We need help," I ground out, my teeth clenched so tight they might crumble to dust. "We need your help... Please."

A welcome yet stern intent settled through my bones, like they agreed or accepted something.

The pain subsided for a split second, and I sucked in a breath. My lungs heaved, my body spent and raw—

Power shot through my arm again and curved my back. Knees buckling, I pressed my free hand to the edge of the pedestal only to be assaulted by more power and pain. My vision blurred, my legs trembled, sending me crashing to the floor, and then everything went black.

147

LENNIE

Death had finally found me. Pain thundered through my mind, and I groaned, pulling my burning hands to my chest as I slumped against the pedestal. Blue light glowed against my clenched eyelids. Who knew you carried your dying agony with you to hell? Maybe that was my penance for all the bullshit and stunts I'd pulled in my time.

Something heavy, yet soft, brushed against the floor behind me, and I stilled.

"Satan, is that you?"

A soft laugh trilled past.

Satan was a woman? No... Wait... That laugh...

Air caught in my throat as I blinked open my eyes. That laugh wasn't possible. Couldn't be here. Had died in a throne room almost a year ago.

I stared ahead at the wall of the Temple cave, too scared to move a muscle.

"I'm definitely dead."

"Far from it, Lennie Martin."

"What the fuck?"

Forget the fear. I needed to see this.

I shifted onto my hands and knees, peering around the pedestal. My eyes widened and I swayed on the spot as I took in a ghost-like Queen Freija. Her thick, navy velvet dress brushed against the floor, her hands clasped in front of her like a respectable monarch, and her copper hair was in a perfect up-do. If it weren't for the hazy appearance and the light glow around her entire body, plus the fact that I'd watched her die, I'd have thought she was in hell with me.

"I imagine it would take something quite miraculous to kill you, dear."

"Is that a joke about my unending run-ins with bad luck? Or are you the ghost of Christmas past? Because if it's the latter, I'd like to go back to Christmas last year. Heidi gave me this ah-mazing tea and my partners rocked my world... seven and a half times. Though, I never told them about the half—it would be a whole thing about who started it and who would be the one to finish me off."

Freija stifled a laugh with her delicate fingers, a faint blush brushing across the tops of her cheeks.

"You shouldn't be able to blush if you're a ghost, right?"

"Rise and let us talk."

I pushed to my feet, swaying like a drunkard as I did. "Am I dead and in hell? Or was there something in the Temple's air that has me tripping out?"

She shook her head.

My eyes bulged once more. "Holy shit, you're actually—" For the first time in my life, words failed me.

She was here. An ancestor. I was communing with an ancestor. In the Temple of the Fae. *Fuck me sideways, I did it!*

I gave myself a high-five and bumped into the pedestal. The thing didn't move, but I took two steps away, eying it warily as if it might zap me into unconsciousness again.

Straightening and pulling on my confidence, I continued my crazy plan. "We need the ancestors' help."

"We heard." She tilted her head to one side. "And saw."

"What do you mean, 'saw?'"

She waved her hand through the air. "We keep an eye on things from our side."

"Like *beyond the veil*?" I said, giving her a haunted edition of my jazz hands. She nodded.

"Are there others watching over?"

"They all do."

I crossed my arms over my chest. "And they sent you as a messenger?"

"We agreed that I might be the best person to converse with you, seeing as we had a prior acquaintance, and my magic now resides in you."

"Partially." I raised a single finger. "You gave some to your baby daddy too."

She inclined her head briefly, but not fast enough for me to miss yet another flush of pink dancing across her cheeks.

"Anyway," I started, not interested in discussing her love life. "You're here to give me a boost? Level me up? Grant me some ancient power that could knock out Veigar with a single flick of the wand—I mean wrist?"

"No need."

"What? Have you not seen what's happening outside? Did my fusing those two shards to the pedestal do nothing?"

She gave me a calm and diplomatic look. "Adding those shards helped you reach us, and can be of benefit if needed."

"Then charge me up, because the need has arisen."

"You have everything you need." She pointed to my chest. "In there."

I snorted. "I mean, Espen will be the first to tell you that my left boob is amazing, but—"

The Queen rolled her eyes, a gentle smile tugging at her lips. "Your heart."

"Oh, okay." I nodded like that totally made sense. *It didn't.* "Care to further explain? There's a history in this town of people and fae not giving me all the details and lessons I need. I think it's time we rectify that."

Another soft laugh trilled from her, and she started pacing, her long skirts brushing against the stone floor. "Last year I requested more power from the ancestors. I feared that forces were out to undermine my reign and harm my mountain. Little did I know that said forces had corrupted members of my own household."

Nora. *Fuck that bitch.*

"The ancestors granted my request, but it was too late." She let out a breathy sigh. "However, that power appears to now reside in you and Halvar... Well, mostly you, it would seem."

"So, you knew shit was hitting the fan?"

"I'd use alternate terms, but yes. The mountain's magic was unstable, the fissure down the fjord expanded at a far more exponential rate than years past, and I grew weaker. I needed power that would hold my mountain together and shield my people from harm."

"You rebelled, though. You illegally transferred that magic to Halvar and, by extension, to me."

A sly yet playful look crossed her features, reminding me that she had been monarch for a very long time and held centuries of wisdom too. She crossed her arms and straightened, those, now ghostly, gray-and-brown eyes staring at me with the force of a sledgehammer. "I did what I needed to do to protect the Fjell Fae."

"Arming a god-like Head Guard and crafting a demi-fae to be his sidekick," I mumbled.

"The latter was certainly a surprise, but one I'm grateful for."

"Really?"

She nodded. "You have a great capacity for love and care. Protective instincts that run deep. I saw those traits during our meetings and have seen them flourish since joining the ancestors."

My chest warmed and I shuffled on the spot, avoiding her gaze. No one aside from my parents and my guys had ever been so bluntly honest with what they saw in me. What I valued so much. Most people saw a tendency for chaos or heard my loud mouth first. But Freija hadn't. She'd seen past that to the core of who I was as a person.

I took a deep breath and looked back up. She smiled, radiating warmth and something I could only classify as regal-ness.

"Thank you," I said. "So, you didn't turn me into a demi-fae on purpose?"

Not a hair moved out of place as she shook her head. "I don't know how it happened, but I have a theory."

"And that is?"

That sly look returned, like she wanted to withhold the information and watch me squirm. "Something you yourself have found in Skolvik."

I refrained from rolling my eyes. Of course, talking to an ancestor would include cryptic messages and lore. That's how it always went in movies. Apparently, the Nordic Fae were no different. But what exactly did the two events have in common? Something I'd found and something she'd given—

"Love." I sighed. "It's love, isn't it?"

"There is no greater power than that."

I had to agree with her there. Although the killing magic I'd used on Wilhelm earlier this year had packed a punch too. Thinking of enemies, we needed to get back to business. I needed to know how exactly we could overpower Veigar before he and his minions decimated my new home.

"Well, I'm sorry for what happened to you and promise to take care of your magic."

She tilted her head in thanks.

"Now, how exactly are we supposed to use this extra power"—I waved at my tits and sternum—"to take out Veigar?"

"Halvar will know. But I'd wager a cunning plan to isolate him, then using the stunning and killing powers, will be your best recourse."

"Oh, I'm familiar with that power."

"Just remember, Veigar has that ability too."

Of course he did.

I pushed my hair away from my face and let out a shuddered breath. Nothing was ever simple. "Any advice on how to deal with Veigar? Any insider monarchy-information?"

She swayed on the spot, dress brushing the floor, and raised her chin. "Men with great power and confidence will brave this world alone. A man with no power and only confidence will surround himself with followers to boost his appearance of power."

"Sage advice. Tracks with Balder." But which one was Veigar?

Freija's image flickered, and she peered over her shoulder before turning back to me. "I cannot help you further. But whatever you do, however you do it, protect the mountain and your people," she said, her voice trembling.

"I have a lot of people in my life I want to protect."

She smiled like she knew and understood that feeling. The need to care for, nurture, and protect that which you cherished most. It was something that had always been part of me, part of who I was. But my community of loved ones had grown to encompass a lot more than my family in Ohio. It now consisted of two—one—handsome fae that would put his life on the line for me, and a village that laughed at my antics while quietly welcoming me into its fold. Not to mention an entire mountain that looked to me as one of their leaders.

"I promise to protect your mountain too," I said.

"Thank you."

She flickered once more, and the hem of her dress faded. We were running out of time. Whichever ancestor controlled this magic allowing her to talk to me, was about to hang up. I wished I knew more about the ancestors.

"You said they... you... watch over us?"

"Mm-hmm."

Hope sprung to life in my chest, and I clenched my hands into fists.

"Did you see if Øyvin was killed? Can you see beneath the water?"

Freija peered over her shoulder as if someone was talking to her from the great beyond. Her gaze turned back to me, her eyes crinkling slightly at the corners. "I cannot say."

My heart beat an unusual rhythm, hope and despair competing against one another. "Please? You must know something?"

Her lips pursed into a firm line, and my stomach sank.

The sad heartbeat won.

Freija flickered a third time, and she glanced over her shoulder before looking back to me, her eyes widening. The air around us took on an urgency as if the line between me and the ancestors was thinning. Time was up.

"One final question before you go?" I asked.

While I had her here, there was one question that had been nagging me for almost a year. And if anyone knew the answer, it would be Freija.

"Proceed."

"How old is Halvar?"

She laughed and a knowing smirk swept across her face. "Now that is something I dare you to ask him some day."

"You want me to die, don't you?"

She chuckled again. "No. But I'd find it entertaining to watch you ask him."

Like mother, like daughter. Aurora had also enjoyed watching me struggle.

"Is he a Norse God?"

"Ask him that too. Goodbye and good luck, Lennie."

She waved her hand and pain washed through me once more. I crumpled to the ground as the world around me turned black.

148
LENNIE

Something hard and cool pressed against my cheek and my bones ached as if they'd been training with Halvar for a week straight without pause. I stretched one leg out from where I was curled up in a ball. A fiery spasm shot through my calf and a whimper slipped past my lips.

"What. Have. You. Done?" Halvar's voice ground out, and I blinked open my eyes. The beast of the mountain leaned against the closed temple door, his arms crossed, eyebrows furrowing so hard they might jump off his face in fear.

Shit.

"Erm... What brings you here on this fine day, good sir?"

The muscles around his left eye twitched as a grimace settled across his features.

I winced. "Please don't kill me. I come in peace."

"Get up."

I rose to my feet and groaned as my body shouted at me. Whatever magic lived in the pedestal had left my limbs feeling flayed. Taking a deep breath, I straightened and faced Halvar head-on with my hands on my hips. "How did you find out I was in here?"

"The guards informed me."

Ah, should have guessed they would report back to him of any visitors to the royal tomb.

"You never said I was banned from entering."

Halvar clenched his jaw. "No. I didn't. You are allowed to be in here. Now, tell me what you did."

"I took initiative. Returned some pieces of stone that belonged there and asked the ancestors for some assistance." I pointed over my shoulder to the pedestal that was now only missing one corner instead of three.

A single silvery brow rose toward Halvar's hairline and the tension in his muscles dissipated as he inspected the temple's centerpiece from where he stood. "I see you've been busy getting help from your partners."

"I did. But Øyvin is missing after the... erm... theft of the Fjord Fae shard."

A line formed between Halvar's eyebrows, and he peered around the room. "Dead?"

My throat tightened. "The ancestor wouldn't tell me what happened to him, but he was sucked into the fjord, and we haven't seen him since."

"So, the ancestors responded this time?"

"She did."

His gaze cut back to me, his eyes betraying a hint of emotion.

"Queen Freija confirmed your suspicions. That I have more royal magic than you." *Don't let it go to your head. Don't let it go to your head. Don't let it go to your head.* "Said she'd visited the ancestors and asked for help last year. They granted her some extra power to deal with the stuff that was happening at the time."

A low rumble sounded from Halvar's chest.

"Did she offer any help?" he asked, avoiding the cloud of emotion choking the room and focusing instead on the battle at our doorstep.

"She recommended a *cunning plan* and the lethal stunning magic I used on Wilhelm. But warned of Veigar's ability to use that power too."

Halvar nodded, his features pinching as his mind turned to thought.

"I'm going to leave the cunning planning part to you. My recent plans *have* worked, but not without an absolute shit storm of chaos."

"That, I can agree on."

I snorted. At least I was self-aware and honest about my modus operandi.

"Come." He stepped aside and motioned to the door. "Let us head to the main entrance. There is something you need to see."

Halvar pulled open the door. I grabbed the abandoned first aid kit, folded it up, and shoved the material into my back pocket before following him through the royal tomb and into the winding tunnels.

The big guy moved like a graceful lump of rock, striding swiftly through the hallways, his broad frame leading the way. We wound up and up until we reached the main entrance where two soldiers stood guard, both bowing their heads to us as we breached the exit point.

I stepped out of the mountain and an orange glow swept across my face. The descending sun had turned red, blocked by an ashy haze. My jaw dropped as I looked across the fjord and found the entire hillside ablaze.

"Oh my god."

Flames engulfed trees and jumped tens of feet into the air, black smoke flooding the sky.

I sucked in a smoky breath. My husband was somewhere in that. I longed to rush over there, to throw my arms around him and shield him from harm. But my rational brain knew better than to act on that. If I did, I'd put us all in danger and put his life even more at risk.

"He can handle it," Halvar said, his tone filled with certainty.

"I don't doubt it. But I'd be lying if I said I didn't want to stand beside him right now."

Halvar grumbled like he understood but wouldn't elaborate. He didn't need to. I knew his feelings toward Queen Freija were the same. He'd loved the woman and would do anything for her. Just like I would for my guys—guy.

My gaze shifted to the fjord and another wave of longing washed over me. *Please don't be dead.*

"How quickly can you call on the killing powers?" Halvar asked, mercifully drawing me from my simmering grief.

Death. I unleashed sparking and searing tendrils down my arms and opened my palms at my sides. Orbs of lightning crackled and popped, promising agony and a swift demise. I glanced up at Halvar. "You tell me."

Halvar let out a low hum of appreciation and turned his attention back to the wildfire. "Good. Very good."

"You're not worried about me being overly juiced up by Freija's magic?"

He peered at me out of the corner of his eye. "Do you intend on harming the mountain?"

"No."

"Then I have no fear."

"What *do* you fear?" I asked, hoping he wouldn't mind me asking.

Another low rumble rocked through the big guy's chest. He pointed to the village where a speck of salt-and-pepper hair in a blue suit sat on a bench looking out over the harbor. "That."

"You have any specific plans on how to handle *that*?"

He crossed his arms. "I do."

"Let's hear it then."

"Veigar's powers are near incalculable."

"But let me guess, you majored in Calculus and minored in Trigonometry?"

He looked at me like I'd spoken a different language then shook his head. "He can muster creatures of fire, shift the earth's crust, summon lava—"

"*Lava?*" There was me thinking huge balls of fire were our biggest threat from the Fire Fae King. But creatures? Lava?

"We must stay alert and spread our forces to protect the region," Halvar continued. "With our combined Fjell and Royal powers, we are entities he has never fought before. Something he cannot entirely account for in whatever plans he has."

"What plans do you think those are?"

He pinched his lips together. "Divide the most powerful."

I looked out across the fjord and valley again. Espen was dealing with the fire. Øyvin had been dragged beneath the water. The Fjell was without a monarch for the first time in what I'd heard was well over a thousand years. Halvar was right. Veigar had spread us out to pick us off, one by one.

The man in question rose from the bench at the end of the dock and sauntered back into the village, disappearing from sight.

"He will start his attack tomorrow," Halvar said, a solemn tone in his voice.

"How do you know?"

"A long time ago, when battles were fought more frequently, he would always send in Herja first. Like a calling card and a warning."

Anger swept through my veins. "What do we do?"

"You protect the village, Lennie. I'll protect the mountain."

149
LENNIE

I ambled down the mountainside, aiming for the place I now called home. Forest gave way to asphalt, and an eerie calm seeped along the quiet streets. In twenty-four hours, the town of Skolvik had gone from a beautiful and vibrant village filled with laughter and life to a ghost town. All thanks to one man and his need for power and standing among a community the humans didn't even know existed.

Turning off the main drag, I strolled down the side street lined with gray cobbles and passed Fisken. The sun had set, a faint glow still peeking above the horizon and the cooler air brushed across my cheeks.

I didn't trust for one second that Veigar wouldn't attack the town in the middle of the night. But dammit, I needed sleep. Talking with the ancestors had done a number on me and the weight of everything that had happened today bore down on me like a mountain. From Øyvin stealing the Fjord Fae shard and disappearing, to Espen and I driving to the stave church to retrieve the Forest Fae shard, and everything after and between.

It was too much for a single day.

And yet, here I was, on the precipice of a battle I felt unprepared for, against an opponent who could wield fire of all things. I dragged my palms across my face.

There was still work to do. There was still a village to watch over. But I couldn't do shit if I didn't lie down. I pushed myself onward, putting one foot in front of the other, and made my way home for a long night of likely restless sleep in an empty bed.

150

ØYVIN

No one was coming.

After over a century of service to the Fjord, not a single soldier, not a single member of my faction, rose from the depths to protect the village and the waters from an invader.

I swallowed the lump in my throat and gazed across the abandoned town, water dripping off my clothes onto the dock.

Stores were shuttered, plants wilted in their window boxes, and streets once rife with joy sat empty.

No one was coming.

I shook my head and straightened. I wanted to yell and scream and tear the fjord apart.

Beg for people to open their eyes and see what Veigar would do to us.

We needed to work with our allies for the freedom we desperately needed. We'd already experienced the losses that came with a power-hungry monarch—we did not need another hegemonic person to take his place.

Fuck. I'd hoped Reuven was different. I'd hoped he cared about the fjord and its well-being. But like so many others, he'd buckled and caved when the pressure mounted.

I wouldn't though. I refused. However much I wanted to dive into the fjord, swim for its furthest reaches and turn my back on everything—I wouldn't. If no others came, I'd stand by myself. I'd stand in the face of adversity. Challenges so insurmountable even a King had bowed to ease the impending blow.

No one was coming.

But I was here.

I'd sworn an oath to protect this fjord, and I intended to keep it. Reuven may have taken my title, but I'd never fall back on my word. Never stop protecting what I cared about.

And it wasn't just the Fjord anymore either. This was my heart's home. The place that brought a smile to her face, a teasing twinkle to her eyes, and made every day worth waking up for.

I took a deep breath and turned to face the village.

Smoke rose from all the forests around town, curling into the gray sky that hung over the scenery like an ominous wave ready to crash and destroy. White and red and blue painted homes sat in its path, bracing for their demise.

"So," a feral voice danced between buildings, echoing out to where I stood on the dock. Even the water beneath me stilled at the cutting tone. "Only one man wished to defy me?" Veigar stepped out from between two buildings and launched a ball of flame at my stomach—

I gasped for air and my eyes flew open. Gone was the barren town above the surface, only mottled gray walls stared back at me.

Chest heaving, I wiped my hand over my forehead, pushing back my limp and sweat-slicked hair.

It was a nightmare. Just a fucking nightmare.

I tilted my head back against the cold stone wall and took another deep breath, trying to stay in the present.

Water dripped to the polished floor somewhere deep within the hollowed caverns beneath the palace, lending an unwelcome percussion to my addled thoughts.

Hours, days. It must've been days since my capture.

No food, just water. Given at irregular intervals to keep me guessing about the time.

It was a good tactic. One I'd used myself when we'd interrogated prisoners with Balder after the battle twenty-one years ago.

But now, here I was, chained to the smooth stone walls of the palace dungeon. A prisoner myself.

Hopefully, stealing the Fjord Fae shard had been worth it. Worth whatever cruelty Reuven and Veigar planned to inflict on me for tampering with their plans. I knew, with every fiber of my being, Lennie and Espen would succeed with our own plans. They worked well together. They'd take care of each other.

Footsteps echoed down to my cell at the very end of the hallway—the darkest one we had, only a tiny sconce of magical light illuminating the desolate square space.

I straightened and moved my hands toward myself, tugging on the chains. The ice-cold metal manacles bit into my skin, cutting off my magic. The unnatural feeling of loss sat in the pit of my sternum felt like my powers had been ripped from my body.

The steps grew closer.

Black boots appeared first.

Navy pants.

Navy uniform jacket.

Cape with lavish silver embroidery.

Here we go again.

Reuven's face materialized from the darkness. His pale features and scar were so much more ominous in the dull light down here. He looked like one of the creatures from the humans' folktales that crept out of freshwater lakes and lured the innocent into their dens.

I sneered.

With a *snick,* he unlocked the iron bars and stepped through the magically enforced door—ripples of light magic and water magic wrapping around the metal beams. If anyone touched them, aside from the monarch, little would remain of their hands.

The door clanged shut behind him. He crossed his arms and tilted his head to one side. "So, Øyvin Håland. Ready to finally explain your actions?"

I stared at the King, my silence filling the space between us.

A smirk twisted Reuven's lips. "Really? Still no apologies for your betrayal? No remorse for what you've done to your people?"

My mouth remained shut, and I cast my gaze to his feet. Emotions I couldn't fully place swam through me on a torrent of anger and confusion. But I wouldn't let him see them.

"Your actions have put the safety of the Fjord Fae at risk."

I highly doubted that, considering *he* was the one who'd allied himself with Veigar. If anything, I'd given us a chance to survive whatever onslaught the Fire Fae King was about to launch at us.

"No?" Reuven said, his voice mocking and calculating. "Nothing?"

I turned away, staring blankly at my dreary confines.

"What if I told you I had your young American partner strapped to my throne and struggling for air?"

My anger ignited. I grit my teeth and faced him. "You'd already be dead if you laid a finger on her."

Reuven grinned like he'd won a game of chess.

"Do you have her?"

The snide grin didn't budge.

"Do you have her?" I growled again.

"Why did you steal the Fjord Fae shard?"

He had to be lying. Espen wouldn't let Lennie be captured... not again.

"Tell me why you thought stealing the Fjord Fae shard was a good idea?" Reuven crouched in front of me. "You defied your king. You defied your own kind. The people you swore to protect. All for what? Love?"

I grimaced. "You know nothing of love."

"I know everything there is to know about love and the sacrifices a man will make to protect it."

My chest rumbled, and I turned my head. I doubted that.

No one could possibly understand what I would do to protect Lennie. I'd sacrifice myself to make sure she lived the life she truly deserved. One that would bring about that unwavering smile of hers. A life where she could take all the photos she'd ever want to, make different types of coffee from the rarest of beans, and dance away to Christmas songs while making a mess of our home. I'd lived hundreds of years. She deserved just as many, if not more, for the troublesome joy she'd thrown into my life in the past year.

I shook my head, needing to quell the emotions ripping through me.

"Disagree with me all you like, Øyvin Håland." Reuven rose back up to his full height. "But the lengths I have gone to protect my own are near incalculable. I've stared into the flame and sworn an oath—"

"And fuck you for it!" I snapped.

Reuven stilled and his lips tilted up at one corner. "I swore an oath to Veigar that was also a *lie*."

Oxygen caught in my throat and my chest tightened. Had I heard that correctly or was I hallucinating after going without food? Or was this a lie? An attempt to get me to reveal our plans with the shard?

"Do you really think I'd stoop to the level of my father?" Reuven's brows furrowed as he squinted at me. "To madness, manipulation, and corruption?"

"I don't believe you," I ground out. I didn't believe in anything other than the love I felt for a woman above the surface who filled my days with smiles and challenges.

He sighed and readjusted his footing. "Let me rephrase then. I'm glad you stole the shard."

What? My shoulders slumped. I must have been delirious from the lack of food.

Reuven nodded like he could hear my thoughts. "You heard me."

This had to be a hallucination. "Explain."

Water dripped somewhere in the distance as Reuven strode back and forth in front of me, his hands clasped behind his back, his broad shoulders relaxed—a man at ease with his burdens. He stopped and faced me once more. "That stone must never get into Veigar's hands."

"Now I really am dreaming."

Reuven chuckled once and shook his head. "Do you really think I'd jeopardize the safety of the fjord? The last time those pieces of the Temple were all assembled, a Fjord Fae King took advantage and become more powerful than the other monarchs. Something we cannot allow Veigar to achieve. Not with his history."

"You're married to Salka," I said. "Isn't that an allegiance?"

"That alliance was forged between Veigar and my father. Not me. It was part of a plan they put into works decades ago in an attempt to rid our world of the female monarchs. A plan that Veigar was manipulating behind the scenes. A plan that my father fell for and foolishly died for."

Fuck. If that was true, Veigar had been playing a long game of chess with everyone, including Balder.

"Ever since I've returned," Reuven continued. "I've made one thing clear—that I would always protect the fjord and its residents."

"You've failed to show it."

Reuven reeled back and pursed his lips. "I've done what I needed to do to keep myself and my people safe."

My chest rumbled in disagreement.

"We may have different methods, Håland. But we're on the same side."

"Prove it."

"I am not an ally of my father-in-law."

"Does he know that?"

Reuven smiled. "Best we keep it that way until the most opportune moment to remove him."

"How does Salka feel about that?"

"Her relationship with her father has always been strained and tenuous. Didn't help when he arranged for her to marry me."

"Trouble in paradise?"

"Leave my marriage out of this, and I won't start asking questions about yours."

I grunted. Fair enough.

"Just know she is *not* allied with her father. Neither is her sister."

I raised my hands, the chains clinking against the stone. "Why should I believe you? You fired me, then dragged me down here and put me in chains."

"You *did* steal the shard. There had to be some kind of punishment to keep up appearances," he replied. "I can't have Veigar getting suspicious."

"I still don't believe you."

He sighed and crouched down, bringing us face to face again. His aquamarine eyes stared back at me, the scar that cleaved his right eyebrow and ended at his cheek shifting slightly. He reminded me of a weathered ship, worn rough around the edges but still afloat and capable of destroying others. Resting his elbows on his knees, he asked, "Did you ever wonder *who* was setting fire to security cameras around the village?"

"Veigar."

Reuven shook his head. "Salka."

I flinched. None of what he was saying made sense. "Why would she burn them? What stake does she have in this?"

"Veigar's orders."

I knew it. "So, you *are* aligned with him."

"No." He rose back to his full height, his cape fluttering around his waist. "We're pretending to be aligned with him until an opportunity to kill him presents itself. Someone has to stop him, and I'm in the best position to do so."

He had a point. If anyone could potentially undermine Veigar, it was the heir who'd been living under his own roof... biding his time. Fuck, he may have not been Balder, but Reuven was just as cunning as his father, if not more so. A man with the entire chessboard in front of him and ten moves ahead of his enemies. I tilted my chin up at him. "Explain."

"You've never been one for patience, have you?" Reuven chuckled.

I shrugged.

"Veigar is an intelligent and unstoppable force. One that anyone in their right mind should be wary of. However, since he lost his wife, he hasn't been the same."

"Depression?" I asked. If anything ever happened to Lennie, I knew I'd sink into absolute despair.

"Madness and delusion. It certainly started out as grief, but after using the Fire Fae shard and communing with the ancestors, he returned to his Small Council one evening and informed us that the ancestors had told him he was meant to return the shards to the Temple and lead all the fae."

Fuck.

"How long ago was that meeting?" I asked.

"Roughly twenty years."

I hung my head. That was just after Queen Ragnhild had been killed by Balder's forces. Veigar had been biding his time for decades, lying in wait until the board was in his favor. Taking the time to plan out his attack and maneuver everyone into position before stepping foot in town. We were fucked, but at least we had one thing helping us. One thing that I had to believe based on the evidence presented to me. We secretly had Reuven.

He pulled a thick metal key from his pocket and shifted closer. "Can I trust you to follow my orders moving forward?"

"Do you have my partner chained to your throne?"

He shook his head.

"Will you do everything you can to protect the fjord and its residents, including the humans?" I asked.

"I swear to you: I will."

"Swear it on your crown."

He swallowed and nodded. "I swear that I will relinquish my crown should I ever fail to protect the fjord and its denizens, both fae and human."

That would suffice.

I raised my hands, metal scraping against stone. "And you have my promise to stand by your side... if you give me back my job."

He smiled. "The position has always been yours."

"Then why did you fire me?"

"Veigar's orders," Reuven replied and shoved the key into my left restraint. "He had a plan for each of the Head Guards. Destabilize internal infrastructure."

"A scary prospect."

"Indeed," he said. "And one that's working. Herja has already set the southern hillside ablaze occupying Espen, and I have it on good authority that Veigar's already attempting to unsettle parts of the mountain."

That was two head guards, plus me, preoccupied and out of the way. But, there was one person that hadn't been accounted for in that calculation: Lennie. That troublesome piece of my heart that lived outside of my body would wreak havoc if something came between her and what she loved. If Veigar crossed her path, then her vocal gymnastics would be the least of his worries, especially since she'd been personally trained by Halvar.

My chains fell and clattered on the floor. I pressed myself onto my feet and rose slowly. My muscles screamed from lack of use, making me sway.

"And Veigar doesn't suspect anything?" I asked, resting my back against the frigid and damp wall.

"Not that I'm aware of. But that's about to change."

My gaze snapped to his. "How?"

His lips curved into a wicked smile. "Have you ever seen what Jörmungandr can do?"

151

LENNIE

The cabin wasn't an option to sleep in, not with the fire this close to town, so I slept at the boathouse, hoping the water wouldn't rise up, drag me into its murkiest depths, and drown me for taking what belonged to the fae of the fjord. Sleep found me in fleeting moments, but every creak and bump had my eyes flying open and sent my heart racing. When the sun finally crept over the mountainside, I clambered out of the lonely bed and texted Espen, Torsten, and Øyvin.

Espen was awake and alive. Watching over the diversions he and a team had created. His added, *I also have news to share when I see you in person,* had my stomach flip-flopping.

Lennie: Are you injured?

Espen: No, but we've sustained some casualties. Will talk in person when this is all over.

Fuck. My gut twisted in on itself, and I got the feeling today was only going to get worse.

Lennie: I'm sorry.

When he didn't reply, I checked in with Torsten. The mountain had suffered some cave-ins overnight and a guard had been killed near the main entrance during a skirmish with some Fire Fae.

Memories of ash mounds flooded my mind. Had the soldier been burned completely? Or had he sustained severe burns? Either way, the loss settled over my shoulders. Even though I didn't know the person's name, they were still one of us, one of mine, a member of my extended fae family.

I brushed aside the awful feeling of grief and sent one final text to Øyvin.

Lennie: Jeg elsker deg.

I didn't expect a reply, and my heart ached when none came.

With a sigh, I pulled on the thick wool pants of my uniform and slid the jacket over my T-shirt, fastening it at the base of my neck. It fit like it had been tailored to my body. Øyvin really had got my measurements right.

A lump settled in my throat at the thought, and I swallowed it down.

Grabbing the dark gray cape, I threw it over my shoulder and secured it with ease.

It may have been the end of summer, but the temperatures outside were cooling and... It felt right to wear the uniform. If I was going to die fighting for my new home today, I'd do so wearing its colors.

I hauled my butt downstairs, the creaky steps wishing me good morning as I descended. The living room sat empty, shadows creeping across the floorboards, trying to hide from the rays of light seeping through the curtains.

As I aimed for the coffee pot, a crack sounded from the hillside outside the boathouse, and I bolted out the door. Smoke drifted past on the breeze, casting a haze over the street in front of me.

I peered up at the hillside. Had another part of the valley fractured?

After pulling on my boots, grabbing my keys, and locking the front door, I ran across the street and fell to my knees in the brush-covered hill. Dried grass and twigs poked at the woven fibers of my uniform like kids begging for attention. I pressed my hands into the ground and pushed a thread of my magic into the soil, hoping my Fjell Fae powers could detect anything.

Warm power danced down my arm and into the ground. What returned was a calm sensation that washed over my skin as if the rock beneath the forest was reassuring me that everything was all right.

I let out a sigh of relief and retracted my hands into my lap.

My brows knit. "But if you're okay, where did the noise come from?"

Spinning and rising in one fluid motion, I turned and stared at the mountain across the fjord. Trees blanketed the slopes, peeks of gray slipped through the foliage, and the cliff where a tiny waterfall usually flew into the fjord lay dormant. Everything looked normal aside from the haze that hung in the valley.

Something flickered in the periphery of my gaze, and I whipped my head toward town.

A puff of smoke rose from the harbor.

"What the fuck is that?"

I clenched my fists and pressed my lips together. It had begun.

Throwing my hair into a ponytail, I ran for the village.

Having risen above the mountains, the red-tinged sun loomed over the smoke-filled valley, looking more like an omen of death than a contributor to life. My cape fluttered behind me, its woven strands catching the falling ash. Clumps of the gray stuff floated on top of the fjord, making the water look like a foamy coffee.

I slunk down main street, my senses on high alert, watching for any movement or signs of flame. That puff of smoke had come from somewhere, but here, in the middle of the village, the trail had blended with the rest of the haze in the air.

A Fire Fae soldier in a red uniform rounded the corner at the other end of the street with an orb of dancing flames in his palm. I stopped in my tracks, sucked in a breath, and coughed it out.

Shit.

His head whipped in my direction and he raised his arm, launching the ball of magic toward me. I tucked and rolled behind the store on my right, my shoulder and hip smarting from the asphalt's blow.

Scrambling to my feet, I leaned against the wooden wall. Was I the only one protecting the village? Halvar wouldn't do that to me, right? He'd send reinforcements.

Someone whistled in the street, and the eerie tune sent a tickle down my spine.

This was like something out of a horror movie. Hopefully I wasn't the ditsy blonde who got herself killed, but the idea that crossed my mind certainly wouldn't help. And yet, it was my best option.

I drew on my Fjell magic and crafted a sharp broadsword. The weight of the stone worked my muscles, perfect for causing injury.

Taking a deep breath, I yelled, "You don't have to do this. Peace is sexier!"

The whistling stopped.

I squatted and raised the sword with both hands, readying to swing.

A wave of heat brushed my right cheek, the one facing the street, and soft steps tapped against the road. *He was close.* And that warmth... That warmth was their calling card. It happened any time I was close to one of them. How hadn't I noticed that sooner?

I braced and flame licked around the corner, singing the building and drainpipe. I took two steps back, narrowly avoiding losing my eyebrows. The Fire Fae soldier stepped past the building, and I charged at him.

He fashioned a flaming sword, and our blades clashed above our heads.

I peered up. "How the fuck is that hard?"

He sneered and retracted. I pushed forward.

We clashed again and again as I pressed him back onto the main drag.

Sweat slid down my forehead and my breaths sawed in and out of my lungs. I readjusted my grip and parried another strike. A clattering noise sounded to my right, but I kept my focus on the man in front—

An arrow shot through his neck and caught fire. The soldier's eyes rolled, and he dropped to his knees. I swung my sword across his sternum and pulled when I felt resistance. The blade carved across his chest and blood oozed from the gaping wound. His body flopped to the ground.

I tilted my head to the sky and swallowed down bile. "That's gross."

The act of killing didn't sit well with me, but I didn't have a choice. Looking back down, a puddle of maroon pooled around him. "Better you than me, buddy," I muttered and wiped my blade across his back.

Cautiously stepping over him, I turned my focus back down the street, no longer empty. Forest Fae and Fjell Fae brawled with several Fire Fae. Magic swirled around them, soldiers dodged blows, and the two local factions worked together—not quite harmoniously, but even with missteps and bumping into each other, they were trying.

With practiced efficiency, the five Fire Fae soldiers backed away and started regrouping. My brows furrowed as they nodded to one another, some form of silent agreement flowing between them.

Four Fjell and two Forest Fae stood between me and the Fire Fae, but didn't block the view as our enemies lifted their chins.

Arms of flame emerged from each of the men, like something was crawling out—

My eyes went wide, and I waved my free hand over my head. "Regroup! Back here! Now!"

The alliance of soldiers spun and ran for me, and we sprinted behind a store.

"Would somebody care to tell me what the fuck those are?" I panted as we lined up against the building, our backs pressed to the wood.

"Fire monsters," a Forest Fae soldier said. Her dark hair was in braids like Ylva's and the sight had me hoping my friend was okay wherever she was. I owed her a beer for losing a bet recently. "They're like lava creatures."

I peered back around the building. There were at least fifteen of the flame aliens, each one sans face or features. Their gangly limbs crackled and sparked, stray embers flying off them like fleas. "I can see that."

"Only the strongest Fire Fae soldiers can summon them," someone else said as I watched the terrors creep down the street. "Rumor has it more than half of their army dies in training because they're too weak to control the monsters."

"So Veigar's forces might be thinner than ours?" I asked, not tearing my eyes from the horrors. Øyvin had suspected as much, but this seemed to confirm it.

"Yes."

Well, that was news I could've done with sooner. And yet, that wouldn't make much difference right now. There were twenty of them, and only seven of us.

"Anyone got any suggestions on how to kill them without becoming a scorched marshmallow?" I asked and looked back at the group.

"Behead them," a Fjell Fae I recognized from the training room said.

I smirked. "Someone went to the School of Halvar."

A brief smile swept across the man's face, and a Forest Fae I'd never met before held up her hand. "This morning's report mentioned the fire beings. You need to take out the Fire Fae, not the creatures. Their lives are tied to their master."

I peered back around the corner. The monsters were maybe ten yards away, but my gaze caught on the line of Fire Fae in the middle of the skirmish. They were protected by a ring of their own making—the monsters acting as a first line of attack and defense. Their focus was locked on the beings' movements. "Oh my god, they *are* controlling them!"

The reports were right, the Fire Fae's monsters were extension of themselves. We needed to take out the Fae.

"Work together, slice through the fire aliens, and get to the Fae." I looked around at the fear-filled yet determined faces around me. "And don't die."

"Yes, ma'am," they replied in unison, and I flinched, peering one last time around the corner. Since when—

A ball of flame shot past my face, and I reared back. There was no time to think about becoming an authority figure. I had a town to protect.

We launched back into the road and attacked the unwelcome beings. I swung my sword at the fire creatures, aiming for their heads. The battle swelled around me, clashing noises and yips of pain filling my ears as I focused on staying alive.

Movement on the far side of the street caught my attention as several more Fjell soldiers appeared behind the Fire Fae, boxing them between us. I breathed a momentary sigh of relief, thankful for the aid.

Windows shattered, flower pots exploded, and screams of pain filled the air. And the smell... I gagged. It smelled like someone had stuck their hand in a bonfire.

People on both sides fell, but only the monsters rose back to their feet, just like the Forest Fae had said they would.

Another fire alien got his gangly arms around one of my Fjell soldiers and the man screamed as his skin melted around his neck. A few seconds later, his head popped off. My stomach churned at the sight.

I beat back another creature and sliced through his arm. He clutched his stump and dropped to his knees, before flopping onto the ground.

"Another sword, please!" Someone in green yelled from beside me and I quickly fashioned another one.

"Here!" I tossed it to the Forest Fae, who plucked it out of the air and stabbed it through a lava creature, making forward progress toward the Fire Fae soldiers in the center. But not enough...

How the fuck did we get to them? We needed something that could strike them all at once. Something like a wave or a storm that could strike them down with a single bolt of lightning.

Lightning.

The monster at my feet started to rise, but I chopped through its chest. I stared at my free hand and a memory from a stony tunnel filled my mind. The faint echo of a wolf in pain sent a shiver down my spine but a smile across my face. I had lightning. Or, at least, some sort of bolt-esque power that Torsten called my death magic.

More yells ripped through the street, drawing me back to the battle.

Another Fjell Fae slammed onto the ground, burn marks flaring across his cheek.

We were losing people. There was no time to wait.

"Back behind me or off the street!" I yelled and pulled on the magic in my sternum. Time to *kill* a few more people out to hurt what was mine. The Fjell Fae at the other end of the street scurried down side roads, heeding my warning. As the last of our team swept behind me, power seared through my body, arcing my back as I screamed and let loose. Lightning shot from my palms with a crack, and I crashed to my knees.

The magical, deadly light shot down the street and wrapped around the remaining Fire Fae. Shouts of agony ripped through the air. Electricity crackled around their middles and contracted as if squeezing life from them. More sparks flew out of their throats as they dropped like puppets with their strings cut.

I lowered my hands to the road, holding myself on all fours as the magic, the power given to me from Freija, appeared to electrocute the men from the inside out.

The last of the soldiers fell, his eyes wide and locked on me, not blinking.

Silence descended alongside the ash.

152

LENNIE

The fire monsters fizzled into smoke and drifted into the haze like they'd never existed, while five red-clad figures lay among other fallen soldiers.

My arms ached like someone had taken a sharp rake and carved them into slices, and a throbbing sensation slowly subsided in my head. I rose to my feet, my vision blurring before refocusing on the carnage that filled the main street through town.

Green and gray capes lay in puddles of blood, a scarlet stream running through the gullies that normally carried rainwater to the fjord. Today they'd be spilling blood into the water.

Soldiers scrambled past me, heading for their fallen friends. I stumbled down the road with them, looking for the injured who might still survive if we got them help. Hair smoldered, blood pooled, and burn marks marred most of the bodies on the street. I pulled my cape over my nose and mouth trying not to inhale the smell of burned flesh.

Joining my fellow fae, I helped turn people over and checked for injuries while keeping an eye on our surroundings—there could be more enemies out there. Aiding in lifting a scarred but breathing Forest Fae, I brought him to his feet and gave him to another Fjell Fae. "I just need to double check," I said with a look over my shoulder to the Fire Fae.

The Fjell Fae nodded and took the full weight of the injured.

I stepped through the carnage and crouched beside one of the Fire Fae. His long black hair hung limp over his forehead, his eyes wide and glassy. Placing my hand in front of his nose, I checked for any breaths. None came.

I moved on to the others, double checking what my gut already knew. The royal magic, my magic, had killed them where they stood. I'd murdered five enemy soldiers with one colossal wave of power. Rising to my feet, I swallowed the growing knot in my throat and suppressed the shiver that threatened to run down my spine.

"I did what I needed to do," I muttered. "I did what I needed to do. I did what I needed to do."

"All dead?" someone yelled, and I nodded, turning back to the fae on my side.

Injured and intact faces stared back at me, and my gut lurched. We needed to get them to safety. We needed to get them out of harm's way before more Fire Fae soldiers showed up, or worse, Veigar. Because if *that* was what Fire Fae soldiers could do, what the fuck kind of magic did Veigar have? No wonder Halvar had been so worried.

I stepped over the dead, looking away from their distant gazes, and focused on the task at hand. Where could I shelter the injured? Where would welcome them—

A light bulb went off in my mind. I knew exactly where we could take them.

"Follow me," I said and hauled ass around the corner and down the street. Oddvar's Café sat up ahead, the white-painted corner-building a beacon of light in the smoke.

"Can someone call for a medic?" I asked. Hopefully the mountain had one to spare for the village as I didn't think Heidi had stuck around. If she had, I hadn't seen her lately.

"Already did," someone replied.

I pulled Oddvar's keys from my pocket and launched up the stone step to the front door. "Thank you! Now, get them inside." I unlocked the door and shoved it open. The bell trilled above me as soldiers streamed past, the injured hanging between them or over their shoulders. One man in particular looked like he was on death's door. Boils and burn marks marred his left side, his uniform singed in spots and melted onto him in others.

Soldiers cleared space and rested the injured on the floor, organizing them based on the severity of their injuries. I motioned to one of the women who'd carried one of the wounded. "Help me flip these tables and make more space."

"Yes, ma'am," she said, and we set to work. Wood scraped against industrial flooring as we flipped over the tables and used them as shields against the windows, chairs clattered as they were moved aside, and the smell of coffee lingered in the air, reminding me of the establishment's proprietor. Oddvar may have been a quiet and introverted man, but part of me knew he would have offered to help those in need. And right now, we had five soldiers in need, one of them seriously so.

"Where's the field medic?" I asked the woman helping me.

She wiped her forearm across her brow. "I was told the Fjell assigned three to the village. One of them is on the way."

The door chimed again, and I whipped my head around and pulled on my magic.

Trygve stepped inside wearing his signature white tunic, flowy pants, and brown apron, with his hands raised above his head. "It's only me," he squeaked.

Half the room lowered their weapons, myself included, collapsing the short blade I'd formed in what must've been less than a second.

"What the hell are you doing down here?" I yelled at Trygve. "You're not a field medic!"

"I volunteered." He wiped his hand underneath his bowl cut like he'd just run a marathon. "I wanted to help you."

"I do have a history with getting injured, but that's not on today's agenda."

"Let's certainly hope not." He smiled. "But I came, and I will help heal our soldiers."

I sighed. He had a right to go where he wanted, where he thought he would be most useful. "Well, you better have plenty of burn cream on hand."

He patted the pockets of his apron and nodded before setting to work. I peered out of the window, keeping one eye on the street and the other on Trygve. He flitted from one person to the other, spending most of his time darting back to the man on the other side of the café—the one with the most severe burns. Would he make it? Would any of us?

A flash of red appeared down the road. "Get down!" I yelled.

Everyone dropped to their haunches and knees.

I peered through a gap between tables. It was a red-uniformed soldier. Not Veigar. But, still.

"Everyone stay down," I muttered.

Nobody moved.

The man crept down the street, passing the café, searching high and low like we might be hiding inside stores or on the rooftops. Which wasn't a bad idea for the Forest Fae archers. If we still had one. They could pick off soldiers from above.

I shook my head.

Where the hell had I learned to think like that? Halvar? No, he didn't talk enough. Espen didn't talk strategy all that often, not unless Ylva goaded him into it. A painful smile twisted one corner of my mouth.

Øyvin.

Øyvin thought like that. Whenever he walked into a space, he checked our surroundings as if scoping out threats. He was a guardian through and through.

I took a deep breath, quelling the rising sadness. That's exactly what I had to be.

We'd taken out five enemies. Now, we had to remove the rest.

The Forest Fae woman beside me readjusted her legs and I grabbed her arm. "Are you the archer? The one who shot an arrow through the Fire Fae's throat?"

"Yes, ma'am."

"Good." I pointed at the Fire Fae disappearing down the street. "Do that again. Go."

She nodded, grabbed a Fjell Fae soldier by the crook of his elbow, and together they ran out of the café.

As they left, another Fire Fae appeared from the right and bolted after them. *Shit. Shit. Shit. Shit. Shit.*

I jumped to my feet and dashed out the door. Someone needed to protect their backs.

Power surged through me, and I swept my hands over each other quickly, crafting a long sword that would put distance between me and the Fire Fae. Careening into the middle of the street, I added some stunning magic and raised the blade.

The Fire Fae soldier screeched to a stop, his eyes wide as they flicked over my weapon. His blond hair reminded me of Øyvin, but his eyes were pitch black.

"Wanna tango, hot shot?"

He cocked his head to one side and sneered.

"I'll take that as a no."

I swung my sword and pushed the magic out of it. A ball of stunning power zipped between us, and I raced after it. One thing I'd learned in training with Halvar and his soldiers was to keep the onslaught going. Keep them on their toes. So, I pushed my legs as fast as they would go and arced my blade through the air as I drew close. The soldier dodged the magic orb but stumbled and lifted his hand above him as he fell back. Fire flew from his palm. I heaved the sword down with as much force as I could and closed my eyes as I made contact. A wet sound met my ears, followed by a bump, then an almighty scream.

I opened my eyes and found blood pumping out of what remained of the man's arm. Falling onto his back, his features contorted in pain as he stared. I flipped my sword, pointing it downward, and gripped it with both hands before plunging it into the man's chest.

He flopped as blood spurted from his new wound.

My breaths came hard as I stared at the damage I'd done. "Holy shit."

I pulled my blade from his sternum and wiped the end across his thigh. A streak of red marred his ruby uniform and blood so dark it was almost black slipped down his sides.

I'd done that.

I'd killed yet another being.

But I'd also protected my own soldiers.

Slow claps sounded behind me.

I spun and sucked in a breath.

Veigar grinned from ear to ear, clapping as he took two more leisurely steps forward. He stopped five doors down. "Impressive."

"You should see what I can do with my tongue."

"I'd rather have it ripped out."

Well, fuck that was graphic.

"Leave Skolvik, Veigar." I raised my sword and pushed more stunning magic into it. The power prickled down my arms, flooding the blade as light glinted off the blood-stained tip.

He flicked open his hands and twin flames filled his palms. "No. This is where I'm meant to be. Where they said I should be."

What the fuck is he talking about. "No, this is not your home. Shoo shoo."

He narrowed his eyes at me, done with my jokes. The next second he threw the fire from his hands at me. I dodged underneath the first ball of flame and smashed my sword into the other. The orb exploded like a firework and small embers rained over my face. My skin stung in all the spots where it made contact.

I wiped my cheeks and pulled back my hand. No blood, but damn, that hurt.

Veigar smiled like he got a kick out of watching people in pain.

Sneering back at him, I collapsed my sword. I needed to keep my distance from him.

Calling on both my Fjell and royal magic, I quickly crafted a small rock in one hand and a ball of stunning magic in the other. Both were smaller than I'd have liked, but as another volley of fire flew my way, I didn't have time to dwell on size.

I launched the rock at Veigar's head, then the sparking orb of light.

Summoning another volley, I winced. They were smaller than the ones before. Was I running out? Had I used up everything on those five fae back in the street?

Two more flames shot toward me. Our brawl continued back and forth. One launching fire, the other rocks and light. My muscles ached, arms spasming and thighs yelling at me as I attacked Veigar with everything I had. His counters were perfectly timed and barely avoided. His hair sat perfectly atop his head, shirt unmarred compared to the debris and dirt on me.

This was easy for him. Too easy...

I furrowed my brow.

His attacks felt basic, limited, like he was holding back. Halvar had said he could wield fire creatures—which I now knew weren't a joke—and use lava. But Veigar hadn't used either with me...

He was toying with me.

I peered at him through wisps of hair that had broken free from my ponytail and growled.

Veigar's lips arched into a menacing grin. He lifted his hand and a ball of flame sprung to life between his fingers. He looked at the orb, then flicked his gaze to me.

I widened my arms, welcoming the fight. "Come on, Asshole! Give it your best shot!"

A low and evil laugh danced down the street from him. His eyes shifted to my right and he threw the fire ball—

"No!"

In horrifying slow motion, the flaming orb crashed against Oddvar's, igniting the wood paneling.

An anguished scream ripped from my throat, and I rushed toward the café. Trygve's wide-eyed gaze peered out the window.

I barreled through the front door as another explosion smashed against the building, shattering one of the windows.

"Get out! Get out, now!"

The fae inside scrambled around, gathering their comrades and stumbling out the front door.

I grabbed an injured soldier by the scruff and hauled him to his feet. The man winced, his green and brown uniform in smoldering tatters. "Move or die."

He whimpered, and I shoved him toward a Fjell Fae just as flames burst through another window and crashed against the counter. I ducked behind my cape and scurried over to the last remaining fae. He lay on his back, staring at the ceiling, boils and blackened tissue mottling his arm and one side of his face. His chest didn't move.

"He's gone." Trygve gently touched his hand to my shoulder. "Come. Out."

I nodded and charged through the smoke and into the only slightly fresher air.

The fae had gathered on one side of the building, out of Veigar's sight. Some scouted for threats, while others could barely stand. Shit. They needed a place to hide. A place where Trygve could work his magic.

I know.

"Get to the boathouse." I shoved my keys into Trygve's trembling hands. "Take care of the injured there."

The boathouse was a short walk from downtown, but far enough away that the maimed and injured shouldn't be harmed or caught in actual crossfire.

"Miss Lennie, we can't—"

"You can and you will, Doc. Go!" I spun to my team. "Take them. Get them to my place."

"Yes, ma'am!"

A moment later, the group of soldiers and patients ambled down the road, heading away from the danger that walked these streets.

I turned back to the carnage that crackled before me. Flames licked up the side of the white, wood building and a charred line of black crept up its cheery facade.

The final window shattered, and I raised my cape, shielding myself from the shards and smoke. The roof let out an ominous groan.

Shit. That was coming down.

I scrambled to the other side of the street, pressing myself against the store. Heat battered against my face as I stuttered a breath, watching the café burn.

I'd failed Oddvar. I'd promised him we'd watch over his precious café. And now look.

The smell of wood, metal, and coffee filled the air along with my failure. My shoulders slumped and I leaned back against the boutique behind me as a tear spilled down my cheek. I'd fucking failed. The one thing Oddvar had asked me to do, and I'd screwed up.

A roar of flame shot up from within the café and the roof crumbled in on itself.

I fucking failed.

But it wasn't my fault.

This was Veigar's doing. Yes, he'd found yet another weakness of mine, but I wasn't the one who set fire to the café. I wasn't the fucking arsonist. He was.

Gritting my teeth, I pulled on the rage that crashed within me, needing to be set free. I'd kill him for this.

I glanced around the corner, an orb of killing magic crackling in my hand.

But Veigar had vanished.

153
LENNIE

The anger within my chest popped along with the crackling of the burning business, and I dropped my hands to my sides with a whimper. I was losing everything I loved. From one of the happiest places I'd ever known to the heart-wrenching loss of my partner. All the pieces of my life were disappearing on me.

Swallowing hard, I crouched, letting the weight of my emotions fill every part of my body. Silent tears streamed down my face as the flames danced before me. The windows on the shop next-door to Oddvar's started turning black, flickers of auburn licking the sills. There was nothing to stop the fire eating its way through the row of buildings.

There was nothing I could do to help either.

No fire truck.

No hose.

No water.

No hope.

Shaking my head, I rose to my feet and stumbled toward the harbor, my mind lost to the darkness.

Mist caressed the streets of Skolvik and curled around buildings, mixing with the lingering smoke and stench of burned timber. Something else marred the air. Something I couldn't quite place. I peered down at my singed uniform and my stomach somersaulted. Wool and flesh. Not mine, thankfully. But the fallen soldiers. That's what I could smell.

My lips trembled, and I brought my fist to my mouth.

This village, these people, the fae, didn't deserve this. This desolation wasn't their fight, wasn't their fault. This was the action of a bored and entitled king whose volatility risked the Fae's exposure more than any other conflict I'd borne witness to in the past year.

This wasn't the stability he said he wanted.

This was utter chaos.

I pulled up beside the concrete planter I'd hidden behind last Little Christmas Eve and leaned my butt against it. Soot buried the delicate pansies in the container, while the tree within it swayed like my confidence as I stared out across the fjord.

The few boats that remained bobbed quietly within the harbor like innocent bath toys as warmth radiated through the village. A light gust of wind brushed through my hair, the flyaways and stray tendrils tickling my cheeks and sweaty neck, like the calm before a deadly tornado set to decimate the Midwest.

This battle would be no different. I could feel it in my gut. Knew it in some deep, hidden part of myself.

Those soldiers who'd just strolled through town weren't the only ones, they were a first wave. A line of fae sent to test us—see what the scenery looked like before focusing and taking the true shot.

I peered over my shoulder. A thick plume of black smoke rose from where Oddvar's lay, and my heart tore into pieces.

Fuck I was failing hard.

I wiped my hands over my face and took a deep breath. "I can't think like that. I can't let him win."

I couldn't. I wouldn't. But fuck did everything hurt right now.

And yet... I could sit by and watch the fire carve through the forests and cascade over the mountaintops. Or I could fight back. Like the rest of the Martin Family, I'd never back down from a challenge, and like my partners, I'd do everything I could to protect my home and my friends.

I looked around me, hoping to find something that might help. Fisken sat empty and locked up. Flecks of ash twirled around the town square and brushed up against the plant containers. Out on the fjord, nothing broke the surface. No one was coming to save us. My husband was caught in his own battle, my partner was missing—likely dead—and I was alone.

But I wouldn't let that stop me.

I couldn't let this village fall to Veigar. I'd promised to protect the mountain and with that came my home, my family. "Fuck it, I may not be a true leader, but I'm not going to let these people down."

Footsteps thrummed behind me, and I spun, drawing a sword—

Soldiers. *Fjell* soldiers. Half of them in uniform sans cape, the other half in black fatigues. A few Forest soldiers too. Their gazes locked on me as if seeking guidance, and I drew in a sharp breath.

The one closest tilted his head in my direction. "Orders, ma'am."

I let loose the oxygen from my lungs slowly as if it might somehow accidentally ignite the cinders around the village.

Anger and rage filled my veins, and my power thrashed within my chest, begging to be unleashed.

No more nice Lennie.

No more quippy little remarks.

I was no longer the innocent tourist who didn't know anything about the world of the fae.

"Ma'am?"

A feminine scream of pain sounded from somewhere in the middle of town, and my head whipped toward the noise. Someone was hurt. Someone—

A jet of orange lava shot toward the sky like the geysers in Yellowstone, and all the oxygen in my lungs evaporated.

Fuck this guy.

I pushed power down my arm and into my sword. Lightning arced at the tip, crackling through the eerie silence that hung heavy over the village.

"We find him," I said. "We find King Veigar and we rid this town of him and his minions. We remove him from the board entirely."

Fuck him for coming for my family. My home. These fae.

I stood among the ring of soldiers like a quarterback hyping up his teammates before the big game.

"We protect the Fae," I added. "Whatever it takes."

"Whatever it takes," the soldiers replied, and together we turned our attention to the battle.

154

LENNIE

Footsteps stomped against the street, the sound echoing off the abandoned buildings. The soldiers in front of me spread into a line, weapons forming from thin air. Blades as long as my arm, rocks so jagged they looked like porcupines, and shields as tall as surfboards filled the line-up. I stepped into the middle, drawing more power into my own sword.

A dense barrier of maroon-clad soldiers marched into the town-square from multiple side streets. I sucked in a breath and steeled my spine.

The fire in the soldiers' palms blazed like torches of a mob.

My men and women shuffled, but held strong, their gazes locked on the oncoming masses.

"Those pointy rocks good to launch?" I asked no one in particular.

"Ready, ma'am," a male voice a few fae down from me replied.

"Good." Adrenaline humming through me, I eyed the scene like one of my brother's football games. "Take out the right side first. Don't let them pincer and force us up the middle."

My order rippled down the line as the onslaught raised their hands and launched balls of fire at us.

I sidestepped an exploding orb and charged to the right. Our line of soldiers clashed against the Fire Fae. I swung my sword as shrieks of pain filled the air. The blade connected and drew blood, rocks flew past my head, and the heat from the Fire Fae battered against me. Sweat pooled around my hairline as I spun and swung, moving like my life depended on it.

Blazing heat encased my wrist. I winced and whirled. Fire Fae.

I swung again and pushed stunning magic down my arm. The fae whimpered, released his grip, and I buried my blade in his stomach.

A roar of anger sounded behind me. I yanked my sword from the fae eliciting a wet *thlum* and twisted. A fiery sword careened toward my face. I caught it in a bloody cross maneuver before pivoting and landing more stunning magic at the fae's face. He dropped like a fly meeting a zapper.

Sucking in a breath, I continued fighting.

Swing.

Zap.

Dodge.

Breathe.

Lunge.

Move. Move. Move.

Blood spattered across my uniform and face, and my hair clung to my cheeks as sweat slid down my temples.

Gray, green, and red blurred into a quagmire of death and destruction.

The line of soldiers that had come down the middle street past Fisken moved in on us, squeezing our left flank.

"Fuck!"

I launched over bodies and embers, splashing through puddles of blood. Numb to my own body and any injuries. I couldn't focus on that.

I had to keep moving.

Keep swinging.

Ducking, I narrowly avoided another ball of fire to the face. A scream sounded behind me, and I shook off the thought of someone else taking the hit.

The magic in my sternum swirled like a twister, ready to attack at a moment's notice.

A wave of fire rolled toward me, and I threw up a stone shield and crouched behind it. The flames licked around the stone, cooking it like a pizza. Pulling my hands off the heat, I pressed my shoulder against it. The smell of singed wool drifted past me.

Shit.

I didn't dare glance at my uniform. I knew what I'd find. Bare shoulder. Crumbling fibers.

The flames died out, and I readied a round of stunning magic. This would have to do. I couldn't chance using more killing magic right now, but we needed to turn the tides. I popped my head around my shield. Other Fjell soldiers prepared their next volleys as the Fire Fae crept closer, using their own flaming shields for protection.

They were going to overrun us if I didn't do something.

I collapsed my sword, rose to my feet, and flung aside the tall shield.

The line of Fire Fae stopped, their eyes trained on me.

Good.

I filled both palms with stunning magic and launched it at them.

One ball made it over the expanse and crashed against a fiery barrier, while the other sailed over the line and landed somewhere behind them. A scream ripped through the air echoing with another noise. Something piercing, wailing even. Was that a siren?

My brow furrowed as I prepared another volley.

Blaring sirens crashed through the town square and the fighting slowed as a firetruck followed by five motorcycles careened from the right and into the melee, sending a line of Fire Fae flying. Which felt a bit ironic. My soldiers and I fell back, using the vehicle's high sides as a shield for a momentary reprieve from fighting.

The firetruck came to a stop and Espen hopped out of the driver's seat. His hair was all over the place, his uniform almost black with some sort of debris, but his eyes found mine in a heartbeat.

My chest spasmed. He was all right. He was alive. He was here.

I stumbled toward him, vaguely aware of the soldiers around me. Yells of "Fall back!" sounded from the other side of the truck, but my focus remained locked on my husband.

He grabbed my hand, yanked me to him, and folded around me. The smell of smoke overwhelmed his usual scent, but I was home. He crushed his lips to mine and it felt like a lifeline. I pushed my fingers into his hair, pressed against the firmness of his body, and bathed in the sweep of his lips. He was here. In my arms.

"Are you hurt?" he asked as I burrowed into him.

"I'm fine."

He brushed his hand down my back. "Good."

"You? Are you injured?"

His chest rose and fell slowly, an extended exhale skimming over my head.

I tensed. "What happened? And where's Ylva?"

His body shuddered.

I pulled out of his arms and looked around. Soldiers on both sides were regrouping. Espen and the firetruck had been a helpful interruption, but we didn't have much time until the onslaught started again. I couldn't see Ylva anywhere and the truck's cabin looked empty, save for an archer who was setting up shop in the backseat with his bow and arrow pointing out the other window. "Where is she?"

"Lennie." The tone of his voice had my head whipping back to him and air catching in my throat.

He shook his head and his lips downturned.

My stomach sank. "No, no, no no nononono."

This... No, it couldn't be happening. She couldn't be gone. "Tell me she's injured and Heidi is stitching her up after giving her some magical tea she steeped this morning."

He swallowed hard like anger and sadness were on the brink of overwhelming him. "I can't."

My heart took another hit, fracturing. I wobbled, and Espen caught me as our breaths came sharp and heavy. She was gone. The tenacious and spirited woman was gone. Espen's best friend. My friend. A fierce woman with a magnificent mind for strategy. I couldn't believe it. It couldn't be true. And yet, based on the pained expression on Espen's face, it was.

I wrapped my arms around him and squeezed. He nuzzled into my neck and breathed in, his chest trembling. If we weren't in the middle of a battle right now, I'd cocoon him in blankets, bake him *sirupsnipper*, and ply him with all the snuggles in the world. It would never make up for the loss, but I'd do anything to soothe the blow a little bit and allow him the space to grieve. But, as it was...

Tears welled in the corner of my eyes, and I brushed them away before they could fall.

"Tell me who did it," I said, my voice unwavering. Whoever had taken my husband's best friend better have met an untimely end or I'd be delivering one.

"Herja."

"Is she dead?"

"Yes."

"Good. Do you need anything?"

Espen opened his mouth to reply as heat washed over the truck. We both peered at the sky. Three orbs of fire flew over our heads and landed on the main dock, singing the wood.

We were out of time.

Another small flurry of fire arched over us, like they were testing their range, and I shoved my sadness into a box. I'd grieve our friend when this was over. She'd want us to kick some ass on her behalf and then wash down the day with some throat shattering aquavit. And fuck it, that's exactly what we would do.

I steeled myself and looked up into my husband's equally tormented gaze. "Any chance there's another truck lying around town that we can use as a lineman against these assholes?"

He pointed to the rear of the truck. "No, but back-up arrived from Alv-dalen."

Four large wolves and a figure in black with bright white hair stepped out from behind the vehicle. "Marius," I muttered, taking in the sight of the small pack with vicious teeth. They must've been the ones on the motorbikes behind the firetruck when it careened into town.

The young Alpha gave me a quick nod as if he could hear my thoughts. "Ylva sent for us. I'm just sorry we couldn't get here sooner."

"I'm glad you're here." Espen patted Marius's shoulder.

"Me too," I added. We needed all the help we could get.

"Aurora is here too," Marius said.

"What?" She was the last person I expected to visit Skolvik.

Espen nodded and looked toward the hillside where his cabin sat. "Her and a few other wolves are escorting Heidi back to my place and setting up a healer location."

Good. Surprising, but good. However, the wolves could probably still get hurt by the fire balls flying around.

"Are you and your crew going to be fast enough to avoid getting burned?" I motioned to the panting pack beside us.

Marius's mouth curled at one corner. "Don't worry about us." He moved a few steps back and shifted into his majestic gray-and-white wolf form. Joints and bones snapped and cracked as the furry creature took shape.

That will never not be weird.

The canine spun, silently communicated something with the pack, and a moment later they sprinted toward the north side of town where the village met the slopes of the mountain.

"They're heading around the perimeter," Espen said, drawing my attention back to him.

"Do you have any other Forest Fae beings to help us? Eagles? Bears? A really big moose perhaps?"

"No." He rolled his shoulders back. "But you've got me."

"Finally. You gonna let the beast out to play?" I'd seen what he could do, but I wanted to know *exactly* how devastating his powers could be, and I wanted them aimed at the Fire Fae King.

His lips tilted into a tiny smile, and he gave me a wink. "Whatever you do, stay behind me."

There was a sex joke in there, but now...

Quiet. It was too quiet.

We both stilled.

An eeriness settled over the town square and nobody spoke, nobody moved. It was like someone had hit the mute button on the TV. That feeling like a tornado was about to blow into town washed through me again, and my body involuntarily trembled.

Espen glanced around frantically, searching for the cause, then stopped. He peered over my head, the muscles in his jaw tensing.

"Espen?" I twisted and looked over my shoulder to see what had caused his eyes to narrow.

The fjord rippled like something was moving beneath the water.

"Stay here for a second," he said and stepped away, walking around the front of the truck. Magic swirled in his hands where he held them at his sides. It reminded me of the movement he'd done on the mountain last year, right before he ripped apart the ground and buried a few dozen Fjord Fae soldiers.

I peeked around the truck. The Fire Fae backed down the streets, hands braced, eyes locked on the water, giddy sneers crossing several of their faces.

My stomach lurched, and I ducked behind the truck again.

Whatever was about to breach the surface had them excited.

Espen bravely turned his back on the Fire Fae, stepped behind the truck, and started barking orders. He moved around the shielded space, the Forest Fae following his commands and getting into various strategic positions, while the Fjell Fae looked to me.

I shook off my anxiety and the crush of emotions the day was delivering. "Listen to him too," I yelled across the square. "That's an order!"

Responses of "Yes, ma'am" met my ears and they all began working with their Forest counterparts again. Several Fjell Fae started making shields for the different groupings, passing them around, while Forest Fae filled quivers with knotty branches they created from thin air.

Espen looked over his shoulder, pride beaming from him.

The water undulated again, and everyone stopped moving.

I stepped up beside Espen and called forward my stunning magic. I still wasn't sure how long I could last using only killing magic, so it was best to save that for later and not potentially run myself dry before I got the chance to kill Veigar.

Ripples grew and the water bubbled in spots on the fjord, small waves lapping against the dock pilons. A moment later a brown-haired head with pointy ears emerged and I sucked in a lungful of smoky air.

The Fjord Fae were here.

"Fuck we're screwed," I muttered and felt Espen deflate beside me as more breached the surface.

We had Fire Fae on one side and Fjord Fae on the other. It was a fae sandwich—the kind I wasn't interested in.

I slipped my hand into Espen's and squeezed. "Do you think you can take out all of them?"

He watched the Fjord Fae closely. "Depends how many there are."

Fjord Fae rose from the deep like monsters, creeping toward shore. Their heads materialized from the water, the group spanning across the entire width of the fjord. They moved as if they could walk on water, using it and the shoreline like stairs.

Their uniforms, all different shades of blue, gave the illusion of an oncoming wave. At the front was their King and Queen. Reuven and Salka moved like graceful statues, scanning the town's harbor front. His cape fluttered around his waist while her dress—the most majestic shade of purple I'd ever seen—flowed from her like a waterfall. Together, they led the masses toward the harbor like war generals.

"Is that too many?" I asked Espen.

"That's an astonishing amount of destruction and decay."

"What do you mean?"

"It's a lot of deaths. Doable. But a lot." His hand squeezed mine again, and I got the feeling he didn't like where this was heading. The ancestors must have enjoyed giving him those destructive powers, found some entertainment in it. Because Espen was not a destructive person. By nature, he wanted to heal and cause the least amount of harm. If given the chance to choose what powers he'd be granted, it would never in a million years be these. Death wasn't cavalier or frivolous. It meant something.

I looked around at the fae on our team. Some cowered at the sight of fae rising from the depths, others narrowed their eyes at them like they were considering how to tear them limb from limb. Most of the latter were Fjell Fae... Probably trained by Halvar. The only way we were surviving this was unleashing my husband and clawing our way out of the skirmish.

Reuven and Salka walked across the water's surface and stepped onto the closest dock.

My muscles tensed.

"Shields up!" Espen yelled and dropped my hand. Turning to me, he added, "Reuven will have stunning magic too. Don't know how long he's trained it or if Veigar may have given him pointers, but brace yourself."

"Don't get zapped. Got it."

He looked back out. "And watch for Salka."

The woman in question glided down the dock, her dress leaving no watery mark in its wake. More soldiers stepped onto the other docks that pierced the shore. Then they stopped, scanning the scene before them.

Espen touched his fingers to my elbow. "Don't die. I'm not done living life with you yet."

"Same." I gave him an emotion-filled smile. "I'm nowhere near done with you. Never will be."

He leaned in and placed a chaste kiss to my lips before breaking away and refocusing on the oncoming royals.

I took a deep breath and pivoted around the edge of the firetruck, watching our back and our front. The Fire Fae relaxed in the side streets. Some leaning against buildings, other crossing their arms and preparing for the shit-storm coming from the fjord. They looked like bored teenagers waiting for a fight to erupt. Especially compared to Reuven and his legion of men and women—their postures braced and ready for combat.

Reuven's gaze slid to the forest fire on the hillside. Blackened trees burned like torches in a picture of orange and smoke.

He wasn't paying attention to me. Salka was, but Reuven was focused on the flames. This was my chance. I pulled stunning magic down my arms, biting into my bottom lip as the magic tingled like pins and needles. Sparks swirled around my fingers, and Reuven's head snapped back to me.

He shook his head and twisted his hands in an ethereal motion in front of his chest.

A droplet of rain plopped on the tip of my nose. Another followed, splashing against my cheek before the skies opened and rain fell like a much-needed storm during a drought.

"What the hell?" I muttered.

Murmurs sprang up from our soldiers.

Espen drew his hands to his sides, readying himself and his powers. Ribbons of sickly-green magic curled between his fingers, and I fought against the urge to run—my inner fight or flight response screaming at me to stay away from the stuff.

Like me, the Fjord Fae didn't move either. Some still in the water, others on the docks.

I peered around the firetruck. Fire Fae looked at each other and back toward the fjord and up at the skies, confusion marring their movements.

"I think we can trust them," Espen said, his voice teeming with an emotion I couldn't quite place.

"Doubt that." I turned back toward the harbor. "They took..."

My words faltered as a navy-clad figure sans cape stepped out of the water and onto the dock beside Reuven.

"Øy... Øyvin."

He was alive. Thank his ancestors, he was alive. Rain dampened his blond hair and shoulders as he unclenched his fists. His eyes found mine, and a whimper left my lips as my knees threatened to buckle. He was there. Right there.

Bows grew taught and soldiers twitched out of the corner of my eye.

"Hold!" I yelled, keeping my gaze locked with Øyvin. "Why'd you keep him alive?"

"Reasons," Reuven replied.

Could they really be on our side? Was that what was happening?

Øyvin gave me a gentle nod and a tiny smile. That was all I needed to see before I started running.

I bolted down the dock and it was as if I'd fired a starting gun. Spouts of fire flew over my head, Reuven and Salka working together with the Fjord Fae to stop them. All hell broke loose, but I could only see one thing. One person.

I launched myself at Øyvin, wrapping my arms and legs around him like a koala, my momentum sending us over the edge of the dock and into the fjord.

The water swallowed us into its cool embrace, stinging parts of my arm, shoulder, and wrists. Øyvin righted us, ensconced me in an ironclad hold, and placed a hand against my lower back as I nuzzled into his neck. A moment later I was dry again and a thin bubble of air wrapped around us, shielding us from the water and providing enough oxygen to breathe.

I pulled back and stared at him. His eyes were so blue, so clear, and slightly hooded as he stared down at me. His skin was paler than normal, sallow, like he hadn't been eating or drinking enough. His gaze flicked to my lips and I surged forward, pressing our mouths together. He tasted like salt and hope. I threaded my hands into his hair and held him against me, needing to meld our bodies together. I never wanted us to be apart again. It had only been days, but it felt like a lifetime.

He touched his lips to the tip of my nose before tilting my head up to his. "Hello, Trouble."

My body shivered at the sound of my nickname.

Other Fjord Fae swam and floated nearby, but in Øyvin's arms, it felt like we were in our own world. A place I never wanted to leave but only add to. All we needed was Espen.

He pressed his fingers to different spots on my body, the rough pads brushing against my skin. "You're hurt," he grumbled.

"Can't feel them."

"That's the adrenaline."

"I'll feel them when we've won. We don't have time right now."

"We really don't," he agreed.

"Reuven can be trusted?"

He nodded.

"Truly, truly trusted? He's not going to flip on us? This isn't a trap?"

"It's a trap," he replied, and my breath caught in my throat. "But not for us."

"What?"

"They've been preparing to flip on Veigar for a while."

"Reuven and Salka? You mean she wants to kill her own dad?" What was it with these fae and killing off their own family members? Sheesh.

He nodded again and trailed his thumb across my cheek before pulling me against his chest once more. "The deception was all part of their plan."

"And they've been working on it for years? Knew this was coming, but didn't warn anyone? Seems like a great time to send a text, letter, or even carrier pigeon."

He stifled a smile. "Veigar thinks he's the chosen one. Believes the ancestors told him not long after his wife died that he would be *the* fae leader."

I snorted. "Has no one told him? I'm the chosen one around here. I even have my own advertisements on store windows."

Øyvin grinned, and my heart sang a little victory.

Something moved beneath us, and I stilled, curling my shoulders and drawing my feet up. "Is that the scaly thing?"

He glanced down and then back to me. "It won't hurt you."

My eyes widened as the *something* moved to my left. Gripping Øyvin for dear life, I slowly turned in its direction.

Staring back at me, with a head the size of the firetruck and a long-ass body like a dragon without wings, was the fucking water snake we'd spotted the other day.

I screamed.

155

LENNIE

Øyvin hoisted me onto the dock as I'd forgotten how to swim thanks to the giant *THING* in the water that looked like it ate fishing boats for breakfast.

I scrambled over the sodden planks and flopped onto my back, droplets pitter-pattering against my forehead. "What the ever-loving fuck is *that*?"

Øyvin pressed his hands against the edge of the dock and hauled himself out of the water in one fluid movement. He crawled over to me and pulled me into an upright position. "That is Jörmungandr."

Yelling and fighting sounded behind me, but I couldn't focus on that. My eyes were glued to the surface, waiting for the beast to slither out and eat me. "Please tell me it's vegetarian."

Øyvin snickered and my heart fluttered at hearing the sound again. His chortles were so few, whenever I got one it felt like I'd won a Hasselblad Award for the best photo of my life.

"It follows Reuven's orders."

"And how long has it been in the fjord? Have you been throwing me in there knowing full well it was down there?"

He opened his mouth to respond, and his eyes blew wide. "Shit," he said, shooting his arms out and using his body as a shield. We crashed back against the dock and a bubble of water formed over us just in time to take a hit from a jet of fire.

My eyes rolled and my head thrummed from being smacked against the wood.

"Sorry," he said. "Stay down. Reuven!"

The fire hissed against the bubble and vanished a moment later. Someone must've taken out the launcher.

I wriggled underneath Øyvin and peered back at the village. A wave of panic washed through my veins and my body trembled. Fire, stones, and smoke were everywhere. Arrows of all kinds flew in every which direction—some smashing through windows, others lodging into victims. Wolves dashed back and forth, snapping at foes. And, in the middle of the melee, stood Espen. His torn police jacket fluttered around his waist like the capes on fae uniforms. Ominous green magic wove between his fingers and power pulsed from him like a steady heartbeat, quaking the ground where he stood. A Fire Fae bolted past Fisken, and Espen unleashed his magic like a whip. A green tendril wrapped around the soldier's throat and yanked. He crashed to his knees, and the ground opened beneath him, swallowing him whole.

My eyes widened.

Espen was death and destruction made real.

"We need to help," I said. "But steer clear of Espen's magic."

Øyvin brushed his nose across my cheek. "Agreed."

We pushed up to our feet and ran back down the dock. Wood gave way to asphalt, and I rolled my shoulders, shrugging off a spell of exhaustion. How long had we been out here? With the cloud cover from Reuven's rainstorm, it was near impossible to tell what the time was.

Battle like I'd never seen before raged around me, with Espen, Reuven, and Salka standing in the middle of it all. Together, they launched an onslaught of magic at the invaders. Salka served up balls of what looked like lava, launching them right at Fire Fae stomachs like a tennis champion. Espen worked in tandem with her, ripping the street beneath her targets open and gobbling them up. Reuven stood beside his wife, half-protecting her from incoming volleys, half-spearheading his own campaign of assaulting soldiers with boiling water. This wasn't my first experience with the Fjord Fae strategy after Torsten was hit last year, but I cringed at the sight, nonetheless.

Øyvin pulled me through the crowd toward the trio, one arm free to shield with me.

We did our best to stay out of the way while helping what forces remained. I crafted boulders, raising them to protect our archers, while Øyvin swirled water around our soldiers, dousing any errant embers.

"All down!" Reuven's voice echoed through the downpour, and Øyvin yanked on my arm, drawing me to my knees.

The Fjord soldiers around us followed suit, encouraging the Forest and Fjell soldiers around them to do the same as the ground rumbled beneath our feet.

"What—"

My question was lost to the wind as the water in the harbor burst upward like a geyser and Reuven's pet snake emerged like a hungry beast set free after its winter slumber.

Jörmungandr sailed over our heads, water dripping from its watery scales as if ancient mythology had come to life before my eyes. I shuddered as the thing that looked like a snake had merged with a really, *really* big dragon rose high into the sky with a deadly roar.

Reuven yelled something unintelligible as the street-sized serpent crashed into town square beside Espen.

A squeal caught in my throat, but Espen didn't even flinch, a renewed battle cry ripping from his throat.

The sea creature's head swung toward Espen, shared a look with him, then slithered toward the Fire Fae that remained, all of which took one glance at the oncoming threat and barreled past Fisken and into town. The beast hurtled after them, Reuven and our forces not far behind.

Øyvin tugged on my arm and helped me to my feet. After the shock of what I'd just seen, I appreciated the help.

We traipsed after them, listening to the battle rage once more. Screams sounded up ahead as if the beast was enjoying its meal.

My hair stuck to my face as the rain poured, putting out the fires that dotted the normally pristine streets. Now, water, soot, and lumps of sludge surrounded me, and my heart beat faster, my feet slowing.

Everywhere I looked, buildings had been bruised, windows shattered, and scorch marks marred doorways. Other structures hadn't been as lucky. Blackened frames of former houses smoldered, several looking more like opened dollhouses—entire sides missing and their contents laid bare to the elements. Rage-fueled tears filled my eyes, but I brushed them away.

"Why would he *do this* to our town?"

Øyvin sighed. "He isn't in his right—"

A flash of red shot out of the camping and hiking store, and Øyvin shoved me behind is back. A Fire Fae raced toward us, his hands raised as flames sizzled in his palms. Øyvin charged, I called forward a tiny dagger, and, within seconds, we had the guy pinned against the building.

Øyvin growled in his face. "I don't think so."

His fingers wrapped around the man's throat, and steam rose from our captive as water trickled out of his mouth. His black eyes blew wide as he scrambled, clawing at my partner before latching both hands around Øyvin's wrist.

A hiss sounded and smoke rose from Øyvin's arm, forcing him to drop the Fire Fae. Øyvin yanked himself free, stumbled back a few steps, and put himself between me and our attacker with a menacing growl.

"You picked the wrong side," Øyvin rumbled.

"I doubt that," the man replied. "Veigar is more powerful than all of you combined."

I huffed. "Then why is he hiding behind his troops? Where is your big, strong, ferocious leader?"

The Fire Fae's top lip curled, and he took a step toward us, flames igniting in his hands once more. I flipped the blade in my hand and prepared to launch as a snarl sounded from our right.

A blur of gray-and-white fur hurtled toward us, latched onto the Fire Fae's leg, and pulled him away. The man screamed as Marius bit at his leg and the unmistakable sound of bones crunching reached me. Not wasting the opportunity, I stepped out from behind Øyvin and threw my dagger. All of Halvar's weapon training came in handy as the blade lodged in the man's shoulder, eliciting another scream as he tried and failed to remove the canine. Phantom pain shot through my own leg, remembering just how painful those wolves' bites were, but this asshole deserved every bit of our wrath.

Øyvin and I rushed forward, and together, the three of us brought down the Fire Fae. He slumped against the broken asphalt, but I retrieved my blade from his shoulder and jammed it into his chest, just in case.

Eyelids fluttered shut. Water dribbled from his mouth. Blood seeped from his wounds.

Marius nuzzled at the Fire Fae's neck then turned to us and made a chuffing noise.

Dead.

Thank fuck.

A howl sounded from somewhere nearby, the eerie sound sending a shiver down my spine. Marius's head whipped in the direction of the noise, ears twitching.

"Thank you," I said.

The wolf looked back at me and his tail wagged once as another howl pierced the air.

"Go. Help them."

He didn't need to be told twice. The wolf bolted, leaving Øyvin and I with the dead soldier.

Yanking the blade from the Fire Fae's chest, I turned and found Øyvin staring down at me. His eyes were hooded, rain droplets resting on the tips of his lashes as a hint of a smile twisted his lips while he scanned me. A wave of heat followed his gaze, my heart beating wildly under his inspection.

"What?"

He shook his head and that smile grew.

"No, really. Do I have blood on my face?" I collapsed my blade and spun to the window in hopes of finding my own reflection.

Øyvin grabbed my arm and tugged me away from our kill. Tucking me against his firm chest, he swept his finger across my forehead, brushing aside errant strands. The touch was so delicate it was just shy of a whisper. "You're perfect."

My knees turned to Jell-o, and my hands pressed against him.

"Are you saying my violent side is a turn on?"

He shrugged and looked down the street, but the twist of his lips gave him away.

"Save it for later!" Espen yelled as he jogged toward us, Salka and Reuven right behind him, the serpent nowhere to be seen. "Back to town square," he added, barely out of breath. "Regroup."

We nodded and followed, my steps faltering here and there, exhaustion starting to set in.

"Are you okay?" I motioned to Øyvin's reddened wrist as we jogged back toward the harbor front.

He grumbled. "Might need Espen's help."

"You know he'll gladly heal you."

Another grumble.

"No point in going on with the rest of your day with what looks like a nasty sunburn."

"Fair."

We regrouped with the other fae leaders in the middle of town square like heroes assembling to avenge their home from the big bad that had shown up and stomped all over their town. Soldiers milled around us. Some attended to wounds, others prepared more shields and blades. I smiled at the sight of all three factions working together.

Øyvin held out his injured wrist to Espen. "Could you help me?"

"Of course!" Espen placed his hands above and below the red marks and his brow furrowed. A translucent energy wrapped around the burn and a wince slipped from Øyvin. The skin shifted from red, to pink, and finally back to its normal state. Espen retracted his hands and bounced on the balls of his feet.

"Thank you," Øyvin muttered and tugged at his sleeves.

"Any time," Espen replied. "Does anyone else need healing?" He looked around the gathered fae. Everyone shook their heads.

Reuven took a step further into the circle and cleared his throat. "We need to implement next steps."

"Which are?" Øyvin and I asked at the same time while Espen listened like a good little school boy.

"Expect another wave of Fire Fae," Salka said, her voice smoky and hoarse. "The next one will have lava."

"How do you know?" I asked.

She wiped the back of her hand across her forehead. "It's father's strategy. Send in the infantry, then batter what remains with swells of lava, with soldiers following after that to dispatch any stragglers."

"Any idea where your father might be?"

"Usually orchestrating from a distance."

I somehow hated him even more.

"Well, I can handle the soldiers in town," Espen said then pointed at the burning Forest. The line of fire had slowed thanks to the rain, but still snuck closer and closer to town. "I can't control that, though, and the barriers we created will only hold for so long."

Reuven straightened. "I'll take care of the wildfire. Please protect the village and fjord."

"Of course," Espen said. "Thank you, Your Majesty."

"We're allies. Call me Reuven."

A quick smile tilted my lips. Even more camaraderie between the factions.

Reuven gave Espen a few sentence run down of their plan and Espen agreed, but asked him to warn the Fjord soldiers of his powers.

"They're well aware," Reuven replied.

Espen's gaze slid to Salka.

"Even in Iceland we've heard tales of what you can do, Espen," she said.

Espen toed the ground. "I'd still prefer any soldiers remain behind me. Seems like when my power is angered, it... Well, things escalate into a rather ugly form of magic."

I eyed my husband, wondering how much *uglier* his magic could get than burying people alive. Was that what the green stuff was?

"Noted." Reuven turned to his Fjord Fae soldiers and barked orders before focusing on his wife. Their fingers intertwined and he leaned in, whispering something to her ear before planting a kiss on her temple.

A flush of pink swept across her face and her gaze softened, adoration shining through. They nodded to each other and then he was running, soldiers following him as he rushed for the forest south of the fjord.

"How many soldiers do we have left here in town?" Øyvin asked Espen.

Espen peered over his shoulder and took a quick tally of the thirty or so soldiers still standing. "Not enough. We're spread thin due to the other fires around the country, but the Fjord Fae will be a massive help."

Looking back over the town square, we still had a decent contingent of soldiers. Many of which leaned against plant containers or sat on what was left of benches, trying to get a moment of rest between the skirmishes.

A lot of them had reddened skin—what I could only assume, from this distance, were burn marks.

I turned to Salka. "You said lava was next? Where will it come from? Who controls it?"

"My father does. He'll likely be at the back of town, trying to usher it through the streets."

"Put a chasm of fire between him and us," Øyvin said, his voice heavy with thought, like he was calculating every move in a chess game.

The quiet queen nodded. "That's always been his tactic."

"Then we need to be more strategic than him," Espen said before sliding out of our circle to a group of nearby soldiers. He knelt beside them and started healing various burns. My heart fluttered and pride welled inside me. Even in the midst of chaos, my dear husband would always help those who were in need.

"We need to get Espen back there," Øyvin said, drawing my focus to the conversation. "Get him behind the lava line and close enough to Veigar to kill him."

"I have killing powers too," I added. "I used some earlier today. Wiped me out a bit, but I've been holding them back to use on Veigar." I turned to Salka and mouthed, "Sorry."

She waved aside the comment.

"Let's get Espen in there first," Øyvin replied. "Then have you slide in behind him with the attack."

I nodded. It was a decent plan. Simple, yet effective. And far from the hare-brained idea of me climbing a nearby roof to zap the king from above. Would I be risking slipping on wet tiles? Sure. Would I be playing and winning a real-life game of *The Floor is Lava*? Yup.

"Can you do the lava thing?" I asked Salka.

Her lips quivered into a ghost of a smirk. "Not quite on the same scale, and not like he can. He can get it going and walk away, watching it tear through everything in its path. My powers aren't nearly that strong."

"Better than nothing, babes," I said and winced at the moniker. "Sorry, Your Majesty. Blame the waning adrenaline and exhaustion."

Her delicate smirk flickered again.

I peered over at Øyvin. He grimaced as if he wanted to slap his hand across my mouth. And, honestly, he probably should. I was running on minimal sleep and zero caffeine. Who knew what shit would come out of my mouth.

Salka bristled and a deep groove formed between her onyx eyebrows. As slow as a cat stalking its prey, she turned and faced the street we'd just run back down.

"Brace yourselves," she said, her voice loud but calm.

A shock wave of heat blew across my face and through my ponytail like someone had opened a gigantic oven. Soldiers stirred from their perches, rising to their feet, and drawing their shields. Espen hurried over to us as another wave of heat blasted past and a new plume of smoke rose from somewhere behind Fisken.

"Keep a distance between yourselves and the flow," Salka said, eying the street.

Øyvin stepped beside me, Espen taking the other flank but putting himself slightly in front. An action so different from his usual request of always walking beside me. It was like this would be the only time he'd step in front of me—when a danger presented itself.

Øyvin, meanwhile, would always have my back. And thanks to our height difference could keep an eye on attacks coming from any direction.

Red and black lava crept past Fisken toward the town square, orange bubbles bursting and sending specks of molten debris into the air.

"Holy fucking shit." The words tumbled from me.

"Soldiers! Cannons!" Øyvin yelled. Fjord Fae fell into line and blasted the oncoming flow. The water hissed as it made contact and steam blended with smoke.

"Spread out and divide!" Espen commanded, and fae from all three factions split up, trudging cautiously down side streets—weapons drawn, Fjord Fae leading the way with shields of stone protecting them all.

Salka and Espen stalked forward, the Queen waving her arms in some ethereal pattern that looked more like a witch casting a spell over a cauldron than a fae drawing on their powers.

I moved to walk after them, but stumbled, catching myself on the arm of a bench. *What the fuck was that?*

Peering at the ground, I searched for what had tripped me up. Was there a random rock I'd missed or had I tripped on my own goddamn foot again? Rain-soaked asphalt stared back at me like it had just played a prank.

Something in my arm spasmed, and I clutched it to my chest.

"Lennie?" Øyvin's voice sounded like it was yards away and under water.

A wave of pain and fear washed through me, bringing me to my knees. The lightning-shaped scar on my left arm pulsed like an erratic heartbeat.

"What's happening to me?"

Lightning cracked out of the forest on the north side of the fjord and shot through the sky.

Air caught in my throat. "Something's wrong."

156
LENNIE

I stared at the spot where the lightning had crackled through the forest as a wave of fatigue washed over me. My butt met the ground, and a shaky breath left my lips.

"What's wrong?" Øyvin's voice changed frequency like it was coming in and out of range on a radio. "Talk to me."

"What the hell?" I mumbled.

A stitch formed in my side like I'd run a marathon, the pain spasming at regular intervals. I hunched over, feeling for injuries, but found nothing. Still, something within me felt off.

I took a deep breath and focused on my magic. The mass of energy was still there but... not entirely. It was as if it were curling into a ball to protect itself. What the hell was happening?

Magical lightning shot out from between the trees on the north side of the fjord once more. My head whipped in that direction, and I narrowed my gaze. It looked like it was coming from the clearing where I'd photographed the illegal magic transfer last year. The spot that had been left scarred, like my arm, by the misuse of power.

Another torrent of electricity forked into the sky.

"Hey guys." My voice trembled as a wave of anxiety overtook me. Since Reuven had run to the southern hillside to ward off the flames, there were only two other beings that could possibly be behind those attacks. "I don't think Veigar is in town."

"I'm more concerned about you." Øyvin brought his finger and thumb to my chin and tilted my head toward him. His lips sat in a firm line, a crease knit between his eyebrows. "Tell me what's happening, Trouble."

"I'm not sure. I think—" I gasped, pain lancing through my body again as thunder rumbled. With a shaky finger, I motioned toward the mountainside. "Veigar found Halvar. I think that's them fighting."

That had to be what the lightning was. Those looked like killing attacks, but stronger. Something otherworldly. And there were two men in the area that I'd classify as not of this world.

"I'm not worried about Halvar. I'm worried about you."

Another pulse of pain ripped through my side as if protesting his statement, and a wave of concern washed through me. "I think we might need to worry about him."

"Doubtful," Øyvin replied. "And I'm not letting you out of my sight."

"Agreed," Espen said as he appeared beside us. A thin layer of rain-soaked ash clung to him like sprinkles on a cupcake.

"I have to do this."

"You don't *have* to leave our side," Espen said.

Øyvin shook his head rapidly.

"You both know I'm the only one here who has that killing power."

Espen's gaze dipped to his hands before looking back at me. "I have destructive powers that can decompose people."

"What!"

Øyvin and I stared at him like he'd grown two heads. Maybe that's what the green stuff was? The stuff that had been weaving around his fingers earlier.

Espen shrugged. "I don't like it. It feels like death, but I could use it."

"Then use it on the lava stuff and whoever might be lingering behind it," I countered.

Øyvin looked as if he was still trying to wrap his mind around Espen's revelation.

Another wave of discomfort ran through my bones, and I stifled a wince. We didn't have time for this. I needed to get to that mountain.

"We'll discuss that news later. I need to get up the mountain. This was always the plan. I have some extra magic juice in me from Freija that could be used against Veigar." At least, I hoped I had. I was pretty sure that was an accurate interpretation of her tale from the Temple, but either way. I had royal killing magic and my partners didn't. *I* had to go.

A rumble sounded from Øyvin's chest, and Espen let out a huff through his nose before pulling me into his arms.

"Lennie." Kiss. "Louise." Kiss. "*Solbakke.*" Kiss. "Martin." He kissed the tip of my nose. "Don't you dare get yourself killed on that mountain."

I grinned.

He nudged me into another pair of arms which spun me until I faced a broad chest. Øyvin pressed one hand to my lower back, the other cupping the base of my head. "What he said." Then he kissed me like it might be the last thing he ever did.

My heart pounded and I felt like a feather drifting on the smoke-filled breeze. Safe, protected, home. This was home.

"Just know I don't like this," Øyvin added with another rumble of displeasure.

"I know." I brushed the tip of my nose against his. "But you're needed down here."

Another crack of lightning lit up the north side of the fjord and shouting sounded from behind us.

I reluctantly pulled back. I didn't want to leave them. But I had to.

The mountain needed me.

Halvar might even need me.

And the town could be protected by my partners. They'd do everything they could to protect our home.

Espen tucked a strand of hair behind my ear as Øyvin let me slip from his hold.

"Follow me when the town is secured." I moved without further thought, my focus locked on the spot where I'd seen the flash of lightning.

With stitches in my sides and a constant tremble of pain through my bones, I bolted through town, ducking and weaving through the streets I now knew as well as the scar on my left arm. Ash-filled puddles lined the edges of the road, some appearing more maroon than others. Plants in window boxes sagged under the weight of the storm and soot, while rainwater rushed down gutters and spouts.

Sweeping through the edge of Skolvik, I barreled down the path past Solveig's house. Boulders glistened along the edge of the fjord and the little bushes that defended the homes looked like they'd been doused in gray icing sugar.

Another flash of lightning ripped across the sky, thunder rumbling in its wake, and I increased my pace. The path may have been slippery, but if I fell, I'd just get back up again.

Reaching the trailhead, I darted into the forest, jumping over logs and rocks, avoiding patches of moss that had grown slick with the downpour. Errant tendrils of hair glued themselves to the side of my face, sweat and rain acting as a natural adhesive. Something moved to my left and I ground to a stop as a fae with pitch black eyes and snarling lips stepped out from behind a tree.

Flames danced across his fingertips.

I didn't have time to think.

I launched for the Fire Fae, pulling on that killing magic that was a necessary evil to protect the mountain and village. Power seared down my arms and I aimed at the guy's head. He reared back at my advance, but it was too late. The magic wrapped around him like a vice and squeezed the life out of him. His body dropped to the forest floor with a dull thud.

"Don't fuck with my family."

I continued up the trail, ignoring the way my thighs and calves screamed at me, refusing to give in to the guilt of taking another life, however necessary. Magic swirled in my chest, slower now, like it needed to recharge after that death. I'd need to be more judicious with its use. Careful not to wear myself out. But most of all, I needed to get to that clearing. I needed to help.

Twigs and mud squelched beneath my feet, rain pelted the trees, and the sky darkened even more overhead as the storm intensified.

Reuven's magic, no doubt.

The sound of a branch snapping had me spinning on the spot, raising my arms into a fighting stance.

Another Fire Fae appeared, and I narrowed my gaze at his his hulking form. This one was bigger than the others in town. Thicker neck. Broader shoulders. And hands that looked like they could stopper a volcano like a cork in a wine bottle.

I drew a sword and settled into my battle stance. "I don't have time for you, Handsy."

He growled and launched a ball of fire at me.

Ducking and swinging, I swerved away from the hit before another orb flew at my face. I spun, but the fire caught my left arm.

"Not again," I huffed as I dodged yet another volley. This guy wasn't letting up, and he'd put me on defense. Football games may have been won with good defensive lines, but I needed to be on the offensive here. I needed to be the one who walked away from this fight.

He lunged, and I swung for his stomach.

Pulling to the side, he sidestepped the blade, but it delved into his arm. A roar of pain echoed around us, and I stutter-stepped as he wrapped his uninjured hand around the sword and yanked.

I flew through the mud and crashed to my knees, pain zinging up my legs. The sword fell to the ground with a muffled thud and panic ran through me. I scrambled through the dirt reaching for the blade. The number one rule Halvar had said when using a sword was to not have it used against you. I couldn't lose it. Couldn't let it fall into enemy hands. Especially hands that big.

Crawling across rocks and mud, I reached for the stone sword, pulling the magic back inside me, the blade disintegrating—

Fingers wrapped around the back of my neck and hauled me out of the dirt. A high-pitched yelp sprung from me and the man turned my face to him. His snarl was all I could see. I grasped at his arms, digging my nails into the stab wound I'd given him. He didn't even flinch. A bubble of hope burst inside me as blood and water sluiced down my back and around my neck where his thumb pressed.

My lungs screamed.

Vision blurred.

This was it.

But if I could… If I could only push some stunning… Magic into…

A ball of light flew over my head and smacked into the Fire Fae's face. The pressure around my throat loosened and I pushed out of his hold, stumbled back, and gasped for air.

"My eyes!" he screamed and pressed his palms to his sockets.

I whipped my head to one side, turning my body sideways so I kept the Fire Fae in my peripheral vision. Torsten stepped out from between two pines, his chest heaving, tawny hair hanging around his chin, eyes locked on the fae he'd just hit.

"I didn't know you had royal magic like me."

He shook his head and mouthed, "I don't."

"What? Then how the hell…"

Oh no, wait. He'd always said he didn't have royal powers, just royal-like light magic. My shoulders fell. "Shit."

He nodded, and I put myself between him and the angered Fire Fae who was now blinking and banking a bunch of fire in his now bloody hands. Both balls of flame flew at us, and I barely got a shield of stone down in time. The thick board of rock thrummed into the mud, shaking the ground beneath us.

Torsten leaned into the shield to reinforce it as a gigantic orb of flames shot at us. The shield exploded with an almighty boom. Rock flew in all directions and we went flying off the trail and into the forest. My head cracked against a tree trunk. Air whooshed from my lungs and my ears rang like I'd just been punched. I groaned and my favorite swear-word slipped from my lips.

A pained moan sounded from my right, and I glanced down toward the noise.

A blurry Torsten came into view—his gray uniform dark and mottled with black, shards poking out of his hair, and blood seeping from his nose and left ear. My stomach roiled.

No. Not Torsten, please.

The Fire Fae roared and circled back as if goading me to try and attack him now that I knew what he could do. It was a wrong move on his part, though.

"I might not be able to save my friend," I yelled and pointed at the fae in red, "but I'm going to fucking kill you."

I was losing friends today. People who'd welcomed me into their lives. People I cared about. My family. I wasn't losing another one.

Rising to my feet, I launched blade after stony blade at the Fire Fae. Magic, stone, and demi-fae worked as one. Launching, creating, and launching again. One hand and then the other.

Handsy was nimble for his size, but I still landed some shots between his own flurry of fire. All I needed was a few seconds, an opening to launch more of that death magic—

Something whizzed past my ear and a knotty branch sprouted from the soft flesh beneath the man's Adam's apple. I didn't bother to look behind me to see which Forest Fae had saved my ass. I took the split second of opportunity and finally launched a wave of my death magic at the beast. The power seared through my aching arms and wrapped around him like thick ropes. They pulsed and tightened. His eyes bugged out even more as he grasped at his neck, mouth opening and closing like a goldfish. He dropped to his knees, then fell on his face, lodging the stick further into his own throat.

"Fucking finally," I huffed.

Turning around, I found Leif on his knees, leaning over Torsten, his own uniform mottled with dark patches that looked alarmingly like blood. He draped his green cape over his husband's abdomen and clutched his hand in his.

I scrambled over to them and knelt beside my fallen friend. "He'll be okay," I said out loud, hoping I was right.

Leif's dark green eyes met mine, and worry struck through me.

"Trygve is at the boathouse. He can help. And Espen. Espen is in the village."

Leif gave me a thin-lipped smile so brief I might've imagined it before he turned his watery gaze to Torsten. "He'll survive. Won't you, my love?"

Torsten's head moved gently as if nodding, his eyes hooded and glazed, scarlet running down the side of his face.

Leif delicately examined Torsten's injuries and wiped his hair off his forehead. He'd turned pale. Too pale. Sweat mixing with rain at his temples. Another dark stain bloomed on Leif's green cape.

I swallowed hard.

"Thank you for saving me," I said, motioning over my shoulder to the dead Fire Fae.

"Not the first time one of my arrows has saved your behind, baby fae."

I furrowed my eyebrows. "What are you talking about?"

"Last year. When Kjetil captured you. My arrow was the one that took him down."

"What? I thought that was Espen."

Leif shook his head. "He was busy. I was watching his back."

"All this time I thought it was Espen who'd saved me."

"Do you really think I'd let the love of Espen's life get killed on the battle-field?"

My chin quivered and my stomach twisted into a mass of knots as I looked to his husband. If I'd made a stronger shield. If Torsten hadn't leaned against it. If he'd let me... Fuck, he needed to survive. But the blood. There was too much blood.

"You need to get that looked at too," Leif said, drawing my attention away from Torsten and nodding at my arm.

I peered down at what was left of my uniform. Large holes had formed in the wool and the skin below bubbled like a severe sunburn. I winced. I couldn't deal with that now. "I have to get up the mountain. I need to get to the clearing."

"Then go, and be more careful. Let the forest serve as your shield. Listen to her, let her guide and protect you."

Sounded like some mumbo-jumbo to me, and yet, I understood what he meant. I needed to put more thought and strategy into my movements, watch my own back, and use the terrain to my advantage. This was my home field. An area I'd photographed countless times. I knew it better than the Fire Fae.

I nodded to Leif and gave him my thanks.

I can do this.

Focusing on the forest, I rose to my feet and stepped toward the trail.

I dared one more look back at my friends. Thick pine branches hung over them like nature's umbrellas, protecting them from the steady rain. Leif lay down beside Torsten and wrapped his arm over him, pressing his hand to Torsten's chest.

My heart shattered as somewhere, deep within me, I knew he wasn't going to make it. Leif may have saved Espen's love, but I hadn't been able to save his. My chest tightened as a tear spilled from my eye. I batted it away. I should've stopped Torsten, should've protected him. Had the power to do so and fucking failed.

Leif's gaze met mine and he shook his head as if he could hear my self-loathing thoughts.

"Go," he mouthed.

Wiping away another tear, I turned back to the trail, stepped over a fallen tree, and continued up the mountain, leaving another piece of my heart behind.

LENNIE

Silent tears streamed down my face as I trudged up the mountain trail as fast as possible. I listened for any other footsteps or noises, following Leif's wisdom to tread lightly and watch my own back.

Leif.

Poor Leif.

Poor Torsten.

If only he hadn't stepped between me and the shield. If only I'd killed that Fire Fae straight away, avoided this mess entirely. A lump lodged in my throat. Head wounds like that were hard to come back from, and with the amount of blood pooling around him, I doubted I'd ever see his teasing smile again.

Another round of tears rushed over my cheeks, mixing with raindrops. I wiped them away as I tucked behind a thick evergreen. I didn't have time for sadness. Didn't have time to mourn. I could do that later. Right now, I needed to focus. I had a mountain and people to protect. I wasn't going to fail again today. Not a fucking chance.

A branch snapped up ahead and I stilled, bracing my back against the tree trunk as moss reached around from the north side to tickle my neck.

Footfalls thumped at uneven intervals as if someone was searching. My heart thrashed against my ribs, breaths sounding too loud as they puffed from my nose.

A Fire Fae slunk down the trail past where I stood.

I stopped breathing.

He scanned his surroundings, hands curved and ready to use his powers.

If he looked over his right shoulder... If he turned even forty degrees in my direction, I'd be caught.

Lightning clattered once again, and thunder rumbled from overhead.

He twisted.

I moved.

Catapulting from my perch, I threw a ball of stunning magic at the soldier. His limbs twitched, body convulsing, before he fell to the ground like a rag doll. Without checking on his condition, I conjured a camera-sized rock and smashed it over his head.

"Sorry, buddy." I threw aside the bloody stone. "You came to the wrong town."

Another flash of light blitzed from the woods up the mountainside and I ran toward it. There was no time to waste. Exhaustion clawed at me and my body ached, but I had to keep pushing, keep moving. I didn't have time to deal with the emotional trauma of killing other soldiers or the bile churning in my stomach.

Dispatching two more Fire Fae in the same way on the hike up, I eventually made it to the clearing where we'd first discovered the scars of Balder's illegal magic transfers.

A battle cry had my steps faltering and my ragged breaths stilling as I ducked behind another tree.

Halvar stood on the north side of the clearing, Veigar to the south on my right, dense pine trees surrounding them on all sides. The land between them looked like it had been torn apart by a massive, scalding rake—soil overturned and flora singed. New marks of royal power slashed through the trees, the silvery light glowing.

Halvar's cape was missing, and his uniform was drenched and covered in woodland debris. A thin cut marred his left cheek, his knuckles bloody and raw as he gripped a monstrous rock axe in one hand while the other wielded a circular stone shield.

Veigar's lips curved into a slick smile. Gone were his sunglasses and suave suits. Instead, his fae uniform, a majestic ensemble of red and black material with gold buttons and epaulets, clung to him like armor. All he needed was a crown and he'd fit the bill for a fairytale monarch.

Shame this wasn't a fairytale, though.

Veigar swung his fiery sword, and a jet of flames shot out of the tip.

Halvar raised his shield, buffeting the blow. His feet slid in the mud, the force of the onslaught enough to shift him backward.

A gasp lodged in my throat, and I crouched behind my tree. Holy mother of Satan, Veigar was powerful.

Stones flew into the air and twisted into a tornado of destruction, churning toward the king. Veigar dodged Halvar's counter like a ballroom dancer, only one rock crashing against his shin. He winced, growled, and unfurled his free hand, launching another barrage of fire at Halvar.

The beast of the mountain crouched beneath it and slammed his axe into the ground. Soil ruptured and the fissure ran toward Veigar. The King's fire stuttered and burned out, and he tumbled to his back.

Yes.

Veigar flipped and rolled to his feet again.

No.

They both stuck out their arms and aimed at each other. Royal power shot from them and crashed in the middle of the clearing. Lightning crackled from the point of impact, stretching toward the clouds.

Fuuuuuck.

That's what I'd seen in town. That was the royal fae powers at work... And Halvar only had a fraction of the royal power Veigar had, yet he could still do that! Was he actually a fae or a god who was really good with rocks?

A boulder sat at the edge of the clearing, branches draping over the top of it, moss clinging to crevasses. If I snuck closer and hid behind it, I could get a better look *and* be nearer should Halvar need back up.

The lightning onslaught ended, both parties' chests heaving.

"You won't last long, Head Guard."

"Fucking try me."

Halvar bellowed like a bear and Veigar cackled, both distracted by each other's new attacks.

Now was my chance.

Dropping to my hands and knees, I crawled over to the recliner-sized rock and pulled my cape over my hair like a gremlin to hide the blonde strands and blend in. This probably wasn't what Leif meant when he said to use the terrain to my advantage, but I was trying my best here.

I crouched behind the boulder, keeping my gaze locked on the two men in the clearing.

Veigar launched a beam of crackling and pulsing royal magic at Halvar. I squinted at the bright light, while Halvar launched his shield like a discus. The stone disk cleaved the bolt of lightning in two before shattering halfway across the field and sending splinters of stone and magic into the air. I turned my face away and narrowly avoided being pelted by the pieces.

Peering back at the fight, I found Halvar with an axe in one hand and a stone hammer in the other. He looked like a Norse god reborn. If any human saw this, they'd think their mythological gods were real and that Halvar was a silver-haired Thor with pointy ears.

The two men continued their dance of death, gliding around the clearing like gladiators. Their steps assured and measured, their movements confident and clear, like they'd been preparing for this fight for centuries. And maybe they had.

A boulder materialized between the two men and a moment later, Halvar's hammer struck it from the top. A massive *crack* pierced the air. Shards broke off the rock and shot toward Veigar.

The King waved his arm in front of him and a surge of heat washed over the clearing. The shards stalled in the air and turned molten. Glowing like deadly fireflies, the fragments hung immobile.

Halvar swallowed hard and grimaced.

"This is the best you can do?" Veigar sneered and waved his arm again.

The lumps of lava flew back toward Halvar.

He batted them away with his weapons, but not without taking a few to his arms and chest.

Shit that had to hurt.

I pressed myself further against my boulder, hoping what was left of my gray uniform camouflaged me. I didn't want to interrupt Halvar or cause him to lose focus, but if there was a moment for me to jump in and help, a moment where I could finally use these killing powers and whatever bonus-ancestor-juice Freija had gifted me, I'd take it.

Halvar's sky-blue eyes scanned the clearing, sliding around, pausing on my boulder for a nanosecond, before continuing their assessment.

Had he seen me?

He swept to his left, cris-crossing his steps. Veigar matched him, coming closer to my hiding spot and giving me his back.

My shoulders curved inward, and my heart raced as sweat and rain soaked every inch of my clothes. *Don't look behind you. Don't look behind you. Don't look behind you.*

"Come along, Halvar." Veigar's voice was filled with malice, goading the man. "Can't you protect your precious mountain?"

Halvar gave the king a death glare that would land me in an early grave if directed toward me.

The earth vibrated and gigantic rock spikes pierced through the soil. Veigar twisted and moved as one of the points jutted up where he stood. The edge caught his arm, tearing through his sleeve as it rose to the sky like a tree, and left a stream of blood in its wake.

The King's chest heaved as Halvar continued his attack.

More spikes retreated and re-emerged.

Balls of fire flew around the field.

Arrow-like stone shards filled the air.

Flashes of royal power shot from one man to the other.

The fight was like a clash of kings. Two powerful beings that refused to be torn down. Halvar raced toward the King, axe raised above his head, hammer across his sternum like a shield.

He swung.

Veigar roared and a blast of fire exploded all around him like a firework.

I sheltered behind my boulder as flames licked around it, heating the stone against my back. Wincing, I breathed through the onslaught and temperature. It felt like I was going to be burned alive and served up as steak.

Mercifully, the flames banked, leaving behind the smell of singed wood and grass.

I peered around my grilled rock.

Trees creaked, threatening to fall.

Pine needles curled.

Halvar staggered back, and I clamped my hand over my mouth to hold back my gasp.

Singed pieces of wool hung from Halvar's arm and leg, the skin beneath red and raw. Burns covered his entire left side as if he'd tried to shield himself from the flames. He groaned and fell onto his back, and my understanding of the world tilted upside down.

"Your dedication was always commendable, Halvar." Veigar's authoritative voice carried around the clearing like a Roman conqueror as he walked toward Halvar, dragging his fiery sword through the battered earth. "You'll be remembered for your bravery and sacrifice."

Remembered?

"Do it," Halvar bit out. "Kill me, and see what happens."

"I'm inevitable, Halvar son of Harald. The ancestors foretold this. Willed this into being. I am to lead the fae to a new dawn." He raised his sword over Halvar, aiming for his chest. The ground quaked.

My eyes widened, and my heart thrashed against my ribs.

Over my dead fucking body.

I launched from my spot and threw stunning magic right between Veigar's shoulder blades. The ball of crackling light landed perfectly and he spasmed, throwing his arms out wide. The blade of flames disintegrated as my own broadsword appeared in my hands, power zipping down it.

He turned on the spot, magic crackling in his palms.

But I was already across the field, already in range, and nothing could stop me.

A roar of anger ripped from my lungs, and I threw all my weight behind my swing. The blade sunk into Veigar's neck, met momentary resistance, then kept going all the way through. His head lolled to one side then popped off as his body dropped to the ground. Empty black eyes stared up into the rain, mouth hung open in shock, and blood streamed from the decapitated head.

Bile raced up my throat and my limbs shook.

"Holy fuck," I muttered as my sword slipped from my grasp. "I just killed the Fire Fae King."

158

LENNIE

I raced over to where Halvar lay on the sodden ground. Welts and scarlet slashes covered his left side in a gruesome tapestry of destruction. His chest heaved, tearing at the delicate wounds, and he winced through labored breaths.

"Oh my shit, I saved your ass!"

He grumbled.

Kneeling beside him, mud caked my knees and water sank further into my already soaked pants. "Holy fuck. What can I do? How can I help? We need a healer. We need Trygve. No. Espen. Espen is closer."

"Well—" Halvar inhaled sharply and groaned. "Well done."

"I'd make a joke about compliments, but now isn't the time."

The big guy rolled his eyes, and my fear of his untimely demise banked... slightly.

Blood seeped from more wounds I couldn't see beneath his tattered uniform and stained the soil underneath him. Injuries I hadn't seen him get. They must've been fighting each other long before I got here.

My hands trembled as I pulled off my cape and pressed it to one of his open wounds. It wasn't clean material, but we needed to stop the bleeding. "Tell me what to do."

Halvar opened his mouth and the ground trembled. His eyes widened with fear and my stomach flip-flopped at the sight.

"What the fuck was that?" I asked with a quick look back at the dead king. "He can't do shit from the great beyond, can he?"

"No. Look at me, Lennie."

I glanced back at Halvar.

"Leave me. Protect the mountain."

"What are you talking about, big guy? I can't leave you here to die. Who would run our Council meetings? Who would scare off the crazies?"

"You'd do fine."

I scoffed, fear nearly choking me at the thought of losing him. "We both know that's a lie."

The ground shuddered again, and an almighty cracked rent the air.

Halvar's lips quivered, his eyes focused above my head, and I slowly turned toward the noise.

It wasn't coming from the clearing. It *was* coming from the direction of the fissure. The one we'd been worried about. The one Veigar had visited the other day.

I sucked in a panicked breath.

"No... This can't be happening."

I'd known the fissure felt off magically, but what if Veigar had shoved lava down there? Salka said he could create lava and walk away from it, letting it do its thing—whatever that meant. My eyes darted between the mountaintop and the town below us, my heart racing wildly. The magic in my sternum curled further in on itself.

Halvar's hand reached up, turning my face to his as another crack sounded, the trees shaking.

"*Run.*"

"But you—"

"Leave me! Save them!" Halvar roared.

Spinning on the spot, I didn't hesitate again, running like lives depended on me.

I bolted through the forest, dodging between trees and over moss-covered boulders, the sodden soil squelching beneath my feet. Rain slashed at my face and my breaths came hard and heavy as I pushed myself to run faster than ever before.

The ground shook again, and I grabbed a tree for purchase, before pushing myself harder. I had to get there in time. I had to do something. Had to some-how stop the land from falling into the fjord or the resulting wave would drown the village and the loves of my life.

A few Fjell Fae soldiers emerged from behind trees up ahead, their gazes flooded with panic. "Ma'am! It's cracking!" One of them yelled, waving his arm above his head.

I careened toward him. "Clear the mountain!"

"But—"

"*That's an order!*"

What the hell had come over me? Maybe it was the trauma of the number of people I'd killed today, including Veigar, or the volume of adrenaline coursing through my veins. Or maybe the fact that I'd just left Halvar to die. Either way, I'd somehow flipped a switch and activated a new *boss mode*.

The soldiers scrambled and dove back into the forest, heading in separate directions.

My feet slid through the soil as I came to a stop at the tree line. The land before me vibrated and small rocks rolled past like tumbleweeds, bouncing down the steep incline. A large groove opened by my feet and I took a step back. "Shit."

This thing was coming down. Now.

I hopped over the cracking soil and ran out onto the middle of the cleared slope, joining the five soldiers huddled there.

"Do you have a report?" I asked the closest one.

She wobbled and readjusted her footing. "The northern watch guards reported significant heat coming from the fissure this morning."

My brow furrowed.

"They think a Fire Fae set an explosive down there," she continued.

"Was that what the cracking noise was?" I asked, putting my back to the fjord and looking up the hillside.

A tall fae with the build of a marathon runner raised his hand. "No, that was the land splintering after the suspected explosion."

"I think it's lava," I said. "Salka mentioned Veigar can walk away from it. Or could."

Five confused gazes stared back at me.

The ground quaked again and we wobbled, holding our arms out to regain our balance.

"Veigar is dead." They smiled. "But his daughter told me he could set off lava eruptions and walk away."

The woman next to me nodded as if a light bulb had turned on in her head. "Like his volcanoes. He can set them off and hide."

I snapped my fingers and pointed at her. "Exactly. I think that is what's happening here."

Soil above us detached from its perch and started sliding toward us.

Two male soldiers dropped to their knees and planted their hands in the ground. Translucent magic ebbed from them, caressing the mountainside as it wove upward, trying to fix the breakage.

"We need to figure out how to secure this," I muttered.

"I don't think we can," another soldier said. "It's almost half a kilometer wide."

I blinked. *Fuck if I knew what a kilometer was.*

"From this tree line to that one," the female soldier piped up, her eyes locked on my face.

Roots snapped, stones skittered down the hillside, and the purple and pink heather vibrated. Something in my sternum spasmed and my left arm tingled. My magic pulsed like it was under attack. Which was weird considering I'd already dispatched Public Enemy Number One. I rubbed the heel of my palm against my chest, hoping to alleviate the pain, but it was useless.

Something was still wrong. That exhaustion I felt in the village hadn't... "Fuck. I'm an idiot."

"Ma'am?"

"Get everyone off the mountain right now."

"We cannot leave—"

"You can and you will," I replied, my voice stern and unyielding, which was kind of new. I turned to the guys with their hands in the ground. "That includes you two, as well."

They lifted their fingers from the dirt. "What about the mountain?"

"Halvar is injured and dying in the clearing down the hill by the scarred trees."

Everyone's eyes went wide.

"Thought that might get your attention. Now, go save him!"

All five of them scrambled off the hillside and back into the forest. Thank goodness. If this went wrong, if my hunch was pure lunacy, I wanted them as far away as possible. Them getting the big guy to Espen would be helpful too.

I turned my focus back to the weakened hillside. The crack yawned open at the top.

"Hello, old friend," I said.

It wasn't Halvar and his fight I'd felt. Our magic wasn't connected to each other like some movie juju or fairytale fate thing.

It was the mountain.

My magic was tied to the mountain.

It always had been. Freija had said so herself. She'd asked the ancestors for more power to save her weakening mountain and passed that along to me.

This. This was what I was meant to use those powers for. To uphold my promise to her and protect her mountain while also protecting what I loved the most.

Another massive crack ripped through the air and the ground started to slide. I teetered and fell to my knees, pain smarting up my legs from the impact.

"All right, Freija. Let's see what you gave me."

Hold. I shoved my hands into the wet ground, pushing underneath the grass and rock-riddled terrain. Stones poked beneath my fingernails and plants tickled my wrists. The magic in my chest rumbled and unfurled like a bear waking from a long hibernation.

Hold. I willed the magic in my sternum to obey, to flow from me like it was the tide itself. That swirling mass of energy cascaded through my arms, painfully zapping my skin as it went.

HOLD.

The mountainside groaned as power seared through me, arching my back and splaying my fingers until it felt like they were being torn from my hand.

"HOLD!"

My vision flashed silver, the ground beneath my fingers shining back at me like a camera's flash. A scream tore from my lips, and I pushed harder. Lines of silver magic crackled out from where I knelt, shooting up the terrain like a spiderweb and pushing the land back into position. Back where it belonged. Back where we needed it to stay.

Muffled voices sounded around me, but I couldn't let my focus drift. I needed to put this piece of mountain back into place before it fell into the fjord and wiped out everything I loved.

Something wet dripped down my cheeks—rain or tears, I couldn't tell. It didn't matter.

I pushed and pushed and pushed. Giving all of myself, all of my power to the mountain.

Everything turned silver. Silver ground. Silver plants. Silver sky. My head lolled forward, my breaths ripping from my chest. The ground shook and moved upward like a puzzle piece returning to its spot.

Good.

My heart beat faster than a camera on sport mode.

My arms burned.

My head was about to split in two.

But it was working. It had to be working. "Please..." The word blended into the ringing in my ears.

If I pushed a little bit harder. Gave a little more.

"HOLD!" I screamed. Power seared down my arms and into the mountain. My hair broke free of its tie and whipped around me in a frenzy. Lightning crackled out of me and thunder rolled through the valley.

"Trouble! No!"

"Lennie!"

A thick wave of exhaustion washed over me, drawing my hands from the soil. My body collapsed backward, rain pelting me from all angles as I tumbled, and silver turned to darkness.

159

LENNIE

A blanket of darkness wrapped around me, but I could feel something... Hand. I could feel my hand and a gentle pressure against it.

Weird. Why couldn't I feel my body?

Weirder still. What the hell kind of dream had I just had? It was strange as fuck. I'd found magical creatures called fae, moved to Norway, and got married. If anything, that was my mother's dream—

"You're not dreaming, Trouble." The voice was muffled, like I was underwater.

The pressure against my hand tightened, and I squeezed back.

"Lennie? Lennie, can you hear me?" another voice said. Male. It was definitely male. Both of the voices were. Low and warm.

My elbow came back online, and I moved my arm.

"She's waking up."

"Stand back, let me check her pulse, please."

"I've had my fingers on it since we got here."

Someone growled.

"Oh, all right. But I wish to examine her when she wakes and has had time to process." A lighter, more old-fashioned voice said. Had I been transported to the 1800's? Doubt I'd do well there. Had they even discovered coffee yet?

"Don't give me that look, Espen," the old-fashioned voice said again. "You may examine her first, but as a Fjell Fae and my friend, it is my duty to check on her."

A door bumped shut.

Espen... I knew that name. It was the man I'd married in my dream. "Was I still dreaming?"

"No, you're not still dreaming, Trouble. Time to wake the fuck up."

Warmth filled my shoulders and chest. I could feel them again. Slowly but surely, sensation returned to my body along with enough brain cells to compute that the life I'd been living in my dream was real.

I peeled my eyes open and squinted against the faint glow of magical lights. A cavern-like ceiling loomed overhead, magical sconces flickered against the walls, and thick wooden chair backs surrounded me like pixies sent to worship their god. Cool stone brushed against my free hand, and my brows furrowed. Stone walls, glowing sconces, big slab table...

Wait a second.

"Did you guys put me on the Council meeting table like an offering?" My voice croaked and I peered at where Espen held my hand. "Yup."

"We got you changed and cleaned up too," Øyvin said from my other side.

That would explain the airy feeling around my body.

Hold up. What clothes?

I glanced toward my feet. They'd put me in a white tunic, billowy pants, and my favorite pair of fuzzy socks. My gaze slid up from my toes, and I flinched.

Halvar stood at the head of the table, arms crossed, eyes locked on me. Scars littered his left side and mottled his face, and part of his beard was missing. The other side had been shaved short to match.

"You're alive," I said to Halvar.

"As are you."

"Thank the ancestors," Øyvin muttered, and my attention fell on him.

The stubble on his chin was scruffier than usual, his hair in disarray like he'd been raking his hands through it, and those eyes... Those oceans looked down at me with a degree of sorrow that wrapped around my heart and squeezed. He'd been worried. Really worried.

I swallowed hard and turned to Espen. An air of hope clung to him and his lips curled into a gentle smile when he caught me looking. But I wasn't fooled by the visible relief. Bags hung heavy under his eyes, and he was still in his police gear, his shredded and scorched jacket slung over the back of his chair.

They both looked like they'd been holding vigil at someone's death bed. *My* death bed.

I wanted to reach out and wrap my arms around them, hold on and never let them go.

"What the hell happened?" I rasped.

"Wait," Øyvin said and disappeared for a moment, reappearing a second later with a pitcher and glass of water. Espen pulled me into a seated position, keeping his hand on my back, as Øyvin handed the drink to me, condensation cooling my palm. "Drink."

I didn't need to be told twice. I tipped the glass against my chapped lips and cool water sluiced down my throat. Saliva returned to my mouth, and I downed the whole thing before passing it back to Øyvin. He set it at the end of the table and turned his focus back to me.

"Thank you," I said. "Now, what happened?"

"What do you remember?" Espen asked.

I opened my mind and recent events came flooding back to me like a river that had breached its banks. The torrent of images and memories—happy and sad, terrifying and jubilant—washed through me. I shuddered and a whimper slipped free. Oddvar's burned. Ylva dead. Forest scorched. Torsten injured. Halvar severely injured too. And, holy hell, I'd killed Veigar.

It was too much. I needed to bury my head in the sand again like an ostrich and ignore my emotions. But I couldn't. Ylva didn't deserve that. The soldiers we'd lost didn't deserve that. The people I'd killed…

I swallowed the hard lump in my throat and let the onslaught in. Let it fill every part of me. From my pinky toes to the top of my head. We'd been through hell, and I had to acknowledge that.

"I remember everything," I blubbered as a tear slid down my cheek.

Espen stroked his palm down my spine, and Øyvin sat down, taking my other hand in his.

"How long have I been out?"

"Two whole days," Espen replied.

The room swayed. "What?"

"You used a lot of magic on the mountain," Øyvin said.

"Did it work? I mean, you're alive, but did it fall into the fjord or not?"

Øyvin shook his head.

Espen rubbed his free hand across my lower back, easing out the tension that had settled there. "You put it back in place. You saved us all."

"Well shit," I muttered. "I definitely tried."

"And you succeeded." Espen bobbed his head from one side to the other. "But there are always consequences to using that amount of magic."

"Like taking a two-day nap?"

Øyvin cleared his throat, and Espen winced.

I narrowed my eyes and looked between the two of them. "What consequences?"

"Try stunning me," Halvar said from the end of the table.

"Umm, what?"

"Stun me."

"I could flash you my boobs. They're quite stunning, just ask Espen. He's really fond of leftie."

Halvar rolled his eyes, and Øyvin muttered something about definitely being awake.

"Use your royal powers, Lennie," Halvar ordered.

"Fine."

I focused on the well of magic in my sternum. It felt different. Weaker. Like it'd been depleted and was trying to refill itself, only reaching a quarter tank so far. Calling on it and picturing a simple ball of light, I flexed my fingers and waited for the magic to skitter down my arm.

Nothing happened.

I tried again. Scrunching my face and closing my eyes, willing the telltale tingling sensation to result in a sparking ball of light in my palm.

Still, nothing happened.

My eyes flew open, and I let out a frustrated sigh. "It's broken."

"It's as we suspected," Espen said. "Try your Fjell powers."

Reaching inside myself, I pulled on a tendril of power and pictured a pebble in my hand. A tickle ran down my arm and a second later a small stone appeared. The royal magic wasn't working, but the Fjell power was still there and healing based on the feeling in my chest. "So, I'm partially broken?" I asked, setting aside the rock.

Halvar grumbled. "Indeed. The royal magic is gone."

My eyebrows hit my hairline. "*All* gone?"

Øyvin examined me with concern etched across his forehead while Espen pressed his fingers against my upper stomach, examining. I didn't complain. I didn't move. I stared at Halvar in shock. "How?"

"You used it all on the mountain," Halvar replied.

Espen's fingers delicately poked and prodded at me. "I still don't feel any changes. She feels fine—" He tapped on my left ribs, and I winced. "Well, except for the bruising."

He pulled back his hands and I raised my shirt, careful not to flash Halvar. A purple bruise bloomed across my left side like lilacs on a summer's day. I'd fought a lot of people, but I couldn't remember anyone getting a hit on me, especially in the ribs. Unless it was from when that stone shield broke against me and Torsten. "How'd I get that?"

"You fell," Øyvin said. "Tumbled a few meters before we could safely get to you."

"What do you mean *safely*?"

"We didn't dare touch you while—" Espen waved his hands beside his head then motioned to his eyes. "Too much power."

More memories flooded back. Painful ones. Silver ones. My vision had turned silver, and a web of power had shot out of me, sailing up the mountainside and hauling it back into place. Protecting everyone.

I huffed.

It was Freija's gift. The magic she'd asked for. I'd transferred it all right back into the mountain. Back where it belonged.

"I think I did my own magic transfer of sorts," I said and looked at the men in the room.

Clear eyes stared back at me, and they all nodded.

"That's certainly what it looked like from the sidelines," Espen said.

"It definitely felt that way too. Ten out of ten, do not recommend." I looked to the silver-haired fae. "Do you still have yours?"

He opened his right palm, and a small ball of crystal-white light appeared.

"Show off," I muttered.

Halvar scoffed and extinguished his magic.

"So, you're the only one with royal magic now?"

He shook his head. "A new light fae has been chosen to take care of the mountain's lighting needs."

"Who?"

"A young Fjell Fae by the name of Sofie."

My stomach flip-flopped as the fact settled in. "Wait, if there's a new light magic Fjell Fae then..." Then Torsten had died. That magic was passed on to another when the former died. My bottom lip trembled, and I clutched my partners' hands. "Torsten?"

Halvar grimaced and another lump formed in my throat. The need to cry creeping closer to the edge of my emotional cliff-side. I'd known it was coming. I'd seen his injuries. He'd have needed a miracle to survive those lacerations.

"Lennie," Espen sighed, his voice sounding heavy. "Leif died too."

"What? He was fine when I left them." Or, at least, that's what he'd claimed. There had been an alarming number of dark patches on his uniform.

Espen brushed a hand over my hair while Øyvin gave my fingers a squeeze. I didn't like where this was going.

"He succumbed to injuries a day after the battle," Espen said. "Too much blood loss. There was nothing I could do."

A whimper slipped out of me. I ripped my hands free and pressed them against my eyes as a sob wracked my body.

"I will leave you now," Halvar muttered and a second later the door to the Council chamber bumped shut.

I don't know how long I cried for. A minute, an hour, a day. But when the tears finally ran dry and Espen stopped rubbing my back, I crossed my legs in the middle of the table. I felt like a wrung-out washcloth—out of magic and out of tears. I'd poured them both on the mountain.

The emotional toll was too much to bear. I'd lost loved ones, failed others, and led people to their own deaths by giving orders while fighting against the Fire Fae.

"I'm a shitty leader," I mumbled and sighed.

Espen pivoted me and pulled me to the edge of the table, letting my legs hang over the edge. He clasped my hands in his. "Look at me, Lennie."

My gaze drifted to his warm amber eyes and the steadfast kindness I'd always find there. Out of the corner of my eye, I caught Øyvin coming to stand beside us.

"You're not a bad leader," Espen said. "Look at everything you've done."

I sniffled. "The café is gone after I promised Oddvar I'd take care of it. Øyvin was captured. My crazy, harebrained—"

Espen squeezed my hands tighter, dislodging my words and train of thought. "You saved people's lives by pulling them from a burning building. You gave them shelter in your own home. Earlier this year, you protected an heir that was about to be murdered. You may not think you're a good leader, Lennie, but your actions say otherwise. And I, for one, am proud of you."

I rested my forehead against his chest. "I barely recognize myself anymore."

"Really?" He tilted my chin with his finger to meet his gaze. "Because I see a woman who went from valuing nature and its beauty through her photographs to protecting it. You haven't changed. You've grown."

I swallowed hard at his observation and leaned into his touch.

"Leadership is so much more than words, Lennie. It's about action too. It's being willing to learn and do better when things don't go right the first time. It's about giving up pieces of yourself to better the lives of those you serve. It's using the tools you have to do the best you can."

"He's right, you know," Øyvin added. "You did everything in your power to save and protect people. That's what a leader does. Something we should all strive to do."

I blubbered and sniffled.

I'd tried my best. Done what felt right. Protected those I could. "It doesn't feel like I did good."

"It won't." Espen tucked me against him, cradling my head in his hand. "Not for a little while."

Øyvin closed in and rubbed his hand across my back. His eyes shimmered with a thousand words he didn't have to say. He was proud of me and loved me more than he could ever put into words.

I sniffed again and pulled back from Espen.

I loved them too. So very much. And perhaps it would take time to wrap my head around everything that had happened and what I'd done. But at least I'd have them to lean on while I recovered.

Sliding off the table, I stepped between the two of them and grabbed the front of their shirts. I pulled them into me and wrapped my arms around their torsos, forcing them into a big group hug. Øyvin huffed, Espen sighed, but they acquiesced and melted around me.

They were both right in their assessments of leadership and the things I'd done. From the inside looking out, it didn't appear like leadership. They were just things I did to help. But, coming from their perspective... Well, I guessed they had a point.

I let out an extended sigh and buried my face against their chests.

Espen pressed a kiss to the side of my head. "Let's go home."

160

ESPEN

The day had come. The day I'd been dreading for the past week: Ylva's funeral.

There was nothing to bury. Her ashes had disappeared into the wind after Herja burned her alive. But it was Forest Fae tradition to bury a soldier killed in combat, and her mother, Gunvor, had requested a funeral. So here we stood in the stave church graveyard, wearing black and shades of dark green, watching over a coffin covered in flowers. It wasn't empty though. I'd placed a wooden sword inside to represent the sharp woman we'd lost too soon. The woman who'd fought bravely until the very end.

Ylva's burial plot sat at the rear of the graveyard near the forest, verdant trees dappling the ground with shadows. It was the perfect spot for her.

I laid a bundle of purple blooms among the other flowers atop Ylva's casket and turned to the gathered crowd. Sniffles and tears filled the air as the mourners watched on, the stave church looming over their backs like a bear ready to attack. Nobody cared though. The sorrowful faces all focused on the coffin beside me.

My gaze found Lennie's and she gave me a gentle nod, willing me on.

I nodded back and cleared the lump lodged in my throat as the group waited for me to start the ceremony.

"Thank you for being here today," I said. "Ylva Nygård was a great friend, fae, daughter, and commander. With a wry sense of humor and unyielding love for the forest she swore to protect, Ylva was the best of us. Someone the young looked up to and the old revered."

My gaze shifted from the mourning masses to Ylva's casket.

"We will miss you more that you could ever know. You were a light that couldn't be tamed. A mind so sharp and strategically inclined. A soul that yearned for peace in an evermore complicated world."

A tear welled at the corner of my eye, and I inhaled sharply.

"A protector through and through. One who made the ultimate sacrifice for her friends, family, and fae-kind. A soldier who wouldn't have wanted to go in any other way."

However much I don't want you to leave. Not so soon. Not now. Not ever.

I took a deep breath and clenched my fists at my sides. "Thank you, my friend."

There was no reply. There never would be. She was already gone.

"Thank you for all the memories. For the laughs and the joy you brought into our world. F-for the—" My throat tightened around my words, barring them from leaving. Leaving like she was. I swallowed hard as a tear tumbled across my cheek.

I can't do this. Flashes of her demise blazed through my mind, reminding me of the end. Her end. Her final moments on this earth.

My tear-filled eyes found Lennie's. She gave me another gentle nod and a loving expression that buoyed me.

With a final look at the casket, I whispered, "Thank you."

I shuffled to the crowd and stepped up beside Lennie and Øyvin. The former looped her arm through mine and pulled me against her side, offering comfort and stability.

More sniffles filled the crowd.

Gunvor stepped forward, having traveled all this way for her daughter, and raised her hands to the trees. They bowed to her as if they were offering their own condolences. Perhaps they were. Gunvor, a tree-speaker, had a rare ability to speak and command the trees. She never spoke of all she could do, but her power was incredible, even at her great age.

Gangly limbs groaned and reached forward as roots rose from the ground and wrapped around the casket like long fingers forming a lattice. Slowly, the tree tendrils lowered the coffin into the hole in the ground.

"Ylva Nygård has served the forest well," Gunvor croaked, her voice carrying through the solemn silence. "May her soul be transported to the ancestors and her power re-bestowed to the woodland she held dear. Trees aid me."

The pines around us swayed, their creaking limbs composing a somber requiem I'd never forget.

Her casket disappeared into the ground and the roots spread out over top it, pushing it further. The Forest and Fjell Fae in the crowd raised their hands and I followed suit, coaxing the soil to fill and cover. Small handfuls from a nearby mound of dirt slid into the hole, eventually filling it to the top.

It was done.

She was gone.

This was the end.

This was goodbye.

My gaze drifted to the stone marker with her name on it.

Ylva Nygård.

Commander and Friend of the Forest.

"Goodbye, commander," I whispered. "You did well."

Another wave of tears streamed across my cheeks and dripped from my chin.

A warm hand cupped my face, and I turned into the heat. Lennie brushed her finger through the tears. "Come on," she whispered. "Let's go home."

I nodded, and with one final look back at Ylva's grave site, uttered, "Goodbye, my friend."

ØYVIN

A week after the battle, the village had been cleared of rubble and bodies, humans slowly trickled back into town, and the final fae memorials had concluded. Skolvik was doing its best to revert back to a new normal. Myself included.

Today, I found myself in the mountain, back in my old role, on a diplomatic mission. Light orbs bobbed around the rocky ceiling like glass floats on water, and thick pillars held the mass of stone above us. Where the Fjord Council chamber was made of polished walls and carved furniture, the Fjell meeting space was a rugged show of power with little nuance.

Seated around the Fjell Fae table were representatives for each of the factions: Espen and Marius, his new second-in-command, representing the Forest and wolves. Myself, Reuven, and Salka representing the Fjord. Lennie, Halvar, and a man named Bodil for the Fjell Fae. And, at the far end of the table, flanked by two male fae with sharp chins, was Embla.

Looking like a harsher version of her onyx-haired sister, Veigar's eldest daughter and the new Queen of the Fire Fae was a formidable presence with a surprisingly genuine smile. Ever since she'd arrived in Skolvik a few days ago, she'd listened, observed, and been amenable to any discussions. Including this one.

The Fjell was putting a lot of trust in Salka vouching for her sister, saying that she wasn't at all like their father, however imposing she might be. But that was the whole point of our meeting together. All four factions needed to reestablish bonds that had been severely broken and could only be rebuilt by trusting one another.

"Thank you all for coming," Lennie said from the head of the table. Pride grew inside me like a wave about to crash along a shore. "I know this is unconventional, but unusual times call for crazy antics. At least, that's always been my philosophy."

Half the room chuckled, and Halvar rolled his eyes.

"I think we can all agree that working together and pursuing our purposes is in every faction's best interest. We don't need one leader; we need a diverse group of leaders who promise to always work in the fae's best interests. *All* fae."

Heads bobbed around the table.

"We have drawn up an agreement we hope you'll agree to. The Skolvik Accord. It's not super long, but details how we should proceed and establishes a Monarch Council with three members from each faction. You should have received a draft prior to the meeting." Lennie looked out over the assembled leaders. "Does anyone have concerns?"

No one spoke.

Reuven cleared his throat. "We, The Fjord Fae, agree to sign the Accord."

Lennie beamed, her body brimming with energy to the point where I could tell she was doing everything she could not to bounce up and down.

"We agree too," Espen said, drawing our attention to him. He smiled. "We promise to always work for all fae. Whatever anyone needs, we are here and willing to help."

I wasn't surprised in the slightest. He'd also told us this morning how the Forest Fae Council had unanimously voted to support the measure.

With three of the four factions on board, that left only one more.

All eyes turned to Embla.

She clasped her hands together and rested them on the edge of the table. "It has been a long time since we've been part of a greater whole, but I do believe we are overdue. The Fire Fae will sign."

I let out a breath of relief.

"Thank you, Your Majesty," Lennie replied. "That means a lot."

The Queen bowed her head in a sign of respect.

A large piece of parchment was passed around, ink and quill provided for each leader to sign. When it circled back to the Fjell Fae, Lennie nudged it to Halvar. He grumbled and nudged it back to her, motioning for her to sign.

"Halvar Haraldson, we talked about this. I will forge your signature if you don't sign it yourself."

He grumbled again and relented, adding two jagged *H*s to the bottom of the page before handing it back to Lennie. She held it up, smiled, and set it aside on a nearby table.

"Now, is there anything else we need to discuss?" she asked, holding her hands behind her back the same way Halvar normally did.

"We have no interest in unchecked power imbalances, nor a retreat from our purpose," Embla said, her voice scratchy and firm. "The Fire Fae have plenty of work to attend to in Iceland. With the tectonic plates moving more each year, we need every Fire Fae we have helping us relieve the pressure being built."

Salka nodded.

"Is there anything you need from us?" Lennie asked.

"Just the Fire Fae shard returned so we can commune with the ancestors and complete my coronation ceremony."

"Of course," Lennie replied.

Halvar silently rose from his seat. He crossed the room and opened a chest near a side door before returning and setting a lump of blue stone in front of Embla. "This is the real stone. You have my word."

Embla brushed her fingers across its jagged edge. "Thank you, Halvar. I trust that you have not been duplicitous."

I did too. No man would dare give her a fake in such a confined space. It would also undermine everything we were trying to do here.

Halvar returned to his seat and Lennie smiled at him like a teacher proud of their student, before turning back to the Fire Fae Queen. "If you ever need access to the Temple, please let us know." She faced the others. "That goes for the other factions too. We can keep the pieces in place or return—"

"Keep them," Espen and Reuven said in unison.

Lennie nodded. It was the best course of action. They'd be safer here and we'd be able to access them if needed, further solidifying our alliance.

Espen straightened in his chair and looked across the table to where I sat with Reuven and Salka. "We would like to discuss aid against the current ground conditions. We were wondering if the Fjord Fae might be able to conjure more rain to help soak the roots while still being cautious around the burn scars?"

"We would be happy to help you, Espen," Reuven replied with a nod.

Amenable conversation continued without any grumbles. In a way, Veigar was getting what he wanted: a united fae. Only difference was we were choosing to work together as separate entities, not one group ruled by one man.

I looked to Lennie. She caught me and smiled.

She'd been right too. All along, she'd said we needed to work together, and here we were doing just that. I returned her smile, proud of all we'd accomplished.

Together.

162

LENNIE

I traipsed up the hillside, camera slung over my shoulder and my rain jacket zippered up tight, protecting me from the cooler temperatures and the damp breeze. Morning had dawned and brought autumn with it like a reminder of seasons and lives ending.

The wind rustled the trees around me as it danced between the pines and muffled the sound of our footfalls against the steep terrain. Espen wandered beside me, surveying our surroundings and searching for spots that might still need healing after the battle a few weeks ago. Meanwhile, Øyvin hiked behind us in his navy jacket, watching our backs like normal, just in case something might jump out and try to kill us.

Everywhere I looked sat reminders of the fae we'd lost in the Battle for Skolvik—as it had since become named. Dozens of Fjell, Fjord, and Forest soldiers had died in the skirmishes, most of them burned to death.

There'd been losses on the other side too. Fire Fae had littered town square, some with severed limbs, others with severe damage to their skulls, others still with arrows sticking out of them like hedgehogs. Apparently, Forest Fae arrows had been doused in so much poison that they could fell a thousand-pound Fjord Horse on impact.

All the bodies had been removed from the village. Some taken into the fjell for burial, some to the forest, and a whole slew of Fire and Fjord Fae had been pulled into the inky depths of the fjord as part of the clean-up efforts.

Mass funerals and memorials had been held, with smaller ceremonies for immediate family to congregate and mourn. I'd attended them all, not in my official capacity as Deputy Head Guard, but out of respect for what I'd asked so many people to do and the orders I'd given that day. Each event had left me feeling like an empty shell.

But the worst ones. The ones that hurt the most, were the ones for my friends.

Ylva's had been first. Facing her mother, Gunvor, had been gut-wrenching, but with a pat to my hands and a hug that reminded me of my own grandmother, she'd said that Ylva had died the way she'd always wanted to: protecting the forest. I'd lost it. As had Espen. We'd held each other for hours after we got home that day.

The next day we'd gone to Leif and Torsten's memorial. I could barely stomach it. They were laid to rest together in a specially made tomb on the side of the mountaintop, near a small patch of flowers, where the forest and fjell converged.

The last few weeks had been hard, but, as Espen and Øyvin had both reminded me: death was inevitable. And those who'd lost their lives had known the risks, yet given themselves willingly to protect what they loved. I couldn't argue with that. I'd done exactly the same.

I'd protected my loves, the place I called home, and the mountain.

The crack was healed, but the humans had been informed that the storm had shifted the earth into a more stable position. Police officers and some geological surveyors had been out to check and deemed the crack and land mass no longer a threat.

I still couldn't wrap my head around the fact that it was my powers, my actions, that had made it so.

"Don't think too hard there, Trouble," a grumbly voice said from behind me.

"What if I was coming up with new ways to suck your cock?"

Øyvin choked on a laugh.

Gosh, I enjoyed delivering shock and awe comments like that. Sometimes he'd respond in kind, other times I'd catch him off guard, like this. It was one of my favorite pastimes.

Espen grabbed my hand from beside me. "You'd better be thinking of ways for my dick too."

I wiggled my brows at him. "Jealous?"

"Sharing is caring, remember?" He winked, and something inside me fluttered.

"Oh, I do."

"So, why aren't we still in bed?" Øyvin asked.

I smiled. "Because the lighting is too good not to be outside today, and we all need a break from town."

It was true. We'd been helping with recovery efforts as villagers slowly moved back in. Oddvar's had been my main focus. The proprietor himself was back and had brought his sons with him when I'd informed him that a lightning strike had caused a fire on the street. Together we'd worked on clearing debris and preparing for the rebuild. But all that work was a constant reminder of what had happened, and honest to hell, I needed a mental health day. A moment of reprieve to do something I loved with the people I loved.

So here we were on a morning hike instead of lying in bed doing unspeakable things to each other.

"Where are you taking us, wife?" Espen's usual pep-in-his-step attitude was slowly returning after the battle, and I knew this hike would do him wonders. It was a chance for him to reconnect and traipse through the woods where we'd spent some of our first days together.

"A little spot Halvar showed me once upon a time."

"When was this?" Øyvin asked as I clambered over a fallen tree with the grace of a potato.

"You were busy. Espen was poisoned"—the man in question quivered then hopped onto the moss-covered log and jumped back down like a freaking gymnast— "and he'd mentioned it was a good spot for a photo."

The big guy hadn't been wrong. It was an epic spot, but a bitch of a hike though.

"Hmmm."

"I know," I replied to Øyvin's noise. "Sometimes the bossman has surprises."

"I think I've had enough surprises for one lifetime," Espen said. "Don't need them from Halvar either."

I snickered and pivoted off the trail, the guys following in my wake. "This way. Just a little bit further."

"Oh, I know where we're going," Espen said as the rocky field turned into a copse of trees.

I wiggled my eyebrows at him.

A few minutes later the trees parted and revealed a view that was surely made by gods. A piece of rock jutted out from the cliffside, looking west down the length of the fjord. Thick, tree-covered slopes rose from the gray-blue water on either side. The sun hid behind a thin layer of cloud, perfectly diffusing the light and casting a soft glow over everything.

I stepped toward the cliff edge and tilted my face toward the sun.

Standing out here with the wind tickling my cheeks and the two loves of my life beside me felt like a breath of fresh air. If I closed my eyes tight enough, I could picture the cobwebs being brushed away and the grief of loss tiptoeing out the front door.

Arms wrapped around my waist, and my eyes sprung open.

Espen glanced down at me. His amber eyes hooded, those soft lips curving slightly. Whenever he looked at me like this, as if I were the most valuable thing in the world, it melted my insides. I swept my hand across his cheek and beard, and he leaned into the touch, his lashes fluttering. The way this man made me feel warm and fuzzy with a single smile was everything I hadn't known I needed in my life. And I'd be grateful for every second I had with him on this earth.

"I love you," I whispered.

He leaned down and pressed his mouth to mine. Our lips moved together, separated, brushed, teased, and nipped in a dance that was all our own. My pulse hummed and my muscles relaxed, content with being here in his arms and enjoying every ounce of sunshine he poured into me. When it felt like I was about to sway and stumble, Espen pulled back and set his hands on my hips. "I love you too. More than you could ever imagine."

"I can imagine every single drop of it," I replied.

"Me too," Øyvin said, and I peered over my shoulder.

Øyvin opened his hand and made a come-hither motion. My body lit up like the Fourth of July in response and I trundled over to him. When I got close enough, he pressed his hands against my lower back and yanked me flush against his chest. I ran my hands over his jacket and settled one against his heart. Its steady rhythm was the perfect soundtrack for today—a reminder of the life we had ahead of us.

I tilted my head up and brushed my lips against his. He breathed into it and reminded me of everything he'd done and everything he would do to keep me happy—even if that meant challenging me from time to time. As our lips moved together in a passionate kiss that would be etched in my mind until death, there wasn't any doubt in my mind that he'd always put me first. Espen too. We were his family now. The fjord had its place in his heart, but the two of us were where he'd always belong the most.

With a satisfied sigh, I wiggled out of his hold and stepped back toward the cliff.

"Don't go too far. We can't have you falling," Espen said.

I smirked and gave them a wink. "Way too late. I've already fallen."

The biggest smiles I'd ever seen beamed back at me, and it took every ounce of willpower not to launch myself into their arms.

"Focus, Trouble," Øyvin said like he could hear me mentally warring with my own desires.

I waved my hand at him, edged out onto the spit of rock, and peered down the fjord toward Skolvik.

There was the mountain that I'd saved from falling, the village where I'd fallen in love, and the hillside where I'd taken that first fortuitous photo and missed my cruise ship. This was home. My home. A place I'd photograph and protect for years to come... Or, at least until we had to move because people were getting suspicious of our lack of aging. There was only so much makeup and miraging could do.

Maybe we'd go to Alvdalen and be closer to family. Maybe we'd head down south to one of the fishing villages. Wherever we went, though, we'd go together. Our little trio. Our little family. The one I'd found in the most unlikely of places.

I drew in a breath and pulled my camera out of its case. Taking off the lens, I shoved it in my pocket and zippered it up. One could never be too careful.

Turning on the camera with a few clicks, it beeped to life.

Peering at the scenery, a smile twisted my lips. I angled the shot, adjusted the focus, and clicked.

163

EPILOGUE

Lennie - Two Years Later

I strode into Heidi's Viking-era hut in the forest after lunch, the smell of herbs and oils bombarding my senses like a camera flash run amok. "Honey, I'm home!"

Heidi scurried over from the sink, frantically wringing her hands in a piece of cloth, her eyes blown wide. "What are you doing here? You're not supposed to stop by until this evening."

"We closed the café a little earlier today seeing as cruise season is over. Didn't Espen tell you this morning when he dropped off Bjorn?"

Heidi swallowed hard and readjusted her long skirt. "He failed to mention it."

"That's all right. I'm here now. Did he behave today? Didn't get into the blue tinctures again?" The staining last week had been a bitch to get off his little hands even with Øyvin's Fjord Fae magic.

"He... um..."

I tilted my head to one side and narrowed my eyes are her. Why was it quiet? Too quiet. My pulse quickened and my hands grew clammy. Whenever it was this quiet in the house, there was a hundred percent chance my son was up to no good. I furrowed my brow and looked around the space. The only things that stared back were shelves full of little glass bottles, herbs drying upside down from the rafters, and a surgical table with dubious stains. No little one in sight.

"Where is he?"

She clasped her hands together and let out a breath. "He isn't here."

"What do you mean, 'he isn't here?'"

Her lips pursed together.

"Heidi... Where is my son?"

"Now, see here, child." She yanked her cloth-come-tea-towel out of her apron and waved it about. "He is a very persuasive man."

No. Please no. I clapped my hand to my forehead. "You didn't. Tell me you didn't."

She shrugged and held up her hands like there was nothing she could've possibly done. Which was a damn lie. If there was anyone other than me who could stand up to the big guy, it would be Heidi.

"How long?" I asked. I'd bet my new house this wasn't a one-time thing.

"Don't be angry, it's bad for your health."

"How long has Halvar been babysitting Bjorn?"

Heidi sighed. "Every Tuesday for the past three months."

"Three months!" I exclaimed. "Do Espen and Øyvin know about this?"

"Øyvin was informed the first day and said it was all right."

A breath whizzed between my clenched teeth. He'd fucking failed to mention anything to his partner and mother of his child. Fantastic.

I stomped to the door.

"Where are you going?"

Spinning in the entry, I replied, "To find my baby!"

I stormed up the hillside and into the mountain, moving like I owned the goddamn place and would steam-roll anyone who got in my way. After coaxing a terrified soldier into telling me where Halvar was, I barreled toward the throne room. Rough stone walls turned to crystalline blue quartz by the entrance where two soldiers stood guard. Their eyes went wide when they saw me. I ignored them. They weren't responsible for this. The big brute with silver hair was.

"Halvar, where is—" I drew to a stop just inside the room, my heart lodging in my throat. "What have you done with my son?"

Halvar beamed from ear to ear, which itself should have knocked me on my ass. But it was what he pointed at that had panic swirling through me like a tornado.

"Look," Bjorn said, brandishing a sharp, toddler-sized stone sword. He waved it around and made a few stabbing motions before holstering it like a soldier... *Where the hell did he get a mini-holster from?* More importantly, why the hell did he have a sword!

I frowned. "Halvar, he's not even two!"

The Fjell Fae snorted at me like I was being ridiculous and swept the tow-haired boy into his arms as if he were his own grandchild. "Bjorn has exceptional Fjell Fae magic. It will not be long before he joins Brokkr and the fae in the forge."

I planted my hands on my hips, careful to keep my tone firm but not too authoritative as I didn't want to scare Bjorn. He wasn't to blame here. It was the stoic beast holding him that was. "Again, he's not even two. And he's part Fjord Fae. Do you really want his unchecked water powers down there too?"

Halvar's mouth fell into a firm line. "We're working on that."

A deep and long breath pressed through my lips as I stared at the rocky ceiling. How was this happening? Being mother of one demi-fae was hard enough, but I was pretty sure I was expecting another. My guess was Espen's considering how much fun we'd had during his birthday yoga session. But honest to hell, how was I going to keep track of two of them when the first was being secretly babysat by a fae who only knew how to raise Fjell Fae soldiers?

"He is doing exceptionally well, and no one has been injured," Halvar said.

"Good, Mamma."

My heart crumpled a bit at the pride emanating from my boy. He was good. As clever as his fathers and a bubbly little thing too.

I knelt and opened my arms. "Come here, sweet pea."

He wiggled out of Halvar's hold and the man set him down. Toddling over to me, he lunged into my arms with a big smile, and I wrapped him into a hug, careful of the stone sword hanging off his hip. Peering over his shoulder at Halvar, I said, "If you put this kid in a Fjell Fae uniform before he turns five, I will personally castrate you."

Halvar rolled his eyes.

Bjorn freed himself from my hug and pulled something from his pocket, proffering it to me.

"What's this, hun?"

The light-blue wool was silky soft against my fingers and— My breath caught.

"Hat," Bjorn said, and my heart stilled. He'd been given a hat. My eyes lifted to the Fjell Fae watching us, wrinkles forming at the corners of his sky-blue eyes.

Bjorn gingerly pulled his hat from my limp hands and yanked something else from his other jacket pocket. "Mamma hat." He passed me a matching hat, only much larger. One that was exactly like the baby fae hats I'd been joking about since I became a demi-fae.

My breaths shuddered as I accepted the simple, knitted hat which rolled up at the brim. Lips curving into a smile, I slipped it on. Bjorn rakishly pulled his onto his head, messing up his hair in the process.

I glanced to Halvar. "I've been waiting a while for this."

His lips turned up at the corners and, for the first time since I met him, Halvar gave me an unfiltered, beaming smile. His cheeks flushed, his eyes crinkled, and warmth radiated from him in waves. "You finally deserved it."

I scoffed and swept Bjorn into my arms, positioning him on my hip. "Say thank you to Halvar."

Bjorn mumbled his thanks between a yawn and rested his head against my shoulder. His long eyelashes brushed across his rosy cheeks. He'd probably fall asleep on the walk home.

I turned toward the exit and Halvar cleared his throat, drawing me to a stop.

"I will see him next Tuesday," Halvar announced, and I spun on the spot. "He needs the training. The sooner he is trained, the safer it will be for him and everyone else."

I bit my bottom lip to keep from grumbling. He had a point. But dammit, I was still bitter that I'd been hoodwinked and left out of the loop on this.

However...

If he so desperately wanted to help us train Bjorn, then I wanted something in return. I wanted the kernel of information I'd poked and prodded people for, searched and questioned for the past few years. Information, it seemed, only one fae had.

"I'll let you train my son every Tuesday on one condition."

Halvar's nostrils flared as he inhaled and crossed his arms. "Name it."

"Tell me how old you are."

His brow furrowed. "That's it?"

"That's it."

Halvar shook his head and sighed. "I'm 964."

"What the fuck!"

Bjorn clapped his hand over my mouth.

THE END

About the Author

Hey! I'm Elle Thrasher, an author of romantic fantasy books.

My books are filled with relatable heroines, swoon-worthy heroes, lots of laughs, and locations that will give you wanderlust.

While I'm originally from the UK, and lived in Norway for seven years too, I now live in the US with my husband and one very fluffy dog. When I'm not writing, I can usually be found drinking a cup of tea, staring at my never-ending tbr, or taking a joke waaaaay too far.

Follow me on Instagram for updates and don't forget to sign up for my newsletter to receive behind-the-scenes info, bonus material, and details about upcoming books!

www.ellethrasher.com

Also by Elle Thrasher

The Cerulean Lazulum Series
(Urban Fantasy)
Cavendish
Hawke

The Nordic Fae Series
(Romantic Fantasy)
The Fae of the Fjord
Christmas on the Fjord
The Fae of the Forest
The Fae of the Fjell